SONGS IN THE KEY OF DEATH

SONGS IN THE KEY OF DEATH

SEAMUS CARRON

YOUCAXTON PUBLICATIONS

OXFORD & SHREWSBURY

Copyright © Estate of Seamus Carron 2013

The authors estate asserts the moral right to
be identified as the author of this work.

ISBN 978-190964-470-0
Printed and bound in Great Britain.
Published by YouCaxton Publications 2015

About the Author

Seamus Carron was born in Blackpool in 1955. Marked as different from an early age, his natural ability did not fit well with the society he was born to.

His turbulent and unusual early life gave way to a degree in Linguistics at University in Dublin. His natural and unwavering desire to make a difference then moved him to the Foreign Office and several overseas postings with the Diplomatic Service, including Pakistan.

What caused his terminal disillusion & rebellion is not clear, but he suddenly gave it all up whilst on holiday in Marbella. They went after him, offered him promotion, but he never returned.

Leaving his career behind, he turned his hand to a wide range of adventures including crewing on yachts, running his own restaurant in Majorca, working in Hong Kong, and teaching English at university in Paris.

In the following years, instead of finding his peace, he became trapped by his demons. A multiplicity of inheritance and experience that saw him at times dead broke and at others living the high life. He lived life on the edge, adapting to what was at hand, avoiding being the target.

How real or imagined his insecurities & failures were we will never know, but the interest of powerful people and agendas was noticeably close during his years of self-imposed exile.

He was a force of nature who loved being the centre of attention. He had a vast repertoire of songs and his rich baritone allowed him to grab every opportunity to sing to an audience.

Tiring of life abroad and homesick, he returned to London in the mid 1990s. This one last chance to find peace was a long haul. He had to re-learn England and was now spiritually tired as well. Eventually he built a career in marketing in the city which offered him a modest income and as much stability as he could tolerate.

Still searching for the answers in life he became a freemason, embracing its rituals and companionship, until work brought him to rural England and Shrewsbury. There he experienced a very different way of life. Quickly turning his back on the city, he settled in Shropshire, found renewed purpose & peace, and took up writing.

He died prematurely, if not predictably at the age of 57, but was it having burnt both ends of the candle of life, or something else?

FOR MY WIFE FRANCES

Chapter One

SHREWSBURY ENGLAND JULY 2005

Janice Hope left her office ready to kill. The next person who pissed her off would receive two fingers in the eyes followed up by an elbow smash to the throat – and it would not take much to piss her off on this sunny Shropshire Friday. After another week of working as a secretary in the pretentious legal practice of Wright Prosser, she had had enough of rebuffing the attentions of the male staff who, basically, wanted to get into the new girl's pants. Her youth, just twenty, meant that even the office junior thought that he had a chance. Her dark hair, dark eyed good looks, which came from an Italian P.O.W. grandfather (or so her mother said) were exotic enough to attract the eye of all the solicitors, with the exception of gay Gavin who lusted solely after her footwear. The fact that she dressed and spoke well made her stand out from the small herd of provincial co-workers and thus generated the occasional smile from the two booze soaked senior partners on their rare visitations to the main office area. Janice's clothes were professionally suited for work but no amount of sartorial discretion that she could afford was able to disguise 5'5" 34-24-34 of femininity.

So the males made clumsy passes and the girls just froze her out, eight thirty to five, Monday to Friday taking dictation about divorce, dues and deaths. If she could not break this cycle she would go mad and she needed this job. She was studying law through the Open University but, Christ, it was hard to hit the books after the mind numbing days of Wright Prosser where she spent an inordinate amount of time playing Dodge the Groper and Smile at Bitches. If she could end the week without bruising a male ego and not giving the girls ammunition enough whereby they could label her either a slut or a dyke she was ahead if the game.

This afternoon she had nearly lost it. One of the largest property development companies in the country had sent a team to them to evaluate their services with a view to making Wright Prosser their sole legal representatives in the UK. Her company's pitch was to be made by Stanley Green who, at just thirty years of age, looked and acted the part of a dynamic but solid legal professional. No one talked the talk like Stanley. However, he had never actually made a power-point presentation before and, in rehearsals, had shown himself to be as technically challenged as a chimp with motor control problems. So Janice had prepared the entire presentation, pressed all the buttons at the right time whilst Stanley did his dog and pony show. The prospective clients seemed impressed and as they filed out for lunch, began to ask Janice innocuous questions regarding life and work in a historic town. Before she could answer Stanley had appeared at her side and said 'Janice, love, lunch will take about two hours. Do you think that you could have a record of the meeting for each of our guests by the time we return?'

'No problem, Mr Green' she replied 'I'll just give the diagrams to Mike in IT and he'll download a record of the meeting to disc and burn as many copies as we require. I'll be five minutes and catch you up at Draper's Hall.'

'That's not what I mean. If possible in the next two hours, I would like you to prepare a written record of the meeting to accompany the audio-visual one. Some clients prefer a more traditional approach. It's just like transcribing the minutes of a meeting. Is this possible Janice?'

'It is if I do it Mr Green. It will be ready when you all return. Enjoy your lunch.'

As the four males left the sole female to cross the t's and dot the i's, that would have been it for Janice had her sharp ears not caught the tail end of a Stanley Green special remark; something along the line of 'not bad spare rib' which generated loud laughter from the visiting team. Now Janice had checked the dietary requirements of their visitors and had been to see the restaurant manager to ensure that the Wright Prosser party received the appropriate level of service so she had also looked over the menu. She was therefore sure that Draper's Hall did not sell spare ribs. So Stanley had probably been referring to herself when he left the office. Jesus! After saving his presentation, you would have thought that he would have had the gratitude to let her enjoy a good lunch (and maybe contribute something to raising the company's image) but no. She was a copy typist and a spare fucking rib!

She had accomplished the task set by Stanley with single minded professionalism; she would not let her emotions show even though she knew she would received no recognition for her work today. The afternoon meeting had been for principals only so she occupied herself with the backlog of her everyday work which had accumulated during her preparation of the Mr Stanley Green presentation. At five o'clock they were still behind doors so she picked up her handbag and left without seeing if their lordships required anything else from their menial. No doubt she would receive grief for this come Monday but, right now, all she wanted was to be in her flat with a glass of rosé and the weekend ahead of her.

At least the weather was with her and, as she made her way down Pride Hill towards her one bedroom flat at the new St Julian's development, the tension of the day started to lessen when six little words of nonsense stopped her in her tracks. 'Dum dum dum dumbdy doo-wah'. It was the intro to her all time favourite song 'Only the Lonely' by Roy Orbison. You hardly ever heard it played by anyone else and here she was listening to it in Shrewsbury town centre – and the busker was good. No amplification, just his voice and a six string acoustic. When he finished the song she applauded, enthusiastically, and then realised she was the only person who had even stopped to listen. The musician was packing his gear away but looked across to his audience of one and gave her a small smile and a nod acknowledging her appreciation.

Janice went over to him rummaging in her bag for her purse so that she could add something to the somewhat meagre pile of coins that he had accumulated.

'I love that song' Janice said 'and you sang it really well. Thank you'

'Thank you' he replied 'Let me guess – it was one that your parents liked; you don't look like the usual Orbison fan.'

'And that's a very polite was of saying that I'm too young to remember good music like that. Anyway my parents were totally non musical and damn! I've no change to give you. How embarrassing.'

The busker had finished gathering his stuff together, snapped the catches shut on his guitar case and said to Janice 'And I'm not worth a note am I?'

For a second she thought that he was serious but then he smiled the warmest of smiles. It was hard to tell his age as he was wearing dark, prescription glasses and wore a low brimmed hat. What hair she could see was dark with no grey in it but what did that mean in an era of male cosmetics? He was dressed in a way that could not date him either. Chambray shirt and blue jeans, both faded but clean, and a good quality brown leather belt that matched his cowboy boots. It was a look that could be carried off by someone as young as David Beckham or as antique as Willie Nelson. She hoped he was closer to the former than the latter.

'Sorry' said the singer 'That was rude of me. Fact is I don't sing on the street for the money. I'm playing a gig in the country tonight and I'm way too early so I parked up and thought I'd spend an hour playing in the sun. That's the first time I have sung 'Only the Lonely' in public.'

'Well, like I said you played it really well. Where's your gig?'

'A place called The Bridges at Rattlinghope. Know it?'

'Only by reputation' replied Janice 'it's really out of the way, about thirty minutes by car and I don't drive. I'm pretty sure there's no bus service between here and there so I have never been. How are you going to find it?'

'Satnav. I always plan my trips as much as possible. This time I've misjudged on the side of caution so I've still got a few hours on my hands.' He paused, looked down at the ground and then looked back up straight into her eyes, waited two beats and seemed to come to a decision. 'I'm Tony. Would you like to come and hear me play tonight?'

Despite her lack of years, Janice was far from stupid or naïve. Her instant reaction to his question was to say 'too damn right I would' but her cautious over-ride kicked in. Was she really about to get in a car with a total stranger, head off to an unknown pub, and not know how she was going to return home after the gig? What did Tony expect from her and when, next, would an attractive musician (who played her favourite song to boot) ask her out? Decision time. He waited for her reply. This was one of the moments upon which vital outcomes turned. The target could disappear from his sights forever, freeze in the glare of his power thereby ensuring its death or take a tentative sniff towards him and stay within his range. He would have bet on the third option. Janice did not disappoint him.

'I'd love to come but, err, it's not that straightforward.'

'OK I understand' replied Tony. 'Now unless you have a prior engagement tonight – here he raised an interrogative eyebrow to which Janice answered with a shake of her head – any problems you have are either logistical, moral or a combination thereof. Correct?'

'Well, yes actually' said Janice.

Tony smiled at her. 'Little things like these we can most certainly solve. But only after I've had a cold one. Where were you headed when you were stopped by the Big O?'

'Home, I'm five minutes walk that way' said Janice, indicating the town High Street.

'OK, my car's in a pay park thataway so why don't we do this. I'll go and stow my gear away while you head home and change. Then we'll meet somewhere you choose and we'll have a drink and make a plan. Fair enough?' Tony mentally held his breath. This was another pivotal moment where he had handed control over the situation to her. There were so many variables, all with different consequences. What would she decide?

'Would you mind if we went for a drink out of town? It's Friday and I really don't want to bump into any of my work mates tonight.'

The prey had just moved squarely into his sights. It would be hard, though still possible, to miss from here.

'No problem' replied Tony 'Where and when shall I pick you up?'

'If you're not from round here I suppose the easiest landmark is the Abbey. It's just on the other side of the English Bridge and it'll be on your Satnav. See you outside there in half an hour or so?'

'Fine' said Tony 'Look out for a silver-grey Range Rover with a lost looking guitarist at the wheel.

He picked up his guitar case and walked away in the opposite direction to Janice. Had she followed him she would have wondered why a stranger to Shrewsbury chose to use the maze of small, hidden alleys and shuts to reach his car and not the few main streets which ran through the centre of the medieval town. The answer lay in the location of the police force's CCTV cameras - Tony was avoiding them as much as possible.

Entering the municipal car park, he found his Range Rover, placed his guitar on the rear seat and headed out of town. He would never operate in such an enclosed environment again for the simple reason that there was nowhere to park that was not covered by CCTV. When he had chosen this place as a hunting ground his reasoning had been that Shropshire was one of the least densely populated counties in England, Shrewsbury was the county town and would, therefore, have a number of live music venues and it was situated in the West Midlands so it had easy access to the motorway network. He had nearly decided against operating here. During his initial reconnaissance he had discovered that Shrewsbury was not a small town; it was a large village. Within the loop of land formed by the River Severn it seemed that everyone knew everyone else. You could still see black and white beamed buildings dating from the sixteenth century standing next to the occasional modern brasserie. The town centre pubs would have been at home in the smallest of rural villages and modernity, in the guise of McDonalds and KFC, had only the smallest of footholds. The highest point in town, overlooking the railway station, was a ruined castle of indeterminate age which houses the regimental museum. What really dominated Shrewsbury were the churches both functional and abandoned. Given the absence of Roman ruins around the town walls, some surmised that Shrewsbury was ecclesiastical or monastic in origin.

Whatever the case, it had been a difficult place from which to obtain a suitable girl with whom he could proceed to the next stage with a reasonable amount of security for himself. But Tony had accepted the challenge and would learn lessons from the experience.

He knew exactly where the Abbey was and how long it would take him to get there so he drove slowly along with river and followed the one way system up past the castle. One of the few good things about Shrewsbury, from his admittedly special perspective, was that there was very little possibility of a traffic jam. Having checked that there were no agricultural shows or folk festivals this weekend, Tony was sure that he would be in place not too long before Janice arrived. It would not be right to keep a lady waiting, and after all he was the one who had time to kill.

At this time of day there had been no problem finding a parking space by the huge, red stone edifice that was the Abbey and Tony waited. There was nothing left to check; his mechanicals were all in place and here she came. He could see her in his rear view mirror and recognised what he knew to be her weekend music gig outfit. Smart black jeans, with a slim black and silver belt, a white cap sleeved T-shirt and, carried at the moment, a black suit jacket with the cuffs rolled up to just below the elbow. Unless she had had a serious growth spurt in the last thirty minutes, she was also wearing two inch heels. He also noted that Janice was carrying a leather bag that was too small to be for sports gear but too large for the usual female paraphernalia. Interesting. Perhaps she thought that she might not be going home tonight. How right and how wrong could you be at the same time?

As she approached the rear of his car he buzzed down the passenger-side window, leaned over and waved his hat out at her. Her face appeared, she smiled and jumped in without hesitation. 'Hi' she said. 'Been waiting long?'

'No not at all' he replied 'So where to?'

'As it's such a lovely day, I thought it would be nice to have a drink outside by the water – do you know the Mytton and Mermaid?'

'I know what a mermaid is and I'll let you explain what a mytton might be. How far and which direction from here?'

'We're only about 10 minutes away, go straight on to the roundabout then straight on again. It's really easy and I'm sure you'll like it.

Tony indicated to pull out and set off from Shrewsbury. He knew exactly where the Mytton and Mermaid was; it was one of the best hotel and restaurants in the area and could not have suited his purposes better. As he had pulled out, he had glanced over his right shoulder to check his blind spot for oncoming traffic, and at the same time, his right hand had dropped to his side where he flicked a switch that started a gas flow. What was seeping into the Range Rover now was a very powerful opiate based mixture based on the synthetic drug Fentanyl. This is 10,000 stronger than morphine and was believed to have been the basis of the weapon used by the Russian special forces when they attacked the Chechen terrorists in a Moscow theatre during the siege of 2002. That day the Russians had succeeded in killing all the terrorists. Unfortunately over 120 hostages also lost their lives and the Russian authorities have never made public the results of the autopsies. Tony was wearing nasal filters, the car doors were centrally locked and he only had to keep his mouth shut for thirty seconds before Janice began to become drowsy. He now put on a flesh coloured full face mask which would have looked horrific close up but, when viewed through the tinted windows of a moving vehicle, appeared quite natural. In reality the mask functioned at NATO CBW standard so Tony was safe, for now.

Janice's chin had slumped onto her chest when she suddenly sat bolt upright, her eyes bulging and she strained forward against her seat belt. Her heart was racing to try and pump blood around her system and get some oxygen into her brain but each breath she took brought her closer to oblivion. Hypoventilation took over and then coma set in. As Tony knew it would. She may have even been dead by then but he could not be sure of this so he continued on the B5061 towards Telford and eventually found one of the secluded spots which he had pre-selected for the next act. Pulling off to the right at the For Sale sign he followed a grass and gravel track to a ruined barn behind which he parked and turned off his engine. He then opened all four doors of the car and listened. All he could hear was the distant drone from the motorway and the odd chirrup of birdsong. Nothing else.

He placed a finger on Janice's carotid and felt nothing. She was either dead or so comatose that she felt nothing when he took her from the car and snapped her neck from behind. Time to hurry. Tony opened the rear of the Range Rover and lifted off the cover to his one large Marshall speaker which was in reality an empty, black box. Into this space he lowered Janice's body, arranging her shoes and personal possessions around her. He removed her mobile phone in case someone should try and contact her. He doubted that this would happen given what he knew of her family and social life but you never knew who could crawl out of the woodwork to raise a hue and cry. Forewarned is forearmed etc. Using a battery powered screwdriver from the glove box, Tony fixed the cover onto the 'speaker'. The car was now totally aired so he mounted up and set off to the south where he would take his trophy and dispose of the rest.

As he motored towards Birmingham and the south he activated the CD player and smiled as he listened to the words – 'Only the lonely, know the way I feel tonight'.

Chapter Two

LONDON 2010

Roger Tucker was a nationally known journalist. His speciality was social and political commentary in the satirical vein. His supporters from the political centre-right loved him. Those on the liberal left would have gladly forgotten their principles and reintroduced hanging in his case because, not only did he make a living exposing the hypocrisy of the left, thus damaging the cause of 'progressive' politics, he also struck a chord with a very broad socio-economic spectrum of people. The newspaper for which he wrote was the most widely read quality journal in the country and he was too famous to ignore. Even the BBC, whom he regularly ridiculed in print, felt obliged to have him as a guest on its most prestigious current affairs programme. In short at fifty, he was an important man.

On this Friday morning in August he was quite a badly hungover man. He had spent last night in the company of three men with whom he had started on his journalistic career so long ago. All of them had cut their teeth in the Alice in Wonderland world of British industrial relations in the 1970's when openly Marxist trade union leaders had almost caused a civil war in the country. Despite the severity of the situation, Roger Tucker had always been able to see the funny side of things. It was hard not to laugh when the leader of the miners union travelled in a chauffeur driven car, employed a personal hair stylist and lived in a luxurious apartment in London's financial sector, all paid for by his comrades' contributions.

When a photo of this same leader addressing the masses with his right arm aloft à la Adolf Hitler appeared it was rumoured that Roger Tucker invented the caption 'MINE FUHRER!' to accompany it on the front page of England's biggest circulation tabloid. The left's lawyers went mental; the print union workers refused to run it so the paper duly appeared with a large space on its front page instead of the photo. A brief editorial explanation was given and another trade union hammered a nail into the coffin of collective bargaining.

Happy days. Roger and his friends had all moved away from pure news reporting but the bond they had formed all those years ago remained firm. They no longer quaffed pints of ale in the evening but had moved onto drinks of higher price and quality. The stories and drinking had continued until after midnight when they had gone their separate ways. Roger had taken a taxi home to his house between Muswell Hill and Highgate. Right now he was thanking God that his wife was with her sister at the villa in Spain. It had been some years since he had last woken to find that he had remembered to hang his clothes up carefully on the floor. He had always believed that only bad quality red wine caused a hangover and that decent Chateauneuf-du-Pape could do a chap no harm. So he could only conclude that bottle number three had been 'off'. How else could he explain the scalpels lancing his skull and the Mojave in his mouth? So he did what he used to do all those years ago as a student and followed the Kris Kristofferson cure – he had a beer for breakfast.

He had no meetings scheduled for today so he would just be passive and wait for the reactions to his Friday column which, he reckoned, should generate more than the usual shit storm of controversy especially his idea that Obama was really Irish because he certainly did not seem to be acting on behalf of the American people.

He performed the usual ablutions but decided that shaving could wait until his hands stabilised. He dressed in jeans and fresh cotton shirt (you could only take on so much of Kristofferson's persona) and sat down to scroll through his emails for anything of use, interest or importance.

It was all fairly predictable. There really were some crazies out there who took the time to compose hate filled messages to him. The joke was that they called themselves, liberal, progressive, of the people, yada yada whilst recommending that he perform physically impossible zoophilic acts. A good deal of the more vicious messages were, in fact, illegal but Roger had long ago ceased to worry about lonely little people spewing out their anonymous bile. Many years ago he had talked with a friend on the Metropolitan Police who had informed him that, if he lodged a complaint, it would of course be followed up. Given the number of people to whom the police would have to give the warning to, it was inevitable that one of the more vicious ones would run screaming to the Guardian newspaper which would be only too happy to run a story that Roger Tucker sets the fascist police on lonely man who was only exercising his democratic right to express his opinion. The fact that the opinion was that Tucker should have acid poured down his throat and have his hands pulverised with a sledgehammer would not, of course, appear in the article.

So Roger Tucker did not overly concern himself with the hate mail he received. But his house was very secure indeed and there was a panic button connected to the private security company nearby.

A large proportion of his emails were from regular correspondents some of whom had put him on to good stories over the years. He had even met a few and he looked forward to the emails that began 'Hi Rog'. These people were like his private intelligence corps throughout the country and they sent him information of the idiocies of how politically correct local government bodies wasted public money. His all time favourite was the London borough council that banned the flying of the English flag on St. George's day as the mandatory risk assessment would prove too expensive but managed to find the money to pay for an 'outreach worker for Rastafarian lesbians seeking IVF treatment'.

Then there were the messages of support and agreement with his articles which were pleasant enough. It proved that he had to be getting it right with some of the people some of the time. There were also some well argued letters which did not agree with him and he spent quite a bit of time with these. At his age it was unlikely that he was going to change his political stance but he did enjoy the challenge of reading something which had been thought out and then dismantling it in a logical and reasoned manner.

Finally there were the missives which did not immediately fit any of his pigeon-holes. These he handled with care. Some of them purported to be stories of great national importance and were actually fictitious. The senders were either mischievous, trying to set him off on a journalistic wild goose chase or devious, trying to damage his reputation. He remembered the Hitler Diaries.

Some started off reasonably enough with good use of English, obviously written by someone who had gone through higher education but, as the letter went on, revealed themselves to be yet another conspiracy theorist. Roger Tucker always thought that if these communications had not come to him electronically then he would have seen an awful lot of green ink, block capitals and heavy underlining.

Right now he was looking at an odd one. On first reading it was a nut job but his gut told him not to dismiss it – and after all these years his gut, even in this morning's delicate state, was normally right. The originating address told him nothing.

FROM: ML@HOTMAIL.CO.UK
TO: R.TUCKER@DAILYPOST.CO.UK
SENT: THURSDAY 19 AUGUST 2010 23.30
SUBJECT: SPEAK FOR US

The main text was like something from Pirates of the Caribbean:-

Dear Mr Tucker – would you be the man to champion England's lost princesses? The quest has held no appeal for those who should have taken it up five summers gone so today royal Vikki's finder gazes west with central resonance to where they lie.

Were Drake to be against the House of Lancs at Plymouth or an untrusted Scottish toiler ply his trade from this rock, then that which binds the slave and half again would find them.

Jekyll's Garden is a public place now and the palace of Diana would weep to see more gaderene disinter the sisters – so, haste with whatever you choose to muster for glory awaits the victor in this game.

Yours aye, ML

A treasure hunt of sorts and the final sentence was telling him to hurry, even though the writer claimed that the challenge should have been taken up five years ago. Odd. Some of the message appeared childishly easy; Jekyll's Garden was obviously Hyde Park and Diana's palace was Kensington so the location was central London. Did this email justify a call to the Metropolitan Police? He could make no sense of the first half of the message and knew that he would need help to decipher it. His newspaper employed some very bright researchers who would no doubt crack this during a coffee break but he then ran the risk of the crime correspondents snatching the story. Did he have a legal obligation to contact the police? What if a person were actually buried, dead or alive, and he made the wrong decision? Looking at the originating details he saw that the information was now nearly ten hours old. Make your mind up time. Despite what his critics thought of him, Roger Tucker did believe that he performed public service so he did not call his editor; he phoned his police friend who had given him advice on how to deal with abusive emails some years ago. This was Detective Superintendent Mark Goodchild who was currently attached to the counter terrorist unit, SO15 and was therefore a very busy man indeed. He and Roger were of an age and went back years to when Mark had been a PC in the old Special Patrol Group. They had done each other favours during this time and not the least of which has been when PC Goodchild had stood over a dazed and bleeding Tucker to face down a screaming mob during the Brixton riots of 1981. This was all the more impressive when one takes into account the fact that Goodchild was armed only with his riot stick and 250 pounds of attitude.

When the two men met up for a drink some days after south London had stopped burning, Tucker had asked Goodchild what he was thinking that night as he faced a crowd which was armed with petrol bombs and machetes. The off duty policeman looked at the journalist and said 'Not for publication OK? This is not an interview.'

'Absolutely not' replied Tucker.

'Well then, what I thought was a line from my favourite Christmas time film; 'Zulu's – fucking thousands of 'em.'

Thus a life or death situation was transformed into a moment of hilarity for the two men and they had remained in touch ever since.

Tucker did not know Goodchild's hours so he called his personal mobile using his own and not his ex-directory landline. After three rings he was answered 'Morning Rog. How are you this fine Friday?'

'A bit dusty round the edges to tell the truth Mark. You free to talk at the moment?'

'Sure, mate. I'm just reading some really interesting guidelines on diversity awareness which is in a language similar to English but not as we know it. What can I do for you?'

'Well,' continued Tucker 'it's a bit of a weird one. I've just received an email, to me, that indicates that something or someone is buried in central London and relates to missing English girls going back over the last five years. I don't know whether to bin it, pass it on to the paper or alert your lot officially.'

'How long is this message?' asked Goodchild

'About 120 words' replied Tucker whose journalist's eye could calculate a word count at a glance.

'Okay. I'm at the office. Forward it to me and I'll run it past a few people and get back to you this afternoon sometime. OK?'

'Actually I'd rather not have a whole lot of eyes on this in case I end up with egg on my face. Could I just read it out to you and have your initial reactions please, mate?'

Goodchild sensed that the journalist was worried about something so he bit his tongue hard regarding Tucker's implied low opinion of discretion at New Scotland Yard and simply said 'OK shoot.'

Tucker dictated the entirety of the email to Goodchild, not knowing that the police officer had developed his own version of shorthand and had copied the message verbatim. After checking a couple of proper name spellings, Goodchild said 'Don't phone your paper. I need to see if someone else here is free. I think I know what this may be but I have to be sure. If things are what I think they are I want you, a printout of the email and your laptop in the Feather's at 1100 hours sharp. Can do?'

'Yeah, but who are you going to talk to? Can't you tell me a bit more…'

Goodchild cut him off. 'Hold it there Rog. You called me, remember? If this is what I think it is, it is not for an open line conversation. It's not even in my area of operations and the one guy I'd let in on your info may not even be available. I'll call you one way or another in fifteen. OK?

'Got it,' said Tucker 'I'll see you in the Feathers at eleven anyway. Lunch on the paper for your efforts whatever the outcome. See you then and thanks Mark.'

Goodchild hung up and consulted his directory. Clarkson,

Derek – Detective Chief Superintendent Serious Crimes Unit. He dialled the extension hoping that he was not going to ruin the day of man whose personal and professional lives were rumoured to be on very shaky foundations.

'Clarkson' replied a bright, well modulated voice which was as close to accentless as one could be. Goodchild thought it unnatural for anyone to sound that chirpy on a Friday morning – without, that is, recourse to booze or happy pills.

'Morning Sir. DS Goodchild here. Could I possibly pop along and take ten minutes of your time? It's a tad pressing.'

He could have been a lot less formal as DS Clarkson was a member of the same Masonic Lodge as Goodchild but, with the press having one of its periodic witch-hunts regarding the Craft, it was better to be discrete in such matters.

'Do you mean now Detective Superintendent?'

'If possible, Sir.'

'Very well. I'll let all the Asian Officers know that you're on their way so that will give them time to hide their prayer mats. See you in a moment then.'

'Yes, Sir. Thank you Sir.' Jesus. Didn't Clarkson know not to make jokes regarding ethnics and Islam? He must be on something or he's after early retirement.

Goodchild left the SO15 offices which were located on the fourth floor at the rear of the ugly glass building that is New Scotland Yard and took the lift to floor seven at the front of the main tower to Clarkson's office. If the opposition, whether Al-Qaeda or the Irish, ever managed to set off an explosive device by the famous revolving sign, it amused Goodchild to think all of the admin weenies who would cop the blast whilst the counter-terrorist unit would be relatively safe from harm. Shame about serious crimes though.

DCS Clarkson's rank gave him his own, small, office and Goodchild knocked and entered when he heard the summons to 'Come'.

'Morning Mark. So, what's so bloody urgent in our respective worlds today? Take a seat.'

'It's a bit out of the ordinary, Sir. Probably best if I just show you. You know the journo Roger Tucker?' Receiving a nod in the affirmative he continued. 'Well we've been mates for years and he called me fifteen minutes ago to ask for my take on an email he received this morning. He wouldn't forward it to us so he read it out over the phone and I copied down what he said. I'm due to meet him at 1100 hours in the Feathers. Here it is.' Goodchild handed his notes over to the senior officer then waited whilst the message was read.

Clarkson looked at the manuscript on his desk with an impassive face. The only tell that he was thinking was the fact that the fingers of his right hand were very slightly rubbing his temple. After five or so minutes he raised his eyes to meet Goodchild's and asked 'Is there any chance that Tucker is having us on here, Mark?'

'No sir – at least not intentionally. I cannot speak as to the motives of ML but Roger would not play with the force. Forget the gadfly image and the Plod of the Week articles; he has a serious side.'

'Well, I hope you're right because I'm going to have to allocate some resources right now and there is no way that it can be kept quiet. Can you be spared from your CT duties today?'

'I'll need to clear it with Commander Pugh but I don't have anything on that I cannot put off until whenever.'

'I'll talk to Barney for you; he owes me one or two, the number of my chaps he's pinched to provide warms bodies for his CT training exercises. I'll see you in the pub as close to eleven as I can make it. Anything else I should know?'

'No, Sir' replied Goodchild. 'Have you, err, worked out what the message means, Sir?'

Clarkson gave a grin which turned into a grimace. His eyes, which had been alive when he had read the message focused on somewhere (or someone) that was not in the room with them. In reply to the superintendent's question he said 'I know where we have to dig. I have no idea what we shall find. And I wish you had picked someone else to wield this particular shovel. See you later, Mark. I have people to call.'

Goodchild made his way back to his desk and checked for messages. None. Good. He activated his voicemail, shut down his computer and went to sit in the toilet to think. DCS Clarkson had kept his transcription of Tucker's words and it was the only copy. Stupid of him not to have photocopied it. Trying to solve the riddle without the words in front of him was not working. He had, in his mind's eye, Sir Francis Drake, Queen Victoria, Scotland and a negro slave. How the hell had Clarkson made a link between such disparate entities.? Too late now. He was due to meet Roger shortly so he flushed, washed and dried his hands then headed for the Victorian darkness of the Feathers public house.

Goodchild found Roger Tucker sat in a corner seat at the back of the main room. At this time of day the place was virtually empty and smelled more of cleaning products than pints. That would change as lunchtime came and civil servants from the various ministries arrived for their breaks where they would rub shoulders with the passing trade that used Broadway as a link between St James' Park and Victoria – Westminster Abbey axis. He noted that Roger Tucker had two pints of London Pride bitter in front of him which was not a good sign at eleven in the morning.

'Morning Roger' said the policeman. 'Drinking for two?'

'Piss off Mark, one's for you. Don't tell me it's too early in the day for one of the Met's finest to have a beer! replied the journalist, who then took a sizeable swallow of his own drink.

'I'm SO15 Roger. If I'm called to an incident with beer on my breath I'll end up mucking out the stables for the mounties. Have you brought what I asked you to?'

'Yes. Here's the print out. Any joy working out what the fuck this character is on about?'

'I reckon I've come to the same conclusions as you but I've shown it to one other officer and he reckons that he's worked it out. He's on his way to meet us now.'

'And who is this genius?'

'DCS Derek Clarkson, Serious Crimes Unit. Know him?'

Tucker's police contacts were extensive at all different rank levels but he shook his head at the question. 'Clarkson rings a bell but not as Serious Crimes. No, I don't know this one. Why did you pick him and what's his form?'

'Firstly, I've know Derek socially for roughly fifteen years and he is one of the brightest blokes I've ever met. Secondly he's totally discrete; compared to Derek, a Trappist monk is the village gossip.'

'So he's a friend then?' asked Tucker.

'No; but he is a brother.' Goodchild looked hard into the journalist's eyes waiting for him to make a comment on what he liked to refer to as the 'All England Association of Funny Handshakes'. When Tucker, wisely, said nothing Goodchild continued. 'Before transferring to Serious Crimes, Derek spent seven years on the child sex crime team. The canteen rumour mill says that he is a burn-out. His wife divorced him and he does not socialise with anyone on the force. When I meet him at the lodge we never discuss police work. He is perfectly sociable with the brethren, likes a drink and that, but seems to have no small talk at all. He only gets animated when he talks about military history of all things. At short notice, I could not think of anyone better to consult and…… heads up; here he comes. Word of warning to you Roger. Never, never use the word paedophile in his presence.'

Tucker observed the man who was approaching the table. Just over six feet tall but stooped at the neck and shoulders to give a very un-policeman like presence, hair more grey than it's original dark and wearing a good quality suit and shirt both of which were just a shade too large for the frame they encompassed. A polyester tie with an emblem that Tucker did not recognise and good heavyweight black brogues which were well polished and broken in. Finally the face. The roadmap of broken capillaries on the cheeks that meant the owner either had a liking for strong drink or was a close relative of Santa Claus. The pale blue eyes were fixed on Tucker and he felt that he was being more than scrutinised. He was being weighed in some sort of balance and the jury was still out. Even without his friend's prior information, Roger Tucker would have estimated that this was a man who had travelled long and lonely roads on which few others ventured and none emerged from unscathed. He doubted though that he would have identified the man as a police officer. He looked more like an oncologist who had lost too many patients.

Mark Goodchild made the introductions. 'Sir, this is Roger Tucker; Roger this is Detective Chief Super Derek Clarkson.' Tucker stood and the two men shook hands.

'Pleased to meet you, Sir. Would you like a drink?' asked Tucker.

'Large vodka and tonic no ice, please. Mark you are officially seconded to me for the next seventy two hours so SO15 drinking rules do not apply. I would advise against drinking pints of beer or coffee as we shall probably spend quite a few hours standing around in a public place without recourse to lavatories. Wouldn't do to be caught short pissing in front of a press photographer eh?'

'Fine, Sir. Same for me then Roger. You can manage the spare pint.'

Tucker went to the bar and was back at the table in less than five minutes. Laying the drinks down he addressed Clarkson. 'Mark tells me that you've solved the conundrum. What's the nutter on about?'

Clarkson took his time in answering. He first looked at Goodchild as if to say 'so you've told a journalist that I've deciphered the message, have you?' then turned his attention to Tucker.

'I would like to thank you for bringing this communication to our attention Mr Tucker. Most journalists would have tried to do something with it themselves or with their papers. You have not told anyone else, have you?'

'No. Mark specifically asked me not to.'

'Good. You get brownie points for that and I shall keep you in the loop as much as I can. There are problems though. This message works on several levels and we don't know what the sender's goal is. He could be aiming to make you and your paper look foolish. Worse, if he thought that you could contact the authorities, he could be trying to make us look foolish. Imagine if we were to evacuate Hyde Park, close down Bayswater Road and dig up a horses arse – all in view of the press. How would we look then?'

'Why would you want to close the park and Bayswater Road?' asked Tucker.

'ML, whoever he is, chose you as the recipient of this message. This person may know that your closest police contact works for SO15. I cannot let my men take a pick and shovel to a patch of royal park which may contain an explosive device Mr Tucker.'

'Shit' breathed the journalist.

'Shit, indeed' said Clarkson. All three men drank, Tucker restarted the conversation.

'So what's all the stuff at the start of the email about? It lost me.'

'It is sophomoric in it's convolutions but actually very simple. I believe that ML wants this spot found and excavated quickly. I don't like someone else pulling my strings hence my caution. In the message, I take 'royal Vikki's finder' to be John Hanning Speke who discovered Lake Victoria in 1858 whilst searching for the source of the Nile. Also consider the subject heading in the email 'Speak for us'.

Speke has a memorial in his name, not in Hyde Park, but next door in Kensington Palace Gardens. It is a very simple stone, red granite actually, and it's most prominent feature is the name

SPEKE in block capitals. The central letter of which is 'E' this being represented in NATO phonetic as ECHO. So there we have our 'central resonance'. Now it becomes even more twisted; bear with me.

Drake at Plymouth is obviously Sir Francis waiting for the Spanish Armada but, if he were to be against the House of Lancaster, he would be for the House of York but the Wars of the Roses finished ninety nine years prior to this battle so what is ML on about. In the email he says 'House of Lancs' not 'Lancaster'. Lancs is the abbreviation for the county of Lancashire also used to denote its cricket team and a 'Yorker' is a style of bowling. You with me still?'

'Yes, Sir' said Goodchild 'but it's a bit of a stretch and I don't see where this is going.'

'OK. Moving on. Who are the untrusted Scottish'? It's the Campbell's because of their treachery when they killed the clan McDonald at the Glencoe massacre in 1692. I find the word 'toiler' a bit odd but one of the many synonyms that springs to mind is labour. So Campbell plus labour equals?'

'Alistair' said Tucker and Goodchild in unison.

'And what did Alistair Campbell do for Tony Blair? He was his Director of Communications otherwise known as a spin doctor and spin brings us back to the cricket and the bowling.'

DCS Clarkson looked at the other two men with his eyebrows raised as if to say 'isn't it obvious?'

Tucker felt in need of another drink but did not want to interrupt the exposition so he waited for the policeman to continue which, warming to his subject, he did.

'What binds a slave? Don't try and be too clever here. The most obvious answer is often the correct one. Chains, gentleman, chains. Which brings us back to cricket'

Clarkson noticed the looks of utter incomprehension on the faces of the other two and realised that he would have to explain something which was, to him, mere general knowledge. 'A chain is an old imperial measure which equates to twenty two yards and half again given us thirty three yards or ninety nine feet. The length of a cricket pitch just happens to be twenty two yards. To conclude; if we measure ninety nine feet from the first letter 'E' in SPEKE's memorial in a westerly direction we dig and find whatever ML wants us to find. Does that make sense gentlemen?'

Tucker replied for both of them 'I understand you interpretation of the email but I feel that I'm missing something here. What is it that is making you drop everything to deal with this message? I don't suppose that Serious Crimes seconds SO15 personnel for the fun of it. What haven't you told me Detective Chief Superintendent?'

'I've not withheld anything that you need to know for your journalistic activities, Mr. Tucker. Right now I am.....'

At that moment Clarkson's mobile must have vibrated in his right trouser pocket as he took it our, stared briefly at the screen then pressed reply and said 'Clarkson. Go ahead John. Dimensions? Depth? No definition at all? The dogs react in any way? OK. I have no choice I am initiating option A. Goodchild is on his way to hold the fort until I can get there. For now we treat this as a UXB. Good question. Call it a fifty yard radius until I or Goodchild say otherwise. Thank you John. With you as soon as I can.'

Clarkson turned to Goodchild and said 'I sent a small team to the gardens with a theodolite, GPR and sniffer dogs. They have located a box measuring about ten inches by five and buried roughly six inches down. The dogs are trained to react to explosives or decaying flesh but neither is indicated at present. This does not mean that they are not. I've a UXB team on standby as well as enough uniforms to secure a perimeter around the object. I am going to close the area down now and want you there to liaise with my office until I can get over. This file contains the details of what you are going to do. Get moving.' Clarkson handed over a manila folder to Goodchild and stood to leave when Tucker interrupted him.

'Is it OK if I go along with Mark, Detective Chief Superintendent?'

Clarkson stopped and looked down at Tucker. If he said no to his request, God knows what might happen. Tucker knew the location of the site and could have photographers and airborne film crews over it before his men were all in place. Tucker knew that he was aware of this, hence the politeness of the request. There was no way that closing down a royal park and a main road which connected central London to Heathrow airport could be kept hidden so news management would become important. Tucker might actually prove useful to him – if Goodchild could keep him under control.

'Well, I did say that you had some brownie points to cash in Mr Tucker so, yes, you may tag along with Detective Superintendent Goodchild. Do not leave his side and please do me the courtesy of letting me know what will appear in your paper tomorrow. I'm allergic to surprises.' With that Clarkson left the pub at a much quicker pace than he had entered it. Obviously he had quite a lot to do as a result of initial outcome of the police search. Tucker smiled at his friend and said 'What now?'

'A double espresso quick whilst I read this stuff then we hijack a car and driver from Serious Crimes and go to play in the park.'

Goodchild read the file in the time that it took Tucker to return with two coffees. He concentrated on Option A and only skimmed the other three scenarios. The operation that Clarkson had put into play was impressive and comprehensive. It was the equal of what SO15 would do to apprehend a subject and bore the hallmarks of something that had been pre-planned. How the hell had this been done in just under one hour?

'Let's go Roger' said Goodchild. 'Wait until we are in the car until you start with your questions.'

'OK for now. But there is still something that you guys are holding back, Mark. Clarkson was saved by the buzz and he didn't convince me with the old 'anything you need to know for your journalistic activities' bollocks.

Goodchild simply said 'Fine' and headed for the door leaving Tucker to catch up.

Chapter Three

London 2010

ML was sitting down to lunch at one of his favourite restaurants in the capital. The Bayswater area was home to many Chinese restaurants which were, to a certain extent, traditional Cantonese in style with air dried ducks hanging in the window. ML had heard rumours of Hong Kong triad involvement in some of the establishments and there had been a spate of unexplained fires in the area about ten years ago. Things were quiet these days so he supposed that the correct amount of 'squeeze' was being paid.

He was lunching with his lawyer today in one of the more upmarket restaurants, the Mandarin Kitchen, situated at the park end of Queensway. As a rule of thumb, the more westernised an ethnic eating place was, the poorer the standard of cuisine. That was most definitely not the case here. The quality of the food was matched by the comfort of the surroundings and the level of service. He could have found more authentic local fare in Chinatown but he did not find gratuitously rude waiters amusing. On his one visit to that area as part of a larger group, he had quietly observed the waiters as they literally threw plates of food onto tables. Little by little the staff had noticed him and sensed his disapproval. Just by looking at their eyes and mentally projecting his complete contempt for them as individuals and a race, he had stopped their antics. He knew that they would have their revenge on him in the kitchen and that he would be lucky if they only spat in his food. So he pretended to take a call on his mobile, excused himself to his table companions pleading a business emergency and left the building, never to return. He pretended not to understand the vulgarities which the staff were saying about him even though all their jaws would have dropped had he revealed to what depths of the gutter his Cantonese could descend. No; why make oneself more memorable than necessary to score points against menials?

His lawyer was always good company. An enigma to just about all who met him (very few could say they knew him), he came across as a blend of Rumpole of the Bailey and Peter Ustinov. A superb raconteur, multi-lingual, well travelled and an avowed epicurean, at sixty five years of age Arthur Blenheim had few peers in international commercial law. As such, he advised ML on how to expand his once small U.K. based publishing company into a multi-national operation which generated a very healthy income indeed. Blenheim's real gift had been to create a corporate structure whereby profits were nearly all banked off-shore and ML was invisible to his senior management. This state of affairs had come about when ML had decided to put his business trust in Blenheim and make him his company secretary and Chief Financial Officer. The two men had agreed a remuneration package and long term business plan that had been equitable and today would see the beginning of its end.

Arthur Blenheim was a large man, just over six feet tall but with the belly of a real trencherman. He was dressed for business today which meant a navy pin stripe over a pink and white striped shirt. He wore a blue tie which bore the strange device of a sword crossed by a quill pen. To those in the know this was the emblem of the Metropolitan Police Fraud Squad and Blenheim did not have the right to wear it. He had, in fact, stolen it from its drunken owner whilst attending a conference on international money laundering at Norwich University. It amused him to wear it now and then especially when some sharp eyed constable saluted him in public and called him Sir. He in turn would touch the brim of his own hat, nod at the lad and carry on his way. To complete his ensemble he wore a monocle which was attached to a length of pink ribbon. This was more normally used to bind together official files, both judicial and governmental, and was the origin of the phrase 'red tape'.

Discretely stifling a belch Arthur Blenheim turned to his host and said 'One of the great mysteries of life is how a nation of a billion souls with thousands of years of history behind it can produce such bloody wonderful food and yet nothing, <u>nothing</u>! a man can drink. I feel that there is something lacking when I have eaten well and can't finish off with a decent bottle of port. Not civilised!'

'At least you won't miss your Cohiba so much.' said ML and instantly regretted it, Blenheim's pink scrubbed face was darkening and his eyes had begun to bulge. 'Sorry, Arthur. Please. I really don't need another lecture on Tony fucking Blair and the health Nazis. Let's have another bottle of Moët.' ML placed the now empty champagne bottle upside down in the ice bucket and signalled for another.

'Would you care to finish off with a soup course, Arthur?' he asked.

'No thank you – the fizz will be sufficient liquid for the present. Now, excellent lunch as ever. What did you wish to see me about. I've cleared my decks for the rest of the day as I think you have something out of the ordinary in mind. Correct?'

'Yes. I want out of the business, Arthur. How much am I worth?'

'I wish you had told me that on the phone and I could have been ready with a more precise answer than I can give you right now.'

'The company's secretary does not know what the company's worth? I find that a bit odd, Arthur.'

'No odder than the company chairman and sole owner not knowing what it's worth, I would say.'

'Touché. Carry on.'

'Physically you don't own very much on the business side. You have always insisted on renting premises both here and overseas. In the current economic climate that is a good thing if you are looking to liquidate – I would not care to be looking for purchasers of office space at the moment; it's a buyers market and will remain

so for the foreseeable future. Anyone who has to sell quickly will
be raped. What you own are your magazine titles and, in a way,
the senior managers who have contracts with the company. The
sales staff are self employed and will follow the money. I take it
that you want to off-load the lot?'

'Correct.'

'Timescale.'

'ASAP.'

'What we have to show to a potential buyer are the financial
track records of all the titles which you still own. We don't have to
mention the failures which went to the wall. We then have to show
future earnings projection and explain the company's structure i.e.
how the overseas managers run their show and what contractual
obligations we have with third parties – printers and distributors
mainly. So it's impossible to say what it's worth. Basic economics;
something is worth what someone is willing to pay for it. Ideally
you would want one publisher who took the whole portfolio off
your hands and paid a fair price for assuming all that. If such a person
were interested I would put a minimum price of £400m on the
deal. You would make more selling it off by geographical area but
the deal would be more complex and thus take more time. Your call.'

'I want to sell it all and I don't care who buys it. The key to
the deal are the Chinese and the Indians. At heart they are the
descendents of coolies and bazaar wallahs. The idea of supplanting
the former colonial master makes their tiny dicks hard. You could, of
course, try to sell it all to a European or American buyer who wants
a presence in the pan-Asian market place. It's a different sales pitch
depending on whom you're talking to. Are you up to it, Arthur?'

'I've never sold anything in my life. I don't think that now is
the time to start!'

'Bollocks, Arthur. Most of life is a sell. The interview board at
university, seducing the pretty girl, promotion in the armed forces –
each one of us is a product of the market place of life. The exterior

we show to that world is our shop window and conversations are sales pitches in disguise. You know the company at least as well as I do. There is only one question which you will not be able to answer; why, if it's so bloody marvellous, is it being sold?'

'Well, I was going to ask you that in good time but, as you've raised the question, why are you anxious to sell? You're a relatively young man, this economy will turn around again. What is the rush?'

'Boredom, Arthur. I've always said that making money is easy and I've proved myself right. I don't manufacture anything, I've not invented something which improves mankind's lot; I simply provide a platform for the people who do so to advertise themselves to their potential customers.

Along the way I employ hundreds of wage slaves and the thousands of manual workers who supply the raw materials to support my vision. With a bit of money and a bit of my brain added to your organisational skills, I'm now worth around £400m. If I were to continue I would be a dollar billionaire in five years; and so what? It's fucking boring Arthur. The Chinese have a very good saying; 'How many chickens can a man eat at once?' I don't need the biggest yacht or the best private jet. At the end of the day, the richest individual in the world will not be able to rival the modern heads of state, be they hereditary monarchs in oil rich nations or the democratically elected heads of government who have access to private 747's. No businessman can approach that level of power so why try to keep accumulating more and more cash when you will always be a financial also ran? I want to travel incognito for a while. You have kept my name out of the public arena for all these years and, to me, that is as valuable as the way in which you have helped the company grow. I'm not Howard Hughes but I'm even more not Richard Branson. You will have to find a reason for the company's sale – the one that springs to mind is that I am in declining health but I assume that would have a negative effect on the selling price?'

'Indeed. We must sell from a position of strength which will not be easy in today's economy.

'Sell tomorrow's, Arthur.'

'Yes. I have some ideas. Bear with me.' Blenheim signalled for a waiter and ordered a bottle of Hennessy five star V.S.O.P cognac. It duly arrived along with two Waterford crystal balloons. He dismissed the waiter and poured a good measure for himself and placed the bottle close to ML, who poured his own but did not touch it.

The lawyer balanced the glass somewhere between belly and breastbone. His small hands warmed the crystal whilst his inclined nose inhaled the alcoholic vapours. He looked like your favourite grandfather who had dozed off after a heavy Christmas lunch but Blenheim was concentrating his mind on information received and how best to carry out the mission. He called the practice olfactory zen.

'Right. I see several ways forward but I cannot do this myself. My own company needs my presence and your business would require my 100% attention. The two are mutually exclusive. Sorry. I trust that you have a PA or something who can carry out the sale for you. I shall, of course, help as much as I can.'

ML focused on Blenheim and spoke in a voice of certitude and seriousness. 'There is no-one else, Arthur. Only we know the company's secrets and I do not have the time to involve myself in its selling. I cannot buy you. You are like me in that, whilst enjoying life's sensual pleasure, you are not a slave to them. Excess is for lottery winners. But I have an offer for you. Sell your company to your partners on Monday − we both know they want it. Devote yourself 24/7 to solving my problem. I will pay you £500k in advance plus 5% of eventual sale price, sum to be deposited in any bank you care to name. Happy retirement, Arthur.'

'I don't wish to retire. I love practising law, I live as well as I please in London and, as you said, you cannot buy me. Again. Sorry.'

'If you earn £20m from the deal and I told you where Carmen lived these days, would that change your mind?'

'How the hell do you know about....where is she....what?' For once Arthur Blenheim was surprised. ML raised a hand and said to him 'Easy Arthur, easy. Before I made you my right hand businessman I had a very extensive vetting done on you. The Carmen affair was tragic and I believe that you were mostly blameless. Her husband manufactured a lot of lies about your goodself and she was put in a position where she had to think that they were true. Her heart was broken as well, Arthur. All I can say at the moment is that she lives alone with her two children. She gets by financially and hubby is no longer on the scene. You could make it all right, even now.'

Blenheim was stunned. Very few people knew of the married girl to whom he had lost his heart some ten years ago. He had been prepared to take her and her children away from the white-trash shit hole in which they existed and give them everything. When she had vanished he had been at a total loss. To have found love so late in life only to have it disappear had damn near killed him. He had received just one message from her, delivered by a trusted friend. There had been no way of replying and he did not have the resources to find her. Not a day passed without him thinking of Carmen and, as years passed, he came to think that the best gift that he could give her was to not try and find her. But if she and the children were just 'getting by' financially and he could engineer a meeting between them, who knows what might happen. At worst he could provide an education and security for the children. He would take the risk of rejection. The scars on his heart had healed and he reckoned that his liver could take another beating or two.

'You're a bastard. Of course I'll do it. I'm going back to my office now to start the ball rolling to sell my company. I'll put out feelers to sell your business within the week and be in touch as and when. You'll tell me about Carmen...?'

'When I have a buyer, Arthur. So chop chop as they say in China.'

'Indeed. Enjoy the fizz' Blenheim rose slowly and left the Mandarin Kitchen without a backward look. On the one hand he was exhilarated at the thought of seeing Carmen again; on the other hand he hated the fact that he was being used by a richer, more powerful man. One with whom he had felt, not friendship, but certainly affinity. Fuck it he thought. Life goes on.

ML poured his Hennessy into the ice bucket and filled the balloon with Moët. Today should see the start of the middle game, if the journalist and his police contacts had reacted as he thought they would. It was a little too early for any major activity to take place and when it did the traffic flow outside the restaurant would be so interrupted that he could not fail to notice even from his screened booth at the rear of the dining room (only a fool would sit next to a plate glass window in central London these days).

ML reflected what he had achieved over the past five years and how he had refined his technique. Haste was to be avoided at all costs and he had been prepared to call off a hunt if conditions were not as close to perfect as he could make them. No predator in nature made a kill on every attempt.

Identifying the target was relatively easy. The same type of girl at the same gig week after week, gazing at the singer with open adoration but lacking the confidence to try and talk with him. She would either be alone or on the fringes of a group but not a member of it. Once initial selection had been made, he then had to find out as much about her as he could whilst remaining invisible himself. He had been tempted to steal a purse on two occasions but there was always the risk of being observed by either someone else at the venue or the ubiquitous CCTV. A lot of these cameras did not even function but it was not a risk worth taking. Patience, always patience. As the evening wore on, drinks loosened tongues and the innocent gave away personal details to whoever they found themselves next to. The best time for this was during breaks between sets. ML did not seek to elicit this information personally but rather positioned himself where he could employ the spy's classic technique of eavesdropping. Once he had a name and address, he could set about building a profile of his target and learn about their routines. He tried to stay out of the town he was going to operate in as far as was possible but when he had to be there he wore what his called his grey man disguise. This he found to be very difficult indeed. Wearing a nondescript suit, shirt and tie, clear lensed glasses and greying his hair was easy. Scuffed shoes and a well used briefcase were adequate accessories. The key to a disguise is in one's comportment and general body language. You had to live the part in order to look it. In ML's mind his role was that of a mid-level clerk in an insurance company who would rise no further. His wife treated him with contempt and they were childless. A mortgage weighed on him so much that his shoulders, rounded from days at the desk, slumped in weariness. He was a loser.

This was so far removed from ML's true personality that he found it a real strain to carry out surveillance and be the grey man as well. He had tried to invent another persona but nothing he could come up with could match this character's level of invisibility. So he carried on.

Once he had found out his target's favourite song (and they all had a favourite) he was ready. Now was when the risks came into play. Would the girl stop and talk with the singer? Probably yes. That was why her favourite song was chosen. Would the loner then enter a vehicle with someone she had only just met? Again, probably yes if he pressed the correct linguistic buttons and she came to believe that everything was her idea and that she was in control of the situation. Once in the passenger seat she was dead but he still had to transport the body across country to fulfil his requirements and dispose of most of it. He was, himself, an accomplished driver with well maintained and properly serviced vehicles but there was no accounting for some of the incompetent cretins using the road system. Foreign lorry drivers who had fiddled their tachograph and were falling asleep at the wheel, boy racers, old age pensioners who had not had an eye test since they had been given their first set of NHS glasses and, of course, your everyday drunken druggie. Any one of these could hit him no matter how careful and observant he was and that would probably be game over. He was armed but had little doubt that in this age of mobile phones, motorway cameras and police helicopters, his chances of killing two or more police officers and evading capture would be minimal.

But, if all risk was eliminated, the project would not be much of a challenge. He had, in his view, done all that he could to remove all physical evidence of what he had been doing but there were still some areas where he had not been able to find out the police's technical capabilities. He was damn sure that their cameras and those of town councils recorded and stored a lot more data than they admitted to. Images of him and his vehicles must be available somewhere. What else had he left to chance?

The restaurant was now nearly full so he settled the bill in cash and went outside to see what, if anything, the boys in blue were up to. Traffic was still using Bayswater Road. He was sure that would have been closed off by now. Roger Tucker's column was out today so surely the first thing that he would do would be to check his emails. The test of his own missive to the journalist was not that difficult to work out; what the fuck were they doing? Carrying out a risk assessment?

Then he noticed the appearance of police officers in their high visibility jackets, which, in his opinion, made them look more like construction workers than the forces of law and order. They were stopping people from entering the park at Inverness Terrace and Black Lion Gates. Looking further along the road he could see more of the bright jacketed police controlling the other entrances on this side of the park and now the traffic was thinning out. It looked as though vehicles were being diverted northwards near the entrance to Lancaster Gate tube station. Now a flat bed lorry carrying crowd control barriers was unloading at the streets which led on to Bayswater Road and two coach loads of constables were being disembarked to man them. Time to go. It is a well known fact that the perpetrators of major crimes of a spectacular nature such as arson, bombings and murder felt a need to view their handiwork or its aftermath and investigation. The police would be systematically filming and photographing the rubberneckers in the hope of identifying a face. They would also check the names of people who were booked into the several hotels which offered a view of the park so, as much as he would have liked to observe the operation, it was advisable to grab a taxi and head for the sanctuary of his home in Clerkenwell.

Chapter Four

Tucker and DS Goodchild had entered the park from its south side using the Palace Gate entrance. They were seated in the rear of an unmarked BMW which made no pretence of being anything other than what it was by virtually continuous use of the flashing lights and sirens. The journey from New Scotland Yard to the park had, literally, flashed by for Tucker though his companion had spent the entire journey on his personal radio speaking in code to God knows who. Although his voice had remained calm whilst on air, it was obvious that Goodchild was becoming frustrated after each call. The journalist had never before heard a DS from the Met refer to fellow police officers as 'fucking useless plods!' It promised to be an interesting day.

The vehicle stopped just past the Round Pond and Goodchild ordered the driver to walk over to the centre of police activity and to inform those present that he was on the scene and would be with them in a moment. He then addressed Tucker. 'Sooner or later, someone is going to recognise you, Roger. I would prefer later. There is an almighty shit storm brewing and explaining the presence of a journo is not going to improve the climate. If I have to introduce you it will be by last name only and I am not going to say who you work for. You do not ask questions and you certainly don't take notes. Last thing; turn your mobile off. Can you live with that?'

'Your driver is now telling your lot that Goodchild of SO15 is here with a nameless civilian. If we play it your way they will think I'm Security Service or something similar. I'm not comfortable with that, Mark.'

'If you want comfort you can fuck off to the Black Lion pub and talk with the red top hacks. Look I'm trying to help here. I'm not asking you to pretend to be one of the funnies. We can't help other people's assumptions can we? You're ahead of the game right now, Roger; don't blow it, eh?'

'OK. But my involvement will be out in the open by tomorrow at the latest. I'll need some photos to go with my story. Can I count on you for that?'

'Yes. I'll tell Press Office to give you an inside track. As Clarkson said, you do have some brownie points. Come on.'

The two men left the car and the scale of the police operation became apparent. From Kensington Palace to the Serpentine water all civilians had been moved away by lines of police officers. No one was being allowed into the park from any perimeter and a police helicopter was patrolling overhead. About 100 yards away from the Round Pond an area 60 feet square had been screened off by light blue plastic sheeting. This was the focal point of activity with at least twelve officers standing around conferring but obviously waiting for something. Goodchild and Tucker set off towards them.

'The first thing that I'm going to have to do' said the policemen 'is to smooth the feathers of the parks police officers. You know about them?'

'Sort of. There is a separate police force for all the royal parks in London. There can't be too many of them.

'No but this is their turf, if you'll pardon the pun, and having this lot descend on them has not happened since the IRA were blowing up guardsmen in 1982.'

'Weren't they consulted?'

'Sort of. We told them that we were coming, what we intended to do and looked forward to co-operating with them. These days SO15 does not so much consult as dictate. Gets the job done.'

As the two men neared the blue tented area, conversations stopped and heads turned their way. A uniformed sergeant intercepted them and spoke to the police officer whom he had obviously recognised. 'DS Goodchild. Good to see you, sir. I'm Mike White. I've been the contact between the Yard and what's going on here. We can't do anything more without your say-so, sir.'

'Thanks, sergeant. Have you spoken with DCS Clarkson yet?'

'No, sir. He's in conference but will call when he heads our way.'

'OK which of this crowd is Park's Police?'

'Their senior officer is in their station which is a couple of hundred yards behind those trees. They've left a PC with us to 'observe and liaise' as necessary.'

'Are they being helpful, sergeant?'

'Well, they are not getting in the way and are walking a loose interior perimeter chatting with our lads. They obviously know the lie of the land and are pointing out potential areas of weakness. They have just asked if we want more bodies bringing in from the other royal parks. I've said that that is your call, sir.'

'No. We can always get warm bodies but I'm not going to strip royal parks of their specialised force. Pass that onto their boss now would you, sergeant.'

Whilst Sergeant White spoke to the constable from the Parks Police, Goodchild ran through a mental check-list of what he had been instructed to do. Clear the area of civilians; establish a secure perimeter; establish contact with Parks Police; proceed with caution; return the park and traffic to normal as soon as possible. His radio communications on the way over indicated that the first two instructions had been carried out but it was always best to be sure. Even the journalist had to be wondering about the speed at which this mobilization had been put into place and asked the question as to why the main man on site was a DS from SO15. Was he being set up as a fall guy if something were to go wrong?

Sergeant White returned and said 'I've had your message passed to Parks, sir.'

'OK. What is the state of play now, sergeant?'

'The Gardens and Hyde Park as far as Serpentine have been cleared of civilians. We have established an exterior perimeter along the Bayswater Road from Orme Square Gate to Lancaster Gate. Manned crowd control barriers have been placed on the north side of Bayswater Road which is closed to traffic between those two points until further notice. On the south side we have officers on all gates between Palace and the Albert to prevent unauthorised access. Traffic along Kensington and Knightsbridge has not been diverted. There is a reserve force of fifty officers at the Hyde Park police station to deal with any unforeseen intrusions. Something has been located buried at a predetermined spot – I don't know how – by the team from Technical Support. I think you need to talk with them now, sir.'

'Good job, sergeant. Would you care to make the introductions please?

All three men walked the short distance to where the Technical Support Unit stood. There were four men and two women all dressed from head to toe in white, one piece suits of a plasticised material. The senior officer turned out to be a civilian whom Sergeant White introduced as Doctor Rachel Watkins. No one shook hands.

'What can you tell me about the scene so far doctor?' asked Goodchild.

Rachel Watkins was short – no more than five feet three – and had to physically look up to speak with most police officers. She wore no make-up and it was impossible to even guess what her body shape was underneath the coveralls. She still had the integral hood up over her head so even her hair colour was an unknown. What she could not hide were a pair of blue-grey eyes that missed nothing and sparked with intelligence. Her face was pleasant but serious and when she spoke there was the trace of a north western accent which had probably been modulated by her years at academy. She also seemed to be fairly annoyed at something and was trying hard to hide the fact.

'What I can tell you is this, Detective Superintendent. This morning my boss <u>ordered</u> me to stop whatever I was doing, organise a team to meet precisely ninety nine feet due west of the letter 'E' in Speke's name on the eponymous memorial where, I was told, something <u>may</u> be buried. I was to 'secure' the area and carry out a preliminary survey for indications of biological or chemical trace. I was told that uniformed units were already in place to mark out a <u>rough area</u> in which we were to work.

Do you know what the first actions of the uniforms were, Detective Superintendent? They started at the monument, guessed which was west and paced out ninety nine feet in their size thirteen's. They spaced out to form a guard around their chosen spot. They might as well have held hands and started a line dance for all they have done to the area.

My team proceeded in a somewhat different manner; using compass and theodolite we calculated the precise location that Scotland Yard had indicated. Using that as a central point, we then conducted a twelve feet square search using GPR.'

'Sorry, doctor. GPR? asked Goodchild

'Ground Penetrating Radar. As used by archaeologists and police forces in the entire civilised world. At the very centre of the grid we can see this.' She handed a multi-coloured print out to Goodchild. On the left side and along the bottom of the page were gradations as in a graph. The majority of the page was black but in the centre, clearly outlined was an oblong shape in blue.

'After GPR found this I used a new bit of kit to make this image. This comes from a thermal imaging unit and tells me that, whatever the box is, its cold – below zero centigrade.

I know of no explosives that operate at that temperature and I can see no wires or attachments to the box so it is unlikely to be UXB.'

Seeing Goodchild raise his eyebrows in non-verbal questioning she clarified 'Unexploded Bomb. I then inserted a methane probe to test for decomposing biologicals. The result is negative. Finally, I sent in the sniffer dogs. Again, negative for human remains or explosives. There is only one further thing I can tell you; this object was buried no more than forty eight hours ago and probably a lot less than that. It was covered by a strip of turf that is slightly different to the park's grass. You can still make out the cut edge of it and it has not yet begun to knit with its surroundings. I could lift it out quite easily.'

'Would that be safe? asked an obviously surprised Goodchild.

'No, it would not.' replied the doctor. 'Our equipment cannot show what is underneath the box. It could be a pressure plate or an anti-personnel mine ready to spring up and explode at a height of about three feet – roughly where a man's testicles hang.' She smiled in a way that conveyed sweetness and sadism simultaneously.

'What course of action do you recommend, doctor?'

'Oh, that's an easy one. We wait until this box warms up a bit then have another look at it and send the dogs in for further sniffing. Twenty four hours should do it.' The smile again.

'Thanks very much for your input so far, doctor. Don't go away. Mr Tucker; a moment please.'

Goodchild and the journalist went back towards their car which had been joined by a large articulated lorry which bore on its sides the words 'Metropolitan Police Mobile Command post'. They climbed the rear steps and Goodchild asked to be put through to DCS Clarkson, who came online almost immediately.

'What do you have for me, Detective Superintendent?'

'The area is cleared and secured. Nothing to add to what you already knew about the package except that it is below zero degrees centigrade in temperature. Doctor Watkins does not repeat does not think that this is an explosive device but her kit cannot see what is underneath the package and would like to wait for twenty four hours to have a look at it again. That is where we are now, sir.'

'If I keep that area closed down until tomorrow, at God knows what cost, and it turns out to be a hoax we are going to look bloody stupid. It will also give various nutters ideas of how to inconvenience Londoners with very little risk to themselves. Any ideas Mark?' It was a sign of the pressure which the senior officer was operating that he had addressed Goodchild by his first name rather than his rank.

'OK. We need to open this thing up soonest but we can't ask a man to do it. If the package is armed with a C4/SEMTEX derivative then there would be nothing left of anyone on top of it even if they were wearing full protective suiting. I need a wheelbarrow.'

'That's what I thought you would say. One's been prepped and is on its way. Should be with you anytime now – hang on – what's the best entrance for the Bomb Squad to enter by? They are nearly at Harrods.'

'Palace Gate, sir.'

'Wait one; Palace Gate.' Clarkson was obviously conducting several conversations at once. 'They are nearly with you. Good job so far, Detective Superintendent. I'm leaving to join you now. Would you help the wheelbarrow team to set up wherever they want to?'

'Yes, sir. I'm heading out now. See you soon.' Goodchild cut the communication and left the command centre, collecting Tucker on the way.

'I know you're just a tad busy at the moment mate, but I've been quiet so far; one quick question please?' asked Tucker.

'Go on then.' said Goodchild as his eyes focused on the far side of the park where Palace gate was situated.

'What the hell is a wheelbarrow? It sounds odd.'

Goodchild smiled for the first time in hours. 'Codenames can be very misleading. When you see it you'll recognise it. And here they come. A convoy of two police cars sandwiching two Transit vans with Metropolitan Police Bomb Squad marked on the sides had entered the park and was heading towards the tented area. Goodchild waved them down and went to talk with them having first instructed Tucker not to move from where he was. After a quick conversation with a Bomb Squad officer he rejoined the journalist.

The two transits left their escorts and drove across the grass to where the centre of activity lay. Once again leaving Tucker alone, Goodchild spoke at some length with Dr Watkins who then disappeared into one of the vans. Ten minutes later she came out accompanied by a man who was dressed in navy blue fatigues which bore no insignia. The two of them, plus Goodchild, then went behind the tarpaulin which rendered them invisible for five minutes after which time they reappeared. Doctor Watkins went to her team, spoke quickly to them with much use of her hands to emphasise her words and they followed her en masse to head towards the command centre.

Goodchild had, at the same time, been issuing instructions on his radio and all police officers in the vicinity of the site began to disperse.

In a short space of time, the only people left at the site were Bomb Disposal, Doctor Watkins, Goodchild and Tucker. The journalist was thinking that he was obviously not only in a position of privilege but also one of peril. If he had been carrying a hip flask, now would have been a good time to have taken a belt from it.

Something was happening at the rear of one of the Transits to divert his mind from objects that explode in public places. The double doors were opened and locked in place; a shallow inclined ramp was attached to the back of the van. From within the van a twin-tracked vehicle began to emerge. It was roughly three feet long and its superstructure was a central column about four feet high from which a variety of rods and different shaped attachments protruded. As the robot cleared the ramp, part of the central column telescoped then bent forward at an angle; at the head of this a camera lens was visible. Curiously, the remote controlled vehicle was a matt silver in colour not police blue or a military camouflage shade. This, Tucker realised, was the wheelbarrow and he had indeed seen it before – in Northern Ireland during the 1970's. There it had been used against suspected car bombs. It sometimes blew the lock off a car door or took out a side window with a single barrelled shotgun blast. This sometimes resulted in setting the bomb off and the destruction of the robot – which was preferable to losing a very brave, if certifiably insane, bomb disposal expert. Later models had been capable of cutting the outer casing of explosive devices then inserting a tube down which water was injected at very high pressure. This often rendered the bomb useless but, as it had not exploded, forensic experts would learn a lot about which IRA thug had created it. This was meant to create a forensically provable case in the future criminal prosecution of the terrorist. Those who believed that story also attached stockings to their bedposts on December 24th.

The robot came to a stop and so it seemed did time as well. Tucker noticed the absence of the high visibility jackets of the police – where had they gone? On the south side of the park they had likewise disappeared from the multiple entrances and he could no longer discern any traffic movement from that direction. For a second it seemed that all was silent but then his senses retuned themselves to the new reality. There was the odd chirp of a bird; in the stillness of the moment a grey squirrel would dart along the ground then up a tree. A great city is never completely quiet and, if he concentrated, Tucker could hear the background whisper of distant, unseen traffic interspersed with the occasional blare of a horn. The helicopter was still on station but at a much higher altitude so that its rotors only occasionally broke the spell.

Goodchild appeared at Tucker's side and said 'Time we weren't here Roger. Come on.' and they set off towards the Mobile Command Centre. 'Clarkson has arrived and taken over thank

Christ. He has had to make a huge judgement call. I personally do not think that this is a classic terrorist incident and it's the content of the email to you that pushes me in that direction. Doctor Watkins team have gone as far as they can in ascertaining that this is probably not a bomb and other sources tell me that there is no radioactive material on site.'

'What sources, Mark?'

'No comment at this time and probably ever on that. There is one last area of risk that we have to consider; biological or a chemical agent. If a big enough one of those went off here we would be in serious shit. There is no prevailing wind today; what breeze there is keeps shifting direction so Clarkson has ordered a half mile radius evacuation of this area of London. There are officers in HAZMAT suits around the park now – you can't see them from here. The sight of those is enough to scare anyone. We are sending the machine in ten minutes from now. Want to stay around?'

Tucker was stunned. All this as a result of an email which had been sent to him last night? Once again he felt that he was not being kept as fully in the loop as Clarkson had promised but events had overtaken any claim he might have had to this story. So it made sense to reply 'Yes, sure. Where is the short-arsed doctor with the attitude by the way?'

'She's at the site with the bomb disposal nutter trying to find a HAZMAT suit that fits. I suppose they come in children's sizes.'

The two men entered the Command Centre to find Clarkson waiting for them. The doors to the lorry closed with a dull thud like that of a commercial airliner. The windows were thick, iodized material and the internal lighting was subdued so that various screens and monitors stood out in contrast. Clarkson rose from a centrally positioned swivel armchair and said 'I'd like you to continue as tactical commander Detective Superintendent. You have seen the site up close and know the people who are going to operate the machinery. I'm here if needs be. Any questions?'

'Has evacuation been completed, sir?'

'Yes. We've put plan Longbow into operation and reinforced it with a door to door check. Mobiles with loudspeakers have done their rounds. If anyone is still in the target area then that is their choice.'

'Who do I talk to on site, sir?'

'You are patched into both Doctor Watkins and the bomb squad commander. Call him John. He is in charge at the site.'

'Very good, sir. Let's get on with it then.' Goodchild took Clarkson's place and donned a microphone headset. In front of him were a bank of screens showing differently angled views of the tented area in front of the bomb squad vans. One camera was obviously fixed to the front of the robot. Goodchild keyed a switch and spoke 'John, this is Command Two; how are you receiving me? Over.'

'Command Two; this is John; receiving you five by five. Over.'

'John, you are clear to proceed with phase one; over.'

'Roger that Command Two. Going to phase one now.'

On the screens the team in the Command Centre could see the robot edge towards the blue tent. On all cameras except that of a rear view one it became obscured from view. The voice of Rachel Watkins talking to John came over the speaker system and into Goodchild's earphones.

'Stop there. Raise the arm. Stop. Zoom in slowly. Stop. You see the two thin red posts in the ground?'

'Yes.' came John's voice.

'If you imagine a line between them that is where the narrow end of the turf strip begins.'

On the screen the grass came into sharper focus and everyone could see a faint, straight line in the ground. Nature does not do straight lines. Then the image blurred as the arm was retracted and another tool was attached to it. The on screen image shook a bit as this was carried out and then came back into focus. In front of and beneath the robocam was a straight edged blade above which were two hooked claws. The blade appeared to be about four inches wide with an equal space between the claws. Very slowly, the arm approached the line in the grass. With minute adjustments of the controls it went back and forwards until the operator was satisfied that the blade was perfectly positioned.

John's voice came over the speakers; 'Penetrating in three, two, one now.'

The blade pushed into the soil at an angle of twenty degrees for a distance of four inches then stopped. The two claws then clamped firmly onto the top of the turf.

John's voice again 'I'm starting a slow vertical lift in three, two, one now.'

The robocam was of no use now as its view of the hole being uncovered was blocked by the strip of turf beneath it. The rear-view camera could not see into the hole because its view was obscured by the robot itself. Goodchild wanted to ask John what he was going to do about the situation but did not dare break the man's concentration. He was also a good enough commander to let his specialists get on with their jobs but this was getting tense. John saved him by transmitting.

'Command Two, I've lifted a strip of turf eighteen inches into the air. This should have removed most weight from the buried object. As nothing has gone 'boom' I propose retiring from the scene then going back for a further visual inspection. Over.'

'Roger that John. Carry on.'

In the Command Centre people looked at the screens which all showed the same images from different angles; the robot was reversing out of the tent screened area and moved back towards the bomb squad vehicles. A strip of turf hung down from its central arm and was carefully laid on a white plastic sheet that had been pre-positioned on the ground. Having completed this task, the robot trundled back to the hole and extended its camera arm into the now excavated area. On screen all that the observers could see was black earth. John's voice could be heard but not as clearly as usual. He was obviously talking with Doctor Watkins about the next step.

'Command Two; I was going to use high pressure water to clear this earth away and have a clear look at the object prior to attempting an extraction. You're scientific colleague says that this would contaminate any evidence at the scene and would prefer me to excavate by touch. I can do the latter but it is clumsy and there is always the risk of damage to the object. Awaiting instructions; over.'

Goodchild looked across to Clarkson who said to him 'Let's get on with it, shall we.'

'Roger that, John. Proceed as the doctor says. Over.'

'Roger, Command Two. Am going in now.'

Once again all eyes were fixed on the screens showing the images from the robocam. The spade-claw attachment was still in place and John was using it to push earth to the rear of the hole at a depth of half an inch at a time. The back and forwards motions of the tool appeared jerky to those watching on screen and the level of tension was palpable. All at once the arm stopped moving and the camera zoomed in on one spot that was lighter in colour than the surrounding black. On screen it appeared to be olive green ominously similar to that of an army ammunition box. The arm started to move again and very quickly the entire box was uncovered. Using the same technique that he had when lifting the turf, John took hold of the object and raised it well above ground without informing anyone that he was about to do so. When it did not explode there was a collective sigh of relief.

'Command Two; object is secure. Am giving it to Miss Piggy who will transfer it to base one for further inspection. Out.'

The robot manoeuvred until it could approach the rear of the second of the Transit vans. When in position, its arms disappeared into the confines of the vehicle. When it came out it no longer held the olive green box. This had been secured in a steel container capable of transporting the most dangerous of materials in safety. Once the door to the container had been locked it could not be opened again until it reached base one where the codes were kept. Even the Transit van was not what it seemed. All its tyres were solid rubber and there were four at the rear instead of two. The chassis was reinforced in order to bear the weight of the secure unit and it manoeuvred like a sow in shit, hence the nickname 'Miss Piggy'.

Little by little the area began to assume an air of normality as the police removed the crowd control barriers and themselves from the scene. Traffic started to circulate once more and most police vehicles, including the Mobile Command Centre, left the park.

A rumour began to go around that this had been an un-announced drill in the event of Al-Qaeda planting a 'dirty bomb' in a public space. More astute individuals would have asked why, if that were the case, was the white clad forensics team still at work behind their blue screens with police officers on foot to prevent the public or the media approaching them.

It was three in the afternoon when Roger Tucker sat down with Mark Goodchild in an interview room at New Scotland Yard.

'I'd love to offer you a drink mate – Christ; I'd love one myself but you need to be an Assistant Commissioner to do that sort of thing these days.' said the policeman.

'Let's piss off to the Feathers then before I file my story.' replied the journalist.

'Well, at the moment you don't have much of a story. The only thing you have that the competition don't is the email from ML that kicked all this off. How about hanging back until a bit later when I can give you a real exclusive?'

'What's on offer here Mark?'

'You'll be the only journalist who <u>knows</u> what was in the box.

If you add that to your eye witness account from the Command Centre plus the fact that you were the recipient of the email I reckon it would be trebles all round at the press awards, don't you?'

'You'll let me be present when the box is opened?'

'No can do Roger. The location – I believe you heard the phrase base one – is top secret and if you even allude to its existence your paper will receive a D notice. If you can hold your water for one more hour – they are working on the box as we speak – you'll be well ahead of the pack. Photos exclusive to you. What do you think?'

Tucker thought that using the threat of a D notice was a bit heavy. The D stood for 'Defence' and was the British government's system of media censorship and very rarely used. A D notice committee, under the chairmanship of a former senior military officer, would convene to decide if the release of a news item would endanger the security of the realm and, if so, issue the D notice to all media outlets. It had no legal standing. Only the courts could issue an injunction banning the publication or broadcasting of certain material. However, any newspaper or television channel that went against a D notice advisory would find itself excluded from those informal government briefings upon which the media relied. It was, therefore, very powerful indeed.

The existence of base one – a top secret site for examining God know what – obviously needed to be kept quiet and was not essential to Tucker's story so he said to Goodchild 'OK. I can live with that. I'm going to give my editor a heads up that I'll have a major story for him later today. When can I expect some visual?'

'I can't give you an exact time, Roger. As I said, they're still working on the box. I'll email you with jpeg attachments when I have something. Are you going into your office or do you intend to file from home?'

'Sod the office; on a Friday? No – I was planning on heading home after phoning in. Why do you ask?'

'Well, you did not hear it from me but Clarkson will be calling a press conference for 1700 hours. You might want to talk to the press office and have a front row seat.'

'God I haven't done a Met media circus in years! Who do I talk to Mark?'

'So you want to be there?'

'Too right. Front and centre. I'll blow those liberal fairies from the Guardian into an alternative universe.'

Goodchild laughed aloud. The left wing press, of which the Guardian was the self – appointed standard bearer, detested Tucker's paper in general and Roger Tucker in particular. This had the makings of fine entertainment indeed.

'Consider it done. I'll tell the press office to reserve that seat for you. Where are you going to be until then?'

'The Feathers. They might even have some food left. I'm running on empty right now and it looks like being a long night.'

'Yeah. I'll have someone come and escort you out. Catch you later.'

Mark Goodchild left the room to begin organising the various elements upon which the press conference would depend but first of all he had to get to base one to witness the opening of the box. A lot of different theories regarding the contents were doing the rounds but Goodchild reckoned that this day was going to hold a few more surprises yet.

Chapter Five

In the Feathers Pub Roger Tucker was scarfing down sausage, bacon, baked beans, fried eggs, mushrooms, hash browns and a fried slice side order – the famous all-day English breakfast; otherwise known as heart attack on a plate. He could never eat this meal without smiling at the memory of a bar in Dublin which advertised 'All Day English breakfast – served 9.00 – 11.30am'. Whatever. He knew of no better remedy for someone who had imbibed rather too freely and needed sustenance to carry on functioning.

His telephone conversation with his editor had been interesting. On being put through to Peter Balls he had been told 'Hi Roger – great column today, love you loads yadda – yadda – yadda but I'm up to my arse in alligators right now. It may have escaped your attention but Central London was shut down today and I cannot get a word out of the Met so be a good chap and fuck off to El Vinos would you?'

'Who else are you sending to the press conference Peter?' asked Tucker innocently.

'What fucking press conference?'

'The Met will be holding a press conference at 1700hrs today regarding today's events and I assumed you would be sending someone along.'

'What the fuck do you mean 'who else' am I sending' Roger? Is it just your shitty use of English or do you mean that you yourself are going?'

'I'm invited Peter. Reserved seat at the front and all that. I'm just having a bite to eat before popping over there.'

'Would you please tell me, in the name of all that is sacred to scribblers such as yourself, what the fuck is going on?'

Tucker ran through the day's events with his editor who let him recount the story without any interruption. When he had brought Balls up to speed he said 'Thatta, thatta, that's all folks!'

Comedy was not going to cut it. The editor, whilst not being the sharpest intellectual knife in the box, was possessed of a low cunning which could detect self-serving the way a vulture finds carrion. 'So your first action on receiving this mysterious email was not to let your paper, your employer, know; it was to call on one of your drinking cronies from the Met!'

'Come on, Peter. At that time there no actual story. Why tie up the paper's researchers on what could have been bugger all?'

'But it wasn't bugger all, was it? Because of this weirdo email, the boys in blue closed down Knightsbridge, Bayswater and most of Hyde Park. God knows how many government agencies were involved. Whilst you have been fucking about with the fuzz, proper journalists have been at work trying to find out what colour of alert we were at, whether or not COBRA was in session, which, if any London hospitals were preparing to receive casualties and do you know what we learned? Fuck-all squared! Then I find someone whose wages I pay has an inside track, is on-site and has not contacted me until he has got himself the best seat at the party that I've not even been told about. I feel that you're doing me up the arse and not having the decency to give me a reach-around, Roger!'

'It's not like that, boss. The way events unfolded and the compromises I had to make in order to keep on the inside meant that I could not call you. Anyway, we are still ahead of the rest and if you shift yourself you can get whoever you want up here saying that you know that Clarkson is hosting a conference at 1700hrs. Don't forget I have the promise of an exclusive on the pictures.'

'Right. We'll talk again about company procedures, I've got work to do.'

Balls hung up the phone without further comment. His rudeness was legendary and Tucker was not in the slightest bit put out by the man's tirade. He looked at his watch and saw that he had at least half an hour spare before making the short walk to New Scotland Yard for the press conference. Time for a nice pint of cool Guinness to wash down the fry up.

§

A short distance (as the crow flies) to the north of New Scotland Yard, but up to an hour away by taxi depending on the time of day and state of the traffic, lies the historic area known as Clerkenwell which, in turn, is part of the London Borough of Islington. This was where ML maintained a Georgian town house in a discrete street named Sans Walk. It was here that ML sat watching Sky News waiting for some sort of announcement regarding the day's events in London. He had turned the sound all the way down so that he did not have to endure the strident tones of the channel's resident harpy. ML was content to watch the rolling news strips as he took the occasional sip from a Baccarat balloon of Armagnac. A Fleetwood Mac CD played in the background and he drifted with Stevie Nicks' mellow vocals.

On screen the good old 'Breaking News' caption appeared. Above the text was the face of the ginger telejournalist whose pop-eyed expression could have been of a pregnant woman with breaking waters. The news was that there would be a live press conference with the Metropolitan Police at 1700hrs – one hour from now for those viewers with numeracy issues he assumed.

'Fine' he thought. 'Let's see what spin London's finest put on their discovery.' Once they showed their hand, he could begin to play his. He settled back in his red Chesterfield club chair, drink in one hand and his mind playing along with the music.

§

Roger Tucker had quaffed his pint of Guinness so quickly that he had time to have another. He was just walking across the darkness of the pub to his table with his glass when his eye caught rapid movement from the entrance doors. It was Mark Goodchild heading his way.

'Having a quick one before facing the press are you? What'll it be?'

'Nothing Roger. Sit down. I've got about five minutes here so listen up. The box was empty apart from some sort of plastic freezer blocks, the kind that you put in your cool bag when you're having a picnic. We've closed down a huge area of London and mobilised hundreds of people for nothing. This has cost millions and some people are wiping egg from their faces. The next material to fly around will be shit, closely followed by blood. Sorry, mate. No press awards scoop for you I'm afraid.'

Tucker looked at Goodchild but could not tell if he was lying or not. He took a long pull of his drink, which tasted more bitter than usual, then said 'I'm not at fault here Mark. Are any fingers pointing in the direction of myself or the email from ML?'

'No and nor will they. If the Met admits that they launched this operation because of an anonymous email passed on from a journalist who, in some quarters, is perceived as enjoying highlighting policing errors, we could look total twats.'

'What line are you going to take, Mark?'

'This was an exercise pure and simple. To keep it realistic we did not notify all and sundry, including our political masters, that this was anything other than the real thing. The scenario is that I, acting on information received, notified my boss. He decided that the threat was credible and put certain plans into effect. Only he and I knew that there was no device buried in the park. He just wanted to test the efficiency of our contingency plans.'

'And me and the email; what about it's existence?'

'It doesn't exist Roger – never did. You can go along to the press conference if you wish but you are to observe only. You will not be able to ask a question or talk about a mystery email. I'd drop this if I were you, mate.'

'Jesus Hairy Christ! Who do you lot think you are? I've already spoken to my editor and he'll probably be sending a big gun reporter to the conference. Have you ever tried to put an angry cat back into a bag, <u>mate</u>?'

'Keep your voice down, Roger. We've spoken to Peter Balls and explained certain things to him. Your email never was. If you want to file a story saying that you were in the park and observed the operation at first hand we can live with that. Your editor will run it by us anyway. My advice is to forget that you were ever involved in this. Oh, and by the way; at SO15 we have experience of putting angry cats back into the bag. Best way is to shoot them first.'

Goodchild glanced at his watch but made no move to leave. He needed to know what Tucker would do next. The journalist drained his pint, placed the glass on the table and seemed to focus on it rather than anything else. He raised his face and fixed Goodchild's eyes with his own. 'Fair enough. I've been around the block enough times to know when not to fight. I won't be at the press conference. I'll talk with Balls regarding the coverage of the story but I reckon you're right; I was never there. I've known you a long time, Mark and I know that you're not a time serving shit so I want one thing from you.'

'And that is?'

'An off the record explanation about the elephant in the room?'

'And which elephant might that be, Roger?'

'Metropolitan Police efficiency. Consider this; at around ten in the morning I call you and tell you the contents of an anonymous email. You tell me to get my backside over here because and I quote 'if this is what I think it is' my presence is required. Two hours, two fucking hours Mark, later you have closed down one of the wealthiest areas in the capital! That would be fast moving in a totalitarian state mate but for your bunch to pull it off – well, you can see how an outsider could begin to wonder whether or not the Met, central government, the Security Service or whoever was expecting an incident. So, someday soon, I want us to sit down and kill a bottle of single malt together and you explain what went on today. OK?'

'Keep next Friday free Roger. I'll be in touch.'

Goodchild left the pub without shaking hands – old friends never did. Tucker had noted that the policemen had not said that he would explain what had happened. It had been worth asking the question though.

The large Victorian clock behind the bar was nearing five so he left his table to be nearer the television screen and watch the fiction that was a live press conference. This needed more Guinness.

§

ML replenished his glass and turned up the sound on his television set as he could see the principal actors shuffling into place. DCS Clarkson read a prepared statement replete with the buzz words of modern day policing; 'in these uncertain times', 'safety of the public is paramount', 'regrets the brief inconvenience to Londoners', 'praise the efforts of all the emergency services' and 'vigilance is the price we pay for freedom'. ML was just waiting for the fool to quote the Metropolitan Police Service's (it was not longer a force) mission statement 'working together for a safer London'. Pass the sick bag. Let's have a group hug. They would most likely prefer a circle jerk but there would be a problem with gender balance.

'So it had been an exercise had it? Interesting. Let's see what questions from the floor would bring.' thought ML.

The journalists having been starved of information all

day wanted raw meat and asked what they though were hard questions. 'Had the Cabinet Office Briefing Rooms (COBRA) been activated?' 'We have no knowledge of ports or airports being closed. Were they? If not, why not?' 'Which government minister was in overall charge of the situation?' And so on. The police killed time by asking for different people to answer different questions but most of the press queries were met with the stock phrase 'We do not, indeed cannot, comment on operational matters regarding national security.' It was like watching Bjorn Borg playing relentlessly from the baseline at Wimbledon. His opponent would try everything to lure him in but, no; the Swede would just keep the ball in play until the other player made a mistake. Eventually the press tired, DCS Clarkson thanked them for coming and they all went away for the weekend.

ML had hoped that Roger Tucker would have made some noise but he was not even sure that the man had been there. Again, interesting. Had the Met brought pressure to bear on the journalist or, more likely, on his paper? At least he knew what stance the Met was taking and he was in no rush to move things ahead just yet. He would wait and see what the Saturday edition of Tucker's paper had to say before proceeding. His lawyer would no doubt have been putting initial feelers out regarding the sale of his business so he could leave contacting Arthur Blenheim until next week. That left him this weekend free; how best to spend it? Tomorrow's press could change his plans. Unlikely but possible. ML provisionally pencilled in a gig in Bristol for Saturday night. There was a good chance that the right people would be there and, if not, other opportunities could present themselves. This evening he would stay home and play for his own pleasure.

In the cellar of his house he had constructed a replica of a pub interior down to the last detail. Tables, chairs, a well stocked bar, mirrors, various bits of pub paraphernalia that he bought from Andy Thornton Ltd and a reasonable sound system.

ML changed out of his city publisher's attire and descended to his private world. Over the speakers came the sound of the background noise of an English pub in the evening. Now dressed in denim, he picked up his six string and sang 'Hello darkness, my old friend'.......He was at ease.

Chapter Six

In a conference room in the bowels of New Scotland Yard a very disparate group of police officers were sat around a large circular table. In front of each one them was a closed laptop and a landline. Looking like a giant alien spider in the centre of the table was the unit used for conference calls. The officers came from SO15, Serious Crimes and the Murder Squad. None of them wore uniform and only one of them knew what the meeting was about; this was DS Goodchild. The door opened and DCS Clarkson, in uniform, entered accompanied by Doctor Rachel Watkins who was wearing a white laboratory coat and a grim aspect. They sat down and all eyes turned to them.

Clarkson spoke 'Is anyone here <u>not</u> aware of what was said at the press conference this afternoon?' Evidently they all knew about it so he continued. 'What was said at the conference was not the whole truth. This was not a planned drill. The operation was carried out as a result of information received by DS Goodchild of SO15. A container was excavated in the grounds of Kensington Palace Gardens and it was not empty. Doctor Watkins was in charge of opening it at Base one. I hand the meeting over to her.'

The doctor stood and spoke without recourse to notes. 'The container is plastic, lined with Styrofoam. I opened it in sterile conditions as it was still possible that a chemical or biological agent could have been present. This was not the case. The box contained five objects. Four of these were plastic cold blocks. They contain a gel which, once frozen, takes forty eight hours to defrost. Normally used to keep drinks cold in a picnic bag. Pressed between these blocks was a small plastic tub, maybe Tupperware, which contained ten separate frozen objects that has been double wrapped in condoms. These objects are human fingers.'

She paused to let the officers take the information in.

During their careers they had come across all kinds of death and depravity so there were no sharp intakes of breath or exclamations of shock. Each of them was analysing the data from their own professional perspective.

She continued. 'These fingers came from ten different individuals, most likely female but I cannot confirm that until later today. Finally, each finger is the third one taken from the left hand, the ring finger. That's all I have at present.' She sat down, Clarkson stood.

'A special unit to investigate and solve this crime has been formed. You are it. DS Goodchild is in charge of it and will report directly to Deputy Assistant Commissioner Addison. Your first task is to select a codename for the operation to which I will not be privy. I'm going back to my roost in Serious Crimes. Lastly Mark; you are going to have to meet with officers in other organisations as well as call on resources from several areas in the Met so you will need a bit more rank. You are Commander Goodchild effective immediately. Good luck and good hunting.' With that Clarkson left the room.

'Bloody wars and dread diseases!' said a saturnine officer from the Murder Squad.

'Excuse me?' asked Doctor Watkins. Goodchild explained. 'It was a toast made by junior British army officers serving in India during Victorian times. Wars and diseases would kill off their superiors so that they could thereby gain promotion. The officer was referring to my sudden elevation.'

'Clarkson's not dead you dolt!' barked the doctor.

'His career is. I hope too many of us don't end up on the abattoir floor with him.' said the same officer.

'That's enough.' said Goodchild stamping his authority on the group, most of whom had out-ranked him scant minutes beforehand.

'I've just come from a meeting with D.A.C. Addison. We are now operation Orion. Some of you know each other some of you don't. We'll do formal introductions as and when each of you speaks. For the moment, we are it. We shall add more bodies as the investigation proceeds and this room will not be enough for our needs. I've sorted out larger offices nearby. If you need anything or anybody just ask me. Do not requisition equipment or personnel without coming to me first; this is not control freakery on my part. It is a security measure. Orion does not exist and if any leaks occur they will be traced to their source. Anyone responsible for a breach will find themselves on secondment to the most backward, uncivilised Commonwealth country that the powers that be can find.'

'Oh no! Not Australia, boss!' This came from the only female officer in the room – a perky looking brunette from the Murder Squad – and reduced the group to stitches. Cries of 'oh my human rights' and 'cruel and unusual punishment' went up. To an outsider, to see senior police officers laughing when they had just been informed of the disfiguration and probable death of ten individuals, would have seemed crass at the very least; certainly in bad taste. This would have been to misunderstand the group dynamic of such people. Most of them, rightly or wrongly, divided the world into three categories. Police, civilians and scumbags. This mentality crossed national barriers and a UK police officer would feel more at ease with, say, his Russian counterpart than he would with someone from the British army and vice-versa.

Goodchild let it run a bit and then interrupted 'OK that's enough. You must have questions. Let's get to it and I'll try to answer them. Take notes on the paper provided if you wish. Hand all notes to me at the end of this session and identify yourself before speaking. Who is first?'

The gloomy officer from the Murder Squad stood up and said 'DCI Jim Cooper, Murder Squad. We have ten fingers you say. Do we have proof of ten deaths?'

Goodchild looked at the doctor who remained seated this time and replied 'No. I have not had time to carry out all the tests I wish to on all the digits but I can tell you this; a finger cut from a live body will show very different histamine levels to that taken from a dead one. So far I have looked into the histamine levels in two digits and both were taken post mortem. I will have results on the other eight fingers by ten o'clock this evening.'

'So, two murders at least.' said Cooper.

'Not necessarily' said Goodchild. 'There are lots of ways that some sick bastard could obtain dead people's fingers and then play mind games with us. Having said that, I would not have asked for the Murder Squad to be here if I did not believe that we were not dealing with a serial killer.'

'And what has led you to believe that?'

'My involvement in Orion began this morning. A journalist contact of mine had received an email which prompted him to contact me. I took it upstairs and the hoo-hah in Kensington was the result. The tone of the email makes me think that we are dealing with a killer. Read it and see what you think.' Goodchild passed a copy of the email to each of the officers who studied it intently, conferring with colleagues from their own unit. Finally the brunette from the Murder Squad stood. She as no longer perky and joking; she was focused and serious. 'D.S. Michelle Stone. I agree, sir. The language is frightening. The writer is fixated on the helpless female; the lost princesses, weeping Diana and disinter the sisters. The binding of slaves is worrying too. I take it that this email gives precise directions as to where the fingers were buried?'

'Yes'

'I'm good at puzzles but at first sight this has me beat. Which genius deciphered it?'

'DCS Clarkson. Don't worry. I'll explain the logic behind it at another time. Suffice to say for the moment that it would be a rare woman indeed who could unravel a conundrum that is based mainly on cricket.'

'The little woman feels so much better knowing that, sir. But this does start to give us a handle on the suspect. Definitely male from one of the few cricket playing notions. Ethnicity can be determined by that of the victims, Doctor?'

'All white.'

'So it's some boring bastard from England, Australia or New Zealand. The language used indicates a certain level of education. We'll have this cracked by; what's that phrase you blokes use instead of end of business hours?'

'Close of play.'

'Yeah. That's the one.'

Goodchild made a mental note about the junior officer's contribution so far to the meeting. It had been insightful, logical and positive. Some of the others had yet to even introduce themselves. The men from Serious Crimes were probably pissed off that their boss was not in charge and was also in the dark brown sticky stuff. They were no doubt blaming him for this unfortunate turn of events. He'd give them one chance to involve themselves voluntarily before cutting them off at the knees and making them man the coffee pot for the rest of them.

One of the officers from the Serious Crimes group cleared his throat audibly but stayed seated. He looked to be round about thirty years of age and was dressed in Ralph Lauren casuals. The man appeared to be anything but a police officer having about him an air of money and sophistication. 'I'm D.I. Martin Carver from Serious Crimes. Commander Goodchild; we've met before during background briefings on A.Q. threat assessments. I'm wondering; a crime has been committed but we don't know what it is yet. Apart from the fact that you were the initial point of contact for the information that led us to find ten buried digits, is their any other reason why an SO15 officer is heading this investigation?'

'Good question D.I. Carver. As of this morning I'm no longer SO15. My sole task is to head Orion and my rank of

Commander is not substantive – although it may become so. I'm not going to give you my CV but I have police experience in areas other than counter terrorism. To be honest, SO15 have been expecting a 'spectacular' to happen in London round about now and certain people thought that this morning's email was the start of it. That is why we were all able to mobilize so quickly. It is also the reason for the secrecy of Orion; terrorism is not always about bombs and bullets. If A.Q. thought they were able to shut down whole areas of London with a single email they could do it again and again. Gradually the population becomes pissed off with its own government and pressures it into making political concessions to the enemy. The inconvenience of air travel is just an added factor in this process – not to mention the purely financial costs we incur as a nation. And here's a cheery thought for you to take to bed tonight; what if day to day living in London were to become so unbearable that major finance houses were to relocate from the City to a country which was not seen as being as cosy with the Americans when it came to the 'war on terror?'

'Cheese eating surrender monkeys for example.' said Michelle Stone.

'For example, DS Stone. So there are the stakes we're playing for people. I can trust why you can see that this team has a former SO15 officer at its lead.'

All the officers appeared to accept Goodchild's explanation. DS Stone, apart from being the only female officer present, was also the most junior. Goodchild could see her eyes looking quickly at each colleague in turn. She obviously had more to say but did not want to appear pushy. Her eyes caught Goodchild's and he gave her the smallest of nods as if to say 'come on, speak.' She caught his meaning and did so.

'Doctor Watkins. Have you finished a tox screen on any of the fingers yet? I know it's early but a cause of death would be helpful.'

'No, is the answer. I'm only using one assistant at the moment for reasons of security. I've known him for years and he is as steady as a rock but moves at a geological pace when I'm not behind him. Once I'm no longer needed here I'm going back to the lab to see what we have. What I can promise you is that the digits will have been printed and compared against your database by tomorrow morning. I shall do the same with the DNA. Tox screening takes longer but we shall work on it this evening; it is the only way that a C.O.D. could show up. If these girls have been stabbed or strangled tox is useless.'

Goodchild addressed the team. 'Does anyone have a specific question for the doctor now? No? OK Doctor Watkins; thank you. I'll pop in and see you later.'

The doctor left without another word or even a glance at the police officers. Her eyes were focused on a place which they could not see.

Looking at the team, Goodchild saw that some of them were reacting to information overload whilst others were hungry for more. It was his first job to manage this. He stood up and stretched, twisting his bull neck from side to side. He looked like a rugby international preparing himself for eighty minutes of mayhem.

'We could talk all night whilst waiting for the lab report and there are times when open speculation, blue skying, brainstorming bullshit can produce results. This is not one of them. I want you all to sign off for the day and be back here by 0800 in the morning. I can't stop you going to your respective annexes (he meant favourite pubs) and discussing this but, for God's sake, be discrete. Use this evening to think. We will have something from Doctor Watkins tomorrow and I want us to hit the ground running. Any questions?' No one had so they all filed out the door leaving Goodchild to tidy up his papers. One minute later D.S. Stone reappeared and said to him 'Sorry, sir. One question. Which is your annex?'

'For the duration of this operation it is the basement bar of the Red Lion in Whitehall. But not tonight. The pubs will have shut by this time I get away.'

'I see, sir.' Would you have any problem with us exchanging personal phone numbers? I may have the odd question that springs to mind outside of office hours.'

Goodchild paused before answering. Very few people knew his private numbers or even where he lived. But Stone's request made sense and she had made the most useful contributions to the day's meeting. He agreed to the exchange then added a caveat. 'You do not give that number to anyone, not even a colleague, nor do you let it be known that you are in possession of it. Having said that D.S. Stone, don't hesitate to call if you think of something; I like the way your mind works.'

Stone nodded her understanding and left the room for the second time that day. She wanted a drink before heading home and if she walked round to the Red Lion in Whitehall she could kill a bit more time and avoid the evening rush at Victoria tube station. Besides which she could check out her new boss' pub; she had never been in it and it had a somewhat dubious reputation. Despite the fact that it had an entrance in Old Scotland Yard, it was not considered to be a copper's pub. Across the road from its Whitehall door was the main building of the Foreign and Commonwealth Office. Further along the street was the monstrosity that housed the Ministry of Defence. Stone thought that the rot of political correctness had begun with that particular name change. It had been much more honest when it was called the War Office. Any pub that mixed the military with the diplomats was also going to have the odd intelligence type around as well so you could never be sure who was who. Stone wondered why Goodchild was going to use it for the duration then realised that his counter terrorist hat was a good fit in the Red Lion. So she set off into the still sunny streets of London walking against the flow of people who were heading towards Victoria and their homes south of the capital.

Chapter Seven

In his large detatched house in the north London area between Muswell Hill and Highgate. Roger Tucker was pacing his lounge with an increasing feeling of frustration which was building towards anger. He had slept poorly in his empty bed despite several large glasses of eighteen year old Macallan. He was showered, shaved and dressed by 0730 which was unheard of for him on a Saturday. The newspapers had been read and he was now at a loss at what to do. The fact that his own editor had rolled over for the government was grating on him and he did not like the feeling. Tucker stopped his aimless movement and sat down in his study thinking chair – a Parker Knoll Recliner which Americans referred to more accurately as a 'Lazy Boy'. He was not by nature an introspective man but he was now trying to analyse himself and his feelings with honesty. Only a naïf would believe everything written in the press and omissions were no different than outright falsehoods. He had handed a first class scoop to his paper and it had not been used. The fact that Central London had been closed off for most of Friday had not even made the front page. What was going on? Mark Goodchild was a mate but Tucker felt that there had been something wrong since they had first spoken yesterday morning. This was why he could not sleep and was now feeling so pissed off. For once he had had the opportunity to be a proper journalist and not just a humouristic social commentator. Sure, he'd made a good living out of irony and satire but that was not what he had set out to do all those years ago as a young reporter. He'd paid his journalistic dues covering the strikes and picket lines of the 1970's and 80's, spending hours in draughty meeting halls being bored to death by the trades union brothers droning on and on about the class struggle and drinking crap beer in even crappier northern pubs with cretins who did not know that Karl Marx and Groucho were not, in fact, related.

Opportunities seldom came along like the anonymous email. He had played it straight and been shafted by… well he could not answer that at the moment. He took stock of his life. Financially he was comfortable with the London house and the Spanish villa both paid for, his bank account was healthy and his accountant had advised him well over the years so that his stocks and shares portfolio was solid. His health was good for a man of his age and profession, especially since he had stopped smoking ten years ago. He could do with being twenty pounds lighter but he was nowhere near being obese and he was not about to forego the pleasures of the table in order to wear skinny jeans.

He had a super wife whom he loved; she had been with him for twenty nine years now and he knew what a lucky man he was. He had never strayed and never even been tempted to. The opportunities had been there and still were; fame is an aphrodisiac to many and even middle aged journos had groupies but Tucker was not interested. Truth be told he would be quite lost without Sharon.

He enjoyed his work. It was literally a laugh and no two days were ever the same. Apart from having to produce 1,500 words of copy twice a week for his paper, he was free to what he wanted. So he managed the odd television appearance, quite a few after dinner speaking engagements and a fair bit of charity work as well. It was not a life to complain about. But he now found himself doing just that. The cavalier way in which his story had been spiked had really got to him and now, in a moment of self clarity, he knew what he wanted – the respect of his profession. No-one was ever rude to his face and he rarely crossed paths with those of the liberal left who might have been tempted to try. He was by far the wealthiest contributor to his paper but he knew that 'serious writers' (and even some sports columnists) regarded him as a figure of fun. It was missing out on the chance to rub their collective, sneering faces in it that accounted for his mood but what could he do now. He was a de facto accomplice in covering up the truth of yesterday's events. Unless Mark Goodchild or ML contacted him he was stuck.

Tucker made a decision. He would write the majority of his Tuesday column today leaving space to insert something more topical into it at the last moment. Then he would get to work on trying to trace the joker who signed himself off as ML. If he could find him before the police did there could be a story here after all.

§

The joker in question was spending his morning in a similar way to Tucker although he had slept well and was looking forward to the day.

After a light breakfast of poached egg on toast with smoked salmon he had skimmed most of the Saturday newspapers to see what he could glean regarding the Met's reaction to his little gift to them. Nothing new appeared in the papers and they all seemed to be following the party line that Friday's events had been a counter-terrorist exercise. Unsurprisingly the only named officer was DCS Clarkson; all other quotes were from a Metropolitan Police spokesperson. Not to worry; there was ample time to stir things up. He would give them the weekend to realise the magnitude of the task that faced them and move on to the next phase of his plan on Monday.

He went downstairs to his private pub and entered the door at the rear of the room marked 'Gentlemen'. Two steps took him to a second door which opened onto a well equipped gym. He picked up a blue spot squash ball in each hand and mounted his running machine which he started at a fast walking pace. As he warmed up he increased his speed and then began to squeeze the squash balls in time to his stride. By the time he stopped running fifteen minutes later he had compressed each ball 900 times and he would be unable to us his hands for anything requiring delicate control for half an hour, but it did give him a phenomenally strong grip which came in useful on all sorts of occasions. He never played music when he ran – he listened to his own internal rhythm and emptied his mind of all conscious thought. Sometimes an idea would germinate during the session and he would let it grow almost independently of him. Many of these withered and died but a few made it to fruition and had proved beneficial to him.

At the time pre-selected by him, the machine began to slow down and then came to a stop. He moved on to the tiled wet-room and enjoyed a steaming hot shower. Finally he went into the drying area where wall and ceiling mounted fans blew hot air all over his body. As he stood and turned in the airstream with his arms held out in cruciform, he wondered what Tucker and his policeman friend were up to.

§

Commander Goodchild had been at New Scotland Yard since 0700hrs. He had been to see that the Orion team's new offices were ready and properly equipped with communications gear, copiers, scanners, shredders and, most importantly, a decent coffee maker. It was odd for someone of his rank to be checking the stationery supplies but it was a job that had to be done and Orion had been set up so quickly that he did not have a dedicated subordinate to do it; so he did it himself but without the team's knowledge – they could assume that the office supply fairy had been. He even checked that both the male and female washrooms were adequately stocked. This area was for Orion's use only and he would see to it that they lacked for nothing. There was even a separate room where team members could eat, catch a quick nap or just get away from the phones for five minutes. Goodchild was determined to give his people whatever they needed to catch ML.

Satisfied with the office arrangements, he called the lab to say that he was on his way over. A male voice answered him with a minimum of human emotion. This, assumed Goodchild, must be the solid but slow assistant whom Doctor Watkins had referred to yesterday. Goodchild had not worked with her before and so far he had found her to be prickly but professional. Perhaps she suffered from small person syndrome or whatever the female equivalent of a Napoleon complex was. In his mind she could be a bloody porcupine for all he cared as long as she produced. If she didn't, she would be out on her very short arse, leaving him to second someone he knew.

Entering the lab he saw that there were only two people present; Doctor Watkins, who was reading a sheaf of papers, and a completely bald headed rake of a man who was staring at his computer screen. The doctor glanced up from her reading and said 'I'll be ready for your eight o'clock meeting Commander Goodchild. That _is_ when you scheduled it for as I recall?'

'Good morning Doctor Watkins; and this is……?' he replied indicating baldy at the computer and implying that some basic politeness would be in order.

'This is Brian Robinson my assistant for Orion.' said the doctor.

Goodchild walked over the man and held out his hand for him to shake. 'Morning Brian. I'm Commander Mark Goodchild – or do I call you Doctor Robinson?' The man looked at Goodchild's huge hand and gingerly grasped just the ends of the fingers giving the policeman the creepiest feeling he'd had in years. It was like the tentative touch of a twelve year old girl at the local youth club dance. 'Jesus, what a pair' he thought.

'No, I'm not a doctor yet, Commander. Just a poor MSc trying to earn my daily bread.' If Robinson had injected the slightest trace of humour into his words they would have sounded normal. As it was, the lack of intonation gave one the impression that this was a robot that had just selected from a programme phrases to use in certain social situations.

'Fine then. I'll call you Brian. Doctor Watkins; I don't want a preview of what you have put together so far – that can wait until you address the team at the meeting which, as you quite rightly said I have scheduled for 0800hrs. I've just popped in to see if you are going to drop any bombshells on us at this early stage. I don't like surprises.'

'I'm sure counter-terrorism officers don't. No, Commander; I've nothing shattering so far. Robinson is following up a weird toxicology anomaly and we may have that result in time for the meeting but probably not. It may be a false trail anyway. So I'll see you at eight. I take it that I shall open the meeting?'

'Correct. See you then.'

Goodchild left the lab and headed back to the Orion offices and a cup of coffee. On arriving he was pleased to see that Michelle Stone was already there and had the coffee machine operating. 'Morning Detective Sergeant. That's the best piece of initiative you could have shown today.'

'Good morning, sir. I bloody well hope not. I've a lot more to contribute than making a brew for the boys, even if I am the low guy on the totem pole.'

'Point taken, Michelle. I'm sure that everyone will muck in and take a turn at it.'

She looked at him with raised eyebrows and a challenging smile as if to say that she'd believe that one when she saw it.

They drank from their respective mugs; his embossed with the badge of the Rugby Football Union and the red rose of England whereas hers was pink and had the words 'Top Bird' all round it. There was no chance of anyone appropriating those by accident.

One and two at a time the rest of the team turned up and

after the good mornings they gravitated to the coffee machine where they realised that they were going to have to make do with Styrofoam cups for the day it being too close to 0800hrs to return to their respective offices for their own china mugs.

Goodchild observed this with interest. One could learn much from the smallest detail and the fact that only he and the most junior officer had thought to bring a proper cup was not, to him, trivial. Foresight, planning, organisation and practicality were vital attributes for the sort of police work that Goodchild was used to – he had not seen much evidence of it from this group so far.

Two minutes before eight Doctor Watkins entered the room minus her lab coat for once. She was carrying an expensive, black leather briefcase which was secured by two combination locks. Picking a seat at the centre of the long conference table, she busied herself opening the case thus giving time for the rest of the team to seat themselves. As they were all waiting for Goodchild to pick his spot he moved first to directly to face the doctor. Once they were all in place she extracted two manilla folders from the briefcase, placed it on the floor and began her report.

'Firstly, there are only two copies of this report; one for me and one for you, Commander.' She passed one of the folders across the table to Goodchild. 'I have done this' she continued 'because of the security concerns that you appear to have. After our meetings, my file will go into my safe – you can do what you want with yours. I shall require guidance as to what security classification to give to these papers. Technically we could keep it as low as 'Medical in Confidence'; there is nothing in here that is in anyway dangerous to the security of the nation. However, Orion exists because ML has made someone over-react and the Met have now lied to the media and the nation, about a pre-planned counter terrorist exercise. You really want to keep a lid on this, I would imagine. I'll leave that one with you, Commander although I shall need a decision at the end of the meeting.'

'No, let's deal with this now, doctor. You raise a valid point. I've not read everybody's personal jackets yet so I don't know as much about you as I normally would – but I will by close of play today. Michelle – you're the lowest rank present. What are you cleared to?'

'Top Secret, boss.'

'Is anybody here cleared lower than T.S.?'

Nobody replied so Goodchild continued 'OK that's easy enough then. For the time being, anything related to Orion is Secret. We may upgrade to T.S. as events unfold but that will do for now.'

A Detective Inspector from Serious Crimes asked 'Why don't you just put T.S. on the whole operation here and now?'

'Apart from the fact that it would be a total abuse of the classification system you mean? There is a practical aspect to this, I can keep Secret material here; once we make is T.S. it has to be held behind three combination protected doors – in reality central registry. I don't intend letting this lot out of my sight. Doctor, would you care to continue please?'

'Of course. I propose to present bare facts and no interpretation. I have my opinions and will give them if you so wish but for now this is what I know. Nor will I explain the details of how I have the facts though, if you wish to hear me bang on about mitochondrial DNA, I shall. If you turn to page one, Commander. The green plastic box which was buried in the park is clean. No fingerprints and no obvious trace at this time. My assistant will find out where and when it was manufactured.

The blue cold blocks which were in the box; likewise clean and again place and time of manufacture will be ascertained.

The white circular plastic tub that was in the centre of the box; clean and we shall find out where and when it was made.

Page two. Here we have ten different packages which we extracted from the tub. Each package consists of two Durex brand condoms, plain in colour, not ribbed or flavoured.

Page three. Ten fingers, each one taken from a different person. Each finger is the third on the left hand, usually referred to as the ring finger. All fingers are from adult females. On pages four to thirteen there is a breakdown of each individual finger by blood type, approximate age and with preliminary tox and trace details. Also photos and observations of the finger's condition.

Each finger was severed from the hand post mortem using a single edged sharp object. The cut was made between the second and the third articulation and was effected in a single blow. Each finger was placed inside the condoms and then frozen. This has been going on for some years as the fingers were not frozen at the same time. The oldest is about five years, newest maybe one year or a little less. Certainly more than six months.

Page fourteen. Identification. We cannot yet identify any of these people. None of them have ever been arrested let alone convicted of a crime – that is what the Police National Computer using AFIS tells us. That is it for the fingerprints. Initial DNA prints show the same negative result. What we have left is familial DNA. A request has gone out and we are awaiting a response.

Page fifteen. Cause of death. Toxicology tests on the fingers have, as yet, not revealed a possible C.O.D. More tests are still underway.

Page sixteen. Further physical evidence. The fingers had not been washed prior to being placed in the condoms and there are many different kinds of trace both on the skin and under the nails. This will take some days to analyse but I can tell you one thing; we do not have flesh, hair etc from a third party.

Page seventeen. Preliminary conclusions. The third finger, left hand of ten young, healthy Caucasian females was forcibly removed shortly after its owner's death. This action was carried out in exactly the same way on each occasion. None of the girls showed traces of illegal drugs but there is an anomaly in all the blood samples which leads me to believe that a poison, so far unidentified, was administered.

That's my report. I'll now go out on a limb and state that you are looking at a single person who has murdered ten young women. Over to you, Commander.'

The team was stunned by the sheer detail of the report. They had watched and listened as the forensic scientist had laid out her seventeen pages of analysis. They could also see the much thicker dossier in front of her which would have all the scientific details of the tests that been carried out. It was an impressive piece of work.

'Goodchild said so. 'Thank you, Doctor Watkins. You and Brian have done an awful lot in such a short time. Very well guys – initial thoughts, questions whatever.'

Michelle Stone was first – which by now did not surprise Goodchild although he noted the lack of approbation in certain areas of the room.

'Could I have a look at the ten pages of details of the fingers, sir?' He passed them over and they all watched as she speed read each one. Finally she looked up and spoke directly to Goodchild. 'I was trying to get a feel for these girls, boss. It's stereotypical, I know, but a lot of young women who get abducted and killed are, by definition, the vulnerable in society. Prostitutes, the homeless, runaways you know. But here we have ten girls who have never come to the authorities attention and are drug free. So, for want of a better word they are normal. Surely someone would be missing them? Just now I was looking at the fingernails. All of them are real – there's not a false one there. With the exception of number three who is a biter, all the nails have been looked after and are freshly varnished. Two of them are clear varnished but the effort is there all the same. There does not appear to be a note of professional manicuring here so the girls did it themselves. Do you see what I'm getting at, sir?'

'Not really, but carry on.'

'They are decent, everyday girls who don't have much spare

money and have just got ready to go out for the night. That's when this shit took them.'

'I see. Anything else?'

'There is no wear and tear on the fingers themselves. These girls were not stacking shelves at Asda or doing anything manual. I'm thinking office workers but not in a bank. Nor would it be anything with direct public contact; when a girl has a job like that, she has to have full war paint on. If you think of the work possibilities for young women at the lower end of the wage scale I reckon that it's pretty limited.'

'Gentlemen – any comments?'

'I think that Michelle has just come up with a very precise victim profile indeed. We can work on that' said D.I. Martin Carver.

'I agree' said Goodchild. Michelle – expand on that and write it up for me today please. Next.'

'Well, as Michelle's going to do the girly profile I suppose the rest of us should try and identify the perp.' This came from DCI Cooper who, as Michelle's boss, should have been pleased with her performance. 'Doctor, in your informal conclusion you stated that this was the work of one man. What leads you to that conclusion?'

Rachel Watkins looked at Cooper for ten long seconds. She could have been preparing to make the first incision in an autopsy and was imagining him as the cadaver.

'I refer you to page seventeen. The exact same cut with the exact same blade, probably a cold chisel, was used on ten occasions. This leads me to believe that it is the work of the same man.'

'But is it not possible......' She stopped him by raising a hand and her voice, 'DCI Cooper – intellectually anything is possible. It is possible that there is a silver tea service going round the planet Venus in an elliptical orbit – I cannot prove otherwise. It is, however, unlikely. The existence of a group of men who employ the same method of removing dead women's fingers, putting them all together and burying them for us I find to be, whilst intellectually possible, equally unlikely.'

Everyone looked at Cooper who had just made himself to look a total buffoon. The silence was becoming uncomfortable until Goodchild broke it. 'Let's take it that we are looking at one perp – profile him people. What's he up to and who is he. Throw some thoughts out guys.'

'Sir, I think it would help if we, or at least I, had sight of the same material as you – especially the initial email' said Carver.

'Fair enough' replied Goodchild who stood and went himself to the photocopier. As the machine was going through its paces he turned to the group and said 'Jim, as the most senior man from the Murder Squad present, what sort of perp do you think we are looking at here?'

Jim Cooper, fresh from his mauling by Doctor Watkins, was aware that he was being given a last chance to redeem himself professionally. He was also being put in a position where he could be shot down in flames by the brighter people in the room. He was not comfortable in this situation but was not able to off-load the decision to a subordinate who could ultimately be blamed for a judgemental error. Damn Goodchild and his SO15 mentality; this was not the sort of policing he was used to. He had to give an answer.

'In the simplest terms, we are dealing with an organised sociopath; one of the most dangerous creatures in the human jungle. Normal rules of behaviour mean nothing to him. As well as being a sociopath, he is also a sexual psychopath and it is rare to find the two conditions together. The choice of finger that he has brutally removed is significant. The act is an affirmation of either his hatred of the state of matrimony or his frustration at his inability to achieve it. He will have some characteristic which, in his mind, makes him unmarriable – he's either physically deformed or impotent.'

Cooper stopped speaking as Goodchild laid a collated sheaf of papers in front of him. He leafed to the copy of the original email and read it. Raising his hand from the text he said to Goodchild 'Would you please explain Clarkson's reasoning when he unravelled this, sir?' Goodchild did and Cooper became even more sombre in mean. 'If you say so. It's all a bit artificial and, unless one were into cricket, history and imperial measurements, it's just not decipherable.'

'Did any of the rest of you see the logic in ML's missive?' asked Goodchild.

Carver spoke up. 'To be honest, sir, it might as well have been written en clair for me. I was a cricketer but the rest of the message is sixth form general knowledge level. I reckon that ML wanted this to be solved very quickly and then we would act on it.'

'Agreed' said Goodchild. 'Why?'

No-one spoke and Goodchild was becoming angry. So far only Carver and Stone had volunteered anything. The rest of this supposedly elite team was sat on the fence. He needed to light a fire under them in order to make them work to the standards that he himself was used to. 'OK. You all have copies of the relevant material now. I want you to come up with a plan to find this fucker. Jim Cooper has started a profile on him and I can't say that I disagree with it at the moment. Put that together with DS Stone's victim profile and we should have an initial plan of action. You have one hour - get to it. Michelle; where are you at with your profile, please?'

'It's done in rough but not typed. I've been writing my girly bit whilst you guys talked.'

'Fine. DI Carver; you've worked with Michelle before have you?'

'Our paths have crossed, sir.'

'OK. The pair of you grab your stuff and come with me. See you in one hour gentleman and I expect a plan.'

With that Goodchild left the room with the two detectives in his wake. They turned right out of the door, went past the entrance to the relaxation room and carried on along the puke green corridor until they came to a single block door with a nine digit entry lock on it. Goodchild keyed in the combination and led the two officers into a comfortably appointed bedsit.

'Have a seat please' he said indicating a four person dining table rather than the three piece suite at the other end of the room. 'I'm going to eat; you two?' They both nodded yeses and watched as Goodchild picked up an internal phone, pressed a button and said 'Hi Dave. Yeah. For three now please. Tough.'

He returned to the table and said 'No special dietary needs, I hope?'

'Sir, the day the murder squad employs veggies it's time to turn to crime' said Carver.

'Michelle, can I have a look at what you have written please? Martin; would you mind getting a brew on? The makings are all round the corner.'

If DI Carver felt put out at being told to make the tea when there as a more junior (and female) officer present he did not show it. Presently all of them were sipping away whilst Goodchild read and reread DS Stone's paper, from time to time making notes on a separate pad.

Someone knocked at the door, three distinct raps. Goodchild left the table and came back with a tray on which sat three plates, each one covered with a large bacon and fried egg toastie. He placed this on the table and then deposited brown and red sauce to go with the sandwiches. The three of them ate in silence (or as silent as it possible with toast) for five minutes then Goodchild asked them 'So why do you think I've cut you two out of the herd?'

Carver replied for them both. 'Herd is the operative word. I've rarely come across such a bovine bunch of bullshitters in my life. Michelle's already come up with some bloody good stuff and my analytical brilliance is self evident. We are your A team, Commander.'

'Fair enough assessment. Ground rules. Fuck rank in this room. I call you Michelle and Martin; you call me boss or arsehole depending on how I'm performing. I'm quite prepared to sack that entire bunch if that's what it takes to get this investigation moving. At the end of the day, this is a murder enquiry and I need your help, but if I have to, I'll call in my mates in SO15 and we will eat them alive.'

'First question. Michelle; do girls always put on nail varnish before going out for the night?'

'If the night is special, then yes. But special does not necessarily mean with a guy – please bear that in mind.'

'Fine. What's our way forward? I assume we send the prints to the central registry of missing persons and see what shakes.'

Carver and Stone looked at each other. Carver said 'You tell him.'

'Boss; there is no such thing as a central data base for missing people in this country. Do you have any idea of the numbers involved?'

'No. Do tell.'

'Around 200,000 people a year are reported missing. The vast majority turn up within twenty four hours. People panic if someone they know breaks a behaviour pattern and, unless a child is involved, the police forces throughout the country rarely allocate resources to a missing person report straight away. You would not believe some of the scenarios we have been involved in. My personal favourite was a civil servant from the Treasury who went AWOL. Wifey on the phone when he did not return from work, absolutely sure he must be dead. Hospitals turned up nothing, colleagues swore blind that they had last seen him in good spirits in the Villiers Arms. The arsehole somehow ended up with a bunch of drunken Paddies in Dublin. He phones Mrs Arsehole three days later.

That is why we don't have a central register for people who are reported missing.'

'Bollocks. Any suggestions?'

Carver spoke up. 'Doctor Watkins has given us a time scale and Michelle has given us a profile. With those we can contact every police force in England and Wales and see who they have missing that matches. We then visit the scene and see if we can pick up a print or DNA sample of the missing person and then get the lab to look for a match. If the trace analysis of the digits that they are currently doing could give us even a rough geographic location, then that would give us a starting point. Failing that, it's a nationwide number crunch.'

'I like it, Martin. Well, I don't <u>like</u> it but I agree with it. We will go ahead on that basis. At least it will give the chaps down the hall something to do. Next question; what is motivating this sick fuck?'

Again, Carver took the lead. 'You are assuming one person here. That is to say that whoever killed the girls, mutilated them, buried the fingers then emailed the journalist is one and the same person. I'm not sure about that; the sexual sadism involved does not square with the tone of the message. 'Speak for us' was the email subject heading. Is it a plea; a command, what? And I have to ask why was this particular journalist was chosen as the recipient of the message. It's a can of worms to me boss.'

'Roger Tucker is a good mate of mine. I've known him for years. You guys only know his public image. In reality he is a straight shooter; in fact he would have made a bloody good copper but he'd never have put up with the PC bullshit we have to. ML must know that he has contacts in the Met – maybe even that he knows me, which is a thought worth pursuing. We have me, Roger and the fingers in London. It makes sense that ML is based in the capital too.'

'But would he necessarily pick his victims from his own manor?' asked Michelle Stone. 'The factor in favour is obviously familiarity with the terrain and the huge number of potential victims in the capital; on the other hand, animals don't foul their own nests. Unless the doctor comes up with something, we need to make a start somewhere. Your call boss.'

'Here's how we shall do it then: Michelle, I'm allocating England north of Birmingham and Wales to you. Martin, you take the rest of England including Birmingham and the metropolitan area. I'll split the guys next door into two groups and they can start the ball rolling to supply you with initial lists which you will prioritise for personal visits. Let's see what we can achieve before the doctor comes back to us. Any questions?'

Carver and Stone looked at each other. The woman spoke up. 'Boss, there are two DCSs in there plus other officers who outrank Martin never mind me. They are not going to be happy acting as our dogsbodies.'

'I'll deal with their poor little egos, Michelle. I can spin it that you and Martin are doing the grunt work whilst they are using their elevated rank and connections to move and shake the nation's police forces.'

'If they don't see through that, boss, they deserve to be traffic wardens.'

'It's just to save face and to get the job done, Michelle. I'll go and let them know now what is expected of them. You two stay here and toss some ideas around. I'll be back at 1230 to take you to a working lunch.' With that Goodchild left. Carver looked at Stone and said 'I don't know if this way of working is unique to him or whether it's S.O.P. for SO15 but I like it. Might apply for a transfer after this show is over.'

'Yeah; it's police work, Martin, but not as we know it. I'll get a brew on.'

And that is how Orion started its first full day of operations with some very surprised senior detectives phoning their opposite numbers around the country looking for un-named, faceless white girls who had vanished during the past five years.

Chapter Eight

Bristol is one of the more interesting of Britain's great cities. Like Liverpool, its wealth had been founded on the transatlantic slave trade but unlike the northern city, it had never developed a heavy industrial base. When the United Kingdom had declared slavery to be illegal in 1807 Bristol still thrived as a trading port but at a much more genteel pace. Situated at the mouth of England's largest waterway, the River Severn, it was always a major player in canal borne trade.

One of its main features is to be found in the city centre, the floating harbour. Around this a lively number of bars, restaurant and clubs has grown up with something to suit most tastes. It was here that ML was strolling on a summer Saturday night at an hour when the sun still shone on the city. He'd driven in and his car was parked near the Cornhill Guest House where he had booked to stay for the night. It was his favourite kind of place; large enough so that he would not stand out in the staff's memory yet not so big that payment of a security deposit by credit card would be required. He had already ascertained that cash was fine with them. This was a follow up visit for him and he did not plan on any direct action but he still preferred to operate under the radar as far as was possible.

As the hour approached eight o' clock the town centre was becoming more and more boisterous. The younger crowd, many from Bristol's large student body, would have been drinking cheaply at home prior to hitting bars and clubs where prices were somewhat higher than the super-markets' loss leaders.

ML made his way towards the venue for the evening, Cromwell's. It was large for a town centre music pub and always attracted a good sized crowd. It had no pretence about it; there were no real ales on offer just a large selection of lagers, alcopops, spirits and industrial strength ciders. Professional door staff kept the idiots out and patrolled the premises on the lookout for drugs or any other problem. Young women came in their droves to drink, dance and let their hair down – they felt safe at Cromwell's. Young women attract young men (and some old fools) so it was a buzzing atmosphere on this Saturday when ML bought himself two pints of Strongbow and edged his way through the throng at the bar towards the rear of the room from where he could scan the audience.

Tony was playing tonight. His gear was on stage and the man himself was at the bar chatting quite happily with the pub's manager. He looked sweaty and dishevelled before he even started to play – perhaps it was the red wine escaping from his pores. Finally he mounted the stage, picked up his acoustic and greeted the crowd. He was more than a musician; he was an entertainer and his act was never the same two shows running. His gift was to gauge the mood of the audience and then give them what they wanted. His repertoire was enormous and when combined with his high level guitar playing, powerful vocals and likeable personality, resulted in a very good act indeed. ML thought that if Tony had hooked up with a decent lyricist early in his career he could have been as big as anyone in the industry. Not his problem. He would listen to the first set and then leave because he could not see his target tonight.

The crowd was lively so Tony went with the flow announcing 'Here's a little song we can all do together; it's about a brothel.' The audience was momentarily bemused until Tony picked out the distinctive opening notes of the music and then launched into the words 'There is a house in New Orleans, they call the Rising Sun.' Instead of singing the next line with its octave leap, he turned his mike towards the crowd who roared the words 'and it's been the ruin of many a poor boy' and they were off on the Saturday evening musical trip. ML could sense that it would be a good one and decided that he might just stay until near the end.

Tony rocked them with fast, demanding numbers that he normally saved until the second set. 'House of the Rising Sun' was followed by 'Summertime Blues' then Pinball Wizard' and, to get the crowd dancing, 'You Never Can Tell'. By the end of the fourth number everyone was cheering, clapping, whistling or roaring approval. The singer downed a pint of still water and slowed the tempo down with some Simon and Garfunkel, Bob Dylan and Mommas and Pappas. As Tony held the last high note of 'California Dreamin'' with most of the crowd joining in, ML noticed a girl at the front of the audience remove a white cowboy hat from her head and wave it in the air. This action revealed a helmet of styled silver grey hair cut high on the neck and sloping down to two points on either side of her slim face. It was his target and he had not recognised her. When he had first seen her in April, her hair had been long, straight and muddy brown in colour. She had been dressed in plain, shapeless clothes and had stood alone at the spot near where she was now, nursing a Coke and staring at Tony like a love-sick puppy. Now she was bouncing away in a form fitting pair of denim shorts and a tight T-shirt with 'Go Go USA' emblazoned across her impressive chest. She looked as if she could be employee of the month at Hooter's; what the hell had happened to her? More to the point, thought ML, how would this affect his plans for her?

At that moment Tony addressed the crowd saying 'Thanks a lot everyone. I'm off to take a quick break now but before I do that I'd just thought that I'd let you know that I won't be here next week. If you want to see me you'll have to get on a plane to Fuerteventura 'cos I'm helping a mate out who owns a bar in Corralejo. So it's a week of sun, sand and sangria for me whilst you lot freeze your woiuits off if the weather forecast is anything to go by. See you all soon.'

Tony made his way to the bar accompanied by applause and much back slapping. ML stayed where he was and started to refine his plans. There was an opportunity here that would be perfect for his purposes. It would require him to take more risks than usual but he was prepared for that. It would also need two other people to perform as he wished them to. Again, this did not daunt him and if luck was not with him he could always return to his original plan. Time to start the game.

ML headed towards the bar with his by now flat second pint of cider in his right hand. Using peripheral vision he steered a course close to his target and timed his arrival next to her with her finishing her bottle of alcopop. Most people on finishing a drink do one of two things; either look for a place to put the empty one down or head to the bar for a refill. The girl chose the latter and turned in that direction just as ML came in from her blind side. Collision, cider all down ML's chest, her apologies, his 'no problem', offers to buy another, 'allow me'. It was as predictable as the outcome of a bullfight. As a result ML and Catherine Taylor-Lodge of White Plains, New York spent Tony's second set together at the rear of the room. They did not talk much until the musician finally called it a night but by then they were used to being in each other's company and chatted freely. ML controlled the conversation with ease. Their starting point had been a love of the music of the sixties, seventies and eighties and especially Tony's interpretation of it. ML segued into the fact that he was looking forward to hearing the man play in a foreign country.

'You're, like going to fly to Spain to hear him play? You <u>are</u> a fan.' she exclaimed.

'Hardly. I'm going to be there anyway. I detest the English winter and always rent a place for six months each year. Guaranteed sun and I can see as many or as few people as I like.'

'Is it like Ibiza? I've never heard of this Fuerteventura place.'

'No. Different ocean for a start. If you look at the early Clint Eastwood westerns a lot of them were filmed in the Canary Islands. They tend to be arid and mountainous. Extinct volcanoes actually.'

'So what's with naming an island group after a little bird?'

'Wrong animal, my dear. The Canary Islands have been home to a peculiar breed of scruffy dog for thousands of years. The ancient Romans noticed this and named the colony after the resident mutts; Latin for dog is canis. Think of the English adjective 'canine'.'

'You know some weird stuff. So what's your story?' You take off for six months a year to do your own thing in the sun – are you one of the idle rich or are you a surf bum or something?'

ML looked at the girl as though deciding whether or not to reply to her question. As if reaching a decision he nodded and said 'Very well; I'm single, solvent and hetero. I most certainly work for my money but, I will admit, in a way that a lot of people would envy. I'm a writer, specialising in food and travel. For six months a year I fly or sail or drive around the world filing reviews to my agent who then has them edited and sold to various publications. Some of these are published anonymously, the rest of them appear under a nom de plume. For the six months I spend in Corralejo I have sufficient articles to send off and keep everyone happy whilst I relax and work on my novel. My name is Dominic Lord.' ML extended his hand to the girl who took it and replied 'I'm Catherine, Catherine Taylor. That sounds wonderful. Have you had a novel published before?'

He smiled, ruefully 'No, probably never will. Scratch the surface of anyone who writes prose professionally, you will find a would be novelist. The truth is that most of us don't have what it takes to succeed in that genre.'

'I don't understand. You write for six months a year, you already have an agent and editor and you earn money at it. What's so hard about the change to a novel for Christ's sake?'

'I take it you know of the writer Stephen King? Yes? He put it very well when he wrote 'writing a novel is easy; you just open a vein and let it bleed.' Not everyone can or will expose their true selves to the world at large and even if they are prepared to do so, the technical skills that novel writing demands are beyond most scribblers. But I keep trying.'

Catherine Taylor, who had, he had noted, omitted her full hyphenated name when introducing herself, was silent. He sipped his drink and waited all the while planning, planning ahead. Finally she said to him 'Are you saying that you're not really good enough to write a novel?'

'What a very direct question! And one that deserves an answer, but I'm afraid that it will have to wait for another time. Would you like to meet again and continue our conversation, Catherine?' He said gently placing the ball on her side of the net.

'Love to, Dominic. When's good for you Mr Writer-man?' came the return.

'I need an early night as I have a breakfast meeting tomorrow. Are you free for lunch at all?'

'Yeah, that's cool. Do you have a place in mind?'

'Funnily enough, I don't know Bristol well. I can find out a decent place from my hotel but perhaps there is somewhere that you'd particularly like to go?'

'I don't go to restaurants often; most of the students can't afford them so when we do go out its usually cheap Italian or Indian food. I'd <u>kill</u> for a really good steak but don't know where to go for one.'

'Leave that to the professional food writer-man. Let's exchange mobile numbers and I'll call you in the morning with details. OK?'

'Sure.' She took her Nokia from her handbag to do the electronic equivalent of exchanging business cards whilst ML searched his pockets.

'Bloody hell!' he exclaimed. 'I've either lost my phone or left it in my room.'

'Try dialling your number; you never know. It might be on the bar or something.'

She offered over her phone. He shook his head.

'You're going to think me dim but I can never remember number sequences – not even my own phone. Look, just write yours down and I'll call you in the morning. Is that OK?'

'Well, this date's getting off to a great start.' she laughed. She took a beer coaster from a table, wrote her number on it and handed it over. 'There you go. Don't lose it.'

'Thank you. How are you getting home? You did not seem to be with anyone earlier on?'

'I wasn't I'll get a cab at the door. There's no way I'd walk round town at night on my own so don't worry about me – I'll be fine.'

'Well thanks for your company this evening; it's been a pleasure. Talk to you tomorrow. Bye.'

With that he smiled at her, inclined his head and turned for the door. He did not look back, Catherine was left with her bottle of bright blue booze and a pleasant feeling of anticipation regarding the next day. Dominic was older than the guys she usually socialised with and his maturity was evident in that he spoke to her eyes and not her boobs. He did not try to control the situation; he'd left the choice of venue up to her after all and he was interesting. Her father would shit martini olives if he knew she had a date with an English writer who looked as though he had a good fifteen years on her. And was cute, too.

So with beauty sleep in mind she finished her drink and headed to get a cab home. Her subconscious played a trick on her and brought a song into her forebrain that she had not heard in years. Joe Cocker is a unique artist and how the hell he came to sing a piece of schmaltz like 'Up Where We Belong' is beyond most people but it did not take a Sigmund Freud to work out why she was humming the shitty ditty when the opening line goes 'Who knows what tomorrow brings, In a world where few hearts survive.' She caught herself and mentally slapped her face. 'God girl; it's only lunch. He's probably going to make money reviewing this place!'

As Catherine was heading home ML was walking back to his guest house. He'd been presented with an opportunity and he intended to exploit it to the full. A lot would depend on tomorrow's lunch but he reckoned he was half way to success. He'd sighted the prey, baited the trap and she was showing interest in sniffing more closely. How closely would she approach on Sunday? What did the change in her clothing and public behaviour mean? It was still relatively early in the evening and he had a lot to accomplish before the night was over. Thank God for the internet.

Arriving back at the Cornhill, he slipped past reception and up to his room. He had, as usual, kept his key with him. Now the tedious but essential detail work had to be carried out. Firstly, when was Tony actually playing on the island? His own website was not that informative with very few dates of English gigs when he would be playing and no news of where he would be during the two week gap that was evident in his schedule. Typical bloody musician. Further searching on the Corralejo website eventually came up with the goods. Tony would be playing at The Rock Café for a week. That gave ML a few days to arrange a villa and flights. No problem. He actually did know the island very well and had several contacts both in the local and ex-pat communities. In the normal course of events he would fly to Lanzarote then take the ferry across to Corralejo. There would be no record of him arriving on the island if he used this mode of entry but it was now a question of timing. He had to be in place before Catherine showed up, if, indeed, she decided to do so and he could not predict her travel plans. The last thing he wanted was for them to be on the same flight. He would sort his flight out later.

Next he called an English acquaintance of his who owned a bar and several properties on the island. Using one of the three pre-paid mobiles that he carried he dialled and, after two rings, a voice he recognised came on the line and said 'The Royalist. King Dick speaking.'

'Richard you reprobate. Dominic Lord here. How the devil are you?'

'Busy, busy, busy. You back in town are you?'

'Busy' thought ML. Of course you are; that's why you picked up after only two rings on a Saturday night. 'No, I'm not on the island but will be soon. I've been trying to reserve my usual place online but it does not appear to be working and I can't raise any Pedros on the phone to say that I'm on my way and will pay cash when I arrive. You don't happen to know what's going on do you?'

'Well, since you were last here a lot of people have gone out of business. Even some of the successful ones. The locals who actually own the commercial properties have hiked the rents up for foreigners and a lot of the latter have said 'sod it' and upped sticks. I'll be honest; I'm struggling myself. How long do you need a place for?'

'At least two months, maybe six.'

'You know that I've got a couple of places, don't you, Dominic?'

'No, I did not know that. I thought the bar kept you in beer and sweeties.'

'I like to keep my fingers in more than one pie. What sort of place are you looking for?'

'Detached villa with secure garaging for two vehicles: minimum of three bedrooms: separate living and dining areas: private outside space and pool if possible though that's not a deal breaker. The main thing I need during the day is peace, quiet and privacy. Any ideas?'

'Depends. Do you want to be near Corralejo or will out of town do?'

'As close to the town centre as possible, Richard. I'm up for some night life this time and I never drink and drive.'

'To be honest, none of my gaffs fit your spec but there is a lot on the market right now. If I sort this at my end would you be able to weigh me in with cash when you get here?'

'Absolutely. Look, I'm flying in this Wednesday, probably Iberia. Can you have something sorted out by then?'

'I'd say so. Look, I'll make a couple of calls and get back to you. If I can't sort it for this week I'll give you one of my apartments gratis until I can but that's just a plan B. I don't foresee any problems really. What number can I get you on?'

ML gave him his Dominic Lord mobile and agreed that they would talk again soon. He was pretty sure that the lure of receiptless cash would secure him the accommodation he required.

Turning back to his laptop he searched the web for steak restaurants in the Bristol area. Having dismissed those which were chain owned he found one that he thought would please young Catherine. He wrote down its number and made a note to call it in the morning.

The last duck that he needed to line up was Ian Williams. Where would he be on a Saturday night? More importantly, how credible would it be for ML, posing as a business lawyer to call him at this late hour? Think – get in character. What hook could he use on the man? Easy money and a free holiday of course. No Welshman was going to turn that down. Using a different mobile this time, ML called the number on Williams' business card. It was answered with a puzzled 'Hello'. He was obviously not used to receiving calls from a 'private number' at this hour on a Saturday night. Background noise indicated to ML that Williams was in a music bar somewhere. No surprises there. He began 'Good evening. Is that Ian Williams?'

'It is. Who's this please?'

'It's Rodney McNaughten, Mr Williams. We met a couple of months ago at Turnmills in London. Sorry about the hour – are you free to talk?'

'Hang on; I'll go outside.'

ML could hear Williams excusing himself as he exited wherever he was. The ambient noise died away and he came back on the phone. 'OK that's better. What can I do for you Mr McNaughten?'

'When we spoke in London I mentioned that one of my clients was thinking of buying some Spanish publications and would be looking at researching the market fairly soon. Well he gave me the green light over dinner this evening and I have to get my skates on as it were. So; question. Are you able to block off the next two weeks and spend them in Fuerteventura for me?'

ML shut up. It is a basic rule of sales that whoever speaks first after a closing question, loses.

Williams lost. 'I've a few other people I'm supposed to be seeing over that time Mr McNaughten. I'd have to reschedule them and possibly lose their business.'

'Of course, of course. And the inconvenience to yourself would be reflected in your remuneration for this initial task. I was thinking £1,500 per week plus expenses. Is that acceptable?'

'Yes' replied the loser.

'Good. I would like to pay you in advance and sort out your travel and accommodation as well. I also need to brief you on what my client requires. Where are you on Monday?'

'I've an early morning meeting in central Manchester but I'm free after that. I could be in London by lunchtime if that would suit.'

'Let me see.' ML did some quick mental calculations. He could travel to Manchester himself which would avoid the question as to 'Mac Naughten's' lack of legal offices. On the other hand it would consume the best part of a day and he did not want Williams to think that he was chasing him. As the man paying the bills he would make the other come to him. 'OK. I think it best for both of us to meet in the business lounge at Euston railway station. That way you avoid the London traffic and can head back north once our meeting is over. Make sense?'

'Yes, that's perfect. If you give me your number I'll call you when I know my arrival time.'

ML dictated a number to Williams, then reviewed the evening's events. It had been a good one. What else could he do? He could light a medium size fire under the police by means of Roger Tucker. The problem was that he was in Bristol and not London. The scope of the government's electronic retrieval capabilities was unknown to him and he did not want to leave a cyber or telephone trail. Tucker could wait until Monday.

ML went to his briefcase and took out a sterling silver hip flask into which he had decanted a quarter bottle of old Calvados prior to leaving London. He poured a large measure into his water glass and sipped away at it until midnight. The glass being emptied, he showered then refilled it before sliding beneath the covers for his final nightcap. By twelve thirty he was in the arms of Morpheus sleeping the sleep of the truly conscienceless.

Chapter Nine

At 1230 precisely Goodchild entered the Orion offices and he did a quick tour of the senior officers' work areas. He saw that they had each taken different parts of the country to target and that some information had already come in. Dossiers were being built. The atmosphere was subdued.

He went along the corridor to the smaller office to find Carver and Stone both on the phone and putting their points across forcefully. Stone's call finished first. She said 'Thank you, sir, I look forward to that very much.' Putting the phone down she added 'You wanker.' She went to the next name on a list and was getting ready to call when Goodchild stopped her with a gesture. They listened in to Carver's end of his conversation. 'No, Chief Constable; I am asking for this information at the request of Assistant Deputy Commissioner Addison. No, sir. I am not going to get him to give you a call. You call him if you wish to but Orion information comes to me. I understand, sir. No. No. May I add that you are the only Chief Constable who has not felt able to cooperate fully with me? As you wish, sir.' 'And fuck you very much, sir' said Carver to the now dead phone.

'Martin; just how many Chief Constables do feel that they can cooperate with you fully asked Goodchild.

'Actually, he's the first one I've managed to speak with, boss.'

Goodchild smiled and shook his head. 'I promised you two lunch. Go out the back way and meet me out front. I need to leave some instructions for the rest of the team. I'll see you in five.'

Goodchild went back to the main office and clapped his hands for silence and addressed the officers before him. 'OK gentlemen – I know it seems like you're shovelling shit uphill at the moment but it's got to be done. I'm out of the office for a couple of hours but am always repeat always reachable on the number on the board.

Keep at it and give some thought as to what else you might need to make this investigation move.'

With that he left them to it and went out of the main entrance to New Scotland Yard where he picked up Carver and Stone. The three of them turned right and carried on past St James Park tube station. Turning right into Tothill Street they came to Storey's Gate which led them into Horse Guards. They arrived at the steps at the top of which was a statue of Clive of India. This was King Charles Street on the right of which was the Treasury and on the left the Foreign and Commonwealth Office. At the end they crossed the main thoroughfare of Whitehall and found themselves outside the deceptively small frontage of the Red Lion. Instead of using the front entrance they went down a small side street and passed through a door that was almost hidden from view. Narrow stairs went down into a long single bar. They were the only people in it apart from a barman who was almost as large as Goodchild. He reached a paw across the bar and said 'Nice to see you again Mark. How's things?'

Shaking the barman's hand Goodchild replied 'It's Saturday; London Irish are playing at home and I'm working. What does that tell you?'

'Oh dear. Best be having a drink then before some raghead nukes central London. What'll it be?'

'Guinness for me. This is Michelle Stone and Martin Carver. May I introduce Joseph Slattery, doyen of London publicans, whose claim to fame is refusing to serve a prominent gay Labour M.P who asked for a shandy by saying, and I quote, 'we don't do fecking cocktails.' He's one of the good guys.

Michelle said 'Pleased to meet you. Will I be thrown out if I ask for a glass of red Burgundy?'

'Sure, no. Different rules for ladies. And yourself, sir?'

'Red Burgundy sounds good to me. Share a bottle, Michelle?' asked Carver.

'Fine.'

Slattery busied himself behind the bar, served the drinks and said to Goodchild 'Are you all eating Mark?' Receiving a yes he carried on 'I've a lovely forerib of beef that I've not carved yet, if you're interested in a Sunday lunch on a Saturday.'

The three police officers agreed to this eminently sensible Irish proposal and took their drinks to the table furthest from the door.

'Cheers, all' said Goodchild. 'How's it going?'

'It's not, boss' said Stone. 'There are forty three different territorial police forces in England and Wales. When we get through to someone senior enough to get things going you can tell what they are thinking; how can we justify allocating the resources necessary to answer Orion's questions. The impetus will have to come from the forty three Chief Constables and we do not have the clout to make that happen. If we cannot even say for certain that a crime has been committed on their patch then they are loathe to jump through hoops for the Met.'

'Michelle's right, boss. You caught the end of my call to the Chief Constable of the Devon and Cornwall force. He just did not get it at all. He actually said 'young people run away to Devon and Cornwall, not away from it.' I know its early days, but the signs are not good.'

'I see' said Goodchild. 'Any suggestions? Anything I can do to help?'

Carver spoke 'In my experience, Chief Constables are territorial and political animals. I think that they all need a kick in their collective arse from the Home Secretary who is, I remind you a woman.'

'The problem is how much of the story can I give her. If I reveal how we came to know of the ten missing women then I have to admit that we lied at the press conference. The alternative is to lie to the Home Secretary and keep her in the dark as to the origins of the fingers. There is no way I can do that. Some pillock in her office would leak it to the gutter press. You can imagine the headline – Serial Killer Takes Ring Finger Trophies. Peter Balls' newspaper would go ballistic at us and the whole sorry story would come out. The Met would look incompetent at best, mendacious at worst; and we would be no nearer a solution. So no politicians. This is purely a policing problem.'

Michelle Stone took a long drink of her Cote du Rhone and said 'There is another way.'

Both men looked at the junior officer with interest. It was obvious that she was not sure of her ground and was sticking her neck out. Goodchild helped her. 'Spit it out, Michelle. All ideas are valid until proven otherwise.'

'You imagined just now a headline which read 'Serial Killer Takes Ring Finger Trophies'. If these girls had been married or engaged it's certain that their other halves would be raising holy hell by now – but that is not what's happened. Therefore they were all single. Are they also friendless? It's possible. Some people are loners, especially in large towns and cities but can they also be parentless? Logically there are at least ten men and women out there whose daughter has dropped off the face of the earth. What have they been doing for the last five, four, three, two years? Come on, guys; put yourself in the shoes of a civilian whose daughter has lost touch with you. What would you do?'

Before they could answer, Slattery's voice from behind the bar boomed. 'Are you ready to eat now?'

'Yes please, Joe' said Goodchild.

Slattery looked down the bar to someone whom the three officers could not see. He raised his fist with the thumb up and said 'You can serve that now, Deirdra.'

A teenage waitress appeared dressed in black and white. Her hair was jet, her eyes the blue of a huskey. As she laid their meals down, the three of them all looked at her hands; no nails, the odd cut and burn mark from her work. And no ring. They ate in silence.

When they had finished their meal and the plates had been cleared away the conversation resumed. Carver took it up. 'A civilian would go to his local police station and file a missing persons report. If they knew where the girl in question was supposed to be living then the station would be contacted. If they did not have a forwarding address for the girl however, it all stops there. If, as we seem to think, this girl has a job then her employers would also notify her as missing. Her flat or whatever would be visited and a missing person's investigation would start. There are a lot of 'ifs' here but we could cross-reference employers and parents who have filed a missing persons report. How long do these cases remain open anyway?'

Goodchild answered him 'They stay open until the person is notified as found – alive or otherwise. But they are not actively followed up unless foul play is strongly suspected. The case files are reviewed every six months in theory.'

Stone joined in, 'In other words the locals give up chasing a ghost who may not even want to be found and we are left with a frustrated parent. What would a civilian do next? If the police are not helping them, who or where do they turn to?' She looked at the other two officers but it was obvious that her question had been rhetorical so they waited for her to continue. 'It all depends on the individual civilian; their educational level is probably the defining factor. I reckon that, the state having failed them, they would go to the fount of all knowledge these days – the internet. If they knew how to search efficiently they could see if their girl was listed in all sorts of areas and, even if she isn't, they could post her details online. I tried to think like someone who is not on the job and the first line of enquiry I came up with was the Salvation Army. But there are other sites out there which we can access.'

'I take it that you've made a start on this, Michelle' asked Goodchild.

'Yes, boss; and it's thrown up some interesting data which we can use. All we need is one index case to get us going and we can start to hunt this bastard down. At first we were all thinking needles in haystacks because of the sheer numbers of people who are reported missing every year – over 200,000. But that is the wrong approach. What we are looking for is people who have remained missing for a length of time – let's say six months up to five years – and who fit the gender – racial profile. One thing in our favour that my search has thrown up is that there is a disproportionate number of ethnics, mainly far-eastern, reported on these sites. I don't know why that should be.'

'I do' said Goodchild. 'A lot of them come from societies where the police are most definitely not the first port of call for a poor civilian. Also, bear in mind that their own immigration status in the UK may be iffy. So, lots of ethnics we can discount. What else can you tell us, Michelle?'

'Obviously we can ignore all the males as well. Some of the sites carry photos and here is where I may be walking on thin ice; we've come up with this profile of a young woman who is in regular employment and takes pride in her appearance. Quite a lot of the photos show women who have some sort of substance abuse problem and I would put them at the bottom of the pile for the time being. I know I'm being judgemental here but it is what my gut is saying to me.'

'No; your reasoning is fine as far as I'm concerned. My question is this; who do you have at the top of your pile?'

'Now and again there is a photo of someone who fits our profile and carries an additional piece of information after the bare factual description. It goes along the lines of 'her family are very concerned about X as her disappearance is totally out of character'. We can find these all over the country and I think we should pursue this line of inquiry as a priority, boss'

'What sort of number are we looking at, Michelle?'

'I have only just started looking but, extrapolating from what I've found so far, I reckon about fifty in England and Wales.'

'Martin, order me another pint of stout please. I think better with a glass in my hand. Good work, Michelle – we are going to run with this. Now tell me what's wrong. You look on the edge of an emotional explosion.'

'I just can't get over the amount of pain out there, boss. Some of the missing were posted ten years ago. It doesn't matter who they are or were; someone cared enough to try and find them. These websites probably represent their best throw of the dice. It's got to me, boss. I know it shouldn't but it has. I've seen some bloody awful crime scenes and helped put some evil shits away. The victims relatives can grieve and then try to move on but this; 'missing persons' seems such an anodyne word for a situation that causes so much hurt. I'm fucking furious, boss.'

'Good. Focus your fury; don't let the red mist take over. It's cold, calculating police work that will solve this. And Michelle? Caring does not equate to weakness in my book.'

She looked at him with a poker face. He had seen right through her and realised why she was emotional. She was worried that a group of senior, male detectives would interpret her caring as being soft and thus render her less effective as a copper. Then he had assuaged her fears with one phrase. She would not follow him into hell – she'd march there at his side.

Carver returned with Goodchild's drink. He took a long draught of it and addressed his two subordinates. 'We are going to spend the rest of the day following up Michelle's idea. Same geographical split as before with one difference; I'll take the Met area. We shall forget Chief Constables for now. Find out who the investigating officer for each case was, see what the case status is and whether or not the person who made the initial missing persons statement is still on the scene. Do not make a song and dance out of this; it is a routine follow up inquiry but get your answers. If the original officer is on the golf course, get him in. If he has moved to another force, track him down. When we have a list of live ones we shall go and see the family and hope that we can retrieve some DNA or some prints for comparison with our ten digits. Cross reference your hit list with anything that DCI Cooper and company come up with. Any questions?'

'When do you think we'll have a full lab report, boss?' asked Carver.

'God moves in mysterious ways, His wonders to perform, Martin. But he is the epitome of blinding clarity compared to a forensic scientist. It'll be here when it's ready but Doctor Watkins is on the case. I'll see her before we wrap up today for a progress report at any rate. Anything else? No? OK. Let's get back to the ranch. You two go on ahead while I sort out the bill with Joe. See you later.'

Carver and Stone took a different route back to the Yard, going via Parliament Square. Despite the large number of tourists gawping at Westminster Abbey and The Houses of Parliament, the streets were relatively easy to negotiate their way through. Very few of Her Majesty's Civil Servants were on duty on a Saturday afternoon. They now had a clear goal to aim for and they headed back with purpose.

Three hours later they paused to take stock and refuel on fresh coffee.

'I'll start' said Goodchild. 'I've had one bite and, to be honest, it's a bit shaky. Sally Greenwood aged twenty two when she vanished in August 2008. Single, lived with her parents in Pimlico, a graduate in graphic design from Westminster University. Worked in a small advertising agency on Old Street E.C.1. Told her parents that she would be late home as there was a works party that evening. There was no party and she is now two years late going home. The original investigating officer reckons that she has buggered off with some bloke somewhere. Her home life was shit and she did not like her work. On the other hand her National Insurance number is dormant; if she is working, it's off the books. Her passport has not rung the cherries either. I'm going to see the Greenwood's after church tomorrow. They are the churchgoers, not me by the way.'

'I've drawn a blank so far' said Carver. 'I won't bore you with the details but I think it's going to be a hard slog for three of us to go through the fifty or so names.'

'I've one possible from West Mercia Constabulary' said Stone. 'Jennifer Duncan, also aged twenty two when she disappeared in May 2007. Her parents live in Telford and Jennifer graduated in Theatre Studies from Wolverhampton Uni. She went to live and work in Brighton as a costume designer and called home every week without fail. By all accounts she was quiet, industrious, good at her job but did keep herself to herself. Sussex Police seemed to have been thorough in their investigation and her parents plastered the town with 'have you seen Jennifer' posters. Obviously all her personal possessions have been returned to the parents by now. I'm going to see them in the morning.'

'Well done, I'd like Martin to go with you. He might pick up something you'd miss and vice-versa. I take it that N.I. and passport did not come up with this girl?'

'No, boss'.

Just then the internal phone rang. Goodchild picked it up and said 'Goodchild. Jesus Christ! Sorry to ask but is this one hundred per cent? Hold on – Michelle; go next door and tell them to wait until I've seen them before they go for the day – OK do you know if this stuff is available in the UK? I'd like you to give and oral briefing to the team now please. No – No write it up for Monday. See you in ten.'

Carver was sat with an inquisitive look on his face. 'Don't ask. You'll know soon enough. Christ I need a drink' said Goodchild. 'Let's join the others.'

They entered the main Orion office and Goodchild noticed a couple of things. It was incredibly tidy. All paperwork had been squared away in preparation for everyone leaving for the day. Furthermore a quick head count told him he was two officers short. 'Who's missing, Jim?' he asked DCI Cooper.

'Dobson and Mathers, sir. I let them go thirty minutes early so that they could make it home to their families at a reasonable time.'

'Right. Well I won't detain you much longer. Doctor Watkins has something that she would like to share with us all and will be with us shortly. Any observations on today's efforts, Jim?

'As you said, sir; we're shovelling shit uphill and I can't see us having any more joy on a Sunday. Perhaps the Chief Constables will be more receptive to our requests on Monday by which time I imagine that they will have spoken to Assistant Commissioner Addison.'

'Right, did you, or any of the team, think of any other approach that could be taken to hurry things along, Jim?

'Ah, no. We stuck to the brief which you gave to us before lunch, sir.'

'Right' said Goodchild for the third time. DCI Cooper did not react thus revealing his ignorance of the rules of baseball and also the United States Justice system. Dead man walking as far as Goodchild was concerned.

The door opened and Doctor Watkins strode in, still wearing her white lab coat. Taking position at the head of the table she began speaking without preamble. 'You are looking for a very dangerous person or persons. Blood analysis of all ten fingers shows trace of a hitherto unknown toxin. It is a version of the FENTANYL based compound used by Russian special forces in the 1998 siege in Moscow theatre. The Russians misjudged the potency of their mix and managed to kill over 100 hostages that day. Without going into detail, this toxin is an opiate. So are morphine and heroin. This cocktail is thousands of times stronger and, I suspect, has been weaponised. And someone in London has access to it Commander Goodchild.'

'What quantity is lethal, Doctor? asked Carver.

By way of an answer she pulled an atomiser perfume spray from her purse, held it up and gave it the smallest press possible. 'Psst; you're all dead. I think it's just as well an SO15 officer is in charge of this.'

'Thank you Doctor Watkins. Do you have anything else for us at this time?

'Not really Commander. I can tell you that the killer did not wash or bag the hands but the trace I've analysed so far does not tell me anything significant. I'll have a full written report for you for Monday first thing.'

'Very well. I'll see you Monday.'

The forensic scientist left the room. The team were in a state of collective shock. Only Carver and Stone were speaking and they were keeping their voices down whilst they conversed animatedly with each other.

'This obviously adds a different dimension to our investigation' said Goodchild 'I'm going to have to talk with the Security Service and S.I.S on this; probably the chemical weapons people at Porton Down as well. It's possible that the counter terrorist unit will take over and that Serious Crimes and Murder Squad will be stood down from Orion. I shall try to call every one of you before midnight tonight. If you do not hear from me then I want you back here at 0800 tomorrow morning. Go home to your families or whatever you do on Saturday nights; this might be your last free time for some while.'

The Orion team filed out more or less together. Carver and Stone made for the other office when Goodchild summoned them back with a gesture. At his nod they sat down with him.

'You two had a lot to say back there. Care to share it with me?'

'Just because a counter terrorist weapon was used to kill these women does not mean that our target is from that world, boss' said Stone. 'It helps us to identify him; you'll know better than us who can get hold of such an exotic means of murder but that's what we still have here – a series of murders. You're not <u>really</u> going to involve the funny folk are you, boss?'

'Not at this stage. I agree with you Michelle. This exotic, as you describe it, gas is an opportunity not a complication.'

'And you are going to take the opportunity to chop off Jim Cooper and the other dead wood aren't you boss?' said Carver.

'Too right. They're good coppers in their own field but they lack the imagination to make a meaningful contribution to a situation like this. I will call them later on to say thanks for their help but SO15 are now the lead section. I imagine that they'll be relieved to be out of it with no loss of face. OK. You've got your road trip to Telford tomorrow and I've my visit to Mr and Mrs Greenwood. Let's meet up at 1500hrs and compare notes. I'm going to have someone standing by in the lab in case we come back with samples for comparison. Anything else?'

'Pardon me saying so, boss; you really have to cover your rear with regards to this Russian type gas' said Carver.

'I know. I'll get a message to Addison but I won't actually see him until Monday. I also need to put a better team together – we cannot do this alone. Grateful if you could put your minds to that for tomorrow afternoon. Good luck with Telford.'

Carver and Stone said their goodnights to Goodchild and headed off in search of a pub where they could unwind and make their arrangements for their trip north in the morning.

Goodchild sat alone rereading the email that ML had sent Roger Tucker barely 48 hours ago. What was this lunatic up to? For lunatic he surely had to be. Was the killer the writer of the email or did ML know who the murderer was and was trying to set the police on his trail in this bizarre treasure hunt scenario? He realised what he had missed when assembling Orion; a criminal psychologist. Who could he find who was discrete? Sod it, he thought. He was in danger of over complicating this, he saw. It was time to take a step back and let tomorrow take care of tomorrow.

Goodchild checked to see that both offices were free from paper lying around that should not be, verified that all wall safe locks were scrambled then switched off the lights and left. He would head over to London Irish Rugby Club for food, drink and conversation which never went near police work. There might even be a decent musician on to further distract him from the ugliness of mutilated girls and Russian gas.

Chapter Ten

ML woke at 0700 and headed for the bathroom. A long shower and a good shave had him ready to face the day.

After a very light breakfast he went online to see if he could find out what had happened to Catherine since he had last seen her to make her radically alter her looks and behaviour. He noted that she still did not have a listing on the social networking sites so he googled her family and there it was. Mummy dearest had dropped dead! A massive cerebral haemorrhage had robbed the world of Elizabeth Taylor-Lodge some two months ago. Catherine had returned to support her 'grief stricken' father Senator Lyall Lodge III but it was obvious that, having secured her inheritance, she had dumped his part of her surname and returned to the U.K. a new woman. Interesting. She must be carrying some heavy emotional baggage. An only child of quite rich parents, she had always toed the line. She had never shone at anything but nor had she ever blotted her copybook which was obviously more important for a political family. She had now become her own woman – hence the transformation; ML could definitely use this.

Time to organise lunch. He hoped that he was not too early to be phoning a restaurant on a Sunday but he was in luck and secured a table for two early in the afternoon. He then spent an hour going through the Sunday Times before calling Catherine. She answered promptly and brightly so ML assumed that she had gone straight home last night.

'Good morning, Catherine. It's Dominic here. How are you?'

'I'm great. Are we still on for lunch?'

'Of course. Do you know the Picture House in Clifton?'

'I've heard of it but I've never been there. I don't suppose it's hard to find; Clifton is not that big an area.'

'It's on Whiteladies Road and I've reserved table for us at 1230. See you there.'

'1230. OK Dominic. Looking forward to it.'

'Me too. Bye'

With a few hours to go until lunch ML called his lawyer to see what progress had been made on the sale of his company. As he'd expected Blenheim was on the case but it was very early days. Still, it was good to keep the old bugger on his toes. He then went down to reception and reserved his room for a further night. He reasoned that Catherine was not keen on the stifling life that she would have had to lead as a daughter of the pompously named Senator Lyall Lodge III and would view most older men as stuffy. Despite having met him in a music venue, she would classify ML as an older man so he would have to appear unstuffy. This would necessarily involve drinking and he could not do that and drive back to London so, another night at the hotel was called for.

He was about to step out of the reception area when his mobile rang. Looking at the screen he saw that the call was coming from Richard in Fuerteventura so he answered 'Dominic Lord.'

'Hello, mate; it's Richard in Corralejo here. I've had a bit of a result on what you asked me about last night. You free to talk?'

'Yes. Please carry on, Richard.' ML walked back to his room whilst his 'mate' gave a glowing description of a centrally located villa which was about fifty per cent too large for him and way over priced in the current economic climate.

'It sounds perfect, Richard. Who do I pay; the owner or an agency?'

'If you pay me, Dominic, I'll take care of the rest. Now, do you want me to pick you up at the airport on Wednesday?'

'If that's not too much trouble I would be most grateful. I'll need you to sort out a car once I'm on the island. Thanks again and I'll see you in a few days time.'

'Yeah; see you at the airport Dominic then we'll get you settled and have a few cold ones. Ciao!'

'Hasta la vista, Richard.'

ML had written down the address that he had been given then opened up the Google mapping service. Calle Carabela, Calle Carabela ah; there it was. He knew it. Not bad. There were some decent properties there and it was in an area where he would have considered buying if things were different. Nowhere is really far from anywhere in Corralejo but this place was so convenient to where Tony was going to be performing that it all had a feeling of destiny about it.

In a positive frame of mind he closed down his laptop and went back downstairs and turned right out of the front door. One hundred yards away there was a taxi rank where he found a vacant cab immediately. He directed the driver in the general direction of the Picture House restaurant without naming it and, having passed it, he made the cab take a left and a right before alighting and going into the nearest pub. Here he ordered a vodka and cola to match the more youthful and sophisticated image he was aiming for. He was getting into character for Catherine.

Finishing his appalling drink, ML walked back to Whiteladies Road and found the restaurant. It was 1215 precisely when he entered to be greeted by a smartly dressed and really quite attractive maitraisse d. She smiled and said 'Good afternoon, sir. Do you have a reservation?'

'Yes. 1230 table for two in the name of Lord.'

The young woman looked in her book, nodded and said 'That's right; would you care to come through to your table, sir?'

'No. I think I'll have a drink at the bar first if that's all right. I'm a tad early.'

'That's fine, sir. Through the archway and on your right.'

ML walked through the subtly lit room which, in keeping with the establishment's name, had a lot of artwork on the walls – some of it quite good. The décor was predominantly grey leather and aubergine fabric, minimalist in style. This had gone out of fashion in London at least five years ago. The provinces – what could one expect? The solitary barman left off glass polishing to serve him. ML asked 'No offence, but can you make a real dry martini cocktail?'

'None taken, sir. How would you like it?'

'Very, very dry. Bombay sapphire, shaken with a twist; no olive.'

'Certainly, sir.' The barman then astonished ML by taking a martini glass from the freezer, adding a dash of vermouth to it, swirling the liquid round then discarding it. He then poured the gin into a stainless steel shaker, added ice and shook vigorously for no more than five seconds before straining the liquid into the frozen glass. Finally he took a paring knife to a whole lemon and cut the twist in such a way that the zest sprayed onto the surface of the drink.

'There you are, sir. I hope it is to your taste.'

ML tasted the cocktail. It was very good indeed. The only places in England where he had had better were in bars where he had instructed the barman as to how he personally liked it made. He did not do so now as he did not wish to leave too strong an impression of himself in anyone's mind. He contented himself with sipping at his drink whilst looking over the wine list. From the corner of his eye he saw two people approach. It was the maitraisse d and Catherine.

'Your guest has arrived Mr Lord.'

'Thank you. Catherine; you look lovely.' He was not just being polite. This was a totally different young woman to the one who had been dancing around in shorts and a cowboy hat last night. She was dressed in ice blue Versace jeans which were tucked into knee length tan leather boots: a cap sleeved, bright yellow top with the discrete double C of the Paris fashion house showed her figure to advantage: she carried a soft leather jacket that matched the colour of her boots. He could not see a label but it was obviously not from the high street. In her other hand she carried a medium sized leather handbag which she now transferred to her left hand so that she could touch him on the shoulder as she gave him a swift peck on one cheek.

'Why thank you, sir' she said, fluttering her eyelashes and sounding like a southern belle rather than the daughter of a New York senator.

'Is that a real American martini I see in front of you?'

'It certainly is.'

'Where's the olive?'

'I don't like the taste of oil in my drink so I always go with a twist.'

'May I?' she said indicating his drink. He passed it to her. She drank and her eyes came out like a cartoon characters. 'Jesus – that's neat gin you've got there!'

'Have you had a dry martini before?'

'Sure. Someone I know mixes his own. He adds vermouth to vodka over ice, stirs it and pours it over an olive. I tried it a couple of times. Can't say I like it but at least I could drink a whole one. This is just, just…' She ran out of words so ML helped her.

'This is something to be drunk with respect. You know that there is a quantity of strong liquor at play with this. The drink you're describing is just as potent but people who imbibe it can fool themselves that it is not dangerous. The famous two or three martini lunches have been responsible for some very odd business decisions indeed.'

'Not just business decisions either. So why do you drink the gin thing?'

'Clears the palate before a good meal and I like the buzz. What'll you have?'

'A gin thing. I promise to respect it!'

They both laughed and contradicting everything he'd just said, ML tossed off the remains of his cocktail and ordered one for each of them.

They moved on to their table and picked up the Sunday menu. It was short – just six starters and five main courses plus four roast meat dishes. ML thought that this was about right for a restaurant of this size and location. He noticed that Catherine's brow was furrowed as she read. This probably meant that she was confused by some of the dishes so he asked her 'Spoilt for choice?'

'I don't know what half the dishes are. I was raised as a meat eating all American girl and I'm a bit lost.

'Well, I brought you here for the steak. Is that still your wish?'

'Oh yeah – the eight ounce, rare.'

'I think you should try the scallops as a starter. We're not far from Cornwall so they should be good. If the stuffed pigs hoof weirds you out you can leave it.'

'I'd noticed that. Kind of Brit surf n' turf. OK. I'll go for it.'

'Any wine preferences?'

'Nope – I'll trust you on that front, Dominic.'

ML signalled to a waiter and asked for a bottle of Montrachet to be served straight away and for a Chateauneuf-du-Pape to be opened for later. He then ordered Catherine's meal and belly of pork for himself with venison Carpaccio as a starter. The restaurant was filling up nicely giving a warm, relaxed Sunday afternoon feel. With the hurdle of menu selection negotiated, Catherine relaxed and under the influence of white Burgundy and ML's prompting was soon telling an interesting edited story about herself. She said her father was 'in politics' rather than revealing his senatorial standing. She also spoke of her mother's recent death and admitted that she had been left financially independent as a result. When pushed on her educational choice she laughed and said 'Staying at school is my way of escaping from my family. All they want is for me to marry the right guy and, by that, they don't mean the right guy for me, they mean the right guy for dad's political career. I've always found studies easy and as long as I can be seen to be pursuing something 'serious and worthwhile' I'm fireproof. So I'm now doing my masters in International Relations, specialising in the socio-economic impact of slavery. That gave me the excuse to get over to England to research.'

'So, what's next – a doctorate? Keep on running until you're a professor?'

'No way, Dominic. I might not even finish up the masters. Like I said, I've got my own money now and I can start living.'

'But, let me guess; you don't know what you want yet, do you?'

'Not in detail, no. I'm more and more drawn to music though. I can sing but I've never had the chance to get up in front of a crowd and really go for it, you know. The feeling last night when Tony was playing – fantastic. Look at his lifestyle. Just like that, he's off to some warm island to play music in the sun, a drink in one hand and no boss to bug him. Every time I see the guy he's smiling – has he got it right or what?'

'Tony is one of the best and could have been world famous if the breaks had gone his way or if he'd applied himself more as a young man. As you say though; he's happy.'

'And you Dominic; are you happy? You're cool, you travel, you sit on your ass for six months a year. What's your story?'

He was saved from answering by the arrival of the first course. The quality of the ingredients was first class and the chef had been intelligent enough not to play around with them. The green apple puree and hazelnuts which accompanied the pig's trotter worked especially well with the dryness of the Montrachet.

As the plates were cleared the conversation turned to the food, which Catherine had enjoyed, and the main course was served before she could continue to question ML. He was enjoying himself. The girl was proving to be unexpectedly good company with a bit of steel to her. But, despite her undeniable physical attractions, this could only ever end one way. He knew her academic achievements and also that she was a millionairess but she was not his equal. He knew of no-one who was so there was no point in speculating about where this lunch could have led in another life. He would play the Dominic Lord role and see what happened to them. He was fairly sure what the outcome would be.

They'd finished their food and the restaurant was now totally full with quite a few people at the bar waiting for tables and the noise level had risen appreciably so they decided to walk to have coffee elsewhere. ML was content to let her lead.

They strolled towards the city centre with the weather still being kind to them. The sun gave ML the excuse to don wrap around dark glasses. Neither seemed inclined to chatter which suited him. From time to time ML would point out a place of interest, usually comparing it to the converted warehouse area of Butler's Wharf in London.

Rounding a corner they came across a large Victorian pub called the Blue Anchor. As they approached it, the double doors opened to let a group of people out and with them came the sound of a band playing 'Bad Moon Rising'. ML and Catherine looked at each other, smiled and nodded. Words were not necessary between them now. Just before they got to the doors he took her arm and said 'I'll tell you now − we won't get coffee in a place like this.'

'Let's get shit-faced instead then!' and so they entered a pub where live acts were the house speciality to judge by the large stage which took up one third of the rear wall. The place appeared to be an authentic Victorian pub. It had the windows on three sides which were etched to a height of six feet making it impossible for passers by to see who was inside. Originally the place would have had a public bar for the workers and a lounge bar for the more affluent. Even these would have been further sub-divided into a smoker's room and a men only bar where snooker or billiards would have been played. A combination of health and safety and equality legislation had put an end to that. The pub companies were happy initially: why have a public bar where the lower orders could drink cheaply when you could pretend that everyone was equal and put the prices up? The large pub companies had bought chain after chain of bars, transformed them into vertical drinking holes and installed MTV. The loans to finance this ran into the billions and the banks were happy to advance the money because it was secured against the property itself. The people from the pubcos who had come up with this scheme had never run a bar in their lives. What they were doing was managing a huge property portfolio in which their tenants paid them rent <u>and</u> had to purchase the pubco product at a price the pubco dictated. And if it did not work out, bye-bye – bring on the next mug. As the value of the property estate kept growing so did the share price. Until the inevitable crash. Pubs were going bust at the rate of hundreds a week as people preferred to buy alcohol from the supermarket for consumption at home (where they could also smoke). Many traced the decline in the pub culture to the Millennium celebrations when companies tried to cash in by charging money for regular customers to go into their local bar. People revolted at this and created their own parties, discovering that it was a better way all round to enjoy themselves.

So a combination of pubco greed and government social engineering had decimated the industry. Only specialist outlets had a chance and music was an obvious choice for a publican. This could take the form of live entertainment, open-mike evenings, jam sessions or – at the bottom of the pile – karaoke.

ML and Catherine did not know what they had walked in on yet but there were two guys with guitars doing justice to Creedence at the moment and that was fine by them.

The bar was half full with most people down near the stage so they had no problem getting a table by a window where the sunbeams shone through the etched glass and then on onto their glasses of Rioja where it created patterns on the marbled table top. The afternoon progressed. It became clear that the guys on stage were a regular feature with a following. They played requests of all sorts, even from the half dozen Irish who had started to drink Bushmills Black along with their Guinness.

Catherine was in her element and started to sing along to some of the numbers. She had not been lying, ML noted. She could hold a tune.

'If you had the stage today, what would you sing?' he asked her.

Without hesitation she replied 'Proud Mary.'

'Go on then.'

'No way – I've never done that; I'd screw up.'

'No you won't. You have the voice. Just make sure hit the first note right and the rest will follow. As long as you remember the words, it'll be fine.'

'I'll sing if you'll sing' she challenged him. He had not yet said that he sang; only that he loved music.

'Deal. You first. I'll go and organise it. OK?'

'Shit. Yeah. OK. What's the worst thing that can happen?'

ML made his way to the stage and when the moment presented itself, had a word with the guitarist who seemed to be organising the show. He went back to the table, sat down and said 'You're on'.

The guitarist stepped up to the mike and announced 'As you know, we encourage people to come and join in with us on a Sunday and this week we are pleased to have a young lady all the way from the U.S of A who's going to sing some more Creedence for us. Come on down, Catherine!'

As she made her way to the stage cheers and whistles went up for the foreigner. No-one would have known that this was her first time singing in public given the confident way in which she took the mike from its holder and nodded to the guitarists to start. What followed rocked the place; she did not just sing the song, she performed it and took the audience with her. By the end of the three minute song she had everyone on their feet singing the chorus 'Rolling, rolling, rolling on the river'. She jumped off the stage and floated back to her seat with cries of 'more' ringing out. She took her wine in a shaking hand, drank and grinned in satisfaction.

'Feels good doesn't it?' said ML. 'Sometimes the first time is the best. What's your encore?'

'Oh no, that's me done, Jesus, that was scary.'

The guitarist was back at the mike. 'Catherine, can we have another one please?'

She stood up and called across the room 'My friend'll give you a song' and indicated ML. Cue more whistling and cheering. ML, still wearing his shades made his way onto the stage where he conferred with the musicians. One of them handed over his guitar which ML strapped on. He then took a tall stool, sat down, adjusted the mike stand and began to speak in an American accent. 'I'm not even gonna try and compete with Catherine – let's slow it down a bit. This song's from the heart. Y'all join in if you know it.'

He had their attention as he began to strum; the other guitarist joined him as they felt their way through the chords. None of the audience could quite work out what the number was. It was there in their musical memory but not quite and when ML sang the first words they all realised where he was going and were pleased.

'Busted flat in Baton Rouge, Headin for the trains, Feelin nearly faded as my jeans.'

Most people identified the song with Janis Joplin out of her head on drugs and whiskey screaming 'nah nah nah nah nah nah nah nah nanna' repeatedly whilst a honkey tonk tries to keep up with her. Kris Kristofferson wrote it as a slow country song and this is how ML sang it in a rich, soft baritone. It made the chorus easy to join in and gave it meaning and pathos so that, when he sang 'Freedom's just another word for nothing left to lose' everyone had a personal moment from their past brought back to them.

When he finished and handed the guitar to its owner then walked back to his seat, he did not receive the ovation that Catherine had. He had not entertained them – he had moved them. A lot of people said 'Well sung' or similar to him and tentatively touched him. He put up with it until he reached his seat. Catherine raised her glass and touched its rim to his. 'Wow' she exclaimed, 'You're good. What's with the accent?'

'Part of the performance, Catherine; that's all.'

'Is that all it is with you, Dominic – a performance? You're good enough to sing professionally. The feeling that came over when you played – you moved people. That's a gift; you can't just learn to do that. I don't know what to make of a man that can do what you do and then say 'it's part of a performance – that's all'. I just don't know.'

'We don't know each other, Catherine. What have we had? Drinks, lunch and a couple of songs. What do you expect?; what do you want?'

His tone was soft and he smiled as he uttered the words but the younger woman felt that she was being weighed in his balance and found wanting. She looked at him as an equal and said 'I want to learn to sing with you.'

He returned her stare, no emotion showing on his face. Finally he nodded and said 'OK. Let's try it. I'm tied up for the next few days but will be in Fuerteventura after that. When you have your next academic break, sort out a flight, give me a call and I'll be at the airport to pick you up. If you like you can stay at my place or I'll organise a hotel for you. Fair enough?'

'Yeah, only to hell with the next academic break. I'd like to be on your island when Tony's playing so I'm going to check out flights for this weekend. Is that OK with you?'

'I'm not your keeper; it's your life, your education and your call. Let me know when you're arriving and I'll be there. So, my place or would you be more comfortable with a hotel?'

'I really don't like hotels but I would not want to impose; I mean, are you sure you wouldn't mind me staying at your place?'

'I never make an offer I don't mean. It will be a pleasure – I'll even cook for you now and then.'

'Well, how can a girl say no to that? Looks like we have a deal Mr Lord! And I feel ready to sing again – how about you?'

'Ah I'm afraid it looks like the Irish contingent is getting into their musical stride. I don't mind listening to the Celts but I'm not going to join in; they always end up being a bit nationalistic.'

'Yeah, I've seen that in New York Irish bars. Let's just listen then. You ready for another bottle, Dominic?'

'Why not?' he smiled and the young American made her way to the bar to purchase more Rioja.

ML and Catherine spent the rest of the evening at their back of the room table enjoying the music and each other's company. The girl was sensible enough to alternate her glasses of wine with large amounts of water so that she did not become too intoxicated. ML, on the other hand, had a high tolerance to all drugs, alcohol included. He was not immune to its effects but he appeared sober at all times. As the evening grew later they snacked on bar food and slowed down their drink intake. At ten o'clock ML saw Catherine to a taxi having said that he had an early start on Monday and they could probably both do with an earlier night with all that they both had to organise in the next few days.

They went their separate ways with the girl promising to call him as soon as she had a flight confirmation. ML returned to his hotel content with the way in which the day had gone. He checked his emails – nothing new had come in so he settled down for the night and looked forward to the next forty eight hours in London.

Chapter Eleven

Mark Goodchild was back in his office by one o' clock on Sunday afternoon. He had spent a frustrating and depressing hour in the company of the missing Sally Greenwood's parents. Their three bedroomed flat in Pimlico was, in reality, a two bedroomed accommodation plus a small store room. There was no trace that, until two years ago, a twenty two year old woman had ever lived there. Not a picture of her was to be seen. What had been her room was bare of decoration and the usual electronic systems that the young surround themselves with. Sally's clothes had been sent to a church charity and the only bit of colour in the room was a small Madonna and child print on the wall above the single bed. Goodchild had seen more cheerful prison cells.

The lounge was equally bare. A photo of John Paul II on one wall and a plain brown wooden crucifix above the electric fire the only adornments. There was no music system or any reading material in view. Goodchild would have bet his pension that the Greenwoods had his and her bibles in the bedroom. They were both slim to the point of malnutrition, quietly spoken and shabby. He was fifty nine years old and worked as an executive officer for the Department of Health and Social Security i.e. he had been promoted three times in forty three years. His wife was ten years his junior and was employed as a teaching assistant at a local primary school. Neither of them owned a driving license or a passport. Their joint income was sufficient that they had no financial concerns. Their flat was owned by the local council so the rent was low – they just had no life.

In talking with them, Goodchild realised that the church was everything to them. Had it not been for the Roman images on the walls, he would have categorised them as members of one of the weirder branches of Christianity to which they were donating a sizable amount of their income. But, no; they were just straightforward Catholics which meant one important thing. Sally, their only child, had been a bit of a surprise arrival. Several possibilities crossed the detective's mind. One, the Greenwoods had sex so infrequently that a single child was a fair return for the effort expended; two, low sperm count or fecundity could account for just one child; three, Mrs Greenwood had been playing away from home and been caught out. Neither parent expressed the emotion one would expect if an only child had disappeared. They did not say it in so many words but the message Goodchild was receiving was that 'it was the will of God and He would look after Sally'. The Greenwood's sex lives were not his concern but this was one of the oddest situations he had ever encountered. Could Mr Greenwood have discovered that he had had a cuckoo in his nest for twenty two years and had something to do with her disappearance? Stranger things had happened and the possibility would have to be looked into. However it did not feel 'right' to him. The Greenwood's claimed not to have known that their daughter owned a passport so she must have always kept it with her – an escape plan? Certainly there was good reason for a young woman who worked in the world of advertising to want to get away from this prison. But total disappearance was drastic and Goodchild had a bad feeling about what had happened to Sally Greenwood. Unfortunately her physical presence had been so expunged by her parents that he had not been able to obtain a fingerprint or trace of DNA for comparison. Hopefully Carver and Stone would have fared better.

§

The other two officers had left London in an unmarked, blue Ford Mondeo at the reasonable hour of eight in the morning. They wanted to arrive in Telford well before the Sunday lunch hour and, as neither of them knew the town, had left quite a bit of a time cushion to find the location.

Carver was driving north on the M6 with his eyes looking at the motorway signs rather than the satnav now. At this hour there was little traffic but he knew that would change as the midlands civilians crawled out of their pits and headed to Wales for a foreign holiday. So they ate up the miles whilst they could.

'What do you know about Telford, Martin?'

'It's one of the 'new towns' built in the 1960's replied Carver. 'Well not built exactly. Basically a road network was constructed to link various villages into one unit. It used to be a mining area – coal and iron – with some heavy industry too. When Telford was created a lot of council tenants from Wolverhampton, Dudley, Walsall etc were relocated there so it's supposed to be a bit grim; think of a dirty Milton Keynes.'

'Sounds awful. Which county is it in?'

'Geographically, Shropshire but when I was researching it last night I found that it is one of those Unitary Authorities – the full title is Telford and Wrekin. Actually I'm painting too dark a picture of the place. There is quite some history here. Ironbridge is just down the road and if anywhere can claim to be the birthplace of the industrial revolution, that's it. The existence of coal, iron and running water plus the genius of men like Thomas Telford made it ideal.'

'Still sounds grim. How far from Telford is St Georges? That's the address I have for Jennifer Duncan's parents.'

'Telford sort of sprawls if you know what I mean. Looking at a map, I've never seen so many roundabouts. St Georges is within the boundaries. We shall see when we get there.'

They lapsed into silence as they continued on to the north west. The sun was now appreciably higher on their right hand side so that Carver donned a pair of black wraparound shades. Stone put her head back and closed her eyes. An untrained observer would have thought her to be sleeping. They would have been wrong. Detective Sergeant Michelle Stone was thinking.

'Coming into Telford now, Michelle' said Carver.

She opened her eyes and scanned left to right. They were on a dual carriageway on either side of which were modern office blocks bearing their company logos – not all of them British. Roundabout followed roundabout and she could begin to work out how the new town had been created. Large, modern office blocks with decent sized car parks. She briefly saw a sign for Cap Gemini. This was service industry Britain.

Carver was now using the satnav to find his way around and Stone thought that he'd made a mistake as they now found themselves on a narrow country lane with a village cricket pitch off to the right to next to which stood a Norman church. He pulled into a pub car park and killed the engine.

'On a job like this, Michelle' began Carver 'there are normally no rules, but this time there are. We cannot let them know that we have a body part.'

'Because we lied to the press' she replied.

'Precisely. We have to play it by ear, assess their personalities and hope that, even after three years, there is still some trace of their daughter in the house. DNA will do; a print from the third finger left hand would be a bonus.'

'I've my forensic kit in the boot if we need it, Martin.'

'And I've my forensics kit plus extras in mine. Don't be miffed if I ask you to run along and fetch it, will you?'

'Oh no – no problem at all boss. I'm just the girly. I'll even make the tea when we get back.' She grinned to show that she understood what his tactic was and that she agreed.

He started the car and pulled out. Five minutes later they were at the end of a cul-de-sac called Orchard Close. Modern, clean semi-detached houses with American style lawns at the front. No doubt there were large English gardens at the rear, some with conservatories and decking. They left the car and walked up an asphalted pathway to the sunshine yellow front door, rang the bell and waited. Their brains had led them to this spot. Their instincts told them that this was where they could start to unravel the web that a killer had woven.

After a moment the door opened to reveal a man who might as well have had 'made by the British Army' stamped on his forehead. Maybe an inch under six feet tall, dark brown hair, cropped close to the skull, gunfighters eyes and a taught body for a man closer to fifty than forty. He was dressed in a mid blue T-shirt with matching slacks and heavy black brogues bulled to mirrors. The final clue was the tattoos on his corded forearms. This was a serious, unsmiling man.

Carver asked 'Mr Duncan?'

'Yes' replied the man in a manner so clipped that it could have been taken for aggression if one did not know the ways of a long serving soldier.

Taking out his wallet and showing his credentials Martin continued 'Detective Inspector Martin Carver and Detective Sergeant Michelle Stone, Metropolitan Police. I believe you've already spoken to DS Stone on the phone.'

'Please, come in' said Duncan stepping back and ushering the two police officers inside. He led them through to a lounge which was illuminated by the sun's rays coming through the front bay windows. The furniture was floral but comfortable – obviously good quality. Everything was in its place with not even a Sunday paper lying around. It looked like a show house so either Mrs Duncan was very house proud or the military did the cleaning.

'Can I get you a drink?' asked Duncan in a neutral manner.

Carver answered quickly. 'A strong cup of tea, two sugars would do me fine.'

Michelle did the mental equivalent of a double take. Carver, like her, was a coffee drinker. He must have a reason so she said 'Same for me but without the sugar please.'

Duncan left the room and they could hear a brief conversation through the open door which must have led to the kitchen. He was back before Michelle could ask Carver about his new taste in beverages.

'My wife will be with us in a minute. Are you going to give us bad news?' asked Duncan bluntly.

'No, Mr Duncan. No news at all. We are pursuing enquiries as the saying goes. I'd rather wait until your wife joins us if that's OK.'

Duncan nodded in agreement and the silence was just growing to an uncomfortable level when his wife entered bearing a large wooden tray on which were set two large mugs of strong tea and two dainty cups and saucers containing visually weaker versions of the same drink plus a plate of various biscuits.

'This is my wife Jenna. Jenna, this is Martin Carver and Michelle Stone from the London police' said Duncan.

Martin stood to shake her hand. Michelle stayed sat and did the same. It seemed to be a household in which traditional roles were adhered to.

Jenna Duncan was in her early forties but looked around thirty five. Short honey blond hair in an urchin style with cobalt eyes and a good sun tan that came from neither lamp nor bottle, she exuded fitness. This was enhanced by the fact she was dressed for the gym in a white top that contrasted well with her tan. Despite the tragedy that had happened in her life, the laughter creases at eyes and mouth had not been erased. Carver found it hard to equate the woman in front of him with whoever had chosen the floral furniture. Then Jenna Duncan started to speak and all was clear; a very slight accent indicated that she was probably German.

'Do you have news of our Jennifer, please?' she asked.

Carver took the lead in replying. 'No, not as such. Let me explain why we are here. DS Stone and I are part of a new unit that has been set up to concentrate on a certain category of missing people, not just your daughter. There is no such thing in this country as a central missing person's registry, as I'm sure you're aware by now. Everything is done at the local level – in Jennifer's case Brighton and Hove which comes under the jurisdiction of the Sussex Constabulary. They did what they could and the efforts which you both made were exemplary. But after a certain amount of time other crimes and events will push the disappearance of one girl onto the back burner. I'm not saying that Sussex Police have forgotten your daughter but, being realistic, she is not the priority she once was.

'They think she's dead or run away don't they Mr Carver?' said Duncan.

'I've no idea what they think, sir. We are here to do two things which I'll come to in a moment; but let me ask you both a question first. Even after three years, you still jump when there is a knock at the door or the phone rings at an unusual hour and you think 'it's Jennifer!' don't you?'

Husband and wife both replied 'yes'; he brusquely, she with a sigh.

'And the hurt goes on each time that it isn't her. I may be able to stop that feeling. What I am going to say next is not very pleasant. Are you OK to stay Mrs Duncan?'

'Jenna. Please call me Jenna.'

'All right, Jenna. We're Martin and Michelle. Are you sure you are up to this?'

'Yes'. She left her armchair and joined her husband on the two seat sofa. 'I am strong – Malcolm is a rock. Please continue.'

'We have files on unidentified people from all over the UK. Some dead, some alive. Sometimes there is a car crash. The bodies are burned or damaged beyond all recognition and the car turns out to have been stolen or bought for cash. We have no way of knowing who the deceased were. Until now, no-one had though of trying to match the DNA of such people to a list of missing persons on a national basis. That is one avenue we are exploring. Secondly, and this mainly a London thing hence our involvement, there are a surprising number of people wandering the streets in a state of bewilderment, without I.D. and who do not know who they are. Some of them are diagnosed to be clinically insane, or a danger to themselves or others. They end up being lost in the system. Again we have all these files and are going to try and match these people with certain categories of missing persons throughout the UK. Are you with me so far?

Malcolm and Jenna Duncan looked at each other as they held hands. They were one of those rare couples who enjoyed a level of communication that bordered on the telepathic. She was strong but was deferring to her man here; gazing up into his eyes willing him to do the impossible and bring their child back.

'So what you're saying is that our girl could be a so far unidentified corpse or a patient in a mental ward. Not the best news I've ever received on a Sunday' said Malcolm Duncan.

'I told you it wouldn't be pleasant but there is another way to look at this. If we can prove that she died in an accident, you can put her to rest, grieve, heal and continue with your lives. If she is in a secure hospital and you saw her that might, just might, bring her back to the real world and would certainly aid whatever therapy she was undergoing. It's why we do what we do, Mr Duncan.'

'You said that 'a certain category' of missing people were being looked at. What do you mean by that Martin?' asked Jenna Duncan.

'To be honest, Jenna, people like your daughter. Stable background, steady job whose dropping off the face of the earth is totally out of character. There are thousands of people who go missing because their lifestyle predisposes that. We cannot chase them all.'

'Where do we go from here? What do you need from us Mr Carver?' asked Duncan.

'Physical evidence to begin with. Without that, it's a non-starter. Did Jennifer come back to visit you after she went to Brighton?'

'Oh yes. She loved it there but came up here for her holidays and always stayed with us' replied Jenna.

Mentally taking a deep breath and crossing his fingers Martin asked the big question. 'And have you kept her room ready for her?'

'We have never given up hope, Martin. It's a cliché, I know, but the room is as it was the last time she was here. I hoover and I air but nothing else has changed.'

'Fine. Would you show Michelle where it is. I'll be with you in a bit.'

The two women left the lounge and mounted the stairs leaving the men on their own. After a door was heard to open above them Duncan sat back, fixed Carver's eyes and with his own and said 'Your story, on the surface, makes sense. But I ask myself, why are two Met detectives in Telford on a Sunday enquiring after a girl who went missing in Brighton three years ago. What am I missing here, Mr Carver?'

'Nothing, Mr Duncan. I've laid my cards, unpleasant as they are, on the table. You're not the only family being visited and the Met does not yet work Monday to Friday so don't go reading too much into us being here on the general public's day of rest.'

Duncan's face revealed nothing but Carver could sense that he was not convinced. Finally Duncan spoke in a low, measured voice, 'You see that woman I'm married to? She is my world. I joined the army as a boy soldier with the intention of doing one stint, getting my HGV license then making a shed load of money driving trucks across Europe. But I found out that I was a good soldier – the life suited me. Started off in R.E.M.E that's Royal Electrical and Mechanical Engineers to you. Travelled all over; Hong Kong, Cyprus, Belize and the B.O.A.R that's British Army of the Rhine to you. I'd made sergeant by then and met Jenna there. She was a tri-lingual translator/interpreter for NATO. All the officers were after her but she chose me – me! She left her own country to live in married quarters in bloody Donnington whilst I ran around doing what we do. Long story short; I left the army, did quite a few different things to make good money whilst Jenna qualified as a teacher. Bought this place and I now own a taxi company doing all the airport runs. I don't have to leave her on her own anymore. Life was great until our girl disappeared but we were, are getting on with it so, Mr Carver, if you do anything at all that hurts my wife I will hunt you down and, policeman or not, slot you. Is that clear?'

' "Slot" me. You did not finish your service career in REME did you Mr Duncan?'

Malcolm Duncan ignored the question. 'Just so we're clear Mr Carver. Shall we join the ladies?'

'No, best not. Women in a girl's bedroom will talk more openly without our presence. Anyway, I've a few questions for you. I've looked over the interviews you and your wife had with the police in Brighton and they seem a bit bare.'

'How do you mean?'

'I don't get a feel for Jennifer as a person – she comes across as one dimensional. Work and that's it. No social life or outside interests, hobbies, sports, anything. Could you comment on that please?'

'Jennifer is a very cautious girl. She saw a lot of shit in Wolverhampton when she was studying and its not her scene to get plastered on booze and drugs are a total no-no thank God. She did go out at college and continued to do so in Brighton but to live music venues mainly. That's her real interest outside her career. She's a pretty good guitarist in fact; used to play for us when she came up for a visit.'

'What style?'

'Oh, I suppose you'd call it folk rock. A bit light for me but I'd love to hear her again if, if.' Malcolm Duncan took a long, deep inhalation through his nostrils as the realisation of who he was talking about and what might have happened to her hit him. He exhaled under control again just as his wife reappeared followed by Michelle Stone. The police officers spoke. 'Boss, could you pop up here please?'

They climbed the stairs together and entered a sun lit room decorated predominantly in duck egg blue. It was well ordered with only one poster on the wall, that of a bare footed Joss Stone. In one corner a guitar case.

Michelle looked at Martin and indicated the poster. 'My namesake. And I can see prints from here. During my chat with Jenna she revealed that her daughter is left handed. Inside that case is an acoustic six string so I'm hoping for something off the lacquered belly of the guitar. There's a toothbrush and a hairbrush for DNA. I've an hour maybe two hours work here Martin.'

'OK I'll take the samples from the Duncans and then try and get them out of the house. In my kit I always carry brown paper bags. Use those for the glasses. They never smudge. OK.'

'OK.'

'Let's get on with it then.'

Michelle left the house to retrieve the forensic kits from the car. Martin rejoined the Duncans in the lounge. They both looked at him, one with expectation the other with barely concealed suspicion.

'Michelle reckons that there is more than enough material in Jennifer's room for us to move on to the next stage. She will spend an hour or so retrieving and cataloguing it before we head back to London. What I'd like to do, if you agree of course, is to take your fingerprints for elimination purposes and also your DNA samples in case Michelle cannot retrieve any of Jennifer's.'

'Of course' said Jenna.

'Prints, no problem' said Mr Duncan 'but why DNA? I don't get that.'

'It's all a bit scientific but, put simply, whilst everyone's DNA is unique, Jennifer's will be a combination of yours. Not fifty fifty but a mixture. It's why some kids look like one parent and not the other.'

'And why some look like the postman' said Duncan. 'OK we'll do it.'

Michelle had dropped Martin's kit off on her way back up to the bedroom and he began by taking bucal swabs of the couple. This was done by running a Q tip round the inside of the cheek; this was then sealed in a container which was labelled and dated. The fingerprints were taken by an electronic digital scanner which surprised the hell out of Mr Duncan who had been expecting a black, sticky mess and a long time scrubbing afterwards.

The jobs done, Martin packed away his gear and said 'Michelle's going to be up and down the stairs for at least the next hour. Do you two fancy showing me a quiet pub nearby where we could continue our chat?'

The Duncan's looked at each other and did their telepathy thing again. He replied for both of them. 'Yes, Mr Carver – we can do that. If we go in your car that means we can both have a Sunday drink for once.' He smiled for the first time during the visit. 'Done. Are you both ready? OK. I'll just let Michelle know what I'm up to.'

Five minutes later Martin was driving the Duncan's down narrow country lanes and, following the husband's directions, leaving Telford behind them. Eventually they stopped at what could only be called an inn. There were no homes in sight so there was no chance of people walking in to call it a public house. It stood proud and alone, set back from the old road (which had once been the only road hereabouts) and was, therefore, in the best traditions of English coaching inns. It was now a bar and restaurant with rooms and was splendid.

Martin bought the drinks and the three of them sat in a quiet spot where the light came through a leaded window. They continued their discussion of Jennifer with Martin only occasionally having to guide the conversation back on track as the Duncan's talked and talked of their daughter – usually in the present tense.

One hour and two pints later and the police officer was no wiser. The missing girl was quiet, had no serious boyfriend, loved her parents and her work in that order, preferred Brighton to Telford (no surprise there) and dreamed of moving to London if the right job came up. Her sole outside interest was music but she had stopped playing and contented herself with the pub music scene on the south coast.

The threesome drove back to the Duncan's home in Telford where Michelle was waiting with her forensic samples all packed up and ready to go. The two detectives said goodbye and promised to be in touch as soon as they knew something, one way or another. Martin tossed the car keys to his colleague and said 'Your turn'.

'You mean you've had a beer or two'.

'Yup. It's a dirty job but - you know the rest. Come on. Let's go and find a pub for lunch. Your choice and the firm's paying'.

Staying on the back roads they came across a grouping of houses which did not appear to be a named village – but it had a King's Head and they availed themselves of a half decent carvery. Half an hour later and they were on the motorway heading south to the capital.

'Apart from prints and hairs what did you find?' asked Carver.

'Nothing and believe me, I looked. All the places a young woman might hide a diary or love letters. Nada. If she kept such things they must have been in Brighton so that's long gone. We'll just have to wait until Dr Watkins and Igor get in tomorrow.'

'Yes. Nothing further we can do today.' But they were wrong.

When they arrived back at their office to stow their gear they saw in large red letters, a message on the white board.

'LAB IS OPEN FOR ORION MATERIAL TODAY – WATKINS 1000HRS'

'Bloody hell, Michelle! Let's shift before she changes her mind.'

The two of them quick marched to the lab where they found Dr Rachel Watkins looking through a microscope and taking notes. After a moment she swivelled her stool around and said 'Commander Goodchild told me that you two were pulling in some Sunday overtime so I thought I'd best be here to sort out whatever you've no doubt been mishandling. What've you got?'

Michelle handed over her samples plus explanatory notes as to their provenance. Martin gave her his control prints and the bucal swabs. The absence of sarcasm from Dr Watkins told them that they had done everything to standard; they did not expect either thanks or praise.

'Tell Commander Goodchild that I'll have a preliminary – stress that word – report for him by 0800 tomorrow. Goodbye.'

Carver and Stone left the lab and returned to their office. It was still only mid afternoon so they decided to work up their report on the day's field trip.

'Martin. All that balls about crispy corpses and loonies lost in the system. I realise that you only invented that to avoid revealing the existence of the ten fingers but you've lied to two grieving parents. Are you going to put that detail into the report?'

'Yes; if only to provide continuity in the event that other officers have to speak to the Duncan's in the future. I'm not happy with it especially as Mr Duncan has promised to slot me if I upset his wife.'

'Slot?'

'Military slang for to personally kill. I've only come across the word a few times over the years. It seems to be a term used solely by the S.A.S.'

'You reckon Duncan's ex-S.A.S then?'

'He may even be a reservist. You could see what sort of shape he was in and Hereford is just down the road from Telford. I'll check him out when I have the time.'

'Yes, I reckon that would be wise. What's next then, Martin?'

'Let's write our reports, check each others work then I wouldn't mind a proper drink if you're up for it.'

'Sure. Let's crack on.'

So as Carver and Stone tapped away on their word processors, 'Dominic Lord' and Catherine Taylor performed to their audience in Bristol and Rachel Watkins worked her magic on three year old forensic samples, the other actors in the play went about their Sunday routines with no inkling of the storm that was gathering and would threaten their very existence.

Chapter Twelve

Roger Tucker was having a productive Monday. Working from his home office as he often did, he had managed to clear all his emails by mid morning and had added a final few snippets to his already prepared page for his paper's Tuesday edition. This he had forwarded to the editor and he was now free to pursue the mysterious ML. Easier said than done. Where to start? He could hardly call the Met and ask what Mark Goodchild was up to. Apart from the fact that the police would not tell him anything, such an approach from a nationally known journalist could have repercussions for his friend. The bottom line had to be what was really in the buried package. If he could find that out it might give him an idea as to who ML really was. After all, the initial email had asked if he could be the one to speak for England's lost princesses; he felt that it was almost a duty to follow this up. Thinking back to his day in Kensington Gardens he remembered the diminutive doctor in charge of the forensics team. Perhaps she could be a point of entry into this cover-up, for cover-up it surely was. He googled Rachel Watkins and was surprised to see that she was the first entry on a hit list numbering 275,000. As Tucker was finishing reading Watkins' impressive CV an envelope shaped icon appeared in the bottom right corner of his screen and an annoying electronic voice announced that he had mail. Switching to his inbox he was shocked to see that the sender was ML.

FROM: ML@HOTMAIL.CO.UK
TO: R.TUCKER@DAILY POST.CO.UK
SENT: MONDAY 23 AUGUST 2010 1105
SUBJECT: SPEAK FOR US

Dear Mr Tucker – are you a knave or a fool? The massive lie emanating from New Scotland Yard and your silence or absence from the press conference indicates that you are one or the other. The riddle was solved and action taken but the truth is still buried. Are you an accomplice to this or are you simply another dupe? I shall tell you plainly what your friends in blue possess; physical evidence of ten dead girls. Ten girls representing thousands they don't even care to search for. It's hard work tracing missing people and it can be ignored as a 'victimless crime' in most cases. But one would think that, confronted with identifiable body parts from ten different people, a bit of an effort might be made. Or are they embarrassed by their record of ineptitude? You have 48 hours before I release this information to the gutter press; and if they are gagged or choose to ignore it I shall simply post it online and let the world beat an electronic path to your door.

Happy hunting, ML.

Tucker's initial reaction was one of shock. If this were true Mark Goodchild and his superiors were out of their collective minds. He could see no possible excuse for a lie of this magnitude. None. Was his editor aware of these claims? Anger was replacing shock in Tucker's mind but he was not, by nature, an angry man and he soon calmed down and began to analyse the email. This was an accusation from an anonymous weirdo. Nothing more at present. But, as a journalist, he had to follow it up. If this were true did he owe Mark Goodchild any favours? If the Met had lied then Mark had played him like a violin. Shit. Where did his editor stand in all of this? For all Tucker knew this email had been blind cc'd to Peter Balls who would be waiting to see how his journalist reacted. Double shit.

Going back to the latest email he composed a brief reply:

FROM: R.TUCKER@DAILYPOST.CO.UK
TO: ML@HOTMAIL.CO.UK
SENT: MONDAY 23 AUGUST 2010 1110
SUBJECT: SPEAK FOR US

Dear ML – I am neither knavish nor foolish and will pursue this. Please define 'body parts' to give me some credibility when I go into bat against the Met. You have thirty minutes before I am incommunicado for the rest of the day.
Tucker.

He pressed send and sat back to wait.

ML was in the first class business lounge at London Euston train station. He had been about to log off when Tucker's reply arrived: he had not expected such a rapid reaction from the journalist. How to respond? ML weighed the pros and cons in his mind and decided on the nuclear option. This message would have the MET and the media at each other's throats.

FROM: ML@HOTMAIL.CO.UK
TO: R.TUCKER@DAILYPOST.CO.UK
SENT: MONDAY 23 AUGUST 2010 1115
SUBJECT: SPEAK FOR US

Dear Mr Tucker – body parts are the third finger, left hand of ten different women. Get on with it if you think you are the man for the job.
ML

He logged off and checked his watch. Ian Williams was due to arrive in forty five minutes so he went to the bar and suffered a railway pub brunch to keep him going until his meeting.

§

Roger Tucker was sat at home staring at his computer screen. The coldness of the message from ML had stunned him. He felt like calling Mark Goodchild and giving him a verbal beating. If this were true, how could the Met sit on something that made the Yorkshire Ripper look like a naughty schoolboy? But his professional, calm head assumed control. This could all be nonsense, designed to create a row between the police and the press. He had to proceed with caution. Tucker knew many newspaper editors in London but he had few real friends so he decided to give Mark Goodchild one more chance. Picking up his mobile he rang the policeman.

'Morning Roger. Your timing is crap. I'm up to my arse in…….'

'I don't care Mark' interrupted Tucker. 'I will meet with you in the next thirty minutes and you will have some explanations for me. I'm calling as a friend not a journalist but if you try to fuck me over again I will reverse those roles. Where's good for you?'

Mark Goodchild's mind was racing. Roger obviously thought that he knew something and Orion might be blown just as they were making progress. Think, think! Putting on his most relaxed voice Goodchild said 'I don't know what's rattled your cage, mate but I don't just drop everything when a journo calls up for a rant. What's the problem?'

'The problem, Mark, is your lies to me, the media and ultimately the public. I want a face to face, Mark and I want it now. If not you can read it all in my paper tomorrow. Balls will publish because if he tries to block me, I'll give it to Rupert Murdoch – he does not give a fuck. So, where's good for you?'

Goodchild realised that Tucker knew something and that they would have to meet. The timing could not be worse. Stone and Carver's visit to Telford had yielded positive results. Rachel Watkins had matched the prints and DNA of Jennifer Duncan to one of the fingers. They now had a place to start from. Michelle Stone's idea for tracing missing people obviously worked and would be expanded upon. The last thing he needed now was a rampaging journalist of Roger Tucker's calibre. Time to bite the bullet but assert control as well.

'I can't do thirty minutes Roger; I've a meeting in ten which is absolutely unavoidable. How about 1230 in the Red Lion, Whitehall?'

'OK. Can do. Downstairs bar I take it?'

'Yes. Can't be seen in public with the likes of you. See you.'

'1230. Don't even think of standing me up.'

'Love you too.'

§

As the journalist and the detective were arranging their meeting; ML was regretting eating in a railway station. A Turkish caff would have been better. To wash the grease from his guts he had downed a pint of chav champagne, otherwise known as Stella Artois. Sitting in the window seat of the bar he was putting on his Rodney McNaughten persona and waiting for the Welshman to arrive.

Amazingly the train was actually on time and Williams arrived at his table smiling ingratiatingly .

'Good to see you again Mr McNaughten. I hope that you haven't been waiting long.'

'No, not at all. I've availed myself of the office facilities to catch up on some other work so I've not had to waste any time. Speaking of which, when do you have to head back north?'

'No fixed time; it all depends on how long our business takes. There are regular trains between here and Manchester. I could even take any northbound train and jump off at Preston which is just down the track from me.'

ML had tuned out this trainspotting drivel and was planning the rest of his day in his mind. Switching back to the here and now he said 'Quite, quite. Very well, lets get on with it. Here are your plane tickets, hotel reservation and cash retainer of £3,000.' He handed a very large white envelope to Williams which the latter opened. Inside were three smaller envelopes which he proceeded to open. ML kept the original large envelope which he ripped apart as if to check that there was nothing left inside. He placed the torn remnants in his briefcase.

'You are staying at the Dunas Oasis which is not the best hotel in Corralejo but it is adequate. I don't expect you to actually eat lunch or dinner in the place because a major part of your job is to visit as many eating establishments as you can. Look at these.'

ML opened yet another large envelope and tipped its contents onto Williams' side of the table. There was a collection of street maps and A5 booklets on the subject of Fuerteventura.

'All these are distributed free of charge around the island' said ML. 'The publishers make their money by selling the advertising space in them with the intention of driving tourists to these destinations. As you can see, they are fairly shoddy and my client thinks that he can do a better job, not just in Fuerteventura, but throughout the Canaries, Balearics and, why not the entire Mediterranean litoral. This is the market tester so, Mr Williams, get it right and you can exchange the rain of Manchester for the sun of the Costas.'

'What exactly do you need me to do?'

'Find out what the advertising rates are, then what these people are actually paying and for how long. Find out if they, as advertisers, quantify how many customers their adverts drive their way. Finally, draw up a hit list of potential advertisers in and around Corralejo – night clubs, bars, restaurants, outdoor activities; anything that wants tourist trade.'

'Basically it's a two week market research job then. No problem. You mentioned expenses. What's the deal on that?'

'This is slightly tricky but only slightly. Keep a daily record of what you spend. You will not always be able to obtain a receipt so we shall have to operate on trust. I am not going to put a limit on expenditure but don't take the piss. You will have to buy drinks for other people to get anywhere but I don't want to see payments to Dirty Dolores for services rendered.'

'Understood. Will I need to hire a car?'

'You won't <u>need</u> to, but you may wish to for a day just to get a feel for the island. The reason I've selected your particular hotel is that it is situated on the top of the main drag into town. You will be able to do most of your visits on foot. If you need to visit a nearby village there is a very good supply of decent taxis. Besides, you do not want to be stopped by the Guardia Civil if you've had even a couple of drinks. Anything you're not clear about?'

'Where do I send my report Mr McNaughten?'

'I suggest that you type it up each day on your laptop or in the hotel office facilities. Forty eight hours after you return I'll give you a call and we'll set up debriefing; you can give me your written report then and I'll reimburse your expenses in whichever form you prefer. Is that alright with you Mr Williams?'

'It's fine, sir. Thanks for the opportunity and I hope that this is the start of a long business relationship.'

ML gathered his papers into his case and stood. Williams did likewise. The two men shook hands, bade each other farewell and ML strode off to the concourse where he was soon lost to view.

§

Across town Roger Tucker had only just sat down with his drink when Mark Goodchild appeared at the bar's discrete rear entrance. The detective saw the journalist and headed directly towards him without stopping at the bar. By coincidence he found himself at the same table where he had lunched with Carver and Stone; he read nothing into this fact.

'Good day to you Roger. I'm sorry to be rude but I have a very full plate at the moment and don't have time to socialise. It's only because we go back so far that I'm here at all. What's up?' asked Goodchild.

Roger Tucker looked his friend straight in the eye. Not many people did this. Goodchild's size, demeanour, scars and rank were very intimidating to most people. At this moment though, Roger Tucker just knew in his journalistic gut that the officer was a worried man.

'Mark, I'm going to be completely honest with you. I'm here as a friend but you are one, just one, lie away from me turning away from you. If you have done what I think you have, you are damn close to not only losing your career but also of going to prison for perverting the course of justice. Are you sure that you don't want a drink?'

'Sure. Say what you have to say.'

'OK Mark. Just remember what I said about one lie. What is Orion?'

Goodchild was a trained professional and never revealed his true thoughts even when interrogating the vilest of criminals and, to his credit, his face showed nothing on hearing a top secret code word from a journalist. Bizarrely his mind flashed to the famous scene in Goldfinger; James Bond is tied down, legs apart as a laser beam creeps towards his genitals. Goodchild found that he could remember the dialogue.

Bond: 'Do you expect me to talk, Goldfinger?'

Goldfinger: 'No, Mr Bond; I expect you to die!'

As the laser beam melts the gold table to which Sean Connery was strapped and Gert Fröbe turns away with disinterest, every male in the cinema was starting to feel empathetic discomfort. Then Bond throws the dice for the last time by yelling to Goldfinger that he knows about the villains planned operation 'Grandslam'. One word and the bad guy has to re-evaluate everything just as one word from Roger Tucker was now forcing Mark Goodchild to calculate whether or not he could risk denying Orion's existence. He needed time.

'I've changed my mind. A pint of Guinness please, Roger.'

Tucker nodded at Goodchild. He knew that his friend did not need the crutch of alcohol and was stalling him but the very fact that he had not denied Orion's existence was an admission in itself. He went to the bar and took his time before returning to their table. Goodchild took a deep draught, set his glass down and said 'Orion exists. All the information about it and even its name are classified secret and above so I cannot legally tell you anything about it or I could, make that would, be charged under the Official Secrets Act. I have to ask you Roger; how did you obtain that name?'

'I'm a journalist, Mark. I've received info that you are not working on counter-terrorism so I waited until I knew that you'd be on your way here and I called SO15. When I asked for you I was told that you were on attachment to something called Orion. Short version; I assured SO15 that my call was personal in nature and nothing to do with CT stuff and could they put me through to the Orion section which they did. Now it's interesting that the Orion person I spoke to revealed absolutely nothing – not even her name; I merely enquired if I was through to the Orion section. All I received in return was 'who's calling please?' so I made up some bullshit about catering services supplies for the new unit. When I was asked for my name and number I said I was P.C Roger Sole. The number I gave was Human Resources. Sorry if I've confused your staff.'

Despite the seriousness of the situation Goodchild had to laugh. 'R Sole of Human Resources? Love it; and don't worry – the woman you spoke to will have seen through that in about five seconds after you got off the line. Who gave you the Orion name at SO15?'

'No idea. I did not ask.'

'I'll let that go for now, Roger. You said that you've received information that I'm not working CT. What information and where from? You cannot withhold anything that might impede the progress of a police investigation you know.'

'The last time I gave information to you the result was a great big fucking lie and me being made to look a cunt to my colleagues. Don't even think of threatening me, Mark; you and your lot are the ones at risk here!'

'Jesus, Roger! Steady on. I was only reminding you of the legal ramifications of your actions. Anyway, my question stands; what do you <u>think</u> you know? What has made you go down this road?'

Mark Goodchild had adopted a conciliatory tone. In effect he was playing good cop bad cop without the benefit of a partner. Roger Tucker regarded the detective for a long five seconds as he decided how to proceed. Finally he spoke in his most serious tone, his eyes never leaving Goodchild's face. 'Remember, Mark; one lie and I'm out of here. Did you or did you not find ten fingers from ten different women buried in Kensington Gardens?'

Goodchild's eyes scanned the bar. It was still a bit early for officials to be lunching but he had to be sure. Seeing nobody that he knew, he leaned forward towards Tucker and softly said 'Yes. Who told you Roger?'

'I've received another email – two in fact – from ML. What the fuck are you playing at, Mark?'

'It's more complicated than it looks but I'll tell you this much; there are national security issues involved and a terrorist angle. Hence my involvement. This is more than a sick serial killer. I need to see the new emails, Roger.'

'And why should I trust you again? Doing the same thing repeatedly and expecting a different result is one definition of insanity. The old 'national security' excuse is wearing a bit thin these days. I'm not prepared to stand back and let us go down the

American route of Homeland Security and the Patriot Act. Give me a reason why I should not go public with this?'

Mark Goodchild realised that he was very close to losing control of the investigation and just when the first break had come his way. He knew Roger Tucker well enough to understand that the man would not be cowed by any threat that he could make. If he arrested him now for withholding evidence and obstructing a police investigation, his paper's lawyers would have him out before you could say 'unlawful arrest' and then the shit would really start to fly – and only ML would be the beneficiary. It was time for diplomacy and truth – two words that rarely appear in the same sentence.

'Roger if you go public with the information that you have now you will be doing serious harm to our hunt for the killer or killers. I'm willing to give you the whole story here and now but, in return, I <u>must</u> see the latest ML communication. When I've finished I hope that you'll agree to keep this to yourself for now. I cannot force you but I believe that once you know the facts you'll agree to work with me and not against me. Fair enough?'

'Can we go on the record here, Mark?'

'No; that's too much too soon. You came to me as a friend and what I'm about to tell you breaks so many rules it's untrue. If you go public at the end of this meeting and quote 'a senior Met official' I'm still stuffed. All I can offer is that, when we resolve this matter, I'll give you personally an exclusive interview prior to an eventual police press conference. What do you say?'

'All right. Against my better judgement I'll listen to you but, I warn you – this will have to be fucking good to keep me from going to press. Shoot. Shit – wrong word to use on an SO15 officer. Carry on.'

Goodchild, by way of reply, went first to the bar for two refills. He was going to need a drink to get through this. Returning to the table, he scanned the room again then began to speak sotto voce.

'For some time now, the Security Services have been warning us that A.Q. or an affiliate thereof was going to carry out a 'spectacular' in central London – most likely an explosive device in a public place. When you showed me your crazy email I thought that this was part of the plot. Derek Clarkson agreed and we set our contingency plans in motion. That is why we able to move so quickly. Once we opened the package and found the fingers, not explosives, we were faced with several problems: firstly the left wing media could have accused us of over-reacting by closing down that part of London: secondly, and more importantly, we did not want to give the bad guys the idea that they could paralyse central London for the cost of a well placed package and an email to the press. So we concocted the training exercise story. Your editor only knows some this but he agreed to play ball with us.'

'The wanker.'

'Perhaps. I've never had the pleasure. Anyway, Orion was set up under my command to investigate the murders and now it gets interesting. Forensics revealed traces in the victims' blood of an opiate gas that does not exist in this country. It is similar to that used by Russian special forces when they took out the Chechen terrorists who had taken over a theatre in Moscow. Do you remember that one?'

'Yes. Complete cock-up. They also killed a load of hostages didn't they?'

'Over a hundred. So who the hell is using an exotic substance like that to kill young women? I now have to let MI5 and MI6 know of this development but they know how to keep their mouths shut. More to the point they have the resources to find out where this drug came from and how it could be brought into the UK.'

'Are you sure that it was brought over here?'

'What do you mean?'

'Maybe the killer operates in Europe and only brings back the fingers. You've not mentioned that you've identified the girls who were killed so I'm assuming they were not on record – or are you holding back on me, Mark?'

'Fuck; we had not thought of that as a scenario. But I don't think it works for two reasons: one, remember the first email. 'Who will speak for <u>England's</u> lost princesses?': two, we have just identified one of the victims – a girl from the north who vanished without trace three years ago. We now have a means of identifying possible victims and matching familial DNA to the remains. We will then examine these groups' lives in detail and look for areas of commonality. We <u>will</u> catch this bastard.'

'Who is the identified victim, Mark?'

'No way, Roger. We have not even told her family yet. That protocol is set in stone.'

'OK. What is the method that you are using to trace these girls whose fingers you have?'

'You do not need to know the minutiae of police procedure at this time. That's the sort of question I'll answer when I go on record, OK. You are now up to speed on what has happened and where we are going. Can I have those new emails please?'

Roger Tucker looked down into the contents of his pint glass as if he could find the answer to his dilemma in the cream and black liquid. The story made sense and he could find no obvious holes in it. If Mark Goodchild was being straight with him then his offer to do an exclusive on the record was a generous one – but it was a case of jam tomorrow. Tucker wished there was someone he could consult on this but the only man he knew that he could trust with this level of information was the one sat across the table from him. He made his decisions. Reaching into his inside breast pocket he pulled out three folded A4 sheets of paper which he handed to Goodchild.

'These are the printouts, Mark. I expect you to keep in touch.'

'Of course. I take it that you received these at home, not the paper?'

'Yes.'

'Then I'm going to have a technical guy go to your place to see what he can see, if that's all right.'

'Sure; you sort it out. You have my numbers. Anything else?'

'There is actually. I'm going to have a criminal psychologist come in to consult with us. As you've been this nutter's chosen point of contact I'm pretty sure he'll want to talk with you. Any objections?'

'None at all. Again you sort it out. Will this guy be a profiler?'

'No; I'm not a fan of that. It seems to me to be American mumbo-jumbo. It used to be called Behavioural Science by the F.B.I. To me it's just stating the bleeding obvious. Silence of the Lambs has a lot to answer for. Last thing, Roger and listen carefully. Do not try and contact ML yourself. Whoever the murderer is, and whatever his mental state, he is organised, resourceful and a stone cold killer. I am not exaggerating when I say that you would be risking your life if you involve yourself any more in this. Are we clear on that?'

'Fine. As long as you remember to keep me informed on the investigation's progress I'll be good.'

'Excellent. Thanks, Roger. I'll be in touch about the techie and the shrink. Bye for now.'

With that Goodchild turned and ascended the dark stairwell into the light and headed back to New Scotland Yard to brief his colleagues on the latest developments. If ML was to be believed, in forty eight hours he was going to release his details to the press or online. How the hell was he going to avoid that from happening?

Chapter Thirteen

As Goodchild made the short walk back to the Orion offices, Tucker hailed a cab to take him home to put the final touches to his regular Tuesday article for the paper. He was glad that he had written the bulk of it already because his mind was reeling from his friend's revelations and satirical irony was beyond him at the moment. The fact that ML had threatened to blow the story if nothing was done in forty eight hours was a major worry. If it came out that Tucker had sat on such sensational information when he could have had a major scoop it would effectively kill any journalistic integrity which he possessed. He could claim that the police had forbidden him to do anything to cover his back legally; he would then be open to accusations of participation in an establishment cover up. Many knives would be out.

On top of that, Mark Goodchild had seemed damned serious when he had warned him about pursuing ML on his own. Roger Tucker was not a coward but nor was he a fool. He had entered a world of which he had no first hand knowledge and it was ML's hunting ground. He hoped the police caught this killer sooner rather than later for more than one reason. To paraphrase Dr Johnson, it's amazing how the prospect of one's own imminent demise concentrates the mind.

A light went off in Tucker's mind which immediately made him see a clear way forward. Dr Johnson was the key. He would write down everything that had happened so far in the form of a diary. This he would update each evening and forward to his office computer where it would be held in a folder accessible only to himself or Peter Balls in the event of Tucker's death. If the police cocked up and ML managed to get to him then he would drown them in their own deceit. As a bonus, if ML was captured, the record would serve as a basis for both his newspaper article and even a book. With a renewed sense of purpose he paid off the taxi and entered his home to start working.

§

Back at New Scotland Yard the Orion team were feeling decidedly less sanguine. Goodchild had not held anything back from Carver and Stone, showing them the print outs of the latest email exchange between ML and Tucker and letting them know exactly how much information he had given to the journalist. After bringing them up to date Goodchild simply said 'Any comments?'

'The first problem is the forty eight hour deadline that ML has imposed' said Carver. 'If he adheres to that we are stuffed and I don't see us cracking the case in that time frame.'

'I've an idea on how to extend the deadline' said Goodchild 'but I'm not going to give you details now as it may not come off. I'll let you know in the morning. What else do we have?'

'It's more a case of what we don't have, boss' said Michelle Stone. 'Martin and I have come up with another fifteen candidates – strong ones – whose family or friends need to be visited. That's about three weeks work for the two of us just to try and obtain samples for the lab; only then can we even start the follow up investigation to try and establish an M.O. which could lead us to finding out who ML is. We need some staff, boss.'

'I've been thinking about that, Michelle. The problem we have is maintaining secrecy on Orion. I cannot believe that someone in SO15 let that word out to Tucker. I'll trace that leak today and stop it. But if SO15 can blab, what chance do we have if I start using locals to do the interviews? None. I'm going to have to call in a major favour from Box.'

Carver and Stone said nothing but their faces were studies in surprise. Box is the insider's term for the Security Service, commonly referred to as MI5 by the lazy or the ignorant. It stems from the term BOX 500 which was its London postal address many years ago. Its current headquarters are at the bleak edifice named Thames House, located on Millbank next door to the Houses of Parliament. The organisation's duties are various but can broadly be described as counter intelligence in the UK. With the increase of the threat of home grown terrorist attacks in Great Britain, the Security Service has increased vastly in size and moved its focus from Northern Ireland to the mainland. For Goodchild to consider bringing them on board was no small move.

Carver spoke up. 'Boss, I can see the rationale for this – you would be using the exotic murder method as a terrorist angle to justify Box's involvement I take it?'

'Correct.'

'But if this gas is a Russian product then surely six are going to join the party too. This could become one unholy mess.'

By 'six' Carver was referring to the Secret Intelligence Service which was often, incorrectly, called MI6. This department was responsible for the UK's overseas intelligence operations and regarded itself as the senior player in the nation's security community. The giant honey coloured ziggurat it occupied at Vauxhall Cross on the south bank of the river Thames was a very public statement of its hubris. Box and six did not traditionally make good bed fellows.

Goodchild addressed Carver's concern. 'I hear what you're saying, Martin; it could become a problem but I won't know until I talk to my contact. I'll arrange a meeting tomorrow morning and I'll keep you in the loop as much as I can. Anything else?'

'Someone has to inform Jennifer Duncan's parents that their daughter is dead' said Michelle. 'I can see a problem coming down the line there. They are going to want a body to bury aren't they?'

'Christ, of course they will! And we don't have one. How did I not think of that?' said Goodchild. 'Martin, you spoke to them the most – what do you think?'

'I think that Michelle and I both have to return to Telford today and speak with the father. We have to be totally honest with him for several reasons. Firstly, simple human decency. These people have really suffered. They put in such an effort to find their girl with no reward that to lie to them <u>in any way</u> would be criminal. Secondly, I've looked into Mr Duncan's service record and there are quite a few missing years that I cannot account for. The giveaway was an entry which has him listed as 'on attachment as an advisor to the Sultan of Oman's armed forces'. Pounds to peanuts that he was in the S.A.S. Simple self preservation dictates that we do not lie to this man. One day the truth about ML will come out and I don't want to be the guy who gave a sealed coffin to Malcolm Duncan for him to bury or burn if, in fact, it did not contain his daughter's remains.'

'I see your point. Do you think he can be persuaded to keep quiet if you tell him the truth, Martin?'

'I'd say ninety per cent yes, boss, but it is a risk. I honestly feel that it's the only way to play this.'

'OK get up there now and let me know what happens ASAP. You will not be able to contact me between the hours of 1800 and 1930, maybe a bit later but keep trying. I will need this information tonight or this afternoon if possible. See you in the morning.'

Carver and Stone left Goodchild alone in the office. The situation was rapidly becoming too complex for him to keep all its strands in his head. The fact that he had not foreseen that the Duncans would want their daughter's remains for burial indicated to him that he was in danger of making a mistake that could jeopardise the outcome of the investigations. Taking a single A4 sheet of plain white paper and an office biro he went about making a 'to do list'. After fifteen minutes and several reorganisations of priorities what he ended up with was:

1. Set up meeting with Box re loan of ten(?) officers
2. Contact Chief Constables for a female forensics officer to accompany BOX at interviews.
3. L.O.I. tonight to review stalling tactics on ML.
4. Choose a criminal psychologist.
5. Have Stone/Carver organise schedule of the fifteen new interviewers.
6. Send Stone and/or Carver to Brighton to look into index victim's past more thoroughly.
7. Preliminary briefing for Asst. Commissioner Addison
8. Have a technical support officer visit Tucker's home

Some of the list he could make a start on, other items depended on the outcome of certain events not least of which was the reaction of the Duncans in Telford. Despite Carver's ninety per cent probability that Malcolm Duncan would play ball, if the bereaved parents created a fuss there was nothing he could do about it. The web that he had woven would disintegrate in the glare of the media's spotlight. He would not even employ the maxim of 'hope for the best, prepare for the worst' for if the worst were to happen the powers that be would want more than his resignation; they would want his head on a plate.

Focussing on doing what he could, Mark Goodchild hit the phones and began setting up all the meetings which would be necessary to get the investigation moving forward. By three o'clock he had managed to arrange a mid-morning meeting with an un-named officer of the Security Service. Goodchild was to present himself, in civilian clothing, at Thames House at ten the next day.

He had thought that finding a close – mouthed criminal psychologist would prove difficult so he'd had a word with Rachel Watkins. The scientist had surprised him with her positive attitude towards criminal psychology and she had phoned him back within fifteen minutes of their initial conversation with the name and number of someone she knew personally and recommended highly. Goodchild googled the name and was pleased to learn that, despite its obvious Dutch roots, Dr Chris van Dyke was, in fact British. Van Dyke had been published frequently over the past fifteen years and, once one penetrated the opacity of the academic titles, it became clear that the man's area of specialisation was the serial murderer. Goodchild phoned him and was able to arrange a meeting for 1630hrs that very day.

His next task was to brief Assistant Commission Addison at 1600hrs so he set about collating his notes. The good thing about briefing someone of Addison's elevated rank was that the operative word was 'brief'. The down side was that some senior officers asked the most bizarre questions and you had to be ready for anything.

In the event the meeting went smoothly and Goodchild was in and out in fifteen minutes. Addison had absorbed the information of the oral briefing and was bright enough to realise that it was still early days but that Orion had made real progress. Once the other interviews yielded solid forensic evidence things should start to happen. The two men agreed to meet at the same time the following day. The only question Addison had asked had been an astute one; how was Goodchild going to make ML extend the forty eight hour deadline? Goodchild said that he was working on an idea for that and would let his superior know the outcome at tomorrow's meeting.

Arriving back at his office, Goodchild checked his watch and saw that he had enough time for one quick call before Dr. van Dyke arrived. He dialled a four digit extension from memory and was relieved to hear the receiver picked up on the third ring.

'Clarkson.'

'Derek; Mark Goodchild. Are you at L.O.I. tonight?'

'Yes I am.'

'Good. It's been too long. I'll see you at six then.'

'Fine. I look forward to it.' Clarkson hung up first knowing that this evening would see him dragged back into the Kensington Gardens debacle. Mark had never called him to see if he was attending L.O.I. before. They were either there at the same time or they were not ergo this was almost certainly police business which his once junior colleague did not care to raise in the office.

L.O.I. stands for Lodge of Instruction. This is where Freemasons meet once a week to learn and rehearse the rituals which they will perform at their quarterly meetings. A large provincial town might only have one Masonic Lodge and L.O.I. will take place in it. However, in London there are so many Metropolitan Lodges that it would be impossible for them all to fit into the Temple in Great Queen Street so L.O.I. often takes place in a private room which is part of a pub or restaurant. Clarkson and Goodchild's Lodge held their L.O.I. in an upstairs room of a pub just behind Saint Paul's Cathedral. One of the rules of Freemasonry is that one does not discuss business in Lodge but L.O.I. is a lot more relaxed about it, therefore it would be an ideal place for Goodchild to consult discreetly with his brother Clarkson.

In Goodchild's office his internal line rang; it was the front desk informing him that a Dr van Dyke was here to see him. Mark requested that he be escorted to his office where he would meet the man.

Goodchild knew from his brief search earlier in the day that van Dyke was forty six years old, divorced, no children and lectured at University College, London. He had not been able to find any record of him having worked with the Met but Rachel Watkins assured him that he was on the list of approved police consultants.

Someone pressed the buzzer outside the Orion office. Goodchild looked at the monitor and saw a uniformed constable and a civilian. He pressed the intercom and asked the modern equivalent of 'who goes there?'

'I have Dr. van Dyke to see Commander Goodchild' said the PC.

'Just a moment.'

Goodchild crossed to the door and ushered the civilian into the secure suite of offices. Van Dyke was small, and no more than five six, completely bald and wearing circular, steel rimmed glasses. His clothing was a mixture of corduroy, flannel and tweed all in natural earth colours. Goodchild was glad to see that he was not wearing sandals or sporting a Greenpeace badge. Despite his name, or maybe because of it, van Dyke was clean shaven. As he sat down with Goodchild his grey eyes were darting everywhere, looking for clues as to what this meeting could be about. His intelligence shone from his gaze and he appeared to be enjoying some immense private joke. Mark Goodchild was relieved that he had remembered to cover the whiteboard and turn all hard copy files face down.

'It's Doctor van Dyke isn't it?'

'Yes – but I'm more comfortable with Chris.'

'Fine. In private I'm Mark; in public I'm afraid it's got to be Commander Goodchild. Now before we go any further I have to make something absolutely clear from the start. This is an extremely sensitive operation and is being conducted in total secrecy – for various reasons. If you come on board you will have to sign both the Official Secrets Act and a legally binding document which will prevent you from publishing, in any way, shape or form, anything that you learn during your time with us. This will be reviewed when the investigation is concluded but, to all intents and purposes, this is an official gagging order. Can you live with those conditions, Chris?'

Van Dyke stroked his chin where the eponymous hair would have been and regarded Goodchild coolly. After a good thirty seconds he answered. 'Before I say yea or nay, could you tell me the nature of the crime that you are investigating, please?'

'No. All I'll say is that it is within your area of expertise and that Rachel Watkins recommended you. Sorry, Chris; I need an answer now.'

Van Dyke's face cracked into a broad smile and he held his hands out to his sides, palms upwards, in a gesture of openness.

'At least Rachel's always been on the interesting cases. OK Commander, I'm in. Bring me your forms and I'll sign away my birthright!'

Goodchild was starting to wonder about Dr van Dyke. How could someone who was privy to the goriest details of serial killers be so smiley and flippant? If the general public ever found out what some of society's monsters had actually inflicted on their victims, there would be riots in the streets demanding the return of capital punishment. It takes all sorts, mused Goodchild. Perhaps this was van Dyke's method of dealing with the dark side of human nature.

Goodchild handed over two forms which van Dyke signed after only the most cursory of glances, raising another doubt in the policeman's mind. He'd have to have a talk with Rachel Watkins about this chap. The forms having been placed in a safe, the two men sat down and Mark Goodchild began to tell the story. Van Dyke listened in silence until Goodchild revealed what the box in the park had actually contained.

'OK Mark; stop there if you would. I can see that this is complex and only likely to become more so. I need to take some notes.'

'That's fine but you will have to leave it all in the office. All your written work, and I include that done on computer must be done here.'

'That's going to limit me a bit, Mark.'

'I understand and, as I explain more to you, I think you'll see why we have to work this way. If your home were broken into and your computer went walkies we would be up to our necks in it.'

'OK. I'll just have to rely on the old grey matter then. So, ten fingers. Ten different women I take it?'

The two men went at it intensely with Goodchild doing most of the talking and van Dyke making copious notes and interjecting with the odd question to clarify some point or other. At five thirty Goodchild called a halt saying 'I'm afraid I have to be somewhere else soon, Chris. If you wish to carry on here I can arrange for someone to let you out later. I'll organise a temporary pass for you tomorrow. Or would you rather head off now?'

'Do you know if Dr Watkins is available for a chat? That would be ideal. If she isn't I'll go for a walk and organise my thoughts for tomorrow.'

'Hang on; I'll see.'

Goodchild punched in the lab's number 'It's Mark Goodchild, Dr Watkins. Dr van Dyke was wondering if you were available for a word. If you could. Five? That's great. I'm shooting off now for another meeting. No, it's not in the Red Lion! I'll wait for you here then. Thanks. She's on her way, Chris.'

Five minutes later and Rachel Watkins entered the room. She walked up to van Dyke and greeted him in a friendly manner. 'So, I take it that you are now part of the Orion family, Chris?'

'Yup; are we dysfunctional, incestuous or mafia?'

'Bit of all I suppose.'

Goodchild failed to follow the doctorial banter and took his leave after instructing Rachel to put anything they wrote down into a Manifoil Mark IV safe and to spin the dial five times before leaving. He then left them to it and hailed a cab to take him to his L.O.I. at St Paul's.

The taxi had just set off when his phone rang. He did not recognise the caller ID and answered, simply 'Goodchild.'

'Boss, its Michelle. We are on our way back, Martin's driving and I thought you'd want a sitrep.'

'Too right I do. How'd it go?'

'It was horrible, boss. Martin did the talking. We'd managed to get the husband on his own and Martin told him everything about the daughter's demise. Malcolm Duncan puts on a very hard front but he's devastated that there's no body to bury. Even though we explained that cause of death was painless, he's obviously imagining all the gruesome scenarios his child might have had to endure before this sicko killed her. Martin played the military card to keep Mr Duncan onside. We have a mission to complete i.e. find this bastard, bring him to book and stop him from doing this shit anymore. Duncan has agreed and we both reckon that he will keep his word and not go public. The problem we have is that he absolutely insists on telling his wife. She was not due back until later this evening and I offered to stay but Duncan said that he'd explain everything to her. He reckons that she is strong enough to understand and will follow his lead on this. I've no idea how she will react so we are at risk here, boss.'

'Let's hope that he knows his wife as well as he thinks he does, Michelle. I'd say that's a qualified well done to you both. I want you to take the night off and pack for five days – Martin too. I want you two in Brighton this week to dig deep on Jennifer. I'll see you in the office first thing in the morning for a briefing. I'll also be introducing our weird criminal psychologist.'

'How weird, boss?'

'He fancies Dr Watkins.

'This I've got to see. Anything else for us, boss?'

'No; you two wind down for the evening. I used to hate those bereavement visits and I know what it takes out of you. See you in the morning, Michelle.' Goodchild switched off his phone and mentally reviewed the conversation. It had not been an ideal result. They had left a lot to chance by not speaking with Mrs Duncan but he had to trust his officer's judgement. Nevertheless it would not do any harm for Michelle Stone to re-establish contact with the woman.

The taxi double parked outside the pub and Goodchild exited as quickly as possible to pay. The ground floor of the pub was busy with the usual mix of City workers who did not want to brave the rush hour yet and were delaying their return home with after work drinking. Only a few years ago the place would have been awash with Champagne; now, in these more straightened times, conspicuous consumption in public was not the done thing. The place still was doing good business and Goodchild had to use his considerable bulk to make his way through the crowd to the end of the bar where his twelve or so brethren were gathered. They were a disparate group as most lodges are, ranging in age from early twenties to some venerable members in their seventies. All the men were white bar one who was of south Asian extraction, Indian or Pakistani – it did not matter. They all greeted Goodchild's arrival with genuine pleasure. His work did not allow him to attend L.O.I. as frequently as he would have liked but when he did his contributions to the proceedings were always useful, especially when he took on the role of Director of Ceremonies. After a couple of rounds of drinks and people catching up with friends that they had not seen for some while, the group decamped upstairs to a private room that was locked from the inside. One member of the lodge remained outside the door in case a member of the public, looking for the toilet, ended up eavesdropping. There is nothing sinister in all these precautions; they merely form part of Masonic ritual.

As the evening went on some of the younger members of the lodge would reappear at the bar where they remained. Their elders were now practising degrees into which they themselves had not yet been admitted. Finally all the group were together again at the bar which was now considerably less busy than when they had arrived. Sandwiches appeared, smaller groups formed out of the larger and Mark Goodchild managed to find himself in a quiet corner with Derek Clarkson. They knew each other well enough not to have to do a verbal ballet before getting down to business. Clarkson cut to the chase immediately.

'What do you need to know, Mark?'

Goodchild quickly ran through the events of the weekend and

today without interruption from his erstwhile superior. When he had finished Clarkson nodded to himself and passed his empty scotch tumbler to Goodchild.

'Get me a refill whilst I think would you, Mark? Glenlivet if you please with a touch of water.'

When Goodchild returned with a good sized measure of malt for each of them Clarkson said 'It seems to me that the investigation is on track. Match a few more missing people to the fingers and you'll be able to start on a profile of the killer or killers. I'm not sure about involving Box as helpers – that's bound to put noses out of joint at the Yard but it's your decision. Where your problem lies is with ML's deadline. I can only think of one way to extend that and that is by communicating with him.'

'What, us, the Met?'

'Not necessarily. How about using your pal Tucker as a go-between?'

'I've only just finished warning him off getting any more involved than he is with this maniac. How can I now go back to him and say 'oh, sorry; change of mind. But would you mind awfully telling lies to a homicidal sociopath who may then hunt you down with a view to performing an ante mortem autopsy on you?'

'I'm suggesting a strategy, Mark. The tactics have to come from you now.'

That last three letter word signified to Goodchild that a baton had been reluctantly passed. Clarkson's brain was still first rate but his spirit seemed crushed and was dragging his body down with it. If any man deserved to be retired on a full pension with PTSD it was Derek Clarkson. Goodchild knew that he himself could never have worked on child abuse cases without becoming either an alcoholic or a murderer. His friend had spent too many years in that thankless battle and was now one of the mentally maimed because of it.

'Thanks, Derek. I'll work on that. Let's get back to the lads shall we?'

With a palpable relief Clarkson switched off from police work and dived into the pool of conviviality that is the truth of Freemasonry.

After a socially acceptable time of talking banalities, Mark Goodchild headed off into the evening in search of another solitary cab ride to start on his journey to where he lived – he never called it home.

Chapter Fourteen

At eight the next morning Goodchild, Carver and Stone were in the Orion offices drinking coffee or tea according to personal preferences and organising their notes before starting their briefing. All three were surprised when the door opened and Rachel Watkins entered accompanied by Chris van Dyke.

'Good morning everyone' said Doctor Watkins. 'I've signed Chris in as a visitor today. Can one of you sort out a pass for him so that he can come and go more freely?'

'Certainly; I'd intended to do that later on. I did not expect him in so early' replied Goodchild. 'Good to see you Chris. Help yourself to whatever you want.'

Van Dyke organised coffee for himself and Dr Watkins who had sat down at the conference table, to the surprise of the three police officers.

Goodchild began by introducing van Dyke to Carver and Stone then methodically went over the history of the case, stated where he believed them to be in the investigative process then threw the meeting open to comments from the group. He did not reveal his conversation with Derek Clarkson.

Carver spoke first. 'Michelle and I will head to Brighton this morning. We have the case notes from the locals and will make a courtesy call on them when we arrive. Malcolm Duncan has supplied us with a list of every contact both social and professional that his daughter had let him know about. There are some on it that the locals don't appear to have known about or, if they did, followed up. Michelle is going to contact Mrs Duncan later today to see what state she's in and try to keep her onside. Finally, we have made a list of fifteen other families that need to be contacted. We've prioritised it with the most likely at the top. I'll leave that with you boss. And that's it from us.'

'Thanks, Martin' said Goodchild. 'Once I've spoken to Box I can move on your list. Chris, I know you've only just come on board but do you have any early thoughts that you'd care to share with us?'

'Nothing that you probably haven't thought of yourselves. I'll be more use to you when we or rather you have identified more victims but, for what it's worth, here goes.

It's well established that serial killers rarely operate outside their own ethnic group. The reasons for this are as much practical as well as psychological. A white male hunting black females in Brixton would stand out like a cue ball. So I'm ninety nine per cent certain that we are looking for a white male. I say male for two reasons. Obviously the incidence of female serial killers is far lower than that of the male. Secondly the language used in the emails to Tucker is very masculine – consider the cricketing metaphors in the riddle. Whilst I am talking about the emails, the vocabulary used and the historical references indicate that ML is either a college graduate or has been otherwise educated to that level. We are looking for a mature, clever killer. As you observed from the physical state of the fingers and, as is confirmed by what we know of Jennifer Duncan, these were not girls from society's underclass; they were decent people and ML was able to become close enough to them to commit murder. He has some sort of charm that draws them in.

Moving on to the fingers. To murder someone is one thing; to mutilate the body and then display what you have done is an entirely different form of psychosis. ML is a sociopath. He may not even be a misogynist. The victims did not have personalities for him – they were merely objects with which he could send his message.'

'You don't see any significance in the specific choice of finger then?' asked Michelle.

'Other than to shock you, or send you off in the wrong direction, no. On the surface ML appears to hate women, the marital state, normal male female relationships. I don't think that's the key to him at all.'

'You said he was sending a message. What is it?' asked Goodchild.

'Catch me if you can. The email was relatively simple to decipher. This is all smoke and mirrors. He is challenging you or your organisation to find him.'

'Hang on there, Chris' interjected Goodchild. 'Don't you think it's a bit extreme to kill and mutilate ten women just to get our attention and engage in a game with us?'

'Serial killers by definition are extreme. ML has chosen to contact you via this journalist chappie. He wants to engage with you on an intellectual level – the murders are incidental. ML is a narcissist, egoist and very sure of himself. When you catch him you will be surprised that he is reasonably wealthy and has being doing this, if not exactly for fun, then maybe to relieve his boredom. If you want a role model to keep in mind think of a homicidal Thomas Crowne but more Brosnan than McQueen.'

'Sorry; you've lost me there. Crowne, Brosnan, McQueen?' said Michelle Stone.

Carver supplied the answer. 'Two films, before your time Michelle. The Thomas Crowne Affair the first starring Steve McQueen in the title role, the remake, Pierce Brosnan. Basically a good looking mega-rich businessman who has it all but is bored so he devises the perfect robbery and gets away with it. The insurance company sends in an investigator to do what the cops should have done. In each film this happens to be a sexy, cerebral female who ends up in Crowne's bed and she then has an ethical dilemma to solve blah, blah, blah. I must say that the prospect of a homicidal Thomas Crowne is as worrying as Gary Glitter being appointed as Chief Boy Scout.'

'All right, Chris' said Goodchild. 'That's food for thought. Anything else that you can give us at this early stage?'

'Well it's not really my place, it's more a police work sort of thing. I would not want to insult you.'

'You can fly a banner from the top of this building saying 'Goodchild Wears a Gimpsuit' if it helps catch this guy for all I care. Spit it out!'

'OK. It occurs to me that you already have the killer on film.'

The three police officers looked at each other in mutual incomprehension. Finally, Goodchild said 'Do feel free to enlighten us, Dr van Dyke. We seem to have overlooked something.'

'It's a simple question of opportunity. The package with the fingers must have been buried during the hours of daylight. The Royal Parks and especially the area close to Kensington Palace are man and dog patrolled at night. It would be a huge risk to scale a wall to bury the evidence in the dark. He also had to do it in a very precise spot. So daylight it is. And that area of the park is under the CCTV view from the camera at the end of Inverness Terrace.'

'Makes sense' said Carver. 'How would he have gone about it?'

'I can think of two straight off' said Stone. 'Think how brazen this guy is. He could hide in plain sight wearing a high-viz jacket with Thames Water on the back: dig his hole with a fake stand pipe next to it, relay the turf and get out before anyone noticed him. If he was approached, I'm sure he'd have the appropriate I.D. The other method would entail him sitting on the grass on a blanket, ostensibly reading and picnicking whilst all the time, carrying out his evacuation whenever the coast was clear. How he did it doesn't matter; we know the precise place and roughly when so we look at all the film and bingo!'

'Or not' said Rachel Watkins. 'It's interesting that a scientist came up with this theory and not a police officer. 'Could not see the wood for the trees' is the phrase that comes to mind. My view is that someone as bright as ML would have foreseen someone eventually coming up with this and taken appropriate counter measures i.e. a disguise. Sorry to be a damp blanket but I reckon that this is all more smoke and mirrors designed to keep you dancing to his tune.'

'Dr Watkins is probably right but it still has to be checked out' said Goodchild. 'I'll deal with that one. OK. Anything else?'

Michelle Stone spoke up. 'When we catch him, Dr van Dyke, what are the chances of him successfully pleading insanity?'

'Stop right there' said Goodchild. 'I'm not going to go down the road of defining mad, bad, crazy, evil, sane or insane. I've seen too much police time wasted on bullshit discussions of that nature. Our job, our only job, is to catch this guy. The courts will process him and the 'expert witnesses' will no doubt add their opinions which will, of course, contradict each other. I'll be happy to discuss metaphysics with you all over a drink or ten when we've put this case to bed. Now, is there anything else? No? OK. Martin and Michelle; give me a quick call at 1530hrs or anytime at all if something breaks. Chris, come with me and I'll sort out a pass for you. Dr Watkins, please call me the instant anything more comes from forensics.'

Goodchild and van Dyke headed off to the admin offices to start the paperwork for the latter's temporary pass. Rachel Watkins went back to her laboratory, leaving Carver and Stone to make the relatively short drive south to Brighton.

The meeting had imbued the small team with a sense of purpose and direction. If Goodchild could obtain some bodies from Box they would also generate some momentum and close the net around ML.

§

At his home in Clerkenwell ML was putting the final touches to his departure.

He'd had a brief chat with his lawyer, Arthur Blenheim who had still not got anything to report at this early stage. He informed Blenheim that he was off travelling for a couple of months but would check his email on a daily basis and get back in touch if a sale of the business appeared likely.

Next was the mundane business of looking for a flight. No scheduled airline has a direct flight from the U.K. to Fuerteventura so he had two options; either fly with Iberia changing at Madrid and Tenerife or grab a last minute place on one of the charter airlines with the hoards of Brits looking for some cheap sunshine. The first option would mean a journey time of up to ten hours but at least he could travel in upper class and enjoy the trip. The second option would mean that he would only be in the air for four and a half hours but God knows in what sort of company he would find himself. Was it worth the anonymity provided by the sweating masses to save six hours? No. At the end of the day he was playing the part of an international travel writer; it would be natural for him to arrive on the national carrier.

The Iberia.com website proved to be one of the more efficient of its kind and a mere fifteen minutes after logging on he was booked onto an early morning flight out of London Heathrow using his Dominic Lord I.D. It was far too early in the day to be phoning Richard in Corralejo so he sent an email instead whilst making a mental note to make a confirmatory phone call later on. It was not unknown for members of the expat community of Fuerteventura to go missing for twenty four hours (or longer).

Should he call Catherine now and let her know of his travel plans? Not a good idea. She now had money and was capable of travelling from Bristol to London and buying a first class ticket on Iberia so that they could arrive together. He'd leave her until tomorrow. As he would Roger Tucker. With the deadline he had set running out in another twenty four hours he wondered what sort of chaos was reigning at New Scotland Yard.

ML smiled to himself. Time for some exercise to clear his mind, then a light lunch then relaxation. He had a busy week ahead of him.

§

Between Westminster Bridge and Lambeth Bridge on the north bank of the Thames is the solid, grey edifice called Thames House. This is the headquarters of the United Kingdom's Security Service. Millions of people see it from the front and from above every week on the BBC series 'Spooks'. It's the only detail that the ludicrous spy show gets right and it must piss off the organisation mightily.

Mark Goodchild had never been there before and did not know what to expect as he climbed the steps to the gigantic double doors which guarded the entrance to this citadel of security. There was a Judas gate set into one of the doors; through it Goodchild could make out men and women walking purposely across a large, dimly lit area which seemed to be about twenty five yards away from where he stood. There was no entrance sign, security guard or doorbell so he stepped inside and instantly recognised the security system in use here. On his left, out of sight from the entrance, were six men all in their late twenties or early thirties. They were dressed in dark two piece suits and grey crew necked sweaters. They were virtually invisible in the shadows and two of them held Heckler and Koch MP5 machine pistols at the ready. God knew what the other four were carrying. To Goodchild's right another young man of military bearing sat high behind a glassed in lectern from which emanated the light of a TV screen or screens. The glass had the dark green tint to it that comes from the heavy duty armour lamination process. Yet another dark suited guard stood behind him. This was the first line of defence and Goodchild was sure that he had been on camera since he had begun the long walk up to the entrance. The business of the Security Services took place in the offices to the right, left and below this atrium. The atrium itself was a killing zone, pure and simple. It was a much enlarged version of the system in use at number 10 Downing St. Anyone who thinks that the safety of the Prime Minister is dependent on a solitary bobby on his doorstep should consult a mental health professional as a matter of urgency.

The man behind the glass looked at Goodchild and politely enquired 'May I help you, sir?'

'Yes. I'm Acting Commander Goodchild, Metropolitan Police. I was told to present myself at ten for a meeting. Afraid I don't have the name of the person whom I shall be seeing.'

The man at the lectern pressed some keys on his hidden equipment. No trace of emotion crossed his face. 'Your ID please, sir?'

Goodchild handed over his badge and papers which were scrutinised very carefully. Finally lectern man said 'If you'd step forward to the white line sir; look straight at the cross on the wall behind me' and a flash went off in Goodchild's eyes 'that's fine. Now approach my desk on your left hand side, place your right hand on the glass plate; hold it still.' The plate lit up in a ghostly green colour and a red line scanned his palm twice. 'Fine. If you'd stand back from the desk, sir. Your visitor ID card will be ready soon. Thank you for your co-operation.'

'Commander Goodchild' came a voice from behind him. He turned round to be confronted with another dark suited security type. 'If you'd come with me, sir?'

'My credentials and ID?'

'Will be returned to you later, sir. This way if you please.'

Goodchild shrugged and followed his escort through an airport – like x-ray frame, a turnstile that the man opened with a swipe card and finally into a small room that contained two bright blue armchairs in a cheap but durable cloth covering and a coffee table on which the day's newspapers were laid out.

'Someone will be along shortly, sir.' The escort left and the door shut with a soft thud. There was no handle on the inside nor were there external windows; but he bet that there was someone behind the mirror or that there was a pinhole camera in the smoke detector. 'Fuck-em' thought Goodchild. It was Tuesday so he'd read what Roger Tucker thought of the world.

Some fifteen minutes later the door opened to reveal a very plain looking young woman who asked Goodchild to accompany her. Once he left the waiting room she handed him a laminated I.D. card which he slipped round his neck. It bore his photograph, name, rank and some numbers which meant nothing to him at all. What one could not miss was the message in large letters which was superimposed on all the other data; DAY PASS – VALID UNTIL 1700HRS ONLY.

Goodchild followed his escort down a corridor at the rear of the atrium where there was a bank of lifts. They went up to the fourth floor and walked for what seemed like an age; the lefts and rights (and even the ups and downs) rendered Goodchild completely disorientated. He would not have been too surprised if they had ended up back where they had started. Eventually his taciturn companion stopped at a door which, like all the others, bore no name or number and gave it three sharp raps.

'Come' called a male voice from the other side so she opened the door and ushered her charge inside.

'This is Commander Mark Goodchild, sir.'

'Thanks. I'll call you if I need someone to see him out.'

The girl left; she had not smiled once during her time with Goodchild nor had she addressed a single word to him. The police officer hoped that she did not represent the corporate mind – set of her organisation or he was facing a long, wasted morning.

The Security Service officer came from behind his battered partner's desk and extended a hand. 'Commander Goodchild, hello. I'm Adam' he said.

'Like fuck you are' thought Mark. Instead he took the proffered hand and replied 'Thanks for seeing me at such short notice. I know how busy you people are these days.'

'Well, I was intrigued when you called me. I had intended contacting the Yard myself owing to something that had crossed my desk recently. Please, do take a seat.'

Goodchild settled into the cherry coloured chair next to a coffee table and he observed his man with a detective's eye. Late forties, thirty pounds overweight for his five nineish, soft hands, balding but what hair remained was coiffed to the point of foppishness. Suit, shirt and tie were high street maybe Marks and Spencer, imitation Gucci loafers and a cheap, chunky sports watch that was probably advertised as a chronometer. The man looked a joke, a weak one too.

But this was Box where nothing could be taken at face value. 'Adam's' suite of offices were large. There was a conference table for ten people in the adjoining room and Goodchild would have bet that the bookcase contained more than reading material. The fact that there was no P.C. in sight and only one telephone for offices this large was definitely wrong. Perhaps there was more to 'Adam' than met the eye. Perhaps this was not even his office. One could be too clever trying to analyse these situations. Goodchild decided to play it by ear.

'So what had crossed your desk that made you want to call us?' asked Goodchild.

'We, and other organisations have a list of trigger words which have been disseminated throughout government agencies. If one comes up, we take a look at it and, if necessary, pursue it further. Your laboratory came up with a complex chemical used by Russian Special Forces against Muslim terrorists. You can imagine that that created quite a stir. I've spoken with Assistant Commissioner Addison and he's filled me in on Orion's function. It's a nasty situation, Commander.'

'In what way?'

'Catching the murderer is one thing and I wish you the best of luck. The cover up you've put in place is something else. The media will have your balls for breakfast if they find out you've conned them. What really concerns me is the presence of this gas in the UK. How did your man obtain it? How much does he have?

Could this be the start of a new form of terrorism? If someone was prepared to die and managed to infiltrate this substance into an enclosed space, thousands could be killed before anyone knew what was happening. The Olympic Games on live TV shown around the world as everyone in the velodrome drops dead – that would shake our society to its core. That is my concern.'

'So our interests coincide then. I have to catch a killer so that your people can interrogate him with a view to finding out where he obtained his gas.'

'Broadly speaking, yes. You asked for this meeting, Commander. What can I do for you?'

Goodchild explained his need for competent officers who could conduct interviews with the fifteen families whilst keeping the truth of the situation absolutely secret. 'Adam heard him out without interruption. Finally Goodchild said 'And that's it. What do you think? Can you help?'

'There actually is a precedent for this; we used to work quite closely with the Royal Ulster Constabulary when we were sorting out the mess in Northern Ireland. Times have changed though. Obviously our main problem is Islamic sponsored attacks in the UK. We are stretched dammed thin at the moment, Commander and to detach any bodies away from other tasks for a police murder enquiry is difficult to justify. Your man, vile as he undoubtedly is, does not fall into a category that concerns my service. Then there is the fact that, by allying ourselves with you, we would risk being tainted with the smell of your initial cover-up.'

'Would you rather be tainted with the smell of thousands of corpses, Adam?'

'The communications from your killer do not indicate that he is about to escalate from serial murder to mass. Nor is there a threat to pass on his material to some lunatics in Bradford. I'm not saying 'no' to your request. I'm going to consult colleagues on it. Anyway as I understand things, time is against you. He has threatened to go public with his story within twenty four hours has he not?'

'Yes he has; I'm working on that. When will you have a decision for me?'

'I'll call you tomorrow afternoon, Commander Goodchild. I shall try and push for this but no promises. Understand?'

'No, I don't. You said that one of your trigger words caused some excitement and that you were going to contact us regarding this gas. You agree that our interests coincide then, in the same breath, you are telling me to hurry up and wait. I've not asked for the moon but I'm being offered nothing of substance so this simple copper definitely does not understand.'

'Sorry to hear it, Commander. Nothing else I can do for the time being so unless there was anything else……..?'

'No. I'll look forward to your call tomorrow.'

The atmosphere between the two men had become frosty. Goodchild was new to negotiating with other agencies at this level and knew that he had come cap in hand. Begging did not become him. 'Adam' punched in a number on the only phone visible in the room and summoned an anonymous someone to see Goodchild out. She could not have been far away for the same girl who had escorted him in arrived just under a minute later. Once again she silently accompanied him back to the reception area, this time by a completely different but equally confusing route. Once there she relieved him of his day pass and returned his own credentials to him. When he thanked her she looked right through him, gave the curtest of nods in acknowledgement, turned on her heel and walked away. Goodchild looked at his watch; he'd been in this building for exactly one hour. As he left it he felt as though he'd just attended a job interview and been found wanting. There was nothing more that he could do about the situation at the moment so he set off at a brisk pace towards his own offices which were only a ten minute walk away. If he had not had so many tasks to complete he would have stopped off somewhere for a drink to wash away the taste that the Security Service had left in his mouth.

The first thing he did when he arrived back at Orion was to contact his man in the Technical Support Unit to see that he was ready to go to Roger Tucker's house. Hearing that he was ready to go at five minutes notice Goodchild said 'Are you able to conduct a sweep of a specific area of Tucker's home to see that it's safe for me to have a secure conversation there?'

'No problem, sir. Bread and butter stuff, that is. I have the kit right here. Want me to take it along?'

'Yes. You're using a British Telecoms van aren't you?'

'Those were my instructions, sir.'

'Good, I'll meet you in the garage in ten minutes; I'm coming too.'

'In my van, sir?'

'God, no. I'm using a driver today. I've yet to meet Tucker and avoid having alcohol with the man.'

'Very good, sir. See you in ten.'

Goodchild then phoned Tucker to make sure that he had stuck to their arrangement to keep himself available to admit his electronics expert. Tucker answered after the sixth ring. 'Roger Tucker.'

'Roger, it's Mark. I've my technical guy ready to go. Can you be available in an hour's time?'

'Sure. I've plenty of things to be doing at home today. How are things at your end?'

'I'll let you know in an hour; I'm coming over too.'

'OK this I've got to see; Commander Mark Goodchild dressed in a set of overalls!'

'Very funny Roger. We'll be arriving separately. See you soon.'

§

Goodchild arrived first forty five minutes later. His driver had dropped him off 100 yards away and round the corner from Tucker's house. Once inside, Goodchild asked for a beer and passed an A4 sheet of paper into the journalist's hand. It read:

DO NOT MENTION ML OR ORION UNTIL MY TECHNICAL GUY HAS CHECKED OUT THIS PLACE FOR LISTENING DEVICES. ONCE HE GIVES US THE ALL CLEAR AND GETS TO WORK ON YOUR COMPUTER I SUGGEST WE SIT IN THE KITCHEN. LET US NOW TALK SHIT UNTIL HE ARRIVES. HE WILL BE DRESSED AS A BRITISH TELECOMS ENGINEER.

Roger Tucker raised his eyebrows and smiled at the message but gave Goodchild a thumbs up to indicate that he understood. He then popped the tabs on two cans of lager and proceeded to interrogate his friend.

'So, Mark; why don't you arrest your old boss?'

'What's the Chief Constable supposed to have done?'

'Not him. The former Home Secretary. The one with udders where her boobs should be. Let me see if I've got my facts straight – She's the Member of Parliament for some dump in the midlands but is allowed to claim expenses to maintain a second residence in London plus all sorts of other goodies. However, if she is sleeping in her sister's spare bedroom I would have thought that that was stretching the definition of the word residence just a bit. When you add in all the TVs, furniture, kitchen appliances which have been installed in her main home in the midlands, not to mention her husband's subscription to 'adult' cable channels, does it not seem to you that there is a prima facie case of fraud going on here, Mark?'

'Prima facie, yes; but it's not my call thank God. We were fucking gob smacked when Gordon Brown appointed her. If I remember correctly her background is as a secondary school teacher; hardly the right preparation for running one of the great offices of state.'

'So why did the mad Scotsman appoint her?'

'There was nobody else left. Just look at the list of people who've held the post during Labour's years in office; there was a blind man who could not keep his dick in his pants, an alcoholic ex-communist, the big fat one who could not be bothered to shave properly. Half of them have been photographed with Fidel Castro. These are the sort of people that Lenin referred to as 'useful idiots'. If the Soviets had ever taken over they'd have that shower swinging from a rope before they got round to Maggie Thatcher.'

'See what you mean; and it meant that Gordon could burnish his equality credentials by saying that he had appointed the first female Home Secretary. The fact that she was completely out of her depth was beside the point.'

'The fact that she was completely out of her depth was precisely the point. Brown, for all his bullying, is basically a weak and insecure man. He did not want a Home Secretary who could threaten him.'

'What a bunch of …,' before Tucker could describe the Labour leadership in more colourful terms the doorbell rang. 'Oh, sorry Mark. I'm expecting BT today. Problem with my broadband.'

'Carry on; I'll drink your beer on my own.'

Tucker went to his front door and verified that someone in a BT uniform was outside by means of his CCTV. Goodchild had followed him and confirmed with sign language that it was, indeed, his man at the door. Goodchild retreated into the house whilst Tucker admitted the technician. The latter had been briefed regarding certain aspects of the situation and he carried out a short conversation with Tucker regarding broadband problems. He then followed Goodchild into the kitchen and began to search the walls and electric sockets using a variety of hand held devices. He scanned the large kitchen window using a light that, to the other men, looked like the laser sights one found attached to certain firearms. Finally he turned on a small, wall mounted TV, tuned it to Sky News and turned the volume up. He beckoned the two men towards him and said 'As far as I can tell, this room is not under electronic surveillance of any kind at the moment. Some bugs are always transmitting and some are voice activated; neither are present here. Some are passive i.e. they emit no energy until whoever planted them switches them on remotely. These cannot be detected but, if one is present and becomes active, this little box's red light will start to flash and you can react accordingly. I advise that you converse quietly and place your table and chairs beneath the TV which you keep at its present volume. I'm assuming that it's natural for a journalist to have the rolling news on all the time.'

'Some journalists, yes' said Tucker.

'OK. I'll get on with the other work then. Talk with you later.'

Goodchild and Tucker looked at each other and, by unspoken agreement, moved the kitchen furniture to a spot underneath the TV. Tucker spoke first 'What's going on here, Mark?'

'I need to stall ML from carrying out his threat to put all his shit on the internet, Roger. I could pretend to be you and email him something in your name to slow him down whilst my investigation continues but, if he were to realise that he was being played, well I doubt if he would react in a favourable manner. In short, I need you to communicate with him.'

Tucker took his time before replying. 'By 'communicate', you actually mean manipulate don't you, Mark?'

'Yes. It's time for us to take control of the situation from him.'

'So you want me to lie and play mind games with a serial killer. The last time we spoke you were at pains to stress how dangerous this arsehole is and that I should be very wary of him. Now you want me to bait him into a trap. What's changed?'

'It's the time limit, Roger. We have to forestall him.'

'All right; how about I give you my email password and one of your merry men can impersonate me whilst I fuck off out of here?'

'Wouldn't work. Firstly, you have a distinctive style of writing; on top of that I'm thinking that ML knows things about you which are not public knowledge. If he were to ask a specific question about you and we could not answer it instantly, we're blown. Sorry, Roger. I need you on this. I can't force you but I do bloody well need you.'

Tucker left the table and took two more beers from the fridge, his forehead creased in thought. Returning to his seat he handed one over to Goodchild and asked 'How is the investigation progressing?'

'I've two experienced officers down in Brighton going through the identified victim's life with a fine-tooth comb. By the end of this week I should have some of the other nine girls identified and we can begin the same process with them. By the end of next week I aim to have enough information to work out how the killer is doing what he does and then our criminal psychologist should be able to tell us what sort of person he is. From there its pure police work to narrow down where he comes from and who he is.'

'You make it sound easy, Mark. You're looking at me carrying on this charade for only three or four weeks? I doubt it. How long was the Yorkshire Ripper at large? How long did Fred and Rose West kidnap, rape and kill? Don't take me for a twat, mate!'

'Sorry. I'm laying out a best case scenario but remember; forensic science has moved on immensely since Sutcliffe and the Wests as has inter-agency co-operation. There is also the fact that this guy has chosen to communicate with us electronically – we still have to see what my guy from Technical Support will come up with. The deck is stacked in our favour and this arrogant son of a bitch does not realise that. What do you say, Roger? Can I count on you?'

'Give me a moment. Neither of us are going anywhere until chummie with the computer gear has finished anyway.'

Tucker took a long pull of his beer, closed his eyes and put his mind to work. He wanted to help. This freak needed to be put away and he had been placed in a position to help to do so. He would also reap immense journalistic kudos when he came to write the story; he could build an entire new career on this case. The downside was the danger. Did he really need this sort of shit at this stage in his life? He would have liked to have consulted Sharon on this one but he could hardly explain this situation over the phone to his wife in Spain. He opened his eyes and observed his friend. Mark Goodchild was one of the toughest men he had ever met but even he was showing the strain. All this had started on Friday; it was now mid-afternoon Tuesday and the detective was looking frayed round the edges. He'd shaved badly the way the elderly do, his eyes had darkening half moons beneath them and even his short cut hair was becoming unkempt. If that was what the case could do to Mark Goodchild, Tucker did not relish following him down the same path. But the small voice of conscience piped up to say 'and if the roles were reversed would Mark Goodchild hesitate to help you? Do you owe him anything for saving your sorry arse in a street riot all those years ago?' Tucker raised his can to Goodchild and indicated that his friend do the same.

'Course I'm in you dopey plod! Skol!' and the two men drained their cans, crushed them then threw them at the waste bin across the kitchen. Tucker's went in for two points but Goodchild's missed.

The technician chose that moment to enter the room and was wise enough to keep a straight face at the sight of a Commander of the Metropolitan Police, drinking beer in the middle of the day with a civilian.

'Sir; if I may, I think I might have something for you' he said.

'Come and join us, please' said Goodchild.

'Ah, sorry to ask, sir; but what I've got is sensitive. Is the gentleman cleared to hear this sort of information?'

'Just get on with it. If I think you're giving too much away I'll stop you.'

'Very good, sir. ML has made no attempt to disguise where he has sent the emails from. I've traced the first one to a cyber café in Camden. It's a very busy spot and not covered by CCTV so I don't reckon you'll have much joy there. The sender was online for such a short amount of time that he will probably have paid in cash. The other two emails are different. They both came from the same location which is the business lounge at Euston Station. This facility is designed for first class passengers and, to keep the oiks out, charges an entrance fee as well as inflated rates for online use. ML may have used a credit card. There will also be a CCTV record held of the entire station by British Transport Police and, if we are really lucky, there will be a TV record of the entrance to the bar area as well.'

'Bloody good work! I want you to get the CCTV images from the Transport Police today. I'll send someone over to the lounge to get hold of the credit card receipts. Call me on this number once you have what you need and I'll see you back at the Yard. If Transport don't jump, get in touch with me and I'll put a rocket up them. OK?'

'Yes, sir. Talk with you later then. Nice to meet you Mr Tucker.' The technician went back to Tucker's office area, packed up his equipment and saw himself out.

'I did not know that the police could find out where an email had been sent from, Mark' said Tucker. 'How does that work?'

'No idea; but if it's been sent there is a record of it somewhere and GCHQ can trace it.'

Goodchild was referring to Government Communication Headquarters in Cheltenham. This was the British equivalent of America's National Security Agency and was basically an electronic eavesdropping facility with listening stations around the world. The giant, toroid shaped building and its banks of super computers had been largely funded by the U.S.A. so Americans worked very closely with British officers and shared in the international 'take' generated from around the world. Australia, Canada and New Zealand were also prime players in the electronic intelligence monitoring game and this international, English speaking organisation was known as Echelon. For it to trace the origin of emails was simplicity itself.

Tucker frowned. 'Is that legal? Could info obtained by GCHQ be used in court?'

'Maybe. It doesn't matter. I'm not looking at producing evidence at this stage; I'm just trying to find the fucker.'

'OK. I'll let that slide for the moment. What sort of message do you want me to send to ML? When do you want it to go out?'

'You have to make him think that you are on the case, kicking police arse and starting to get somewhere. Keep it as factual as possible but do not give him anyone's name and definitely do not use the word Orion. Tell him that you lit a fire under me and recount our meeting in the Red Lion. Again, do not name the location. Admit to knowledge about the Russian type gas; he'll know that we can trace that anyway. Flatter the shit; play to his ego; ask him for help and instructions as to how <u>he</u> thinks you should proceed. Anything to buy us time, Roger. Do this without me present; it must be in your own words but once you've written it, send it to me before you transmit to him. All right?'

'Fine. When do you want this?'

'Tomorrow morning. I don't want him to think that his communications via you are making us jump though hoops. Let's leave it to the last minute and gain as much time as we can. Look, Roger, I've still got a mountain of things to do today so I've got to be off. Thanks for taking this on; call me if you have to.'

'Will do. Let me see you out.'

The two men parted at the front door. Goodchild headed off to his driver for the return to New Scotland Yard from where he could organise obtaining credit card details from the Euston Station business lounge. He would also have to brief Addison at some point in the afternoon and also field calls from Brighton and, no doubt, British Transport Police. He felt like a hamster on a wheel. If he could not get some help from the Security Service tomorrow he would be in danger of having to start anew. How much time could Tucker buy from ML? He realised that it was a huge risk for the investigation to be so reliant on a civilian's contribution but this was the hand that he had been dealt. He would not fold now.

Chapter Fifteen

ML had had an early night and was up well before dawn for the journey to Heathrow. Even first class passengers had to check in an enormous amount of time prior to take off these terrorist days but ML did not mind; he simply factored it into his plans. The idiots who kicked up a fuss regarding airport security amused him. If they were given the choice of flying on a plane where all luggage and passengers had been carefully scrutinised or another where it was just a case of rocking up with your ticket at the last minute he was pretty sure that they would be damned grateful for option number one.

Normally ML only took carry on luggage as waiting for the carousel to disengage the bags from the hold would mean him standing in one place under surveillance cameras for longer than he was comfortable with. He always brought new clothes and toiletries at his destination. On this occasion, however, he had some special items that he could not transport in the cabin so he had checked in one suitcase in addition to his two suiter and small sports bag.

He had travelled to the airport in a chauffeur driven Mercedes S class from one of the many private hire companies in London. The drivers of such vehicles were used to not talking to their charges which ML found preferable to the garrulous black cabbies whose non-stop verbosity he found intrusive.

After a painless check in with the charming girl at the Iberia desk, he went to the Executive Lounge where he enjoyed an excellent English breakfast, read the morning papers and was seated in the Boeing 757 by 0715. First class was half full and business class looked to be very busy indeed. He assumed that most of these passengers would be leaving the airport at Madrid and that not many would be accompanying him on his journey to the Canary Islands.

The flight attendants closed the door, checked everyone was belted in, made sure that the overhead lockers were closed then went into the emergency procedures song and dance routine (in English and Spanish). The plane was taxiing on time and launched itself into the air only five minutes later than the stated ETD. Once the seatbelt signs were off he took his sports bag from the locker and retrieved a thick paperback written by the ever entertaining Nelson de Mille. He was pleased to see from page one that he would be flying to Madrid Barajas in the company of John Corey so at least he's be assured of a non PC joke or six.

Two and a half hours later they had landed and ML disembarked for his first layover of the day. It was now ten thirty in the morning local time and there are a lot worse places in the world to kill time than the first class lounge of Barajas airport. ML settled down with the day's copy of El Pays newspaper and a café solo with an enssimada to give him a taste of Spain. Once he had finished and had cleansed his lips of the dusting of fine flour that the frangible delicacy always deposits upon you no matter how fastidious you are, he used his mobile to call Catherine in Bristol. The electronic voice informed him that his call could not be taken at this time which meant that she was either in a lecture or asleep. He sent her a text saying that he was en route for Fuerteventura and would call her later. He returned his attention to El Pays and carried on killing time.

§

In London it was time that was killing Mark Goodchild or rather the lack of it. He was on his own at the moment and his lack of resources meant that he was doing the work of ten men. He was aware that if he pushed himself much more he would inevitably make mistakes and, at this level, that was not an option. Addison had not said it in so many words at yesterday's short briefing but he had made it clear that Goodchild was very much under the eye on this case.

Carver and Stone had reported in. There were proceeding in a detailed, methodical manner and did not appear to have upset the local constabulary yet; give it time thought Goodchild. He wanted them back at Orion by Friday at the latest.

The results from Euston Station were worrying him. It looked like ML had paid in cash for a start; that had always been a possibility and Goodchild was neither surprised nor disappointed. What was more perturbing was the fact that the CCTV system had been playing up for the period before, during and after the transmission of the two emails, both in the computer suite and the bar area. From the time that the lounge opened the recording was perfect until fifteen minutes before ML's first transmission. Then the cameras showed only snow and white noise, for an hour and ten minutes when they came back on again. Goodchild did not think that this was a coincidence. The British Transport Police who watched the screens in their control room swore that their screens had been fine on that day so Goodchild concluded that ML not only had access to exotic toxins, but also possessed high tech electronic spyware of some kind. He felt that this investigation was descending into a Mission Impossible scenario.

This morning he had reviewed the images taken of Kensington Palace Gardens and, sure enough, there he was. It had not taken long to find film of someone who had laid a green blanket on the grass and sat down to enjoy a picnic and read a book for an hour in the late afternoon. The subject moved his bulk around a lot and was mostly viewed from the back. On the few occasions when his face edged into shot it was clear that he was wearing wrap around dark glasses and a full beard. A broad rimmed Aussie style bush hat also hampered clear identification. He had entered the park from the north side and headed off towards the south east, probably divesting himself of various elements of his disguise along the way prior to leaving by any one of the many exits. In brief, ML rarely let himself be seen and when he did appear in public he wore camouflage or even a disguise. The man was like a chess grand master who saw several moves ahead and played his game accordingly. Goodchild felt as though he were treading water until he received replies from Box or something positive from his team in Brighton. For the sake of doing something as well as trying to build up a more complete picture of ML, he took the technician who had visited Roger Tucker's home off all other duties and ordered him to concentrate on analysing the images from Euston Station. The man seemed pleased at the prospect of doing something out of the ordinary and had promised a preliminary report by the end of the day; more waiting.

With time on his hands, Goodchild sat at his word processor and typed up a complete report of events from the moment that Roger Tucker had first contacted him less than a week ago until the present time. He omitted nothing and in his summary he even stated that he had conferred privately with Clarkson but had withheld that meeting from the Orion team. He did not state why he had done so.

The nature of the information was so sensitive that Goodchild had no hesitation in according it a Secret classification. He entitled the document and its attachments Orion: Situation Report; the sole recipient was Deputy Assistant Commissioner Addison. He printed off two copies, placed one in his own safe and the other in a Metropolitan Police khaki envelope with 'Secret' labels plus Addison's name and rank. He walked the envelope up to the deputy assistant commissioner's office and handed it over to the uniformed sergeant who acted as Addison's secretary.

'See that your boss has at least thirty minutes with that before our 1530 meeting would you? It's important' said Goodchild.

'I'll try, Commander; it won't be easy' replied the sergeant.

'Important issues never are. Make it happen, please.'

Goodchild turned and left. He went back to his office to check to see if Roger Tucker had sent him anything yet. On finding nothing he left the building and headed to the Red Lion for an early lunch. If anyone wanted him they could call his Blackberry.

§

At his home in north London, Roger Tucker was struggling to find the right words for his message to ML. This was frustrating; words were the tools of his trade and he liked to think that he utilised them better than most. Once he had decided which subjects to tackle in his newspaper column and which angle to take, the language just flowed, the stream of words being almost automatic. Obviously his years of experience helped but Tucker had always enjoyed this ease of usage. Now, when more was riding on it than merely raising a smile on the face of middle England (whilst infuriating the middle left), he found himself suffering from what he supposed was writer's block. 'Don't overanalyse this' he told himself. Mark Goodchild wanted him to reply to ML because of his 'distinctive writing style'. What a laugh that was; a five year old whose first letter began 'Dear Santa' would be of more use than his efforts of the last two hours. If he tried to be honest and totally natural then 'Dear Psychonutter fruitcake' would probably not have the effect that Goodchild wanted. If he became too serious though, he reckoned that ML would realise that he was not working independently of the police. What was required was a balanced piece of writing; this was what was proving difficult for Tucker who, after all, had made a career out of humouristic polemic. He thought about calling Goodchild and explaining the problem but dismissed the idea almost instantly. He did not want to appear to be a weak sister to his friend and it was ludicrous for a journalist of his standing to ask a police officer for writing advice. It would be like Marco Pierre White asking bin Laden if he had any nifty recipes for belly of pork.

When in doubt, have a drink was the journalist's motto so Tucker took a beer from the fridge and applied his mind to the problem. As he paced the length of his lounge downing his brew it came to him that he was like an actor on stage learning his lines. That was the answer! Get into character; imagine what a conversation with a police officer would have been like if he had done what ML had demanded and had not had access to Mark Goodchild. He drained the can and opened another his mind racing along this new course. If he had have met with someone from Scotland Yard there would have been threats, an argument, counter-threats then a compromise. He would have left the meeting and found a quiet spot where he could write up some notes whilst the details were still fresh in his mind.

Tucker put his beer down and ignoring his P.C., grabbed an A5 pad and began to write as quickly as he used to when he was reporting on strikes and urban riots. Thirty minutes later and he had the guts of his next email to ML. Another half an hour and he had crafted a draft email to ML. He was about to send electronically to Goodchild when he paused. The ease with which the police technician had traced the origins of ML's emails had surprised him and made him wonder whether or not their adversary had access to technology that could read what he proposed to send to Goodchild. Thinking it better to err on the side of caution he called his friend's cell phone.

'Goodchild'

'Mark; its Roger here. Can you talk?'

'Yes; I'm just about to order some lunch. What's up?'

'I've drafted an email to our mutual friend for your approval but I'm not sure whether or not it's safe to transmit to you, if you know what I mean?'

'Good point, Roger. Go to your kitchen and read out what you've written. We know that room is clean and if someone can break the security on my kit we might as well pack up and go home anyway.'

'OK, here goes; Message begins:

ML, I've been on the case and am being hit over the head with the national security stick. I'm persona non grata at the Yard and my contacts are not returning my calls. I eventually managed to pressure them into an off the record meeting which took place on neutral ground. I've no idea with whom I met; I don't even know if he was police or Security Service. My pitch was that a serial killer was at large and that this information was being withheld from the public which could be detrimental to catching the killer. The government man patronised me with the old 'I don't know all the facts' routine so I revealed that I knew about the ten fingers from ten different women. What other facts did I need? What was to stop me from printing my story there and then? After a lot of bluster he came up with the national security story. Apparently these women were killed using some substance connected with Russian terrorism. I thought that he was talking about Alexander Litvenyenko and the polonium poisoning event but he claims that it's bigger than that. 'What's bigger than using radioactive substances to kill people?' I asked. He would not be drawn but I have to say that, from being an arrogant H.M.G. security type, he had changed into a worried looking civil servant. He claimed that a high level investigation was in progress and that any press coverage at this stage would endanger its outcome. I agreed to sit on this for a week and he promised to get in touch with me when he could.

I've come to an impasse. My police contacts are giving me the cold shoulder and I've never had occasion to deal with the intelligence/security community. I'm willing to pursue this but I need more information. Who were these girls? What is the Russian connection? If you can help me, I'll take the fight to the police: Message ends.

What do you think, Mark?'

As usual, Goodchild had been taking notes in his own shorthand. He now reviewed these looking for weak points in the proposed message; he found none. Indeed, Roger Tucker had been very clever. He'd found a way to buy at least a week's time and, by hitting the ball into ML's court, maybe even more.

'I like it, Roger. Send it off mid-afternoon and print a copy for me. I'll get it next time we meet. How are you fixed for tomorrow?'

'I'm busy in the morning putting the final touches to my Friday column; after that, I'm free. Lunch?'

'I'll let you know. Thanks, mate. That's a good piece of work. Let's wait and see how ML reacts. Talk with you soon.'

Both men ended the call feeling better than when they had begun. Goodchild felt that he was now taking control and, if he used the time Tucker had bought well, could start to identify the killer.

Tucker, like most human beings, enjoyed being praised by someone he respected. He went to his computer and updated his diary of events which he then forwarded to the secure file at his newspaper.

§

In Madrid the final call for Iberia 123 to Fuerteventura via Tenerife had just been made. ML strolled over to the first class boarding line and called Catherine. This time she answered and was almost gushing in her pleasure at hearing his voice. 'Dominic! Great to hear from you. Don't tell me you're back in Bristol.'

'Not quite. I'm in Madrid. A spot of business came up so I'm taking advantage of circumstances and carrying on to Fuerteventura later today. How are things with you?'

'Same old, same old. I've lost any enthusiasm I ever had for studies and students. I've an idea of what I want to do but I don't know if I have the ability.'

'Only one way to find out, Catherine and that's to try. Mind if I ask what it is?'

'Ah, can I wait until I see you again, Dominic? It is something I'd like your opinion on but I want to see your face when I tell you.'

'How very mysterious. Fine. Hasta la vista wherever the vista may be. I'm starting my long break today. I'm even going to review the island's eateries.'

'I am still invited to stay aren't I?'

'Of course. Just let me know your flight details and I'll meet you at the airport. If I'm on another island I'll have my pal Richard pick you up. When were you thinking of coming?'

'As soon as, Dominic. Are there daily flights?'

'From Bristol. No idea. The only direct flights are on the package tour deals, Thomas Cook, Thomson that sort of thing. Any other airline will involve at least one airport change. I'd suggest going online and seeing what's available; failing that, go and see a travel agent.'

'OK. How can I contact you? Phone or email?'

'Best to phone on this number. I try to avoid computers when I'm on the island. Talk with you soon, Catherine. They're calling my flight.'

'Bye'

ML checked in and smiled to himself as he walked along the airway towards the front of the plane. He would have bet that he would see the young American by Saturday at the latest. He settled into his spacious seat and retrieved his book wondering how Mr Corey was going to solve the mystery of how a 747 fell out of the sky over New York.

§

At three in the afternoon in London, Mark Goodchild received a call from 'Adam' of the Security Service. It began with a lot of cloak; Goodchild felt that the dagger was not far away.

'Commander Goodchild, good afternoon. Adam calling as promised. Is this line secure at your end?'

'Wait one; I need to divert to another unit.'

Mark punched a button and dialled a four digit number which caused the second phone on his desk to ring. He picked it up and then disconnected the first phone. 'OK we are secure now. What can I do for you?'

'Forget we ever met would be good but I doubt if you ever forget a face Commander. Look I'll come straight to the point. We've had a meeting to discuss your request for some officers to help in your investigation and the answer is definitely no. Apart from our service becoming embroiled in what it a potentially disastrous cover-up on the Met's part, we simply do not have any spare capacity. You've worked SO15 so you should be aware of the true level of terrorist threat we are dealing with these days; if we had our way we would be recruiting more officers not loaning out the ones we already have. Sorry. On a more positive note, we are looking into this bloody gas the Russians use with such alacrity. We are liaising with VX and also the Defence Research Establishment at Porton Down. I'll let you know if anything comes of it.'

'What or who is VX?'

'Secret Intelligence Service. Those chaps who work in the tarty ziggurat on the south bank. VX stands for Vauxhall Cross which is their address.'

'Jesus, you people.'

'Adam' laughed. 'It's better than what we used to call them. During the cold war they were known as Tsar which stood for Those Shits Across the River. I'll be in touch if I have anything for you. Good luck.'

'Thanks. You too.'

Goodchild hung up and disconnected the secure line. He felt crushed. Just when he'd seemed to be taking the initiative 'Adam' had cut him off at the knees. He was due to brief Addison in fifteen minutes and this was not going to look good at all. If he did not get some more bodies to help with the investigation then the Orion team was in for a long slog indeed. He quickly wrote up the details of the conversation that he had just had. This was not for the record; there was no point. 'Adam's' existence was as deniable as sex with Monica Lewinksy. He would use the notes as an aid memoire later.

Goodchild tidied his desk and closed down his computer. The empty offices and silent phone lines only served to remind him of how dead his investigation was right then. There was no way that he could put a positive gloss on the drab picture that Orion was at the moment – and spin was not part of his style anyway. Time to take his lumps. Picking up the notes of his conversation with 'Adam' he headed up to Addison's office. On arrival the sergeant waved him straight in saying 'He's expecting you, Commander.'

Addison was sat in an armchair by a coffee table with Goodchild's summary report in his hands. 'Sit down, Mark. Tea? Coffee?'

'Nothing for me thanks, sir.'

'Right. Thank you for putting this together. It's always useful to have the entire story laid out in a chronological order. It enables me at any rate to highlight what is important in the investigations process. You've made a good start, Mark. I think that you are heading in the right direction. A couple of questions though; Carver and Stone seem to be the only full time members, apart from yourself, of the Orion team. Why have you dismissed Jim Cooper and the others?'

'They are all good coppers, sir but they are not used to this sort of work. They resent sharing authority and do not really see the need for secrecy. Sooner or later that resentment will turn into complaining and what we've decided to keep to ourselves will become too widely known.'

'And yet you have let a journalist be privy to everything we know?'

'No choice, sir. He's a friend to whom I've lied once and I could not see any other way to stall ML until I've received some more evidence to link the habits of the victims.'

'I see. And that, I assume was Clarkson's idea?'

'Partly, sir. I do do some of the thinking myself from time to time.'

'I'm sure you do, Commander. A word or advice; Clarkson was one of the best but he has seen one dead child too many. The kiddie fiddlers have crushed his spirit and he is now a functioning alcoholic – he will not be with the Met for much longer one way or another. Do you understand me, Commander?'

Yes, sir; I won't be consulting him again.'

'That's probably for the best. Any news from Box regarding your request for some more helpers?'

'Yes, sir. They contacted me just before our meeting and I'm afraid that their answer is an unequivocal no. They have said that they will follow up on the Russian gas angle and will be talking with Porton Down and VX as they call the SIS.

'Yes; the secret world does like its sexy acronyms doesn't it? So, Commander; no additional bodies, nine as yet unidentified victims and an unknown time limit from ML. Where do you go from here?'

Goodchild had noted that his superior had used the personal pronoun in the second singular. First plural would have been more encouraging.

'I'm leaving Carver and Stone in Brighton for one more day. I want them back here by Friday for debriefing. In the meantime I'm going to second three bright young detectives and split them between us and make a start on the list of possibilities that Sergeant Stone has drawn up. I won't be giving them a full background on the case; they are only to assist us. That's just three visits per team so we could cover that in one working week. It'll stretch us and I'll need Rachel Watkins dedicated to Orion to the exclusion of all else. That's all I have, sir.'

Addison removed his designer glasses and busied himself polishing the lenses with a silk cloth taken from a rigid, black case. He held them up to the light and, not satisfied, repeated the operation. After a couple of minutes of this business he replaced the glasses on his face addressed Goodchild. 'Mark, the situation is far from ideal but I would say it's a case of 'so far, so good'. It could all change with an email from ML to your journalist buddy, or God help us, one to the media. We could not squash it again. This case will make or break you, Mark. You will either come out of it smelling or roses or the stuff they put on flowers to make them grow. If you need anything from my office just ask. Good luck and, obviously, keep me informed.'

'Yes, sir. Thank you, sir.'

Goodchild left Addison's office thinking 'roses? It's the pricks I have to watch out for'. He headed back to his own desk and checked his messages. Seeing nothing of substance he phoned Roger Tucker to verify that he had transmitted the email to ML. Tucker confirmed that he had and that no reply had been forthcoming. The two friends arranged to meet for a late lunch the next day and said goodbye.

Goodchild needed to get out of the office to clear his head. He's had enough shit for one day and the only police officer he would have shared his thoughts with had been branded a booze hound. He knew that he could go over to Roger Tucker's house as Sharon was still in Spain but that would inevitably mean a serious whiskey session which was not advisable when he was heading the hunt for a serial killer. Reluctantly he decided to head home to his semi-detached house in Reading; his very empty semi-detached house since the divorce five years ago. Thank God she had left him to set up home with an estate agent. Once he'd recovered from the surprise and, to be honest, the shame of her new partner's profession he realised that it demonstrated how shallow his ex-wife's values were. Goodchild had never before experienced schadenfreude until the property market went into freefall. It was with amusement that he viewed the closure or downsizing of estate agents' offices in the town. It did not change the fact that he lived alone and that his life revolved around work and London Irish Rugby Football Club but it did help him to remember what a lucky escape he had had. Thankfully there were no children involved; neither he nor his wife had ever pushed the subject. Perhaps they had never, in their deepest hearts, really committed themselves to each other. Truth was, he did not know and it was all in the past now. He was alone but not lonely and that suited him. Perhaps there was a woman out there for him but he was not inclined to go looking for her. If she appeared, great; if not, he'd carry on as he was – a very private man.

§

Two and half thousand miles to the south another very private man was disembarking from an Iberia 737 at Fuerteventura airport. The last leg of ML's flight from Tenerife had been uneventful and brief. The plane had only been half full so he'd retrieved his hold luggage rapidly and entered the well lit, airy and very modern arrivals hall. As ever it was busy with package tourists arriving from the UK and Germany in the main. He scanned the sea of faces as he made his way through the throng and quickly spotted his contact Richard. It would have been hard not to. Richard was a shade under six feet tall and weighed in at around 250 pounds. His russet hair was cut en brosse, its colour matching the freckled skin of its owner. The muscular physique was clad in a white T-shirt which bore the image of a bulldog who, in turn, was wearing a union flag as an accessory. Bold type declared Richard to be a 'Great Briton'. White Reebok's and soccer shorts were part of the ensemble as was enough gold chains and rings to finance a coup d'état in a minor African nation. Richard was looking at the new arrivals intensely but failed to spot ML until he had walked right up to him and addressed him. 'Hello, Richard. Thanks for meeting me.'

'Fuck me!' said Richard in a broad east end of London accent. 'You look different every time I see you, Dominic. How was the flight?'

'Long. Can we move please?'

'Sure, sure. Give us that case and we'll get a wiggle on.'

ML surrendered his main case to his greeter and the two of them donned sunglasses to head out into the late afternoon glare. The temperature was a comfortable 25°c and the air was dry and still. The sky was cloudless which made the range of extinct volcanoes stand out, their dull brown slopes contrasting with the dazzling blue of the air. They loaded ML's belongings into a newish looking black BMW X5 with tinted windows. As they set off for the short drive to Corralejo ML said 'I hope that this is your vehicle and not one you've obtained for me, Richard.'

'Yeah, it's mine. What's wrong with it?'

'Nothing if you want to be taken for a pimp. It's not exactly low profile, is it?'

'And I am? Fuck it, Dominic. It's all part of the image. And it has its uses. Hiding in plain sight if you know what I mean.'

ML looked across at Richard and said nothing. He did not want to let the man think that he was interested in the shadier side of his life so he let the comment slide. Twenty five minutes later and they were on the outskirts of Corralejo. Richard avoided using the main street and took a more indirect route down Avenida Rey Juan Carlos to drop ML at his rented villa.

'You'll want to shower and change I suppose after all that fucking about in planes. I've switched everything on, there's an instruction list on the kitchen table. You up for drinks and dinner later so we can sort out details?'

'Yes; good idea. I'm actually feeling pretty good. I'll pop over to your bar eightish and we'll take it from there if that's all right with you.'

'Fine. Here's your keys. The alarm is set to 8-6-4-2 at the moment so you will want to do something with that. See you later then.'

Richard helped ML to the front door of the villa and drove away to his own place which lay only 200 yards to the east on the other side of the main drag. ML then made a tour of the property inside and out. He was impressed; Richard had come up with the goods – as he should have for the price he was paying. There were two large bedrooms with en-suite facilities plus a further two doubles and a family sized bathroom. ML unpacked his belongings in the room which overlooked the pool area then took a long shower to wipe away the fatigue generated by ten hours of airports and planes.

Richard had stocked the fridge with the basics and had also laid in a reasonable selection of drinks. ML fixed himself a gin and tonic and sat down to familiarise himself with the list of how the mechanics of the house functioned. Simple stuff really but he did not want anything to break down and have to call someone in to fix it. Staying low profile in a place as small as Corralejo was difficult enough – he did not need any complications so it was worth the effort to read boring details like how the pool pump worked. Finally satisfied, he dressed in grey chinos, deck shoes and a light blue polo for his evening with Richard. The last thing he put on was a lightweight, navy coloured jacket. He wore this not for reasons of warmth but as the masculine equivalent of a ladies handbag. The interior zippered pockets contained his ID, two cell phones and credit cards. The outer pockets carried weapons although not even a police inspection would detect them. His trousers were where he stashed rather a large amount of high denomination euro notes. This was discrete and not really necessary – street crime is virtually unheard of in Fuerteventura; but ML always sought to have the edge in any situation.

He reset the alarm to numbers of his own choice and headed out into the early evening light for his meeting with Richard.

Chapter Sixteen

It was early evening in Brighton and Carver and Stone were entering their last venue of the night in their search for Jennifer Duncan. It had been Michelle's idea to come to the Proud Brighton Ballroom in Saint George's Road; Martin Carver had said nothing but he did not have to – his body language spoke volumes. Everything they knew about the victim gave an image of a mousey little introvert who played folk rock guitar as her only pastime. What, wondered Martin, made Michelle think that she would have been attracted to this temple to transvestites and 'alternative' comedy?

They had all but exhausted the bars, pubs and clubs in the town which featured live music. The problem they had was that, after three years, all the staff had changed with many having moved up to London. The people who owned or managed these places tended not to interact with the customers that much and were of no use to their enquiries. They were sometimes able to say where their former staff had moved on to, if one of them had asked for a reference. Carver and Stone did not relish following up such long shots but acknowledged that it might come to that. The other source of information would be the regulars who frequented the music bars. Jennifer had disappeared on a Thursday so the police officers were readying themselves for a big push the next night.

At the moment they were in the office of the manageress, Roxy, explaining why they were there. The women listened patiently then spoke, not unsympathetically 'Brighton does attract a lot of young runaways but your girl does not appear to fit that category and I must say, from your description of her, she does not sound like the sort of person we attract. This is very much an extroverts type of place; cabaret, dining and dancing – retro if you like. There would be no point in talking with the staff either. Three years ago this place was called Hanbury's; it was still a ballroom or sorts but had become shabby. The Proud organisation took it over, refurbed and employed completely new staff. Sorry.'

'I see' said Michelle. 'Do you have a list of places where the Hanbury staff went to? Did any of them ask for references for example?'

'Yes and we would have stated that so and so had worked here from such a date until Proud took over. My HR manager can give you those names tomorrow if you wish.'

'That's fine. Do you mind if we spend some time in the club? We are still trying to get a feel for Brighton night life.'

'Be my guest. Here.' Roxy handed over a gold coloured plastic card to Michelle. 'Have supper, drinks, whatever on the house. If I don't see you before you leave just give the card to whoever is at reception.'

'Thank you very much. Hope to see you later' said Michelle.

Carver and Stone left the office and went into the ballroom. At this hour the place was only half full so they had no problem securing a balcony booth which overlooked the dance floor, stage and main bar area. The predominant décor theme was black gloss, chrome and mirror balls. Martin Carver could barely conceal his disgust at what he felt to be a waste of their time. Michelle Stone picked up on this and said 'Take it easy, Martin. I've a feeling about this place; we just need a bit of patience. Fancy some food?'

'Might as well. I'm declaring us officially off duty and will have Sussex chicken with a bottle of Laurent Perrier Rosé. Yourself?'

'Seabass for me and I'll share the pink fizz. Bit on the extravagant side for a drink though.'

'Mirrors on the ceiling, pink champagne on ice, as the song goes. The choice of drink may create an intro with some of the more exotic clientele. I've not ordered this crap for pleasure, Michelle.'

She looked at her colleague with new eyes, realising that, although their paths had crossed professionally a couple of times, she knew very little about Martin Carver.

'Question, Martin. When we visited the Duncans in Telford you asked for strong, sweet tea and I know you're a coffee man. What was that about?'

'Empathy. Duncan was military and the British Army lived on strong sweet tea. If they can, they'll add whisky to it and the resulting brew is called gunfire. Just by asking for that drink put Malcolm Duncan more at ease with us.'

'Clever. Does your every move have a goal in mind? Do you ever switch off from being a manipulative detective?'

'Look in the mirror and ask yourself that question, Michelle. Enough of that for now; why on earth have you brought us here? Even that tart of a manageress thought it was a non-starter.'

'Bear with me, Martin. Can we have a time out until after we've eaten? Just look around this place; observe the people and see if you can come up with a reason why Jennifer would have come here.'

Carver took a deep breath and nodded 'OK'. He was not happy and was not hiding the fact. To his credit, he remembered that it was Stone's lateral thinking that had enabled them to identify the only victim so far. He was prepared to give his junior officer some latitude.

Supper was served quite promptly and was of an acceptable standard. Carver relaxed and ordered a second bottle of Laurent Perrier. He had decided to go with the flow and see what happened. The lights dimmed at eleven o'clock and a single spotlight hit centre stage. He half expected a Joel Grey impersonator to introduce Sally Bowles and take them all off to the fun place that was Nazi Berlin's cabaret land. Not quite. What he got was a group of transvestites and a lead female doing 'Chicago' and the song 'All that Jazz. Perhaps manageress Roxy chose the cabaret.

The song ended and Michelle leaned over to Martin and asked 'What did you see?'

'Black stockings, sequins, bowler hats and short skirts – and that's just the men.'

'Ok put those elements into one word; what do you come up with?'

Carver took his time as he formulated a response. The dominant theme was black and sexy but that was not what Stone was aiming at. He closed his eyes and visualised the stage scene. Commonality; what did the ensemble share? Got it! 'Costumes; they were all wearing costumes.'

'Exactly; and Jennifer Duncan's job was …?'

'Costume designer! Bloody hell; that could be the link. We need to know who supplied the cabaret outfits to – what was the name? – Hanburys. Roxy won't have that info so we'll have to track it down tomorrow. What's your thinking here Michelle?'

'I don't believe a musical person with strong parents who graduates in theatre studies then relocates to what is probably the most bohemian town in England would be a mousey introvert. The poster on her wall is of Joss Stone who is a very strong individual with a unique voice. Jennifer could not attain that degree of musical accomplishment but maybe, just maybe, she could receive adoration vicariously by clothing the performers. She may have come here for the visual aspect of the show, not the musical.'

'I can see that. We need to run this past van Dyke, Michelle. Let's call it a night and get back to the hotel before some fat, middle aged tranny gives us the obligatory Shirley Bassey impersonation.'

'Deal. We can walk it from here. There's a short cut that bypasses the Lanes. Nightcap at my place? I've got the 'Junior Suite'.'

'Sound good. Let's go.'

Carver and Stone left the ballroom pausing only to return Roxy's pass at reception. On exiting the building Stone led them left and left again. Soon they were away from the bright lights of the beachfront area and heading inland to their hotel. Each kept their own council as they mentally reviewed the way ahead that costume design might lead them. Suddenly Carver's left hand took Stone by the right elbow and he stopped her forward progress whilst turning her body towards his. He placed his right arm around her shoulders, leant into her face and breathed softly.

'Don't worry; there are three numpties who have been following us since we left the club. They have now reappeared twenty five yards ahead on the other side of the road where the street lamp is out. This is obviously their hunting ground. With the greatest of respect, Michelle, they probably think we're two gay guys.'

'Maybe they think you're a prettier than the usual dyke. What's the plan?'

'Follow my lead. If it comes to it, I'll take the two on the right first then move on the one who will be facing you. Keep clear of me by a yard if it kicks off and only come in if I go to the ground. Your main job is to watch our six; I don't think there's any more than three but let's be aware. OK?'

'Why don't we just declare we're the police, Martin?'

'Because then they'll attack and we'll have to play by the rules and arrest them. I don't think we have time to spend helping the locals with their enquiries; nor would Goodchild be too happy if we made the front pages. If you're not up for it we can go back the way we came.'

'You are fucking joking. Let's go lover.'

Carver and Stone broke their clinch and carried on walking up the ill lit back street lightly holding hands. Martin was in fight mode and the effects of over a bottle of champagne felt non-existent to him although he knew that his reactions would be off by a fraction. Michelle, with her much lesser body weight, would be more impaired he knew. He would need to be at his best in the moments ahead.

As they progressed further into the gloom of back street, three bodies detached themselves from the shadows and crossed over to block their way. The one on their left was an obese monster of well over six feet tall; his long, lank hair hung in strands over a pock-marked face and he was hyperventilating already. The one on their right was rail thin, of medium height and was dancing from foot to foot like a small child desperate for the toilet. This bag of nerves kept his hands in his pockets and glanced repeatedly at the person who stood in the middle of the trio. The male in the centre was the little group's leader. He was a low life sack of shit like the other two but he possessed an air of native cunning and, hence, superiority about him that made him stand apart from his buddies. His eyes glittered from recent amphetamine use so this was probably a straight forward rolling to finance further drug purchases. The first words spoken by the threesome's main man dispelled this notion.

'Good evening you fucking faggots; what will you do for us to avoid severe pain?'

'Martin seemed to go weak at the knees and replied in a tremulous voice 'No, no. You've got it wrong. We're not gays. We're straight.'

'We'll see about that. Get in there.'

The group's leader indicated an overgrown piece of waste ground where the wire link fence had been torn apart. Martin and Michelle looked at each other and exchanged the tinniest of nods then Martin went back into his terrified civilian act.

'No, we don't need to do this. I have cash on me and can get hold of a lot more within the hour just let…'

'Shut up, you cunt' said the same person who then clicked his fingers. On command, the skinny member of the group produced a switchblade which he clicked open. 'As I said, in or we shall slice your fucking eyes out where you stand and take your purse anyway.'

Martin and Michelle went through the fence and then turned to face their captors. There was nowhere to run, one could not reason with the retarded so each of them knew that the situation was going to end in violence. The pack leader spoke again. 'So how do you get hold of a load more money for us, money boy?'

'We've more or less spent up having dinner but we can each take out £300 from an ATM and the same again at one minute past midnight. It's 1130 now so we'll have to hustle to get this done.'

'That's it? Twelve hundred pounds and we don't mark you. Tell you what: twelve hundred, your little friend shags my little friends and you give me the world's best blow job. Fair enough?'

Michelle's eyes opened to their upmost extent and her jaw dropped in shock. Martin stumbled backwards as though confronted by Satan himself. The three thugs laughed like drains and advanced line abreast stroking their crotches.

'Hold it' said Martin. 'I've one more thing to bargain with. May I take my wallet out please?'

'Slowly.'

Martin did as he was told and from inside his black, leather billfold he extracted a dark coloured credit card.

'I'll bet that none of you have ever seen one of these.'

'What is it?'

'It's an American Express Black Card.'

'So fucking what?'

'This is the world's most exclusive charge card – in any twenty four hour period I can charge up to one million dollars worth of goods and services. It's not even made of plastic – this is anodised titanium. I propose that we all head into London and first thing in the morning, I go on a spending spree for cars, jewellery or whatever that you can convert into cash. What do you say?'

'Let me see that thing.' The group's leader held his hand and Martin moved towards him to give the card over but appeared to stumble on the uneven ground. As six eyes watched him clumsily regain his balance they did not see or really feel him flash his hands across the foreheads of the two more slightly built men. They only realised that something was amiss when their eyes were filled with their own blood. The large lout on the left did not react at all – he merely stared at his fellow crims as they attempted to clear their vision and he did this with both feet planted firmly on the ground. This meant that when Martin stamped down on the side of the fat one's leg, it snapped clearly at the knee joint and he was definitely out of the game. Moving quickly but unhurriedly, Martin stepped behind the two bleeders and felled them both with a single punch to the base of each skull. Finally he moved behind the now prone porker who was vomiting with shock and knocked him out in the same manner. Seven seconds from start to finish.

'Michelle, go and keep watch while I tidy up.'

'Roger that.'

Martin retrieved his card, wiped as much blood off it as he could then wrapped it in a handkerchief and placed it in his trouser pocket. He then took the switchblade and cut through the web of flesh that connects the thumb and the first finger on both hands of his would-be assailants. They would be out of the mugging game for some time as that particular wound takes an age to heal, if indeed it does.

He now left the waste ground and caught up with Michelle. They set off at a fair but unhurried pace. Along the way Martin took a pack of paper tissues from his colleague which he used to clean the switchblade of blood and prints. The used tissues he pushed down a sewer drain and he used the last one to cover and carry the knife in. After a further hundred yards of walking he dropped this in the gutter and kicked it into the large opening of one of the town's storm drains. The only words the officers had exchanged since the attacked had been when Martin had asked Michelle for the tissues. Their hotel was now in sight and he addressed her in low but urgent tones. 'When we enter the hotel head for the public toilets. Once you're there lock yourself in a cubicle and give your shoes a thorough scrub – including the soles. Then go up to your room and wait for me. I'll ring your mobile before I come up. OK?'

'Where are you going to be?'

'I'm off to the gents to do likewise and also scrub my nails. We cannot do this in our rooms as the sink traps can retain blood and I don't want us walking any forensic trace over the carpets. It's not perfect but it's the best I can come up with on the hoof.'

'All right; I'll see you soon and you can explain where you learned your version of police work.'

It was fifteen minutes before he called her room. She was waiting for him so he went along for what, he was sure, was going to be a difficult conversation.

Michelle opened the door at his knock and turned her back on him leaving him to follow her in. She sat down in one of the two armchairs and picked up what looked like a tumbler of whisky.

'There's a mini bar on your right. Help yourself unless you'd prefer something from room service' she said.

'First things first' he said. 'Check my face out, please.'

'What!?'

'I want you to get as close to my face as you can and inspect it for the smallest spot of blood.'

'Jesus Christ! OK, come into the bathroom; the light's better.'

They went into the surprisingly spacious en-suite where Michelle proceeded to examine Martin's face from hairline to collar. She finally said to him 'I can't see anything but people have been convicted on microscopic amounts of blood that the naked eye can't detect. I'm going to wipe you down with make up remover using loo paper which I will then flush away. After that you will have to wash your face with ordinary soap and water. OK with you Mister Forensics expert?'

'Fine. Let's get it done.'

Five minutes later they were finished. Martin went to the mini bar and made do with a brandy of dubious provenance. He then sat in the other armchair and waited for the inevitable questions.

'What did you use the flick knife for, Martin?' asked Michelle.

'I cut them. All of them.'

'Could you be a bit more specific please? I mean what did you cut? Their carotids, their jugulars? Or did you just split their noses the way we used to in the good old days?'

By way of reply he held up his right hand with the four fingers together and the thumb extended at right angles. 'I sliced this web of flesh here. They will not be holding any offensive weapons for some considerable time. The recovery process will be painful and of sufficient duration to give them time to reflect on the error of their ways.'

'For fuck's sake, Martin! I can just about, just about handle the way you dealt with those three scumbags although the phrase 'excessive force' does spring to mind; but the knife work was premeditated, grievous bodily harm. Who the hell trained you? The Taliban?'

'You deserve an answer; the brief version is that my chosen career was the army. I ended up as a Captain in the Royal Military Police. I've served in various overseas posts as well as the UK. Along the way I picked up some combat methods that don't appear in government training manuals. As soon as that shit pulled a blade on us he crossed a line, and yes, I went in hard – I've learned from experience that it's the best way. I admit I dispensed summary justice by cutting them but what would have happened if I'd just left them there? The local police would have interviewed them at whichever hospital had to patch them up and they would have claimed that they had been mugged by six very large bikers and could they have some compensation please? Even if they hadn't pulled a weapon and we had arrested them you know that the chances of them doing time would have been minimal. I don't go out at night looking for muggers to sort out – I'm not a sadist. Anyway, that's my explanation for tonight's action.'

'Why did you leave the army? I would have thought it would be more suitable to someone with your morality.'

'What do you mean by that?'

'Soldiers have an even more black and white view of the world than we do. It's them versus the enemy and they are allowed to kill the enemy. Isn't that your view of things?'

'You don't know me or the army well enough to make such a statement. In all my years in the army I never once fired a weapon at another person. I was a military policeman carrying out specialised police work. I might be investigating theft from an armoury one day and tracking down a deserter the next. Or, if I was really lucky, get to stop a hundred drunken squaddies and sailors smashing up a bar in sunny Cyprus. Laugh a minute being an MP.'

'My question stands; why did you leave?'

Martin Carver finished his drink and stared into the bottom of the glass. Not finding an answer in that particular crystal ball, he went to the mini bar for a refill. He drank again but did not sit down, choosing to speak whilst maintaining a distance.

'In 2003 I was in Iraq. By then our main task was to train the locals into some sort of cohesive force in preparation for when we left. One day, in a shit hole called Majar al-Kabir, a mob of around 400 rag heads surrounded a building where there were six redcaps. Normally I'd have backed our people to be able to keep a rabble like that at bay until more force could be brought in to assist. That day we had the Parachute Regiment in town so it should have been no problem. Unfortunately our comms systems were incompatible; worse, the MPs were inadequately armed and had limited stocks of ammo. Result: six dead redcaps. A total cock-up.'

'Were they friends of yours?'

'I only knew two of them well. That is not the point. They should not have been placed in that situation to begin with. The politicians and even some senior officers tried to shift the blame onto the dead MPs themselves. It took years for an inquest of sorts to take place and that only came about because the fathers of two of the dead just would not shut up and forget it all. It was not until this year that eight Iraquis were arrested for their involvement in the killing and it was the Americans who did that – our government would prefer to pretend it never happened and if we ever do get a conviction I'll show my arse in Harrods' front window. The taste it all left in my mouth was nearly as bad as this brandy's.'

Neither officer spoke for a minute. They sipped their drinks in silence and the tension which had been stifling the room started to dissipate. Finally, it was Michelle who spoke.

'I suppose we'd better get out of Dodge first thing tomorrow then.'

'No, not first thing. We have an HR person to see about former Hanbury staff. If Roxy has left a message and at least one of us does not turn up it will look odd. The hospital staff will not let the local police interview the three stooges whilst they're recovering from concussions so we should have until noon tomorrow until they have any sort of description of us. If we are not seen together we minimise the chances of being stopped. I reckon that you should take a taxi to the ballroom after breakfast and obtain what we need. Change your appearance as much as you can from last night's. I'll go and make a courtesy call on the locals to say thanks for all their help and that we'll be in touch. Whoever finishes first calls the other's mobile and I'll come and pick you up. OK?'

Michelle nodded her agreement so Carver continued.

'I'll phone Goodchild with an update and I reckon he'll want us back in London. If he doesn't summon us I'll say we've done all we can down here and need to use the Police National Computer to check the whereabouts of Hanbury employees on the night of Jennifer Duncan's disappearance.'

'Sneaky. One last thing; can I have a look at your Black Amex that doubles as an offensive weapon?'

'I'm afraid not; I've posted it back to myself in London. It's not a real charge card anyway. Christ, if a copper owned one of those he'd be under internal investigation, before you could say 'police corruption'!'

'You don't miss a trick, do you? OK. I'm whacked; it's been quite a day one way or another so I'll see you at some stage tomorrow then.'

'Yes. Goodnight, Michelle.'

Carver went straight back to his own room leaving his colleague to her thoughts. It was obvious to him that she was far from happy with his actions this evening but had decided not to pursue the matter further – for the moment, anyway. He had hoped that they could continue to function as a team; only time would tell.

Chapter Seventeen

As ML walked slowly towards Richard's bar, he reflected on the very mixed feelings which he had about the island of Fuerteventura. He loved its physical aspect; it was bare, very little grew here and the only animals one ever saw were the scraggy, local goats. The place's volcanic origins were evident even though all thermal activity was long extinct. The extensive, sandy beaches, yellow on the east coast and black on the west, were pretty much unspoiled. The locals had managed tourism in an intelligent manner, eschewing the construction of forests of tower blocks in which they could cram in hordes of northern Europeans from whom they could squeeze cash at the expense of the environment. There were literally a handful of hotels which exceeded five stories in height and no more could be built.

In general, the tour companies organised things so that the British stayed in Corralejo on the north of the island whilst the Germans based themselves in Jandia at the extreme south. In between the two lay the capital, Puerto Rosario, where the locals got on with their lives. It was a system that functioned well for all concerned.

Then there was the downside, which ML was enduring now. Licenses and leases had been given and sold with little thought as to what kind of establishments might come into existence. The result was an alcoholic bedlam of bars and eating places mostly crammed along Corralejo's Main Street each one competing for the tourist business. Every few yards a young Englishman or girl would try and entice the passer-by into their establishment in a variety of ways. These ranged from a polite invitation to look at the menu to the more aggressive approach of thrusting a flyer into the mark's hand offering special deals for that night only. The youngsters engaged in such activities would claim, with straight faces, that they worked in public relations.

ML was approached less frequently than the average tourist, dressed as he was in more formal clothing and also having a certain air about him. He did not look like the man who would be swayed by the offer of a free T-shirt if he drank seven pints of lager. If someone did block his way he would politely state that he thanked them for their offer but that he had a dinner reservation in the old town. These dubious 'marketing' activities were intrusive enough to dissuade ML from having purchased a property in town.

This evening he arrived at Richard's bar relatively unmolested and was looking forward to catching up with what had been happening in town since his last visit. The Royalist was actually one of the more pleasant bars in Corralejo, hidden away in a small side street which led to one of the quieter beaches. It consisted of a single room of about thirty feet on a side which was divided up by chest high partitions to give each nest of tables an air of privacy. A well stocked, horseshoe shaped bar was one of the Royalist's two dominant features. The second was Richard himself. As soon as ML opened the door he could see that business was good. The bar was three quarters full with most customers being middle aged tourists but with a fair amount of locals mixed in despite, for them, the early hour of eight in the evening. The latter had probably not even thought about dinner yet whereas the British would have long finished their hotel buffets and were now out looking for some entertainment.

ML found a stool for himself at the bar, ordered a bottle of Mahou and then waited for Richard to finish his conversations with two ladies of a certain age when he could politely join him. After five minutes he did so.

'Evening, Dominic. All rested up and ready to go are you?' said Richard.

'I'm fine but fancy a quiet one tonight. Have you a live act on later?'

'Yeah; guy and a girl. He's keyboards, she's guitar and vocals. Rockabilly country and not bad.'

Not bad from Richard meant very good indeed. The reason that ML had got to know the larger than life Londoner was the man's incredible knowledge of popular music. He openly admitted that had first opened a bar so that he could drink what he wanted and, more importantly, listen to what he wanted to and if you did not like his taste you could piss off to the disco.

Over the years ML had spent many an hour in the Royalist listening to Richard's CDs. Now and again he would have to ask who the artist was and he'd buy the person's collection on his return to the UK.

Live music was not a regular feature of the bar; Richard refused to book people from the island circuit but would allow acts to audition at his convenience. If they passed the test he paid them a fair amount but nothing went from his pocket to an agent's. An act that could say that they played the Royalist was greatly enhancing their CV.

'So you'll have to be here later on when it becomes busy' said ML. 'How about an early steak dinner nearby and you can be back here in an hour or so?'

'Get your coat – you've pulled!' laughed Richard. 'Let me just brief the Pedro and we'll split.' He left ML to finish his beer whilst he explained to his local barman that he would be back soon and not to steal <u>too</u> much in his absence. He then came around the bar and headed back to the main street with ML. This time none of the barkers even tried to talk to them; Richard would go where Richard would go and this evening they climbed the steps to El Toro Negro where a booth at the rear of the restaurant was given to them. It was not so much secluded but, if it had not been for the small oil lamp on the table, they would have been invisible. Perfect as far as both men were concerned.

'How's the villa?' asked Richard.

'Just right' replied ML. 'But the garage is empty.'

'I'll have that sorted by mid-afternoon tomorrow at the very latest – probably sooner but I don't want to make a promise and then not keep it. If you need to be anywhere sooner...' ML held up his palm and interrupted. 'No, no. Tomorrow afternoon is absolutely fine by me. Now, let's sort out payment. As I said on the phone, I don't know how long I'm going to be staying so what I think is fair is this.'

ML handed a white envelope quite openly to Richard. 'That contains the equivalent of three months rent; one in advance, another month in lieu of notice in case I have to curtail my stay unexpectedly and a further month against damages. On this date each month I shall give you a further months rent and we'll keep it rolling like that. I have included a ten percent finder's fee for your trouble, Richard. No – don't argue; we all have to make a living. This other envelope contains a further sum which I would like you to hold against utility bills and possibly extras such as pool cleaning etc. All payments are in cash – God bless the 500 euro note eh? - and we'll do another accounting at the end of my stay. Is that OK so far, Richard? '

'Yeah; works for me, Dominic.'

'Good. That just leaves the car. How do I pay for that?'

'Let's deal with that tomorrow. It all depends on what sort of deal I can swing for you. OK?'

'Fine. Do you think that you could wave a gold bracelet in the direction of a waiter; they seem unwilling to approach this table for some reason.'

'Hah! Well I've got the Pedros trained not to interrupt me business meetings until I'm good and ready. What do you fancy?'

'A bottle of Marques du Riscal and a 16oz entrecote medium rare should do it for me. No starter, no fizzy water.'

Richard looked across the restaurant and raised his head slightly. The manager came over accompanied by two waiters and a lengthy conversation in very measured Castillano ensued. Richard's working class demeanour disappeared when he spoke Spanish and it was obvious to ML that he was accorded no little measure of respect in this town.

The Spaniards went away; one came back, served the wine with excessive ceremony and then left the two Englishmen to resume their conversation.

'Any special plans for this visit, Dominic or is it just your usual chill out time?' asked Richard.

'Actually I am going to do something out of the ordinary this time round. I've managed to obtain a commission to review not only the eateries of Fuerteventura but also to write about the music scene on the island.'

'Bloody hell! That's great work if you can get it. How can I help?'

'Thought you'd be impressed. This is something I've wanted to do for quite a while now and normally you would be the ideal chap to chauffeur me round and point out the good, bad and indifferent but, given that you are a prominent music bar owner yourself, I really can't use you.'

'But you don't publish under your real name, Dominic! No-one would ever know. Come on; I can be bloody useful to you.'

'I'm sure you could but you're wrong; someone always knows, especially in Spain. Think about it. Especially amongst ex-pats.'

Richard sipped his wine with closed eyes as he thought the problem through. Finally he smiled wryly and said 'Yeah. Fucking denuncio. If I received a decent review and I'd been in your company for several months some bastard would go to Guardia Civil and denounce me. They would have no option under Spanish law other than to shut me down whilst an investigation was carried out and that could take forever. Even if I were found innocent I'd receive no compensation and the bastard who had denounced me would remain anonymous. Bollocks!'

'Precisely. Neither of us could afford to run that risk. Ah, here comes the food.'

The two men ate their simple but adequate meal and made as much small talk as they ever did. It was easy for ML to steer the conversation in the direction he required and, by the time their platters had been cleared away, he knew which places in Corralejo were 'in' and which were struggling. They were dawdling over coffee and 103 brandy when ML's mobile sounded. He looked at the screen and saw that it was Catherine Taylor.

'Sorry, Richard. I really have to take this call.'

'No problem I'll get the bill.' Richard waved at a waiter whilst ML spoke into his cell.

'Hello there. Where are you calling from?'

'Hi Dominic. I'm at Bristol airport about to embark for Madrid. I won't bore you with my itinerary – it's a nightmare – but the bottom line is I get into Fuerteventura tomorrow afternoon on Iberia 307 from Lanzarote. Can we meet?'

'Of course. I'm due to take delivery of a car tomorrow so a run out to the airport and back should do it good. Will you have much luggage?'

'Just one case in the hold and one carry-on. I'll buy new stuff out there as and when I need it.'

'Yes; that's the system I use myself. OK. I'll pick you up at the airport tomorrow, see how you feel and we'll take it from there.'

'Look forward to it. See ya, Dominic.'

'Bye.'

Anyone listening to ML's side of the conversation (and Richard had been) would have thought that it was between two business acquaintances, most likely of the same gender. ML did not think it necessary or even desirable that Richard knew that he was going to greet a young woman who he had only met socially.

'Richard, I've someone coming out to see me on business, landing tomorrow afternoon sometime. Any chance of you expediting the vehicle before noon tomorrow?'

'I can't promise. Look, I won't be driving again tonight. Here's a spare key to my wagon. It's parked round the back of the bar. If we have not met up by the time you need to move tomorrow, just take it. All papers are in the glove box so no problem if you're stopped by the Guardia.'

'Fine. I'll call you if I have to do that so for God's sake keep your bloody phone turned on, will you.'

'It's always on, Dominic, but I don't always hear it. I run a music bar, remember?'

'So put it on vibrate and stick it in your front pocket.'

'Do what?'

'Give me your phone.' Richard handed over a new model Nokia to ML who played around with the settings for less than twenty seconds. 'Now, put that in your trouser pocket.' Richard did so and ML dialled his number whereupon the phone's owner jumped up from the booth with a cry of 'Fuck me!'

'OK Richard. I take it that you won't be missing anymore of my call from now on?'

'Too right. I can think of a few uses for this baby from now on.'

'I really don't want to know, Richard. Look, it's been a long day and we both have things to do in the morning so I'm going to head back to the villa and leave you to it. See you tomorrow.'

'Yeah; I'll try and get an early one too. If it looks like being a late one at the bar I'll have Pedro lock up. Mind how you go.'

They went their separate ways into the still warm evening – Richard calculating how best to profit from Dominic's stay and ML reflecting on how to deal with Catherine's imminent arrival. She was at least forty eight hours in advance of the schedule he had planned for but there had been no way for him to stall her. She was on her way and that was that. Deal with it.

ML took a tour round the outside of the villa then entered, set the alarm, showered and went to bed. He would be up and rested tomorrow whilst most of the island was asleep. He would need to be alert; not only was Catherine Taylor due in on the next day but the obsequious Williams was also due to arrive to begin his market research for 'McNaughten'. To top it all, Tony the musician was supposed to start his stint this weekend. Lots of balls in the air but ML had known that this would be the case.

Chapter Eighteen

Martin Carver had taken breakfast as early as possible then checked himself and Michelle out of the hotel. He did not want either staff or guests to see the two of them together and have the idea of them as a couple in their minds. Sooner or later the local police would be paying this establishment a visit looking for a white male and his girlfriend who had been involved in some rather spectacular nocturnal violence. Far better for them to fold their tents as individuals.

He drove across town to the local police station and presented himself to the front desk without an appointment. At that hour the senior officer present was a sergeant and the arrival of a Detective Inspector from the Met was well above his pay grade. Praying to whichever god looks after policemen, he admitted Carver to the station canteen and left him with tea and the morning newspapers whilst he went to find a senior officer.

It was nearly an hour later when the sergeant returned to escort Carver upstairs to the office of DCI Finnigan. Carver had made no comment on the fact that he'd been left cooling his heels for so long and it was a very relieved sergeant who headed back to the canteen to grab a brew for himself.

DCI Finnigan was in uniform and looked as though he could do with a visit to the dry cleaners and about twenty four hours sleep. He had the manners to apologise to Carver though.

'Sorry to leave you hanging around, Inspector but we have a bit of a flap on at the moment.'

'Anything I should know about?' he asked professionally.

'No, just some local nastiness that the media has got its teeth into. It's all a bit weird – even for Brighton.'

'Weird, how?'

'As far as we can make out, three of our local scumbags were attacked in the street last night. They are all in hospital with severe concussion: two of them have been slashed across the forehead, the other has a badly broken leg. All of them have had their hands cut between the thumb and forefinger. The tendon damage is considerable. What do you make of that, Inspector?'

'I'd say lock up all the Graham Greene fans.'

'I beg your pardon?'

'Graham Greene; Brighton Rock? Ring any bells?'

'None.'

'Very good book. I actually read it in school. Superficially it's about a nasty little shit called Pinkie who runs a protection racket using acid and a straight razor to enforce his will. The real message in the book is the nature of good and evil plus the role of religion. It was made into a film just after the war and remade this year – Helen Mirren, if I remember correctly.'

'Oh fuck! Are you sure about this?'

'Broadly, yes. Google it and see what you get.'

Finnigan attacked his keyboard and, the more he read, the wider his eyes grew.

'No-one has picked up on this yet, Inspector. But there is bound to be some journalist who will. This is going to cause one almighty shit storm – what the hell do I do now?'

'It depends on what your three victims are saying; were they mugged for money or drugs? Is this gang related? The likelihood of it being psycho-religious nutters is statistically small but I reckon that you might want to bring the film's and book's existence to the attention of whichever poor sod has to face the press – it would not do for them to look better read than the police, would it?'

'Indeed. OK thanks for that. Now what can I do for you?'

'Nothing. I just popped in to say thanks for the professional courtesy which your force has extended to the Met. Our enquiries are progressing and we may well be back. You're obviously busy so I'll get out of your hair and I'll leave you to it.'

'Our pleasure, Detective Inspector. If you do come back give me a call and we'll try and have a drink together.'

'Of course.'

Finnigan rose from his desk and escorted Carver to the station exit. The two men shook hands and Carver strolled to his vehicle whilst Finnigan all but jogged back to his office to make sure that his superiors were up to date on classic twentieth century English literature.

Carver called Michelle Stone's mobile and she picked up straight away. 'Hi, it's me. Where are you?'

'I'm sat in the lobby with my luggage. I've done a morning's work already.'

'OK be outside in ten and we'll get moving. See you then.'

Owing to the vagaries of the Brighton traffic system which had obviously grown up around the horse and buggy rather than the motor car, it was actually closer to twenty minutes before Michelle dumped her bags in the car and they set off north. Martin pulled over once they were outside the city limits. Michelle had an A4 envelope in her hands and Martin pointed to it asking 'What did you get?'

'This is a list of ex-Hanbury employees who gave Proud Brighton as a contact point for a work reference' said Michelle.

'How many are there?'

'Eight. That includes two agencies – both London based.'

'Fine. That's more than do-able. Time to call Goodchild.'

'There is one more thing; I spoke with the woman who employed Jennifer Duncan. She confirmed that Jennifer worked on the costumes for the Hanbury. She could not say whether or not the girl ever went there though she thought it unlikely given that Jennifer was quote 'the quiet type'.'

'I'll concentrate on the positive aspects of what she had to say. Good work, Michelle.'

Carver took out his cell phone and dialled a pre-set number. He was quickly put through to Goodchild.

'Morning, boss. Quick progress report. We've struck out on the music bar front. Staff have moved on and, after three years, the managers who are still in place cannot remember Jennifer. They did not recognise the flyers that her parents distributed first time round so no surprises there. Michelle has found another route that appears promising though; she's discovered the most famous place where Jennifer's costumes were worn. It's a show bar called Hanbury's. That closed down and changed hands. All the old staff were let go but Michelle has a list of those who used it as a reference. We reckon that Jennifer would have gone to Hanbury's to see her creations at work as it were and that one of those staff members might be able to tell us more. Yes, boss. N.I. numbers, addresses'. Carver looked at Stone who nodded in the affirmative, 'yes, we have those. About an hour and a half if we don't break any laws. On our way, boss.'

'Well?' asked Michelle.

' "Well done you" says the boss. He wants us back at the Yard now to start the follow-up. He's also got some warm bodies interviewing the other potential victim's families so we're moving. Christ, we're due a break.'

With that Carver pulled into traffic and headed north to London and the next stage of the investigation.

The first fifteen minutes of the car journey passed in silence. Carver concentrating on motorway driving whilst Stone studied the paperwork she had obtained from Proud Brighton's HR department. There was still a frost in the atmosphere between the two officers. Finally he said to her 'This is your lead, Michelle. How do you think we should follow it?'

'Let's start with the phones for the individuals. It's just a matter of locating each one and then having a face to face with them. The two agencies I'm not sure of; I've never had to deal with a recruitment outfit before. I just have a feeling that they might scream client confidentiality if we cold call them. Any views on that?'

'There is a fair bit of pressure we can bring to bear on agencies. Very few of them can withstand an in depth look at their procedures especially in the hospitality trade. We have to accept all sorts of new Europeans here as workers but their papers need to be thoroughly checked. Tell you what; once we get back, I'll take on the two agencies while you make a start on the individuals. If your people are London based get them in to the Yard and we can save ourselves some time.'

'Makes sense. How were the local plods?'

'Plodish. I told them that we might be back. They seemed distinctly underwhelmed.'

'They weren't chasing around hunting for the midnight slasher then?'

'If they were they did not say so to me. Forget it, Michelle. It's in the past.'

She turned her head to her right and looked directly at him, her face completely blank. Carver concentrated ahead but his excellent peripheral vision made him aware of her scrutiny. He knew that he was in for a long day and that pressure was building inside his partner. Whether that would dissipate over time or be held back for an almighty explosion he could not tell. One thing was certain; he was not going to force the issue.

The end of the run into London proved to be smoother than usual, mostly because they did not have to stay on the M25 orbital for very long. Once they had parked beneath New Scotland Yard they headed straight into the Orion offices where Goodchild was waiting for them.

'Morning you two. You made good time.'

'Yes; pretty smooth all the way. What's been happening during our absence on the UK's gay Riviera?' asked Carver.

By way of reply Goodchild gave each of them a copy of the briefing paper which he had submitted to Addison. He then enlarged upon what he expected Tucker's holding email to ML to achieve and finished by describing how he had teams of two officers interviewing people who had reported a lost one missing who fitted their profile.

'Comments, Martin, Michelle?'

'I don't see what more any of us could have done so far, boss' said Carver. 'Anything new from forensics?'

'No and Dr Watkins has exhausted that area. We are still waiting for more information on the make-up of the poison but that is coming from the secret world so don't hold your breath.'

'Yes; I can't believe how the Security Service have played this boss' said Michelle. 'They should be going all out to find someone who has access to, what is technically, a weapon of mass destruction.'

'They probably are in their own way. They are not renowned for sharing' said Goodchild.

'Anything from van Dyke, boss?' asked Carver.

'Nothing more than what he said at our last meeting. He reckons that he needs to know about more victims, their occupations, their interests before he can make up a pathology for the killer.'

'Bollocks. If we had that information we'd have the bastard ourselves. I don't see what van Dyke is bringing to the party, boss.'

'He's our condom' said Michelle. 'Better to have one in your purse and not need it than to need it and not have one.'

'Quite. Anything else you'd like to ask?' said Goodchild.

'A lot is riding on your mate Tucker, boss' said Carver. 'The holding email was good but how solid is he? He could blow us out of the water anytime he wanted to.'

'I think he's fine. I count him as a friend and I don't think he'd shit on me without giving me chance to get out of the way. As it happens I'm meeting him for lunch in an hour so if you two could avoid the Red Lion today that would be helpful.'

'Anything to help, boss' said Carver.

'Michelle; I reckon that your hit list of people will most likely be busy on lunchtime shifts right now so why don't we grab a bite in the Feathers then come back and hit the phone?'

'Sounds good to me. I'll see you in there in ten. I've a couple of personal calls to make.'

Michelle left the two men on their own in the Orion office, Carver looked at Goodchild and said 'Personal calls, my arse. Why can't she say that she needs a piss?'

'Professional pride, Martin. How is she performing by the way?'

'She's very good. She thinks laterally and is also quick on her mental feet. We are lucky to have her and it's crazy that she's still a D.S. I'd be putting her up for promotion.'

'That's good to hear. If we crack this case I reckon that will be a racing certainty. If we don't...'

'Yeah, I've always liked the uniforms that the security guys at Toys-R-Us wear. OK. I'm off. I'll see you when I see you, boss.'

§

Whilst Carver and Stone were eating in the darkness of a London pub, ML was standing in the sunlit glare of the arrivals lounge of Fuerteventura airport. He was always amazed at the progress that the Spanish had made in airport design. Their busiest tourist destinations used to be taken from a circle of hell that Dante had not imagined. Nowadays they were models of efficiency designed to move tourists from plane to transport with the minimum of fuss. Even the taxi drivers at certain destinations appeared to be working to some sort of coherent plan and as for eating and drinking; all Spain's international airports put the UK's to shame.

He had verified by phone that Iberia 307 was on time and had set off intending to arrive fifteen minutes after its landing so that he would spend the minimum amount of time standing around in a public space. Richard had not come through with his vehicle so he had driven the man's pimp-mobile to the short stay car park. On reflection he was glad that it would be these license plates that any security cameras filmed and not ones that could, at a later date, be associated with himself.

With his back against a pillar he scanned the new arrivals from behind his wrap around Oakleys and there she was, her silver grey hair still cut in a graded bob. The loose fitting white cotton harem pants and the sky blue cheesecloth blouse that she was wearing did nothing for her figure but, he imagined, they'd be damn comfortable for flying in. Espadrills as well. Sensible girl. She had a largish brown leather bag slung over one shoulder and in her other she was pulling along a black Samsonite suitcase on wheels. This model did not look expensive and would be unlikely to attract the attention of larcenous airport staff but, ML knew, it had very secure locks indeed requiring time and effort to force them. All in all, Catherine was showing herself to be an intelligent traveller.

She was scanning the line of meeters and greeters some of whom were holding up small signs bearing the names of those whom they sought. Obviously this was not his style and Catherine raised her line of sight and saw him. She was not sure until he raised an arm in salutation and smiled that it was him. Then they walked to each other with their own expectations.

'Give me your case and let's get out of here.'

'Sure. Nice to see you too, Dominic.'

All across the concourse people were hugging, kissing, faux-kissing and crying. ML looked like a driver who had come to collect his charge. Which was, of course, his intention.

They made the brief walk to the oversized vehicle in under five minutes. Whilst ML loaded Catherine's bags into the capacious rear, she turned in a three sixty with her eyes fixed on the skyline. 'God, Dominic; the air's so clear. How come I can't smell anything though? I know that the sea is just over there.'

'The air's clear because there's no industry to speak of. Think of Fuerte as a large, desert island. If you headed east the next stop is the Sahara. As for the lack of sea smells that's easy; what most people think of as the smell of the sea is actually the odour of decomposing marine vegetation.'

'You know some weird shit, Dominic.'

'Hey! I'm Mr Travel Writer man, remember. Get in and I'll lead you to a warm shower and a cold drink.'

'Sold to the lady in the straw hat.'

They climbed up into the front seats and set off north to Corralejo. The sky was cloudless with the sun still high but beginning to drop behind them. Catherine looked across ML to see the remains of ancient lava flows then they came to a long stretch, mile upon mile, of white gold sand that ran down to the sea. There were no hordes of tourists lying in serried ranks of sunbeds desperately seeking suntans such as she had seen on visits to mainland Spain. Here people were actually engaged in physical activity with kite flying appearing to be the most popular. Windsurfing looked to be a big hit too and some of the participants were attaining very high speeds before performing acrobatics as well. It was not what she had expected and she was pleased. She was equally glad that 'Dominic' was not someone who felt that he had to talk to fill a silence. Indeed she doubted if he did small talk at all; the 'how was your flight, what's the weather in the U.K.?' bullshit that meant absolutely nada as far as she was concerned. No; she was more than happy just to soak in her first impressions of a new place. There would be time enough for talking in the days and nights to come.

After twenty minutes of driving through semi-wilderness (albeit on a well maintained tarmacked road) signs of construction began to appear.

'Looks like there's a lot of building work going on round here' she said.

'Not really. All these shells were abandoned three years ago and the tower cranes dismantled. The tourist boom has come to an end for the time being. That's one of the themes I'm going to be writing about.'

'So unemployment and hard times for all the locals I suppose.'

'I don't know yet. They have different expectations of life out here and Lehman brothers means nothing to them. Look at that.'

ML pointed to large amusement park that had appeared on their left. 'When that opened it was a major money spinner. It's basically a fun fair built around water. As the seas around here are too rough for children, this was ideal but it totally changed the demographics of tourists coming to Corralejo plus, if people are spending the day here, they are not spending in the bars and restaurants in town so, if this place went bust, not many locals would shed a tear. Anyway, we all think it's a fucking eyesore.'

'And your point is?'

'That, for this island at least, it is not all about making a fast buck. OK on your right is the main drag, high street, whatever. Formally Avenida Generalissimo Franco. We'll visit it later. I'm going to take the next street along because it's easier to access where I live from here but, if you ever get lost, just find that avenue and you can't miss the villa.'

Five minutes later and they parked beneath a frangipane strewn pergola in the grounds of ML's rented residence. The smell of the flower could overwhelm that of the duty free perfume department at the airport and it was a relief to enter the climate controlled interior of the villa. ML carried Catherine's case upstairs and led her to the east side of the building.

'This is your billet. I'll leave you to unpack and freshen up. Drinks by the pool whenever you're ready.'

'Thanks, Dominic. I won't be long.'

He turned and left her with the briefest of smiles. She watched his back as he walked away from her then mounted a second flight of stairs which must have given onto the square, central tower that she had noticed on arrival.

Turning round she surveyed her room. Cream coloured stucco walls with dark wooden beams predominated. The bed was enormous and made of more dark, heavy timber, the floor light brown marble with a pleasing speckled effect. Catherine slipped her shoes off to feel it cool on the soles of her feet. There were windows on three sides of the room which had venetian blinds, again in wood, rather than the traditional Spanish external ones. These she opened to admit sunlight into what had been, until then, a dim, cool cavern. Each view gave her a different aspect of Corralejo. The window on the left hand wall overlooked the villa's entrance and the view extended to what she assumed was the length of the main street. The window opposite the room's door indicated that the villa was someway up a quite steep hill. The view dropped down over several properties until it reached the main street and thereafter went out to sea. If she looked to her left she could just make out the island of Lanzarote in the distance. The window on the right hand wall next to her bedhead was a full length affair and had a Juliette balcony. It was directly above the villa's swimming pool but when she looked up to the horizon she was treated to the sight of an enormous volcano whose caldera had collapsed on the side which faced her.

Catherine had travelled quite a lot for an American but it had always been in the sanitised security of five star hotels in London, Rome, Paris. This was really abroad and she was not sure about the emotions she was feeling at that moment. It was beautiful but she felt like she was about to burst into tears. 'What the hell is wrong with you girl?' she thought angrily. Shaking herself mentally she went into the bathroom, where she stripped, dumped her clothes into a tall wicker basket and opted for a power shower rather than a soak in the bath. Finished, she dried herself on a large fluffy towel that she took from the heated towel rail. She was then debating about what to wear and how much make-up to put on when a sudden splash sounded from the pool. Walking to the balcony she saw 'Dominic' performing a slow, strong front crawl and that solved the sartorial selection for the time being. Minutes later she arrived poolside in a red and white batik sarong. ML turned at the far end of the pool and stopped when he noticed her.

'If you're intending to swim, I warn you; the pool's heating isn't on at the moment.'

'Don't worry about me, Dominic. It'll take more than a little cold water to make this girl scream.'

With that, Catherine dropped the sarong to reveal that she was clad in a crimson one piece swimsuit á la Baywatch. She arrowed into the water leaving barely a ripple and proceeded to swim two lengths of the pool submerged. On surfacing, she began to swim in the same style as ML and with equal aplomb; she was obviously at home in the water.

ML left the pool and showered by the side before entering the changing rooms which were located under a canopy of bright purple Bougainvillaea. When he came out dressed in fresh khaki shorts Catherine was just hoisting herself onto the edge of the pool.

'It's refreshing but heated might be better for the evening, you know, Dominic.'

'I'll see to it. Drink?'

'Beer's fine by me.'

ML went into the kitchen and came back with four bottles of Estrella Dorada in an ice bucket. He sat down on the sun lounger next to the one on which Catherine was lying, opened two and passed a bottle to her.

'Cheers and welcome to Fuerteventura.'

They touched bottles and drank deeply in the afternoon sun.

'What do you think so far, Catherine?'

'It's a lovely island but in a strange way. I mean it's so dry, barren almost. All those dead volcanoes. Then I end up in a Spanish hacienda which is quite charming. I'm very glad I came, Dominic. Thank you.'

'My pleasure. A beautiful place like this needs a beautiful woman in it.' He said these words accompanied by a smile that was so natural that it was impossible for Catherine to feel either threatened or offended.

ML continued to speak 'I want you to treat this place as your own. Mi casa really is su casa. Here is a set of keys for you and if you enter or leave when I'm not here this is the alarm code. Can you remember that?'

'No problem. Four digits make for a simple mnemonic.'

'Good. Now there are only two house rules. Number one – absolutely no drugs, not even weed. OK?'

'No problem; it's not my thing anyway. And number two?'

'You are bound to meet young people out in the clubs and bars. I'm afraid that you cannot invite anyone back here, day or night. I keep quite a low profile on the island and this is my private refuge. If you are not going to make it back at night, just leave a message on my mobile. Is that OK?'

'Sure but you make it sound like we won't be seeing each other very much.'

'We'll see each other as much as we can and wish to, 24/7 in someone else's company does not often work. Married couples in the same office are nearly always a disaster. I enjoy your company, Catherine or I would not have invited you here but there are no strings attached and you are a free agent. OK?'

'Understood. What's the plan for today? Is there one?'

'Not really. You have to get into the island rhythm of life which basically means everything happens much later then in England, especially meals. Are you hungry?'

'Not drastically. Iberia put on a pretty decent lunch and beer tends to fill me up.'

'In that case let's finish these, put some walking shoes on and I'll show you town whilst it's still light. All I have to do at some stage is change my car for something less, ah, ostentatious.'

'I was kinda wondering how that beast fit in with keeping a low profile.'

'That beast as you so rightly describe it belongs to my pal Richard. He's promised to deliver me something more suitable later today.'

Catherine nodded to signify that she was listening even though she was now sat back on her lounger with her eyes shut facing into the sun. From time to time she drank from her bottle and her lips always drew back to rest in a lazy smile, a young woman at ease with her world.

ML's polarised glasses showed him that her skin was already catching the sun. She was naturally sallow and would probably turn the colour of honey eventually but if she did not dress within the next half an hour she was going to need to apply some sunscreen.

ML rubbed some Nivea factor 20 onto his forehead and face. Catherine turned to him and said 'It's not that hot is it, Dominic?'

'You'd be surprised how strong the sun is at this latitude. The breeze keeps the air temperature down but, as I said, over there is the Sahara desert. We are soaking up some serious UV right now. When I walk during the day I always wear a hat.'

'OK pass the cream. Nothing more undignified than a peeling nose. I'm done here, Dominic. I'll just go and change and you can show me Corralejo.'

'Don't forget your sunglasses. I'll see you in the lounge when you're ready.'

Catherine stood and snapped off a salute to him then turned to make her way back into the villa. ML tidied up the debris from their drinks and followed her in.

Ten minutes later they were outside the building both dressed in shorts and T-shirts and sporting dark glasses and hats, his an

Aussie bush style whilst hers was a classic straw Panama. They could have been anyone.

'Down this hill is the main street, as I said before' said Dominic indicating the steep slope to their right. 'I want to go back the way we drove into town so that you can see the whole drag in one go. Ready?'

'Yup.'

They set off back up the hill at the top of which lay some uninteresting scrubland. By turning left and left again they arrived at the ugly water park but the view was worth it. They were at the foothills of the volcano that Catherine could see from her bedroom and from there the main street descended arrow straight to the port a mile and a half to the north. The mountains of Lanzarote were visible through the heat haze which rose from the baking soil. ML and Catherine began their descent.

After the stark, natural beauty of the island, man's additions to the environment were superficial, tawdry and, hopefully, temporary. ML pointed out hotels and apartment blocks that had been quickly built and now lay abandoned not ten years later. All the bars and restaurants had some sort of international theme – one could dine from Mexico to China but not Spain. The first place with a purely Spanish sign on it was a large supermercado.

'Why is there a supermarket in the middle of a tourist resort, Dominic? asked Catherine.

'Well there are people who actually live around here, a lot of the locals. Then there are people like me who either own property or have taken out long term rentals. Finally there are the tourists who have opted for a self catering holiday. They don't buy much food but by God they stock up on beer and water. Even the people who have booked an all inclusive break need to buy sun-cream and sweeties from somewhere.'

'What does 'all inclusive' mean?'

'If you look around you can see people wearing a brightly

coloured, plastic wrist band. This serves as ID at their respective hotels and means that all their food and certain drinks were included in the price of their holiday. For families on a budget it makes economic sense but some people are just bloody mean. They steal the breakfast croissants and doughnuts to have for lunch on the beach later. They will never see the inside of a bar or a restaurant where they have to pay.'

'I don't get it; what's the point of flying all this way to live like that?'

'Cheap flights, cheap booze and guaranteed sun. That's all it takes to keep a working class Brit happy and look at this.'

They had stopped outside a large entrance to a self proclaimed Sports Bar. 'In there they can watch all their football games on Sky TV and then there is even a separate room where they can bet on UK horse racing. Rule Britannia.'

'Jesus. Where's Tony going to be playing?'

'Just down here. There it is across the road; Rock Café.'

'It looks empty.'

'It's open but there is no live music until eight at night. Things don't start moving until around ten. I've made enquiries and Tony starts his gigs this Friday. We might pop in when we make our way back home. Shall we carry on?'

'Sure.'

They strolled comfortably in the warmth of the day and ML pointed out the various small shops where a girl could buy clothes, shoes, bags etc. He also indicated the small side streets which led off the main street where less tourist orientated Spanish bars were located. Finally they passed a petrol station.

'This is one of the main reference points in town' said ML. 'It's known as Music Square and, as far as I can work out, it's an open mike facility for Spaniards of very varied ability. The restaurants are of a pretty decent standard by the way. Ready for a drink?'

'Sure am. Which bar?'

'None of these. This way.' ML led Catherine across the square then through a narrow back street which opened onto a cobbled path which was obviously for pedestrians only.

'Corralejo started life as a tiny fishing village and this is it. People still live in these little houses and they still work the sea from here. I'm taking you to one of my favourite places on the island; most tourists take a look at it and keep walking which suits all concerned. Here we are.

They walked into a bar which was smaller than Catherine's bedroom at the villa. A Zinc counter ran the length of one side. Six men were perched on bar stools at it. The body of the bar was taken up by six tables and twenty four chairs and that was it. The décor was murals of sea scenes from the turn of the last century and the stuffed head of a swordfish was mounted on one wall. A television mounted high in one corner blared out the Spanish version of MTV. Everyone ignored it choosing instead to look at the two foreigners who had entered their domain. All conversation had stopped.

'Jeez, Dominic; is this where the knife fight starts?'

At that moment a man appeared from an area behind the bar which was not visible from the front. He was in his fifties, square of build with hair more grey than black. His face was the colour of well varnished teak and looked just as hard. He looked from ML to Catherine and back again and then grinned, showing that he possessed a full set of teeth with two of them being gold. The only adjective possible for the character was 'piratical'. His bass voice boomed out 'Señor Dom! Com esta?'

'Muy buen, Miguel; y usted?' replied ML. The two men clasped hands, clapped one another on the shoulder and began a rapid fire conversation in Spanish. After a couple of minutes of this ML held up his hand to halt his friend's speech and said to him 'Momentito, Miguel. Sorry, Catherine, I never asked but do you speak Spanish?'

'No, Dominic. Not a lot of call for it in New York. Florida, California and all those happy places maybe, but in civilisation we stick to English.'

'OK. I'll introduce you. This is Miguel who owns this place, amongst others. Miguel, yo presento una amiga de inglaterra; se llama Catherine.'

The Spaniard took her hand gently in his work roughened fist and said 'Encantado, Catherine.' He then indicated that they all sit at the central table which they did then he and ML went off into another two minutes of expressive Spanish which increased in volume and seemed to require much arm waving in order to communicate. ML turned to Catherine who had obviously decided to go with the flow.

'Miguel wants to know what you would like to drink. I said you'd be fine with a cold beer. He say's that's not good enough for a lady of your obvious quality and that only his best wine will do for you. Your call.'

'Never argue with locals I say. Bring on the wine, Dominic.'

ML turned to Miguel, smiled, nodded and said 'Vale, amigo: tinto por favor.' The owner disappeared behind the bar and busied himself amongst his bottles. A teenage boy appeared and left a plate of hunks of something that was white and purple along with some bread and a couple of forks.

'Eat up, Catherine. Speciality of the house.'

'What is it?'

'Fresh octopus' said ML taking the first forkful and placing it in his mouth.

Catherine speared a piece and looked at it closely. The circular suckers on the tentacles were clearly visible. 'I just know that this is going to be gross' she said then rapidly placed a forkful in her mouth and began to chew. ML watched her expression as she masticated the rubbery meat and finally swallowed it. 'That's not too bad; there's not much taste and it's quite clean. Not something I'd order though.'

'Yes; in itself it has little flavour, a bit like snails in France. It all depends on what sauce it's served with. You have to remember how poor this island used to be. Those murals are not romantic invention; that's how these people use to survive. Look closely; woman and children are pushing the fishing smacks over wooden rollers and down to the sea. Octopus was just another protein source. Now Miguel gives it to friends.'

'Well you certainly seem to get along quite well with the guy. How come?'

'An Englishman who speaks the language correctly and does not patronise them is a rarity. I've also done him a couple of favours over the years.'

'Like what?'

'No big deal but they are personal. We'll be having lunch here on Sunday by the way. His wife makes the best seafood paella I've ever eaten. Ah, here's the wine.'

Miguel placed a bottle and two glasses on their table and then had another animated conversation with ML in his native language. At the end of this he turned to Catherine and said 'Hasta luego, senorita.'

'Hasta la vista, Miguel' she replied to his evident delight.

'See, you do have some Spanish, Catherine.'

'Nope. I remembered that from the Terminator film. If your friend had replied to me I'd have been stuck. OK less talking, more drinking.'

Catherine poured two glasses which they raised to each other. 'How do you say 'cheers' in Spanish, Dominic?' she asked.

'Salud. It means health.'

They drank and Catherine's eyes widened in surprise.

'Jesus, that's good stuff. I didn't expect that in this kind of place, Dominic.'

'Hmm, yes. Not bad at all. This is actually a fairly common brand – Campo Viejo, roughly the equivalent of a French Côtes du Rhone. You can find it in any supermarket but the way to get a superior wine is to look for the word Reserva on the bottle or, as we have here, Gran Reserva. If you follow that rule you won't go wrong.'

'It's a bit weird though. Cheap octopus and top of the range red wine together.'

'That's because you're here. If I were on my own I'd be drinking the roughest red from a ceramic pitcher and turning my teeth purple so you've saved me from that.'

'Sexist pigs. I might like the rough red stuff too.'

'They're being gentleman in their own way. And, as you said, don't argue with the locals. I think we need some more food if we're going to start on wine this early. Do you want me to order or would you like to have a look at what's on offer at the bar?'

'It's your turf, Dominic. I'll go along with what you order - as long as you promise to tell me what everything is and how to say it in Spanish. I hate not being able to understand what people are saying around me.'

'Spanish lessons it is.'

ML caught the eye of the young barman who came to their table and wrote down the food order. As soon as he left for the kitchen ML looked at Catherine and said 'Is now a good time for me to ask what your career plans are or would you rather tell me at a later date?'

Catherine finished her glass then refilled it and topped up ML's. She looked directly into his face with all traces of frivolity gone. This was obviously important for her.

'I want to sing' she said. 'I also want to try and write, maybe even learn an instrument.'

She paused, waiting for a reaction from him. He gave her nothing. 'Well, at least you didn't laugh at me. What do you think, Dominic? Say something, dammit!'

'Why? What aspect of music makes you want to take it up as a career, Catherine?'

'Performing. When I sang in that pub in Bristol I've never felt more scared and alive before. I could feel the people responding and I was in a position of power – and it was more than that. Those people and me were… communicating. No; wrong word. I'm not expressing myself very well for someone who has pretentions to be a performing artist am I?'

'That's only because it's new to you. I've been in the same place, years ago. I understand what you're trying to say. Change the word 'communicating' to 'communing' and you're closer. It's still not the right one though.'

'What is? Help me here, Dominic. It's important to me.'

'Fair enough. Communing is a bit of a dippy-hippy non word and does not define what you have with an audience. Catherine, you were having sex with them as all real rockers do. There are singers with the most fabulous voices like a musical instrument but, when all is said and done, they are playing for themselves. In England such a person is known as a wanker. You, on the other hand, fucked the audience's collective brains out and got something back in return – am I right?'

'Uh, yeah. I definitely had a healthy afterglow on me when I jumped down from that stage. Was it like that for you, Dominic? Your first time.'

It was ML's turn to seek refuge in his wine glass. He too drained it, refilled then replenished Catherine's. His eyes focused on another time, another place and a half smile grew on his face.

'My first time, Catherine? I'll tell you about my first time, another time. Food is arriving so now it's time for a Spanish lesson.'

The barman gave each of them an empty plate then proceeded to cover their table with small dishes of various hot and cold fare, which ML explained and named for Catherine. Another bottle of Gran Reserva appeared and the conversation changed to Spanish cuisine, its variety, history and why it was nothing like Tex-Mex. No Spaniard would eat something made from maize – that was what they fed pigs on so burritos were most definitely out.

The evening progressed comfortably with Catherine enjoying the experience of multiple new taste sensations. From time to time a local male would come to their table and greet ML in a friendly fashion. None of them spoke in English. The bar was becoming very full and the music on the television had been replaced by the build up to a Spanish football match which held no interest for either of them so Catherine and ML decided to move on. He settled the bill and they left the locals to their sport.

'How are you feeling, Catherine? It's still early but you've had a long day' asked ML.

'Well my ears are ringing from the noise level of your friend's bar, and the booze is starting to take effect. Something quiet would be nice at the moment' she replied.

'In that case we'll avoid the main street; all the barkers will be at work by now. Let's take a walk by the beach and grab a coffee. We'll take it from there.'

'Sounds good to me.'

They turned left out of the bar then right along the seafront. They passed many smaller restaurants which then gave way to modern apartment complexes. The sun was nearly gone leaving the sky streaked in orange, purple and grey. The sandy parts of the shore were now empty of people as the temperature dropped to a level where clothing was necessary. From their left came the gentle noise of the sea meeting the sand. It seemed to be telling them to hush. From their right came the beat of Europop, thankfully muffled by the buildings which lay between them and the main street. Catherine and ML strolled in silence.

They came to a large circle which looked like a turning place for cars. ML stopped and said 'Decision time. If we carry on it's twenty minutes walk until the Bahia Ocean hotel for a coffee or we turn down here into tourist town. Lot's of places for a coffee or if we carry on to the end of this road we'll find ourselves back home. What would you like to do?'

'To be honest, Dominic I'd like to have a lie down for while. It has been a long day and we do have the weekend coming up. Is that OK?'

'Of course it is. Let's call it a night. We can have a drink back home if you like or you can just go to bed.'

'Great. I think I'm going to crash until morning.'

'Come on then let's get you home.'

It only took five minutes to reach the villa. Catherine went straight upstairs where she undressed then slipped under the sheets and drifted off to sleep with a smile on her face. Not surprisingly she dreamt of octopus.

Downstairs ML was examining the paperwork that Richard must have posted through the door. It pertained to the white Range Rover which was standing in his driveway. The hideous pimp-mobile had gone, presumably back to the Royalist. ML decided to go over to Richard's bar and thank him in person. It would help his cover to be seen in town on his own and there was no chance of Catherine joining him; the mild sedative he'd added to her last glass of wine would keep her asleep until morning.

After going to his room and changing his clothes for a more businesslike look, he set off into the night to visit Richard's bar. Hopefully there would be some decent musicians on.

Chapter Nineteen

Mark Goodchild entered the dimly lit downstairs bar of the Red Lion at two fifteen in the afternoon. Most of the Whitehall regulars had headed back to their desks, the days of two hour lunch breaks a thing of the past. He saw that Roger Tucker was at the bar deep in conversation with Joe Slattery, a pint of Guinness in hand.

'Afternoon, gentlemen' said Goodchild. 'How are you both?'

'Is he not the politest policeman you ever met Mr Tucker?' said Slattery.

'Probably means he wants something Joe; lunch on my paper's tab no doubt' said Tucker.

'Fuck the pair of you. Guinness please, Joe'

'Are we going to eat or drink lunch, Mark?' asked Tucker.

'I would dearly love to get shit-faced with you now, Roger but no can do. I've already eaten and need to have a clear head for when something breaks. The fourth estate can, of course, do what it wants.'

Slattery served Goodchild his drink and Tucker opted for the steak and ale pie. The two friends moved across the bar to a table.

'Thanks again for that email, Roger. It's a good piece of work which may buy us the time we need to track this bastard down.'

'No problem. Here's a hard copy I printed off for you. So much for the paperless society, eh?'

'Thanks.' Goodchild took an envelope from Tucker that he placed in an inside jacket pocket which he then zipped shut.

'How's it going, Mark? Anything you can tell me at this stage?'

'There are always going to be things I can't share with you, Roger. You know that. But I'll give you everything I can – you're owed that much. As to how it's going; I still only have one solid lead. I've got my two best officers following that up. The rest of the team are banging away, doing the door to door stuff to try and develop some more. If we could identify two more, or even one more victim, we'd be on our way. It's a matter of time, attention to detail and all the boring stuff that gives results. Cases like these are not solved by some illuminating flash of brilliant insight from a super detective; that's strictly for the TV.'

'Anything more on the poison?'

'Not yet. There are other agencies working on that and I doubt if their priorities are the same as mine. Nothing I can do there. I'm still waiting on a tech report on why CCTV at Euston Station did not work when we needed it to.'

'What are you on about?'

Goodchild looked at Tucker and realised his mistake. 'Shit of course – you don't know about that' he said. Goodchild quickly explained about the surveillance cameras at Euston being out of service at the vital time when ML was presumed to have been there. To his surprise Roger Tucker began to laugh.

'It's not bloody funny, Roger. Chummy surfaces in public again and we don't get an image of him. Sorry, but I fail to see the joke.'

"Scuse me, mate. I was thinking of something that used to happen years ago in a pub in Upper Street. It was an ordinary north London boozer; wooden floors, pub grub and some decent real ales. I used to meet a guy there who worked for Islington council and he gave me no end of stories of how the left wing lesbians were running the place into the ground. Anyway, this guy was a really easy going gentleman of the old school but he had two pet hates. Horse racing and football. If we were having a meeting in this pub and either of those two sports came on the TV the screen would go blank for several minutes then come on again, cut out and so on until the manager got pissed off and unplugged it. I noticed that it only happened to the gee gees and football. Rugby, cricket, athletics, motor racing – none of these were affected. As I got to know this guy better he explained his philosophy to me. Basically, if the peasantry want to watch horses they can piss off to the bookies and if the sub-peasantry want to watch girly ball they can piss off to the stadium. Eventually I asked him how he was fucking with the TV and he showed me this gadget he had – no bigger than a zippo. He'd switch it on and slip it inside his sock. Then all he had to do was tap it with his other foot and it sent out a signal that scrambled the TV. Hilarious. It would appear that ML has a more sophisticated version of this kit which is not quite as funny at all.'

'I've never heard of anything like that. Do you know where your man obtained it?'

'No, but I can ask.'

'Don't put yourself out; I'm sure my technical services chap will know. If I need you to follow it up I'll call.'

For the next quarter of an hour Tucker ate and they shared small talk regarding the trials of keeping their weight down as middle age began to makes its presence felt.

Once the plates had been cleared away they found themselves to be the only customers left in the bar. Tucker sat back in his chair and reached into the side pocket of his jacket. 'Bugger it' he exclaimed. 'I still forget that I don't smoke any more.'

'How long's it been?'

'Five years. I can go months without even thinking about a cigarette then I go into an automatic smoking mode. You know – a decent meal, a beer, company from the past. It needs a smoke to complete it.'

'Don't worry, mate; they say the first twenty years are the hardest.'

Before Tucker could reply Goodchild's mobile rang. He looked at the screen and pressed green to receive.

'Yes. Go on. That's bloody marvellous, Michelle. We'll discuss that when I get back. Keep at the others and I'll be with you in thirty.'

Goodchild put his phone away and his face underwent a subtle change. He looked like a prosecution lawyer who had spent time asking questions of a glib and slippery defendant. With one well placed verbal trap his prey was left with nowhere to go, his evasive options had run out and the hunter was moving in for the kill.

'Come on, Mark; spit it out. What was that all about?'

'That was the office. We've had a break. Not a huge one but it bears out that we are on the right track. I've got to get back there but reckon I can manage another beer. You?'

'Allow me.' Tucker went to the bar and returned with two more beers. 'I've left the company credit card behind the bar so you can sod off as soon as you have to. Anything more you can tell me, Mark?'

Goodchild drank half his pint in one go before replying. 'Someone who knew our identified victim three years ago is coming into the office within the hour. Apparently they were 'confidants' whatever that means and he knew all her secrets. The guy sounds like a gold mine. Happy days.'

'Indeed. Look, Mark; if there's any way I can help, just call. I can't make my editor perform to order but I do have a certain influence. It can't hurt to have a national newspaper in your corner.'

'Appreciate it, Roger. I don't know how this afternoon's going to go but I'll be in touch. Thanks for lunch.'

'No problem. When I publish my best seller about this case I'll recoup it a thousand times over.'

Goodchild gave Tucker an old fashioned look that spoke volumes. He drained his glass and headed up the stairs and out into the afternoon sun without another word. Ten minutes later he was entering the Orion offices to find Martin deep into a conversation on the telephone and Michelle reading the file on Jennifer Duncan.

'Hi, boss' said Michelle. 'Let me…' Goodchild held up a hand to stop her.

'Let's wait until Martin's free and we can discuss this together.' He sat down with her and they waited until Carver had hung up on his call, made a few notes and then came over to join them.

'OK Michelle. Let's hear it from the top please' said Goodchild.

'I've tracked down a Mr Brendan Fitzgerald who used to be head barman at Hanbury's. He is currently bar manager at the Blue Boy cabaret bar on Old Compton Street. He claims that he knew Jennifer Duncan very well, that they had many a long talk together and that he'd be more than happy to help us with our enquiries.'

'What's your impression of Mr Fitzgerald, Michelle? Is he the real deal?'

'First impression is that he is as camp as a row of pink tents but he does not come across as an attention seeking queen. Lots of girls have a gay best friend in whom they confide. Just because Fitzgerald lives and works in Soho does not make him unreliable. I've not been able to check yet but he claims to have worked at the Blue Boy for the past two and a half years. That indicates stability to me, boss.'

'Hmm. Well he's due here soon; you've spoken to him, Michelle – we haven't. How do you think we should play this?'

'I think that I should interview him and ask his permission to record it. I'd like you two to observe from behind the mirror and to come in if you feel it's necessary. It's a play it by ear scenario, I know, but he's been open with me so far. I don't see a reason to change that now.'

'Agreed' said Goodchild 'Do you have an interview room set up?'

'Yes, boss. Number three is ours for the afternoon.'

'Good. Martin; you're quiet today. Anything I should know about from your side of the room?'

'Nothing substantive at the moment. I do have one thought though; I reckon that my time would be better spent manning the phones than watching Michelle's interview. We've those guys out in the field trying to crack the other nine victims. It would be pretty dumb if one of them called in for instructions and there was no-one here to instruct.'

'Point taken, OK, Martin; you do that. I'll observe the interview. You can review the tape later on if necessary.'

The phone at Michelle's desk rang. She hit the speakerphone button and said 'DS Stone'.

'This is Constable Hemmings at post one, Sergeant Stone. I have a Mr Fitzgerald here to see you.'

'Thank you, Constable. Would you have him escorted to interview three please and I'll be along in a minute?'

'Will do, Sergeant.'

Michelle broke the connection, picked up her handbag and headed for the door. 'I'll be back in five, boss. I just want to freshen up.'

As soon as the door closed behind her to two men looked at each other. 'Not a fucking word please, Martin.'

'I was not going to say anything derogatory or sexist, boss. In fact I think it sound police procedure to empty one's bladder prior to interviewing someone. Brendan Fitzgerald; I wonder if Gerald fits Brendan? Good luck with this one, boss.'

Goodchild kept a straight face until Michelle returned. She had obviously spent time fixing her hair and make up. Collecting a dossier from her desk she looked at her superior officer and nodded. The two of them set off to meet someone who, they hoped, could fill in the gaps in their knowledge of Jennifer Duncan's private life.

Stone and Goodchild observed Fitzgerald from behind the two way mirror. The man was dressed in form fitting black jeans and a white Ralph Lauren polo. An expensive looking blazer jacket was draped over the back of his chair. He sat with one knee crossed over the other and from time to time examined the back of his fingernails or brushed an imaginary piece of dust from his leg.

'I can see how Brendan got on well with someone who made frocks for a living' said Goodchild.

'Come on, boss; he's not that bad.'

As if to prove her wrong Fitzgerald stood up from his chair, advanced to the mirror in very small steps and proceeded to examine his teeth. He then licked his fingers and patted his already immaculate eyebrows into place. After one final pursing of his lips and a pose, he skipped back to his chair. The two police officers, having been no more than twelve inches distant from this display, looked at each other in stunned silence.

'Would you please begin the interview, Michelle before he starts an aerobics workout? Christ, we can sell this tape and retire on the proceeds.'

Michelle left Goodchild and entered the interview room. Fitzgerald sprang to his feet.

'Good afternoon Mr Fitzgerald. I'm Detective Sergeant Stone. Sorry to have kept you waiting.'

They shook hands and sat down facing each other across a lightweight Formica table.

'This interview is not being recorded Mr Fitzgerald...'

'Please; call me Brendan' he interrupted.

'OK Brendan. I'm Michelle. As I said, this interview is not being recorded but I would like your permission to do so as it will make things easier when I review your statement. Would that be alright?'

'No problem. I'll do anything I can to help you find Jennifer.'

Michelle left the table and crossed the room to a shelf where the recording equipment was set up. She pressed some buttons then retook her seat and spoke up. 'DS Michelle Stone Metropolitan Police in interview suite three. Interview is with Mr Brendan Fitzgerald of 14 Old Crompton Street, London W1. Mr Fitzgerald has verbally agreed to the interview being recorded.' She paused and opened the dossier in front of her. After a brief pause that felt like an age to her, she'd marshalled her wits and began.

'Brendan; when we spoke on the phone earlier today you told

me that you knew Jennifer Duncan well. Would you tell me how you met her?'

'About three years ago I was head barman at a club in Brighton called Hanbury's. Jennifer used to come in two or three times a week and we just started to talk. You know; barman customer sort of chat. She was very shy but little by little we became friends and it turned out that she was the girl who made most of the costumes for the artistes! Well, I love cabaret and we could talk for hours about film and theatre and costume and design. We even went out a few times on my night off.'

'Did she ever come to Hanbury's with anyone else, Brendan?'

'No. She always arrived and left alone.'

'Apart from yourself, did she talk with any other members of staff?'

'No. She sat alone, watched the show and chatted with me between the acts if I was not too busy.'

'I find that a bit odd, Brendan. I mean Jennifer's costumes would have been a main part of the Hanbury show. Surely the management would have wanted to look after her or the performers want to comment on her work.'

'You're right. Jennifer could have had VIP treatment whenever she wanted but that was not her style. When we got to know each other she made me promise not to tell anyone at the club who she was.'

'All right. So she's a loner. What was she like apart from shy and self-effacing? Did she drink?'

'Just enough to be sociable at Hanbury's. It was like she was still at work when she went there. On the occasions when we went out together she did enjoy a drink but she was not one of these staggering, vomiting ladettes one sees in town at the weekend.'

'Did she talk about how she got on with her parents? I mean she could hardly have travelled father away from Telford than Brighton.'

'You're confusing two things there, Michelle. She hated Telford, Wolverhampton and the entire Black Country. She loved her parents. No; she loved her mum and respected her dad. I remember that Jennifer carried their photos in her wallet. Her mum was a stunner, a more modern Grace Kelly if you know what I mean. Dad looked a bit scary. His photo was 'if you see this man do not approach him'. Psycho killer eyes.'

'What about friends? Had she kept in touch with anyone from college for example?'

'Again, no. She got her qualification then flew the nest, got a job and was starting to make a name for herself. Brighton ultimately would have been too small for her.'

'Did she ever talk about re-locating?'

'No. She was contentish for the time being. I'm sorry; I'm not being much help here, am I?'

'You're doing fine, Brendan. OK. Apart from work and the costume related interests you two talked about was there anything else that she was into?'

'Oh yes; music. In a big way. She played guitar and went to live gigs all over the place.'

'All over Brighton, you mean?'

'No. Au contraire, Michelle. The night scene in Brighton did not suit her but she would travel hundred of miles to see an act that she liked. I remember that she tried to fix it that her visits back home coincided with a gig she wanted to go to.'

'A gig in Telford?'

'No silly. From what she told me the troglodytes of Telford have not progressed past druidic chanting. She used to go to nearby towns for her music fix.'

'Which ones?'

Fitzgerald seemed about to reply then he froze. A look of puzzlement appeared on is face. 'Shit! I can't remember. I've gone blank. Perhaps if I saw a map it might come to me.'

'OK. Not to worry. We'll come back to that later. Let's change tack a bit. What about her love life? Was Jennifer seeing anyone?'

'This is a bit complicated. The short answer to your question is no. Jennifer is straight. I've taken her to gay bars and she made it clear that girls did not interest her. Whenever Jennifer went out she would attract attention. She made her own clothes and had her own look which made her stand out from the crowd. Combined with, I don't know how to describe it properly, a sort of stillness, a self containment – she was literally attractive. She did not want for offers but rebuffed them all – I've seen her do it. Some of the guys she turned away were good looking, well mannered, not pushy. God, I should have her luck! I asked her once why she preferred going out with me when she could have one of those hunks. And do you know what she said? She was in love with someone else!'

'Who was she in love with, Brendan?'

'A musician! A fucking bar bum as far as I could make out. This was why she travelled up and down the country – just to hear this guy play. For all her talent, Jennifer was just a downmarket groupie.'

'Does this musician have a name?'

'Tony.'

'That's it. Just Tony? No surname, no band name?'

'From what Jennifer used to say, the sainted Tony played solo; he's a singer guitar player. That's all I know.'

'So you never saw him play yourself?'

'No, I just had to hear how wonderful he was from Jennifer.'

'Was she actually seeing him, Brendan?'

'Come on, Michelle. You're a police officer; ask the real question. Were they having a sexual relationship is what you really mean.'

'All right; were they having sex?'

Brendan looked down at the table for a few seconds then raised his eyes to meet Michelle's his face devoid of any expression.

'According to Jennifer, they'd never even spoken.'

'As you said, it's a bit complicated. Could you elaborate on how this sort of love affair worked?'

'I don't know where she first heard Tony play but she told me she'd never seen anyone like him. Apparently it's not one thing about him that made her fall for the guy – it's more like he's greater than the sum of his parts. Good vocals, good guitar, energy, humour and he plays the sort of music Jennifer likes.'

'And that music is…?'

'Various old stuff; rock and blues mainly. Not my cup of tea anyway.'

'Did she describe what Tony looked like?'

Fitzgerald paused and thought before answering.

'Not that I remember or at least not in precise descriptive words. For some reason I have the impression of a large, long haired white guy with no dress sense. Once, when we were talking about music, Jennifer said that Tony's voice could be as deep as Johnny Cash's. I joked about him dressing up as the man in black and she became all defensive about him saying that image was not important to Tony, his music was what mattered yadda yadda yadda.'

'And this is the man she followed round the country but never spoke to. Surely he must have noticed her. Did she have an autograph or a photo of him?'

'Funnily enough, I asked her the same thing. She said that she always sat at the back of the room – Tony did not know she existed as far as she knew. I know that she did not take a photo of him and I don't see how she could have an autograph if he'd never spoken to her.'

'Yes, quite. Brendan, I want you to take you time on this next question. Put yourself back into a time and place when you were in Jennifer's company. What was Tony's surname?'

Fitzgerald closed his eyes and sat as still as a statue. Michelle found that she was holding her breath. 'It won't come to me, Michelle' he said. 'Sorry.'

'Don't worry. We're not done yet. Can you name one or more towns that Jennifer travelled to hear Tony play?

Fitzgerald closed his eyes again and thought. 'Sorry, Michelle. I can't be sure. If I say something I'd only be guessing. It's three years ago after all.'

'Think calmly, Brendan there must be something. You remembered that she tried to make her visits home to Telford coincide with Tony's gig somewhere nearby. I'm going to go and get a map for you to look at. Would you like a drink?'

'A coke would be lovely please, Michelle.'

'OK. You think back to your conversations with Jennifer and I'll go and organise a few things.'

Michelle rejoined Goodchild in the observation room. 'What do you think, boss?'

'Good work. He obviously gets on with you and this musician is definitely a person of interest. Pity he can't remember the name. I'll go and get a map whilst you grab his drink. See you back here.'

Michelle went down to the Orion offices to get a coke for Fitzgerald whilst Goodchild went to central registry to check out a large scale atlas of England and Wales. They met up in the observation room less than ten minutes after Michelle had left interview three. Neither officer said it but they were both aware of the fact that they were following a definite trail that could lead them to Jennifer.

'OK. Michelle; get on with it. I've had another idea. I'm going to ask Martin to phone the Duncan's and see if 'Tony' rings any bells with them. If it does and they remember where she went to see him I'll come in on your interview. OK?'

'Fine by me, boss. Good luck.'

Michelle entered interview three and handed Fitzgerald his canned drink plus a plastic cup. He ignored the latter preferring to drink from the can. Once he seemed settled Michelle said 'Any names come to you at all, Brendan?'

'I'm afraid not. I've tried and tried but it's just not there.'

'You might be trying too hard. Let's try this. I've an atlas here and in the annex there is a list of counties plus their towns in order of population numbers. I'd like you to go through it and see if anything jumps out at you. Jennifer lived in Telford so let's start with Shropshire. Limit yourself to towns with a minimum of ten thousand inhabitants.'

Fitzgerald looked at the list and started to nod to himself. 'Right' he said. 'Some of these I can discount because I've never even heard of them. Where the hell is Market Drayton? I'm not sure and I don't want to start you off in the wrong direction but I've a feeling that Jennifer mentioned Shrewsbury and Bridgnorth. That's it.'

Michelle made a note of the two towns on her pad then stood up. 'Thanks, Brendan. I'm going to give these to a colleague. Whilst I'm gone I want you to carry out the same exercise for the five counties contiguous to Shropshire. Here's the list.'

Fitzgerald looked at the sheet of paper that Michelle handed to him. Cheshire, Staffordshire, Warwickshire, Worcestershire and Herefordshire. At least another fifty places to try and remember or eliminate. Michelle left him to it and headed back to Orion where she found Goodchild and Carver in conversation.

'He reckons she might have mentioned Shrewsbury and Bridgnorth' she announced. 'Have you spoken with the Duncans yet, Martin?'

'I'm just about to call them. Thanks for this. What's he doing now?'

'I've got him looking at the five counties contiguous to Shropshire; see if anything there rings a bell.'

'What about cities? Birmingham, Wolverhampton all those fun places?' asked Goodchild.

'I'd hoped not to have to go down that route, boss. It would be needle in a haystack with the amount of bars we'd have to canvas. But I'll do it if nothing comes from the county level. I'd better get back to him. Good luck, Martin.'

Michelle went back to interview three to find Fitzgerald pacing up and down the room in a state of some distress. His hair was unkempt and his brow was damp with sweat despite the room being quite cool.

'Michelle, it's no use!' he cried. 'I know some places but not in a Jennifer context. I've had one memory or half memory but I can't recall the precise details.'

'What is it, Brendan?' said Michelle. She'd stayed standing, making no attempt to get Fitzgerald to calm down this time. Something was cooking in the man's head and she wanted it to come to the boil.

'She went to see Tony at a rugby club. I can't remember which one but it is a big one. The weird thing is that Jennifer said the club was a London club but not in London. Neither of us knows anything about the game so it did not really register. I'm sorry. I'm all done here, Michelle. I'm back on duty in two hours and need to change and calm down first. May I go now, please?'

'Of course you can, Brendan. You're here voluntarily and we do appreciate you coming in. Believe it or not, you've been a big help.'

'Really?'

'Really. Is it all right if we contact you on your mobile if we have any follow- up questions?'

'Sure, but I do turn it off when I'm working.'

'Well we can always come and visit you if it's urgent.'

'God, just don't send a young bobby in uniform. I'd never hear the end of jokes about handcuffs and truncheons!'

They both laughed and Michelle escorted him off the premises then hastened back to interview three to retrieve the tapes. Having done that she went directly to Orion to share her latest piece of information. She knew very little about rugby but she knew a man who did.

Goodchild and Carver were sat at a computer which the latter was operating.

'There's just too much info; the names too bloody common. Why couldn't she be in love with someone called Adolf?' complained Carver.

'What's the problem, gentlemen?' asked Michelle.

'Martin's spoken with Malcolm Duncan' replied Goodchild. 'The name Tony means nothing to him or his wife. He did, however, say that Jennifer went into Shrewsbury now and again for music gigs. He can't remember the names of the venues. Martin is googling Tony/Shrewsbury/Music and we are being swamped by shit.'

'There are ways round that but something else has come up that I need your input on. Brendan remembers that Jennifer went to see Tony play at a rugby club. He doesn't remember which one but recalls that it is quite 'a big one in London but not London'. Does that make any sense to you, boss?'

'Too right it does!' said Goodchild leaping to his feet. 'London Wasps play in High Wycombe, Saracens play in Watford and London Irish, God bless them, play in Reading. I'd put my money on London Irish.'

'Why them, other than the fact they're your team, boss' asked Carver.

'A few years ago we were given a new nickname; Not-Nots. That's because we're not in London and not many Irish play for us. Jennifer could have picked up on that. Let's go and see Mr Fitzgerald, Michelle.'

'Ah, I've let him go back to work, boss. He was in a bit of a state and I wanted to keep him sweet in case we needed to re-interview him.'

'Jesus Christ! If he were any sweeter we could chop him into pieces and sell him as Pick and Mix. Call him and then put me on please, Michelle.'

Michelle dialled Fitzgerald's mobile and put him on speaker-phone. After three rings a tentative voice answered 'Hello, this is Brendan. Who's calling please?'

'Brendan, hi. It's Michelle Stone here. Are you OK to talk?'

'Sure, Michelle. What's up?'

'I'm with my boss and he'd like a quick word with you. Hold on please.' Michelle stood away from the speaker and Goodchild took over.

'Mr Fitzgerald; my name is Commander Mark Goodchild. Sergeant Stone has updated me on your interview and I have a quick question for you. Please take your time and think before you answer. The rugby club where Jennifer went to hear Tony: was it, by any chance, called London Irish?'

The answer came back instantly. 'Yes, Yes it was! Ooh you clever, clever man. How did you know that?'

'An educated guess Mr Fitzgerald. Thank you very much for your help and good day to you.'

'My pleasure, Commander. Bieee!'

'You know he's going to dine out on this forever don't you, boss?' said Carver. 'The day a full Commander of the Metropolitan Police phoned little old Brendan. It's not unknown for the journalists to frequent the Soho gay scene.'

'It's a long shot of that happening. We can cover with an on-going missing persons story if we have to. I'm going to talk with London Irish. I'll have Tony's details within an hour. Michelle – you said you can sort out the shit that Google throws out. Get on with it. Find out which venue Tony was playing three years ago in Shrewsbury and also if he's booked to appear anytime soon. In fact try and find everywhere this guy has played for the last five years then cross reference the dates and places with missing girls, Martin – you help her. I'll see you in an hour's time if not sooner.'

Goodchild left the main Orion office to use the phone in the private annex. He was about to use his personal contacts at his rugby club for official business and did not want his junior officers listening to his private conversations.

Fifteen minutes later Goodchild was back with Carver and Stone who were at the same computer station where Michelle's fingers were flying across the keyboard.

'Come up with anything?' asked Goodchild.

'Not yet' replied Carver 'but it's only a matter if time. Michelle's been using search engines other than Google and we're narrowing the hunt down. Don't ask me how it works but it does.'

'I don't care if she uses black magic as long as we get hold of this guy. See if this helps.' Goodchild handed a slip of paper to Michelle who looked at it and raised her eyebrows at him.

'This is the name of a singer who plays twice a year at London Irish and has done for at least the last five years. The club secretary will be back to me with more details ASAP. See if you can beat him, Michelle.'

She attacked the keyboard single minded intensity. Images came and were deleted with what seemed like reckless haste until she stopped and sat back. 'Come and have a look at him, boss' she said.

Goodchild went round to her side of the screen. 'Meet Mr Tony Guest' she said. 'Live at the Shropshire Hunt public house six months ago. Big bugger, isn't he?'

'Yes. If that's a normal bar stool he's sat on then he's well over six feet. The twelve string looks like a banjo in his paws. Can you compare him to the images we have from the park, Michelle?'

'I can't. Someone in Dr Watkins team will be able to. I'll get that going. He has his own web page but it's pretty basic. Here, I'll pull it up.'

The screen changed and more images of Guest appeared along with biographical details.

'This is not much use to us. I need to know where this joker is going to play next and where he lives. Martin – check CRO to see if this guy had any prior form. If he's clean, tax, National

Insurance, electoral register the lot. Find me his address. This bugger could be from anywhere. Shrewsbury to Reading has to be 100 miles easily. I'm going to check out this Shropshire Hunt pub, see who the licensee is and try to get a handle on Guest that way. Carry on and shout if you need anything.'

'Boss; not being funny or anything but are you comfortable with online searching?' asked Michelle. 'I'm only asking because Martin's pretty damn slow and, well.'

'I'm a middle aged dinosaur?'

'No; it's just that I can pull the pub info in about thirty seconds.'

'Pull it then, Michelle and then print out what you find so an old man can have something tangible to refer to.'

The three police officers went about their separate tasks in their different ways. At seven in the evening they reconvened to pool their information.

Michelle went first and handed her male colleagues printouts of what she had. 'As you can see, he first appeared at the Shropshire Hunt five years ago. He must be good because he has had a regular spot there ever since and usually plays every other Thursday. The pub is tenanted with the parent pubco being Marston's Brewery. Current licensee is Mr Kenneth Round who has been there for the last seven years when the pub was refurbished. I have not spoken to him as I don't know how you want to play that one, boss. I've been to see Dr Watkins or rather her assistant who is the resident electronics whiz. Having examined and compared videos of Guest with those taken of our mystery park man, all he will say is that it could be the same man. I pushed him to be more positive but that is as far as he is prepared to go.'

'Thanks, Michelle' said Goodchild. 'Martin; what do you have for us?'

'Quite a lot. I'll need to collate it all and type it up but for now I'll just present what I have got. Tony Guest, born 1970 in London, went to school there and left age 16 without any qualifications at all. He went straight into the music scene and has made a living as a session musician and performer ever since. He's self employed paying schedule D tax and insurance. He cleared £60,000 last financial year. Has been married for the last fifteen years to Gillian, no children. He lives in a converted barn near the village of Upton Magna – where do they get these names from – and has nearly finished paying off the mortgage. He has travelled extensively throughout Europe and, apart from his solo work, he also plays with a band for larger events. So far, so normal. What I find bizarre is that he has never come to the attention of the authorities at all.'

'Why's that bizarre, Martin?' asked Goodchild.

'He's a travelling musician who spends just about every evening in a pub or bar. He must drive thousands of miles a year to get to his gigs but he has never been involved in an RTA, never been breathalysed nor found to be in possession of the smallest amount of dope. He's never even had a parking ticket. He's either very lucky, very careful or has another identity when he's on the road.'

'I see what you're getting at, Martin' said Goodchild. 'Let's give him the benefit of the doubt for now. I don't have too much to add at this stage. My contact at Irish confirms that he lives in Upton Magna; they pay him by cheque so he is legitimate there. He is also one of their most popular entertainers. Everyone seems to like him.'

'Have you heard him play, boss?' asked Stone.

'No. I tend to drink in a quieter part of the clubhouse when I attend. Here's how I want to proceed; Martin, I want you to set off now for Shrewsbury. Book into a hotel and tomorrow see what you can find out about Guest, especially if he is due to play at the Shropshire Hunt anytime soon. See if anyone there remembers Jennifer Duncan as well. Do not go to his home in Upton Magna until we have more details. OK?'

'Fine. If I get a move on I can even visit some town bars tonight.'

'Michelle, I want you glued to the computer and try and find where and when Guest has been playing for the last five years.

Cross reference to missing girls on the list of nine. I know it's a shitty job but you're the best able to do it. Let Martin know when you come up with anything. Martin; how long will it take you to type up Guest's biographicals?'

'Half an hour max, boss. It's just a cut, paste and print job.'

'Do that before you leave for Shrewsbury then. Leave it in my in tray and I'll use it to prepare a report for Addison. Any questions?'

'No. I'll call you when I've spoken to the publican.' Martin got to work at his keyboard and ignored the other two officers.

'I'm going to have some dinner, boss and then pull an all nighter here. I'll sleep in the annex and should have something to send up to Martin tomorrow morning' said Michelle.

'Good idea. I could do with some protein myself. Where were you thinking of eating?' asked Goodchild.

'Something fast and nearby. One of the Angus Steak Houses on Victoria Street or similar.'

'Let's use the Orion contingency fund and do a bit better than that. How about the Texas Embassy?'

'Heard of it, but never been there. Trafalgar Square isn't it?'

'Close by. It's number one, Cockspur Street. We'll grab a taxi. Ready?'

'I'll just fix my face and I'll be right with you, boss.'

Goodchild glanced over at Carver as Michelle left the room. The man remained fixed at his work station and gave no indication that he had heard the exchange between his superior officer and the female detective sergeant. He was, thought Goodchild, either the most concentrated policeman in the Met or the most diplomatic.

Michelle returned and, as they made to leave, Goodchild called out to Carver 'Talk with you later or tomorrow, Martin.'

Carver lifted his head from the screen and nodded; 'Yes, right. Watch out for the jalapenos, boss.'

Goodchild and Stone left Orion with the former feeling glad that not much bypassed Carver's attention.

Chapter Twenty

Catherine woke on Friday morning with the sun on her face and the sound of water splashing in her ears. For a few seconds she experienced the sense of dislocation that comes from being in a strange bed and not remembering how one had ended up in it. As her eyes adjusted to the room her brain kicked into gear and she stretched under the white cotton sheets. She was in Fuerteventura and had managed to get drunk on her first night! God knows what Dominic thought of her.

Her head felt fine but her mouth was feeling pretty rank. She could see that she had dropped all her clothes onto the room's armchair and that she had placed her jewellery and watch on her bedside table. Looking at the watch she saw that it was ten thirty in the morning. She must have been tired but, hey ho, she was on holiday so what the hell. Entering the bathroom she examined her face in the mirror and was confronted by a panda with a purple tongue. She'd not taken off her make-up and the Campo Viejo Gran Reserva had left its mark. Time to hit the shower. Fifteen minutes later and she looked and felt ready to face the world. A quick glance from her window showed her that the noise to which she had awoken was that of Dominic performing slow laps of the pool. She went downstairs to join him.

'Good morning Dominic' she called as he stopped at the far end of the pool.

'Hi' he replied with a smile. 'Sleep well?'

'You bet. That Spanish wine was stronger than it tasted.'

'Not really; you'd just had a really long day of travelling and it all caught up with you.' He climbed out of the water, picked up a towel and walked towards her. 'What are your plans for the day?'

'I need to do a bit of shopping first. T-shirts and toiletries basically so I thought I'd head on down the main street and look at those stores you pointed out yesterday. What are you up to?'

'I've some business calls to make so I'm going to be here for the next few hours. After that I have to research a Spanish seafood lunch in town. It is Friday after all. Do you want to join me for that?'

'Love to – as long as I don't have to eat octopus!'

'No problem. I'll see you at La Dorada at one thirty. It's marked on the little map I've left on the dining room table. If you want breakfast there's juice and fruit in the fridge. Last thing; don't forget sunscreen and a hat for when you're walking around.'

'OK will do. Juice sounds like a good way to start the day. I think I'm dehydrating already.'

'That can be a problem even if you don't drink alcohol. There are some bottles of mineral water in the fridge. You could take one of those with you for your walk into town. OK catch you later.'

With that ML went inside and mounted the stairs to his quarters. After showering and changing his clothes he lay on his bed and listened. Marble floored villas were cool but they also had a tendency to cacophony. He had left his door open and could see Catherine in his minds eye as she moved around the kitchen. Each small sound, even the opening of the fridge door, reached him. He waited. Finally the front door opened and closed. After a beat of ten he went to the top of the villa's central tower from where he could observe Catherine as she descended the hill to town. Satisfied he returned to his room to move his project forward.

Opening his safe he took out an unused and untraceable mobile phone. Consulting a list he dialled the required number which was answered after only a slight delay. 'Hello' came a voice which managed to convey mystification and interrogation in only two syllables.

'Mr Williams; is that you?'

'Yes. Who's calling please?'

'Rodney McNaughten here, Mr Williams. All settled in are you? Hotel all right is it?'

'Everything is fine, sir. I got in last night. After breakfast I took a walk into town to get a feel for Corralejo. I'm back at my hotel at the moment planning an itinerary for the coming days.'

'Good man, good man. Look, Mr Williams; something's come up that I need you to be aware of. My client has heard that one of his competitors has someone running around the islands doing what we've asked you to do. Nothing wrong with that. Business is business. What we don't want is our interest in this particular market to become known so discretion on your part is important. As I'm sure you've already seen, it's a small place and people dining alone stand out.'

'What are you advising me, sir?'

'Two things. Watch out for someone watching you. The company we're concerned about is American and we know that they normally use females for this kind of job. If you could find her and find out what they are up to that would be a bonus – and you would be in line for one.'

'I don't suppose you've any ideas of where this mystery woman is staying do you, sir?'

'Not yet, but we have a good idea where she will probably spend her evenings. The American company is involved in marketing rock music and research shows us that there is only one sizeable rock venue in town.'

'I passed it this morning, sir, OK. I'll visit it tonight.'

'You will visit it every night until I instruct you to the contrary. I shall call you as and when I can to check the state of play. Goodbye.'

ML broke the connection leaving Ian Williams to wonder how he would identify one unknown American woman from amongst the hundreds of foreign tourists who would be out and about in the evening.

§

In London Michelle Stone woke in a single camp bed in the Orion annex. It was seven in the morning, her head was clear and her first considered action was to look across the room to the other bed where Mark Goodchild had spent the night. It was empty, the sheets folded and no clothes were in sight. She could not hear any sounds from the bathroom so she concluded that her boss had quietly made himself scarce.

Leaving the bed she found a note on the dining table that read 'back with bacon toasties at 0730 M.G!' 'I should have been a detective' she thought. Hastening to the bathroom she performed the usual start up functions for the day and thanked the god of female police officers that her short hair only required a brisk towelling for her to be presentable.

She was sat at her computer composing an email to Martin Carver when Goodchild returned bearing breakfast.

'Morning, boss. I'll get a brew on.'

'Thanks, Michelle.'

By now she knew how he liked his tea and it seemed perfectly natural for her to make it for him. She returned with two mugs to the table and they fuelled up for the morning.

'I tell you what, boss. You get a girl breakfast, you make your own bed and you don't snore. That's pretty near perfection in my book.'

'You're easily satisfied then.'

'Am I?' she replied with a challenge in her eye.

'Shit; that came out wrong. I meant it doesn't take much to please... oh for God's sake! Eat your bloody toastie.'

Michelle could not obey the instruction as she was laughing too hard. 'Oh dear, boss. Am I that terrifying?'

'Nothing scares Goodchild of the Yard, I'll have you know. With the possible exceptions of having to attend courses on equality, diversity and how to embrace the trans-gender community.'

'With you there, boss. I've got all the equality I need. Anything come in from Martin overnight?'

'No. He didn't leave London as early as he had intended to. I reckon he stayed here until we were on our way back from dinner, keeping Orion manned just in case something came in. I should have thought about that; it gave him a bloody long day.'

'He'll survive. What time do you think he'll visit the pub?'

'If it were me I'd leave it until about nine. If it opens at ten thirty or eleven the landlord will have to be up to oversee the cleaners and see that everything is in place for the day ahead. What info did you pull on the place, Michelle?'

'It appears to be well run. Given that it's a High Street pub in a market town there have been very few incidents there in the seven years that it's been open under the present management. The odd complaint about noise on the music nights – from neighbours each time. No violence and they've only called for police help three times and on each occasion the call was enough to make the problem go away and he phoned back to say that assistance was no longer required. The landlord and his wife attend the pubwatch meetings where they participate positively. In a word, the local law like them.'

'OK. Email that to Martin now. It'll give him a steer on how to approach the man.'

'On it, boss.'

§

One hundred and fifty miles to the north, Martin Carver was having a final cup of coffee to complement the excellent cooked breakfast he had enjoyed in the dining room of the Lion Hotel. He was sat in a window seat with the sun on his face as he read the daily paper. Goodchild's friend Tucker was not really on form today, his page containing lots of small, disparate stories none of which set a tone. Sure, each was amusing in its own right but they lacked the substance of the journalist's usual work. Carver mentally excused the man his slip in standards knowing, as he did, the pressures under which he had been operating recently.

Putting down the national paper he picked up a copy of the Shrewsbury Chronicle that the friendly girl at reception had obtained for him. Reading through the 'What's on in Shrewsbury' section he was glad that he was not a young man growing up here. Most of the advertised restaurants seemed to be Indian/Bengali and night life was seventies-eighties retro clubs plus some karaoke or open-mike pub venues. There were live music acts but they were few and far between in the town itself. He needed some local knowledge; perhaps the receptionist would help. She seemed the accommodating sort and had managed to slip into conversation that her shift finished at three this afternoon.

Carver's Blackberry buzzed to announce an incoming email. He saw that the originator was Sergeant Stone. 'Good timing, Michelle' he thought to himself. The content was useful. It indicated that Kenneth Rounds was a publican who would not be averse to talking with the police (which was not always the case in Carver's experience). The Shropshire Hunt public house was literally one minute walk up the hill from his hotel so, armed with the information contained in Michelle's email, he went back to his room to prepare for his meeting.

A bare two hours later he was on the phone to Michelle who was still in Orion.

'Michelle, Martin here. Is the boss there?'

'No; he's out and about seeing people. I'm holding the fort in case anything comes in from the field teams. Nothing yet. How are you doing?'

'I've just come back from interviewing Ken Rounds – thanks for the email by the way. The man's a straight talker but it's not been a productive day so far. I showed him a photo of Jennifer Duncan and it did not ring any bells. Rounds says that he never misses a music night so Jennifer cannot be a regular or he would have remembered her. He showed me his booking diaries going back five years and our friend Guest is in there quite a lot. It's not exactly every second week because sometimes there are other events on like folk festivals or concert in the square – all sorts of rural crap. Anyway, Rounds will give me copies of the diaries after lunch. The main piece of our news is that Guest should have been playing next week but has cancelled. Apparently he's gone to run a mate's bar in Spain for two weeks; Rounds was not sure of the details because Guest left a message with Mrs Rounds and she does not really get involved in the music side of the business. Short version is that Guest is not due to play here for another two weeks.'

'Where in Spain is he, Martin?'

'Don't know. He's only gone in the last 48 hours as far as Rounds knows so immigration can get that for us. Or we could contact Guest's wife. I'll need to speak to the boss before I do that.'

'Yes. Well he said that he'd be back by eleven so I can go and get a change of clothes. Apparently he keeps a spare wardrobe in his own office in case of emergencies. I'll have him call you as soon as he shows up.'

'Thanks, Michelle. I'll wait in my room for his call then I'm going back to the pub to view the CCTV footage of the nights when Guest was playing, see if I can spot any groupies.'

'God, that's going to take forever.'

'No it won't. The hard drive is wiped every month so I'll be lucky if there are even two sessions with our man. The more I think about it, the more I reckon I'll have to talk to his wife. I can't think of a quicker way of finding out all the different venues where Guest performs. We'll need to identify them and look at their CCTV records as well. Has the…'

'Hang on, Martin. The boss has just come back' interrupted Michelle.

Carver waited. He could just about hear what Stone and

Goodchild were saying as she brought the senior officer up to speed on his visit to Shrewsbury. Finally Goodchild came on the line.

'Good morning, Martin. Michelle's filled me in on what you've been doing. What's your plan now?'

'I need to have another go at Ken Rounds when he's not distracted trying to get his pub ready for opening and I also need to look at his CCTV records. I'll probably bring his computer back to London tomorrow.'

'Good. I've been talking with London Irish and they are sending their system to me today. As far as talking to Mrs Guest is concerned, I agree that it would be the quickest way forward but can you do it without alerting her?'

'Depends; worst case scenario is that they are in it together. Unlikely, as Guest performs solo but I would be helpful if Michelle could dig up some biographicals on the woman for me. When I was an RMP, tracking the movements of AWOL squaddies was our bread and butter so I'll apply those techniques to Mrs Guest.'

'OK. Martin, Michelle's on it as we speak. Anything else you need?'

'Another eight hours sleep would be nice. This is all starting to catch up with me. I nearly dozed off on the drive up last night.'

'Stay the night in Shrewsbury and travel back tomorrow morning then. All three of us need to be sharp for then. We might even have a lead from the other teams around the country by then. I'm surprised we've not heard anything back by now.'

'If I were you, boss I'd chase them up late this afternoon. Find out why they are not sending anything back. If it's a case of people moving house after a daughter has disappeared or they have expunged all traces of a girl's existence then a different approach is required. We need to be creating a history and database. We may even have to widen the search parameters.'

'I hear what you're saying, Martin. Talk with you later.'

Carver could not do much until after his meeting with the

publican and Michelle sent him information on Mrs Guest so he went for a walk around the town centre to get a feel for the place. He found it odd with black and white beamed buildings hundreds of years old being sandwiched between the ugliest glass and concrete monstrosities that had obviously been constructed using the cheapest materials possible. The architectural vandals of the nineteen sixties had obviously been busy.

Traffic was, for the most part, single lane and therefore one way with the main shopping area being pedestrianised. As he neared the railway station he came across a splendid grey stone building outside which was statue of Shrewsbury's most famous son, Charles Darwin. On closer inspection Carver saw that this was the town library though it had obviously not always been so. Lack of time prevented him from investigating further so he retraced his steps to the Shropshire Hunt where Ken Rounds awaited.

Along the way his Blackberry sounded to indicate another incoming email from Michelle Stone. 'Interesting' he thought on reading it. Gillian Guest was an admin officer at RAF Shawbury. That meant that she would have signed the Official Secrets Act. She also put in two nights a week voluntary work at the local hospice – possibly when her husband was out playing guitar.

He phoned London. 'Michelle; Martin here. Thanks for that. Do you know which nights she works at the hospice?'

'No' replied Stone. 'It varies. I suppose you'll just have to phone her or turn up on the doorstep and take your chance. Have you worked out an angle yet?'

'More or less. I want to sort my meeting with Ken Rounds first. Last question; isn't RAF Shawbury where Prince William learned to fly helicopters?'

'Hang on. I'll check. Yes; you're right. Harry was there too. Why do you ask?'

'No reason. I just like to know things. Anything new at your end?'

'No. We're sat here waiting on your results, Martin.'

'I'll crack on then. Talk to you later.'

Carver made his way along the High Street until he arrived at the Shropshire Hunt. It was one of the town's black and white period buildings, probably even a listed one. He entered the small, single roomed establishment and wondered how it could function as a music venue. There was no stage and if there was room for more than fifty people under the fire safety regulations he would be very surprised.

The landlord was behind the bar putting change into the till. There were two male customers who eyed him openly the way country folk do when seeing a stranger and one twenty something barmaid who looked like a fashion model on her day off. She approached him and asked what he'd like to drink. 'Nothing for the moment thanks. I'm here to have a meeting with Mr Rounds.'

Rounds looked over his shoulder. 'I didn't expect you back until a bit later' he said. 'I've not finished doing those copies yet.'

'Not to worry. If we could go to your office whilst it's still quiet there's a couple of other things I'd like to ask you about.'

'All right. Hold the fort, Lucy. Carol's due in in half an hour but if things get too busy just give me a bell' he said to the girl. He then came from behind the bar and led Carver through a door marked private which gave on to his accommodation and office area.

Once they were sat in the small work space Rounds asked 'What else do you want to know, Detective?'

'I'd like to view whatever CCTV footage you still have on an evening when Tony Guest was playing and I'd like to do it with you present. I'll have questions to ask you whilst we're looking at it. Is that OK?'

'Tony's gigs start from between eight thirty and nine and go on until eleven or even midnight. That's a lot of viewing and I've got a business to run.'

'I understand that, sir and I'm trying to cause as little inconvenience as possible. But if I have to, I will close your pub, remove all the records and equipment I want then take you to London where we can continue this conversation in surroundings considerably less comfortable than a country pub.'

'You can't do that!' gasped an outraged publican. 'You have not even told me what this is about – who, if anyone, is being charged with what!'

'I'm conducting a nationwide investigation, the details of which are none of your business. This matter does have national security implications and is being headed by <u>Commander</u> Mark Goodchild at New Scotland Yard. Would you care to phone the Commander right now and tell him what we can and cannot do, sir?'

'Jesus, there's no need for all that. Let's get on with it.'

Rounds pressed some buttons on a keyboard and the CCTV monitor switched from the live scene from the bar to another one in which the lighting was different and more people were present. 'I've double checked my records and I'm afraid that Tony only played one gig in the last month' said Rounds. 'He cancelled four weeks ago because he had to do a recording session down south and he's missed his last gig owing to this bar he's gone to run in Spain.'

'Does he cancel a lot then?'

'No; Tony's one of the more reliable musicians I know so I did not kick up a fuss when he said he had to go off for a while.'

'You said that you did not know where in Spain he's gone to. Do you remember where the recording session took place?'

'No. I don't think he told me, to be honest.'

'Fair enough. Let's watch the gig then.'

Rounds had been scrolling back through the images and stopping to check the date and time references. Finally he found what he wanted and froze the screen. 'Here we are' he said. 'That's Tony Guest.'

On the screen was the image of a man carrying a speaker

through the main entrance to the pub. From the overhead angle it was obvious that he filled the doorway.

'Big bugger, isn't he?' said Carver.

'Certainly is. Hands like shovels. God knows how he can play some of the delicate stuff he does.'

'OK. Let me look at all the other camera angles. Not many people in are there?'

'It's early. Tony turned up at eight that night. If we play this through we'll see the place fill in the next thirty minutes or so.'

'Do it but speed it up until just before he starts to play.'

There followed the always comical sight of people going about their normal business but in the staccato manner that high speed replays input to them. Guest set up his equipment then went to the bar where he shared a drink with the landlord. He was joined from time to time by other people who had a brief talk with him then found a place to sit until the show started.

'OK. Mr Rounds. All these people who have come up and spoken to the singer; do you know them?'

Rounds rewound and played at normal speed, 'Yes, I know all of them by name' he said. 'They're all regular customers who've been coming in for years.'

'Do they only come in when Guest plays?'

'No, these are proper regulars who live locally. That girl there used to work behind the bar for me.'

'Fine. Start up again. What I'm looking for is someone who only comes in on the nights Guest plays. Stop the machine if you spot someone who fits that bill.'

Images jumped across the screen as Guest began his first set. The pub was nearly full now with all seats taken and a few people standing at the bar. Rounds stopped the machine. 'There. The girl with the big glasses and ginger hair' he said.' She hardly ever misses a Tony gig and that's the only time I see her. Vera, Veronica something like that. If Tony had a fan club, she would be its president.'

'She's sat with some other people. If she with them or are they just sharing a table?'

'I'm pretty sure that's her husband or significant other with her. The other couple I don't know. To be honest, it's a bit embarrassing. She virtually drools when Tony's on, she claps too loudly and is forever trying to buy him drinks. Groupie syndrome.'

'Anyone else? Take your time.'

Rounds looked from camera to camera, shaking his head in frustration when a frown crossed his brow. 'Yes. There is another one. This guy here in the corner of the snug bar. He's not at every Tony gig but they are the only times I've seen him.'

'What do you know about him?'

'Not a lot. He drinks Fosters and keeps himself to himself. I've served him a couple of times but he does not make conversation. He's creepy in a quiet sort of way. I'd put him down as a gay boy who fancies Tony.'

'OK. Let's continue.'

They went to the end of the evening's recording but Rounds did not see anyone else who matched Carver's criteria.

'I'd like you to think about this another way' said the detective. 'Can you think of anyone who was a regular at Tony Guest nights who stopped coming without warning? Go back as far as your memory allows you, Mr Rounds.'

'Do you mean stopped coming to the gigs or stopped coming to the pub entirely?'

'The latter as in disappeared.'

Rounds concentrated, visibly so. Over the years some regulars had dropped away. They'd moved house, lost their jobs and changed life styles, married and really changed lifestyles. Some had even died. No matter how hard he tried, he could not come up with someone who had only come to Tony gigs but who had inexplicably disappeared.

'Sorry, detective. It's not coming to me. Do you mind if we break for a drink? This is driving me mad with frustration.'

'Yes, let's do that. I've no more questions anyway. I've a few more things to see to in Shrewsbury before I head back so if I could pick up those copies and your CCTV at seven tonight that would be useful.'

'They'll be ready by then, Detective Carver. Let's go and have that drink.'

In the end the drink turned into a late lunch. Carver thought that if the cook ever left and set up a shop in London then he would make a fortune, his menu being both adventurous and very well executed.

Carver tried to elicit more information from Rounds but to no avail. The publican was trying to help but the information just was not there. He could not name a single pub that Guest played in but was able to state that they had an agreement that he did not play in any other Shrewsbury bars so that saved Carver the trouble of canvassing them all. As the detective was leaving, having arranged to return later in the evening, he felt a weariness settle on him. It was years since he had had to do this kind of spade work and he knew that his analytical talents were not being utilised sufficiently. If Mark Goodchild did not sort out a real team soon they were not going to make any progress before ML began to go public.

He made his way back to the Lion Hotel where he extended his stay for another evening. The friendly receptionist, who introduced herself as Kate, asked him if he knew his way around the town.

'This is my first visit' he said. 'I've some business to take care of this afternoon then I'm going to do a crawl of the music bars of Shrewsbury. Back to London in the morning.'

'What's your line of business, Mr Carver?' asked Kate.

'I'm a Detective Inspector with the Metropolitan Police.'

'Well you're probably not too weird then. I'm not working tonight and I know all the music places in town. Would you like me to show you around?'

Carver looked at her. She was pretty in a coquettish sort of way but he had ten, more likely fifteen, years on her. Still, local knowledge was always useful. Self justification is a wonderful thing.

'I'd like that, Kate. I'm Martin, by the way. I should be finished by about six, so if I give you a call around seven we can meet up and take it from there.'

'Sounds good to me'.

She wrote her mobile number on a piece of hotel stationery and handed it to him with a smile. Carver tucked it in his breast pocket. 'I'll see you later then' he said and headed for the stairs.

As he walked up to his room, he reflected on how easy it had been to end up going out with a girl not too different in age from Jennifer Duncan. Kate did not know that he was a police officer. Just because he was presentable and staying at a decent hotel did not make him safe. Food for thought.

Once in his room he decided that he really had to speak with Gillian Guest so he did the simple thing and phoned her home, reasoning that as an employee of the Royal Air Force she was unlikely to be working from nine to five. He was in luck; the phone was picked up and a female voice answered 'Hello.'

Putting on the thickest Birmingham accent he could muster, Carver replied 'Duz you fix toilets?'

'No, I don't. You have the wrong number.'

'Sorry, pet.' Carver hung up having kept the phone conversation as short as possible. He rinsed his mouth with Listerine to remove the odour of beer and went to the hotel car park to retrieve his vehicle. Upton Magna was roughly five miles west off the old A5 towards Telford. Gillian Guest should still be there by the time he arrived.

Ten minutes later, thanks to light traffic and satnav, he was parking outside an impressive looking barn conversion set in about an acre of land. He'd prepared himself for this interview because, in his opinion, the investigation was in danger of stalling and a lot was riding on his tracing Guest's movements. Leaving the car he walked up the gravel drive. It was so quiet out here that, if she were in, Gillian Guest must have heard his approach. There was no bell visible on the large wooden front door so Carver used the round metal knocker to rap three times. The rapidity to which the door opened confirmed that his arrival had indeed been observed. He was faced by a small, slender woman in her early forties, about five two in height brown hair and wearing quite thick glasses. Her clothing was country casual; Cotton Traders ladies rugby shirt and well worn blue jeans. A pleasant, pretty face which looked up at him with an air of polite curiosity.

'Good afternoon, ma'am,' he said. 'I'm Detective Inspector Martin Carver from the Metropolitan Police.' He offered over his ID which she took from him them then handed back. 'I'd like to speak with Mr Tony Guest if possible.'

'You'd better come in Inspector. Would you care for some tea?' she said in a pleasantly modulated voice.

'Thank you; yes.'

He followed her through to a large, modern kitchen dining area which gave onto a patio at the rear of the home.

'I'm Gillian Guest. I'm afraid that my husband's not at home right now. Can I help?'

In all his years of turning up on people's doorsteps unannounced, Carver had never met anyone so self contained. Most civilians reacted with the phrase 'has anything happened?' or something along those lines. Only people who had practise in how to deal with the authorities were this calm. In training he'd been shown film of the traitor Harold 'Kim' Philby running rings around MI6's most experienced interrogators. This was not what he had expected.

'When do you expect him back, Mrs Guest?'

'Next week, Inspector. Sugar?'

'Two please. Where has he gone Mrs Guest?'

'Fuerteventura. A friend of his owns a music bar there and his main performer has had to go away for a short while. Tony has agreed to replace him for the duration. You do know that Tony's a musician, don't you?'

'Yes, I do. I should have phoned ahead. This is quite inconvenient.'

'Inspector Carver; I've let you into my home but you have to tell me what this is all about. Is Tony in some sort of trouble?'

'No, not at all. We need his help to try and locate someone else. I'm afraid I can't tell you any details because, well I don't want to come across as melodramatic, but there are national security aspects to this case.'

'National Security! Tony?' laughed Mrs Guest. 'That really is too good. Tell me, Inspector; do you know who I work for?'

'No, I don't' he lied.

She rose from the table and went across to a work surface where she had left her handbag. From it she extracted a laminated card which bore her photograph. She handed it to Carver.

'Ministry of Defence. Let me guess; Donnington?'

'Not even close, Inspector. RAF Shawbury. I would imagine that my security clearance is at least as high as yours. Now, would you care to tell me why you need to see my husband or would you prefer to wait until next week?

'If I had the time I'd prefer to fly out to Fuerteventura and interview him over a jug of Sangria but that's not going to happen. OK here goes. There is a small group of men, no more than four of them, who are using the identities of musicians to move money around. A lot of people are being paid in cash in your husband's industry and not all of them are meticulous in recording it or paying their tax.'

'I can assure you that Tony is. I'm both his secretary and accountant.'

'Excellent. You will be able to help us then. I've been running round the country building up a profile going back five years of a whole group of musicians – pardon the pun – and finding out where and when they performed plus how much they were paid. This information is then used by our number crunchers in London as a means of cross referencing with other cash deposits made by our mystery men. Don't ask me how it works; I just have to find the information.'

'Where does national security some into it?'

'Terrorists need bank accounts and have to explain the origin of money going into them. Cash deposits of £200 per day would be easy for a musician to justify. If we can show that these accounts are not those of musicians, then where is the money coming from?'

'Come with me, Inspector' said Mrs Guest, who led him through the lounge and into a home office somewhat more auspicious than the one in the Shropshire Hunt.

'All the information you require is here in three different formats. Firstly there is a paper copy, which is obviously how we started. One day I hope Tony will write his life story and I've transferred everything onto hard drive. Finally we have it all backed up on memory sticks which are kept in the safe in case some oik steals the computer one night. Take your pick.'

Carver could not believe his luck. His story had more bullshit in it than a Tony Blair speech but this woman had come up with gold dust.

'If only all members of the public were this efficient, Mrs Guest. Thank you. I'll take the memory sticks and they will be returned to you ASAP. There's just one thing; could you keep my visit to yourself please? I include your husband in that, by the way.'

'I understand, Inspector. Tony never asks me what goes on with the military and I never ask what goes on when he's on tour. At the end of the day, he always comes home to me.'

'He's a lucky man, Mrs Guest.'

'We're a lucky couple, Inspector. I'll see you out.'

Carver drove back to Shrewsbury feeling that he had finally accomplished something. It was tempting to turn around and head down to London but he knew that fatigue was not far away. No. Better to have a power nap and a shower ready for the evening with Kate. She looked like she gave good reception.

Chapter Twenty One

Catherine had enjoyed a quiet day with ML. They had sat at a shaded table at La Dorada where they had taken their time over a seafood lunch. Sole with a prawn and champagne sauce had been a definite improvement on octopus.

La Dorada was also an excellent place from which to people watch. Despite the mob of fat foreigners who broiled in the sun at the terrace tables, many obviously local people made their way into the darkness of the bar. There, some of them ate small plates of Canarian delicacies washed down with regular glasses of vino tinto whilst others sat at plastic tables drinking beer and playing dominoes, their voices at full volume.

The restaurant faced a small, sandy cove where local artists had created the day's sand sculptures and waited by their works for tourists to throw a few euros their way.

Small children played in the shallows as this was one of the few parts of the coastline where tide and wind were not a danger.

The angle of the sun was moving so that even their table in the shade was about to receive some rays so, at ML's suggestion, they headed back along the beach to the villa for a siesta. As they walked back together Catherine realised that she did not feel like a tourist, certainly not an American one. This was a new experience for her and it only took a moment for her to understand why. It was not so much her as it was him. Unless one knew Dominic one would never guess that he was English. He was wearing trousers and a polo as opposed to the shorts and T-shirts of his compatriots. His physique was trim without a trace of a beer induced paunch and his hair was short, but styled in contrast to shorn. Then there was the ease with which he ordered food and drink in Spanish. The locals obviously respected him and she, as his companion, was being treated accordingly.

Catherine thought back to when they had both sung on stage at the music pub in Bristol. She would bet that everyone who had been present that day would remember Dominic as an American. The man was a chameleon. 'Who was the real Dominic?' she wondered.

No matter. For now she felt at ease as she walked back to the villa for the second time that day. 'Do you really take a siesta, Dominic?' she asked him.

'That depends on how much I've had to drink with lunch and what else I have to do. Today I have to write up my notes on La Dorada then I plan to have a few beers by the pool once the sun's a tad less fierce. What about you? Any plans?'

'I feel great. Lunch was just right so I'm going to swim for a while then work on my tan. We also have to plan tonight don't we?'

'We do indeed. I'll see you by the pool in an hour or so.'

They had arrived back at the villa by now. Each went to their rooms where Catherine changed into her swimsuit and ML reviewed his progress so far. In general he was content; he was still dictating the pace of events but the British police could not be stupid forever. Once they had Tony Guest's name connected with one girl's, it would not take long for it to be linked to the others. Or should not take long. The more he studied police tactics and procedures, the more he wondered why people did not take up crime as a career. So called 'clean up' rates were a joke with crimes against property not exactly high on the police's procedure list of priorities. There were pubs all over inner city Britain where one could place an order for the goods one wanted to 'fall off the back of a truck'. Crimes against the person only rated slightly higher. Conviction rates for rape were scandalously low as were murders amongst the ethnic minorities. The only area where it seemed that the police stirred themselves was the prosecution of the new category of 'hate crime'. It had reached the stage where infant children were being placed on a register for calling another child gay, black or paki in the playground.

ML believed that only stupid people were convicted of serious crimes. The process was Darwinian in its logic; the drunk, the drugged and the dysfunctional were behind bars. Those on the outside had learned from their mistakes.

So ML was not overly worried about London's finest descending on Corralejo anytime soon. The only thing nagging away at the back of his mind was the lack of communication from his lawyer, Arthur Blenheim. He would need to chase the man up before long even if it meant him having to accept a lower price for his company.

ML fired up his computer for a quick check of his emails. emails. One from Tucker, who seemed to be getting nowhere fast. He would let the situation stew for a little longer; he would be stirring it again soon. Nothing from Blenheim. Then he logged on to the ITV news website to check on the current affairs in the UK. Again, nothing. He changed into a pair of shorts and went down to join his house guest.

'Hi. Not too hot for you?' he said.

'No. This is just right. The walls keep the breeze off so I'm aware of the real temperature here. It would be damn easy to get burned on the beach, I reckon.'

'Would you like a beer?'

'No thanks; I'm going to save myself for tonight but if you're headed to the fridge I'd take a still water.'

'OK. One agua sin gas coming up.'

ML went inside then returned with the two drinks. They drank in silence each sat up on their own sun lounger, appreciating the late afternoon sun.

'What's the plan for tonight then, Dominic?' asked Catherine.

'Well we both came out here to listen to Tony sing so that's the only fixed point in my agenda. After tonight, I have places to visit professionally so it may be my only chance to see him with you. And I'd like to do that.'

'How do you say 'me too' in Spanish?'

'Yo tambien.'

'Yo tambien, then.' She smiled at him, aware that their relationship had shifted ever so slightly. She was also aware that she was alone with an attractive man whilst wearing a minimal amount of clothing and with her visible flesh glistening with coconut scented oil. If she asked him to rub some lotion on her back now, the outcome would be pretty much assured. But did she want that and would a new level of relationship spoil or enhance their time together? 'She who hesitates is lost' is balanced by 'fools rush in where angels fear to tread'.

'We have a decision to make, Catherine.'

She made the mental equivalent of a gulp and said 'And that is?'

'Where and when do we eat, of course. It would be crazy to spend the night in the Rock Cafe without food inside us. The place will be packed this evening so, if we want a table, we'll have to arrive early and eat there. That means rack of ribs, down and dirty and American or we can go somewhere else and risk having to spend all night on our feet. Your call.'

'Hey! Down and dirty and American does it for me. I'd even wear the T-shirt!' she laughed. The moment of sexual tension had passed and there were many days and nights ahead of them.

It was still light a few hours later when they made their way to the Rock Cafe which was less than five minutes stroll from the villa. ML was wearing dark glasses and a black fedora which matched his fresh jeans and short sleeved shirt. Catherine had joked that he looked like Johnny Cash after a makeover.

The terrace outside the bar was large with all the tables absolutely full of young people enjoying the last rays of the sun. External speakers blasted out a selection of old rock classics at a volume which made conversation difficult, so everyone's voice was raised as they tried to communicate. It made for a lively early evening atmosphere.

ML and Catherine went up the few steps which led to the bar's entrance. The inside was deceptively large with a long, curving counter on the left balanced by a well raised stage to their right. The main body of the room was taken up with wooden, circular tables for four people and there were small booths lined across the rear wall. ML steered Catherine to one of the latter.

'It's not the best view of the stage' he said 'but we are out of the speakers' line of fire. Also the ladies rest rooms are just over there to your right.'

'Seems fine to me. We can always move later on if we want' she replied.

A young waitress came to their booth and took the order in Spanish. As she left them she treated them to a dazzling smile and looked a much happier person than the one who had initially approached them.

'I have got to learn this language!' said Catherine. 'Whatever you said to her, you've made that girl's night.'

'Fuerteventura likes to take the tourist dollar but does not want to sell its soul the way some of the other islands have. This place is an alien creature for that girl and she will have to put up with a lot of shit here. Basic politeness and even an attempt at speaking her language will go a long way; being fluent knocks them out.'

'So what's the best way to learn, Dominic?'

'That depends. Do you speak any foreign languages?'

'High school French; that's it.'

'That's a good start. Without knowing it, you already have the grammar. French and Spanish are both Romance languages and…'

'Whoa there! What has romance got to do with it?'

'Not romance as in love ever after, flowers and moonlight' laughed ML. Romance as in coming from the ancient Romans i.e. Latin. The main Romance languages are Italian, French, Portuguese and Spanish. They have very similar grammatical structures so now all you have to do is build up a vocabulary and practise.'

'That's all, huh? Devour a dictionary then make a fool of myself mispronouncing everything.'

'There are many ways. Listen to the television news in Spanish so that your ear becomes accustomed to the sound, the tune of the language. Read the newspaper aloud. One huge advantage is that Spanish is totally phonetic – what you see is what you say. Can you imagine how difficult it is for someone to learn English? If you take the letters OUGH and put a different consonant at the beginning you end up with words which sound totally different COUGH, DOUGH, ROUGH being just three. Go into a cafe and ask what something is called – people love to teach their own language; it's a subject they know.'

'OK. I see where you're coming from. Any other tips?'

'Don't be afraid of making mistakes. It's not a matter of intelligence to speak another language; it is, quite literally, child's play.'

The waitress returned with four bottles of Mahou beer and their order of sticky chicken wings, ribs and fries. All decorum went out of the window as they got down and, if not dirty, certainly American.

As the plates were cleared away, Catherine declared 'Damn that was good!'

'Pig and poultry are always a good bet in Spain' replied ML. 'Both beasts tend to be corn fed. Anyway, it looks like the evening is almost about to get going.'

The band was setting up on stage. It consisted of a rhythm guitar and a keyboards who were doing something musical together, a bassist who was tuning a walk, and a drummer who was, predictably having a beer. Then Tony Guest appeared carrying a lead guitar which he plugged in and picked at, adjusting the machine heads until he was satisfied. The house lights went down, the external speakers fell silent and he addressed the audience.

'Good evening ladies and gentleman. If you've come here tonight to listen to Carl Canty well, you're shit out of luck. Carl's had to go home for a couple of weeks and I'm the closest thing to a musician the bossman could find to stand in for him. My name's Tony Guest, these are the four horsemen of the apocalypse for all I know, but we are here to rock you tonight. I now declare this bar a Julio Iglesias free zone – hit it!'

And with that the band went into Status Quo's Rockin All Over the World.

ML looked at Catherine and put his mouth close to her ear. 'I hope this doesn't mean Tony's going to play to the limitations of the others or we're in for a very long night' he said.

'The crowd love it though.'

'This lot would love Hi Ho Silver Lining! We'll see.'

As the evening progressed it became obvious to anyone who had seen Tony Guest play before what was happening. He had not had enough time to rehearse with the others and was going through their repertoire to gauge their competence level. Little by little he increased the complexity of the songs, built the atmosphere, all the while communicating with the band members as to where they were going.

By the time they took a break, the house was rocking and the band were enjoying themselves instead of just going through the motions. It had been an impressive piece of work by the new man.

Catherine was glittering with happiness.

'This is so much better than seeing him in a Bristol pub' she exclaimed. 'I can't wait for the next set, eh Dominic?'

ML forced a quick smile and just nodded at her.

'Dominic; are you OK? You're looking a bit shaky.'

'To be honest, my stomach's not feeling too good. I had a small doubt about the clams at lunchtime. Hopefully it'll pass.'

'God! Do you want to get some fresh air? It's quite hot in here now and if you're feeling sick…'

'Look Catherine; I don't want to spoil your evening. It's your first Friday night, you're enjoying the music and that's why you came out here after all. If it's all right with you, I'm going home to take a pill and lie down. You're quite safe in this area and, if you do have any problem, call me and I'll be here in five minutes. OK?'

'No! I feel awful partying on if you're not well. I'm taking you home.'

'No, you're not. What are you going to do? Sit and watch Spanish TV whilst I lie in bed? One of us might as well get some fun out of the night. How much cash do you have on you?'

'Not much but I have my cards.'

'Always try to pay in cash. Card cloning machines are starting to appear even here. Take this.' He handed her two one hundred euro notes under the table. She was about to protest but ML stopped with a raised hand and a smile, 'I know, I know; you can pay your own way and all that' he said. 'We'll sort out the finances tomorrow. That's just to get you through the evening without using your cards. I'll see you in the morning, Catherine.'

ML stood, turned and made his way through the crowd to the exit without another word. His haste was not generated by a stomach upset; he'd spotted Ian Williams at the far end of the bar and was anxious to leave before the Welshman saw him with Catherine. It was unlikely that he would link ML with the Rodney McNaughten persona he'd used at Euston Station but he needed to leave the way free for him to approach the American girl as he'd been instructed.

ML passed within two feet of Williams' back on his way out, the latter being occupied in the ordering of a drink. His departure went unnoticed. All his players were now in place and he could do no more except return to the villa and wait. The middle game was progressing well.

§

As ML was making his way back home, Martin Carver was experiencing Shrewsbury night life with Kate.

The evening had started well. Ken Rounds had kept his promise to prepare the copies of his music bookings so Carver had been able to collect these along with the CCTV material at seven o'clock. Having deposited all this in his room, he phoned Kate and, half an hour later, they met up at a town centre pub called the Bull. This lay on a small cobbled street called Butcher Row which he'd arrived at having walked along Milk Street and then Fish Street. 'Welcome to the countryside' he thought to himself. There was even a long narrow passage called Grope Lane which made him wonder what commodities had been sold there in years gone by.

The Bull was clean, pleasant and not too modern. There was a young man playing acoustic guitar in an accomplished manner and singing songs he'd written himself. The lad had the talent, he had the looks; would that be enough to make it in the music business? Not if he stayed in Shrewsbury was Carver's opinion. He would have liked to have spoken to the singer to try and get a feel for how the music scene operated out here in the sticks but Kate was determined to show him as many different venues as possible and dragged him off to the next pub as soon as they had finished their drinks.

And so it went on; a classic young person's Friday night pub crawl with the establishments ranging from the acceptable to the deplorable. Kate knew people in every one and the more white wine she consumed the louder she became. The demure, efficient receptionist was turning into a monster who appeared to be in training for the Great Britain Olympics drinking team. Carver was glad that he had eaten a decent lunch as dinner on a Friday night did not exist on Kate's agenda. When he had suggested it she'd replied that they could always grab a kebab later on. That was when Carver knew that he going to cut the evening short at the earliest opportunity. This came when they were in a night club called C-21, a charming little place situated next to the public toilets near the Abbey.

The club was packed with a young crowd, many of whom seemed to work in Shrewsbury's bars and restaurants. He and

Kate found themselves at a large semi-circular booth at which maybe ten people were squeezed in. By now his local guide had switched from white wine to Sambucca and quite a few of her friends were knocking back the exotics as well. Carver reckoned that they were about thirty minutes away from a demonstration of synchronised projectile vomiting so he pulled the old 'I must take this call' trick and walked away from the table with his phone clasped to his ear talking into a silent unit.

He rejoined the table and tried to explain to Kate that he was needed back in London and would have to go.

'It's past fucking midnight' said the young lady. 'What sort of office calls at this time of night?'

'The Metropolitan Police, darling. Remember? Are you going to be alright getting home or do you want me to call a cab for you now?'

'Sod off, Martin! Night's just starting. I'll see you next time you're up this way.' With that she took his head in both her hands and kissed him with such enthusiasm that he felt that his face was being sucked off. When she finally came up for air he waved goodnight to the assembled company and made good his escape. He hoped that the hotel bar was still open as he needed a drink to take away the taste of second hand Sambucca. He hated aniseed.

The following morning he was up, showered and packed by seven o'clock. He enjoyed a good breakfast in the hotel restaurant and was checked out and on his way back to London half an hour later.

The traffic gods were kind to him and when he passed the huge RAC building in Birmingham without encountering any major jams he felt confident of arriving back in the capital in good time.

Just after ten he walked into the Orion offices to find Goodchild and Stone sat side by side watching a computer screen.

'Morning, all' said Carver. 'What's on the box?'

'Hi, Martin' said Goodchild. These are the CCTV records of Guest from London Irish. We've only just received them so no news yet. How was Shrewsbury?'

'Productive I think. I've the Guest CCTV pictures from the Shropshire Hunt here and also records of when he played there going back for five years. Last but definitely not least is this memory stick which Gillian Guest gave to me. She does all his admin work so what we have here is a record of his financials and locations of where and when he played.'

'That's good work, Martin' said Goodchild. 'We've a lot of cross referencing ahead of us but I've a good feeling about this. What impressions did you pick up from Shrewsbury?'

'It is so provincial it's not funny. The youngsters are bored stupid but they are not in the same boat as the kids on inner city council estates. The town itself is lovely but all there is to do is drink. Yesterday my hotel receptionist made a date with me – I doubt if she's twenty five yet. She dragged me all over town until she could hardly stand. If I'd been a wrong'un she could be floating down the River Severn now. It's mad. Anyone who is a bit out of the ordinary can sweep these girls off their farmland feet – a musician could get away with murder.'

'So you've spent Friday night on the piss with a Shropshire lass. Martin. I look forward to seeing your expenses claim. What did you make of Mrs Guest?'

'Very controlled, very smart and, I reckon, very straight. She offered up her husband's records in any format we required; paper copy, hard drive or this memory stick. I've asked her not to let anyone know about my visit including her husband. I think she'll play ball.'

'What makes you think that?'

Carver recounted the terrorist cash laundering story that had used on Gillian Guest and how he had pretended not to know that she worked for the military.

'Can you smell something, Michelle?' said Goodchild.

'Yes, boss. It's the unmistakable stench of bullshit!'

'Yes, well bullshit or not I've got the info I need but I was thinking on the way back down; these CCTV images we have from the Shrewsbury pub and the rugby club in wherever it is are no real use to us. They only cover the last month and these murders have been going on for years. Do we really think that he'd take more than one victim from the same place? Somehow, I doubt it. If even two girls had gone missing and their last know location was, say, London Irish Rugby Club the common denominator of Guest being the singer would have come up wouldn't it?'

'Shit; you're right Martin' said Goodchild. 'The way forward is obviously to try and match dates when girls disappeared with venues that Guest played at that time. It shouldn't be that difficult so let's set it up and get on with it. Michelle; how does this memory stick work?'

'Pass it here, Martin. We'll only need two people to do this, boss. To start with, one can call out the dates and places where our potential victims went missing and the other checks the stick data to see where Guest was that night. When we get a match we call the team who have been tasked with that person to go all out for primary DNA, familial DNA and fingerprint retrieval. How many matches would we need before we can pull Guest in for questioning?'

'I'll go for it if we can find three occasions when Guest was in town and a girl went missing. If we can tie a victim to a venue as well that will strengthen our case. This is all circumstantial, not to say theoretical at the moment.'

'OK. I'll bring up the info from the stick; Martin, are you ready with our list of victims?'

'Yes. Where do you want to start?'

'Jennifer Duncan. What date did she go missing?'

Carver leafed through the dossiers in front of him until he came to the one concerning the girl who had disappeared from Brighton. 'She did not turn up for work on Monday 21st May 2007. Her employer phoned her a couple of times and contacted the parents on the Tuesday when she had still failed to come in. Her father phoned the police that afternoon who entered her flat to find her gone. We know the rest of that story. She had been at work on the Friday so that gives us three evenings when something could have happened to her: Friday 18th, Saturday 19th and Sunday 20th. Where was Guest booked then?'

Michelle Stone's fingers flew across her keyboard making both of the older, male officers very aware of how policing had changed in the twenty first century. 'On Friday he was booked at the Turk's Head in Bridgnorth, Shropshire and on Saturday he was down for London Irish Rugby Club. Sunday is marked as free. What do we make of that, gentleman?' said Michelle.

'We cannot tie Jennifer Duncan evidentially to the rugby club. During the initial investigation Sussex Police looked into her phone and credit card details. Her last phone call was on Thursday afternoon to her mother and on Saturday morning she withdrew two hundred and fifty pounds from a Brighton ATM near the railway station. That is the last time we have for her. It looks like she took the train to Reading to see her unrequited love perform, paid for her food and drinks in cash then was killed. If Guest is our man he then had Saturday night and all day Sunday to do whatever he does and dispose of the body. No way of proving it though.'

'That's a good summation, Martin' said Goodchild. 'I'm going to go to the club this afternoon and do some digging. The first XV are at home today so all hands will be on deck. I can find out who was working the bar that night and show Jennifer's photo around.'

'Does your club have female staff, boss?'

'It does. Why?'

'Perhaps it might help if I came along and asked them a few questions too. What do you think?'

'Good idea, Michelle. OK, what's next, Martin?'

'Let's try this one. Lauren Prospero. Reported missing Tuesday June 17th 2008. A medical secretary at Stafford Royal Infirmary.

Lived alone on the outskirts of Stafford itself. Similar scenario to Jennifer Duncan; failed to report for work on the Monday, her line manager let it slide until Tuesday whereupon she called Lauren's mother. No reply from her mobile so Staffordshire police were informed. On entering her flat they found it full of her personal possessions, her passport was there, her jewellery was there but she wasn't. Lauren was last seen at 1700hrs when she left work for the weekend. So, Michelle, where was Guest on that particular weekend?'

Once again she attacked the keyboard and after a few seconds she sat back from the screen, a look of puzzlement on her face.

'What's wrong, Michelle?' asked Goodchild.

'Well we have him there all right. He was free Saturday and Sunday but, on the Friday night he's down as playing at a venue in Stafford, get this, the Whore's Bed! How did a name like that get past the licensing magistrate?'

'It didn't' smiled Carver. 'Do your internet voodoo and I'll bet you that you'll find that Stafford has a pub called the Boar's Head.'

Thirty seconds work later and Carver was proven right. 'Either that was a Freudian slip by Mrs Guest or she was making some sort of statement when she entered the info. Do you reckon that she believes her rock god husband is playing with someone else's instrument?'

'Could well be, Martin' said Goodchild. 'All I care about is that we've put two names into the system and we've found Guest was present when both those girls went missing. Carry on with the list, I'm going to contact whoever is checking out Lauren Prospero and light a medium sized fire under their backsides.'

Fifteen minutes later Goodchild strode back into the main room a look of satisfaction on his face.

'We are on a roll, folks. Some scrote from Staffs police is on his way in with Lauren Prospero's DNA and some objects that may contain partial prints. Doctor Watkins will take charge of that side of things as soon as the cretin arrives. Hopefully we'll have a match with one of the fingers this afternoon.'

'Excuse me, boss' said Michelle. 'If this officer is bringing us this material, why is he a 'scrote and a cretin'?'

'Because the little shit was going to have it couriered to us so that he could go and watch Stoke City play girly ball!' thundered Goodchild. 'How are you two getting on?'

'After our brilliant start' replied Carver 'we've hit a brick wall. None of the other eight girls we had on our hit list went missing when Guest was in the vicinity. Michelle's come up with another idea though.'

'If we assume that Guest is the killer' she continued 'then his modus operandi; appears to be to take the victim on a Friday or a Saturday thereby leaving him Sunday to dispose of the body. If I work backwards from his booking records and apply those parameters, cross reference to girls who were reported missing in those areas at that time then I can work up a new list of people to visit and then try for more physical evidence.'

'Sounds like a hell of a task, Michelle. Can you really do that?'

'The data is all here, boss. It's just a matter of processing it. Martin and I could have this done by lunchtime.'

'Get it done then. I'll give you until twelve thirty then you and I are off to Reading. I really would like to find a witness who could place Jennifer Duncan at the club when Guest was playing there and I reckon you interviewing the female employees is a good idea. Martin; call the field teams who are or were going to follow up those prospects that you've now eliminated. Stand them down for the rest of the day but let them know that you'll have new targets for them; possibly by tomorrow, definitely by Monday.'

'If you don't mind me saying so, boss. I think that's a mistake. You're betting everything on Guest being our man and that these girls were only killed at places where he was playing. One thing I learned in Shrewsbury is that musicians sometimes just show up at their pals' gigs and jam for the fun of it. Imagine that Guest played a gig down south on a Wednesday night, he then stays over and travels who knows where. He could be taking girls from where he was officially not present. I think the field teams need to pull in all the physical evidence they can, boss.'

Goodchild paused before replying. Carver's point was a fair one. In fact there was no flaw in the argumentation. The only worry Goodchild had was putting too much workload on his small number of field teams. He was going to really push them when Michelle Stone produced her new list.

'All right, Martin. I see your point. Don't stand them down but speed them up and make them aware that there is more to come. Michelle; I'll see you at twelve thirty.'

Goodchild left them to their allotted tasks and went for a walk. He needed to get out of the windowless Orion office and clear his head. He was experiencing the loneliness of command. With Clarkson persona non grata there was no one with whom he could share his thoughts or even use as a sounding board for his ideas. Michelle Stone was bright but she was a detective sergeant who did not have the experience to appreciate the political aspects of this case. He was glad that Assistant Commissioner Addison was not in the office this weekend although he would not be surprised to receive some sort of communication from the man at some stage.

He would also be hearing from Roger Tucker some time soon. It was the weekend, his friend's wife was still overseas and no doubt he would like to have a drink or two and try to pick the policeman's brains. Escaping to Reading suddenly looked like a very sensible move.

His walk had taken him to the foot of Clive Steps and he would either cross over to St James' Park to soak up the sun or turn right to the Red Lion to soak up a pint of Guinness. No contest – Michelle could drive him to Reading.

Chapter Twenty Two

Catherine woke slowly on Saturday morning. The blinds in her room had not been fully closed and the sun's rays from the window behind her head were slanting across the room to create a different light effect. She picked up her watch from the small table next to her and noted that it was past ten o clock. She would have rolled over for another half hour of dozing but the fullness of her bladder made a bathroom visit a matter of urgency. Once up, she remembered that her host (friend?) had been taken ill last night and there was no noise coming from the house or the pool. Feeling guilty. She showered, brushed her teeth and dressed in double quick time to go and see how he was.

The ground floor of the villa was deserted so she went out the pool area where she found him lying on a sunbed reading a paperback.

'Good morning, Dominic. How are you feeling?'

'Hi. A bit delicate but a lot better than last night. How was your evening?'

'It was great! Tony pulled the stops out for the second set, the crowd wouldn't let him off the stage. I'm sorry you missed it.'

'Not to worry. He's here for a week so I'm sure I'll catch him before he goes. I'm just sorry to have left you all alone on your first night out.'

'Actually, I met someone. Not long after you left this English guy came over and asked if the seat was spare so I had to say yes. He turned out to be a marketing consultant or something. Anyway, his work takes him around England, he's really into music and he's seen Tony play in a few different places up and down the country. We had quite a good chat when there was a lull in the music and, truth be told, there were a lot worse people who could have joined me.'

'Are you seeing him again?'

'Shit no! It wasn't like that. Ian, that's his name, Ian's sweet but, well, boring, I suppose. He wasn't really at ease with me, you know. More of a boy than a man. He did offer to walk me home but I put him off and sort of left it that I might bump into him around the island.'

'OK. I feel better that you were not totally left alone. I'll buy the chap a beer if you ever introduce me to him.'

'Talking of beer, have you had breakfast?'

'Yes. Camomile tea and toast; but you go ahead if you want.'

Catherine went into the villa and returned with a can of San Miguel which she popped and took a good pull from.

'So a girl who has beer to start the day doesn't shock you then, Dominic?'

'We've all done that at some time in our lives and I'm an equal opportunity drinker. I even know a song about it.'

'Beer; for breakfast; no, I don't know that one.'

'Wait here then, and learn.'

ML went inside and came back carrying a six string acoustic. He drew his fingers across it at once, decided then it was sufficiently in tune then launched into a lazy country rhythm and sang 'Well, I woke up Sunday morning with no way to hold my head that didn't hurt. And the beer I had for breakfast wasn't bad, so I had one more for dessert.' At the end of his couplet he smiled and winked at Catherine who laughed and applauded in delight. ML then carried on until he had sung all five verses.

'That's a sad, sad song, Dominic. Who's it by?'

'It's called 'Sunday Morning Come Down' and was written by Kris Kristofferson. A lot of people think it's a Johnny Cash number but they're wrong.'

'That's the second time I've heard you sing about loss and loneliness. It doesn't fit with someone who's a fan of Tony's style of music.'

'Just coincidence, my dear. That and the song happened to fit into the conversation. People tend to read too much into song choice sometimes. Quite often a man just wants to sing, or his mood and frame of mind influences what he wants to express. Then there's always the drink.'

'Tell me about it. Remember those Irish guys in the pub back in Bristol.'

'Yes. I rest my case.'

'Anything planned for today, Dominic?'

'I'm not intending moving from here for some while, if at all. To be honest, I don't want to be far from a loo for the rest of the day so I'm just going to stay here, read, drink tea or water and try to be all right for tomorrow.'

'Fine. I'll just chill by the pool too but I'll skip the tea. Do you reckon you'll be up for the music tonight?'

'We'll see how it goes. I don't want to start popping pills then putting alcohol on top of them. It's best to let these ailments run their course. You know your way round enough now to do your own thing so don't worry about me. I promised you the best paella for Sunday and we won't miss that.'

'Oh yeah; the octopus tavern or whatever it's called. I'm looking forward to that. Remind me to go easy on that special wine though; it really did a number on me that time.'

And so they continued, comfortable in each others company – sometimes chatting, sometimes not. He read, she swam. They discussed music with ML playing for her from time to time. They moved into the shade as the sun reached its zenith. At one thirty Catherine left the villa and came back with Chinese food from a small restaurant she had spotted on the main street. ML smiled and ate steamed fish with plain rice which she insisted would be the best thing for someone in, as she put it, 'his condition'.'

'You make me sound as though I'm pregnant!' he joked.

In mid afternoon Catherine retired to her room to sleep off

the beers she'd consumed during the day and with a view to being fresh for a Saturday night at the Rock Cafe.

§

In England Goodchild had returned from his walk to find that Carver and Stone had indeed managed to create a new list of times and places where Guest had been playing and an unresolved missing persons report had been filed.

Over the last five years the man had played just under a thousand gigs that they knew about. Most of these had been in the Midlands but quite a few were in and around London. The size of the venues ranged from small country pubs to large town centre theatres plus everything imaginable inbetween.

The bad news was that the list contained just over a hundred names. Goodchild was stunned.

'Is there any way we can thin that number down, guys?' he asked.

'Eventually, yes' answered Michelle. 'But I've approached it in a different way. I decided to find out if this percentage was significantly above the average – it's as close as dammit to ten per cent. If I took another singer who played a similar number of gigs over the same time scale, what percentage would come up with an unresolved missing persons report?'

'Good; it's like a control group in a scientific experiment. How did you create one, Michelle?'

'I went back to a contact I have from when I worked in Serious Crimes. It was one of the most boring cases ever but it involved organised benefit fraud on a massive scale – millions of pounds a year. It was Martin's bullshit with Gillian Guest that gave me that idea. To cut a long story short, there was this accountant who saved his arse by co-operating with us and we still keep him on a short leash. I called him and asked if he did the books for any jobbing musicians who worked around the country on a predominantly cash in hand basis. The greasy little bugger had dozens so I asked him to select those who worked two hundred times a year between London and Manchester and to send me their details by email. He sent me the info on nine individuals which we've cross referenced with the regional police forces missing persons list and the percentage we arrived at is between one and three per cent.'

The room was silent as Goodchild absorbed this new information. 'Is there any way to explain this anomaly other than the fact that Guest is guilty?' he asked.

'Martin and I were kicking some ideas about when you came back. We need to examine and compare the data a bit more.'

'Martin, you get on with that. Michelle, time for us to leave.'

'Be right with you, boss.'

Michelle left the two men on their own. Whilst she was gone Goodchild said to the younger officer 'Anything you need, Martin?'

'No, boss. Michelle's set the system up so even a chimp could operate it. What time does the oik from Stafford get in with the DNA on the Prospero girl?'

'Anytime now if he doesn't get lost in the big city. As I said, he'll report straight to Rachel Watkins and she'll call down here when she's done her tests.'

Michelle reappeared carrying an over night two-suiter and a laptop. She set up the portable computer at an empty desk then went across to her own work station and did mysterious things on her PC.

'OK, boss. I've now cross loaded all the data Martin and I were working on onto my laptop so I can do some work in the car on the way to Reading. I don't know what time we'll finish at your rugby club so I'm prepared to book in somewhere and crunch some numbers this evening as well. Ready when you are.'

Mark Goodchild did not reveal to Michelle that he'd planned on her doing the driving and thanked the stars that he'd only had two beers in the Red Lion. He led the way to the car park.

As they set off west in an unmarked he turned to her and said 'Before you start in on your computer, would you tell me what ideas you and Martin were discussing?'

'Sure. At first sight, Tony Guest has a very different profile to the people that my tame accountant sent to me. Apart from the pub nights, Guest has quite a lot of corporate work. This usually takes place in large cities which more or less guarantees a missing person hit. London Irish is not the only rugby club he plays either. He's done Leicester, Sale, Bath and Northampton that I can remember. Again, big places that will be more prone to generate missing persons reports. The nine characters we checked out as a control are not like that. They play the same number of gigs as Guest but they are all in small, out of the way places – much less likely to be showing up in the statistics.'

'So you're telling me that Guest's figure of ten per cent is a false positive thrown up by the size of places where Guest plays?'

'Maybe. Put it like this; if we put into the computer dates and venues of an Elton John world tour and cross reference it with reports of young men going missing I bet the figure would be approaching one hundred per cent. We would not then go and interrogate him would we?'

'I see what you mean. Anything else you can tell me?'

'Not until I've played with the data a bit.'

'I'll let you get on with it then.'

The rest of the journey passed in silence save for the clicking of the keys on Michelle's laptop. Initially Goodchild found this distracting to the point of annoyance but, after a while, he ceased to notice it. He reckoned he must be adjusting to the sounds of the twenty first century.

When they pulled into the car park of the Madjeski stadium she put the laptop in its case and waited for instructions. She felt sure that she was going to receive some and was not disappointed.

'We are on duty here, Michelle so despite all the rugby bonhomie, backslapping, people calling me by my first name and offering drinks I'm ' Commander or sir' until I tell you otherwise. OK?'

'Fine by me, sir. Will my computer be safe in the boot of the car or should I bring it with me?'

'Bring it with you, sergeant. We'll put it in the club secretary's safe.'

The two of them entered the Madjeski West Stand entrance and Goodchild led the way to what was obviously a private member's lounge. He introduced Michelle to the club secretary and explained what the two of them proposed to do. The man's name was Patrick Kearns and he was a living testimony to the hardships of playing in the front row of a rugby scrum. His ears made cauliflowers look like orchids and his nose was more broken than a politician's promise. Perhaps to dull the pain that he had endured throughout his playing career, Kearns had self prescribed copious doses of ethanol which was evinced by the fractured capillaries of his face. Then again, perhaps he just liked a drink.

He summoned a younger committee member over and instructed him to escort Michelle to his office where she could deposit her laptop and bags. Once she had gone he addressed Goodchild.

'Jaysus, Mark but you're looking awful serious. Can I help you in any way?'

'You've been a huge help already, Pat. I know it's a big day today and I don't want to disrupt the club but I do need to talk to the catering staff who were here on the nineteenth of May three years ago. Sergeant Stone will be doing the same thing. She is not known here as I am so if you could make people aware that she is here with your blessing that would speed things up for us.'

'Tell you what I'll do, Mark; I'll assign young Declan to escort and introduce her round the stadium. That should do the trick. Do you mind me asking what this is all about?'

'I don't mind you asking, Pat but answering's the problem. Between you and me, we're looking for a seriously sick bastard who abducts and kills young women.'

'That won't go any further than me, Mark. Good luck; call me if you need anything but now you'll have to excuse me as I've got to go and be nice to those cunts from Harlequins.'

Kearns left Goodchild at the members bar to wait for his sergeant's return. He could feel the atmosphere building as the pre-match drinks were consumed, old friends and adversaries met up to exchange banter. God, he loved this. When Goodchild had played the game, rugby had been an amateur sport – at least in England. As such, it had attracted a body of predominantly white collar people who could afford to give up the time to train and play. Once money had been placed on the table things had changed with a rapidity which few had foreseen. London Irish had gone from playing at a council owned piece of land in Surrey to sharing a state of the art soccer stadium in Reading. The rugby world cup was the third most popular televised event after soccer and the Olympic Games. It made Goodchild smile to think that the top players were now millionaires, doing exactly what he used to for the sheer love of the game. And yet the spirit of the game remained. The fans were not segregated, foul language was not orchestrated and the youngest child would watch a match in total safety. Goodchild had once; in a drunken discussion with colleagues from SO15, tried to put forward a social model for a nation run along the same lines as the world of rugby. The discussion had foundered on the rock of whether or not all men were equal.

Michelle returned with Declan. Goodchild took her to one side to explain what she had to do and arranged to meet her in the same spot in an hour's time. He then thanked the young committee member for giving up his time (and the enjoyment of watching the match) to escort his colleague and headed off to start his questioning.

The Madjeski stadium is tiny compared to the likes of

Twickenham or Old Trafford but it does not lack in its hospitality facilities so Goodchild and Stone had their work cut out to visit them all in one hour. The staff were uniformly helpful but none of them could recall seeing Jennifer Duncan. The two police officers were not surprised; it had always been a long shot that someone would remember one face from three years ago.

'What do you want to do now, sir?' asked Michelle Stone.

'I want to watch the second half of the game but I suppose I'd better give Martin a call and…' Goodchild's mobile had rung. He looked at the screen and it was apparent that he did not recognise who was calling him.

'Goodchild. Hello, sir. I'm at Reading trying to match the whereabouts of one of the victims with those of a suspect.'

Michelle was listening and watching. It was probably Assistant Commissioner Addison calling.

All of a sudden, Goodchild froze in place, a look of shock on his visage. He closed his eyes, grimaced, opened them again and strode to the most isolated corner of the room to continue his conversation. Michelle observed him from a distance. For whatever reason, her superior officer did not want her to hear what he was saying and she had to respect that. She did not like it though, feeling that she had contributed more than enough to the investigation to merit trust.

Goodchild put his phone away and just stood there with the expression known as the thousand yard stare. After a minute of this, Michelle crossed the room to him. He did not seem to notice her approach.

'Commander Goodchild' she said. 'What's happened?'

He came to, as though waking from a dream. Seeing her he said 'Derek Clarkson's dead. His cleaner found him this morning. No signs of foul play unless you count an empty bottle of scotch. Preliminary diagnoses is multiple organ failure. I reckon the autopsy will show it was alcohol induced. Fuck it all.'

'He was a friend wasn't he?'

'Yes and they are fucking rare in the modern police service. He was the only officer I could go to and trust. Shit, what a shabby way to die. The waste – the waste of one of the best minds in the force. We shat on him after Hyde Park, Michelle. In the States, burned out policemen, and it is nearly always men, eat their guns. We do it less spectacularly with booze.'

Michelle thought that her boss was on the verge of falling apart which would be disastrous for him in a public place where his name and occupation were well known.'

'We've done all we can here, sir' she said. 'What say we decamp somewhere quieter and raise a glass to an absent friend?'

Goodchild nodded his acquiescence and the two of them made their way to the car where she relieved him of the keys. He sat in the front passenger seat still lost in his private thoughts.

'Could you just hang on a bit longer, sir? I'll just pop back and get my things from the secretary's office' He let out a sigh to indicate that he had heard her.

Michelle then speed walked into the stadium and was back in the car a scant ten minutes later.

'Where to, sir? I don't know Reading at all.'

He directed her in a monotone until they were on the outskirts of town in a residential area.

'Pull over behind that red Focus, Michelle.' She did so and waited; he seemed as though he still had something to say.

'Look at it, Michelle. Number forty. A crappy, semi-detached post war home. Three bedrooms plus a garden and garage. All paid for; current value – who the hell knows in today's market. That's what I have to show for nearly twenty years on the force. Pathetic.'

Goodchild picked up a small black box from the cup holder behind the gear stick, pressed a button on it and the single metal gate on his driveway swung open. At his direction Michelle drove into the property and stopped whilst the main gate swung shut once more. Using the same black box, Goodchild opened it like a cigarette case to reveal a nine digit key pad on which he entered a sequence of four numbers. Ahead of the car the garage door opened in an over and under operation. Michelle drove very gingerly into the large, dark space which became even darker as the door closed behind them. Now the only light came from the cars instrumentation panel. Goodchild did something else to the black box and bright light flooded the garage.

'You can switch off the engine now, thanks. Follow me.'

There was a second door on the left hand side which Goodchild opened by using his keypad. He entered and Michelle followed him into a medium sized but well equipped modern kitchen.

'Fridge is there, drinks cabinet is in the lounge through to your right. Make yourself at home and I'll be back down as soon as I've made some calls.'

He left her standing in the kitchen and mounted the stairs to what, Michelle assumed, was his home office. She was a detective and decided to take this opportunity to detect, or at least have a nosy. There are certain areas in a person's home which are highly revelatory of their personalities and one is the fridge. Goodchild's contained the very basics; butter, milk (full fat), bacon, six cans of Guinness and six cans of a German lager. The freezer yielded Tupperware boxes labelled; curry, bolognese, beef stew and white, sliced bread. In cupboards she found, pasta, rice, egg noodles and a good selection of herbs and spices. This was a single person's kitchen; someone who cooked but was not a gourmet. Whenever they cooked it was done in quantity with the surplus frozen for later use when time was short. She reckoned that Goodchild did not spend much time at home.

The other area in a home which tells much of a person's character is their book shelf. Taking a lager from the fridge Michelle went into the lounge to see what she could find.

The room did not contain anything that could be considered

feminine. No plants or flowers, the furniture was a three piece, green leather Chesterfield, a very solid looking, dark wood coffee table on which were issues of Rugby World. There was a large, wall mounted flat screen TV but, oddly, no DVD player. Finally, the book collection, housed in an enormous mahogany coloured bookcase. To her surprise it seemed to have the complete works of several authors, all in paperback and all showing signs of having been much handled. There was Tom Clancy and Frederick Forsyth (no surprise there) but also Stephen King and Arthur C Clarke. There were books by authors whom she'd never heard of and writers whom she thought would be present but weren't. She looked for but did not find anything by Thomas Harris and, on skimming the back cover synopsis blurb, realised that none of the works were in the crime fiction category.

By far the largest category of books were reference tomes on military history. Present also were a sizeable quantity of Jane's weaponry and war material literature. To round off the library there was a Times Atlas of the World and, quaintly, Mary Berry's Complete Cookbook.

Michelle had built up quite a detailed picture of Mark Goodchild since they had pulled up outside his home. She wondered if he would have left her alone in his den to snoop, as he surely would have expected her to, if he had not been in shock over Clarkson's death. She was still thinking on this when she heard a heavy door slam upstairs and the sound of Goodchild descending. Stepping away from the bookshelf, she sat down in a club chair and busied herself with her drink until he reappeared.

'Sorry to leave you alone' he said. 'I've spoken to Martin; the Prospero girl is a definite match for one of our victims. Martin's going up to Stafford to interview people at the Boar's Head as we speak but it looks pretty certain that there is a pattern developing here. He also said that he's just sent you an email with a revised list of potential victims based on what you two were discussing this morning. If we compare that with whatever you were working on in the car on the way up, we should have a manageable list to send out to the field teams tomorrow. Are you still up for working this evening?'

'No problem. Where shall I book into?'

'I've an office and a spare room here if you're comfortable with that.'

'Makes sense to me; it'll save time and we can head back to London first thing' she replied without hesitation. 'Who's minding the fort if Martin's in Stafford?'

'Addison's staff are taking Orion calls until one of us gets back to base. They'll just record messages unless something urgent comes up. OK, Michelle. We are off duty for a couple of hours so my name is Mark until further notice. I'm going to call a cab and we'll sample the bright lights of Reading where we shall raise a glass to Derek Clarkson. OK with that?'

'Fine; I'll just go and get my things from the car'. She stood up and made to go towards the kitchen where the connecting door to the garage was located. Goodchild stopped her.

'This house is a bit more complex than it seems. If you start opening doors without doing certain procedures, bells will ring at the local station and they'll be an armed response unit round here before you can say 'Heckler and Koch'. It was installed when I was appointed to SO15 so I'll come with you.'

Goodchild led the way and entered combinations in two hidden keypads before they were able to enter the garage. Michelle retrieved her laptop and personal possessions whereupon he showed her his office (another keypad) the bathroom and a spare bedroom. He then went back downstairs to wait whilst she got ready.

He was astonished when she reappeared ten minutes later in a smart, dark blue skirt suit, black stockings, short heeled black shoes and a bright red cotton top. She had applied a discrete amount of make-up and fluffed her hair.

'Excuse me, miss' he said. 'What have you done with my police officer? I know I had one not ten minutes ago but she seems to have disappeared.'

'It's me, Mark; I'm in plain clothes tonight!' It felt distinctly odd to use his given name for the first time. He was covering it well with bluster but she could tell that he was knocked off balance.

'I cannot believe you changed so quickly. My ex-wife used to…' He broke off the sentence not wishing to make comparisons between his ex and Michelle. She was not going to let him get off that easily.

'Go on, Mark. Your ex-wife used to what?'

'Whenever she went to the bathroom I knew that I had time for a couple of beers and several Chapters of a book before she was finally ready to go out.'

'Ah, but was the result worth the wait?'

'Men have a phrase to describe beautiful women who are brainless; 'the lights are on but there's nobody home'. What's worse is when the light's are on, someone is definitely at home but that person is not very nice at all. It's no use to have hair by L'Oreal and heart by Lucretia Borgia. Change subject?'

'Sure. Is the cab on its way?'

'I'll call it now. I did not expect you down so soon!' They shared a smile.

Twenty minutes later the cab had dropped them off just outside the town centre. Reading was one of the strangest towns that Michelle had ever been in. It was a mix of modern office blocks housing some of the most high-tech companies on earth and the remains of a ruined abbey that had to have been at least eight hundred years old. It seemed soulless to her.

They strolled towards the centre in silence, Goodchild lost his thoughts and Michelle comfortable to leave him with them. They passed quite a few pubs which would be considered 'traditional' with names like the Nag's Head, each extolling the virtues of the real ale on offer but Goodchild did not even glance at these. He finally led her into one of the Litten Tree outlets much to her surprise, and they took a small corner table at the rear of the cavernous room. Fake Tiffany lamps and faux, stained glass windows abounded; the music volume was just about at a legal level and all the promotional offers were for the fluorescent alcopops favoured by teenagers intent on getting wasted as quickly and cheaply as possible. To make it worse there were large TV screens around the place where Sky was continually updating the day's soccer scores. This held the attention of the spotty faced youths who made up most of the clientele at that hour.

Goodchild returned from the bar with two pints of Guinness, two large whiskies and two bottles of Grolsch.

'It's happy hour – two for the price of one' he explained before downing one of the Guinness and both whiskies. He stared at the second empty whisky tumbler for a long moment then upended it on the table.

'Are you going to get absolutely shit faced, Mark? I don't mind but I do like to know what I'm getting into.'

'No, I don't intend to. One last drink for Derek will do tonight. No doubt there will be a wake sometime next week plus whatever the Lodge puts on. I got a bit maudlin and twisted back at the club and that really isn't me, Michelle. Bemoaning my lot is bollocks, self pitying bollocks. There are ten dead girls to avenge whose families, as you pointed out yourself, have gone through a damn sight more pain than I have. I'm not going to trap the killer if I'm suffering from alcoholic poisoning. Having said that, I do intend to wind down tonight which will involve more drinking than you are used to so don't try and match me.'

'Macho SO15 pig! Just because you're double my weight and God knows how many year's older than me doesn't mean that it's a given that you can metabolize alcohol more efficiently than me.'

'On your own head be it then.'

'I take it you don't want to talk shop then?'

'Not unless you have come up with a blinding insight as to how we can tie Tony Guest to the murders, Michelle − no.'

'Fair enough. So, why did you choose this place? I'd have put you down as a man who liked a proper pub without TV's all over the place.'

'Correct. No-one I know will ever come in here ever and that suits me tonight. My contemporaries at the club will do their drinking there and the majority of the youngsters don't even know who I am.'

'Sorry to interrupt but that statement implies that you are, or at least were, someone of note around here.'

'Before the game became professional I did turn out for the first fifteen on a regular basis. I was known as 'The Unlaughing Policeman'.'

'Do you still play? You look fit enough.'

'Thanks, you flattering wench. No, I stopped twelve years ago − neck injury. It doesn't bother me but it can't take the pressure generated by a scrum. The idea of quadriplegia is not an appealing one. What about you − any sporting interests?'

'Long distance running, mainly on roads.'

'What, marathons?'

'Yes, I've done that distance but I really prefer to run alone. I live in Crystal Palace so I do some track running there as well.'

'My God! I'm drinking with someone from south of the river. My career will be ruined if this ever gets out.'

'If you can get away with living in a semi-detached in Reading I reckon you're pretty bloody bullet proof, Mark.'

'Touché' he said and raised his glass to her. The evening continued in like vein and, for a few hours, they were no longer police officers, just a man and woman who, either by choice or circumstance, had ended up living quite solitary existences.

By eight o clock the bar was becoming uncomfortably crowded

so they left and found a back street trattoria where they were served food that the colosseum cats would have refused.

Back on the street the town was becoming more animated with groups of males and females engaged in a tour of the bars prior to ending up in whichever late night drinking establishment suited their needs.

'Not exactly our scene, Michelle' said Goodchild. 'Fancy a final drink at my place?'

'As long as you have something better to offer than cheap lager then that's fine by me.'

He smiled down at her. 'I reckon I have something to suit your tastes. Come on.'

He took her to the mini-cab office from where they were driven to an address round the corner from where Goodchild actually lived. Once the taxi had left, they walked the short distance to his home where he went through the rigmarole of locks and alarm systems necessary to secure entry. Once inside he went round closing all the blinds before switching on some lights.

'Follow me' he said.

Goodchild opened the door to a large storage cupboard under the stairs which contained bits of cleaning equipment, raincoats, bags and other items which made up the flotsam and jetsam of domesticity. Turning to the wall on his left, he exposed another hidden keypad which he activated. The entire wall, which was inch thick steel, slid to the right where it disappeared. In its place was a flight of stairs leading down into darkness. Goodchild flicked on a switch and turned to Michelle. 'Come on down but mind your step – there are no handrails here' he said before descending.

She followed him down and found herself in a large room, roughly eighteen feet square and seven feet from floor to ceiling. The contents were interesting to say the least.

In one corner an upright fridge quietly hummed. Next to that was a collection of weapons ranging from a Browning nine mm

Hi-power pistol to an M-16 assault rifle via a Mossburg pump action shotgun with it's barrels sawn off. Ammunition for this collection was contained in army green lockers which rested on a wooden trestle to keep them off the ground. Another wall was taken up by TV screens which were, at present, dead and what looked like a command post standard communications system which was also switched off for the moment.

The centre of the room was taken up by a three seater, leather settee in black and a coffee table that could have been the brother of the one in the lounge upstairs.

But the piece de resistance had to be where Mark Goodchild was standing. In the space formed by the rear wall, the floor and the underside of the stairs, someone had installed a triangular shaped wine rack which contained row upon row of reds.

'Pick your jaw up off the floor and tell me what you think, Michelle.'

'Alice and rabbit holes spring to mind. Let me guess; guns, cameras and booze. You bought this from the estate of an alcoholic, voyeuristic mass-murderer who you once pinched and/or shot. How am I doing?'

'Not even close. This was built as a safe room for me when I joined SO15. The screens are linked to CCTV pinhole cameras throughout the house and its exterior. The weapons are all registered to me.'

'You can't have a sawn off registered to you, Mark!'

'Well, yes. I did omit informing the locals about that small modification. Moving on; if you look up in the left hand corner you will be able to make out a ring bolt. Turn twist and drop and there's a trap door opening into the garage – which is also a lot stronger than it looks from the outside.'

'So this is your panic room. I can imagine you locked in here with Jodie Foster.'

'Goodchild of the Yard does not panic! Although being locked up with a militant American lesbian might prove a bit of a strain on the nerves. Anyway, we're getting dangerously close to talking shop here. What'll you have to drink?'

'A red Bordeaux please, Mark. And I bet that wasn't put here by the Home Office either.'

'No; all my own work. Best thing I ever did in retrospect.'

'Oh, why's that then?'

'Well my ex was not allowed down here. I did tell her that there was classified material stored here and my personal weapon but one day she 'found' a credit card bill of mine and she wanted to know why I had paid Berry and Rudd the wine merchants two thousand pounds. Here you go – cheers. I tried to explain that it was not for drinking and that I was laying down the wine as a financial investment for the future. I guess she didn't believe me as she was gone within a month. So here's to Berry and Rudd.'

They drank their claret. It was the best red wine that she had ever tasted and she wanted to ask him what it was but the conversation had moved on to another path that she wished to follow. They were still standing as they sipped their drinks.

'Why did you buy it, Mark? Two grand for wine is a lot. Was it an investment?'

He sat down on the settee with his glass and the bottle. She joined him.

'No, it wasn't a fucking investment, Michelle. Those were dark days. We'd no sooner sorted out the bloody Irish problem when the Muslims start their holy war. Jehadis and martyrs from Bradford! What a mess. If I screw up at work, people die. It's that simple. It's better to be single than to come home to get earache from your wife, husband or significant other. So I would lock myself down here and drink a bottle of good wine until she either went out or passed out. Then I would emerge and get six or seven hours in the spare room. Pretty pathetic, eh?'

'No and what's more you know it's not. Pass the bottle. Are you seeking my approbation?'

'Probably.'

'Good' she took his glass from his hand and set it down on the table. Then she took a mouthful of wine from her own glass, knelt next to him on the settee and, taking his head in both her hands, placed her lips on his. As his mouth opened she let the liquid flow into him and then followed it with her tongue. He responded. She withdrew.

'Open a bottle of port please, Mark. Not a special one – one ready to drink.'

He did as he was asked and returned to the settee but Michelle was on her feet already. She took the bottle from his hand and moved towards the stairs.

'I'm going to introduce you to a new form of terrorism, SO15' she smiled.

'What's that then?' replied Goodchild.

'It starts where my mouth full of port meets the end of your cock and we take it from there until the explosion. See if you can counter that!' and she trotted up the stairs in her stockinged feet.

Given that Goodchild had to secure several electronic locks before joining her, he made admirable time in reaching the bedroom where Michelle Stone was already under the duvet with the port in her hand and a smile on her face. She had not turned all the lights out so she watched him as he pulled off his clothes (undressed would be too formal a word to describe the high speed strip that Goodchild performed) then jumped in with her.

Over the next hour or so he re-discovered the joy of sex where each person gets to laugh as well as rut. Much port was spilt but enough was consumed so that all exertions of the evening ensured a good night's sleep. The morning would take care of the morning.

Chapter Twenty Three

The sound of classical Spanish guitar floated through the warm air of Corralejo, rising and falling but always progressing as a boat sails across water. Little by little the notes insinuated themselves into the subconscious mind of Catherine Taylor until she awoke from sleep to blink at the Sunday morning sunshine. The music stopped then restarted with the guitarist seemingly searching for a series of chords that he could not quite find. After two more false starts, he had it and the music continued its journey.

She went to her window to look down on the pool area from where the sounds were coming. She was only half surprised to see that it was Dominic that was playing. It was more surprising to observe that he was dressed in a bright white, heavy cotton dress shirt, black jeans and matching cowboy boots. And it was absolutely amazing that this was happening at the ungodly (or certainly, unSpanish) hour of nine in the morning.

After a quick ablute, she descended to the patio to see what was going on.

'Morning, Dominic.'

'Buenos dias, guappa.'

'Euh, yeah, that too. Bit early for all this isn't it? You look like you've been up for some time too.'

'I have. Sorry to have woken you but if I'd let you sleep on you'd have had to rush to be ready for lunch.'

'Lunch? These guys have lunch at two o clock don't they? What's the freaking rush?'

'Ah, it's slipped your mind that I'm taking you for the best paella ever today.'

'Oh shit, yeah. I did forget. Is that why you are in semi-formal attire shall we say?'

'Correct. The great and the good of Puerto Rosario beat a path to my friend's humble door every Sunday. They will be dressed to the nines, especially the women so, out of respect for the house, I make an effort too.'

'OK I can do that. What sort of style should I be looking at here, Dominic?'

'If you have something that would be suitable for an evening cocktail party that should do the trick. We need to arrive no later than twelve to secure a table so you will have time to do your hair and nails. That all right?'

'Easy. I've a classic little black dress and some decent gold. I can be ready in an hour. Right now I need some O.J.. Can I get you anything?'

'Soda water with a slice please?'

Catherine fetched the drinks and sat down with ML.

'How was last night?' he asked her.

'It was good. Tony's really getting into it and word is getting round – the people were spilling onto the terrace. Sorry that you weren't there though; how are you feeling?'

'I'm fine; really looking forward to today. I'm sorry to have left you on your own for the second night running. I'm not being the best of hosts am I?'

'Don't be silly! You've been great and, anyway, I wasn't alone. That guy Ian showed up and sat with me like a chaperone all night.'

'Did he now? An admirer already then is he?'

'I don't think so; in fact I reckon he might be gay. Most young guys talk to my boobs before they even see me – he doesn't. When Tony's playing though, he can't take his eyes off him. Weird. Still, he knows a bit about music so we can talk and the fact that I'm sat with a guy keeps the creepazoids away.'

'Have you arranged to meet him again?'

'No – same as before. See you when I see you sort of thing. So, what's with the Spanish guitar thing? You going to play for the crowd today, Dominic?'

'No, not today. I'm not good enough yet. It's not as fanatical here as in Andalucia but they do take their guitar very seriously. It's more than an art form; it's part of their culture and national identity so one does it very well or not all. One day.'

'I'm sure. What's the plan for today then?'

'Once you're ready we'll drive into town and go for a bit of a stroll round the local bars. Then we'll make our way to Miguel's and eat. After that it's go with the flow until we either stagger or take a taxi back here.'

'Why are we driving into town at all? You'll only have to pick the car up tomorrow? We could just walk there couldn't we?'

'Well my thought was that if you're wearing a LBD you'll probably be wearing shoes with some amount of heel. A sprained ankle can ruin your whole day and you've seen the crazy paving around here.'

'Good point. Considerate, too. OK. I'll go in and get ready and see you later.'

She left him in the shade by the pool. It was a pleasant temperature at this time of day and on the coast the perpetual breeze would have been quite cooling but the sun was climbing quickly so staying out of it was the sensible option.

ML resumed his guitar playing, sometimes just picking riffs which he repeated again and again until he was satisfied with the result, sometimes playing a longer piece which held itself together as a coherent tune. He played from memory with his eyes closed and the slightest of smiles on his face. An observer would have thought him able to continue for as long as he wished – a man alone with his music. This would have been wrong; ML's playing was almost automatic. What he was actually engaged in was an internal debate regarding the fate of his house guest. Details, decisions, doubts and dilemmas. Throw the dice or rig the deck? Death in the key of D.

'Hi, Dominic. How do I look?'

He stopped playing and opened his eyes, his smile gone in an instant. She had appeared at his side without him noticing, all his senses letting him down. The height of the sun told him that he had been lost in his thoughts for over an hour. That had never happened to him in his life and he felt a physical dislocation from his surroundings for the briefest of moments before he gathered his wits together to really look at Catherine. She was stunning. Her silver hair was perfect, so he assumed that she had packed the electric kit that women used to obtain such an effect. Her eyes had been made up with a blend of black and sparking pearl which served both to enlarge their size and match her hair colour. This effect was amplified by iridescent pearl lip gloss. The editor of Vogue would have shed blood to have such a face on the cover.

She was, indeed, wearing a simple black cocktail dress, strapless with the line broken by a silver lamé belt. Her shoes were two inch black suede with a single strap on the ankle. Her only jewellery was a discrete silver necklace and a modernistic silver bracelet on her right wrist.

'I've changed my mind' said ML. 'We are not going to drive to the old town; we are going to walk down the main street just to observe all the car crashes. Catherine, you are absolutely beautiful.'

'Gee, thanks. Glad you like it.'

'I thought you were going to wear gold?'

'Change of mind. It's a matter of accessories. Don't ask; it's a girl thing.'

'Seriously, though; if you have jewellery in your room you might wish to put it in my safe. This place has a good alarm system but it's not Fort Knox.'

'Yeah, that's a good idea. My passport and driver's license too, I guess. Let's do that now before we go out.'

'OK bring down whatever you need to secure and I'll show you the system.'

Catherine went up to her room and returned with a small, leather purse which contained her documents, a variety of rings, chains and two expensive watches. She handed it all over to ML.

'If a crook is determined enough and has sufficient time, he will nearly always get what he wants. So we have to put ourselves into his mind set. If, and it's a bloody big if, he gains access to the house without setting off the alarms, he will go to the bedrooms and see if we have been dumb enough to leave valuables lying around. Finding none he will then start looking for the safe. There is one in my room but it contains little of value. However what will he find in the lounge behind this painting – ta dah – a very professional combination safe. The total amateur is now pissed off and will shit on the bed and steal my suits but it's unlikely that a total amateur could have bypassed the alarms so he will come prepared. It is possible to drill the lock on this model of safe if you have the right equipment and the time, so imagine our crook opens the safe, which I'll do using the combination. What do you think is inside, Catherine?'

'Diddly squat?'

'No; try again.'

'A booby trap?'

'Good idea but I don't know what the Spanish legal system would have to say about that. So, no again. What Pedro the prowler finds is a thousand euros, a Rolex watch and, praise the Lord, a little cellophane baggie of white powder. The Rolex is fake and the powder is for unblocking drains. God knows what it does to nasal passages. Anyway, Pedro is out of here temporarily happy. The real safe is here!

ML counted six marble tiles in from the far corner of the room along the wall then a further four in towards the centre of the room. Inserting a stiff knife between two tiles, he prised it up from the floor to reveal another combination lock.

'If our thief gets this far he deserves the damn money. The

combination is 19-48-68-0. You turn the dial five times to the right so that nineteen aligns with the centre mark, then four times to the left for forty eight, then three times to the right for sixty eight, then twice to the left to finish on zero. Once to the right and… it's open. Pass your purse to me.'

He dropped the small bag into the safe then scrambled the dial and replaced the marble square which concealed it.

'All safe, pardon the pun. Ready to go, Catherine' he asked.

'Yeah.'

'OK. I'll lock up and see you at the car.'

ML took the wheel and they turned left out of his driveway then took a right to follow the northern cost road which lead them part the Bristol Playa hotel complex and into Corralejo the back way. This was not a part of town frequented by tourists. The bars were small and dark, their habitués older males. The modernity and money of main street did not seem to have had much of an impact on this particular barrio.

At this hour on a Sunday there were few people up and about but eventually they came to a large corner bar called Casa Rincon where a dozen or so local men were drinking and eating tapas. All eyes turned in their direction as they entered and conversation stopped. As they took seats at a window table a local in his early twenties fell to his knees, clutching both hands to his chest and cried out. 'Ayuda me, senorita! Ayuda me! Es mi corazon, mi pobre corazon.'

The bar erupted with laughter and shouting. Two men dragged the first to the far side of the room where they proceeded to cuff him round the head and force beer down his throat.

Catherine turned to ML and said 'What the hell was that all about?'

'The young man was asking for your help. Apparently he has a problem with his heart. That's a word you'll hear a lot in Spain. I swear that every Spanish song ever written contains the word 'corazon'.'

Chapter Twenty Three

'Well, I think he deserves a reward for his courage. Is it OK to sing in here.'

'Go for it.'

Catherine walked to the bar where she ordered two beers which she took back to her table then, one bottle in hand, she approached the young man who had a 'heart complaint'. She looked down at him for a long moment and let the silence build then, a cappella, sang 'Every night in my dreams, I see you, I feel you.' She went all the way to the end of the Celine Dion number, holding her own breast whenever she came to the line 'my heart will go on and on'. When she finished she blew a kiss to the young man then returned to her table and ML. The bar erupted in applause and cheering. She remained the epitome of calmness. ML knew better.

'How's your heart rate?' he asked.

'Off the scale! I can't believe I just did that – stone sober too. The locals seemed to have liked it.'

'You will be the talk of the town, literally. What other tricks do you have up your metaphorical sleeve?'

'Hell, who knows? I'm taking my lead from you, Dominic. Make it up as you go along and see where it leads to. What did you think of the song, by the way?'

'Well sung, but every time I hear it I think of a joke. Celine Dion walks into a bar and the bartender says 'Why the long face?''

'I don't get it.'

'Don't worry, it's an English thing. Shall we leave before your public demands an encore? I don't really fancy a Sunday drinking session with this lot.'

'OK, Dominic; onward and upward.'

They left the Rincon to applause and ML promising to return soon with 'la inglessa hermosa' or the beautiful English girl. After a leisurely stroll around the back street and no more musical interludes they found themselves once more at the small Spanish fishing bar where they took a table next to the open French doors.

Miguel came out to greet them which involved ML in translating all the compliments the man wished to pay Catherine. Unsurprisingly the Gran Reserva came out again. It was going to be one of those days.

The atmosphere was calmer than on the last occasion that they had been in the bar. The clientele were more well to do and, as ML had foreseen, well dressed in their Sunday finery.

A large, dark skinned, jolly woman who was Miguel's wife shuttled back and forth between the kitchen and a small house directly across the street. Apparently she needed two places in order to produce her famous paella.

The barman approached with a plate of octopus for them but ML spoke to him before he could place it on their table.

'What did you say to him?' asked Catherine.

'I politely declined his excellent cephalopod and asked if it were possible for the beautiful lady to try their grilled sardines. Hope you like eating with your fingers.'

'Sardines, huh? And the new experiences just keep on coming.'

The afternoon passed pleasantly. The locals smiled at them thinking they made a handsome couple but, once it was clear that Catherine was unable to join in the conversation, they were left to their own devices.

The paella did not appear until one thirty by which time every seat was taken. The sardines had been good; meaty and simply grilled with sea salt. The main dish was visually spectacular with brightly coloured crustaceans competing for space with various molluscs on a bed of saffron rice whose golden hue was encrusted with the red of the peppers and the yellow of the cut lemons.

ML and Catherine had a so called medium serving each which was enough to fill them. She declared that it tasted as good as it looked and asked him if she could obtain the recipe.

He laughed. 'There is no recipe; the dish is different every week. She puts into it whatever her sons bring her back from the sea that morning. I can tell you the basics of making paella myself – it's not difficult – but you have to find the meat and fish you want to use and then work out their different cooking times so that it all comes together. Therein lies the only difficulty.'

'OK, Dominic, I'll hold you to that. After you have taught me to speak Spanish you can give me cookery lessons.'

'Not forgetting learning a musical instrument of course.'

'No; I said that more as a joke than anything. Singing is what I love and I need to work on it, I know. I just don't know which route to take. Any ideas, Dominic?'

'Tough one; so far I've heard you sing Proud Mary by Credence and My Heart Will Go On by Celine Dion. You could not have more contrasting songs unless you plumbed the depths of rap or punk. The problem is that you performed both equally well. Which did you enjoy singing the most?'

'Proud Mary. It has energy, it's easy to sing and the crowd gets into it too. Doing Celine is a damn sight harder. Having said that, I know that it shows off my voice more. I don't know.'

'Here's a question then; could you imagine listening to My Heart Will Go On and similar songs for ninety minutes?'

'Jesus, no! I'd slit my wrists after half an hour.'

'And that's why Celine varies her live act so much. I heard her sing in Vegas a few years ago and that is one of the toughest gigs going. She knew that they were all waiting for the 'Titanic' song and that she'd get a standing ovation as she does every evening but she gave them all the songs she's known for plus other people's material. Do you know 'I Drove All Night' Cindy Lauper?'

'Yup.'

'Well Celine did that to a disco beat but still showing her vocal power. Made Lauper sound like an asthmatic frog.'

'So what are you trying to say here?'

'That if you have a good voice you don't have to confine yourself to one style. But you do need a vocal hook.'

'What does that mean?'

'It means that you have something in your voice that is unique to you and immediately identifies you as the singer in a listener's ear. Abba for example. Those two Swedish girls had good voices, they were multilingual but, if you listen carefully, they always slightly mispronounce a couple of words. This has the added advantage of being quite sexy. It's like when I visit the States; some woman is guaranteed to say 'Oh my God – I just love your accent'. I never point out that, from an English perspective, it is actually <u>she</u> who has an accent.'

'I think I get this. It's like Ricky Martin doing his La Vida Loca crap. Because it's different, it's definitely him and sexy. I'd never thought of that before.'

'Difference is the main element of a sexual attraction. Just think of a group of single males and females, all looking and acting more of less the same, the chat up lines are all same old, same old and then there's a new kid in town. He or she will be the centre of attention and, unless they have obvious physical or mental defects will be de facto attractive. There may even be a biological imperative at work here. It makes sense to enlarge the gene pool.'

'Is that your line when you hit on a girl, Dominic? Want to come back to my place and enlarge the gene pool? That would only work in San Francisco.'

'I'd have to explain what a gene pool was for a San Franciscan. No; can't see that line ever working.'

The two of them returned to the subject of female vocalists past and present to see if there was anyone whom Catherine deemed a suitable role model. It was a search doomed to failure; she was too much her own person.

The afternoon continued in a relaxed and happy manner with the cast of characters changing continuously. Nearly everyone who entered the bar had something to eat and the stock of fresh fish which was displayed on the counter was dwindling rapidly.

ML settled the bill which resulted in Miguel arriving at their table with a bottle of deep brown liquid and three glasses.

'Here we go – another mystery Spanish drink' said ML.

'You really don't know what it is?' asked Catherine.

'No, all I know is that we have to drink it in one or he will be offended. He's been doing this to me for years. Don't worry; I haven't been sick yet. Cheers.'

The three of them raised their large shot glasses and knocked back the liqueur. Miguel waited for their reaction not even trying to hide his amusement.

'That is lovely' said Catherine. 'What on earth is it?'

'It's caramel vodka and should have been banned under the dangerous drugs act' replied ML.

He spoke in rapid Spanish to Miguel who passed the bottle to him so he could read the label.

'Yes indeed. It's so sweet that girls love it. It also happens to be eighty proof. If you had a session on this stuff it would be a short one with a severe hangover guaranteed. Your only hope would be that you'd become so out of it that you'd end up in hospital getting to know the medic with the stomach pump.'

'But it tastes so nice. One's not going to kill me, is it?'

'Of course not but you can see how one could turn into several. In alcohol terms, you have just downed the equivalent of three large whiskies.'

Miguel interrupted then by speaking very slowly to Catherine. Taking his enquiry to mean 'had she enjoyed the drink' she gave him a thumbs up and said 'Muy bueno, Senor Miguel' whereupon he refilled her glass to the brim.

'Nice one, Catherine. He just asked if you'd like another and you accepted – in Spanish!'

Miguel raised the bottle to ML who covered his own glass with his hand. They exchanged words rapidly and Miguel went to the bar to fetch two fresh glasses for the men and a bottle of

103 Spanish brandy. Sunday lunch was in danger of becoming Sunday bender.

'Do I have to down this in one, Dominic?'

'No; sipping is acceptable. That's what we will be doing with this ciento tres. I would advise you to take some water though.'

'Yes; good idea. Will I be alright after this?'

'You're with me. You'll be all right.'

'If a guy had said that to me in the States I'd have called him a patronising chauvinist. How come I don't feel offended when you come out with a macho comment like that?'

'I'd say that it would be more useful for you to think about it then answer your own question.'

Catherine looked at him and realised that he was right. So, what was the answer? In all the time she had spent in his company he had never shown himself to be macho. He encouraged her to do her own thing and had set out a bare minimum of house rules. At the end of the day, she was on his turf here and she did feel safe in his company. She supposed that the real question was where did justifiable self confidence cross the line into arrogant chauvinism.

'That was rude of me, Dominic. I apologise. Would it be okay if I paid for a last round of drinks with Miguel then we went home for a siesta?'

'A woman paying for his drink? I'll have to negotiate this but I'm sure it'll be all right. You're not planning on having another of those caramel vodkas are you?'

'No; I need to slow it down a bit. Champagne?'

ML smiled and nodded in approval. Turning to Miguel he explained that he lady wished to express her appreciation for his hospitality by buying drinks for him, his wife and the bar staff. Freixnet if possible.

Miguel responded by kissing her on both cheeks and bellowing orders to his staff. In minutes all service had ceased as the barmen, Miguel and his wife were at Catherine's table toasting her health, her beauty and her friendship. ML had to interpret all this (and her responses) all of which took time so that, an hour later, three bottles had been consumed.

With much cheering and applause following them, ML and Catherine bade the company farewell and retraced their steps back to the villa.

Her balance was only slightly off as they linked arms and took the coast road that avoided the main street. Driving was not an option. ML was aware of her impressive breasts bumping into his side rather more often than lack of equilibrium would dictate. This he put down to lack of subtlety on the part of the young.

Arriving back at the villa the first thing they did was to kick off their footwear and enjoy the coolness of the marble floor on their feet. His boots had become hot and her shoes were killing her.

'I'm going to grab a shower and then catch some sun by the pool' said ML.

'Sounds good. Eh, would it be okay if I were to lie out there topless!' asked Catherine.

'We're not overlooked by anyone so no problem at all. I might even take to you to the nudist beach one day.'

He turned his back on her and went into the kitchen to get a cold drink from the fridge. As he was seeing what there was to choose from her heard her voice shout from the dining area 'Shit!'

He went out to her. 'What's wrong?!'

'Damn zipper on this dress is bust or stuck or something.'

'Let me take a look.'

The zip was on the side of the dress and hidden by a double fold in the material. It was also small and difficult to manipulate. As he was trying to do this in close proximity to a very sexy young woman with his cock getting stiffer by the second it was well nigh impossible. Catherine moved her stance slightly and her hip bone came into contact with his hardness. She stoked it with her fingers through his trousers.

'Now that's what I call a giveaway, Dominic.'

The zip gave, the dress dropped to the floor leaving Catherine naked save for a black cotton thong. ML's right hand went between her legs to stroke her lips in turn through the material. She was soaking. 'So's that, Catherine.'

She undressed him totally and slid off her thong and placed her hands behind his head to pull his mouth down onto hers. He responded to her hunger with control. He broke the kiss, placed his hands beneath her buttocks and lifted her onto the dining room table.

'Lie back and hold onto the side' he instructed. She obeyed. He walked up between her legs, placed the backs of her knees on his shoulders and slid inside her. Catherine was young, tight and wet; he was thick, engorged and experienced. It made for very good sex. He established a rhythm to suit her which made her orgasm suddenly and noisily. He slowed down to watch her catch her breath as she looked up at him along the length of her body.

Still inside her, he placed her legs around his waist, bent his head to hers for her arms to clasp the back of his neck then he stood up and, taking most of her weight by putting his hands under her buttocks again, proceeded to walk through the house, up the stairs and into her bedroom with his cock moving deep inside her all the time. By the time she was placed on her bed she had orgasmed again and was moaning with her eyes closed when he knelt behind her and took her from the rear. As his cock moved in and out of her in long controlled strokes, he put his finger in his mouth to wet it then drew gentle patterns on her anus. Her moans were becoming gasps, her head was whipping around like that ugly kid in The Exorcist so he increased his tempo and exploded inside her to coincide with her third climax of the afternoon.

They lay in bed with their different post coital thoughts. He hoped that he had not done too much and scared her off. Young

Americans were an unknown species for him. She hoped that he did not think her a total slut and distance himself from her. He saved the situation by gently taking her chin in his hand and saying. 'You're beautiful, that was magic, thank you.' He kissed her gently on the lips and stroked her hair. 'I'm going to take that shower now. See you by the pool?'

'If I can still walk, yeah. See you in a few minutes, Dominic.'

After showering, Catherine decided not to bother with swimwear at all and just wrapped herself in a diaphanous sarong. When she arrived at the pool she noticed that the sun loungers had been repositioned so that two of them were next to each other. Dominic (as she thought of him) was lying on one of them with an ice bucket full of San Miguel cans at his side. He looked up as her shadow fell across his torso and said 'Hi there. Fancy a beer?'

'Only if you promise to get me drunk and take advantage of me' she replied with a smile.

He returned the smile and popped a can for her. Catherine unselfconsciously dropped her sarong to the ground, took the beer and lay down next to him. They spent the late afternoon sipping their drinks, doing a few laps and occasionally exchanging kisses which were not passionate but promised more to come.

They barely spoke such was the level of comfort that they had attained. It sufficed for ML to raise the bottle of sun lotion in Catherine's direction for her to nod and turn over for him to oil her back. Although they were physically close, neither crowded the others space. After a while she fell asleep, supine, her legs slightly parted, as relaxed and defenceless as a human can be.

ML continued to drink and reflect on what had occurred. It had always been a possibility that she would fall for him. He was well aware that he was attractive to a certain kind of woman. He had not anticipated it happening so quickly and he certainly had not expected to develop any feelings himself for this innocent abroad – but he was. His face showed no expression as he looked down on her perfect sleeping form. His mind was contrasting the many different scenarios which he could bring about after today. Very few of them ended well for the young American.

Chapter Twenty Four

Mark Goodchild awoke at seven on the Sunday morning and surveyed the wreckage of his bed. The room smelled like a pub before the cleaners had had a chance to do their job. The realisation of what he had done began to sink in and he was pleased to find that he could not care less. For an officer as senior as him to be having a relationship with a sergeant directly under his command was a career ending disciplinary offence. He would do it all over again in a heartbeat.

The bedroom door opened and Michelle walked in looking only slightly worse for wear. She crawled in under the covers, put her arm around his chest and said 'Good morning. How are you feeling?'

Thinking that the question could be answered at multiple levels on 'the morning after' he opted for a safe response and said 'I'm fine. You?'

'Great. I've been to the loo so we're okay.'

'Sorry; I don't follow you.'

'Oh yea you do. Big, strong rugby guys like you wake up in the morning with a big, strong hard-on and all you want to do is bounce on a small person like me who has a full bladder. So, I've been to the loo.'

'That's an extremely unfair generalisation and…' His protestations had to stop as her hands were around his cock which was proving him a liar. She swung her left leg over him and guided his shaft inside her and then proceeded to perform a pole dance on him which would have made her a star from LA to Thailand and most points in between. When he came he understood why the French called this 'la petit mort'. In fact any greater intensity and he reckoned he'd slip into cardiac arrest.

Once they had regained their breath, Michelle looked across to him and said 'I guess we have to go back to being police officers now, Mark.'

'Yes, we do. Ten families demand it.'

'Is there anything for us or was last night just last night?'

'Do you think I make a habit of taking my sergeants to bed, sergeant? Aaaargh!' he screamed as she bit quite hard on his right nipple.

'Try again' she purred.

'Sorry. Wrong answer. I'm flippant when I'm cornered. We're close to catching this freak and once it's over I'm going to insist on taking at least two weeks of the leave I have accrued. I'd like to share that time with you and we'll take it from there. Fair enough?'

'Where were you thinking of going?'

'The Basque Country. Beautiful place, great food and honest people. It's basically France without the French and Spain without the Brits.'

'Sounds perfect. I'll have to read up on it or you'll be playing tour guide. What's the plan for today?'

'Let's get cleaned up and hit the road ASAP. There's a caff on the edge of town that does a nice fried breakfast then we'll head on back to the Yard to check the messages from yesterday. I also need to speak with Martin at some stage as do you I suppose.'

'Yes. I've narrowed the target list for the teams to follow up tomorrow into a more manageable number but I need to cross-reference it with Martin. I was going to do this last night but something came up.'

'And we both know what the something was. I'm escaping to the safety of the bathroom. There's toiletries and towels in the shower next to the second bedroom. See you downstairs in a bit.'

He bent down and kissed her mouth softly. She was equally gentle in her response but it still took an effort for them to break the contact and head off to their respective bathrooms.

Half an hour later they were demolishing enormous plates of bacon, sausage, tomatoes, mushrooms and fried bread washed down with mugs of strong, sweet tea. Suitably refuelled, they set off east for London with Goodchild driving and Stone reviewing her notes on her laptop. It being Sunday, they made good time into the capital and headed up to the Orion offices in a positive frame of mind.

The uniformed sergeant from Addison's staff who had been on shift to field calls was happy to be relieved of duty so that he could spend some of his Sunday with his family.

Goodchild and Stone logged on to their computers and began the day's work. Between them they prioritised a list of potential victims for the field teams to follow up on. They only needed Carver's input then they could finalise it and give it a green light.

'Shall I give him a call, boss?' asked Michelle.

'No. He's been working hard at this and, for all we know, could be in the middle of an interview right now. Martin'll make contact when he has to.'

'I've nothing to do for the moment. I think we should start putting our minds to how we are going to proceed if we decide that Guest is our man. Imagine if Martin turns up with a photo of him and Lauren Prospero together, taken on the last night she was seen alive; we'd move on that, wouldn't we?'

'If he were the last person to see her alive then, yes. But he could easily say that lots of girls want their photos taken with the singer and that she did not leave the pub with him. Nor can we link him to Jennifer Duncan. Apart from what Brendan Fitzgerald told us we have nothing. So, no; I would not move unless we had something more solid.'

'What would constitute 'solid' for you?'

'A third victim ID that tied in with a gig by our friend. Three goes beyond coincidence and I'd definitely have him in and sweat him. Or at least have Chris van Dyke do a psych evaluation. You never know; the right approach and he might just give us chapter and verse of what he's been up to for five years.'

'We're relying on the field teams to come up with another ID then. OK, let's look at another detail which we have not really covered. All this started with the email to your mate Tucker. If Tony Guest is our killer, who is ML?'

'Good question. It has to be someone who knew <u>exactly</u> where the box was buried and what it contained so it's either the killer, who we believe to be Guest or … Christ! The bastard has an accomplice.'

'This is what I meant when I said we should start putting our heads together. I suppose we now need a list of Guest's known associates. I'll get on that in a moment. Another question; any thoughts as to what 'ML' stands for?'

'No. It could be anything from Music Lover to Mutilating Loony. I don't think it's worth speculating on that at this time, Michelle.'

'Perhaps it might be worth running it past van Dyke?'

'OK. He's not exactly been over utilised so far. I'll sort that one out. In fact we could do with an Orion meeting on Monday.'

'I still cannot get my head around the original email. It's a challenge to solve this case, in effect denouncing the uselessness of the police. Why would either the killer or, if he has one, his accomplice start us on the hunt?'

'I don't look for reasons, Michelle. I just try and catch the sick bastards. If you or I try to understand the workings of the mind of the criminally insane then we'll fail. Take it from me, they inhabit a planet where our rules of logic do not apply. It's also why I am somewhat reluctant to use people like van Dyke. If you really can understand those who commit monstrous acts then it follows that you have a bit of the monster in yourself.'

'I'll have to think about that one. There is another thing; according to the schedule of gigs that Martin obtained from

Guest's wife, the guy is due to play in Birmingham Monday week. I've checked flight manifests from Fuerteventura and our guy is booked to fly direct to Manchester on a flight with an ETA of 1630 hours. His vehicle is parked in the long stay area at the airport so it's feasible that he could be home with his wife by 1900 hours – and guess what they are going to talk about? Martin's visit.'

'And if he is our boy how is he going to react? I suppose that depends on whether or not it was he who sent the email to Roger Tucker. If it was him, this could be part of his game and he will have foreseen it and play things cool. Something makes him believe that he is untouchable. If, however, Guest is not ML then anything could happen. At the very least he is forewarned that we are interested in him or he might panic and try to bolt.'

'So we need a plan in place ASAP. Also, have you thought of the possibility that he may phone his wife now and again?'

'I did and discounted it. From what Martin said after meeting Gillian Guest he does not even call her when he's on the road in the UK. She knows how to get hold of him if something urgent came up; there are no children for him to call home to and he does not strike me as the kind of man to phone from Spain to say 'missing you babe' so I've taken that risk.'

'Big risk, boss. If he disappears because wifey phoned him and said that the police had paid her a call – well, I don't have to paint you a picture but I much prefer you with your balls where they are.'

The phone rang and Michelle picked up.

'Hi, Martin. Yes, we both are. Do you want a word? He's right here. All right; see you then.'

'That was Martin. He's on his way in and has info on the Prospero girl that he wants to talk with us about. He thinks he should be with us in about fifteen. I'll use that time to make a start on finding out who Guest's buddies are.'

'I've a couple of things to be getting on with as well. Looks like it could be a long Sunday, Michelle.'

It was, in fact, closer to thirty minutes later that Martin Carver entered the Orion office. He was his usual well dressed self, clean shaven and groomed but tell tale signs of darkness had appeared below his eyes indicating the onset of fatigue. Neither Stone nor Goodchild commented on that fact.

'Good morning, Martin' said Goodchild. 'How was Stafford?'

'Long, but rewarding. I managed to interview six people who knew Lauren Prospero from the hospital where she worked. These ranged from consultant doctors to other medical secretaries and they all said the same things about her. Fantastic at her job, well liked as a person, very pretty but did not know it, quiet to the point of shyness. The only subject about which she would become animated was music. No known boyfriend or girlfriend for that matter. She never went to staff drinking parties, saying that she had to be home to look after her elderly parents. Then I visited the Boar's Head where the landlord remembered her well, the reason being that he asked to see her ID the first time she came in. Now get this; the landlord is a William Shakespeare nut and for him, Prospero means the Tempest which apparently was Shakespeare's last play. Lauren had never read 'the master' in her life, much to the landlord's horror so he took it upon himself to try and educate her. Whenever she came in, he would make a point of serving her himself and try to interest her in this one particular play. She politely declined his offer of going to the theatre with him. 'I think she saw me as Caliban' he said to me. Sad old git. Anyway, I put up with half an hour of his crap until I struck lucky. He had some photos of her. Look at these.'

Carver handed over six photo's of varying quality. They were all interiors of a busy pub at night. In most of the shots the customers were sat at their tables drinking, looking at something to the left of the camera which was not in shot – presumably the musician.

In two of them quite a few people were on their feet dancing. Again, the musician could not be seen.

'There is a common denominator in all these which, unless you're told what it is, would take a while to spot' said Carver. 'So I'll tell you. This girl here, here, here, here, here and here is Lauren Prospero.'

In two of the shots the girl was at the rear of the bar sat behind a table so all one could tell about her was that she had shoulder length, straight brown hair and was wearing a dark blue jacket over a turquoise, crew necked top. In another two of the shots she was closer to the camera and sat in such a position that one could see her from head to toe. Her hair was a fair bit shorter and looked more styled. She was wearing the same jacket as in the other two shots but now one could see that it was part of a trouser suit. The turquoise crew neck had been replaced by a red blouse of a material that had a sheen to it. In the last two shots the camera has caught Lauren Prospero dancing. Her hair was now so short that it could be called elfin and was subtly, but well made up. She was wearing a halter necked dress in an expensive looking black material that ended half way down her thighs which were clad in sheer, black tights. For the first time, she was smiling – a broad smile that showed both her teeth and her happiness.

'Bloody hell! Why are there no shots of the musician?' exclaimed Goodchild.

'Because the pervy landlord only wanted to snap the girl' replied Carver. 'But, for my next trick, we turn the photos over and hey presto!'

On the back of each photo someone had written a date and the single word 'Guest'.

'I've checked with the list of gig dates that Gillian Guest gave me; they match' said Carver.

The room went absolutely quiet as each of the three officers evaluated this new information.

'Well done, Martin' said Goodchild. 'Do you have anything else for us — like how did you obtain this in one visit and the local yokels didn't during the initial missing persons enquiry?'

'The locals missed it for a couple of reasons. None of Lauren's colleague's knew that she had any social life. She'd told them she went home to her elderly parents. That was not true. Her parents live in Swindon which is about eighty miles south of Stafford so I stopped off on the way back here. The father is a forty five year old fireman and I reckon he's not quite kosher. He said all the right things but there was no sincerity to him. From the look of him he pumps iron and guzzles ale. A bully, I'd say. The mother is a broken woman, either through the loss of her daughter or living with her pig of a husband. I wish I'd had you with me, Michelle, to split them up. Anyway, they showed me a photo album with the usual family snaps in them. Lauren was an only child and in every photo her father is touching her in what I would describe as a propriatorial way. The photo that they gave to Staffs police was the most recent they had of the girl so she would have been just coming up to eighteen. The police cropped Lauren's image from this to use in their search. Here's the result.'

Carver took an A4 piece of paper from a folder. It was the standard 'Have You Seen This Girl?' sort of thing plus a contact number to call. In the photo Lauren looked like a grumpy adolescent.

'To be fair to the locals' continued Carver 'they visited every venue where music was played, including the Boar's Head, but who the hell was going to recognise her from that?'

'A question, Martin' said Michelle. 'Why did the landlord not pick up on the girl's name if he had been so taken by it?'

'I asked him that and he has no recollection of the police ever enquiring after Lauren. He does take one day off a week — either Tuesdays or Wednesdays or he could have been out doing his banking or the cash and carry run. Whatever. If the locals spoke to someone it was a member of staff. I think we need to have a look at the Staffs police file, boss.'

'Correct. I'll organise that today. OK, Martin. I think that you need to get off home now. You've put in a lot of hours and miles; you'd probably like to get to your own bed.'

'I'd love to but there's still more to do today. I'd sleep better if I knew what you were planning to do with this info, boss.'

'Nothing for the moment, Martin. I'm calling an Orion meeting, to include van Dyke, for 0800 tomorrow morning. I'll see you then.'

'Are you planning on pulling Guest in for questioning, boss?'

'Michelle; update Martin on what we were talking about. I'm going upstairs on some other business. I'll be back in twenty minutes and I expect you not to be here when I return, Martin.'

Goodchild rose and left the room at a brisk pace, not giving Carver a chance to say anything more.

'What the fuck was that all about, Michelle?'

'Derek Clarkson was found dead at his home yesterday. They were good friends for years so I reckon he's taking it hard and trying not to show it.'

'What happened?'

'Addison phoned him when we were at the rugby club. I don't know the details and the P.M. has not been carried out yet but, reading between the lines, the poor bastard drank himself to death.'

'Is the boss functioning?'

'Yes. We finished what we had to at the rugby club – no joy there by the way – then we went and had one drink in Clarkson's name. That's it. I don't know if he went home and got hammered but he picked me up from the Holiday Inn on time and has not spoken about it since.'

'Fair enough. OK, update me then. Why is he not going to pull the singing arsehole in?'

Michelle went over the ground that she and Goodchild had

covered whilst waiting for Carver to arrive. At the end of her dissertation her colleague shook his head slowly.

'So, basically what you're saying is that the circumstantial evidence we have is not sufficient to warrant pulling Guest in. But if we had just one more piece of evidence then we would. Am I understanding you correctly?'

'Yes, Martin. That's about it.'

'Have a look again at the photos where Lauren Prospero is dancing. Turn them over. The date is Friday the thirteenth, two thousand and eight. How odd is that, Michelle?'

'I don't get you, Martin. You're not going all superstitious on us are you?'

'Not at all; but that date was the last on which the girl was seen alive. See you tomorrow.'

Carver picked up his briefcase and laptop then left the room without a backward glance. Michelle sat, stunned, looking at the date on the back of the photo then turned it over to look at the image of the beautiful, happy, young woman who was dancing her life away.

'Bloody fucking hell! I'll get this piece of shit if it's the last thing I ever do' she said aloud.

Putting away her anger, Michelle Stone applied herself to the task of finding out who Guest's closest friends were. She was still mixing online searches with phone calls when Mark Goodchild came back to the office.

'How's it going?' he asked her.

'Nothing exciting. I've been drawing up a CV of Guest since he was a kid and trying to see if he's still in touch with some pal from his formative days. That's when the strongest bonds are made and if he has a buddy who helps him in serial murders and mutilations it would make the Kray twins look like casual acquaintances'.'

'Makes sense; come up with anything?'

'Just the one so far; a Gary Raven. Same age as Guest, went to school with him but stayed on an extra two years to take his A levels – he passed in Biology, Physics and Maths. Could have gone to college with his grades but went into music the same as his pal. He is a member of the same band as Guest but spends most of his time on the solo circuit. Briefly married, now divorced, no kids. Lives about a mile from where he grew up in Barnet, North London. Raven's criminal record is interesting and he's been bloody lucky to avoid going inside. Seven counts of possession of cannabis; he's always had just too little to have been prosecuted for intent to distribute. He's racked up so many points for DUI and speeding that he received an eighteen month ban in 1990 but he saved his best for the year after; he appeared in Crown Court on a charge of grievous bodily harm. A pub fight turned into a near riot and a guy was hospitalised with brain damage; he recovered but it was Raven who was in the frame for line dancing on the victim's head whilst wearing cowboy boots. The prosecution only had one witness and he failed to turn up on two consecutive occasions so the case was thrown out. A warrant was issued for contempt of court but the locals did not find the missing witness for another three months. He turned up dead in a squat in Camden with a body full of smack and the needle broken off in his arm. Coroner's verdict was death by misadventure.'

'This stinks.'

'Like a Syrian sewer. Raven had pleaded not guilty. He admitted to being in the brawl, along with about twenty other people, but denied kicking anyone. Since then he has not even gone through a red light.'

'Learned his lesson, cleaned up his act or is he just more careful? I think it would be useful to see if he just happened to be playing gigs in the same towns as Guest and at the same time. Can you pull that sort of info from the net, Michelle?'

'I'll try but I doubt it. I reckon his tax records would be more revealing. Probably too much to hope that Raven has someone like Gillian Guest keeping a record of what he had been doing for the past few years. I'll get on it anyway and let you know, boss. You sticking around today?'

'I'll be in and out. I'm going to be involved in organising Derek Clarkson's funeral and I'd better write up a progress report for Addison. I've a feeling that he might want it for Monday morning.'

'Why don't you see if he'd care to attend the Orion meeting tomorrow, boss?'

'Never happen, Michelle. We are deniable and someone in his position is going to keep his distance from us. Because of the lies we told at the very start of this investigation, we have painted ourselves into a corner. If Clarkson had not been known for his drinking, I'm sure he would have been the fall guy here. As it is, if I'm not careful, it'll be my turn in the barrel.'

'Oh, I see – I think' said Michelle in a suddenly small voice. 'I'm not used to the political side of police work.'

'Put in long hours, solve cases, keep your nose clean and get promoted. Politics will then follow as sure as bullshit follows lawyers.'

'I'll crack on, then. See you later.' She turned back to her computer and continued her searching.

Goodchild left her to it and went to his own office to contact his Lodge brethren to organise Clarkson's funeral. He was pretty certain that his friend had no close family and he was equally sure that the Met would not exactly be honouring the man's memory.

It was two hours before he returned to Orion where Michelle was still at her keyboard typing up notes she had made during her search.

'Ready to take a break, Michelle?' he asked.

'Give me five minutes and I'll be done. Then we can go and drink lunch.'

'Fine. I'll get a warm body down to monitor the phones and I'll see you in the Feathers for beer and a debrief.'

'Or wine and a working lunch. See you in a bit.'

She went back to her work then closed everything down and tidied her desk locking all her loose papers in the safe just as a uniformed sergeant of about fifty years of age arrived. He had obviously pulled this sort of duty before as he was carrying a thick paperback to pass the time with. Michelle quickly briefed him then headed off to the Feathers for lunch.

Pubs in central London on a Sunday can be a gastronomic nightmare. Many of them go for the carvery option which often means slices of roast meat that has sat under the warming lamps for so long that it tastes of sawdust and the vegetables, already overcooked in the English fashion are beginning to take on the consistency of soup. Mark and Michelle struck lucky with good slices of pink sirloin served in soft, warm baps with homemade horseradish. They found a quiet corner table to eat their food and drink their respective drinks – Guinness for him, red wine for her. They'd been working non-stop all morning and breakfast was a faint memory; the fuel was needed.

Once they'd finished, Goodchild asked Michelle to tell him how far she'd progressed.

'Before I talk about Raven, boss, there is one thing I must point out. You remember the photos of Lauren Prospero where she is dancing?'

'Of course.'

'Well the date on the back was Friday the thirteenth; that was the last day when anyone saw her alive.'

'Fuck-a-doodle-doo! I'm going senile. When did you notice this, Michelle?'

'I didn't; Martin pointed it out to me when you had left the room. You'd put his nose out a bit when you ordered him to go home.'

'I'll put him in fucking traction if he ever keeps information from me again! What's he think he's playing at? Bloody prima donna. OK, in and of itself, this is not important. On the other hand, it is another piece of very strong circumstantial evidence against Guest. Moving on; what about Raven?'

'He pays his taxes and has an accountant whom I've been unable to contact. Mobile is switched off, landline goes to answer phone. It is Sunday so he could be on a golf course or something. He is in North London as well, so someone could pop up and see him tomorrow if I don't manage to talk to him today. Obviously I don't want to leave a message or it might find its way to Raven.'

'Have you been able to place Raven in the same town as Guest? Where was he when the Duncan and Prospero girls vanished?'

'No joy yet, boss. Gary Raven is an unusual name and I cannot find any reference to a musician called that anywhere. It's possible that he has a stage name. His accountant will know if that's the case. Sorry.'

'How does Raven seem to you, Michelle? You've been looking at him for a couple of hours now.'

'At first sight it's a case of clever, bad boy who saw the light and cleaned up his act. But, once you look more closely, there are indicators that something is not quite right. His declared income has only been around the thirty – thirty five thousand mark over the past five years or so, either he doesn't do many gigs, or he's paid a lot less than his friend Guest. His credit rating is acceptable, he has the full range of credit and debit cards plus he owns his house outright.'

'Foreign travel?'

'Lots. He takes the ferry to Calais four times a year. Once he's in France he can drive anywhere within the European Union and we would have no way of knowing where he went – as long as he was paying in cash to keep under the radar. I've also got him as a visitor to India and Sri Lanka every other year.'

Chapter Twenty Four

'How about Thailand or Turkey?'

'Negative; it does smell of drugs though.'

'Maybe. What I'm also thinking is the countries of eastern Europe which are now members of the EU. If Raven were floating around there using cash not cards he would be close to Russia where the basic poison was produced that killed those hostages in Moscow.'

'And Raven was an accomplished science student who may have developed his skills over the years. Jesus – this can't be a coincidence. What now?'

'Back to the office. Give me two more hours searching for a Raven – Guest link. I'm going to call all the field teams for an update – they've gone too quiet for my liking. Then we'll call it a day. We need to be fresh for the morning.'

'As opposed to sexually exhausted and hung-over?'

They were comfortable enough with each other to smile at the previous evening's fun and games. For the moment they were managing to keep their personal and professional relationships in separate boxes but knew that the situation would have to be addressed one day. For the time being they were two adults with an important, stressful job to do who had snatched some time together. If they had had an everyday occupation their mutual attraction would not have been an issue. As it was, they walked the short distance back to New Scotland Yard together, but apart, to resume their hunt.

Two hours later they went their separate ways; Michelle to Victoria Train Station and thence to Crystal Palace, Goodchild by car back to Reading. Each was on the others mind as they tried to concentrate on processing the plethora of information that the investigation had yielded so far – although there is a school of thought that states that one can never have too much information.

Back at their respective abodes, each followed a very similar route. Pour a drink, review the case notes and try to think of a way forward. Whenever one of them stood up to take a break or replenish a glass, they were tempted to phone the other. Neither did for reasons that the other would have found silly. So, on that Sunday night, each slept alone thinking that they had done the mature, responsible thing and was able to drift away with Morpheus, looking forward to the morrow.

Chapter Twenty Five

The days for ML and Catherine were developing a rhythm of their own. They had not even gone out for the music on the Sunday evening, content to stay by the pool until the drop in temperature necessitated the donning of clothes. ML had made the short run to the Chinese restaurant for take away this time which they ate in the villa's kitchen.

Afterwards he gave her her first guitar lesson, resulting in the predictable complaints of how much the strings hurt the tips of her fingers. But she persisted and proved a competent pupil, finally mastering, sort of, a three chord change that had a sound approaching what one could call music.

Intelligently, she quit whilst she was still ahead, handing the instrument back to him so that he could play for her. She sang along and learned new songs from him; he showed her how to harmonise and their voices went well together. The beer gave way to wine and the wine took them to her bed where he made slow love to her, using classic techniques of tongue and fingers to give her two orgasms before he entered her, finishing the night in rapture.

Now it was Monday morning. ML was just putting the final touches to a mixed fruit salad when Catherine padded barefoot into the kitchen.

'Hi' she said.

'Hi, yourself. How are you today?'

'I'm good. Don't deserve to be after what I drank yesterday but, yeah, I'm good. You didn't wake me.'

'You looked so peaceful and were smiling in your sleep so I thought I'd leave you to rest whilst I prepared some breakfast.'

'He prepares breakfast! Are there no ends to this guy's talents? How the hell have you escaped marriage Mr Lord?'

'I keep on moving; makes me a hard target to hit.'

'I see; typical commitment-phobia. I knew it. At least you're not perfect then.' She smiled as she uttered the words but he could sense the insecurity that behind them. Time for some charm, he decided.

'No; you're wrong there, Catherine. Please excuse my flippancy. The simple reason I've never married is that old cliché 'I've never met the right girl'. My lifestyle has precluded me from getting to know anyone well enough to even contemplate marriage but I have no fear of commitment per se. Having said that, I'll admit that I have not gone out of my way to look for a wife but if it happens, great; and I'd try and be the best husband I could.'

She looked at him carefully. He was speaking more seriously than ever he had and she saw a vulnerability in his face that had never been there before. As an intelligent, modern, young woman she was sure that she knew the truth of the matter; he was not scared of commitment. This self confident, multi-talented man of the world was terrified of rejection.

She walked towards him, put her palms on the sides if his face and looked up into his eyes. He knew that she was about to declare her love for him or something along those lines so he bent down and covered her mouth with his to give himself time to think.

Suddenly the most Godawful noise came screeching from upstairs; it was the sound of electric guitar as played by punk rockers.

They broke the kiss and ML shook his head with a rueful smile. 'Sorry, Catherine' he said. 'That's my phone for London calls. I must take this. Hold that thought.'

He bounded up the stairs leaving a bewildered American in the kitchen. Five minutes later he was back. He walked right past Catherine to the fridge from where he took a bottle of Freixenet Cava. He then picked up two champagne flutes and sat next to her on the lounge settee.

'Good news, I guess, Dominic. What the hell was that noise?' she asked.

'My mobile is linked to speakers and certain people I know have their own musical settings so I can tell who is calling. That particular racket was The Clash playing 'I Fought The Law'. The caller was my business lawyer and, yes, it was good news. He's just set up a deal for me which means I'll never have to work again so, cheers, my love.'

They touched glasses and drank. She looked at him and said 'What did you call me, Dominic?'

He paused as if doing a mental double take. 'God, sorry. It just slipped out; it felt the, I don't know, the natural thing to say.'

'Dominic, Dominic; you're starting to sound like Hugh fucking Grant and he's a jerk. You can say 'love' to me as much as you want on two conditions – A. you mean it and B. I get to say it back to you.'

He raised his eyebrows as thought surprised then drained his glass and placed it on the coffee table. Catherine followed suit.

'Those are fair conditions. What's not fair is that I need to be in London yesterday so I'm going to have to get moving now. Sorry.'

'Can I help? Can I come with you?'

'Thanks but there's not point in you spending half a day on a plane – you would hardly see me in London anyway. I'm going to sort out a flight now and I'll be back in twenty four hours. OK?'

'I guess so. Will you call me?'

'Of course I will. Right now I need to call someone else though. I just hope he's out of his pit.'

ML speed dialled a local number and was in luck; the man he wanted picked up on the fifth ring.

'Richard; it's Dominic. Good morning. Look, sorry to bother you at what, I know, is a terribly early hour for you but I require some help rather urgently. I need to be in London ASAP and I seem to remember that one of your contacts is a tame travel agent. That's right; time is more important than comfort here so if one of the cattle carriers that flys direct has a spot, I'll take it.

If all else fails would you get me an open return, first class, on whichever flight will get me to London the quickest. No. Hand luggage only. That's right; price is not an issue here, Richard. I'm packed already. Thanks, Richard; I'll wait for your call.'

ML finished the call and noticed that Catherine had replenished their flutes.

'That was interesting' she said. 'Your man Richard didn't ask many questions, did he?'

'Richard is one of those expats who lives on the margins of society. I don't ask him questions and pay him in cash for any services he renders me. He's one of the good guys and useful to know; having said that, I do keep him at arms length. OK. Time to pack. See you in a moment.'

ML mounted the stairs two at a time and was back in five minutes flat carrying a sports bag, his laptop and a two suiter. He placed it all by the front door then sat back down with Catherine.

'Look, I'm sorry to have to leave you like this,' he said 'but it can't be avoided. Are you OK staying here in the villa on your own or would you prefer a hotel until I return?'

'I'm fine here, Dominic as long as you're cool with it' she replied.

'Of course I'm fine with it. You know how to set the alarms and how to open the safe, don't you?'

'Yeah. I've got those covered. So, when exactly will you be back?'

'It all depends on flights. I need to meet my lawyer for a comprehensive briefing on what he has set up. If all goes well, I'll sign some papers Tuesday and get the first available flight back that afternoon so I reckon I'll be here tomorrow evening. As I said, I'll call you.'

'You'd better, pal' she said punching him playfully on the shoulder. Before he could respond ML's phone rang. He looked at the screen and was pleased to see that it was Richard.

'Richard; that was quick.' ML was silent as his fixer went into a long explanation about local aviation.

'I'm amazed, Richard. I did not know that Fuerteventura <u>had</u> VIP facilities. How much? One way only. OK. I'll take it. Tell them to warm the engines up or whatever they do. Would you take me to the airport, Richard? Good man. Yes. See you outside in ten. Bye.'

'Unbelievable' said ML. 'There's a private Learjet 55 doing nothing at the airport and is flying back to London for servicing today. It would have been empty but its mine for seven thousand five hundred Euros – cash. Bargain!'

'So you're just hopping on someone else's Learjet are you?'

'Not at all. It belongs to a charter company based in London and would have been flying back empty otherwise. I'm merely buying the pilots (and Richard) a rather large drink.'

'You don't really live like other people, do you Dominic?'

'If only you knew. Now; go and enjoy the music tonight. I'll call you as soon as I know what time I'm returning on Tuesday. On Wednesday I'm going to drive you around the island and we'll take things from there. Now come and kiss me before Richard arrives.'

She moved into his arms where they embraced with a restrained passion which would have progressed to who knows where if a car horn had not sounded from outside. Breaking away ML said 'Mi casa es su casa – don't forget to lock it. Hasta manana, guapa.' Then he stooped, gathered his luggage and was gone.

Catherine bolted the door and went back to the kitchen where she poured the wine away. It had lost its sparkle without Dominic in the room – plus she had not had brunch yet. She dutifully ate her way through the fruit that his hands had prepared for her; hands that had played her body as skilfully as they had played the guitar. Nothing in life had prepared her for a man like this. She felt that all she needed was a scruffy little dog and she would be Dorothy, caught up in a tornado, not of magical wind, but of emotion. The man she was falling in love with had just left her alone in a foreign country whose language she could not speak.

By rights she should be just a tad pissed off at Mister Dominic Lord but she was unable to be so. She washed the dishes and glasses, took a San Miguel from the fridge and walked out onto the pool area. Admiring the colour of the bougainvillaea and inhaling the heady scent of the frangipane she said aloud 'Beats the shit out of Kansas, Toto.'

§

In London the Orion team has assembled. In addition to Goodchild, who was chairing the meeting, Martin Carver, Michelle Stone, Doctors van Dyke and Watkins were present.

'Good morning everyone' he started. 'Thanks for arriving so promptly. I spent a good deal of yesterday putting together everything we know about this case. I stress the word 'know'. These are facts, not conjecture; there will be time for that later today. I want you to read the document in front of you and come back to me with comments, opinions and ideas. You may annotate your copies if you wish as they will remain in this office at the end of this meeting. Officers Carver and Stone; you will be familiar with nearly everything in the dossier but try and imagine that you are seeing it for the first time. I'm going to leave you to it for half an hour. Anyone want some food?'

Only the police officers answered in the affirmative. Neither of them were particularly hungry but knew that events could take an unexpected twist and leave them running on empty very quickly so they took on fuel when they could. It was the equivalent of a combat soldier sleeping whenever an opportunity arose.

Goodchild left them to it. The four people leafed through the papers in silence with the two academics making the most notes.

Van Dyke was not very good at controlling himself with his body language and facial expressions revealing that he was not at all comfortable with some of the material in front of him. Both

Carver and Stone picked up on this and exchanged a look that spoke volumes. They did not like the civilian being privy to all their operational secrets.

Carver thought that Goodchild must be mad to allow van Dyke such access. Perhaps he knew something that he and Stone didn't.

If Rachel Watkins had noticed anything she had given no sign of it, keeping her head down to speed read then stop to make a note regarding something that had caught her eye.

The four people in the room had finished their perusal of the dossier at more or less the same time and were reviewing their own notes when Goodchild returned carrying a small cardboard box from which emanated the unmistakable odour of bacon and toast. He handed a sandwich to each of his officers then demolished his own. Carver cleared the mess away and all eyes turned to Goodchild.

'Right; Doctor van Dyke. I'd like to hear from you first of all' said Goodchild.

'Before I start - is this meeting being minuted?' asked the criminal psychologist.

'No, it's not. This is an informal meeting where rank means nothing and anything can be said by anyone. In the business world it called brainstorming I believe. All right, Doctor?'

'Call me Chris, please. I won't pretend that I'm comfortable with this. It's obvious that the media have been lied to and if that ever comes out then you three will be lucky to get jobs as security guards in Toys-R-Us. I'm safe – I'm just an academic called in to consult but what about your position, Rachel? If the shit hits the fan some is going to stick to you.'

'I'll look after my own position, thank you Chris' said Doctor Watkins. 'I run a forensic laboratory where politics has no place. I'm sure that the police have thought this through.'

'Well' continued van Dyke 'something that stands out a mile is that the security services want nothing to do with us despite the, ah, exotic C.O.D. You are very isolated, Commander.'

'Thanks for your concern, Chris. Anything else now that you have got that off your chest?' said Goodchild.

'Well, the circumstantial evidence indicates very strongly that Guest is our man. However, he does not match my profile at all. At our first meeting I stated that the killer would be educated to graduate level; Guest left school at sixteen to pursue a career in music. It does not fit. I based that profile on the original email to the journalist, Tucker. Looking at Guest's CV I cannot see where he ever had the time or, indeed, the ability to amass the knowledge required to compose that original message. If it were not for the fact that he happened to be playing in towns where a couple of girls went missing – and bear in mind only one of those is certain – then he comes across as a good guy; a happy-go-lucky, singing fool, with a great, big heart.

His friend from schooldays is a totally different animal. Obviously bright – he chose not to go to university – anti-social and violent. We need to know more about him. He escaped the GBH charge by the skin of his teeth. If I were interviewing him, I'd dearly like to ask why he did not pursue a career in science. What made him turn to music? Was it the drugs which he perceived to be part of the lifestyle or the power that a musician has over an audience? The sender of the email is a classic case of narcissism. What is Mr Raven's view of himself? How did he cope in his formative years having such an unusual name – a name which most erudite people would instantly associate with Edgar Allan Poe. I'd be interested to know if Raven had a habit of getting into scrapes which did not come to the police's attention. We need to know a lot more about him.'

'Do you think that Raven and Guest could be operating together?' asked Goodchild.

'It's not impossible but it is unlikely. Serial killers who operate in pairs exist but are rare. There is almost always a sexual motivation at work. Think of Fred and Rose West or Brady and Hindley in this country. The same applies in the USA. Two males killing together is rare and usually stems from a severe mental disorder. The bond between a pair of serial killers is extremely strong and can be formed by marriage or a profound experience two people have undergone together; a prison sentence for example.

Whoever killed our ten victims is what is classified as an organised serial killer, one not motivated by sex but something else. In this country I can only think of one example of a pair of organised serial killers and that is Burke and Hare. Their motive, as we know, was financial gain.'

'So what you're saying here' interjected Carver 'is that the evidence points to Guest, your original profile was wrong and you don't have enough info on Raven to make any intelligent comment.'

Van Dyke was stunned into silence by the bluntness of Carver's appraisal. As a respected academic he was used to deference not criticism. He looked around the table but no help came his way. The Orion Team waited for him to respond.

'Well, you could put it that way.'

'No 'could' about it, sunshine, I just did' said Carver with barely concealed hostility.

'Very well; I doubt very much that a jobbing musician who left school at sixteen wrote that email so, with your evidence pointing strongly towards Guest, logically a third party is involved. Your work has only uncovered Raven and, superficially, he fits the profile of someone clever at covering his tracks. I can say no more until I have more material to work with.'

'I think you are underestimating Guest, Doctor van Dyke' said Michelle. 'Just because he left school at sixteen as an academic zero does not make him stupid. After all, whilst you have memorised facts and figures for your profession, he has memorised hundreds of different songs which he then has to interpret and perform whilst playing a musical instrument. Could you get up in public and do that?'

'It's nonsense to compare our respective fields, sergeant. His is, supposedly, art, mine is scientific.'

'That sounds like intellectual snobbery, Doctor' said Carver. 'Not all of us are convinced that what you do is scientific. The FBI are talking about closing down the behavioural science unit at Quantico you know.'

'OK that's enough' said Goodchild. 'Chris; thanks for your contribution. Doctor Watkins; the floor is yours.'

'I have very little to add to my original comments' said the diminutive doctor. 'I, like you, Commander prefer to deal in facts but we have a case here where the absence of data becomes a fact in itself. It is a given in forensics that a killer will interact with his victim and in doing so leave some trace of himself behind. As well as this, the victim must interact with the environment in which they are killed and pick up trace of that environment. I have to tell you that none of the ten digits show trace of another human being on them. The digits have not been washed; they all bear trace of substances which we all pick up during the course of a day or night. This varies from furniture polish to make up to wine and spirits. No two victims' fingers had picked up exactly the same thing.' Rachel Watkins paused to let her audience think about what she had just told them.

'What do you infer from that, Doctor?' asked Goodchild.

'Firstly, the victims did not know what hit them. There was no struggle between them and their killer therefore they were either rendered unconscious prior to being poisoned or the gas hits them from a remotely controlled delivery system which allows our murderer to keep his distance during the very short time it takes to act.

Secondly he must have a disposal site for the bodies. The two girls you've identified are from opposite ends of the country and this singer travels all over the place. If he is the killer I would say that it's likely that the other eight victims are from a widespread geographical area. I refuse to believe that he has dumped ten corpses, minus a digit, and we have not come across one therefore he has a disposal site, therefore he transports the bodies to said site, therefore you should be looking at his vehicle which, I see from your dossier, is sat at Manchester airport.' Doctor Watkins voice had risen in intensity as she laid out her thoughts. She had not called the police stupid incompetents but the insinuation was there.

'You're right, of course Doctor' said Goodchild. 'I take it that you want his vehicle brought back to London for examination?'

'Correct. If you can lay on a car transporter plus crew I'll head on up with one of my people by train today to supervise the transfer back here.'

'I'll sort out the transporter within half an hour. You get yourself and your person to Gatwick by official car and I'll have a chopper waiting to get you to Manchester. It's about time we speeded things up. I'll sort out the paperwork so that Greater Manchester know what's what. Martin; Michelle; get on the phone and light a medium sized fire under the field teams. Stress that I am becoming seriously pissed off at what appears to be a lack of urgency on their part. Once you've done that, I'll want one of you to do a pub crawl around Barnet. What is Raven's stage name for God's sake? Once we have that we can see if he crosses paths with Guest other than on the occasions when they play in their band. For what it's worth here's what I think. There are too many coincidences in play here. I don't give a shit about Guest's lack of education or, for the moment, who ML is. The simple fact is that, of the two victims we have identified, one was obsessed by the man and the other vanished on the same night that she attended one of his gigs. We have to work to find one more link between Guest and these girls. I don't care if it comes from Doctor Watkins examination of his vehicle or Martin and Michelle killing their livers in the line of duty but find it we will. And then we pull him in for a quiet chat.'

'Extradition or pick him up on his return to Manchester, boss?' asked Carver.

'The latter – less complicated. He's due back next Thursday so it's not long to wait.'

'Imagine that we establish another link in the next forty eight hours though' said Michelle. 'Would you be comfortable leaving him out there on his own for two or three days during which he could disappear?'

'Good point. I'll give it some thought. OK everyone; get to it. I'll be back soon. Chris, come with me please.'

Goodchild left the office with Doctor van Dyke in tow. They walked to the bank of lifts and headed up to Goodchild's new office near the top of the building. 'Take a seat, Chris; this won't take long.'

The academic sat on a straight backed chair in front of the policeman's impressive desk. He'd seen smaller conference tables at his college. Goodchild installed himself on the other side of the desk in a large, comfortable looking, black leather swivel chair. It had been ergonomically designed to alleviate the back pain that was his inheritance from his rugby years. After all, Rank Hath Its Privileges.

'You probably felt a bit bullied back there, didn't you Chris?'

'I've worked with police on numerous occasions over the years. I've never been spoken to like that. I'm aware that not all police officers believe in the work of criminal psychologists and I can live with that but Carver's level of aggression is, frankly, unhealthy.'

'Unhealthy; that's a strange choice of word. What do you mean by it?'

'Carver is a man with issues.'

As soon as Goodchild heard this phrase his mental shutters closed down. He knew he was about to be given a liberalist, psychobabble lecture and he was going to have to sit there and take it.

'He barely controls his anger – in the bad old days he'd be the copper who supervised the suspect who fell down the stairs and broke his nose. He resents the fact that we now have a police service and not a police force. Added to this is confusion about his sexuality and you have a potentially explosive individual.'

'Sorry; could you rewind to the sexuality bit please?'

'He is a good looking alpha male who most likely regards himself as a 'man's man' but he is just that little too careful in the way he dresses and grooms himself. He may feel that he has bisexual tendencies and is ashamed by that which in turn manifests itself as anger. In reality, Martin Carver is gay and you should keep him on a tight leash.'

For a second Goodchild had a mental image of gays and tight leashes which was not at all pleasant. He felt like taking a leash and throttling the pretentious poseur with it. Instead he smiled and said 'Well, thanks for you input, Chris. I asked you in here to reassure you that I appreciate the work you are doing for us and will be in touch as soon as we have more information for you to look at.'

'Thanks; that's good to know.'

'Let me see you out – your pass is not valid for these floors.'

Goodchild escorted van Dyke to the main reception hall, shook his hand and bade him goodbye. To his departing back he breathed 'You arrogant cunt.'

Once back in his office he began to carry out the tasks that would have been better done by an administration aide. The plus side was that a call in person from a Commander of the Met did tend to result in swift action so it did not take him long to organise vehicles and a helicopter for Rachel Watkins and to have the Greater Manchester police prepped for her visit as well. All that being done, he descended to Orion to see how his officers were getting on. It had been a pretty good start to the week he thought. Now he had to keep the momentum going and try to obtain a positive result by the end of it.

When Goodchild arrived back at Orion neither of his officers were on the phone. They were both at their computer stations carrying out research of some sort. He went over to their desks and said 'Where are we then? Have you contacted the field teams?'

'Yes, boss' said Carver. 'They all assured me that they are hard at it and will report back here if they get the slightest sniff of anything.'

'Thereby passing the buck' said Goodchild. 'OK. What else do you have for me?'

'We think it best if I stay here, boss' said Michelle. 'If we get a shout from the field one of us will have to make a visit and my people skills are more suited to dealing with bereaved relatives than Martin's.'

'What do you plan to do in Barnet, Martin?' asked Goodchild.

'Exactly what you suggested, boss. Trawl the drinking holes. I have a request though. I'd like to take someone with me who both knows the manor and is familiar with the drug scene. An added bonus is that I won't be done for drink driving.'

'Do you have someone in mind, Martin?'

'Yes. DS Chris Fearnley – used to work with me in serious crimes and has done undercover work for narcotics. Very bright, streetwise and someone I work with well.'

'You've worked with Chrissie?' exclaimed Michelle. 'We were on the same intake together. I wondered what became of her.'

'She's doing fine despite some guys having it in for her after the incident with the unarmed combat instructor.'

'What incident is that, Martin?' asked Goodchild.

'Well, I was not there boss and she's never spoken to me about it but…

'I was' interrupted Michelle. 'The self defence instructor was a pig. He played up to all the macho guys saying that, in the interests of equality, he was going to batter the girls just as hard as he'd batter the men; and he did. One girl had her nose spread across her face and quit the force. Of course, guys were hurt as well but all the females felt that this shit was trying to break us and complaining would have been worse than weakness. Anyway, one day he was going one on one with Chrissie. Have you ever seen her, boss?'

'Nope.'

'Five ten, one hundred and fifty five pounds, blond and blue eyes. She can stop traffic without make-up or minis. She is also seriously smart. So she has to face this inadequate arsehole who's sole talent is hurting people. He gives her the short rubber stick that represents a blade and tells her to come at him so he can demonstrate how to stop a knife attack. Well, Chrissie danced around him for five minutes until he was soaked in sweat whilst she remained the ice queen. Every now and then she would manage a small touch on his hands, arms or back as she avoided his lunges. It was obvious that, as he tired, she was going to hit a vital spot so he called a halt to it. He said that in a real life situation, back up would have arrived by now and the ballerina would have been tasered until she was even more stupid than she already was. He then made them swap roles to show how crims really use knives. He had his breath back by now and took his time. Chrissie started to take the piss out of him, calling him fat, middle aged, impotent and finally she said 'if a piece of shit like you had managed to get into Met you'd be a uniformed PC until the day you retired'. That bit was a tad too close to home and the guy lost it. He flew at Chrissie and next thing we knew he was on the floor in agony and she was left holding the rubber stick. Somehow she's managed to dislocate the guy's wrist, elbow and shoulder with nobody seeing how it had happened. The official line was that he slipped and landed badly. Chrissie would not speak about it but I know that she was put on some unofficial shit list; there's no way she should still be a DS.'

'And this is who you want to go drinking with in Barnet, Martin?'

'Definitely. The question I have is how much can I tell her

about Orion. I don't really want to tell her a load of lies and say that we're just looking into the background of one Gary Raven – she's way too bright to swallow that.'

'What are you suggesting? Tell her all and second her to Orion?'

'That would be my strong recommendation, boss. I think Michelle would go along with it.'

Both men looked at Michelle Stone who took her time before answering Carver's question.

'Chrissie would have been the number one recruit in my intake. Intelligence, courage, physical skills – she has the lot. Where she missed out was in team working. No-one got close to her and every rookie has a buddy or it's hard to get through. Nobody disliked her but she always marched to the sound of her own drum, if you know what I mean.'

'Well she plays my kind of music' said Carver. 'Let's face it; we could do with another body on this team. Your call, boss.'

'What is she doing now, Martin?'

'Her lot have just busted a ring of coke dealers based around the Canary Wharf banking scene – very sensitive politically is the rumour. Chris is collating the paperwork for the CPS on the fifth floor and is going quickly batshit.'

'All right, Martin. Your request for a drinking partner is approved – she is to be seconded to Orion for the duration so bring her down here for a full briefing right now. If her superior has a problem with that, refer them to me. Move it. Barnet awaits.'

Carver left the room and Goodchild took the opportunity to question Michelle Stone.

'Any reservations?' he asked.

'About Chrissie Fearnley? None at all. About her working with Martin – some.'

'Such as?'

'We all know that he comes from a military background and violence is their choice of first resort. I'm not sure that two police officers who are quick to use the physical are the right team to conduct discrete enquiries in north London.'

'Do you know something specific about Martin, Michelle?'

'Please don't ask, Mark or I'll have to lie to you – if only by omission. He's never done anything to my knowledge that would compromise the investigation. Can we leave it like that?'

There was silence between them then. Goodchild saw that, by embarking on a relationship with one of his team, he had limited his own ability to command it. In effect, Michelle was making an operational decision on his behalf.

'All right then, Michelle. But when we put this investigation to bed I'm going to ask you about Martin Carver.'

'Deal.'

The subject of their conversation reappeared in the office accompanied by a tall blond woman wearing black jeans, a white T-shirt and a black leather bomber jacket. Detective Sergeant Chris Fearnley. Goodchild looked at her and tried to work out what was missing from the image. Then he got it; it was the first time he'd seen a woman enter a room without a bag or purse in her hand.

'Good morning, sergeant Fearnley. Thank you for coming. I'm Acting Commander Mark Goodchild.' They shook hands. 'I believe you already know Michelle.'

'Hiya, Rocky. So this is where you ended up. Special Operations!'

The two men looked at each other then at Michelle. As one they said 'Rocky?'

'Here's the deal guys' said Michelle 'you don't call me Rocky and I don't call you Chrissie or the nicknames written on the walls of the Ladies for you two characters. OK?'

The other three smiled and mumbled their agreement (with the men wondering what the hell the female graffiti said about them).

'Good to see you again, Chris' said Michelle. 'It's been a while.'

'I'm afraid it's going to be a while before you two can catch up with your induction nostalgia' said Goodchild. 'We need to brief Chris in now. Chris; nothing you hear in this room is to be spoken of outside. If you don't feel comfortable with joining Orion after your briefing that's fine. The injunction will still stand. Martin, I'd like you to conduct the briefing with Michelle drawing the relevant photos and statements from the file to back you up. I'll be back in an hour.'

After Goodchild had left, the briefing began. Chris Fearnley asked no questions, took no notes. She simply sat and listened, absorbing the information like a super efficient sponge. When it was over Carver said 'Any questions, Chris?'

'What the fuck have you got me involved in, Carver? The best incentive I've ever come across is that we have to catch this arsehole or else we all go to prison. Jesus!'

And then she laughed and the other two joined in with her. They were still laughing when Goodchild returned. He looked at the three of them until the noise subsided.

'I take it that Chris is now fully briefed?' he said.

'Yes, boss' replied Carver.

'Are you happy to join Orion, Chris? I mean it won't interfere with your career as stand-up comic or anything?'

'I'm in, boss.'

'OK. Well if you and Martin could spare the time to fuck off up to Barnet, I'd be most grateful.'

Carver and Fearnley left the office quickly. Goodchild's face broke into a broad smile.

'I think that our new team member is just what we need right now. Get a body from Addison's office to man the phones, Michelle. I reckon we owe ourselves lunch.'

Chapter Twenty Six

ML hailed a black cab on Farrington Street and directed it on the short journey to Ironmonger Row. Once the car had departed, he set off on foot towards City Road and one of his favourite establishments in London – Colonel Jasper's Wine Bar. Part of the Davy's group, CJ was a haven from the mass of plastic pubs which had infected the City. There was still sawdust on the floor, real ale in the barrels and good beef in the kitchen. Its only nod to modern times had been when the chairman had decided to apply for a spirits license so that women could have a gin and tonic with lunch. Prior to that decision, the drinking choice had been limited to ale or wine.

ML entered the discrete door next to Moorfield's Eye Hospital and descended the steps into the dark, but welcoming rooms. The uniformed porter bade him good day and escorted him to the private booth which he had reserved. He was an hour early for his meeting with Arthur Blenheim and spent it reviewing the papers which his lawyer had given him the previous evening.

On the face of it, Blenheim had set up a very good deal with an American publishing house for the purchase of ML's entire portfolio. The clever part was that ML had the option of first refusal to buy back any publication of the portfolio which the Americans should wish to sell in the future. ML had no intention of buying anything but, by agreeing to this clause, he was in a position of strength when dealing on price.

His booth, was in fact, a private room within the main bar area. It could comfortably seat ten chairs and was a bit of a goldfish bowl, albeit a soundproof one. As a card carrying member of the Davy's group, ML had been able to reserve the room with a single phone call. He now sat awaiting his lawyer with a decanter of vintage port in front of him. How much longer would he be able to enjoy simple pleasures such as this, he wondered. Were he to proceed in his endeavour as planned, he would have to leave the country. Was it worth it? The choice was still his. The British police would never trace the ten dead girls to him but the Americans would bring forces into play that could well change the game considerably. It was not too late for him to alter tack, take the money that Blenheim had negotiated and set out on a completely new life which would not involve his leaving London. But doing what? Mentoring Catherine in a musical career? To what end? It would also prove impossible to remain anonymous in such a role and he had striven all his life to remain invisible whilst discretely amassing a considerable amount of money.

He was still determined to expose the ineptitude of the British police but was it necessary to compare them with the Americans in order to do so?

At the back of his mind ML knew why he was having doubts. It was nothing to do with a concern over the superior investigative resources the American agencies would bring to bear. He welcomed the challenge and his original plan had taken them into account. No; the totally unforeseen element was the feelings which he had begun to have for Catherine and it was as 'Catherine' that he thought of her, not 'the American' or 'the prey'. She was a flesh and blood real person with whom he was enjoying spending time. But how much more time did he wish to spend with her? A day? A summer? A year? A life? Was this last so preposterous?

He did not have to rush his decision. If he were to adhere to his original plan then he had to be back in Fuerteventura within twenty four hours. The discovery of VIP facilities at the island's airport facilitated this (and why had he not known of this before, he wondered) so he would wind up his business today and return to Fuerteventura by tomorrow morning at the latest.

The door to the private booth opened and Arthur Blenheim entered, suited and booted in his lawyer's pinstripes as usual.

'Good God!' he exclaimed on seeing the decanter. 'Am I to assume that we are drinking lunch?'

'And a good day to you too, Arthur' replied ML. 'I don't want to be soporific when we conclude our business with the Americans so I've ordered some snacks for us to soak up this rather fine port. I hope we shall have a chance to dine later on but if not, let our last drink together for a while be a decent one. Shall I pour?'

'Me dear chap, please do. Are we going to go through the paperwork here?'

'No, I've already done that and am entirely satisfied. The only thing left to do is for both parties to sign the contract, then to transfer the money to the account you've set up and then we shall conclude our personal business. Are they happy with doing an electronic transfer of funds?'

'Absolutely. They thought that, as Brits, we would require banker's drafts or some such.'

A discrete rapping came on the glass panelled door to the booth and, after a few seconds pause, two waitresses clad traditionally in black and white, entered carrying trays on which were a selection of first class hors-d'oeuvres. The woman deposited the plates of food, flatware and cutlery then left.

'We are meeting the Americans in the Thistle Barbican' said ML. 'Is that where they are staying?'

'No; they are at Claridges around the corner from that bloody ugly embassy of theirs. Makes them feel safe, I suppose.'

'Good. I don't want to talk to them any more than I have to, Arthur. Would you let them know that I cannot stay long and will not be insulted if they bugger off back to wherever after we've signed. Nor do I want any group photos of the happy occasion. In other words, I want you to run this meeting. Once we are on our own, we'll go to the business centre and I'll transfer your funds and give you the dossier on Carmen. OK?'

'Fine' said the lawyer through a mouthful of smoked salmon and quails egg. 'They're going to think it a bit odd that you don't want to celebrate a deal of this magnitude though.'

'Like I care, Arthur. Let them put it down to English eccentricity. More port?'

The two men worked their way through the food which, as ever in a Davy's establishment, was spot on. Both knew that their lives were about to change and it was unlikely that their paths would cross again but they did not feel the need to articulate this. Despite the closeness of the business relationship which they had enjoyed over the years, they were not friends. Neither man was given readily to friendship, albeit for very different reasons, and the emotional incontinence displayed by the lower orders who followed 'reality' TV was virtually incomprehensible to them. So they ate and drank until it was time to leave for their meeting at the Thistle Barbican, a mere five minute stroll away along Lever Street.

This modern hotel is cunningly named. It is not located in the upmarket and arty Barbican area at all. It is half a mile to the east and is in the middle of a council housing estate. There is nothing wrong with this sort of housing and its population per se but arty it is not, so calling the two square blocks which made up the hotel the Thistle <u>Barbican</u> was, at the very least, misleading marketing. Having said that, it is clean, has good conference/business facilities and its location suited both ML and Blenheim.

The meeting went off without a hitch thanks to the skills of the British lawyer and his American counterpart who, it became clear, had also received instructions from his boss to expedite the business as quickly as good manners required. One hour after the principals had been introduced the contracts had been signed, monies transferred and congratulatory toasts made. The Americans departed in two hired Mercedes limos having brought a team of six to the signing and ML was free to fulfil his promises to Arthur Blenheim.

It did not take long to calculate what five per cent of the sale price was and to move it electronically to a numbered account in the Cayman Islands. ML looked at the man who was no longer his lawyer and said 'Congratulations Arthur. You are now wealthy, unemployed but I'm sure that you won't be idle.' He took from his briefcase an oversized manila envelope which he opened and emptied the contents onto the table between them. They consisted of three A4 envelopes which were, for the moment, sealed.

'Arthur; I truly wish you luck and happiness in your quest. This information regarding Carmen's whereabouts was correct as of yesterday. The people I employed to find her are no longer on the case, I've paid them off and you will not find their details in those envelopes. It's all up to you now.'

Blenheim placed all three A4's inside his own briefcase without opening them. That he would do in private then decided how to proceed. Turning to the man who had been his employer until a few minutes ago he said 'I suppose I should thank you but I'm feeling a bit nonplussed at the moment. Instead I'll just say goodbye and good luck in whatever you choose to do next.'

'Goodbye, Arthur.'

The men looked each other in the eye and shook hands firmly, silently reinforcing the truth behind their words. Then Arthur Blenheim picked up his briefcase and marched off towards what the fates had in store for him.

ML paid for the few remaining hotel charges in cash then stepped outside to the cab rank. Within ten minutes he was back at his place in Sans Walk from where a couple of phone calls set in motion his transport arrangements for his return to Fuerteventura – private car to Heathrow and a Learjet to the island. He used a different aviation company than the one on which he had left the day before for no other reason than that it was his habit to vary his travel methods and identities as often and as much as he could. If, one day, he were to be hunted, why make it simple for his pursuers? In reality ML knew that the electronic trail which one left when travelling internationally was readily accessible to the authorities but that could work in his favour. By establishing a certain image of himself using identities which would one day be revealed he could, by changing his methodology radically, evade pursuit until he reached safe haven.

He'd chatted briefly with the two pilots and the stewardess prior to take off, establishing himself as a polite but private man who required a minimum of attention. He informed the three crew members that he intended to work during the flight but would take a break at 1800hrs ZULU for whatever light refreshments the company had to serve as long as they did not include offal or cheese (which he considered to be dog food and mould). If he required anything else he would call for it.

The crew were pleased to have such an undemanding passenger and at 1600hrs precisely the Lear leapt to the sky, climbing towards its cruising altitude of forty thousand feet then heading south towards the Canaries. Once it had levelled off, ML went to work on his laptop and started to split up the funds which Blenheim's efforts had secured for him into smaller amounts (small being a relative word) and into various shell companies which he himself had set up post 9/11. He had known that the Americans would one day get round to blocking the terrorists ability to move funds across the planet so he'd decided to have his companies in place in case the day ever came when they were needed. That day had come and it had been his biggest headache in organising this aspect of his new life. It was Arthur Blenheim who had, indirectly, solved the problem for him. One evening after a particularly fine dinner at Rules in London, Arthur had told a story which he had heard at a conference on international fraud. This was Arthur's world and ML had only been half listening until the subject of identity change had come up. Apparently this had been the downfall of a very clever fraudster who had managed to con a group of property speculators out of twenty something million pounds. The problem had been what to with the electronic loot. He could hardly stick it in his local Barclays and he wanted it out of the UK but accessible to himself alone. He sought (and paid for) advice from the criminal fraternity but, despite his cleverness, made a total pig's ear of things and was nabbed by Her Majesty's finest. Found guilty of various charges, he managed to bargain a sentence of five years by paying back as much as he could which involved him selling his home and various vehicles. His wife grabbed as much as she could, divorced him and flew off to Marbella, presumably to find a more competent criminal. When he came out of Ford open prison he had the clothes on his back and less than four hundred pounds in a Post Office savings account which he proceeded to drink.

ML engineered an 'accidental' meeting with him and discovered that, whilst inside Ford, he had honed his skills at prison university. He had learned from his mistakes, which is not the same as being rehabilitated. He now knew where he had gone wrong procedurally and would not make the same errors after his next successful con.

It was obvious that his real problem was the bottle and his new best friend was only too happy to keep it replenished whilst he soaked up a lifetime's worth of information of how to hide large sums of money all over the world. Thus it was that ML cruised the skies in a private jet moving funds into secure locations ready for his future use whilst the man who had taught him how to do it lived in sheltered accommodation which the state gave him because of his self confessed alcoholism.

ML finished his financials more quickly than he had anticipated so he unbuckled his seat belt and went for a short walk. The seats on the Lear were very comfortable but he had still been hunched over a keyboard for nearly ninety minutes and he needed to stretch. He was twisting his torso left and right when the stewardess came through the curtain which separated the crew from the passenger cabin.

'Is everything all right, sir?' she asked.

'Fine. Just a but stiff from staring at a computer screen for too long.'

'Can I get you anything, sir?'

'Tell you what, a cold bottle of beer would go down well before I eat. I'll leave the choice to you.'

'Certainly, sir'

ML went to the area of the cabin which was laid out like a lounge and was soon sipping an ice cold Löwenbrau. He lay back with his eyes closed for a moment thinking that this was the only way to travel for a man such as himself.

Draining the beer, he used the jet's phone to call his man Richard on his mobile. He was answered very quickly indeed.

'Richard; it's Dominic. Did I vibrate you?'

'Too right you did. I've just slopped San Miguel all over me shoes. Where are you calling from?'

'Several thousand feet above the Atlantic en route for Fuerte ETA seven your time tonight. Any chance you could come pick me up?'

'No problem. Which flight are you on?'

'Private plane – so I'll see you at the VIP area. No luggage so we'll be out as soon as I clear customs. OK?'

'Excellent. All this VIP bollocks is going to ruin my low profile lifestyle though!'

'Maybe it'll attract a more upmarket clientele to the bar, Richard. See you later.'

ML broke the connection before Richard could begin to talk bar business. The stewardess began to lay the dining table. When she finished she turned to him and said 'I've prepared a Greek meze for this evening, sir' Would you care for some wine?'

'Yes but nothing too smooth. What's the roughest red that you have on board?'

'Well, when I've looked after Greek passengers they've always liked Bulgarian Bulls Blood. Would that suit, sir?'

'Good God! £4.99 from the supermarket. I have not even seen it since I was a student. Bring it on and let Bacchus weep with envy!'

The meal was ideal for a solitary person flying. It killed time with all the different bits and pieces which appeared from the gallery and there were no sauces that could cause a catastrophe should they hit clear air turbulence. As the girl cleared the dishes away, ML discretely slipped her a five hundred euro note.

'That's just for you' he said. 'The two chaps at the front are amply rewarded already.'

'Thank you, sir. I hope to see you again.'

'Who knows? May I have a Metaxa now please?'

'But of course, sir.'

The rest of the flight passed uneventfully with ML nursing the coarse Greek brandy until they landed smoothly at Fuerteventura. He shook hands with all three crew members and wished them a pleasant overnight stay on the island.

With his one bag he strolled through customs and immigration to where Richard was waiting for him. After perfunctory greetings the two men got into the pimp mobile and were at the bar thirty minutes later. At this early hour there were no customers so ML and Richard sat on bar stools together with a cold beer each.

'You know, Richard' said ML. 'Even with the most luxurious aircraft in the world and no hassle about baggage or customs, it's still a relief to be back on the ground and having a beer at a bar.'

'I would not know, Dom, me being a simple sod who's never flown in a private fucking plane. What's all that about anyway? I know you got a great deal on the way out but that bird was from a different company and if you paid full whack then we are talking serious dosh.'

'You don't miss much, do you Richard? Let's just say I decided to treat myself and leave it like that shall we?'

'Fine, fine. You'll tell me when you want to. Everything all right with the villa is it?'

'No problems at all. You did well finding that for me. I'm looking forward to spending the summer there.'

'Good. How about a cleaner, laundry, a pool boy – that sort of shit?'

'Yes; I'll need all of that. How much notice do you need to set that up?'

'Twenty four hours, mate. Unemployment is a major problem in Spain right now. I've got hot and cold running Pedros looking for work all the time.'

'I'll give you a call tomorrow then to sort something out. I'll have been there a week tomorrow so that bloody fine dust, sand, whatever it is will be starting to accumulate and the PH values in the pool will need checking. Who will you use; an agency?'

'Fuck, no. I'll use my bar staff and one of their family. I take the piss out of them but they are sound enough. I've never even had so much as a bottle of beer go missing either.'

'Fair enough. Would you excuse me, Richard? I've just got to step outside and make a business call to someone.'

ML went into the still quiet street and dialled Catherine's mobile. She picked up quickly.

'Hello?'

'Hi Catherine; it's me. I'm back. Where are you?'

'I'm at the villa getting ready to go out. I can wait for you then we can go together. How long will you be?'

'About thirty minutes. I've a bit of business to finish up in town then I'll be with you.'

'You're in town already? Not the airport?'

'That's right. My flight got in an hour ago. Richard picked me up.'

'Oh; I see. OK. I'll just wait for you here then. Bye, Dominic.'

'See you soon, Catherine.'

ML had detected an unspoken criticism in her tone of voice and choice of words. She had obviously thought that he should have called her as soon as possible and also to head straight for the villa and her. He'd wondered if she would react like this and, at least subconsciously, had tested her. There had been no reason to lie to her about having business in town; he could just as easily been at the villa in the five minutes it took to walk from Richard's bar. Some of the gloss had come off the hitherto shiny Catherine Taylor. The defect could prove fatal.

Catherine herself was not unaware that she had made oblique criticism of Dominic and wished she could have the moment back again. The man had flown thousands of miles at a moment's notice to sign a life changing deal then turned around and flown right back as he'd promised he would. He must be tired, in need of a shower and all she had given him was negative vibes because he had not come bounding back to her like a dopey dog. 'You can be some kind of stupid, girl' she said aloud. For second she hoped that maybe he hadn't picked up on her disappointment but then reality kicked in. This was Dominic she was talking about; she could not fool him with coquetry, flattery or anything. She hoped that she had not blown her chances of something other than a summer fling with him.

When ML finally arrived back at the villa she was waiting in the lounge. He closed the heavy wood door behind him, dropped his bag on the floor and strode across to where she sat. Catherine rose, searching his eyes for a hint of how he felt but could detect nothing. He bent to her mouth and kissed her long and slowly whilst his arms held her in a firm embrace.

'I missed you, Catherine' he said simply. 'It's good to be back.'

'I missed you too, Dominic' she replied. 'I'm sorry I was so bitchy on the phone but…'

He silenced her by placing his fingertips onto her lips. 'Stop right there. I totally understand. I call you 'my love', we make love, I fly away then, on my return, I don't come straight back to you, I do something else. It must have felt like being stood up on a date.'

'Well, yeah. I was sort of disappointed you know.'

'So I deserved a bit of bitchiness. That's forgotten now. I need a shower then we'll go wherever you wish to.'

'Great. Can we do wings, ribs and rock again?'

'Certainly. I'll be back down as soon as.'

He kissed her quickly on the lips then went upstairs to shower and change. Once in his room, ML closed the door, opened his personal safe as opposed to the one in the lounge and took out yet another different cell phone. He punched in a number after consulting a list and was answered after four rings.

'Ian Williams' came the sing song voice of the Welshman.

'Williams: Rodney McNaughten here. How are things going over there?'

'Fine, sir. I'm making real progress.'

There followed a long silence which ML finally broke. 'Could you possibly find it in your heart, Williams, to give me a verbal sitrep with special reference to American females? Would that be alright with you?'

'Oh, sorry sir. Let me get my notes. Right here we go.'

Williams then whined his way through a list of what he had done chronologically since his arrival the previous Thursday evening. ML endured it thanking God that it was only five days worth. The speaking clock was more interesting that Williams. When he had finished ML asked 'This American girl you've been seeing; what colour is she?'

'She's white, sir.'

'Right, that's that then. I'm cutting your trip short, Williams. I want you back in the UK no later than this Friday evening. If you can visit a few more establishments other than this Rock Bar that would be good but the main thing is that we meet on Saturday at the latest.'

'But I was contracted for two weeks work, Mr McNaughten' came the whine.

'Quite; and you shall be paid for two weeks even if you only carry out one. Try and change your return flight. I'll call you on Friday to arrange a meeting. Any questions?'

'Do you want me to look out for this American female, sir?'

'Absolutely not. Our information is that she is a negress who is now in Mallorca. In fact avoid that Rock place totally. Your face must be getting known by now.'

'Understood, sir. We'll talk on Friday then?'

'That we will, Williams; that we will.'

ML stepped into the shower feeling sure that there was no chance of his bumping into Williams this evening. Even if he did it was unlikely that the Welshman would recognise him as Rodney McNaughten the London lawyer but why risk it. All he had to do now was survive wings and ribs on top of Greek meze.

Half an hour later he and Catherine entered the Rock Café where they took the same booth at the rear in which they had sat on that first Friday evening together. Catherine remarked upon this saying 'So much has happened since then that it seems like a lifetime ago.'

'What short lives we lead, Catherine' said ML raising his glass to her.

The evening progressed predictably. Tony and the band now had their act together. The word had gone round Corralejo's small expat community and what would normally have been the quietest night of the week instead saw a packed house ready to party the night away.

Catherine wanted to dance but ML used the crush of people as an excuse to stay sat in his booth. She mock pouted at him but he was thinking, amongst other things 'many a true word spoken in jest'. He kept up the conversation and said all the right things to ensure that Catherine enjoyed herself. By midnight she could no longer handle the volume of beer so she switched to tequila with predictable results. At two in the morning she weaved her way unsteadily back from the rest rooms to take her last shot of the night. It was almost pure rohypnol; ML had doctored her glass during her absence.

The band had finished for the evening and the crowd was thinning out. Catherine's eyes were just starting to lose focus but she was compliant and ambulatory as ML guided her out of the bar and back up the street towards the villa. There were couples staggering around, singing and looking in far worse state than they did. The police cruised up and down the main street and never gave them a second glance.

'What a great night, Dominic' slurred Catherine as she collapsed onto the couch. Her eyes were open but she was not really seeing anything; she was awake but not aware of her surroundings. The so-called 'date-rape' drugs really do put people into a mental state similar to the hypnotic. Only someone who has been hypnotised can truly understand what that means.

ML finished locking the villa and setting the alarm system. He then lifted Catherine from the couch and carried her upstairs into her room where he placed her gently on her bed. He began to undress her which was slightly problematic as her body was now totally relaxed and uncooperative but he stuck to his task.

'Ya gonna fuck me, Dom? Eh? Ya gonna fuck me?' said Catherine.

'Whatever you want, Catherine' he smiled at her.

'Oh yeah, fuck me, Dom; please fuck me.'

She was now naked and lying prone on the bed. ML stood back and observed her. Within minutes the girl was deeply asleep breathing loudly through an open mouth. ML went to his own room from where he returned with a can of what appeared to be an internationally known brand of shaving foam. Once again he picked up the American in his arms and carried her like a small, sleeping child, this time into the en-suite where he laid her gently in the bath/shower unit. He placed the canister between her feet and, having removed the cap, twisted the nozzle one hundred and eighty degrees then pressed it. Only a faint hissing noise resulted but ML stepped back hastily and closed the plastic shower door which ran all the way to the ceiling. The rubber, waterproof seal should have been enough to keep the gas in the cubicle but ML took the added precaution of closing the bathroom door behind him then placing a wet towel along the small gap between door and floor. He then went to the kitchen to grab a beer and wait.

Fifteen minutes later he went up to the en-suite with a wet cloth over his nose and mouth. He activated the extractor fan system, opened the windows which gave onto the front garden and left the room, closing the door behind him. Five minutes later he returned to check on his efforts. He hoped the gas had killed her otherwise he'd have to break her neck. It did not really matter as long as the autopsy on the finger showed that she had ingested the lethal substance.

With the windows open, all he could smell was frangipane. He closed them. Catherine could smell nothing. Her pupils did not react to the light he shone into her eyes, her carotid did not pulse. She was dead.

ML returned downstairs. He was on automatic pilot now having planned for this scenario since he had first viewed the villa. From the trunk freezer in the utility room he took sack after sack of ice which he then placed in the tub with the corpse. Once it was covered her removed the finger using a pair of secateurs he had found in the gardening shed. He wrapped the digit in two condoms from a pack that he had purchased in London. He then placed it in a small plastic tub and left it in the kitchen freezer. Finally, he turned all the air-conditioning units in what had been Catherine's part of the villa to their coldest settings, turned off the lights, closed the door and said aloud 'Now you're fucked.'

Then he went to bed. He knew that he had a lot to do the next day, disposing of bodies when you're away from your own territory can be daunting. He would need a good night's sleep.

Chapter Twenty Seven

On Tuesday morning, as ML was preparing to meet his lawyer and convert his publishing empire into hundreds of millions of pounds worth of cash, on the other side of London the Orion team had come to a grinding halt.

Carver and Fearnley had hit lucky with the third landlord whom they had talked with during their tour of Barnet drinking holes. His face betrayed him when he was shown a mug shot of Gary Raven and, although initially reluctant to help the police with their enquiries, proved a fount of knowledge once Chris pointed out that the majority of his clientele looked as though they should have been at school rather than his pub.

'Were I to conduct an ID check right now as you or your staff should have done, I reckon the median age would be sixteen' said Chris. 'So that's an eighty pound fine for each member of staff, up to ten thousand for your good self and your license is fucked.' This reasoning brought out the good citizen in the landlord.

Gary Raven's stage name was Steve Strong and he rarely played in Barnet. He was a local face and rumoured to be the sort of guy to go to if you wanted to purchase tobacco and alcohol without the inconvenience of contributing to Her Majesty's Revenue at the same time.

Carver had called Michelle Stone AKA Rocky with the stage name then he and Fearnley left the pub. On the way out Chris made eye contact with a large man wearing motorbike leathers who was the centre of the young girls' attention. She motioned him outside, showed him her police credentials and had a quiet word in his ear. Carver did not know what she was up to but he left her to it and went to the car to wait. When she reached him she took the wheel and set off eastwards towards the Old Bull Arts Centre where she stopped.

'Any reason why we've stopped here?' asked Carver.

'I fancy a drink and I know a decent place or two round here. Also if Rocky, sorry, Michelle comes up with something on Raven we might be able to search his flat which is walking distance from here.'

'Fair enough. What did you say to biker boy back there by the way?'

'I told him that there had been a report that there was a hidden camera in the ladies loo and that, whilst we had not found any evidence of such an item, he might like to take the girlies somewhere else. That should screw the creep's business plan.'

'That might just screw the creep's ability to move without a wheelchair.'

'You reckon? Let's get that drink.'

Half an hour later Michelle called them to say that she had a list of places where Steve Strong had played during the last three years and not one of them coincided with a location at which or even close to where Tony Guest was playing on the same date.

So now they sat in Orion with Michelle, trying to come up with a plan that did not rely on the efforts of others. Goodchild was expected any time now having left a message that he was in the forensic garage with Doctor Watkins and Guest's vehicle which had arrived last night. If the forensic team could find some trace of one of the victims then they would move on the musician but this still did not change the fact that they were, once again, in a reactive mode. This went against the grain for all three officers.

The main door to their windowless office opened and Goodchild entered. He looked fresher than he had been doing and was dressed in a well cut blue suit, bright white shirt and mid-blue tie. His hair had had been trimmed and his black brogues polished. He could have passed for a senior Conservative politician.

'Good morning, everyone' he boomed in a disgustingly hearty

manner. 'Chris, you are the newest member of our little family. A fresh eye, fresh mind and all that. What are your thoughts so far?'

She did not hesitate before replying. '<u>Little</u> being the operative word, boss. What the hell are we playing at with us four trying to coordinate a nationwide search and, at the same time, going out on the road ourselves? This operation should have ten times the number of officers allocated to it than is has.'

'I could not agree more Chris but there is no way that size of operation could remain confidential. The counter terrorist aspect of this investigation supersedes the ten murders for the time being. I know that's distasteful, but it's reality. Once we have proof that Guest is our man then nothing will stop me from bringing him in. The top floor can deal with the politics of the case. We'll just bring the guy to trial.'

'Well we've certainly made a rod for our own back – and to mix metaphors, we're fighting with one arm tied behind…'

The phone rang and Michelle picked up 'Yes, he is. Hold on please; for you, Martin.'

Carver took the call and started to scribble notes on a pad. His body language communicated tension and urgency to the rest of the team who were now tying to work out what the unheard side of the conversation was. After a few minutes of him listening he said 'That is of great interest to us, sir. I, or a colleague, will have to travel up to see you and retrieve the material. May I have a contact number please? Thank you. I'll be in touch within thirty minutes if that's convenient.'

Carver hung up then consulted his notes 'Michelle; where was Guest playing on the weekend of July twenty second 2005' he asked.

'On the Friday he was at the Bridges in Ratlinghope, nothing booked for Saturday or Sunday. Monday he played with his band at a wedding in Wandsworth.'

'Where is Ratlinghope?' asked Carver.

'Shropshire, south Shropshire to be precise. It's about ten miles from Shrewsbury. What's going on, Martin?' asked Michelle.

'That call was from a Mister Fullerton Prosser, senior partner of Wright Prosser solicitors of Shrewsbury. He'd been having a drink in the Shropshire Hunt pub and overheard the landlord talking about my visit last week. He had a word with Mister Rounds and obtained my name from him. One of his secretarial staff vanished that weekend, never to be seen or heard of again. Twenty years old, single, no family apart from a mother who was in a care home. The firm reported her missing to the police on the Wednesday morning. Apparently she'd had some sort of row at work and stormed off without saying goodbye. Not all that happy was Mister Prosser's impression of her. After two weeks they cleared her desk and boxed her stuff. They still have it.'

'This could be number three' said Goodchild. 'Who fancies a trip to the country?'

'I'd like to get a feel of the place, boss' said Chris Fearnley. 'But then Martin knows his way around already. Which is the most effective use of resources?'

'Both of you go. I'm authorising the helicopter. Things are moving now and I can't have two officers stuck in traffic behind tractors or whatever they drive in yokel town. Doctor Watkins might come up with something whilst you're up there as well. Find out what you can about the girl – what's her name, Martin?'

'Hope. Janice Hope.'

'God, is that a sign? OK get gone. If you need to stay over do so but let me know so I can organise transport with the locals. West Mercia isn't it?'

'Yes, that's them' said Carver. 'We should be with Prosser by early afternoon I reckon. Shake a few trees, see what falls out, grab Hope's effects and be back here in time for tea.'

'If her effects have anything with a print or useable DNA on it I want you back ASAP and Chris can stay up there to work the locals and get a profile of this girl. Go for it, Martin. We're close, I can feel it.'

Carver and Fearnley squared away their desks and, after a quick call to let Fullerton Prosser know that they were on their way, the two officers left Orion to make their way to the helipad at Battersea on the south side of the river Thames.

As the black and yellow aircraft was speeding northwards, Goodchild called ahead to the local police to organise a reception for Carver and Fearnley. Fortunately there was a small police station in Shrewsbury town centre which had its own sizeable car park so that the two officers from London were escorted to the firm of Wright Prosser not ten minutes after landing. A Detective Inspector delivered them to the door then left them to their own devices.

Fullerton Prosser was in his sixties, lean of build, white of hair but sharp as a scalpel. He took Carver and Fearnley into his private offices and offered them tea which they declined. Both officers were impatient to move ahead. Sensing this, Prosser opened a cupboard and extracted a brown, cardboard box about one foot square and sealed with brown, plastic tape.

'This is what you came for, officers' he said. 'All that was left in young Janice's desk.'

'Have you kept it in here for the past five years, Mister Prosser?' asked Carver.

'Yes, I know that may seem odd but it served to remind me that the firm failed that young woman.'

'Failed? In what way, sir?' said Carver again.

'She was only twenty years old and family circumstances had precluded her from going to university but she was definitely bright enough. I knew that she was studying law through the Open University and, with the right help, would have made it. Unfortunately few people looked beyond her physical beauty to see the real person there and she had no friends at the firm. On her last day she had done outstanding work which was not acknowledged by her line manager and, by all account, left in a bit of a temper. I feel that if we had a system of mentoring younger members of staff they would be happier and more productive. I'm a voice crying in the wilderness on this issue but I kept her possession to remind me of what loneliness can lead to.'

'Do you have a list of the contents of the box, sir?'

'Yes. We are lawyers after all.' Prosser handed an envelope to Carver from which he took a sheet of paper. He read it quickly.

'Chris; there's potentially useful stuff here. The likelihood of prints is high and there could even be DNA. I want to take this straight back to the lab. I'd like you to interview staff who were here at the same time as Janice then think about visiting this pub in Ratlinghope.'

'If you think it's worth it. We don't even have a photo of this girl, Martin. I don't suppose your personnel department has a snap of her, Mister Prosser?'

'Sorry, no. We do not photograph our secretaries.'

'I'll work around it. OK. Martin; you get gone and I'll call in later to let you know what I'm up to.'

Carver said his goodbyes and allowed Prosser to see him out bearing the box which he hoped would match up with one of the, as yet, unidentified digits.

Meanwhile Chris Fearnley was allocated a small office and began the process of talking to staff who had known Janice Hope.

After two hours of this she was losing the will to live. The younger female staff could barely hide their dislike for the vanished girl. She was described as 'being above herself' and 'aloof'. Reading between the lines, Chris realised that beauty and brains were a drawback for a girl in this small town of small minded mediocrities.

Every male she spoke to began by describing Janice Hope as a physical object. Their lust for someone not long out of school was pathetic. Only Stanley Green gave a different take on her, unbelievably saying that he barely remembered the girl; 'just another typist. They come and they go, you know'

Chris Fearnley thanked Fullerton Prosser for his help and left the offices just as the staff were finishing for the day. She decided to retrace Janice Hope's last journey from the office and phoned the local police station for some help. Within five minutes an extremely tall and very young uniformed constable arrived to give her the benefit of his knowledge of Shrewsbury's highways and byeways.

'Janice Hope lived at Century House in Saint Julian's' she said to the nervous young bobby. 'I'd like you to take me there by the most direct route.'

The two of them walked along the pedestrianised Pride Hill which was busy with people who had just finished work for the day and were now heading for the car parks or the train station. During the five minutes it took to negotiate the street, Chris noticed three different street musicians playing for change.

'Seems to be a very musical town, Shrewsbury' she said to her guide. 'Are there always buskers here?'

'More often than not, ma'am; especially in decent weather' he replied.

At the foot of the hill they turned left into the High Street which was the same as any other in middle England; banks, building societies, coffee chains and charity shops. At the end she noted the Shropshire Hunt pub where Martin Carver had interviewed the landlord. They now came to a steep hill called Wyle Cop which led down to the river. More pubs appeared, none of which looked as though they would appeal to an attractive intelligent young woman on her way home from work. At the foot of the hill the pubs gave way to artisan jewellery shops and here the road split in two and there was Century House where Janice Hope had lived.

The walk had taken ten minutes. During it Chris had seen nowhere that would have enticed Janice in. The coffee shops were outrageously expensive for a young secretary and the pubs all looked like male drinking dens.

Chris tried to put herself in Janice Hope's shoes. It's Friday, a summer's day and you've just finished another shitty work week with an argument. What would you want to do? A drink would have been good but between the office and the flat there is nowhere suitable. Therefore the options are a drink alone at home or go to the other side of town where Martin had said the more youthful bars were located. But if Janice had taken the latter option she would have risked bumping into her work colleagues which was probably the last thing the girl wanted. So she was more likely to have gone home to do a Bridget Jones, but somewhere along the way she had gone missing. If she had made it home she'd gone out again. When, where, why and with whom?

Chris felt that she was missing something, some small piece of local knowledge that would fill in the blanks of the picture she was constructing of Janice Hope's last hours.

Releasing the young constable back to his duties, Chris retraced her steps back up the hill, along the High Street then stopped where the pedestrian precinct began. Nothing had jumped out at her to say that this was the spot where Janice had met her abductor – if indeed he existed. The girl might simply have packed a bag and gone walkabout, but Chris doubted it. The local police had found Janice's passport and quite a lot of personal possessions in her flat when they had finally entered it. No; Chris was fairly certain that she had disappeared from this area on that Friday.

Taking out her cell phone she called the direct line to Orion in London. Michelle Stone picked up. 'Michelle; Chris Fearnley' she said. 'Martin's on his way back in the chopper now. I'm going to spend the night here and do some digging. Could you tell me the name of that hotel receptionist that Martin went on the piss with?'

'Hang on, Chris; I'll check the file' replied Stone. 'Here it is. Kate Pigeon.'

'Pigeon? Jesus, wait till I see Carver. The number of plump breasted bird jokes must be endless! Thanks for that, Michelle.

I'm going to try and get a room at the Lion Hotel. Are you guys going to be burning the midnight with the Janice Hope material?'

'Yes; Rachel Watkins and her people are pulling overtime on this. I'll call you when we have more news.'

'Fine. Talk with you later.'

Chris Fearnley had seen a largish department store on the High Street and made that her next stop. She would need some fresh clothes for the morning and some basic toiletries. She'd travelled up at such short notice that she did not even have a toothbrush to her name. Once supplied, she headed back to the Lion Hotel where she booked a single room for one night.

The receptionist informed her that Kate Pigeon had finished her shift some two hours ago and would not be back until the following afternoon at three. At Chris' request the receptionist phoned Kate and let the police officer speak with her. After quickly explaining who she was (and saying hello from Martin Carver) Chris arranged to meet the girl at the Shropshire Hunt pub in an hour's time. She then checked into her room and took a long shower more for the sake of relaxation than cleanliness.

Forty five minutes later she was sat on her own with her back to the wall in a position from which she could observe anyone who entered the pub. She sipped her, surprisingly decent, Rioja and crowd watched. It was still early in the evening and the clientele looked as if they'd all come straight from work to throw a few cold ones down before heading home. It was an eclectic mix of people ranging from smartly dressed shop girls, to casually clad middle aged males whose solo topic of conversation appeared to be football. The atmosphere was friendly and the background music unintrusive. She judged it to be a well run establishment for a market town.

A young woman entered the door at the other end of the bar, stopped and looked around. She was in her early twenties, smartly dressed in a black two piece skirt suit but with just a tad too much make-up and hair extensions. Half the people in the pub seemed to know her and she had a dazzling smile for everyone. From where she was sat Chris was able to lip read and saw a young man greet the newcomer as 'Kate' so she left her table to introduce herself.

'Hello there' she said. 'Are you Kate from the hotel by any chance?'

'That's me' she replied brightly.

'Hi; I'm Chris Fearnley. We spoke earlier. May I buy you a drink?'

'Sure. I'll have a white Zinfandel, thanks.'

The two women made their way back to Chris' table and the police officer began the slow process of extracting information from someone who was not aware that she might possess the answers.

'Thanks for meeting me at such short notice, Kate' said Chris. 'I'm sure you've other things you'd rather be doing on a night off than talking with the police.'

'No problem. I hope I can help with whatever you're looking for. Plus, to be honest, it breaks the routine. I had a great time with Martin even if he did bail out early on me.'

'Older bloke; can't handle the pace any more.'

The two women laughed and raised their glasses in an unspoken toast to female solidarity. Chris got down to business.

'Look, Kate; the reason I'm up here is connected to Martin's investigation but separate from it. Five years ago a girl called Janice Hope vanished. I don't suppose you know that name do you?'

Kate thought then shook her head. 'No; not a name I recognise'

'Not to worry. Janice was twenty years old and worked as a secretary at Wright Prosser solicitors in town. From what I've learned, she was very pretty, intelligent but did not get on with her colleagues. On the last Friday on which she worked, there was some sort of a row in the office and she went off in a temper. She was never seen or heard of again.'

'Shit! Twenty years old. That's awful.'

'Yes; she lived in a small flat at Century House in Saint Julian's and I've been trying to trace her last movements. My thinking is that it's Friday, she's had a crap day and she wants a drink. The trouble is I've walked the most direct route from her office to her flat and cannot see anywhere that a girl like Janice would stop. Are you with me, Kate?'

'Yeah. What route did you take?'

'Down Pride Hill, along the High Street then down Wyle Cop to home.'

Kate shook her head. 'That's not the way she would have gone. First off, she wants to get away from the office rapido so she would avoid Pride Hill and the High Street. They're both full of numpties at the best of times but on a Friday afternoon it's worse. Secondly she sounds like she'd have wanted a decent place to have a drink. Did she have much money?'

'Not that we know of. She did not earn that much and her rent was quite high.'

'Then I reckon there's only two places she would have gone. Do you want to see them? It's easier if we just walk there than if I describe it.'

'Yes; if it's not too much trouble.'

'No worries; lets drink up and I'll take you to the nice bars.'

The two women finished their drinks and headed out into the early evening sunlight. The streets were busy with people taking advantage of the pleasant weather and there was something of a party atmosphere in the town. Walking past yet another church they came to a set of traffic lights.

'OK. Chris; this street is called Dogpole…'

'Dogpole?'

'Yeah, Dogpole. Don't ask me why 'cos I've not the slightest idea. Anyway it becomes Saint Mary's Street and then connects with Pride Hill. On the way there is Cromwell's bar, restaurant and hotel. A lot of young people use the bar.'

Chapter Twenty Seven

'Let's take a look then.'

The building was just fifty yards up the street on the left hand side. They entered the centre doors then turned right into the deceptively spacious bar area. All the tables were occupied so Chris and Kate took their wines into the garden at the rear where they found a small table.

'Everybody seems to be in couples or small groups' said Chris. 'I didn't notice anybody drinking alone. Would a single girl come in here?'

'You're right; probably not. Sorry; I wasn't thinking. I can go more or less anywhere 'cos I know that I'll bump into friends or family. I also know a lot of the staff. It would have been difficult for the girl you're trying to find.'

'Don't worry, Kate. By eliminating places I'll get closer to the truth. Before we move on to your next choice of venue, what can you tell me about the Bridges at Ratlinghope?'

'Great place! I've only been a few times 'cos it's like, a bugger to get to, you know. The live music can be a bit folky but, when they have an open-mike night, it's ace.'

'How would you go about getting there?'

'You need a car but then you can't drink so you'd have to book a room for the night. A taxi will take you there but it's not cheap and you're not guaranteed to get one back to town. Every time I've been lucky enough to have had a lift there and back.'

'I see. OK Kate; imagine it's a Friday, about five on a summer's evening. Where would Janice have been likely to meet someone who'd give her a lift to the Bridges?'

Kate took a swallow of wine and though before answering. 'It would have to be one of the music pubs' she answered. 'The Shropshire Hunt where we just were or the Bull where I'd planned on going next.'

'Drink up, girl, I want to see it whilst it's still relatively early.'

Drinking up proved no problem at all for Kate who soon

found herself in the company of a Metropolitan police detective in the Bull for the second time in a week.

Having ordered two more wines, Chris joined Kate and observed the bar.

'Nice place, shame about the people' she said. 'Why are all these old scrotes in here, Kate?'

'Several reasons; they spend their days going from pub to pub via the bookies and end up getting banned from the decent places. Also there's a beer garden out back where they can work on their lung cancer.'

'Marvellous. So where are the musical types?'

'I can't see any. Perhaps they don't have an act on tonight.'

'Not to worry. Tell me, Kate; do you go out to the local pubs when there's live music on?'

'If it's a good act and I'm not working silly shifts, then, yes.'

'And who is your favourite act?'

'That's easy; Tony Guest. The guy is a legend. It's always a good gig with Tony.'

'Where does he play?'

'Well in town he keeps to the Shropshire Hunt. He's usually on every second week. He's also involved with the Bridges but I don't know when. Apart from that, I don't know. Why are you asking about Tony anyway?'

'I'm just trying to build up a picture of how a good musician operates in this neck of the woods – it's not about Tony himself.'

'Oh, I see.'

'Did you ever see Tony play in the street, you know, like the guys on Pride Hill?

'You must be joking! No way. The guy is a total pro, he's cut CD's, played big concerts – we're lucky he plays a local pub at all. There is such a thing as musical street cred you know. He's a lovely guy as well.'

'OK Kate; I've no more questions for you. You've been very

helpful anyway. May I buy you dinner? The last thing I ate was a toasted sandwich this morning.'

'Yeah, that's cool. How about going back to Cromwell's? We should be able to get a table at this time of day.'

'Fine by me. Lead on.'

The two women retraced their steps and were seated immediately at a table for two in a corner. Chris Fearnley had switched off as much as she ever did. An idea had begun to percolate through her brain but she could not pursue it until she spoke with the team in London. The trail on Janice Hope was five year's old and as cold as a tax inspector's heart so she put everything on intellectual hold and settled down to dinner.

The two women were not very disparate in age but were miles apart in life experience. Despite this they go along well to the extent that Chris found herself advising Kate on how to become a police constable (although she did not tell her of the grief a name like PC Pigeon could cause her). They were onto their coffee and liqueurs when Chris' mobile rang. She saw that it was the Orion number.

'DS Fearnley' she answered.

'Chris; it's Martin here. Can you talk?'

'Not at the moment. I'll call you back in fifteen. Which number can I reach you on?'

'Reply on this one, Chris. Talk with you soon.'

Carver's voice had been under control but she knew him well enough to realise that something major had occurred. She signalled the waiter for the bill and said to Kate, 'I'd love to stay and chat but that's the office. I need to get back to my room and call them. This is my card. If you're ever in London give me a call and we'll catch up.' She handed over a white and blue business card which Kate put in her purse.

'Chris, say hello to Martin for me will you' she asked. 'I liked him.'

'Of course I will. Must dash now.'

She walked quickly to the door pausing only to take a receipt from the waiter for her expenses. Five minutes later she was in her room at the Lion, composing herself before calling Carver.

He answered after one ring . 'Hi Chris. You free now?' he asked.

'Yes. What's up?'

'Doctor Watkins has worked her voodoo and lifted some partial prints. She hates to commit but she says that she had an eighty five per cent probability of a match with one of the digits. She's still working on the rest of the material to try and improve on that. DNA is proving more difficult but she reckons that she'll have a result by mid afternoon tomorrow.'

'It sounds pretty strong, Martin. What's Goodchild Saying?'

'Not a lot. He's writing everything up for Addison and has a meeting with him tomorrow morning. That's the good news; here's the bad. Guest's car was totally clean. It had been recently valeted but there were still traces of hair and whatnot on it. None of it matched any of the victims.'

'Shit! So where do we stand now?'

'Goodchild has ordered that Guest's car be returned to its space at Manchester airport. I infer from this that we are not going to Spain to pick him up.'

'OK. I need to talk with Goodchild. I've an idea of what happened to Janice Hope. It's a bit tenuous and I need to do a bit more digging but I'm going to travel back on the first train in the morning and run it past you first, Martin.'

'Now you've got me intrigued. Care to give me a hint as to what this idea is?'

'Not yet. Oh, by the way; Miss Pigeon sends her best to you.'

'Who?'

'Kate; the young hotel receptionist you went on the lash with. Don't tell me you didn't get her last name?'

'Nor keep her number. I reckon that one could out drink Goodchild. See you tomorrow, Chris.'

'Yes; I'll call when I have an idea of an ETA. See you tomorrow.'

It was still light outside when Chris Fearnley left the hotel again to begin a recce of the town centre. She had no particular plan in mind but this was how she operated best. By getting a feel for a place she was able to put herself in the position of a criminal or a victim. Then she could start to hunt. She thought that she was a pretty good huntress.

Chapter Twenty Eight

ML awoke on Wednesday morning and began the process of erasing all traces of his and Catherine's presence from the villa.

He arranged for Richard to send his cleaners round the following day to give the place a thorough going over from top to bottom and also to launder all the sheets, pillowcases and towels. He himself then cleaned Catherine's quarters and his own, paying special attention to wiping all surfaces which either one of them could have touched.

He washed and polished all glasses, plates and cutlery in the kitchen then took all the empty beer and wine bottles to the disposal bank at the top of his street.

Catherine's clothing, make up and assorted personal effects were double wrapped in heavy duty rubbish bags in which ML had already placed a paving slab. Fortunately for his purposes, Catherine had travelled light and this parcel fitted neatly behind the front seats of the Range Rover. He would use her single suitcase for himself.

As he went about his business he was as meticulous as he could be, even going so far as to wipe down the arms and legs of the poolside furniture. But he was under no illusion that a really professional forensics team would, eventually, find something. He was counting on the fact that no such team would ever have the opportunity to investigate this property; thus all his efforts were being made to mitigate the effects of a worst case scenario.

It was early evening before ML decided that he had done all that he could so he went to check on the state of the dead body.

The ice and the air-conditioning meant that rigor was only just stating to fade. This was fine by him. All he had to do now was wait for the dusk to fall so that, by the time he reached the site that he'd selected for the body's disposal, it would be full dark. With nothing else to do for the time being he went for a walk along the sea front to clear his head. He'd spent a lot of time in the company of other people recently and, whilst he did not consider himself to be anti-social (in the conventional sense of the term), solitude was his natural condition and the one in which he did his best thinking.

The logistics of what he had to do next were simple but not without risk. Driving the back roads of Fuerteventura in the dark was inherently dangerous. There were idiot tourists in hire cars, full of sangria and stupidity. A bigger worry would be a spot check by the Guardia Civil. It was the latter eventuality which had made ML decide on a non-alcoholic day until he had taken care of his business.

Arriving back at the villa, he lay down to doze and wait for dusk to fall. He did not sleep; he did not dream. He played a form of relaxed, mental chess with himself in which he imagined possible future scenarios and how he would manipulate them. The exercise was akin to wandering round your own mind palace and rearranging the furniture.

Time passed. ML sensed the changing light and went to Catherine's former room where he switched off the aircon. Entering the bathroom, he lifted her slight frame from the tub and placed it on two large bath towels for it to dry. He then carried the corpse downstairs where he put it inside a blue, nylon sleeping bag which he zipped closed then laid in the rear of his car.

The sleeping bag suited the outdoor image of the Range Rover. Now, as dusk fell, he drove south on the FV101 which led him to Villaverde then La Olivia. When he saw the signpost for Tipdaya he turned west and found himself on the dusty track that finally reached the coast. Heading south once more, he found the spot which he had selected during a daylight reconnaissance two years ago. The cliffs were shear here although a mere one hundred and fifty feet in height. The sea had eroded a channel into the land some three times that in length but only twenty five in width. The result was that the Atlantic Ocean surged in and out perpetually against the land, leaving no boulders and certainly no beach. It was ideal for his purposes. Working quickly, he unloaded the sleeping bag, placed it between the vehicle and the cliff top then unzipped it three quarters of the way round. He placed one of the many black rocks which he found lying around, this one weighing, he judged, about fifty pounds in the bag with the corpse. The next step was to stab the corpse with a razor sharp hunting knife just above the pubic bone then carve up until he hit the sternum. This meant that there would be no accumulation of bodily gases which could result in flotation. He closed the bag and cut a four inch slit into it to allow access to the bottom feeders. The lot was then tipped over the side of the cliff and the knife was flung far after it. He did not hear a splash as the sea was too noisy nor did he see the impact as it was too dark, but he knew that the operation had gone well. Finally, he retrieved Catherine's bagged personal effects and sent these down into the dark to join their erstwhile owner. Disposal had taken just under a minute.

ML returned to his vehicle, performed a careful three point turn and retraced his route back to Corralejo. There were no dramas on the way; perhaps they were reducing the number of Guardia Civil patrols to save money these days was a thought that crossed his mind.

It was still relatively early as ML parked up at his villa so he headed back on foot to the main street to see if he could catch Richard and set in motion his departure from Fuerteventura. As he opened the door he could hear Toby Keith singing how much he loved this bar which meant that the boss was choosing the music and, sure enough, there he sat, glass in hand, large as life and twice as ugly.

ML took a seat at a corner table and waited for Richard to join him which he did fetching two cold one with him.

'Didn't expect you tonight, Dominic' he said. 'Everything all right?'

'Yes, fine thanks, Richard' he replied. 'Something has come up though which necessitates a change in my immediate plans. Long story short; I'll be leaving tomorrow night for the Far East and won't be back this side of Christmas.'

'Do what? What about the villa and the car?'

ML took a draught of his beer and smiled inwardly at the transparent avarice of his good friend Richard.

'It's not a problem. You organised everything in good faith and it's not your fault that I have to shoot off at short notice. If you can let it out again and recoup some of my outlay, well, that would be fine and we can settle up next time I'm here. If you can't, you can't and I'll just have to take the hit. Either way, you're covered aren't you?'

'Well, yeah; but you've paid a lot of dosh for a week's accommodation, mate.'

'Not your problem, Richard. One request though. Your staff are due to come in and clean tomorrow. I'd be grateful if they could hold off until Friday when I won't be here.'

'No worries. Leave it to me. Anything else I can do for you? A lift to the airport?'

'No thanks, Richard. I'm good. I'll leave the car keys in the upstairs safe and all the combinations will be written down so that you can reset them. Thanks for everything and I'll be in touch in a few month's time.'

ML stood, shook hands with Richard and left the bar without any further words. Richard returned to the bar calculating how best he could profit from this unexpected windfall. A few more mugs with more money than sense and he could retire.

At that moment his mug was entering the packed Rock Café.

He had a small gift from Bristol to slip into Tony Guest's guitar case before they both left the island. If all went to plan it would prove decisive in his game plan.

§

Chris Fearnley took the earliest available train from Shrewsbury to London on Wednesday morning. She travelled first class in the hope that no one would sit at her table and disturb her as she tried to put together the various thoughts which were now running around her brain after her visit to Shropshire. Being the latest member of the Orion team did not make her feel in any way inferior to those who had been in on the operation from the start. Indeed, in her mind, she had the advantage of a fresh perspective on things and she honestly thought that her colleagues had become bogged down in the minutiae of the case. Obviously the small details were vital when presenting the matter to the Crown Prosecution Service and, ultimately, a jury but she felt that the big picture was out of focus in this particular investigation. At the earliest reasonable hour she called Martin Carver on his cell phone and arranged for him to meet her on her arrival back in the capital.

She was off the train as soon as it stopped moving and marched straight across the concourse of Marylebone station to where Carver was waiting in the early morning sun.

'Hi, Martin. Thanks for meeting me' she said. 'Where are you parked?'

'Well, as you said you wanted to talk and have some breakfast before we go back to the Yard, I've left my car at the Landmark.'

'Good call. Let's go.'

The two officers walked the short distance to what is one of London's less fashionable but more efficient hotels. After making a sizeable dent in the pig dominated breakfast buffet Chris Fearnley began her pitch.

'There is one thread running through this case and I can't believe that we're not pulling on it as hard as we can.'

'And that is?'

'Music. Everywhere we look there is music or musicians. The girls we've identified had sad, lonely lives and their only social activity appears to have been live gigs. This guy Tony keeps popping up but we've done nothing about him and…'

'Hang on, Chris; you're contradicting yourself. Orion's work has brought Tony Guest to our attention and it's only a matter of time before Goodchild…'

'Goodchild's eye is so far off the ball that he's not even in the game anymore, Martin!'

'What are you on about? The guy is a total pro and, given the constraints under which he had been operating, he's done a hell of a job.'

'You really don't see it do you, Martin?'

'No. See what, exactly, Chris?'

'Acting Commander Goodchild is banging Detective Sergeant Stone.'

Carver did not react immediately to this bombshell. He stared at his colleague and mentally evaluated the possibility that she was right. Finally he said 'Did Michelle tell you this herself?'

'No. She doesn't have to. It's obvious to anyone who has a basic knowledge of gender interaction and office etiquette.'

'Which is why I can't see it, I suppose. Shit. If you're right this is a real mess.'

'I am right, Martin. Look, the bottom line for me is this. There is some sick bastard out there kidnapping, killing and cutting up women. He then makes a game out of it and is leading us a merry dance indeed. I have the feeling that we are being set up to look like idiots and don't intend to end my career as the butt of a joke. Don't get me wrong; I want to bury this son of a bitch but not at any cost. The press are already too involved for my liking and if they tumble to the fact that the man leading the investigation is banging one of his junior officers, well. You can imagine the fallout, Martin.'

'What course of action would you recommend?'

'Haul Guest's arse in and roast it. See how he reacts to pressure and let him know that he's under the eye. None of these weirdos are as smart as they think they are and, once they start talking, well you know how it goes. You can't shut the fuckers up. The best they can hope for is to be sent to a hospital for the criminally insane rather than to do hard time. What have we got to lose, Martin?'

'OK. I've listened to you and don't necessarily disagree with what you're saying. Let me bring you up to speed with where we're at as of now. Guest is due to fly in to Manchester tomorrow afternoon ETA 1615hrs. His vehicle will have been returned to its parking space by then. He will be under visual surveillance from the moment he disembarks. Goodchild has used the anti-terror laws to obtain permission to monitor all phone calls to and from his cell and his home land line. We are very close to doing what you have just outlined but it's Goodchild's call. Happy?'

'No. What will we know in twenty four hours that we don't know now? We should be squeezing this guy's nuts and seeing what sort of noise he makes. What do you think, Martin?'

'Off the record, I'm with you on this. All the circumstantial evidence points to Guest and I'm sure that Michelle's efforts are going to give us more of the same, digit by digit. But it all seems too easy. A guy who has been making girls vanish over a period of years just suddenly jumps onto our radar screen – I'm finding that a bit much to swallow. On the other hand, if it walks like a duck, has webbed feet and quacks, it probably is a duck. Or so the theory goes. We can only wait and see what the surveillance turns up, Chris. It's still Goodchild's show.'

'All right. I'm going to play devil's advocate and imagine that Guest is not our man. I'm going to go over the case files and look at alternative scenarios. You OK with that?'

'Yes but let's keep it between ourselves. You don't want to be caught pissing on Goodchild's chips if he turns out to be right. Ready to go?'

'Yeah; lets.'

Carver and Fearnley left the Landmark from where he drove them back to New Scotland Yard. They passed the short journey in silence. He was still absorbing the information that his superior officer was having a relationship of some kind with a junior whilst she, focusing on the case, was thinking of an alternative killer to Tony Guest. She was fixated on the musical aspect to the investigation but was finding it hard to answer the question 'if not Guest then who? If not a musician, then what?'

Back at Orion they found Michelle Stone manning the office alone, hammering away at her keyboard. 'Hi guys' she said. 'Anything new from our friends in the north, Chris?'

'I'll let you know. I've got to shift through some shit first. Where's the boss?'

'He's upstairs briefing Addison. They've decided to use the counter terrorist team to observe Guest. That's how this all started anyway.'

'Jesus, that's a bit of a stretch!' said Fearnley. 'How the hell can he justify using CT for a serial killer – a suspected serial killer at that?'

'The justification comes from the email and the package in the park. The reason why we're using CT is practical. Guest will be flying in to Greater Manchester and, we think, will then go home to wifey which comes under West Mercia although nobody knows what this joker will do after he lands. In the absence of a UK version of the FBI the CT team cuts across all the jurisdictional bullshit.'

'Who's liaising with the locals?' asked Carver.

'Addison will talk to the relevant Chief Constables. Hopefully we won't be tripping over northern plods.'

All three officers went to their respective work stations and busied themselves with various tasks. All their minds were, in reality, several hundred miles away and hours into the future when Guest was due to land at Manchester International.

At just before 1300hrs the next day Goodchild strode into the office, grim of aspect but fixed of resolve.

'Good afternoon, everyone' he said. 'Update time. Doctor Watkins and her people are still working on the material Martin brought back. She will interrupt us as soon as she has something positive to report. In other words, don't be calling her every half and hour asking what she has. Secondly, Guest's flight is on time and he is confirmed as being on board. The lads and lasses from SO15 are in place at Manchester airport and the commo people are coming in here in thirty minutes to set up a dedicated and encrypted voice link to them. So, if you want lunch, sort it out amongst you after this meeting. Any questions?'

'What do you think the suspect is going to do, boss?' asked Fearnley.

'The natural thing would be for him to get into his vehicle and head on home to his wife. If he is our man then I have no idea what he is going to do.'

'Honest answer' said Fearnley. 'Contingency plans in case he does not go straight home?'

'From the moment he goes through immigration he is under the eye. There are teams of spotters at arrivals, obviously in the car park and also at the train station which is quite close to the airport. We have three cars to lead – follow him. Finally there will be helicopter surveillance. He is landing in daylight, weather conditions between Manchester and Shropshire are clear; I reckon we have him. Comments?'

'It's a miracle, boss' said Carver.

'What is?'

'Clear weather in Manchester! That place makes Seattle look sunny.'

The weak joke generated more laughter than it merited but served to relieve the tension that had built up in the room. Chris Fearnley volunteered to go and buy some food to see them all through the hours ahead. Her offer was accepted. They all knew that she would not return with salad and yoghurt.

Chapter Twenty Nine

Tony Guest stood at the baggage carousel waiting for his one piece of hold luggage to come around and inwardly cursing Islamic terrorists who were responsible for his delay. He could have quite happily spent a week in Spain with only the contents of a small bag that would have qualified as hand luggage but, because of Abdul bin Hijacker, he would not have been able to carry a razor or shaving foam aerosol. So he waited. Such is the fate of those too vain (or too mean) to invest in disposable razors and locally purchased toiletries for a couple of weeks away.

Finally his bag appeared and he used his height to reach past a fat family to lift it with ease. Heading towards immigration he could not help humming a few bars of the song Homeward Bound to himself. 'My suitcase and guitar in hand; and every stop is neatly planned for a poet and a one man band'. – pretentious Paul Simon bollocks was his real opinion of that particular piece.

The horde of returning tourists shuffled through the lanes at the terminal like sheep on their way to the abattoir. Finally it was his turn to present his passport and, despite his height, he found that he had to look up at the unsmiling face of the uniformed official who was now inspecting his document. What he could not see was the button on the side of the computer that had been pressed to alert the team behind the one way glass that he had arrived.

On the other side of the glass a senior immigration official spoke to a plain clothed Detective Sergeant from the CT team.

'Your Mr Guest is at desk number three' was all he said.

The CT officer observed for a couple of seconds then put a small black radio to his mouth. 'All units this is Kestrel repeat Kestrel. Subject Ninepin has arrived at immigration desk. He is at least six three, shoulder length mid brown hair, wearing blue jeans and a turquoise short sleeved shirt with a pattern of bright red flowers. Subject ninepin is carrying a large, black sports bag, a plastic duty free bag and a black guitar case. Kestrel out. Let him through please.'

The immigration official pressed a button three times to silently signal the desk officer to allow Guest to proceed. The Detective Sergeant nodded his thanks and made his way to the arrivals lounge where some of the team were in place.

Also in place was ML who had arrived in his rented jet an hour beforehand. On seeing Guest emerge from customs he headed for the Post Office at the front of the arrivals hall at Terminal One and posted his small package to the American Embassy. He then made a call from a one time cell phone then walked off in the direction of the railway station from where he would travel back to London. He would buy a ticket for cash and hope that there were seats available in first class. Logic told him that there should be at this time on a Thursday afternoon. Anyway, he had made all the moves that he could for the moment. Now it was up to others to respond.

In the arrivals lounge two men with throat microphones were watching Guest as he exited the customs area. One of them activated his mike and spoke.

'Nest this is Bird One. Ninepin has left customs and is on his own. Wait one. Ninepin is using his cell phone. I cannot see if he is sending or receiving. OK. Call has been terminated. Ninepin heading towards the front of the arrivals hall; he is not, repeat not heading for the long term car park. Over.'

'Bird One this is Nest. Can you still see Ninepin? Over.'

'Roger, Nest. He is heading to the information desk. Will – what the? Wait one, Nest. We have a problem with local officers. Out.'

In the command centre which was located in the back of an articulated truck about half a mile from the airport, the team commander known as Nest said aloud 'What does he mean 'a problem with locals'? Jesus! Kestrel, this is Nest. What is your location? Over.'

'Nest, this is Kestrel. I have left the terminal and am on my way to you. ETA five minutes. Over.'

'Kestrel, return to arrivals. We have had a break in comms with Bird One. Some problem with local officers apparently. Find out what you can and report back ASAP. Nest, out.'

In the arrivals lounge a uniformed PC was standing his ground against two men claiming to be from the Metropolitan Police's Counter Terrorist Unit. The latter two were trying to forcefully but discretely make the PC fuck off and let them carry on with their job. The young PC, complete with his high visibility jacket, was trying to clear the area because a bomb threat had been received. He had not used the words 'bomb threat' yet as they tended to frighten the general public but, having scrutinised the identification docs of the two men with the throat mikes and earpieces he now informed them why he had to ask them to leave the building. The senior member of Bird One had a brain wave.

'Look constable; you're doing your job but think it through. Bomb threat and CT from the Yard just happen to be present. Coincidence, do you think?'

'Well, when you put it like that' said Manchester's finest.

'Good lad. Now carry on getting the public safe and leave us to do what we have to do.'

'Yes, sir. Good luck, sir.'

'Have you kept sight of Ninepin through all that shit, Roy?' the team leader asked his colleague.

'Just about – there's bodies moving all over the place. Everything is closing down. Shops, the info desk, the lot. Look! There he goes – right out the front door.'

'Nest this is Bird One. There has been a bomb alert and Terminal One at least has been cleared out. Ninepin is leaving by the front door now. Request instructions – over.'

'Bird One this is Nest. Bird Two has Ninepin. Stay where you are in case he doubles back. Nest out.'

In London the Orion team had listened in to the radio exchanges coming over the loudspeakers from Manchester. There were also eight flat screen TV screens mounted high on one wall showing various images of the airport area. Three of them were currently blank as they were connected to mobile units which were not yet moving.

'I don't like this' said Goodchild. 'Comments anyone.'

'It cannot be coincidence' said Carver. 'But there's our target on screen two looking as lost as everyone else. Plus he's hardly wearing camouflage, is he?'

'Quite right, Martin. So something may be, probably is, going on but we don't know what it is. Michelle; call Manchester and find out what you can about this bomb threat. We'll just have to wait and see what develops.'

For the next 45 minutes flights stacked up over Manchester as they were refused permission to land. Some were diverted to other airports as their fuel began to run out. Road access to the entire complex was closed down which resulted in huge tail backs on the nearby motorway network. Several hundred people who had been cleared out of the arrivals area found themselves corralled by police in the area immediately across the road from the main airport building. Tony Guest was amongst them. Like many others he sat down on his bag and made calls on his cell phone. For the CT officers responsible for keeping in contact with their subject it was a nightmare situation. Guest would disappear from view then stand up again unexpectedly. When he sat down their directional microphones could not focus to pick up what he was saying. In short; it was chaos.

Finally the police announced that the airport was open to the public and slowly life got back to normal.

Nest this is Bird One 'Am following Ninepin on foot. Subject appears to be heading for the long term car park. Over.'

'Roger, Bird One. Maintain visual and contact me if subject changes direction. Bird Three – are you ready over?'

'Roger, Nest. Bird Three is in place. Over.'

'All units, this is Nest. The plan has not changed despite what has happened during the last hour. Keep focused and we will not drop the ball. Nest out.'

In London Chris Fearnley laughed out loud.

'Something funny in this situation that I'm missing, Chris?' asked Goodchild.

'I was just wondering why, in times of stress, men tend to use sports analogies. 'Drop the ball' bollocks.' She replied.

'You're right, Chris' said Carver. 'It would be far better to have a girl in charge who could say 'stay alert everyone and we won't ladder out stockings'.'

'Fuck off, Martin!'

'OK guys. Watch the screens' said Goodchild. 'Subject has just appeared on number six. That's the car park. Yes; he's entering his vehicle and moving off. Bird Three is following. Stay back you clowns! That's more like it. OK. OK. Nest – this is Eyrie. Is the Hawk up? Over.'

'Eyrie, this is Nest. Roger that. Hawk is up and holding until we know which direction Ninepin takes. Over.'

'Thank you, Nest. I'll leave you to it. Eyrie out.'

The Orion team sat back and listened to the brief radio exchanges coming from the north of England. It was soon obvious that Guest was using the motorway network and heading in a south westerly direction which would be the quickest route to where his home lay. Images were now being relayed from the helicopter designated Hawk with the mobile units driving a mile behind, and thus out of sight of, the subject.

'Boss, I've some info on the bomb scare if you want it now' said Michelle.

'Might as well. Shoot.'

'A brief call to the Manchester Evening News at 1630 hours. Voice described as male, accentless English, well educated. Said that there was quote an explosive device in the arrivals hall Terminal One unquote then rang off. The newspaper has a standard protocol to follow if it judges the call to be legit. They did and called airport security directly so they bypassed our colleagues in Greater Manchester police.'

'Was the call recorded?'

'No, boss. M.E.N is a glorified local rag.'

'So, all that chaos was the result of either luck or good planning. I'm starting to feel twitchy about this. Michelle, follow up with the paper. Who took the call, was the time logged precisely, what made them think it was real. You know the drill.'

'On it, boss.'

'Martin, Chris; I reckon he's headed home and won't resurface until late tomorrow. I'd like you two fresh for whatever happens next so get off now and I'll see you in the morning. If anything breaks during the night, you'll be contacted. All right?'

'I don't need telling twice. See you tomorrow, boss' said Carver.

'Wait for me, Martin' said Chris Fearnley. 'I've an awful thirst on and it's not ladylike to drink alone.'

Carver and Fearnley shut down their computers and left the offices together. Goodchild and Stone continued with their respective tasks. At 2000hrs Goodchild received a call informing him that Guest, as expected, arrived home where his wife was waiting. After assuring himself that SO15 had adequate surveillance in place and then standing the helicopter down, he organised for Orion calls to be routed to Addison's staff with a standing order that he himself was to be notified if anything of immediate importance happened. He then readied himself for the drive home. Michelle Stone accompanied him.

§

The American Embassy in London occupies a large part of Grosvenor Square and is one of the ugliest buildings in London. Some say that the Americans did this to spite the Duke of Westminster who refuses to sell them the freehold to this prime piece of real estate, making them pay rent like anybody else. The story goes that, when the American State Department said that all their other missions around the world were owned by them outright, the Duke replied that the same would apply in London once the United States government returned to him the title of all properties seized from his ancestors post 1776. As this comprised of a large section of the eastern seaboard, the Americans refused the Duke's offer and continued to be tenants in an ugly, enormous but well positioned property. Many an Ambassador to the Court of Saint James had enjoyed the facilities of Claridge's just around the corner.

Whatever the building lacked in architectural beauty it made up for in efficiency. Every working day at 0900hrs a red van bearing the insignia of the Royal Mail drew up at the rear of the embassy and, under the eye of two US Marine security guards, delivered the day's post and received the outgoing material from the mission which was destined for UK addresses only.

In these days of ever more creative criminals who wished to attack the United States wherever they could, all post was security screened before it went anywhere near an official's desk. The first procedure was to pass the item through a fluoroscope, similar to those used at airports to examine carry on luggage. After that there were other procedures used to detect the presence of explosives or toxic substances. Once an envelope or package had been deemed to be safe, it would be stamped to indicate that it had passed scrutiny and then forwarded to the relevant section in the embassy.

On Friday morning Dan Grofinius had the mind numbingly boring yet vital task of manning the fluoroscope. He was half an hour into his shift when he spotted something that made him do a double take then hit the large red button that stopped the conveyor belt. He rewound slowly then stopped the machine again.

'Jesus H – this is weird' he said to nobody in particular. By now the entire post room staff were looking at him. It was not unusual for the line to stop; all sorts of sad cretins sent fake bombs to the embassy but Grofinius' reaction indicated that this as something of a different order.

'Hey, Mikey' he called to a colleague. 'Can you come and take over here? I've got a situation.'

'Okey Dokey, Dan' said Mike Gagen who heaved his 240 pounds of weight across the room and replaced Grofinius at the screen.

Dan Grofinius had removed the package from the belt, looked at the addressee and punched in a four digit internal number.

'Legal Attaché's office' said a well modulated female voice.

'Hi; this is Dan Grofinius in the post room. We've received a package addressed to the Legat that he needs to come down and see right now. Can I speak with him, please?'

'I'm afraid he's in with the Ambassador for the next forty five minutes. I'll let him know you called.'

'Hold on; who is the ranking officer with whom I could speak right now?'

'That would be Jim McCarthy.'

Grofinius waited through five seconds of silence before taking a deep breath and saying 'Would you be so kind as to put me through, please?'

'Certainly' came the cheery, mindless reply.

'Legal Attaché's office, Jim McCarthy speaking.'

'Hi; this is Dan Grofinius in the post room. We've received a package down here addressed to the Legat that he needs to see ASAP. Now, I'm told that he's in with the Ambassador for a while and that you're the ranking guy for the moment. Could you possibly come down here, sir?'

'On my way.'

'Well at least someone on the FBI team has their head screwed on' thought Grofinius. Five minutes later he spotted a tall, slim guy with short, blond hair, steel rimmed eyeglasses, grey suit, white shirt and red tie. He had Bureau written all over him and was heading his way.

'Dan; I'm Jim McCarthy. What's the problem?'

'If you'll come over here, it's easier to show you.' Grofinius took the FBI agent to a long table along one side of the post room. 'This is the package. As you can see, it's a standard, padded envelope – what the Brits call a jiffy bag – and it was posted in the UK first class. I can't tell where or when as the post mark is smudged but, no doubt, you guys can overcome that. Its hand addressed to the Legal Attaché using his job title, not his name. What made me call you is what the fluoroscope shows us. Watch.' Grofinius, wearing purple surgical gloves, picked up the yellow package and placed it in a second, more compact machine. 'All I can tell you from this is that the bag contains a CD case and the case appears to contain a finger, probably a human one. There is nothing to indicate the presence of an explosive device and I have not tested for anthrax or any other nasties.'

'Why not?'

'Some of our tests could compromise the integrity of the package and I reckon that your lab has better equipment than mine. I'll carry out a full range of tests if you wish or I'll release the package to you to do whatever you want to. Your call, sir.'

Jim McCarthy looked at the x-ray image in front of him. 'I don't see any metal or solid objects in there, Dan' he said. 'You don't reckon it'll go 'bang' if we open it?'

'No, sir; I don't. If there is anything nasty in there it's very small indeed.'

'Like anthrax spores?'

'Like that. Yes, sir.'

'OK. Good job, Dan. I'll take this off your hands and see what my lab guys make of it. Would you put it in a bag, please?'

Grofinius placed the package into a brown, paper bag which he handed over to the FBI agent after making him sign for it thus absolving the State Department of any responsibility for harm which might befall members of the Bureau as a result of handling material which had etc, etc, etc.

McCarthy headed back to the Legal Attaché's section and briefed the technical team on the situation. They went to work immediately and had extracted the CD case fifteen minutes later. It was Postcards of the Hanging by the Grateful Dead.

'As far as I'm concerned' said the lab technician 'there's no reason not to open this case up.'

'Do it' said McCarthy.

The technician popped open the case. In the round hollow where the CD should have been, lay a small, human finger – pale from blood loss but with its manicured nail still intact and vibrant in a shade of coral pink.

'Process that as far as you can but start with print identification.'

'On it, sir.' The technician lifted the finger out of the case using sterile tweezers and placed it into a Petri dish. He then walked over the magic machine known as IAFIS. This stood for Integrated Automated Fingerprint Identification System which the FBI operates 24/7 every day of the year, including Christmas and Thanksgiving. It is the largest biometric database in the world, housing the details of around 100 million individuals – not all of them criminals. If you do have a criminal record, then IAFIS will spit out your details in about ten minutes or so. If your details are on file for another reason, say you were in the United States military or had worked for the Federal government in some capacity, then things might be a little bit slower – say an hour.

So when the technician announced that he had a match after

only three minutes, McCarthy was pretty sure that someone had mailed a felon's finger to them.

'OK. Who is the crim missing a finger then?' he asked.

'Ah, not a crim, sir. This print belongs to someone on our VIP list. She's Catherine Taylor-Lodge – daughter of Senator Lyall Lodge III of New York. We have her down as a student at Bristol University.'

'Right – everybody stop what you're doing; this just turned political. Is there a note with the CD case?'

'Yes, sir' replied a second technician. 'Very simple in content you might say.'

McCarthy went and looked at an A4 piece of white paper on which someone had written ONE OF YOURS, WE BELIEVE.

'Right, guys. This stuff is all going to Quantico for a full examination. Pack it all up after you have taken photos for our records. Correct me if I'm wrong but we do not have the facilities to test whether or not that finger came from a live or a dead body do we?'

'No, sir. We don't. It was decided that if we ever needed a test like that carried out urgently we could either use the British police facilities or, if time were not a factor, fly body parts Stateside.'

'OK carry out as instructed and not a word of this to anyone. I'm going to see the Ambassador. With that, McCarthy exited the lab and headed for the top floor where the big dogs had their kennels.

The Ambassador's office was guarded by Marine security staff and his PA Marion Keller. McCarthy would have preferred hand to hand combat against the marines than trying to dominate Ms Keller. She looked up from her reading when he arrived at her desk. 'Yes, McCarthy?' she said atonally.

'I need to see my boss and your boss together right now, Marion. Would you let them know I'm here, please?'

She looked at him without a change of expression. 'They've said no interruptions, Mr McCarthy.'

'They will want to know what I have, Marion. It's a matter of national importance and every minute will count.'

Once more she scrutinised him then came to a decision. 'Wait here, please. I won't be long.'

She left her desk and went past the marines and entered the double doors into the Ambassador's private office. McCarthy noticed that she did not knock. She was back out in thirty seconds and beckoned the FBI agent towards her. 'Good luck – I hope for your sake you were not exaggerating' she said quietly before closing the doors behind him.

He strode across the large room to where his boss and the Ambassador were sat drinking coffee. They did not offer him a cup and he noticed that a sheaf of papers which lay before them had been turned face down.

'I'm sorry to interrupt your meeting but something has happened that you both need to know about before I take further action.' He then quickly outlined the morning's events starting with the call from the post room at 0930hrs.

'I don't understand;' said the Ambassador. 'Why are the fingerprints of the Senator's child on a criminal database?'

'IAFIS is not solely for criminals, sir' replied McCarthy. 'It also carries the biometric details of federal employees and, what we informally call, VIP list. Whilst US nationals resident overseas are not <u>obliged</u> to register with their Consulates, they can if they so wish. This would help in time of evacuation/repatriation or in identification in the case of accidents or, God forbid, a kidnap. Looking at the girl's file it's clear that her father insisted on her registering before he agreed to her attending college here.'

'He would. I've met the man. Very protective type. He's going to go ape on this and he's a close supporter of the President. This is your world, gentleman. What do you advise before I call DC?'

'I would hold off on calling Washington until we know whether the finger was removed from a live or a dead body. It's the first thing the Senator will ask' said the legal attaché.

'And how quickly can we find that our, Kevin?'

'If I send the material to Quantico via military courier, about ten hours. If I call in a favour from the Brits, about thirty minutes.'

'That's a big time difference. How much detail would you have to give to whoever your contact is?'

'My contact is the Commissioner of the Metropolitan Police at New Scotland. He's one of the good guys, not a political appointee like we had when Tony Blair was Prime Minister. I would tell him all we know, Ambassador, for the simple reason that whether this girl is dead or alive, we will need local help to find her. Best to be straight with them from the start but to ask for discretion until we have at least notified the father.'

'That sounds reasonable to me, Kevin. OK run with it and keep me informed. I'm here all day. We'll find time to talk about that other business another day. The Lodge situation is your number one priority. Jim – good work.'

'Thank you, sir.'

The two FBI men returned to their own part of the building and started things moving. The Legal Attaché, Kevin Ryan, contacted Sir Alan Sampson at New Scotland Yard and requested the urgent use of their lab facilities. This was immediately agreed to and Ryan said that he would be arriving within the next half an hour.

'Jim; give me a printout of the girl's photo and passport details. Also her last known residential address' said Ryan.

'Got them here, sir' said McCarthy having anticipated this particular request.

'Thanks. I want you to start on building a profile on the girl's habits, friends, the usual. I know it's summer break but do your best. I'll give you a call as soon as I've finished at the Yard. Anything else you can think of right now, Jim?'

'No, sir. Your car is waiting for you in the basement.'

'Right. Talk to you later.'

With that the Legat left the room and took the lift to the basement where an agent was waiting to drive him. Their journey was a short one going south along Park Lane then skirting the rear walls of Buckingham Palace before turning left into Victoria Street which took them to New Scotland Yard. The Americans were moved swiftly through the security checks and, a mere twenty minutes after leaving the embassy, Kevin Ryan found himself seated with Sir Alan Sampson. Tea having been offered and declined they got down to it.

'Jim – if I may say so, you sounded somewhat fraught on the telephone' said Britain's top police officer. 'All I know is that you need information on an unspecified body part. My head of forensics will be here in a couple of minutes; is there anything else that you would care to tell me?'

'The body part is a human finger belonging to an American citizen resident in the UK. We received it in the post this morning and have identified it as belonging to the daughter of a United States Senator. Before I inform the gentleman of this fact I would like to know if the finger was cut from a living or dead hand.'

Sir Alan looked at Kevin Ryan and was thankful not to be in his shoes. 'Are there any other tests you would like us to perform on the, ah, specimen?'

'No, thanks and I would be grateful if you did not try. Once your folk have answered my initial question I'm sending all the material I have back to Quantico for a full examination. I would also like to request total discretion from you and yours until we have spoken with the Senator.'

'Goes without saying, Kevin.' The intercom on Sampson's desk buzzed. 'Yes?' said the Commissioner.

'I have Doctor Watkins here, sir' came his secretary's voice.

'Send her straight in, please.'

Seconds later the door opened and the diminutive figure of Rachel Watkins appeared. If she was intimidated by being summoned to the most important office in the building she did not let it show.

'Doctor Watkins, thank you for coming. I'm afraid we've no time for chit chat today. I want you to perform one test and one test only on this specimen.' Sampson indicated that his visitor hand over the package to the doctor. 'We need to know whether this came from a living or dead body. How long will you need?'

'Free histamine test is simple and straightforward. I'll take this now and can be back in ten minutes with that information.'

'Good. We shall wait here for you, doctor.'

Rachel Watkins left the Commissioner's office without another word as though requests at this level were an everyday occurrence for her.

'Kevin – I've cleared my decks for the next half an hour. Given what you've told me so far this is going to be bloody serious. How can we help?'

'This is a nightmare, Alan. The Senator represents New York State and is in the current President's party. As such he is important and knows it. He is recently widowed and his daughter is/was his only child. The US media will be all over this – human interest and all that sort of thing. The best I can hope for is that this is a kidnap situation and not a murder. Either way, I'm going to need the help of your people to go door knocking and provide local knowledge, Alan. I take it I can count on that?'

'As far as I'm concerned you can. Where was the girl studying?'

Kevin took a dossier from his briefcase and glanced at it. 'University of Bristol is our information.'

'That comes under the Avon and Somerset Constabulary. I know the Chief Constable there very well – a good man in a crisis. What else can you give me regarding this unfortunate girl?'

In answer, Ryan handed over a slim dossier to the Englishman. Sir Alan's face did not show any emotion as he scanned the document but, inwardly, he was amazed at the details that the American embassy held on one of its citizens. Address, phone numbers, next of kin, full face and profile photos, passport details

– all fairly normal. But blood type and dental records as well seemed a bit morbid.

'Where are you in your investigation, Kevin?'

'We're not. All this started when the package arrived at the embassy around 0930 today. Once your lab tells me what I'm looking at I'll put some pre-set plans into operation. I'll be in charge over here unless Washington decides otherwise. It would be useful to have one of your senior staff to act as liaison, Alan.'

'Yes, quite. Who that will be depends on what we are dealing with so I'm afraid we'll have to wait on Doctor Watkins's results. Do you think that there may be a terrorist angle here, Kevin?'

'I doubt it. If you look in the dossier you'll find a photo of the only note that came with the package. The original will go to Quantico. 'One of yours we believe' does not sound much like the work of any terrorist group I know of. It's more like the taunting of a very sick mind and that worries me big time.'

'Indeed. The photo of the envelope; were you able to ascertain place and time of posting? I can't make out what this says.'

'No. It appears that the franking on the padded envelope was smudged. Quantico will clear that up for us.'

'We could do it very quickly here, Kevin.'

'I should have brought it with me. Too late now. I have to send as much as I can as soon as I can to the States. You know how it goes, Alan.'

'Yes.' The English policeman was too polite to mention that the influence of politics on the judicial process was much more persuasive in the United States than in the UK (although it seemed to him that his own country was hell bent on imitating the worse aspects of political life from the other side of the pond). 'I note from your file that Catherine is not in halls.'

'I'm sorry – what does that mean?'

'I mean that she does not live on campus' said Sampson translating. 'Hers is a private address. Most girls that age house share to save money and to have a support network. There does not appear to be a list of house mates here, Kevin.'

'It's obviously something we need to look into. If she is sharing it's not to save money. Her family are rolling in the stuff. When I get back to the embassy we'll start phoning around. Someone will need to go to Bristol and interview tutors, lecturers, friends, the whole nine yards.'

'I'll find someone to accompany your someone. Despite the Senator's elevated position, you do not have the authority to conduct unilateral enquiries over here you know.'

'Yeah, I know. And you know the pressure that's going to come down from on high. If the Senator calls the President and he calls your Prime Minister and he kicks the ass of your Mayor well, guess who gets it next?'

'Quite. Have your people called any of the contact numbers for this girl?'

'They will be trying that, or will have tried that now. I left instructions for them to call me if anything came to light. The fact that they've not gotten back to me makes me think that they've not been able to speak with anyone yet.'

'So we wait. Sorry to have to ask this, Kevin but have you given me all the information that you currently have?'

'I've given you everything that I can, Alan. And I'm not playing word games here. OK?'

Before the Commissioner could reply to what he thought was a rhetorical interrogative there was a quick rap on the office door which then opened. Doctor Watkins marched in clad in lab whites this time. She placed the package which she had been given just ten minutes previously along with a closely typed, A4 print out headed UK Confidential in pink, capital letters on the desk.

'Gentleman; I'll be brief. The finger was cut post mortem. That is certain. I know that is all you asked me to test for but the free histamine procedure does throw up additional information which may be of use to you. The finger belonged to a white female aged between roughly twenty to thirty years of age. I have decided to classify this information as confidential for the time being as I do not have any information which would warrant a higher classification, I have kept a copy for my own files. Will there be anything else, Sir Alan?'

'Not for the moment, doctor. Thank you for your help.'

She nodded and left the room as quickly as she had entered it. Sir Alan scanned the paper she had left on his desk then handed it over to his American visitor who did the same.

'Third finger, left hand' said Ryan. 'I knew this was a sicko S.O.B.'

'So it would seem, Kevin. I take it you will be heading back to the embassy now or are you going to go to Washington yourself?'

'I'm staying in London. I'll have an agent take all the evidence to the States. Thanks for your help on this, Alan. We'll talk later when you've decided who your liaison guy will be. I'd better be off now.'

The two men shook hands and the American picked up his driver from the outer office. Once they were safely on their way back to Grosvenor Square, Sir Alan returned to his office to think. After a minute he punched in an internal number which was picked up almost immediately.

'Watkins' came the one word response.

'Doctor Watkins; Alan Sampson here. I don't suppose that you have sufficient material left over from the sample you were given this morning to conduct one more test would you?'

'That would depend on the test, Sir Alan.'

'I was thinking of looking for traces of the toxin used in the Orion killings, doctor?'

'I thought you might. As I know precisely what to look for I can have a yes or a no in five minutes, Sir Alan.'

'Excellent. I would like you to call me on 2337 once you have your result, doctor.'

'I'll be back to you as soon as I can' and she hung up on the head of the British police force to do what she had known she would have to since the moment she had seen the shrivelled finger.

On the other end of the line, Sir Alan Sampson stared at his telephone in puzzlement. It was not possible that someone would hang up on him – was it? Mentally shaking his head he punched another internal number.

'Deputy Assistant Commissioner Addison's office.'

'Alan Sampson here. Where is he?'

'He's gone down to Special Ops, sir. Due back in twenty minutes.'

'I want him in my office in ten and I want Commander Goodchild with him. Organise that, will you.'

'Yes, sir.'

This time Sir Alan hung up. He went back to his desk to think through as many possible scenarios as he could arising from the unexpected arrival of the Americans into the Orion case. The odds of two people lopping off young girls' ring fingers were too long for him to even consider and he was fairly certain that the toxicology report would reinforce his view. The major negative in this new development was that he would be obliged to alert his political masters about Orion which would surprise them to put it mildly. There, were, however, positive aspects to the situation and he noted these down in his personal shorthand.

When the door to his office opened to admit officers Addison and Goodchild, Sampson glanced at the wall mounted clock, noting that they were precisely on time.

'Gentlemen – please, take a seat.' Sampson remained behind his fortress of a desk rather than move the three of them to the more relaxed 'conversation area' of the office. Obviously this was serious business.

'I would like to talk with you regarding the state of play in the Orion case' began Sir Alan.

Chapter Twenty Nine

'Sir, if I may' interrupted Addison.

'No, you may not, Oliver. Just listen. This morning I received a call from Kevin Ryan, the Legal Attaché at the American embassy. He had received an object in the post – a finger – and wanted us to test it to see if it had been taken from a live or a dead body. Doctor Watkins tells us that it was the latter. That was all Ryan wanted from us and the finger plus all other material is now on its way to their laboratory in Quantico. Ryan informed me that they had identified the finger as belonging to one Catherine Taylor – Lodge, the only child of Senator Lyall Lodge III who is, in turn, a close political ally of the current President. The young lady was studying at Bristol University so it looks like we are going to be involved in a high profile, very public murder investigation. Just to make matters more interesting, Doctor Watkins carried out a further test at my request and the finger contains traces of the same poison found in all your victims, Commander. For the moment, the Americans are unaware of this. So, that's the latest development. How do we act on it, gentlemen?'

'What details do you have for this girl, sir?' asked Goodchild.

Sampson passed the American dossier to Goodchild who sped read it. 'May I use your phone, sir?'

'Be my guest' said the commissioner not realising that he had just used a most inappropriate word.

Goodchild picked up the internal phone and dialled. 'Michelle, it's me. Stop whatever you're doing and check if the following person left the UK for Fuerteventura in the past two weeks.' He then dictated Catherine Taylor-Lodge's passport details to Stone. 'Begin with flights from Bristol. If that comes up dry expand the search to all international airports. If she did not go to Fuerteventura, try Spain then France. If that does not work out, search everything you can. I'm in the Commissioner's office; call me on my mobile when you have something. Clear?' He placed the receiver back in its cradle and sat down.

'If this American girl was on the island the same time as Tony Guest we have a decision to make.'

'You're the person with day to day control of Orion, Commander' said Sampson. 'What do you think is going on here?'

'According to the Americans they received the girl's finger this morning via the Royal Mail. The envelope could have been posted yesterday but Guest was under surveillance from the moment he landed until when he arrived home. Having said that – sorry, Sir Alan; how much detail do you know regarding events at Manchester yesterday?'

'I know of the operations existence but I have not yet read the action report.'

'OK. Guest was observed to either make or receive a call on his cell phone. Not long after that Manchester airport was evacuated because of an anonymous bomb threat transmitted via the Manchester Evening News. It's possible that Guest was briefly out of our sight during the crowd confusion that the evacuation caused. I'll need to go over the CCTV images again. Finally, there is a Post Office in Terminal One.'

'If we accept that as being what happened it makes Guest look pretty stupid, doesn't it?' said Addison. 'He would know that we'd be onto him sharpish yet, as far as I know, he's still at home.'

'Maybe not' said Goodchild. 'If I put something in the normal post on late Thursday afternoon I would not expect it to be on someone's desk the following morning. I would reckon Saturday if I were lucky, more realistically Monday. Perhaps the Royal Mail expedites post for diplomatic missions more efficiently than it does for the general public.'

Normally the Royal Mail was a good target for humorous comment but none of the three officers were in thigh slapping mood that morning.

Mark Goodchild's mobile rang. He looked at the screen and answered 'Yes, Michelle?' The two senior officers were silent as they observed the younger man's body language and listened to his end of the conversation. 'Good work, Michelle. If you can canvass hotels without creating a fuss then do so. If not, leave it. I'll be with you soon.'

He terminated the call and addressed his bosses. 'Catherine Taylor-Lodge flew from Bristol to Fuerteventura via Madrid and Lanzarote eight days ago. She'd booked for an open return and was not part of a package group so was not pre-booked at any of the main hotels. Detective Sergeant Stone is following up on where she might have been staying. Gentlemen, I think we have to arrest Guest now and get someone down to Fuerteventura. We shall have to liaise with the Spanish authorities, carry out a forensic search of Guest's accommodation and do that now before the FBI send an invasion force to the island. I want this arsehole for the murdered English girls. I know that the circumstantial on Catherine is the strongest but I would like to use that as a lever to make Guest cough. If he cops to the UK killings then we will try and sentence him. Otherwise we'll let the Yanks have him and he can spend the rest of his life in a federal penitentiary singing sweet soul music with Bubba and the Baboons.'

'We would not hand over a UK citizen to another nation when there were charges here to face, Commander' said Addison.

'Sir, the Americans are of the view that certain crimes committed against their nations interests wherever and by whoever they are carried out will be tried in a United States court. Anyway, all that is politics and way above my pay grade. May I go and arrest him, sir?'

Sir Alan stood up and walked to his window which gave a good view towards St James' Park and Buckingham Palace beyond. His duty as a police officer was clear but only a fool could be ignorant of the political ramifications this case would throw up. He'd kept the government in the dark from the beginning and his officers had lied to the media regarding what had been found in Hyde Park. He could deal with that but the American angle was tricky to say the least. He could say with a straight face that he had not been given all available information by Kevin Ryan but, sooner or later, he would have to come clean with the Americans. Just when could he say to them 'What – you're looking for a man who kills girls with a foreign poison, cuts off a finger for fun and had a link to an island off the coast of Africa? Why, we arrested one just like that on Friday, just after your Legal Attaché's visit. Small world, eh?'

The evidence would probably be sent to the States using a military flight out of the giant USAF base at Mildenhall. The material would yield up its secrets sometime tonight GMT and then the Department of Homeland Security was going to scream international terrorism and perform a rodeo in a Meissen factory. It would be best for all concerned to avoid that.

His other problem was that the Mayor of London, the Home Secretary and the Prime Minister were all overseas on holiday. The latter two were due back this Sunday evening and the Mayor, although nominally his immediate boss, did not really matter. Timing was against him. He did not fancy trying to explain the complex events that were now unfolding over the telephone. At the end of the day he was a British policeman and that decided him.

'Commander Goodchild. Bring Guest to Paddington Green station and formally charge him with the UK murders. Close his house down and carry out a full forensic search. Have an officer meet his wife at the airbase where she works and keep her away from the media. I want all this done quietly and out of the glare of the TV cameras. Don't mention the American girl until I give you the go ahead. I'm going to try and stall Kevin Ryan and set up a meeting with the PM and Home Secretary for Sunday. Questions?'

'So, no deployment to Fuerteventura then?'

'Not yet. Select a team and find out where Guest was staying whilst he was on the island. Again, wait for me to give the nod on that.'

'Right. I take it that you want him in Paddington Green to play up the terrorist angle, sir?'

'Yes. That's why you became involved in this bugger's muddle to start with isn't it, Commander?'

'It is, sir. If I might make a suggestion; I think it would be useful in the short term if Guest were to assist us in our enquiries. Once we formally charge him the clock is ticking before an appearance in court and he will probably hire a lawyer. Why not keep things informal and only charge him if he proves unhelpful? We could buy ourselves some time and keep this out of the press until next week.'

I hear what you're saying, Commander but I'm afraid that I cannot think of short term advantages here. Have him arrested, brought to London and charged. Carry on.'

Goodchild picked up the dossier that the American had left. Sampson made no objection so he took it with him back to the Orion offices to set in motion the next phase of the operation. God knows what the team were going to think of this latest development. As the Commissioner had so eloquently described it, it was a real 'bugger's muddle'.

Chapter Thirty

As soon as Kevin Ryan's car had left New Scotland Yard he had started making phone calls. He'd given Special Agent McCarthy a heads up that he would be taking all the evidence to the Bureau's main laboratory at Quantico whilst Ryan remained in the UK to coordinate the coming investigation.

Ryan had spoken with the Ambassador and sought, and received, permission for McCarthy to use the Embassy's Gulfstream V 1550. This aircraft was based at a private hanger at Heathrow and could cruise at 575mph with a range of over 7,500 miles making it the equal of a Boeing 747. The material would be undergoing tests late this afternoon Washington time and preliminary results could be expected by the end of the working day there. Ryan foresaw a late night ahead for himself.

On arrival in his office he summoned McCarthy to join him which he did immediately.

'All set to go, Jim?'

'Sure. Always have a get out of Dodge bag in my office. What are my instructions?'

'You'll be met at Andrews and escorted to Quantico – chopper or car I don't know yet. I'll have contacted the forensics team so they'll have cleared the decks for your arrival. Stay at Quantico until someone tells you otherwise and feel free to call me if you need to. OK?'

'Yeah, fine. I'll be off then.'

'No. Wait one. I've booked a call to the Director and I want you here whilst I make it. You never know – once he hears what's happened he might just countermand all my instructions. Take a seat.'

Two minutes later and Ryan's secretary's voice came over the speakerphone. 'I have the Director on line one, sir.'

'Put him through please, Mary-Beth. Director? Good morning, sir. Thanks for getting back to me so quickly. Are we secure?'

'Yes we are, Kevin. So, what's so urgent in London, England that I need to re-jig my morning schedule?'

'I'm about to give you a lot of details, sir. You might care to record my call before I send you a written summary.'

'All right, Kevin. Let's assume that my memory does not function so well these days. We're recording.'

In London the Legat winced at the barbed comment but proceeded to recount the day's events starting with the arrival of the package and ending with the fact that Jim McCarthy was ready to fly to the capital with the evidence. The Director had not said a word during Ryan's summary and remained silent at the end of it. Over the speakerphone came the noise of a pen scratching on paper.

'Mind telling me why you involved the Brits at this early stage, Kevin?' said the FBI Director.

'Time, sir. You are not going to be able to sit on the fact that we identified the finger as belonging to the Senator's daughter at 1030 this morning, that's 0530 your time. The Senator's first question will be is she dead or alive. I figured you'd want to have that information, sir.'

'I see. You also saw fit to let the Brits know Catherine Taylor-Lodge's identity. Why?'

'Again, time. We are going to have to work with them on this. By giving them maximum info from the very start they'll have no excuse to drag their bureaucratic feet as the investigation proceeds.'

'How much have you told the Ambassador, Kevin?'

'I briefed him before I visited Scotland Yard then I asked for permission to use the Gulfsteam. He knows that the finger belongs to Senator Lodge's daughter but not that she is dead.'

'Keep it that way unless he asks you a direct question. If he knew all the facts he would probably cable the Secretary of State and I can do without her input today.'

'Understood, sir. I'll make myself busy setting up initial enquiries regarding Catherine's habits and I'll let you know as soon as I have a liaison contact at Scotland Yard.'

'That's fine, Kevin. We'll talk again later today or tonight. I've got a difficult phone call to make now. Catch you later.'

Down the road at New Scotland Yard Mark Goodchild was making his most important phone call for some time. He could not afford the smallest slip in Guest's arrest procedure and would have been far happier being at the scene himself or even sending Martin Carver who had, at least already visited the premises. As it was, he was now giving a final briefing to the DCI in charge of the SO15 team who went by the code name Nest.

'Right to re-cap. I want a hard entry, armed police shouting their heads off, Ninepin down and cuffed, then bring him to Paddington Green. Try not to shoot him, Nest.

'Roger that, sir. Anything else?'

'I want all his clothes and personal effects, especially anything that looks as though he brought it back from Spain, sent down to London ASAP. The forensics people can take their own sweet time over a detailed search of the house. Lastly, has everyone been briefed on the possibility of toxins being present?'

'Yes, sir. Don't worry – we've all been here before.'

'OK. Nest. It's all yours. Out.'

In his mobile command centre Nest had sound and vision of his subject. During the night, microphones and mini-cams had been fixed to windows on the ground floor. Mrs Guest had left for work at 0700 but their subject had stayed in bed until 1100. An SO15 sniper was watching him from a tree perch just over 1,000 yards away.

At noon the sniper radioed Nest to say that the subject had finally finished his ablutions and was descending the stairs.

'Sir, we have him in the kitchen making coffee. Go or not?' asked the assault leader.

'Not yet; I hate kitchens. Too many knives and pots of boiling liquid.'

The tension was building with each passing minute. Guest poured himself some juice then took his drink through to the lounge.

'Nest – subject is seated on the sofa with his back to the front door. Situation optimal for us. Your instructions?'

'Go, go, go.'

Tony Guest never knew what hit him. One moment he was reclining on his old, brown Chesterfield with his eyes closed, mentally rehearsing an addition to his repertoire (Dedicated Follower of Fashion); the next, the world was a confusion of men in black who hurled him to the floor and twisted his arms behind his back, all the while screaming unintelligibly into his ears. Guest was reminded of a bad experience at an AC/DC concert many years previously. Finally he was hauled to his feet, still in a state of shock and with his wrists shackled behind his back. He was surrounded by men in black coveralls, some with black helmets on, others wearing what looked like ski masks. All carried firearms. A man appeared amongst them dressed in smart but casual civilian clothes. This one spoke directly to Guest but so rapidly that the latter could not follow. He knew what it was though through viewing the cop shows on TV that his wife enjoyed so much. It was the British equivalent of what the American's called a 'Miranda'. He had just been read his rights and the only words he recognised were 'Anthony Leonard Guest' and 'murder'. He vaguely registered the fact that the names of three women had been uttered by the plain clothes officer but the shock of the moment precluded him connecting them to himself.

The next thing he knew was that he being half carried into a waiting van. The vehicle had a double door and he was pushed through them both. It was, in reality, a locked cage on wheels with plastic benches along two sides. The doors closed behind him and the van set off.

Three hours later the vehicle stopped for the first time. It reversed a few yards and the engine was switched off. The doors opened and Guest looked out at the unsmiling faces of two uniformed police officers, one wearing sergeant's insignia. The sergeant beckoned him forward and he was helped down the van's steps then guided along a corridor into a reception area. It was a modern, brightly lit space but with no external windows. Police officers milled around on their business but Guest had had time to calm down and noticed the curious glances that were directed his way. He did not think that these guys were his fans.

A desk sergeant signed some paperwork which Guest assumed was to acknowledge receipt of one bewildered musician currently possessing all his limbs, teeth and reproductive organs. From the reception area he was taken to a small room where his cuffs were removed. This was done, not to make him feel more comfortable, but to facilitate the taking of his fingerprints. The process was a clean one. He placed his hands, palm down on clear, plastic plates which were part of a portable machine. A green light came on and scanned his extremities, not unlike a photocopier machine. Once this process had been completed to the operator's satisfaction he was made to sit on a stool and his photograph was taken from the front and both sides. The handcuffs were reattached and, for the first time since his arrival, someone spoke to him.

'Open your mouth wide, please. I'm going to take a swab for DNA purposes' said the same WPC who had operated the print machine.

Guest complied without complaint. Several if his buddies from the music scene had been busted for various minor offences and on each occasion the police had insisted on a DNA swab – even from guys who were never even charged. Despite the vociferous efforts of the human rights lobby, the British government continued to build up its DNA database. Guest figured that someone facing multiple murder charges would be wasting their breath by not co-operating at this stage.

The final stage of Guest's induction to the system was humiliating though not completely unexpected. He was taken into a small, windowless room where four large, shirt sleeved policemen awaited, one in each corner. In the centre of the room was a white stool behind which stood a slim young man who wore a white coat and, in common with the burly bobbies, latex gloves.

'Please be seated' said white coat in a firm but civil voice. 'I am now going to search your head for foreign objects. If you move, you will be restrained.'

Guest said nothing and sat patiently whilst white coat combed through his hair, looked in his ears and examined his teeth. After each process, boxes were ticked on a form that one of the policemen kept on a clipboard.

White coat left the room and returned immediately carrying three transparent plastic bags.

'Please place your shoes in one bag and all your other clothing in another' he said.

Guest stripped to his boxers and bagged his possessions as instructed.

'I said all your clothing.' The civility had gone from white coat's voice. Guest took off his boxers and placed them with his other clothes.

'Now, stand still.' White coat examined every inch of skin on Guest's body even down to behind the scrotal sack before writing on his form 'No tattoos or other distinguishing marks.'

'One last thing to be done. It is not pleasant either for you or us but it is obligatory. I am going to perform a rectal examination on you. If you cooperate and relax as much as possible then we will be done quickly. If you choose to be obstructive then restraint will be used on you but, rest assured, the examination will be carried out.'

Guest took a deep breath and stared down at white coat seething with impotence but managing to hide his contempt from the functionary.

'Get on with it' he said.

Five minutes later it was over and he was handed a white coverall made of what appeared to be very strong paper and similar slippers. His original guards reappeared and escorted him to what was, according to the sign on the door, interview room four. Here he was left, alone once more.

Goodchild, Carver and Fearnley were observing Guest from the other side of a two way mirror. They were joined by white coat. The law prevented them from observing a strip search covertly, but there was nothing to stop them from talking to the person who had conducted said search.

'So, Doctor,' began Goodchild 'what are your first impressions of this guy?'

'The first two words that come to mind are 'intelligent' and 'vain'. The cameras show that he spent the journey to London with his eyes closed. He did not show sign of panic in the van nor scream and shout. He conserved himself.'

'Like a soldier' said Carver. 'Sleep where and when you can. You never know when you might next have the chance.'

'Precisely. He is a large man who looks after himself physically. He is not a hairy hippy; that look is the result of expensive barbering. The really significant factor is that it is rare to find someone of his age and social background not to be tattooed – especially someone in the music industry. No; he likes his body as it is. Also, his eyes miss nothing. They scan and evaluate surroundings and situations. Despite the humiliation of the body search, he gave in with only token resistance. He would have liked to have assaulted me but realised that it would have been counter-productive. Be very careful with this man, Commander. I would not like to find myself alone with him. Anything else?'

'No – thanks for that. We'll probably talk later.'

The three Orion members turned back to the mirror and observed their prime suspect. He was sat at a plain, white table and staring into the middle distance, his face expressionless.

'Any opinion, guys?' said Goodchild.

'He does not look like a master criminal who's just had the world come crashing down around his ears, does he?' said Chris Fearnley.

'Nor does he look like some poor itinerant songster who's been banged up in London for killing three birds he's never heard of' said Carver. 'Where's the panic, the sweat, the protestations of innocence. If I did not know otherwise I'd say he'd gone through military counter – interrogation training.'

'So who should have first crack at him?' asked Goodchild.

No one spoke. This was an extremely important decision. It was often the case that a subject would open up right at the start of the interrogation process if the interrogator were skilful enough. The converse held true; a clumsy approach could lead to a subject making a Trappist monk seem like a gossip columnist.

Finally, Carver spoke up. 'I've an idea, boss. I could conduct a non interview interview.'

'And what the hell is that?'

'It's like when someone replies to a job advert by telephone and they're talking away to someone they think is the receptionist when, in actual fact, they have called a dedicated line for the head of HR and they're already at first interview stage.'

'Sounds devious. Military?'

'No; commercial. People show their true colours like that. It's also used to weed out applicants who can't string two words of English together.'

'I like it. How do you propose using it in this situation? What's the legal status of this technique?'

'It has no status; it does not exist and we cannot record it. Think of it as me going on a recon mission and you will use the information later when, as the superior officers you engage the enemy formally.'

'All right. How are you going to work this?'

'Chris and I have done this dance before so why don't we just do it and you watch, boss. If you want to call it off at any stage just walk in through the door.'

'My turn to be the incompetent cretin is it, Martin?' asked Fearnley.

'Yes. I know more about his era of music than you. Shall we?'

Martin and Chris left the observation room. Goodchild was watching Guest through the mirror when the door to Interview 4 banged open and an angry DI Carver burst in and shouted 'This is unfuckingbelievable, sergeant!'

A flustered DS Fearnley followed him in saying 'I'm sorry, sir; I'm new here and'

'Never mind that!' said a now icy toned Carver. 'Go and find the relevant officers. I'll wait here. Jesus.' He sat down across the table from Guest whilst Fearnley disappeared at speed.

'Sorry about that, Mr Guest. You should not have been left on your own. There will be someone with you shortly.'

'What's going on?'

'Sorry, sir. I should not talk with you. There has to be a minimum of two officers present to interview a suspect.' Carver took a black, leather bound note book from his hip pocket and began to flick through it.

After five minutes of being ignored Guest said 'Bollocks'

'Beg you pardon, sir?'

'Bollocks. You're play acting. You've been watching me from behind that mirror and this some weird interrogation technique.'

'You've been watching too much Law and Order, sir. We don't use two way mirrors. We view and record everything on digicams. There's one in each corner of the ceiling if you look. When they're on you'll see a little red light. Likewise your interview will be sound recorded on this piece of kit here. But, as I said, there needs to be two officers present and I should not be talking with you so, if you wouldn't mind.' Carver went back his note book.

Guest looked around the room. Mounted high in two corners of the space were, indeed, a couple of small cameras. Like the sound recording equipment on a shelf to his left, they did not appear to be functioning. He looked at the man on the other side of the table to him. He seemed way too cool to be a cop – unless he were vice or something.

'How come you knew my name?' asked Guest.

Carver closed his notebook and let out a long suffering sigh. 'Because it's written on the charge sheet which is on the cover of the file which sits in a holder which is attached to the wall outside this interview room, Mr Guest. O.K?'

'Sorry – it's just that I'm confused. Yesterday I was flying back from Spain after a week's gigging and next thing I know I'm being jumped on by the Men in Black. Where am I? Can you answer that for me at least, please?'

'No reason why not – you'll know soon enough. This is an interview room at Paddington Green police station in London.'

'Why here? Is this where the three women are from?'

'No, Mr Guest. This station is normally used to house terrorist suspects. I imagine that you are here because the crime you're accused of is going to make a big splash in the media and whoever is running your case wants to keep the reptiles at bay for as long as possible.'

'Reptiles?'

'Journalists and talking heads.'

Guest nodded as if acknowledging the wisdom of such a tactic on the part of the police.

'I didn't do it, you know.'

'No Mr Guest; I don't know and I'm not really interested. Guys who abduct and kill young women are fairly commonplace in our society. Three is not even that big a number and not really important – unless you're one of the three of course. My field is a tad more important than sexually inadequate murderers.'

'So what do you do, big man?'

'Well let's say that my aim is to keep the trains and planes running on time. Talking of which' – Carver looked at his wristwatch – 'where the fuck are your people?'

'Look, man; I've not done anything. I'm a musician not a murderer.'

'Yeah, yeah, yeah. The prisons are full of innocent people Mr Guest.'

'My name's Tony; would you call me Tony?'

Guest was nearly begging Carver to use his given name. It seemed as though it were the most important thing in the world for him to be humanised and not be regarded as a 'sexually inadequate murderer.' This, of course, had been Carver's intention and he now had the choice of assuming the role of Guest's pal or of being the stone cold cop. He would have felt more comfortable if he'd had more time to set this up and know that he had an experienced colleague to play against. Well, he hoped Goodchild was paying attention on the other side of the mirror.

'O.K then – Tony it is. But I still can't discuss your case. That's for <u>your</u> protection by the way.'

'Fuck all that, man. What's your name anyway?'

'Call me Martin. Excuse me if I don't shake hands.'

Guest looked down at his wrists which were now cuffed in front of him. 'Yeah, a bit difficult to be civilised when you're in chains.'

'That sounds like it could be the basis of a song, Tony.'

Guest's face went blank then, slowly, a smile spread across it. 'Yeah – something Country. It's Hard to Say Hello When You're Handcuffed!' He sang the line in a generic CW style. To his amazement, Carver followed up with what would be line two in a pleasant tenor. 'And the Sheriff's got a Shotgun to your Head.'

'Cos Those Chains are there to Keep You in Your Place, Boy' continued Guest.

'And If You Move the Man Will Surely Shoot Your Dead' finished Carver.

'I don't believe it!' exclaimed Guest. 'I've spent hours with professionals trying to write verses that scan. Off the top of your head, just like that? Damn, that's good.'

'Don't get carried away, Tony. I'm not looking to change my day job. So, what sort of music do you play?'

'Whatever the crowd wants, I've got a semi-regular set of venues around England that I've built up over the years and I more or less know what each place wants. This gig in Spain was a favour for a friend and was a bit more complex as I had to front a band of guys who weren't that experienced. It worked O.K. though.'

'Plus the sun, sea and sex eh?'

'I wish. By the time I crawled out of my pit in the afternoon I had just about the energy to crash out on the balcony and re-hydrate in time for the evening's set. Back in the day I would not have been waking up alone but, shit, I've slowed down some I must admit.'

'So it was just work all night then back to the hotel? That's not very rock and roll, is it?'

'Not even a hotel. My buddy Jake gave me the run of his apartment on the beach looking out to Lanzarote…..'

On the other side of the two way mirror Goodchild and Fearnley were observing Carver at work.

'This is brilliant stuff, Chris. He's got the guy's address in Fuerteventura, contact names, itineraries; Guest is eating out of his hand. Have you seen him do this before?'

'Not exactly like this, boss, no. But close enough. By the time Martin's finished with this mutt he'll be ready for phase two which is where you, or someone you choose, comes in. It will be time for a hard, formal interview that will be useable in court.'

'Where did he learn this stuff, Chris?'

'You'd have to ask Martin, boss.'

'I'm asking you, Chris.'

Goodchild had spoken in his best command voice. Chris Fearnley looked him squarely in the eye and said, 'Firstly, sir, you're assuming that I know where Martin learned his interview technique. Bear in mind the possibility that you may be wrong. Secondly, sir, if I did know then you would have to think that Martin had entrusted me with that information and that I would be willing to break that trust. There you are very definitely wrong, sir. I think now might be a good time for me to get this information to Michelle and see if she can verify it, sir.'

It had been a long time since anyone had stood against Mark Goodchild. He could break a junior officer in more ways than one but he realised, as he locked eyes with Chris Fearnley, that she was not in the least intimidated by him.

'Very well. Get that over to Michelle. I'm going to conduct the next interview myself. I want you in there with me, and Martin to observe from in here. How much longer do you think he'll be?'

'Hard to say. You can, of course, walk in and take over when you want. Martin will stand up and stretch when he has decided that he's had enough time with the subject.'

'O.K. Hurry up getting that stuff to Michelle and get back here ASAP.'

Chris Fearnley nodded then exited the room leaving Goodchild alone to continue observing Carver and Guest. She was back in under five minutes.

'How's it going?'

'Amazing. If they had guitars then these two would form a duet. Martin's had him singing 'Freedom's Just Anther Word for Nothing Left to Lose.' Guest nearly broke down. They've discussed what Johnny Cash's music would have been like if he'd been black; they've compared the merits of different international airlines and airports. It's a lot of bullshit but, amongst all the crap, there are nuggets of gold. Guest is revealing a hell of a lot about himself to us without knowing it. Martin seems to be able to talk about any subject under the sun; I've never seen anything like this. We missed a trick not recording this for our own evaluation purposes.'

'It was set up too quickly, sir. I'm sure Martin will have something to say about that later on. Oh, oh. There he goes.'

On the other side of the mirror Carver had stood up, put his hands behind his back and stretched his upper body.

'Chris, it's time. I've decided to be a real pig in there and I'm going to be quite rude to you as well. I want to see how he reacts to a woman being verbally abused. Can you play the meek and mild little lady for me?'

'No problem.'

'Let's go then.'

Goodchild entered the interview room with Chris Fearnley trailing in his wake. He was wearing full Commander's uniform including hat and black, leather gloves. Carver stood up immediately.

'Thanks for babysitting, Inspector. You may go now' said Goodchild.

Carver left the room hurriedly without a glance at Guest.

Goodchild removed his hat then placed it upside down on the table and put his gloves inside it. He sat down opposite Guest then said to Fearnley 'Remove the cuffs, sergeant then start the audio-visual recording equipment.'

'Yes, sir.' She did as instructed then made to sit down next to Goodchild.

'No, sergeant. Under the circumstances I think that it would be more appropriate if you observed from that position' said Goodchild pointing to a chair at the rear of the room behind Guest.

'Sir.' Chris went and sat in the indicated place.

Goodchild cleared his throat and began to speak. He began by stating the date and the time then continued 'We are in interview room number four at Paddington Green station. This is interview number one of Mr Anthony Leonard Guest, Orchard Place, Upton

Magna, Shropshire. Interview is being conducted by myself, Acting Commander Mark Goodchild, Metropolitan Police 9039. Also present is…'

Goodchild turned his head towards Chris Fearnley and raised his eyebrows. When she did not speak he made hurry up motions with his right hand and stared at her as though she were an imbecile.

'Oh: Detective Sergeant Chris Fearnley, Metropolitan Police 2420' she stammered.

'Mr Guest' continued Goodchild, 'you were arrested at your home today on suspicion of the murders of Jennifer Duncan, Lauren Prospero and Janice Hope. Were you informed as to your rights?'

'I've no idea. There was so much shouting……..'

'Very well' said Goodchild cutting him off. 'You have the right to remain silent but anything you don't say now but you bring into evidence at a future date may be used in court against you. Do you understand this, Mr Guest?'

'Yes.'

'We have a mountain of evidence that implicates you in the murders of these three young women, Mr Guest. As we speak, forensics specialists are examining your home, your possessions and your clothing for conclusive physical proof of your guilt. They never fail, Mr Guest. Once we have identified the prime suspect they always find a link. You know that. Anyone who reads the news or even just watches T.V knows that. So, I have only one question for you. Why? Why kill harmless, single women whose only link to you was that they liked your music? Tell me, Mr Guest.'

'I've never heard those names in my life! I've not killed anyone and I don't give a fuck about your forensics geniuses – does the name Barry George not mean anything to you?'

Goodchild appraised the angry man facing him. The happy

go lucky singer who had chatted with Martin Carver had been replaced by a very different personality, one who clearly thought that attack was the best form of defence. Time to give him some rope.

'Yes, the name Barry George means something to me. What does it mean to you, Mr Guest?'

'Some time in the nineties – I don't know the year – there was a T.V presenter called Jill Dando. She fronted travel shows and also 'Crimewatch.' She wasn't any kind of expert; just blond with teeth and tits. Anyway, she was killed on her own doorstep in London – one close-up shot in the head, execution style. No witnesses, no clues; a nationally known personality killed in broad daylight and you lot were running around like headless chickens. If I remember correctly, the suspects ranged from a professional hit by the Serbian mafia who were pissed off by her poxy T.V. show, to someone she used to fuck before she was famous. Because the great British public liked her, you lot were under pressure to get a result and you ended up with some poor schmuck who lived locally, bit of a weirdo who lived alone and claimed to be Freddie Mercury's cousin! That was Barry George and your forensics pointy heads found a microscopic trace of gunpowder on his clothing to seal the deal. But you fucked up, didn't you? The defence has its own forensics experts and they shot your so called evidence down in flames. So don't waste your time trying to intimidate me with your scientists. CSI Shropshire wouldn't know the difference between poison and pig shit.'

'Why did you mention the word 'poison', Mr Guest?'

'No reason.'

'It's just that poison was the murder weapon in all three cases. Freudian slip on your part?'

'No, dozy; poetic. Poison and pig shit. Both begin with the letter P. Writers call it alliteration. You can find it in most good dictionaries.'

'Leaving forensics aside, we have sworn testimony that these girls were always present at venues where you were performing. They travelled some distance to see you, Mr Guest. We even have evidence that one of them was in love with you.'

'It happens, but it's not the person they fall for; it's the image. Part of being a good performer is just that – the act you put on. The real me is not the guy the audience see on stage.'

'Spare me the psychobabble nonsense, Guest; I'd hardly classify singing in the Shropshire Hunt on a Thursday night as being 'on stage'. Anyway, the image the victims had of you is irrelevant. We can place all of them as having been fans of yours and last seen alive at one of your gigs. You're toast, mate.'

Guest glared at Goodchild and, for a second, it looked as if his anger was going to boil over. Then he seemed to deflate. He slumped back in his chair and shook his head. His voice took on a tone of resignation.

'That all sounds very thin to me. I'm sure that there are quite a few people who were regulars at those venues and who are still walking around drawing breath. Obviously you're under pressure to find a multiple murderer and I've been in the wrong place at the wrong time; we're back to Barry George again, minus the bullshit forensics. I can't see a jury swallowing this crap, sunshine.'

'You're a cold one, Mr Guest. Don't you care about the families of the victims? If you deny the murders then it follows that you won't tell us where the bodies are. The dead are dead but their friends and family still hurt. Stop the brave act; we will prove our case. The law states that, if you confess before trial, then the judge has to reflect that when sentencing – although not always in murder cases. Showing remorse for the bereaved would help you too. What do you say, Mr Guest?'

'Let me get this right. You are trying to say that you have proof, with more on the way, that I am a cold blooded multiple murderer. You're certain that it's me and that I've disposed of three girls' bodies. However, if I repent – go completely against my murderous character – to help the bereaved 'find closure' is, I think, the phrase in vogue, then all will be well. Are you on fucking drugs? There is no logic to your proposal nor any common sense. You've just let slip the fact that you don't even have any bodies so this is, in reality, a missing persons case. How the hell did a cretin like you make the rank of Commander?'

'Have it your way. Detective Sergeant Fearnley; is there anything that you would care to ask for the record?' Goodchild's facial expression made it clear that he did not expect a serious contribution from the junior officer. She spoke in a quiet voice.

'Mr Guest; why don't you like women?'

Guest had to turn ninety degrees in his chair to look at her before replying.

'I like women fine, darling. I'm married, as I'm sure you know. Your question makes no sense at all.'

'I beg to differ, Mr Guest. You describe Jill Dando as 'blonde with teeth and tits'. That's close on misogynistic when referring to a murder victim. A man who truly liked women would have described her as attractive with a good figure and a nice smile. Your vulgarity shows your opinion of women.'

'No it doesn't; it shows my opinion of the plastic princesses who make it in the entertainment industry. All those bints reading the news or presenting the weather – do you think they would be on TV if it were not for their looks? And they have the cheek to sue their employers for unfair dismissal when they reach a certain age and the years have taken their toll. They want to have their cake and eat it. My business is the same. If you don't look good on MTV then forget a career in music. There are top earners out there who cannot sing a note but whom the camera likes. If they had not made it in my industry then they'd have ended up as soft porn stars or married to a footballer. You know that's true, darling.'

'So good looks and talent are mutually exclusive in your opinion, Mr Guest?'

'No, but it's a fucking rare combination. Joss Stone is an example of a girl with the lot. But all the little girls who want to be famous don't have her as a role model – they know they can't sing like her. No; the underclass wannabes want to emulate Cheryl Cole where talent is replaced by titty-tape.'

'So what do you think of the women who come to see you sing?'

'Christ, it's amazing how one little word can reveal so much about someone. Come to <u>see</u> me sing? You go to <u>hear</u> someone sing, love. You go to see someone <u>perform</u>! You do understand the difference, don't you?'

'All right, Mr Guest; I'll rephrase the question. What do you think of the women who make up your audience?'

'God, this is becoming fucking boring. There is no 'one size fits all' description of a particular singer's fan, whether it's me or Robbie fucking Williams. People turn up for every reason under the sun – some of them, believe it or not, just to do with liking the sounds.'

Just as it seemed that the interview was losing momentum there was a knock at the door.

'Come' called Goodchild.

A uniformed constable in white shirt sleeves entered and handed a note to the senior officer. Goodchild looked at his watch then spoke for the record.

'Interview suspended at 1745 hours.'

He beckoned to Chris Fearnley who crossed the room and deactivated the recording equipment. He then showed her the note that had been delivered.

'Take Mr Guest to a holding cell, sergeant, then come back here. Constable, see that he is fed and watered right away; I'll be talking with him again shortly. Dismissed.'

The two officers escorted Guest out of the interview room leaving Goodchild on his own. He looked across to the mirror and said 'Come and join me, Martin.'

Carver duly appeared and sat down with his direct superior.

'I have to meet the Commissioner in thirty minutes, Martin. What are your initial thoughts?'

I think we should wait for Chris to get back, boss. Let's compare all our notes at the same time.'

'Bloody hell! What is it with you two? Are you joined at the hip or something? I asked her a simple question about your interview technique and she refused to 'break trust' or some such bollocks. Have I made a mistake allowing her on to the team, Martin?'

'You've just seen her begin to work on Guest, boss. I think you can answer your own question.'

Goodchild looked squarely at Carver who looked back at him. The Commander had adopted the less formal hierarchical methods that had suited him in C.T. work for the Orion investigation but, under pressure, was falling back on more traditional policing procedure. He had not missed the fact that Chris Fearnley had started to call him 'sir' rather than 'boss'. That meant that she was reacting to his change of stance and Carver was not too far away from acting likewise. He felt that the Orion team was losing cohesion at this crucial moment and he was not sure how to reinstall it. He made a mental note to talk to Michelle about it later on – if he survived his meeting with the Commissioner.

'Very well, Martin; we'll wait for the sergeant's return and hope that she won't be too long.'

As it happened, Chris Fearnley reappeared two minutes later so the atmosphere in the room had not had time to fester.

'That was quick, Chris' said Goodchild.

'They're on the ball here, being used to dealing with terrorists and other high risk scumbags. So; what have I missed?'

'Nothing. We were waiting for you to get back so that we can all compare notes together. You start, Martin. What do you make of chummy?'

'I've never fancied him for the English murders, circumstantial evidence notwithstanding, and nothing I've see or heard since he's arrived back in the U.K. has changed my mind. On the contrary, his behaviour at interview leads me to think that he is not directly involved in the killings. Look at the guy. If he were guilty he should be shitting himself, screaming for a lawyer or 'no commenting' us to death. Instead we have a guy who only got excited when he created a four line country verse with me. He would talk music until they have Miller time in Mecca; it's his major interest but does not make him limited or stupid. He hit every ball you two threw at him and was not in the least bit intimidated. When you accused him or misogyny, Chris, he should have backed right off but, instead, he justified his use of language. At the end of the day he is a product of his time and environment, as most people are. The most we can say is that he is not politically correct and that's not a crime. Yet.'

'Thanks, Martin. Chris?'

'I agree with Martin. Look at the profile of our killer. Organised, socio-psychopathic, cold. Tony Guest does not fit that picture. I've been round more murderers than I care to think about and, I don't know about you, but for me there is a certain 'feel' about them. I'm not talking about spur of the moment killings, normally spousal. I mean the calculated taking of life of another human being. Guest does not have that 'feel'. He is passionate, alive, clever, brave even. If he does not confess, then I cannot see a jury convicting him on what we have.'

'Never mind the jury for the moment, Chris. Do you think that he's innocent?' said Goodchild.

'I do.'

'And what about the American girl? How do you two think he's going to react when we raise that particular issue?'

Well we won't know for sure until we do' replied Carver. 'If our opinion is correct he will probably say he's never seen or heard of her. Then again she may have made herself known to him at one of his gigs or talked to him in Spain. I can't see him saying 'oh yeah; I killed that one, guys' you know.'

'I'd have to go along with that' said Chris.

'I don't believe this' said Goodchild. 'You two wanted me to haul Guest in even before we knew about the American but now you're blowing off the biggest piece of information that we have as though it doesn't exist. How much circumstantial do you need?'

'It's called circumstantial for a reason, sir' said Chris. 'Coincidence does exist. I sometimes feel that we've been fitting the person, i.e. Guest, to the crime and not really pursuing the cases to a logical conclusion.'

'I think you are both wrong. Suspend your commonly held belief for a moment and imagine that Guest is our guy. We agree that he's clever but with limitations. He has not make it in his chosen 'profession' and I'd say that if it were not for the solidity of his wife he'd lead a fairly miserable existence. So his arrest was a shock to him but he's had time to prepare for such an eventuality. Anyone who does not suffer from a God complex would admit that they might be picked up during our investigations and prepare accordingly. He also had all that time on his own during the journey down to London to get ready for the fight. We should, in retrospect, not have allowed that. Better to have kept him off balance. So, if he's guilty, just how clever is Guest? What's our next step, folks?'

'Obviously to bring the American into the equation' said Carver. 'The question is how do we do it.'

'I'd like you to do it, Martin' said Goodchild. 'Problem is you've set yourself up as being not of this investigation.'

'Oh I think Chris and I could come up with a solution to that little problem, boss. I reckon we could manipulate him into demanding that I and I alone conduct the next interview. I still think we're barking up the wrong tree though.'

'Be that as it may, I'll leave you two to sort something out. I'm off to the top floor. I'll see you both back here and we'll discuss our next step. Oh, and touch base with Michelle; she probably thinks we've forgotten her.'

Goodchild left Chris and Martin. They looked at each other for an intense moment before the woman spoke. 'He either wants, or is under orders to, wrap this up ASAP. He has stopped analysing and is going to use the Yanks to bring this to an end. What do we do, Martin?'

'For the time being we do as we are told. I need to be the one to talk with Guest. The poor fucker will hang himself if he doesn't learn to control his mouth. We'll let events run their course but I'll tell you now, I'm not happy. I'm going to revisit the entire Orion file and see what we're missing. Out of motive, means and opportunity we only have the last of the trinity against Guest and that's not enough for me.'

'A parallel investigation? Not the first time, is it, Martin? Need a hand?'

'I need two. I'm fucking useless with computers. Think it through, Chris. I appreciate the offer but this is bound to become political. The Met is going to take some very serious flack when the truth starts to come out. You're at real risk of being collateral damage.'

'Good job I've got a tin hat to protect me from the shit that rains from on high then, isn't it?'

Chapter Thirty One

On high, or at least on the top floor of New Scotland Yard, Sir Alan Sampson was waiting for Goodchild to arrive. He had just spent a very tricky few hours dealing with the fallout of the Orion case and hoped that he could use what remained of the day to impose some sort of order onto the chaos that had started with the American Legal Attaché's visit that morning.

Fortunately Kevin Ryan was an experienced professional who knew how to play the game at this level. The man had not even expressed surprise when Sampson had 'suggested' that it would be in both their interests (and that of their respective organisations and countries) for them to meet, off the record, in a public place.

So he had found himself facing the Legat at Speke's Monument in Kensington Palace Gardens barely five hours after their initial encounter at New Scotland Yard. If the FBI officer thought it odd for the Commissioner of the Metropolitan Police and a knight of the realm to be dressed in tan chinos, green polo and wearing wraparound shades then he kept it to himself.

The two men walked together in the late afternoon sun in the direction of the palace looking for all the world like a pair of middle aged businessmen exchanging pleasantries. Their back-up staff observed them from a discrete distance.

Sampson told Ryan how Orion had come into existence and held very little back. He even admitted to the receipt of the original email but did not reveal the recipient's identity, saying instead that it came from a 'trusted source.' When he revealed that Guest was in custody and pleading innocence to the killing of the three English girls he stopped his pacing and looked Ryan squarely in the eye.

'So when you asked for our help this morning, Kevin' he continued 'I had no idea that the two cases could be connected.'

'Come on, Sir Alan. Last night there was a major operation at Manchester airport. You must have known about that.'

'I knew that a murder suspect was flying in from Spain and was going to be placed under rolling surveillance. The only reason I knew, I might add, was that the officer in charge thought that his team could have ended up operating in several different policing jurisdictions and I contacted certain Chief Constables to make them aware of his presence.'

'O.K. I'll buy that. But when I gave you a girl's finger, are you telling me that you did not make a connection between that and what your Orion people found in this park?'

'I am, Kevin. Look, Orion was set up in a rush by our counter-terrorist division. Not even our political masters know the details and some of my officers have lied to the media regarding what was found here. For better or worse, I was kept in the dark as well. If the man behind Orion had told me that this had been anything other than a CT exercise then I would have told the Home Secretary, our version of your Sec State for the Interior I believe, and we both know how leaky politician's offices are. Come on, Kevin; does the Director of the FBI know every details of every operation being carried out in his name?'

'Point taken. So when, exactly, did you make the connection, Sir Alan?'

'This afternoon. I'm not going to give up any names but an Orion member made the link and contacted me. I've spent the day getting up to speed on this and the suspect was arrested on my direct instructions. Interrogations will continue tonight and I'm inviting you or one of your staff to observe but unofficially at this stage.'

'It's not that I'm ungrateful but I have to ask, why are you letting me have all this now?'

In answer, Sampson handed a sealed envelope to Ryan.

'Inside that is the chemical formula for the poison used in

the English murders. The substance is Fentanyl, an extremely powerful opiate which some lunatics take recreationally. One of its derivatives is known as KOLOKOL-1 which we suspect the Russian Special Forces used in their attack on the theatre in Moscow when Chechen terrorists took it over.'

'I remember. They killed everyone including a couple of hundred hostages.'

'Quite. Putin was in charge and it's proved impossible to get to the bottom of what happened. Some accounts have the Special Forces spending their time putting bullets in the skulls of sleeping terrorists instead of evacuating the civilians. The local hospitals were not told what gas had been used so the Russians certainly weren't going to inform us. Perhaps your people have more information. Anyway, if you test your girl's finger for that substance and it is present then we have a very strong link and should be able to convict this chap for multiple murder. You and I can liaise to wrap this up. What we don't need is your Department of Homeland Security seeing international terrorists under the bed – which they will if KOLOKOL-1 becomes common knowledge.'

'O.K. Sir Alan. I've got to get back to the embassy and send this info to Quantico. What's your next move?'

'Back to the Yard, change kit, early private dinner then home to my wife. I am contactable on this number. Please keep it to yourself.'

The Englishman handed over a business card to the American who placed it in the wallet that contained his gold coloured FBI credentials.

'You said I could attend the interrogation of your suspect in an unofficial capacity. When will that take place?'

'I think we'd better hold off until you have your lab results don't you, Kevin? If she was not killed by KOLOKOL then it's back to square one isn't it?'

'Maybe but I doubt it. It would be one hell of a coincidence, no – make that series of coincidences for your suspect not to be our perp too.'

'Coincidence exists, Kevin. Let's not try and make the crime fit the suspect eh?'

The two men shook hands and went their separate ways. Sir Alan felt secure that he had bought a few hours time by giving the chemical details of the poison to the Americans and, as a bonus, gained credibility by inferring that his people had not already ascertained what had been used to kill Catherine Taylor-Lodge. Now he had to push the investigation forward as far as possible before the FBI carried out their own tests and came back to him with all guns blazing to obtain access to Guest.

His intercom buzzed and he was informed that Goodchild had arrived.

'Send him right in, please.'

He was standing to meet his junior officer and took him to the less formal seating area of his office.

'How's it going, Mark?' he said without preamble.

'No change, sir. I conducted the first formal interview with DS Fearnley in attendance. I played the bad cop to Carver's matey act and Fearnley batted her eyelashes and did little Miss Muffet. He's denying everything and is arrogant as hell; even went so far as to say that, without bodies, all we have is a missing person's enquiry.'

'If he believes that then he is not au fait with British law. What's your take on him, Mark?'

'Manipulative, glib, clever up to a point. He thinks we are a bunch of plods and that he can run rings around us. He has not even asked about a lawyer and we're not going to raise the issue. It's interesting that he has not asked after his wife either.'

'Yes, yes; it's all <u>interesting</u>, Mark. Do you think he's our man?'

'I do, sir' replied Goodchild without hesitation. 'When we started the investigation, I brought in a Doctor van Dyke who is a criminal psychologist. His profile was not all that useful and I have my doubts about the man anyway but he did say that the killer's motive was basically ego. He wants to prove he's better than us. That would fit with what Guest has shown of himself so far.'

'Again, interesting but it will not secure a conviction. What is your next move, Mark?'

'Carver did an excellent job on Guest and we want to build on the rapport which he was created. He and Fearnley have assured me that they can manipulate Guest into demanding that he will only talk with Carver and sideline myself for the moment. Once our meeting is over, sir, I intend putting this into motion. Would you care to observe?'

'I'm tied up elsewhere I'm afraid, Mark. Take Addison along but don't let him into the interview room; my orders, OK?'

'Yes, sir. Will that be all, sir?'

'Not quite. I'm not going to tell you how to proceed with your interview but I'd like to give you something to think about. I don't hold out much hope of the arrogant Mr Guest confessing unless it is to his advantage. Now, at some stage this evening the Americans are going to contact me to say that they have discovered the nature of the exotic poison used to kill their Senator's daughter and they will demand to see our prisoner. My thinking is that Guest would far rather be detained at Her Majesty's pleasure than to spend time in the United States prison system.'

'I see you point in a general way, sir, but it's still a hard deal to sell to a man like Guest.'

'Come on, Mark. You all keep saying that what matters to him is music. Just remind him of the Birmingham six and the singing horse.'

Sampson looked at his watch and said 'Sorry, Mark; I'm late now. I'll be in contact later on once the American eagle starts screaming. Don't forget Addison.'

As he had spoken these final words he had guided Goodchild to the door and seen him out. The Commander made his way to the car which would return him to Paddington Green station trying to work out what singing fucking horses had to do with anything. If he'd had the time he would have asked Michelle Stone but, when he went into Oliver Addison's office to give him the good news, he found himself hi-jacked by the Deputy Assistant Commissioner and on his way north before he could do so.

On arriving at the rear of Paddington Green, Goodchild and Addison made their way to the observation room next to Interview 4 where Carver was waiting.

'O.K. guys; have you organised things so that he asks for you, Martin?' said Goodchild.

'Well, in a general sort of way, yes, boss' replied Carver. 'Basically, you and Chris get in there with Guest and, before anything is on tape, you act such an utter arsehole that he refuses to talk to you. Can you do arsehole boss?'

'Just wait and see what I put on your next fitrep, Martin. All right; I reckon I know what buttons to push on this monkey. For your information, Sir Alan is going to call me once the Americans verify that their girl was killed by the same shit as ours. Expect the FBI to descend around 2200 hours – no later than midnight at any rate.'

'Sir Alan is going to call you, Commander?' said Addison. 'Just what is my role here?'

'You are to observe interview proceedings from this office on the Commissioner's behalf. That's all he told me sir.'

'Very well, Commander. Carry on.'

Goodchild and Fearnley left the room the reappeared on the other side of the mirror. The female officer dialled an internal number and spoke briefly then she and her superior conferred quietly (to the frustration of Addison and the amusement of Carver).

The door to interview four opened and Guest was brought in by two shirt sleeved constables.

'Put him there, please' said Goodchild indicating the same bare chair that Guest had occupied before. Chris Fearnley took a clipboard from one of the constables and wrote on it before handing it back to him whereupon he and his colleagues left.

'What was that you were writing, sergeant?' asked Goodchild distractedly. He was sat at a different desk to Guest with a thick file in front of himself.

'I was signing for the prisoner, sir.'

'Just like DHL, eh? I hereby acknowledge receipt of one sack of shit guilty of murdering songs in a public place. Jesus, the fucking paperwork these scumbags generate!'

'Sack of shit? Scumbag? What happened to Mr Guest you two faced moron?'

'You're 'Mr Guest' when an interview is being recorded. Right now I'm in the real world, shithead. Which involves signing off papers designed by lawyers to look after the interests of various perverts, psychos, paedophiles and chronosomically challenged cunts like you.'

Guest just smiled. 'Let me guess; you don't like paperwork.'

'Correct.'

'Hardly surprising for someone whose collar size is larger than his I.Q. If you study hard and pass the exam you might get promoted to sniffer dog.'

'Do you know what I'm wasting my time on here, sonny? These are compensation claims from prisoners who say that they were injured whilst in custody and that we failed in our 'duty of care' towards them. There is one wanker who claims that he can never work again after his hand was crushed by a cell door slammed by another prisoner. The little faggot reckons he'll never be able to blow dry again. Just have to make do with blow jobs, I suppose.'

'That's a really weak attempt at intimidation you clown. Is that the best you can do – indirect threats to my hands?'

'What have your hands got to do with anything?'

'I'm a musician; I play guitar. You know that.'

'For all I know, or care, you're the idiot who bangs the cymbals once every half an hour. Don't need all your fingers for that do you? You could retrain if you had an accident.' Goodchild's turn to smile.

'Fortunately I would not need to. As I said, I play guitar and not too badly I'm told. But music comes from here.' – Guest laid his fist on his belly – 'The other officer, Martin, he gets that. I sing, mister man, I sing. And no slamming door can take my voice away.'

The room went silent. Guest stared at Goodchild defying him to gainsay his words. The latter stared back and, very slowly, a fierce grin spread across his face. His shoulders began to shake with repressed mirth, he began to laugh from deep in his chest and he finally stood up and faced the wall. When he turned around, Goodchild's eyes were wet with tears.

'You think you are so clever, don't you? You and, yes, people like Martin Carver because you 'appreciate' music. You have not got a fucking clue about real life.'

Goodchild went back to his pile of papers muttering to himself 'I'm sure I saw it here; where the fuck is it?'

Guest looked across at Chris Fearnley whose skin had visibly paled. He caught her eye and raised his eyebrows in a mute plea for information. She lowered her gaze to her lap and shrank in on herself.

'Here it is!' cried Goodchild. 'The Singing Sambo. Of course that nickname never made it into the media. This black bastard worked in a nursery; everybody loved him because nothing was too much trouble. Nappy need changing? No problem. Some rug rat puke up his banana mush? Here, I'll clean that. But his real gift was that he could calm the most fractious little shit by singing to them. Lullabies from Lagos or some such happy crappy. Long story short; he left his cell phone lying around, a co-worker found it and discovered his personal collection of kiddy photos. When he was remanded in custody to await trial, it became clear that he was going to walk on a technicality so the good inhabitants of Her Majesty's Prison, Belmarsh poured drain cleaner down his throat. He survived, but I don't think he'll get an audition on the X Factor anytime soon. So my point is, shithead, that even a voice can be broken.'

Silence descended onto the room once more. Goodchild sat back with a look of self satisfaction to put that of Piers Morgan in the shade. Chris Fearnley was, to all intents and purposes, invisible. Guest was in shock.

'You are an evil man' said the prisoner 'and I will speak no more with you.'

'That is absolutely fine by me. When the sergeant activates the recording equipment and I ask my very reasonable questions you can do your impression of an I.R.A. hard man and say 'no comment' as long as you like. That is the tape which the jury will hear and the prosecution will be able to paint you as uncooperative. It will all help to send you down, musician.' Goodchild spoke the last word of this statement in such a way and with such a sneer on his face that it made the profession of musician seem to be on the same level as that of the guy in charge of the sheets in a Harlem whorehouse.

'O.K. sergeant. Can you start.....' Goodchild's question was interrupted by his cell phone which must have been set to vibrate because no ring had emanated from it prior to him taking it from his pocket and regarding its screen.

'Sergeant, I've got to make a call in private. Can you keep an eye on this? I'll be back in five or ten.'

'Yes, sir.'

Goodchild picked up his files and left the room without another word. Chris rose to her feet and took the seat at Guest's table.

'Nice guy your boss, eh?' said Guest.

'He's not paid to be nice; he's paid to get results.'

'Well he's not going to get a result from me. I meant what I said; that's the last word I speak to that fascist bastard. I've done nothing and that's what will come out in court. I'll let everyone know why I'm not speaking and the shit will fall his way. What do you think, sergeant?'

'I think that you don't understand how the system works and Commander Goodchild does. You will not be allowed to get up on your hind legs and accuse him of insulting you - there is no evidence. All the jury will see are the tapes that he allows into evidence. If you refuse to speak you are within your rights. But, logically, an innocent man would welcome the opportunity to put his side of the story to us. You really should speak to him, Mr Guest.'

'No fucking way – that's final.'

Chris sat back in her chair creating a distance between herself and the prisoner. She was subliminally isolating him. A man alone will reach out for human contact especially in extremis. After two long minutes of silence, Guest began to crack.

'I'd talk with you, sergeant.'

'Can't be done. I'm too junior and the Commander would not make an exception for me. Sorry, Mr Guest.'

Silence, utter silence, resumed. The wall clock was electronic and made no sound. Chris Fearnley was aware of the red second hand sweeping round the white face of the time piece. She wondered to herself whether or not an audible chronometer would put more psychological pressure on the prisoner - the Metropolitan Police's version of Poe's beating heart. Again, Guest spoke first.

'Does Inspector Martin have the seniority to conduct the interview?'

'Inspector Martin? Oh, you mean Martin Carver. Yes he does but he'd not part of my team. He does... well, other things. He just did us a favour when you were left on your own.'

'Look; I'll speak with him. He understands where I'm coming

from and, no offence to you, but I doubt if many people in this organisation could do that. Could you see if that's possible? Please?'

Chris looked at Guest and tried to keep her face neutral, all the while evaluating the man in front of her and trying to work out who was playing who.

'I'll make some calls, Mr Guest. Don't get your hopes up is my advice.'

She picked up the phone and punched in an internal number. After what appeared to be a brief volley of telephone tennis she had a result.

'Inspector Carver? This is DS Chris Fearnley. We met… Yes, that's right. Could you pop down to Interview Four ASAP. We have a bit of a situation that you might be able to help us with. Thank you, sir.'

She hung up and started to arrange the paperwork in front of her into neat piles.

'Well?' asked Guest.

'He's on his way. I'll explain the situation when he arrives and we'll take it from there.'

Shortly afterwards, Martin Carver entered the room.

'Hi, Tony' he said. 'Still with us then?'

'Well the conversations are so stimulating that I can't bear to tear myself away.'

'I'll bet. So what's going on, sergeant?'

Chris gave a rapid, if bowdlerized, account of Guest's interview with Goodchild culminating in the former's affirmation that he would happily answer any questions that Carver had but that was all he was willing to commit to at present.

'Tony; you really can't pick and choose who interviews you, you know' said Carver.

'I'm drawing a line here, Martin. I've cooperated with all your procedures and I've not even tried to involve a lawyer yet – I emphasise the word yet. I will not put up with bullying and abuse

– your colleague gave you a very watered down version of what your boss has been up to. If the police want me to continue to communicate then I'll do it via you. If that's not on then I'll call a lawyer in and you can talk his language.'

Guest folded his arms across his chest and sat back in his chair with an air of finality. He was neither threatening nor cowed. Just a man who had made his mind up – or so he thought.

The door opened to admit Mark Goodchild who was moving at speed.

'Inspector; would you mind telling me what you are doing back here?' he asked.

'Best if we step into another office, sir' replied Carver who held the door for Goodchild to exit. He followed him out and returned a few minutes later.

'Chris – looks like we are working together on this. The Commander has gone to process the paperwork and I'm going to conduct the interview with your help. Tony; you've got what you wished for and you know the saying about that I'm sure.'

'Yeah. Be careful. So, shall we start?'

'Not yet. I've got to read up on the case before I can talk sensibly with you. This could go through the night so I reckon it would be best if you went back to your holding room and grabbed a bit of rest. Make sense to you?'

'Yeah, O.K. Look, thanks for taking this on. You're going to get grief from your boss, aren't you?'

Carver laughed. 'No. I've turned it round on him. I'm doing him a favour is how he sees it. The fact is the guy is a monumental prick who is crap at interviewing but would never admit it. I've implied that he's too senior to be spending his time on just one case; he should be operating at the strategic level. I've also let him know that I will keep away from the media and he can do the T.V. stuff. That he is good at.'

'Fine. I'll try and get some Zs then.'

'That's best. Chris, could you get Tony to his room then come back here to bring me up to speed, please?'

'Yes, Martin.'

Chris Fearnley and Guest left. When she returned Carver put his fingers to his lips and made the sign of someone walking with the first two fingers of his right hand. She nodded, put on her jacket and they left the station together in search of a pub. Once they were some distance away from Paddington Green and walking along the Edgware Road Carver said

'There's something about that station that I don't like. It does not feel like a proper British nick if you know what I mean.'

' It's the terrorist background, Martin. I hear what you are saying.'

'I always worry that funny people can hear what I am saying whenever I visit that fucking place. You know Goodchild used to be based there, don't you?'

Chris turned towards Carver and nodded. 'Yes. Because of the amount of time he spent in Muslim coffee shops, one of his nicknames is Laurence of Belgravia.'

Carver laughed. In this part of London it was not uncommon to see foreign males sat in the street sharing a hookah. In the summer months when the middle east was too hot, hordes of Gulf Arabs descended onto this part of the capital the women showing only their eyes and thus known as BMO's – Black Moving Objects. Carver wondered what would happen if the African-Caribbean community ever started to wear masks and smoke exotic substances in public.

At length they found a bar whose interior could not be viewed from the outside. They entered to find a dimly lit room given over to discrete booths, low level muzak and a clientele trying hard to be well dressed but merely looking expensively uncoordinated. Nobody stood at the zinc covered bar except for a couple of attractive cocktail waitresses who looked to have more class to them than the customers.

Neither officer had been here before nor had they heard of its name but it took their practised eyes seconds to spot the unmarked door which would lead to other floors and the single bruiser who was trying to guard it whilst remaining invisible.

'For fucks sake, Martin. You really know how to show a girl a good time.'

'Sorry. They really should have a flashing neon sign saying 'Hookers R Us.' Let's relax.'

One of the waitresses approached, showing no surprise at the presence of a couple in the establishment. She'd seen stranger clients.

'What would you like, sir; madam?'

'Well, miss' said Carver 'we have to talk to a cowboy tonight so give me a bottle of José Cuervo Gold, the fixings and two Corona chasers. Put this on Mark Goodchild's tab. Thanks.'

The waitress returned to the bar without batting an eyelid but Carver noticed that she took he time preparing the drinks order whilst the barman disappeared from his post. In the background, the bruiser's head turned in their direction as his right hand went up to the side of his face. He was obviously wearing an earphone and was receiving a message. The Spy Shop on nearby Park Lane had probably sold it to him.

The waitress made her way back with their order on a matt black tray. She placed the drinks in front of them and moved like a feline back to the bar.

'She the manager or added security, Martin?'

'Hard to tell. Certainly a fighter. That dress is velcroed together and would rip off in a second. I think the tray has an edge to it as well but it's hard to tell in this light. Here comes someone from upstairs. Cheers.' The two of them did the salt, drink, lemon ritual followed by a swig of beer from the bottle as a thirty something man made his way towards them from the back of the room. His acne scarred, dark skin was the only notable feature to him. He was otherwise so nondescript that he would best be likened to a

North African accountant who had seen better days. Stopping at the table he coughed as one could imagine Uriah Heep doing.

'Excuse me; I'm told that you wish to put your drinks on the tab of Mr Mark Goodchild. I'm afraid we have no-one of that name on our members list.'

'Really?' said Carver. 'He must be using another one for this place. He did recommend you to us.'

'And you are?'

'We work for the same organisation as Goodchild – show him.'

Chris opened her jacket slowly and laid her I.D. wallet on the table. Carver noticed an increased alertness in the waitress and the bruiser.

'Wave off your dogs, lad. We're not here to hurt you,' said Carver.

The man made a sign with both hands below his waist level and everyone, except him, relaxed.

'O.K. What do you want from me?'

'Nothing tonight. We're just here to let you see our faces so we don't have to do this dance on future visits. Tonight, just give us privacy and we'll see you again soon for a more detailed conversation.'

'And I assume that you too would like to open a tab, correct?'

'How kind.'

'Under what name shall I put it, sir?'

'Goodchild of course. Oh, one last thing. A business card with your cell number on it please.'

The man extracted a small plastic box from a side pocket. It contained cheaply printed business cards on one of which he wrote down a private number and handed it to Carver. The latter did not even glance at it, instead just passed it to Fearnley who slipped it into her jacket.

Nobody spoke and the combined gaze of the two police officers persuaded the bar manager (if such he was) that his presence was no longer required so he retreated to wherever he had come from.

'Was that you being you or did you have reason to believe that the Commander used this place?' asked Fearnley.

'Mostly the former with about ten per cent of the latter. You never know and I am aware of Goodchild's patterns. There will be a place within walking distance of Paddington Green that he regards as a safe base – this fits the parameters. We'll try another direction on Monday. Hang on – I'm vibrating.'

Carver took his cellphone from his hip pocket, looked at the screen and answered. Chris Fearnley listened to his end of the brief conversation.

'D.I. Carver. Has she released it to you yet? That makes sense. Fair enough – has Goodchild been told? All right – I'll leave that up to you but keep trying. Who else is in the loop on this? Try and keep it to that until the boss says otherwise. If I don't hear back from him in two hours Chris and I are going to interview Guest again and we shall put this to him. Thanks, Michelle. Yes, that makes sense to me.'

Carver refilled the shot glasses and they drank again. After they put their beer bottles down he turned to Fearnley and said 'That was Michelle. Doctor Watkins has found something hidden in one of Guest's guitar cases; the one he took to Spain with him. It's a torn beer coaster advertising the Bristol Beer Festival for this year. On it was written a phone number. It belongs to Catherine Taylor-Lodge – it's her cell number.'

'That's pretty damning. Whose handwriting for the number?'

'They're still checking but if it's either Guest or the girl, he has a problem. The hits against him are accumulating. The Yanks will be all over this like lions on raw meat. Shit.'

'Are you starting to doubt his innocence, Martin?'

'I don't want to and his reaction to this evidence will be vital. I've got to put it to him fairly but I'm not here to defend him. Nor are you, Chris. Our guts may be wrong this time and we could end up being cut by Occam's Razor.'

'Yes, you're right, Martin. Let's forget the bastard and let the Americans have at him. More beer?' Chris had uttered the sentence with an utterly straight face, knowing what Carver was really thinking. Until proven guilty to their satisfaction, Tony Guest had two allies.

She raised her empty Corona bottle in the direction of the pantheresque waitress and indicated that she required two more. Once these had been served (along with a smile as fake as an Italian war hero) she resumed her conversation with Carver.

'So you're delaying the next interview for two hours; why, exactly?'

'Firstly to give Goodchild time to get up to speed – Michelle says she'll find him. Secondly, to give the forensics people time to work on what they have. It's all grist to the mill. Finally we have the time. The Americans chose not to use U.K. facilities to analyse what they received in the post. Even if they drive it to a military base and fast jet it to the States they still have to get it out to their lab at Quantico and I've been there. It's a pig of a drive even for the FBI. Bottom line is that it will be very late this evening before we have to deal with them. Time's with us for now.'

Carver was wrong; time was most definitely not with them. It was not his fault entirely. He had tried to imagine how the Americans would most quickly transport their evidence back to Quantico for analysis and had not been aware of the existence of the embassy Gulfstream. He compounded the error by thinking that the package would travel from the airport to the FBI building in Virginia via the same means that he had taken when he had visited the academy. He was guilty of applying British methodology to an American problem – one which had political aspects to it to boot. The Director of the FBI, having informed Senator Tyall Lodge III of his daughter's death, had been obliged to promise that the full force of the FBI's resources would be employed in finding her body and tracking down the guilty party. These resources were formidable so a helicopter was waiting at Andrews AFB to transport McCarthy and his material to the waiting laboratory. On top of all this, a strong transatlantic tail wind had shaved nearly 30 minutes off the Gulfstream's flight time so the American authorities were marshalling their forces much more rapidly than Martin Carver had anticipated.

At 2200 hours London time, Kevin Ryan was still in his office at the American embassy and had just finished talking on the phone with his Director. An encrypted email was on his screen from the same person. Ryan printed it off the better to absorb its contents. Like many of his generation, society would never be paperless.

Once he was satisfied that he knew all that he could for the moment he phoned Sir Alan Sampson's private cell number.

'Sampson.'

'Sir Alan; this is Kevin Ryan. Is there any way we can make this call secure?'

'Good evening, Kevin. I'm afraid not is the answer. I'm not in a location where our facilities marry up with yours. If you can wait, say 45 minutes I could manage it. Failing that we could rely on circumlocution.'

'O.K. here goes. I've just finished speaking with my company's CEO and he has sent me our latest results and a request that I carry out more purchases in the U.K. We are certain that your tri nationals stopped operating because of the same market forces used in the sole American exemplar. As a result of this I would like to meet with the U.K. supplier with whom you are in close contact at this time. Where and when could you facilitate such a meeting, Sir Alan?'

'I'll need to talk with subsidiaries. Are you still in your office?'

'I am.'

'Very well. Sit tight and you will be contacted securely to organise the meeting. Would first thing in the morning suit you, Kevin?'

'I was thinking of a bit sooner than that. The British press may have gone to bed but I'd hate for the New York Times, the Post or the Wall Street Journal to get hold of this. After that you get CNN, Sky – God, even the BBC might wake up.'

'Point taken, Kevin. I'll see what I can do.'

Sir Alan Sampson broke the connection and swore softly to himself. He knew that he had just been threatened and there was not a damned thing he could do about it. The Prime Minister and the Home Secretary were still abroad so it all rested on his own shoulders. He racked his brains trying to find a way to buy some more time and in the end decided on the functionary's default option – when in doubt, delegate. He called Addison who was still at Paddington Green reading the Orion files.

'Oliver. Sir Alan here. Any progress?'

'Not really, sir. Carver has disappeared with his sergeant, officially to get up to speed on the case. The prisoner's back in his box and will be interviewed as soon as Carver returns.'

'Where is Commander Goodchild?'

'I don't know, sir. Perhaps he's back at Orion. They are still working on the data regarding the other seven girls, sir.'

'Right. When Carver arrives have him call me on my private line. No belay that. You call me then put him on. Understand?'

'Yes, sir.'

'Now patch this call through to Orion and I'll see where our Acting Commander is.'

Addison did as instructed and Detective Sergeant Michelle Stone found herself taking a call from the Metropolitan Police Commissioner – which definitely got her attention.

'Sorry, sir. As far as I was aware Commander Goodchild was still at Paddington Green directing the Guest interview.'

'Well he isn't Detective Sergeant. Do you think you could tap into the junior rank's grapevine and find him for me please? And, when you do, tell him to call my private number.'

'I'll shake some bushes, yes, sir.'

'If that's code for phoning all the public houses he likes, I don't want to know. Just sort it, and sort it now.'

Again Sampson broke the conversation before the other party had time to acknowledge him. Michelle just looked at the phone and said 'Fuck you very much, sir' before dialling Goodchild's personal cell.

'Hello you. What's happening?' he said.

'Hi. I've just had Sir Alan on the phone. He's trying to find you. Everything all right, Mark?'

'Never better. Martin's getting to Guest and I reckon we'll have a result very soon indeed. Then we can charge the bugger and go on leave. What did Sampson want?'

'He wants you to call him on his private number. He did not sound a happy bunny, Mark. He was trying to stay cool and calm but I could tell that something's rattled him. Listen Mark – I've been trying to get in touch with you for half an hour. Rachel Watkins' lot have turned up a significant new piece of evidence. You won't believe this one.'

'What is it then, Michelle?'

She described the finding of the torn beer coaster in Guest's guitar case and what was written on it.

'Right – that nails the bastard even if we can't state it's his handwriting one hundred per cent. Most people print a number in such circumstances' said Goodchild. 'Who else knows about this, Michelle?'

'Outside of the forensics team only Sir Alan who will probably tell Addison. I've just got off the phone from telling Martin. I assume that he'll tell Chris. That's it, Mark.'

'Fine; I'll call Sampson now. By the way – does the phrase 'Birmingham six and the singing horse' mean anything to you?'

'Well the Birmingham Six are that bunch of Paddies who were given life sentences for setting off bombs in pubs on behalf of the IRA in 1975. They were released on appeal in 1991 after their convictions were deemed to be unsafe. Like, you'd confess to murdering more than twenty innocent people if you had not done it? As for the singing horse; there is a story about an Arab who was caught in the act of stealing something from his Sultan. When the Sultan said 'give me one good reason why I should not have you executed immediately?' the thief replied 'Oh, Sultan; it is known that you own the most magnificent horse in all the land. I am a magician and, if you give me a year, I will teach your horse to sing.' The Sultan agreed and the thief was sent to live in the royal stables where, each morning, he would sing to the Sultan's horse. After a week of this, one of the guards said 'everyone knows that a horse can't sing. You're mad.' The thief replied 'I have a year which I did not have before and who knows what tomorrow may bring. I might die, the horse might die, the Sultan might die and, who knows – the horse may learn to sing. Why the weird question, Mark?'

'Just something Sampson said to me. Thanks for that, Michelle. I'd better call him now. I've no idea what time I'm going to be free. What are your plans?'

'Well, as we are nearing the end of this part of the course, I thought it best to stick around so I've a change of clothes with me and I'm going to crash out on the camp bed in an hour or so. See you for breakfast?'

'I'll call you first. Goodnight, Michelle.'

'Night, Mark.'

They both put their phones down reluctantly.

Goodchild was tired of the machinations that this case had pushed him into and was not looking forward to a late night conversation with the Commissioner. He'd rather have called it a day, taken Michelle to supper and then to bed. He could even had foresworn the supper bit. But, as she had said, they were nearing the end of this part of the course and his engrained professionalism would not allow him to drop the ball (just mix metaphors) so he called his boss as instructed.

'Sampson.' came the brusque reply.

'Mark Goodchild here, sir. Orion says you wish to speak with me.'

'Yes, Mark. I've had Kevin Ryan on at me demanding access to Guest tonight. If we do not accede to this 'request' I have a feeling that the media will be in a feeding frenzy before you can say 'press leak'. You need to call him at the embassy within the next thirty minutes maximum.'

'Very well. Have they given you any additional information arising from their examination of the evidence?'

'No. All he said was that they were certain that the same substance was used to kill the Senator's daughter and the British victims.'

'Well we knew that would happen, didn't we? I'll talk with Carver and then I'll call the FBI. I'm not going to let them dictate how we run an investigation, sir. They will be welcome as observers at the interview stage for now but that is as far as I'm willing to go unless they want to share their forensics with us.

'Nothing wrong with a bit of quid pro quo, Mark. By the way, Oliver Addison informs me that Carver and his colleague have gone walkabout.'

'Don't worry about Carver, sir. He won't be far. Look, I'd best crack on if I'm to meet the Americans' deadline. Anything else, sir?'

'Not for now, Mark. Don't hesitate to wake me if you have to. Goodnight.'

Goodchild had to admire the way in which his chief had managed to say 'I'm going to sleep now; don't dare disturb me' but at the same time cover his arse by making himself <u>officially</u> available. What a pro!

Ten minutes later he was back at Paddington Green where he found Martin and Chris going over the files, discussing various scenarios and deciding how best to proceed with Guest.

Chapter Thirty One

'Hi guys' said the senior man. 'Where's Addison?'

'Gone home, boss' replied Carver. 'To be fair, he's been here since 0800 and he does have a wife and kids waiting for him in leafy Surrey.'

'Whilst we sad, single sods carry on at the coal face' said Chris. 'The joys of being married to the job.'

'Yes – as demanding bitches go, she runs my ex a close second' said Goodchild. 'O.K. here's where we stand. The Yanks want to have access to Guest having discovered how their girl died, I'm due to talk to their FBI head man in London within the next fifteen minutes.'

'Hang on, boss' interrupted Carver. 'How can they have that information already? Their people could not have left the embassy before 1300 hrs, surely.'

'The Americans move bloody quickly when they have to – and I suppose the death of a senator's daughter would light a fire under them. I've also always believed that they have technology that they don't share with their closest allies. Anyway, the fact is that they have confirmed the poison's presence and are jumping up and down. I can only stall them so much and I'm going to have to let them know about the beer mat very soon. Martin – the ball's with you. Can you get him to confess to the U.K. killings?'

Carver's eyes left Goodchild's and went out of focus. The few people who thought that they knew Carver would have recognised the look. He was thinking hard, deeply and rapidly to come up with an answer to an important question. The outcome of the investigation could turn on his response and he did this in thirty seconds with his eyes unfocused but open. Some officers, both police and army, who had seen Carver in this state referred to it as 'doing the mystic.'

'I can get him to confess all right, boss. That's not the problem. What I have to do is make him confess twice; once, to me in private and the second time to the camera for the record. I don't think that you, or anyone other that Chris, should witness the first.'

'For fuck's sake, Martin. This is Paddington not Abu Grahib!' exclaimed Goodchild.

'Don't worry, boss. I'm, not about to connect his nuts to the mains power. It's just that I'd like you to be able to say 'no' to future questions in court with a clear conscience and no risk of perjuring yourself.'

Goodchild gave Carver an old fashioned look and let the bullshit slide.

'O.K. This room will now be locked so you can operate as you think best. I expect the Americans to be here in around thirty minutes from now. I'll call you once they are ready to talk to Guest. Anything else, Martin?'

'Just buy me as much time as you can, boss. If I can get him on tape I'll call you. Let's get on with it.'

Chapter Thirty Two

The FBI does not work bankers' hours. Around the world, 365 days a year and 24/7 their agents are operating at one level or another so it was not surprising that there were six people still at their desks in the American embassy in London, when Kevin Ryan entered the Legal Attaché's department just after 2200hrs on a Friday night.

'Listen up, everybody' he called. 'I've just got off the phone with Commander Goodchild of the Met. The Brits have some new evidence to show us and they won't discuss it on a landline.'

'Probably scared that the gutter press have compromised their comms systems' came a voice from one of the staffers.

'Whatever' said Ryan. 'I'm going to shower and change then head on over to Paddington Green to meet with this guy then try and get access to the mutt they have in custody. Anthony – you'll come with me.'

Anthony Connolly nodded at his boss thinking to himself 'what you really mean is, Anthony; you are my designated driver.'

'O.K. I'll be back in fifteen' said Ryan who then strode with purpose to his private office. He planned on looking his alert best for his meeting so a shave and a shower was logical. He always kept a change of clothes in his office just in case some clown spilled coffee on him five minutes before a television interview or a meeting with some self important Brit who'd been educated at a college which was three hundred years older than Ryan's own country.

Two miles away as a London pigeon flies, Tony Guest sat on one side of a table faced by a worried looking Martin Carver and Chris Fearnley who was a study in neutrality. They were back in Interview Four.

'Tony, I'm going to remind you that you don't have to speak

to me. We are not recording yet and I would prefer to keep things like that for the moment, but it's your call' said Carver.

'Whatever, man' replied Guest. 'I just want out of here rapido. You know I've not killed these girls, Martin.'

'O.K. I'm going to ask you a couple of questions off the record, Tony. Then I'll decide how to proceed. Have you ever seen this girl before?' Chris took two photos of Catherine from a folder and placed them on the table. One was a standard passport image whilst the other had been taken at the American embassy. Both showed an unsmiling young woman with long, mid brown hair and minimal make up. It was a very forgettable face.

Guest took his time, looking intently at each image, his brow furrowed in concentration.

'She's not someone who I recall seeing, Martin. She is a bit, well, plain really though, isn't she?'

'Fine. Next question. Do you know a girl called Catherine Taylor-Lodge?'

'Nope – and that's the sort of name you would remember, isn't it?'

'Quite. Last question. Have you ever met or talked to an American student, probably in her early twenties, at one of your gigs?'

'American? I don't think so. I've chatted to Aussies, Kiwis, South Africans, all sorts of Europeans but not an American. They don't seem to be on the same sort of circuit as me.'

Carver looked at Fearnley and something passed between them. Even Guest noticed it.

'Tony. I believe you and so does Sergeant Fearnley. Unfortunately we don't have much influence in what is going to happen to you and you are in shit up to your chin and in about thirty minutes someone is going to stand on your head.'

'I told you; I don't even know those three girls and...'

'Tony. Tony' interrupted Carver. 'Forget them for now; they are our problem not yours. Yours has changed and it is a twenty four carat bastard. Catherine Taylor-Lodge was the daughter of a very important US Senator. She was a student at Bristol University and may have attended your gigs in that city. We have evidence that she has been murdered in the same manner as the three English girls and the last trace we have of her is that she flew to Fuerteventura the day after you did. So that puts you and this girl in the same place at the same time twice. Any decent lawyer could persuade a jury that that was pure coincidence but, unfortunately for you, there is more. Chris.'

Chris Fearnley took two more photos from her folder and placed them on the table.

'These are front and back images of a beer mat which promotes the Bristol Beer Festival' said Carver. 'The actual object is still undergoing forensic examination at New Scotland Yard. The number which has been written on the mat is Catherine's cell phone. The mat was found in an inside pocket of your guitar case, Tony. Anything to say, Tony?'

Guest's eyes remained fixed on the photos but he was not seeing them. As some of the police had already noted, he was not a stupid man and he was trying to think his way though the situation in which he found himself.

'Martin – how much can you tell me about these murders?' said Guest.

'Tony, I could give you the entire file and it would not help you. I've just given you some facts – facts that will damn you if we can't find an explanation.'

'There is only one explanation, Martin. Some fucker hates me so much that he is willing to kill and then plant evidence pointing to me as the killer. Martin – I get on with most people. In my job I have to be professionally likeable. I don't know anyone who dislikes me enough to scratch the paintwork on my car let alone do this.'

Guest slumped back in his chair, his shoulders sagged and the self confident stage performer looked a beaten man.

'Sorry, Tony but it's all about to get a whole lot worse. The FBI are on their way here now. They want to interview you and we are going to have to share all our evidence with them. Obviously the senator will be applying pressure to the Bureau and they are really pulling the stops out on this. They were straining at the leash to get at you <u>before</u> the beer mat was discovered so imagine what they'll be like when we share that piece of information.'

'What'll they do, Martin?'

'I'll answer that for you, Tony' said Chris. 'They will ask to interview you, which request we will agree to. We have no choice but there will always be a British officer present if you agree to be interviewed. Any such interview will be recorded. What I expect them to do is to demand your extradition to the United States so that you can be tried for the American girl's murder in federal court. Catherine Taylor-Lodge and her family are residents of New York State which does not have the death penalty. It does, however, have some damned nasty maximum security prisons like Attica and I'm certain that that is the sort of place where you would end up.'

'Jesus Christ! Would the British government agree to an extradition request?' said a visibly rattled Tony Guest.

'I really would not like to say' replied Carver. 'Because of the senatorial aspect here, this would be decided politically. Senator Lodge is close to the US President and pressure would certainly be brought to bear.'

'My view is that Cameron would give you up if their side presented a reasonable argument' said Chris. 'Your life would be put under a media microscope so if you've spent years travelling around banging young girls expect it to come out. Likewise any drug use. I doubt if the great British public will have much sympathy for you and, without that, the government would have no political problem handing you over.'

'I'm fucked.'

'Looks that way, Tony. Sorry, mate' said Carver.

'Is there any way I can refuse to talk to this Yank, Martin?'

'Sure. You are in Britain with British rights so you can say 'no comment' to everything he asks – you can keep totally schtuum, which will piss him off but it won't stop the extradition process.'

'Fuck it, Martin! I don't know the girl! There must be something I can do – help me, man.'

Again, Carver and Fearnley looked at each other. She nodded to him in agreement to a question that had obviously been previously posed. Guest noted the exchange.

'You're going to have to trust me with you life, Tony' said Carver. 'Chris and I believe you and are going to go out on a very shaky limb for you. If you fuck us, we'll lose everything including our liberty. But we are ready to risk it.'

'You came in here with a plan, did you?'

'Yes and no. We had to see how you reacted to the information about Catherine Taylor-Lodge. If you really did know her, you should give up music and become and actor.'

'So what's the plan, guys?'

'The only place where we can put you where the Americans cannot get to you is in a British prison. I want you to confess to the murders of the three English girls and I want you to do it now, on tape. You will then be formally charged and enter the system. It will take months for this to get to Crown Court. When it does, you will have to plead guilty but refuse to answer any questions regarding why or how you carried out the killings. You will not comment on where the bodies are, nor will you answer questions regarding other possible victims.'

'And what happens to me?'

'If you were to plead not guilty but a jury found you otherwise you would be looking at three life sentences with a recommendation that you serve a minimum number of years, that number being up to the judge. By pleading guilty you oblige the judge to take that into consideration. You'll still get life.'

'Martin – I didn't fucking do it. You're asking me to confess to a horrific crime and to accept being banged up for God knows how long.'

'You said it, Tony. God knows how long. Chris – tell him about the Sultan's horse.'

Chris Fearnley told the story and told it well. The two police officers saw that Guest was starting to see where they were coming from.

'So the moral of the story is that you never know what tomorrow may bring' said Carver. 'In the 1970's some Irishmen living in England were arrested for planting bombs in pubs which resulted in the death and maiming of dozens of innocent people. They confessed, under duress. After years of campaigning they were freed. I hope you won't have to spend years inside, Tony but I won't kid you – it's a possibility. The alternative is an American prison for as long as you can survive it. What do you say?'

'You're asking a lot, man. How do I know that this isn't some scam to get me to confess to a crime that you can't solve otherwise?'

'Because, you dopey bugger, in a very short space of time you are going to be confronted by the Effa Beeya Eye and you will then be flying solo. Plus, you can change your plea whenever you like – which would drop Chris and me in deep doo-doo. I don't like doo-doo Tony.'

'Fuck it! What do we do?'

'In five minutes we go to record. We will role play your confession now but we are going to have to improvise once the tapes are rolling and we have to get it right first time. I want you out of this building before the FBI arrive. If that's not possible then you invoke your right to silence. Get it?'

'Got it. Let's go.'

Carver coached Guest through his 'confession' with Chris Fearnley chipping in when required. After a couple of false starts Guest understood what was needed of him and the process assumed a more natural air. Finally the police officers felt that it was time to record.

'OK Tony – ready for your close up?' said Carver.

'One moment'. Guest closed his eyes and took a deep breath. When he opened them his face had taken on a look which neither Carver nor Fearnley had seen before. The man across the table had become a captured killer; in acting parlance, he was 'in character'.

The prearranged verbal dance began with Carver leading and Guest following but only someone privy to the plan would have noticed. Fearnley played her part by signalling to Guest whenever he had to resort to 'no comment'. She did this by silently blowing in the direction of the prisoner's face thereby giving neither the audio nor the video recordings any indication of her involvement.

At 2237 hours Carver formally ended the interview. Guest was taken back to his cell whilst Chris Fearnley went to organise the paperwork necessary for charging him.

Carver then telephoned Guest's solicitor and informed him of his client's predicament and his desire for legal representation. The lawyer was a specialist in contract law as it pertained to the music industry but worked for a well known London based firm which would be able to send someone over right away. This was not what Carver had wanted to hear but there was nothing he could do about it. He had just ended the call to the solicitor when his cell phone rang. The screen showed that it was Goodchild.

'Martin Carver.'

'Martin – its Goodchild here. Are you free to speak at the moment?'

'Yes. Sir.'

'Excellent. I'm in the conference room on the first floor along with the Legal Attaché from the American Embassy. When can you get away from the interview and give us an update on how things are going?'

'I can come up right now, sir. The interviews are over. Sergeant Fearnley is charging Guest and I'm waiting for his lawyer to appear.'

'What on earth has happened, Martin?'

'He confessed, sir. We are processing him now.'

'Get up here immediately please, Martin. I need bringing up to speed.'

In the conference room Kevin Ryan and Anthony Connolly exchanged looks.

'I take it that there has been a development, Commander' said Ryan.

'Apparently the prisoner has confessed. Detective Inspector Carver is on his way up to brief us now.'

'That's damn quick. Can I get to talk to this guy tonight?'

'I don't see why not but why do you want to? If he's confessed on tape what more could you want?'

'Mark, there is a hell of a lot we want. A body to send back to her father for a start. An explanation as to why he killed her and there is also the small matter of jurisdiction. This is a United States citizen, temporarily resident in England, murdered by a UK national probably in Spain. I'm pretty sure that the best way forward will be to get this mutt to the US. After all, the murder was not committed in this country, was it?'

'Well Catherine's wasn't as far as we know, but there are...'

They were interrupted by the arrival in the room of Martin Carver. Goodchild introduced him to Ryan then they all sat at one end of a cheap conference table and went to work.

'How many girls has our Mr Guest admitted to killing then, Martin?' asked Goodchild.

'Three, sir. Janice Hope, Jennifer Duncan and Lauren Prospero. When I asked him about further victims in the UK he said 'no'. When I pressed, he went the 'no comment' route. He denies talking to any American girls at his gigs. When I showed him Catherine's photo and gave her name to him he claimed that they meant nothing to him. I pushed on the American girl by showing him a copy of the beer mat. He denies all knowledge of it. So he is being charged with the three specimen murders only at this time. As we match the other fingers to missing girls we can add them to the charge sheet. Finally, he stated that he has nothing more to say to us until he has spoken to his lawyer. That's it for now, sir.'

'Who's his lawyer?'

'I spoke to the solicitor who handles his music business. Obviously he'll be of no use here but he works for Irwin Mitchell who are bloody enormous. Someone from there will be arriving tonight to talk to Guest.'

'We'll have to live with that. Recommended plan of action, Martin?'

'Keep him here over the weekend. Magistrates court on Monday where he will be remanded in custody – obviously no question of bail. Crown Court – the Old Bailey, I imagine – in three to four months time. As we have a confession all his brief can do is go for mitigating circumstances or some sort of insanity defence. Whatever – he is going away for a long time.'

'Right; I'm reasonably happy with that. A pity he would not cough to the American girl. Sorry, Kevin.'

Ryan looked at the two British policemen and tried to work out how to deal with them. He outranked them and was close to the top of a vastly more powerful organisation. He was also in their back yard and would need them. They came across as two honest cops but the French did not call England 'Perfidious Albion' for nothing. During his tour of duty in London he had felt subtly snubbed on several occasions. People from the so called upper classes would listen politely to what he had to say, smile then utter the single word 'quite' then change the subject. He reckoned they thought him a red faced Mick not two generations out of the bogs of Kerry.

'No, don't apologise, Mark' he said. 'In fact it's probably for the best. You guys have him in custody which will give my people the time to mount a thorough investigation of what he's been up to in Bristol and in Spain. By the time we've finished we'll have so much proof that he'll have to give up what happened to Catherine as well. We might even find some missing English girls along the way. When can I talk to him?'

'We have to wait until he has seen his solicitor' said Goodchild. 'After that, we'll ask him if he wishes to speak with you.'

'Ask him?' said an astonished Ryan. 'How about you sit his ass down in an interrogation room and tell him that a representative of the United States government has some questions for him. Come on, guys; we work in law enforcement not social services.'

'Quite' said Goodchild to Ryan's annoyance. 'Even self confessed murderers have some rights in this country – as I'm sure they do in yours, Kevin. I've found that asking is better than ordering, especially when there is no way in which one can oblige someone to obey.'

'OK. OK. Can I view the tape of his confession then?'

'Yes, we can do that later on. It's with the sergeant doing the charging procedure at the moment' said Carver.

'You only have one copy?'

'Of course not. There is a master copy which is in our registry now and can be added to after future interviews. There is the working copy that the charging officer has in her possession to maintain the evidence chain and there is one final copy which we will give to the accused's solicitor. When we've finished here I'll arrange a viewing for you.'

'So for now all I can do is wait around for this guy's lawyer to appear and even then it's not sure that he'll agree to speak with me. Is that your position, gentlemen?'

Goodchild answered for the both of them. 'That's the state of play right now. If you want the use of an office to communicate with your embassy or your headquarters in Washington I can organise that for you.'

'Thanks – that'll kill some time until this guy's lawyer shows up I guess. Where do I go?'

'Martin – would you wait here and let front desk know where you are? When the lawyer arrives have him brought up and I'll join you. In the meantime, I'll sort Mr Ryan out.'

'Yes, sir.'

'Right; Kevin, if you'd come with me.'

Goodchild escorted Ryan into a well lit sub-basement which hummed with that low key activity common to all efficient communications centres. He showed him into a windowless room and explained the capabilities of the various systems, some of which were familiar to the American.

'If you need anything just raise the receiver and you'll be in contact with an officer from next door. I'll let them know you're here. As you can see, there are dedicated secure lines to various locations but not FBI H.Q. All lines are secure and the room itself is Tempest protected so, make yourself at home and I'll come and get you once this lawyer arrives.'

Goodchild left Ryan in the communications mini-suite. The door did not have an inside handle and Ryan was certain that it was wired for sound. The American composed himself and then called his office in Grosvenor Square. Once he had established his identity he recorded a report for transmission to Washington. After recounting how things stood regarding the British prisoner and the new evidence that Scotland Yard had discovered he went on to explain that he was still waiting for the arrival of the prisoner's lawyer and that this was very much an interim report with more to follow shortly.

'I am dictating this message from Paddington Green police station which the British use to interrogate suspects in terrorist cases and the communications equipment is secure by local standards. As such this document is to be classified Secret – USUK Eyes Only. Given that I am having to wait for a lawyer to appear, I do not anticipate gaining access to prisoner Guest this evening, if at all. The lawyer will surely instruct his client to invoke his right to say nothing. In view of this, I make the following recommendations; despatch a team to London, England to aid and assist my staff in establishing Catherine Taylor-Lodge's movements prior to her leaving for Fuerteventura. At the same time despatch a team to Fuerteventura to conduct an on site investigation into the woman's activities during her time there and see if we can find further links between her and Guest. I suggest that the team stages through the United States naval base at Rota, Spain and that our Legat in Madrid liaise with the Spanish authorities. Finally, we should brief the Attorney General's office on the situation and look for an early decision regarding jurisdiction and future extradition of Guest to the United States for prosecution under Federal Law.'

Ryan was certain that a transcript of this communication would be in Goodchild's hands pretty damned soon and, from there, would make it up the food chain to Sir Alan Sampson shortly afterwards. This was one of the reasons why he had metaphorically flexed his muscles in his recommendations. Once the British were aware that teams of FBI agents were about to descend on Europe to do their jobs for them and that the A.G. was being primed to kick ass, then they might stop fobbing him off and get their act together.

Ryan was only half right. Goodchild had indeed seen a transcript of his message but had no intention of bringing it to Sir Alan's attention this evening. That could wait until tomorrow at a civilised hour. Instead, he had shared the information with Carver and Fearnley. The three of them were sat in the conference room waiting to hear that the lawyer from Irwin Mitchell had finished with his client and could meet with them and the FBI.

'Any idea why Guest uses this particular firm Martin?' asked Goodchild.

CHAPTER THIRTY TWO

'No. Chris – how about you?'

'I've checked them out briefly – they are huge and are actually northern based. Manchester, believe it or not. They also have offices in Spain, Malaga and Madrid to be precise. Coincidence?'

'That is rapidly becoming my least favourite 'C' word. Who is the brief, Martin?'

'A certain Gordon Roberts – nobody special. He just happened to be the guy on call for criminal tonight. He seemed pleasant enough, professional attitude, about what one would expect from a firm this size. I doubt if the case will remain his for very long once they grasp its magnitude.'

'Remind me; where are their London offices?'

'Holborn, E.C.1. at the end of Gray's Inn Road. Traditional lawyer land.'

'And here was me thinking that that was under a flat stone at the side of a cess pit' said Chris Fearnley.

'Such cynicism in one so young, Chris' said Goodchild.

Before they could start a debate as to the most suitable location for the abode of defence lawyers the internal phone buzzed. Goodchild answered. 'Thanks. Bring him up. The Irwin Mitchell chap is on his way up. Chris; play nicely.'

Gordon Roberts was shown into the room. The man was in his late forties, rotund to the point of obesity but impeccably turned out even at this time of night. His jowls shone pink from recent shaving and he did not waste time on pleasantries.

'You've done quite a number on my client.' he began, not taking an offered chair. 'I'm at a loss as to why he is insisting on pleading guilty to three charges of murder when all evidence is purely circumstantial at this stage. There are also massive questions to be answered, not the least of which is how a musician has access to a substance which, according to your information, is only used by the Russian Special Forces. I take it that you will be transferring him to Belmarsh or some such prison for the weekend?'

'Actually, no' said Goodchild. 'We are going to keep him here until Monday when he will go to Marylebone magistrate's court. After he enters his plea – well let's not get ahead of ourselves by trying to second guess the workings of the judiciary.'

'You're not hanging about, are you, Commander?'

'Once you've looked at the recordings and digested the dossier we've given to you I think you'll understand why. Now – is Guest willing to talk to the FBI regarding their missing citizen? The Legal Attaché from their embassy is in this building waiting to see him.'

'He'll have a bloody long wait then. My client denies all knowledge of missing Americans and will not speak with their government's representative. That is final.'

'Would you be so kind as to let the FBI chap know that yourself Mr Roberts? It would be helpful, you know.'

Roberts blinked theatrically then looked to his right and left before saying 'Sorry; I though you were talking to an invisible moron. I'm not here to be helpful to you, Commander. Tony Guest is paying my fees. If the Americans won't take your word regarding my client's intentions that really is not my problem. Now; there will be people from my office who will wish to talk with Mr Guest prior to his court appearance so they will expect him to be available to us over the weekend. If you decide to move him somewhere else, please inform me first.' Roberts handed his business card out, one to each officer. 'I'm done here for now. Would someone please escort me back to reception?'

'I'll see you out myself Mr Roberts' said Goodchild to the lawyer's surprise. He was more used to being shown the door by uncommunicative constables.

'What happens now, Martin?' asked Chris once they were on their own.

'That's up to Goodchild. I reckon that we are going to find ourselves with new duties which will be as far away from Orion as he can make possible. Think about it, he has a confession, Sampson and therefore the politicians are happy. He has the lying to the media to explain but Oliver Addison is the Met's go to guy when it comes to spin and I'm sure that an explanation has already been worked on.'

'What about the Americans?'

'Precisely. They are going to make noise at all levels and we, the Met that is, will have to give them all necessary assistance. That could be our way forward, Chris. One or both of us to help with the UK end of their enquiries would be logical. I cannot see Sir Alan letting the FBI loose on the British plods, can you?'

'I've given up trying to work out the thought process of our senior officers on this one, Martin. There is one other option; did you know I spoke Spanish?'

'I see where you're going with this, Chris but it's a big jump. The FBI will work with the Guardia Civil, if anyone. I cannot see a justification for us to get involved with the investigation of a dead American girl in the Canaries, can you?'

'Give me time – I'll work something out. What…'

Goodchild entered the room and crashed his huge frame down onto an office chair.

'Pompous fat shit. Thank God I won't have to deal with Gordon fucking Roberts anymore' he growled.

'What's happening, boss?' asked Carver.

'Nothing much. The Irwin Mitchell lot will be in and out all weekend trying to squeeze more info out of Guest. We won't be privy to that obviously but I'm going to be available in case any Orion input is required. You two have the weekend off and I'll see you back at the Yard 0800 Monday. You've both done well on this and I shall so inform Sir Alan tomorrow.'

'Promotions and trebles all round then boss?' said Chris.

'I'll guarantee the drinks but the other – well, who knows. I'm heading back to the yard now to give the same message to Michelle. She deserves a break too.'

'There are still seven fingers minus their owners, boss' said Carver. 'What are we going to do about that little matter?'

'Michelle's system has proved its usefulness so it's just a matter of time and legwork to continue that side of the investigation. I'm going to suggest to Sir Alan that we disband Orion and allocate a new group of officers to follow up on the remaining – victims. You know; it's possible that the three girls we've identified will be the only ones we ever manage to match.'

The room became silent as the three of them thought through the reality of that last statement. They all knew that the clear up rate for people killed from outside their family or social circle was appallingly low and Michelle Stone's best efforts might already have yielded their results. But the files would remain open and would be revisited periodically. One day, maybe years down the line, a cold case team would find a link that had evaded Orion.

The trio of police officers split up and went their separate ways. Normally the entire team would be having a congratulatory drink together now that someone was in custody and had admitted their crime. But these circumstances were different as they were all aware; there were too many unanswered questions for them to feel comfortable and they knew that the way ahead was unclear. Carver and Fearnley had their own agenda which carried risks which they thought they knew. They were both bright enough to admit that there were still unseen elements to this case which might elude them which could result in an innocent man being locked away for years.

Goodchild also had an agenda and, for once in his life, it was a selfish one. The death of his friend and mentor Clarkson had affected him deeply. The initial shock and pain had not diminished – only morphed into something more lasting and, potentially, more destructive. He had made his mind up to leave the force and build a new life for himself. How the powers that be would react to that he could not guess. Would they be relieved that a potential political embarrassment removed himself from the game or would they try and keep him close by making his promotion to Commander substantive with the promise of more to come? Then there was the question of Michelle. They were good together and he could see how she would be good for him in the longer term but, realistically, what did he have to offer her? He was world weary, disillusioned and, let's face it, a damn sight older than her. He needed to get to know her away from the confines of the police force before he could dream of a future for them as a couple. The standing down of Orion and the hiatus between now and Guest's trial would give him that opportunity.

In the bowels of Paddington Green station's sub-basement Guest lay on his bed with his fingers laced behind his head and his eyes closed. He could not sleep as the hatch in his cell door opened every 15 minutes for a police constable to look at him. Suicide watch, he supposed. 'They really do not know me at all' he thought to himself.

His mind wandered, which was hardly surprising after the day's events. His lawyer had promised to contact his wife and try and arrange a visit before his initial court appearance on Monday. He doubted if she would make it. He could not get the Americans out of his brain and it was not Johnny Cash's bullshit about Folsom Prison that ran through his head. No; it was the sensitive figure of Tim Robbins being gang buggered in the Shawshank Redemption that played and preyed on his mind. If he remembered rightly, old Shawshank Penitentiary was in New York State. Did it still exist? The way his luck was running, it probably did. What was the catchphrase Andy Dufresne used in the film? Yes. 'You've two choices. Get busy living or get busy dying'. The wit and wisdom of Stephen King. Guest knew he would not survive the American penal system and that was why he had seized Martin Carver's offer no matter how crazy it had at first appeared.

He knew that he was facing a long time of solitude and he was, by nature, a gregarious man. He would have to find a way to use his mind or he risked cracking under the strain, admitting his lies and then the American's would be waiting for him. He'd read of prisoners who played endless games of mental chess or recited huge works of literature (often the Bible) to themselves. That was not his world. His world was music so he decided to create his own jukebox. He would fill it with all the songs he'd heard or could learn or even write then find a way of allocating them numbers which he could somehow generate randomly (dice?) and then listen to them. He decided to begin the process logically and place the groups in alphabetical order. Unfortunately this gave him ABBA as his first selection so he decided to create his list in reverse order. Thus it was that Tony Guest spent his first night in solitary listening to the greatest hits of ZZ Top.

Chapter Thirty Three

On Monday morning Roger Tucker was putting the final touches to his article for the following day's edition of his paper when his eye was caught by a breaking news caption flashed up on SKY TV. 'Musician charged with multiple murders' was alliterative enough to grab his interest so he turned up the set's volume to listen to whatever detail SKY had. The telejournalist outside the court had a lot more questions than answers. The bare facts were that a British musician named Tony Guest, aged forty one and a resident of Upton Magna, Shropshire had been charged with the murders of Janice Hope, Helen Prospero and Jennifer Duncan in three different incidents sometime during the past five years. Photos of three young women appeared on screen as the talking head went on about the possibility of a serial killer who preyed on his fans. Guest was remanded in custody for four weeks when he would reappear before magistrates to be sent for trial at Crown Court sometime in the future. The Metropolitan Police would be issuing a statement at 1400 hours.

Tucker decided to crack on with his work. The breaking story may or may not be linked to Mark Goodchild's case and he would have more to go on in just over two hours time. If this was connected to the events that had started with his receipt of the ML email, then he was well ahead of the pack when it came to producing a more in-depth story. It would not do to go off half cocked though so he resolved to keep his journalistic powder dry until he knew more about the situation.

In Clerkenwell ML had just finished dressing after a shower necessitated by a vigorous gym workout. He reckoned that today would see the Americans enter the game when their embassy received it's morning mail and that Anglo-US relations were about to be subjected to some severe stress. So he was more than a little surprised to see the same TV news flash that Tucker was even then watching.

Putting his surprise behind him he began to work through various scenarios which could have resulted in Guest's arrest. Obviously he had been picked up, transported to London, interrogated then formally charged sometime between Thursday evening and midnight Friday. Otherwise his appearance in Magistrate's Court would not have been until tomorrow at the earliest. ML wondered what had made the police act now. Had their investigations resulted in such an amount of circumstantial evidence that they felt justified in arresting the man? Possible, but not probable. So; there was an outside element at play here and that could only be the Americans. If the Royal Mail had delivered his package to their Legal Attaché by Friday morning then it followed that the Americans would have known Catherine's identity pretty damned quickly and, hopefully, lit a medium sized bonfire under the Met's collective backside. Yes; that had to be it. The FBI had forced the hand of the British police and all sorts of shenanigans were no doubt going on between Scotland Yard and Grosvenor Square (with Downing Street and Pennsylvania Avenue yet to join in). The question now was how best could he make use of this development. It had not escaped him that only British girls had been cited as murder victims. How long before Catherine's death became public? Personally he gave it no more than 48 hours. If his idea was correct then surely the Senator must have been informed over the weekend. Perhaps it was time to stir the soup again. Like Tucker, he resolved to wait for a few more hours and see what the Met had to say.

Deputy Assistant Commissioner Addison had been selected to face the media. This was a world in which he was normally at home but, today, he felt on hostile ground. The big guns of the press and television were facing him and his performance would be scrutinised by his peers and superiors. He could not lie and he had little room to spin. All that he could hope for was that the media had such little knowledge of the background to this case that their questions could be easily dealt with.

Addison sat behind a long trestle table with a large set of screens behind him which bore the police crest and its mission statement 'Working Together for a Safer London'. The serried lights of the TV cameras hindered his view of his questioners and also generated enough heat to make him sweat. The combination of physical discomfort and nerves made him want to vomit.

After an opening statement (which was basically what had been transmitted from outside the magistrate's court) he looked up and said 'I will now take a few brief questions. Please excuse me if I do not answer them all but this is an ongoing enquiry and I cannot say anything which might prejudice the forthcoming legal proceedings. Who's first?'

All hands went up Addison selected the representative of ITV.

'Guest is accused of three separate murders and, as such, would fit the definition of a serial killer. How many other victims may he have been responsible for?' said the well coiffed and suited personality.

'The team which conducted the enquiry that resulted in Mr Guest's arrest is currently investigating a further seven deaths' replied Addison.

The room erupted and it took a uniformed sergeant a good minute to restore order. Addison's perspiration rate increased; this was not how press conferences were normally conducted in London. He indicated that the woman from the BBC should ask the next question. She chose her words carefully 'Are you saying that you have discovered ten dead bodies but only identified three of them?'

'No – I did not say that at all.'

'Well, how many bodies <u>have</u> you discovered?' she added quickly before he could move on to another questioner.

'None. Our enquiries and the arrest are result of us uncovering body parts rather than complete cadavers.' Addison silently prayed that the media would not pick up on his use of the word 'uncover' as opposed to 'discover'. They didn't.

'What was the cause of death for the three victims with whose murder Guest has been charged?' asked the verbose woman from the Guardian newspaper.

'We believe that all three were poisoned.'

The press conference then entered the jungle of murder minutia and Addison handled it with ease. By getting the major television channels and a liberal-left 'serious' newspaper out of the way at the start he could now field questions from the popular press who wanted to know about types of poison, sexual assault, were the victims prostitutes and/or drug users. This was meat and drink to a police officer who'd spent many a day on residential courses devoted to PR and media relations. He was congratulating himself on a job well done and saw that time was nearly up.

'All right ladies and gentlemen; I'll take one more question.'

'If I may' came a strong, polite voice which managed to cut through the hubbub without seeming raised. It belonged to Dawson Wilkes, the crime correspondent for Richard Tucker's paper. Right wing, usually but not blindly pro-police, he seemed the ideal person for Addison to give the final question to. He acknowledged him with a nod.

'You said, Deputy Assistant Commissioner, that you enquiries and the arrest are as a result of – and I quote 'the uncovering of body parts rather than complete cadavers' unquote. Would you tell us what, exactly, these body parts are?'

Some of the media regarded Wilkes in disgust, judging his question to be inappropriate and insensitive at the least. Others, more experienced, thought to themselves 'fucking good question. He must have some inside information to ask it'.

The brightly lit room was silent as all present waited for Addison's reply. Finally, it came.

'Fingers. We have uncovered ten different fingers.'

'Fingers. That's all?' asked Wilkes.

'That's all' said Addison who then stood and left the room with his aides.

At his North London home Roger Tucker exploded. 'Fucking bastards!' he exclaimed to no-one in particular. He dialled Mark Goodchild on his cell and was rewarded with an automated reply saying that he was not available. Tucker then called New Scotland Yard in an attempt to track down his friend through normal channels but to no avail. He even called Goodchild's unlisted home number where the answer phone kicked in. He declined to leave a message. Having exhausted all available means to get in touch with Goodchild he called his own office and was put through to the editor, Peter Balls.

'Hello Roger' he said. 'What can I do for you on a Monday afternoon?'

'You can tell me what the fuck Wilkes is doing at a Met press conference on what is my story.'

'Don't fucking swear at me you cunt. Wilkes is this papers senior crime correspondent. You are the house comedian.'

'Dead girls; missing fingers. Ring a bell, Balls? I brought all this to you weeks ago and it's on file. If it weren't for my link to Mark Goodchild we would be sucking hind tit on this story so what's going on?'

'Since when did you bring me anything about missing fingers? If you were the genius with the inside track to Goodchild you wouldn't have to fucking ask what was going on, would you?'

'I can't get hold of him, Balls. He's not answering any of the numbers I have for him and the Yard are saying nothing.'

'Where are you now, Roger?'

'I'm at home. I've just submitted my piece for Tuesday. Why?'

'Well, why don't you pretend that you're a journalist and get off your fucking arse and track your buddy down, you know; like we did in the days before internet and cell phones. I doubt if it would be too much of a problem for you to go on a fucking pub crawl, would it? That's where I'd look for a washed up copper.'

'Washed up! Goodchild? No way – unless you know something I don't, Balls.'

'What I know that you don't is bigger than a banker's bonus – and that's fucking obscene. Look – get hold of Goodchild and, if you can find anything out from him that will add to the story I'll put you on it. Fair enough?'

'I'll be in touch.'

Talking with Peter Balls always raised Tucker's blood pressure especially on the rare occasions when his boss actually had a valid point, which was the case here. Without Goodchild he really had no leverage into this story. It was time for some thought prior to action so Tucker took a can of Red Stripe from the fridge and sat down in his favourite club chair to sip and seek a solution.

A quarter of an hour and one can later, Tucker had decided what to do. The pub crawl was a non-starter given the number of establishments where Goodchild could be in London. Nor would going to the man's rugby club in Reading be likely to produce a result. Goodchild's crowd there would make the Metropolitan police seem like loquacious luvvies. If anyone was likely to be able to get a message to him then it was the Irish publican, Joseph Slattery. Time for another visit to the Red Lion in Whitehall.

Before leaving his house, Tucker checked his computer to see if any new emails had come in. There were four new messages, none of which required his immediate attention. He was just about to log off when the machine gave a muted sound and a new message appeared accompanied by a red exclamation mark to indicate urgency and/or importance. It was from ML and was very brief.

HELLO ROGER – YOU ARE BEING PLAYED. ON RECEIPT OF THIS LEAVE YOUR HOME AND CALL THIS NUMBER. I SHALL ONLY WAIT FOR TWO MINUTES. ML.

The number was that of a cell phone. Tucker did not hesitate. He could imagine why ML had put a time limit on him and was willing to play his game if it gave him some new information. The 'you are being played' statement had definitely pressed the right button.

Pausing only to set his alarm system, Tucker left his front door, walked down the short garden path and turned left away from the main road with its traffic noise. He checked the clock on his cell phone (did anyone use a watch these days?) and saw that ninety seconds had elapsed since ML's message had come in. He had entered the number into his own cell as he'd read it and now pressed green to call.

'Roger – how prompt. I'd expected you to send an acknowledgement of receipt before calling me.' The voice was electronically modulated and could have been any English speaking person, young, old, male or female.

'Ah, I did not think of that. The message came in and I grabbed my phone and went out. What do I call you?'

'You don't and I have little time to spare so just listen to me, Roger. I take it that you saw the press conference at 1400 hours?'

'Yes, I did.'

'It was interesting for what was missing rather than what was said. Where was your friend Goodchild I wonder?'

'I don't know. He seems to have dropped off the face of the earth.'

'Hmm – and he now has far to fall. Be that as it may, Roger. You have done reasonably well so far but the powers that be are not being straight with you, are they?'

'What do you mean?'

'I mean that you should have been at the press conference, Roger. You are being sidelined just as your friend is. Would you agree?'

'That's one way of looking at it I suppose. Mark and I both have bosses we have to report to and they don't have to tell us everything.'

'Roger, Roger, Roger. Are you telling me that you are the loyal company man? Peter Balls is a vulgar boor, not fit to sharpen your pencils in my opinion. Is he, I wonder, trying to make a name for himself on the back of your efforts and acumen, Roger?'

'It wouldn't surprise me. Not much I can do about it though.'

'Oh, I don't know about that. What if I were to give you a piece of information that your boss does not have but that the boys in blue are desperate to keep quiet?'

'I can see how that would be useful. What's the price for this?'

'Good man, Roger – there will be a price but it is one which you will be able to afford. I want your word that, if I ever summon you, you will come to me, alone and without informing anyone as to what you are doing. Deal?'

'What's to stop me agreeing to this then going back on my word when the time came?'

'How does the continued consumption of oxygen on your part strike you?'

Tucker paused for thought the way one does when a psychopath threatens to kill one. But he wanted the information so he said 'Point taken. We have a deal. I'll bring a long spoon.'

'Very droll, Roger. Now, listen. No lies were told at the press conference but the sin of omission was committed. The man in custody is suspected in the death of an American girl, a member of an important political family to boot. She was resident in England as a student and the American embassy have proof of her death. It is certain that they will have contacted Scotland Yard by now so at least two national governments are sitting on this information.'

'By saying 'at least two' you imply that there may be more. Could you clarify that?'

'It is highly probable that the girl died in Spain. That's all I have for you, Roger. Use the information well.' The line went dead. Tucker returned home as quickly as he could trying to recall the conversation as closely as he could. Once back in his home office he hastily wrote down every word he could remember, then he went to work in a more methodical manner. What he wanted was a verbatim transcript, or as close as he could manage, of his conversation with ML. Once satisfied that he could not improve upon what he had written, he took a fresh sheet of paper and tried to analyse the person who had just threatened to stop him breathing. The electronic masking of the voice proved a real hindrance in reading the nuances of speech which could have proved useful.

Whoever he was, ML was bright and well educated. His vocabulary alone showed that. He was also quite mad. Normal people don't insert death threats into their terms and conditions of doing business. If ML ever did summon him, Tucker would be in a difficult position to put it mildly. He would cross that bridge when or if he came to it. Right now he had to decide what to do with this new information. Normally he would have contacted Mark Goodchild but he'd already spent enough time trying that route today. ML's news was about an American, resident in the UK so it seemed logical to approach the US embassy for verification of what could become a major news story. Unfortunately for Tucker he had no inside contacts in the diplomatic community so he was forced to rely on his wits and experience to navigate the waters of American bureaucracy.

He phoned the main embassy number and asked to be put through to the consular section. Once connected to someone he assumed to be at the foot of the totem pole, he said who he was and who he worked for.

'I'll put you through to media relations, Mr Tucker' said a female consular official who sounded as if she were not old enough to order a drink in her native land.

'No, don't do that. I'm a journalist but this is not a media matter yet. It concerns the murder of an important American citizen in this country. I'm trying to be discrete here so could I speak to someone in authority in your department please?'

'Please hold, Mr Tucker.'

After waiting for two minutes the same young woman came back on the line. 'I'm having difficulty locating the Consul, Mr Tucker. Could you give me your number and we'll get back to you' she gushed.

'I'll gladly give you my number but I'm not going to sit around waiting for you guys to contact me. Once I hang up my phone, my next calls will be to professional friends at CNN and Fox News. They will lead their murder story with the fact that, despite this girl's death, the United States Consul was unavailable for comment. Your call.'

'Please hold, Mr Tucker.'

This time it was over five minutes before someone came back to Roger Tucker. The voice was male and strong. Definitely somebody senior.

'Mr Tucker – the consular section say that you have some information regarding a citizen. What exactly do you have for us, sir?'

'Well a question to start with. You know who I am and who I work for. Would you mind telling me who you are, please?'

'My name's Kevin Ryan. I'm the Legal Attaché here. Now what's this about?'

'I've received information from a source close to the Tony Guest case which indicates that one of your citizens is also missing, believed killed, by the same man. Scotland Yard made no mention of this at their briefing this afternoon and I'm trying to find out (a) if this information is true and (b) if it is, what the British police are hiding it for?'

'Where does your information came from, sir?'

'I'm not going to answer that just yet Mr Ryan – you know I don't have to. But I'm not going to obstruct a murder enquiry for the sake of a story. All I ask is that people play straight with me. So – has my informant given me true information so far?'

Kevin Ryan had little time for the press. He would happily use them if it were in his own interest but he really did not like the boot being on the other foot and right now he felt that his ass was being kicked. If the pussies in consular had not said that this Brit knew people at CNN and Fox he would not have spoken to him. As it was, he was glad that he had. To Ryan's knowledge, no-one outside of law enforcement knew about Catherine Taylor-Lodge's link with Guest so this Brit journalist might prove useful to him.

'Your information is correct, sir. The FBI is conducting an investigation into the murder of a US national resident in Great Britain. Scotland Yard are aware of this and are providing full assistance.'

'My information is that the victim was a member of a prominent American family, Mr Ryan. Would you care to comment on that?'

'Damn! How much does this guy know?' thought Ryan. Catherine's identity was sure to leak in Washington or New York later today. Would it help the FBI if he were to give this information to the UK press first? He made his decision.

'The deceased's name is Catherine Taylor-Lodge, only daughter of Senator Lyall Lodge III of New York. Do you have any information as to what happened to her, Mr Tucker.'

The revelation that a US Senator's child was the victim had really focused Tucker's attention. This story, linked as it was to a UK serial killer, was going to be huge. He was not going to let anyone else take the credit this time so he was going to gather as much information as he could prior to filing his piece with Peter Balls as a fait accompli. With this in mind he proceeded to dole out more facts to Ryan.

'I've been informed that it is probable that Catherine died in Spain. Does that tie in with your information, Mr Ryan.'

'All I'll say to that is that it is one line of enquiry which we are pursuing at this time. Now – I ask again; where is a civilian receiving this level of information from? I assume you have your contacts at Scotland Yard.'

'Yes, well, I used to assume that too but my guy appears to have evaporated.'

'Yeah? Who's that?'

'Commander Mark Goodchild. We go back a long way. Do you know him, Mr Ryan?'

'We've met once. I went to see him when Guest was brought into custody. Look, Mr Tucker; I realise you have your job to do and you've been straight up in calling the embassy before going to print and I hope you feel I've been equally fair in answering your questions. Is there anything else you can tell me?'

'Not regarding Catherine, no.'

'So how did you get involved in this whole Tony Guest case? I've quickly checked you out on line and crime is not your area, Mr Tucker.'

'I'd need to consult some people before I let you known how I got involved in all this. As you say, I have a job to do and I'm going to get the Yard to comment one way or another on my new information. Who do you normally deal with over there, Mr Ryan?'

'Sir Alan Sampson' said the American without missing a beat, knowing that involving the name of the most senior police officer in the country would bring home to this journalist that he was playing in the big leagues now.

'Thanks for that. It should be fun trying to get him to answer my phone call.'

'That's why they pay you the big bucks, Mr Tucker. I've a feeling that you and I will be talking again soon. This is my personal cell number. Please keep it safe.'

The two men exchanged details then finished their conversation on a cordial note – false but cordial nonetheless. Tucker was satisfied, ML's information had checked out and he'd managed to extract further detail from the Legal Attaché. Ryan was less happy. The unexpected appearance of a British journalist with inside knowledge had blindsided him for a moment. Hopefully he had made an ally of the man and he might prove useful as a Trojan horse inside the maze that was Scotland Yard.

Tucker reviewed the notes he had taken whilst talking with Kevin Ryan. He thought about googling the man's name but knew from experience that he would receive millions of hits to such an everyday name. No doubt some whiz kid at his office would be able to narrow down the search in seconds but this was not a skill that Tucker had nor envied. It was sufficient for his purposes to know that Ryan's contact at the Yard was the Commissioner himself so, bearing that in mind, he rang the general number for the Metropolitan police and asked to be put through to Sir Alan. He ran into the expected brick wall. The most he learned in ten minutes of telephone hop-scotch was that the Commissioner was in a meeting and said meeting would be over when the Prime Minister decided it was over. Changing tack, Tucker asked to be put through to Deputy Assistant Commissioner Oliver Addison. This man's office seemed to be guarded by a woman who made Cerberus seem like Scooby Doo. Tucker's limited supply of patience was running out so he went for broke. He'd either be put through to Addison or they'd refer him to the press office.

'Look, darling' he said 'Let me explain it to you very, very simply.' He could visualise the police officer gritting her teeth at one sentence which managed to imply that he was a sexist, patronising bastard who looked down on the police in general (and policewomen in particular). 'The reason I'm asking to speak to your boss specifically is that he fronted the press conference on the Guest case today and I have further information regarding this case. Don't ask me what it is; it's way above your pay grade. Now, I've just got off the phone with Kevin Ryan - he's the Legal Attaché at the American embassy by the way – and he was quite willing to chat with me. Kevin's point of contact at the Yard is Sir Alan but I can't talk to him 'cos he's in with the P.M. so I'm doing you the courtesy of giving you the same opportunity as I gave to the Americans. I can go to print with what I have now and say that there was no-one available for comment at the Metropolitan police or you can put me through. Your choice, love.'

'I'll see if he's free' came a voice shaking with the effort of remaining polite.

Another few minutes of waiting ensued. Tucker wished he were a lawyer with a stop clock ticking on his desk to indicate the amount of billable time spent on every phone call made. Finally, a voice sounded in the receiver.

'This is Addison.'

'Olly! How are you? Thanks for taking my call.'

'Have we met, Mr Tucker?'

'No – but I saw you on TV this afternoon.'

'And you think that gives you the right to call me 'Olly' do you?'

'Well, you look like an Olly to me. Oliver would be far too pompous and a man does not rise to your level in the service by being pompous now, does he Olly?'

'I'm told that the Americans have given you new information regarding the Guest case and that you wish to share that information with us. Correct?'

'Nowhere near, Olly. I received information from my original source which I verified with Kevin Ryan. I'm now giving you the opportunity to comment before I go to print.'

'By 'original source' do you mean the sender of the email that started all this?'

'Spot on, Olly – I knew there was more to you than just being a spin merchant.'

'What is the nature of this information, Mr Tucker? How and when did you receive it?'

Roger Tucker proceeded to mix the message from ML with the additional details which Kevin Ryan had furnished. Together it amounted to a considerable body of work.

'Mr Tucker' said Addison. 'Your usual contact over here is

CHAPTER THIRTY THREE

Mark Goodchild. Why have you not spoken to him regarding this development?'

'I've tried, Olly, I've tried but he's not answering any of the numbers I have for him and no-one seems to know where he is. I did note that he was not part of the press conference this afternoon though. Is he still on the case or have you taken over the running of Orion?'

'I cannot comment on operational matters, Mr Tucker. Look, I think it best if you pop in and see us. We need to talk about this and I will make sure that Sir Alan is aware of your input too.'

'Olly – I've given you all the information I have. You can check with Kevin Ryan if you doubt it. I'm asking you now, on the record, for the Metropolitan Police's comment on these new revelations.'

'I have no comment to make at this time…'

'Are the Met helping the Americans with their enquiry into the murder of one of their citizens?'

'I have no comment…'

'Yes, yes. Do you confirm that Catherine Taylor-Lodge, daughter of Senator Lyall Lodge III is the subject of a missing persons or murder enquiry?'

'Tucker, you know I cannot comment right now. If you would…'

'Stop right there Deputy Assistant Commissioner. My paper and I have been doing all the giving since day one on this case. We are getting nothing in return and I for one am not going to end up standing without a chair when the music stops. I've a feeling that's the position Mark Goodchild finds himself in right now. I've all but finished my story for tomorrow's edition and your pathetic 'no comment' will fit nicely next to the American's more helpful input. If you have anything to add, Mark has my numbers. Have a nice day… Olly.'

Tucker stood up and wiped his brow. He had just pissed off a very senior police officer and one who was very well connected to the media world indeed. But at least he had managed not to swear or overtly insult the man so his backside was professionally covered. The next stage was to write the bloody story so he sat down at his word processor and went to work whilst the conversation (and the buzz it had given him) was still fresh in his mind.

Despite the wonders of spell check and his own years of copy writing, it was still half an hour before Tucker was happy with the piece he produced. He then phoned Peter Balls.

'Yes, Roger – I've received your wonderful copy. Highly informative and amusing now what do you want? A blow job?' said Balls with his customary charm.

'You might want to pull that piece Peter. Something's come up which might render its inclusion inappropriate.'

'Fuck me – I bet you can't even spell inappropriate. I didn't think the word was even in your vocabulary. What are you on about, Roger?'

'I take it that tomorrow's front page will be dominated by the singing serial killer who was the subject of the Met's bullshit press conference today?'

'That's the plan at present. Why?'

'Think back to how the story started. I've received another communication from ML. In short the guy the Met have banged up is also the prime suspect in the murder of the daughter of a US Senator – New York no less. The Yanks and our lot are working together on this but they conveniently kept schtum about it at the media briefing this afternoon.'

'Shit! Are you sure? Someone's not pulling your prick here are they, Roger?'

'I'm sure. I've verified my info with the Legal Attaché at the American embassy and he's given me the dead girl's name. This guy, Kevin Ryan, liaises directly with Sir Alan Sampson so he's not some monkey, Peter.'

'OK, Roger. Write it up and send it over. What do the Met have to say for themselves?'

'I spoke with that clown Addison. 'No comment at this time and could I pop in for a chat' was his line. Sir Alan was, I'm told, with David Cameron this afternoon but I don't think that there is any significance for us in that. I cannot find Mark Goodchild anywhere so bugger all is coming out of the Yard. I've already written the story and I'm about to send it to you.'

'Good man. I'll get on it myself.'

'Two more things, Peter. This story goes out under my by-line with my photo. I'm not sharing it with Wilkes or anybody else. Understood?'

'Christ, Roger. He's the senior crime correspondent, he's going to have some input and check with his sources at the Met. I've got to let him look at this.'

'He can look all he wants and if he can talk to someone more senior than a Deputy Assistant Commissioner I'd be very fucking surprised indeed. The front page is mine; if he wants to write about 'serial killers I have known and loved' he can do it inside the paper as 'additional reporting by Dawson Wilkes'. If you don't like that, just run my Tuesday fun piece and then play catch up with the rest of Fleet Street – I reckon the American media will break this soon anyway.'

'With a little help from you if you have to no doubt. OK, Roger; it's yours. You said there were two things. How else are you going to fuck with me today?'

'Leaving aside the fact that I'd hardly describe giving you and international exclusive as 'fucking with you', I thought I'd better warn you that I had to play a bit of rough with Oliver Addison and his staff so be prepared for some attitude from the Met once they get their act together.'

'OK. Thanks for that. What are you doing for the rest of the day? I might need to go over some of your copy with you.'

'I'm going to try and find Mark Goodchild. There's something odd going on there and he is a friend. I'll have my Raspberry on me if you need to send me a she-mail or whatever the jargon is, Peter.'

'Fine. Well done, Roger.'

Tucker looked at his phone in astonishment. Balls had broken the connection first as he always did but he had, ever so slightly, praised him – and not for the purposes of damnation. God! That was a first. Feeling good about himself and life in general he fired off his story to the office then left his home to search for Goodchild.

Peter Balls summoned some of his senior correspondents to his office. Apart from Dawson Wilkes he also included those reporters who covered the diplomatic and home affairs beats. At the last minute he decided to brief his chief show business writer to supply background on the world that Tony Guest inhabited. They all went to work beating the bushes of their different but now overlapping fields trying to find out what was going on between Scotland Yard and the American embassy. Half an hour before the deadline for the next day's edition they reconvened with the editor. They had little to report.

The Metropolitan police referred them to Addison's office. The man himself was not available and all enquiries were met with the comment that the paper had already interviewed the Deputy Assistant Commissioner so why were different journalists tripping over each other's feet? Which was actually a pretty fair question.

Kevin Ryan had been busy. He had called the consular and media relations staff together to let them know, to a certain extent, what was going on and to instruct them to refer all enquiries to his office. From there he politely said to all callers that these enquiries had already been dealt with and that a full statement would be issued 'shortly'. In other words, and by coincidence, the FBI and the Met were singing from the same hymn sheet.

Peter Balls was not displeased by this result. He did not want to make too much noise at this stage; that might have alerted his competitors that something was going on and his goal was to have a front page exclusive for the next day's edition. Once he went to print the television channels would pick the story up and throw their resources at it. The late evening news would be obliged to use his paper as the quotable source for the story of the day. No doubt they would be screaming at their Washington staff for information from the senator's office and then the American media would start their normal feeding frenzy. International serial killer, young women (sex?), politics, police incompetence and cover-ups and show biz. This story had it all and Peter Balls was going to be the man who broke it. He loved it.

At New Scotland Yard Sir Alan Sampson and Oliver Addison were reviewing the situation. The latter had a sheaf of papers showing the list of callers from Tucker's paper who had requested further information on the Guest story throughout the day.

'So what do you think is going on here, Oliver?' asked the commissioner. 'This is your world, not mine.'

'If I were you, sir, I'd prepare myself to enter this world some time this week. Once the American media get hold of this, which will be about 2100hrs tonight our time I reckon, then we will be forced to go public. The one thing I can't understand is why nothing has leaked from the senator's office yet. Anyway, to answer your question, sir; I think that Tucker has submitted his story to Peter Balls and Balls is using real journalists to verify the information.'

'You don't consider Tucker to be a 'real journalist' I take it?'

'Never in a million years. He is a clown but a dangerous one with a platform. He panders to the prejudices of right wing middle England and lends an air of respectability to racism, sexism and homophobia. He is also an irritant to police forces throughout the country.'

'Hmm – so he manages to be right wing and anti law and order at the same time. That's quite a trick. OK. This article is going to appear tomorrow whatever we do. What is our exposure, Oliver? Worst case scenario, please.'

'The fact that we lied to the press and the public over what we found in Hyde Park is hugely damaging at a national level.

The Orion team was way too small to conduct an investigation into ten deaths. If it were to come out that the under resourcing of Orion contributed to an American senator's daughter being killed then political pressure from the very top – and by that I mean their President and our PM – would mean that heads would have to roll.'

'Do you envisage that being at a ministerial or mayoral level?'

'No, sir. The media will try and say that the politicians were not aware of what the police were doing and are therefore incompetent and culpable. However, they have an easy out on that; Clarkson cut them out of the loop once he'd decided to close Hyde park and the lie just fed upon itself until we've arrived at this point.'

'And Clarkson's dead. That could be useful. But we cannot credibly lay all the blame at one man's door. Wasn't he close to Goodchild?'

'I believe so, sir. I read and re-read the Orion file and the irregularity of police procedure from the outset stands out.'

'In what way?'

'Think of the chain of events, sir. ML sends a cryptic email to a so-called journalist who then contacts his friend in the Met, Goodchild. Goodchild goes straight to <u>his</u> friend, Clarkson and the next thing you know is that Operation Longbow is launched without consulting people higher in the chain of command. Were you aware, sir, that Clarkson was a functioning alcoholic?'

'No, I wasn't.'

'He was due to retire and allowances were made because of his exemplary service record. To be quite blunt though, he literally drank himself to death. We hushed that up for everybody's sake.'

'All right, Oliver. I can see a way forward on this. I'm going to have to brief the Home Secretary and the mayor now. She's OK but the mayor is bound to try and use this to further his own political ambitions. Thanks for your input, Oliver. It's been most useful.'

'Sir, if I may – I think that you're going to have to let the Prime Minister know or at least the Cabinet Secretary.'

'Why? I've spent a good part of the day already with Mr Cameron.'

'The ministers who will be in the firing line will be the Home Secretary because she's in charge of the police but also the Foreign Secretary because of the American involvement. Apparently this senator is politically important to Obama so don't be surprised if the really big guns aim our way. In my view it would be best to let the PM know ASAP and he can decide who to notify.'

'I suppose you're right. Is there anything positive that I can tell the Prime Minister?'

'Let him know that Goodchild's Orion team have been replaced. We now have fifty officers looking into the seven unsolved murders and we have offered the FBI fullest assistance into their investigation into Catherine Taylor-Lodge's killing. We also have a Spanish speaking officer to liaise with the Guardia Civil.'

'Good, good. What are Goodchild and his people doing?'

'They are compiling a report for my attention detailing everything that has happened in this case up to and including Guest's confession. DS Fearnley is the officer I'm sending to Spain. I'll notify her tomorrow morning. DS Stone is taking two weeks leave beginning a week today and DI Carver is going on secondment to the Diplomatic Protection Group. I wanted to consult with you before deciding on what to do with Goodchild, sir?'

'Give him two weeks leave as well – he's just buried his mate Clarkson after all. By the time he returns the dust should have settled a bit and we can plan for a more long term solution. Oh and make sure I receive a copy of the Orion report when you do, Oliver. That'll be all.'

'Thank you, sir.'

'Addison left the Commissioner's office feeling pleased with himself. He was adept at reading between the lines when senior officers spoke and he was sure that his own position was safe. The same could not be said for Goodchild. Addison reckoned that his chances of survival were on a par with those of the last case of Guinness at an Irish wake.

Chapter Thirty Four

For once in his life Mark Goodchild left New Scotland Yard at a civilised hour but not before arranging to meet Michelle Stone in the Shakespeare pub by Victoria station. She left a diplomatic fifteen minutes after he did and was pleased that he was so tall otherwise she would never have spotted him in the packed bar. Lots of office workers thronged the Shakespeare prior to enduring the misery of the commuter trains that headed south to the coastal towns of Dover, Brighton et al stopping at every Sussex sheep dip on the way. Some people's lives were so sad that they had established regular card schools to break the tedium of the twice daily journey.

Goodchild was at the bar and had kept an eye out for Michelle. As soon as he caught her eye he waved and, through improvised sign language, ascertained that she too would like a pint of Guinness. He was soon politely, but forcefully shouldering his way through the crowd with four pints of the black stuff in his paws. She took one from him and they found a space (or rather Goodchild's bulk created one) by a pillar and they savoured their drinks.

'Couldn't take it any longer then, Mark?' she said through a cream covered top lip.

'It's not the fact that we are finished with Orion that gets me, Michelle' he replied. 'It's the fact that Jim fucking Cooper has been put in charge. The man who put the plod in plodding. Jesus!'

'Look at it this way; our brilliance cracked the case. It now takes a clerical worker to do the follow up.'

'Yeah, that's one way of looking at it. It still feels like a kick in the nuts though. I mean – I sacked the useless twat in the first place. He could barely keep a shit eating grin off his face towards the end of the day.'

'Mark, after a kick in the nuts you can fight back. What you should be worried about is the blade between the shoulders.'

'I'm not stupid, Michelle. Someone is going to lose their head over this and I'm first in line. By throwing Jim Cooper and fifty officers at this the Met are tactically admitting that I got it wrong first time round.'

'But what else could you do? Derek Clarkson set all this in motion then dumped it in your lap.'

'Derek's not around to comment on that though, is he? I went to his funeral last week.'

'Shit. Sorry, Mark. I forgot about that.'

'Nothing to be sorry for, love. It was a cracking send off. There were a hell of a lot of retired officers of all ranks there. I was the most senior serving policeman though. Neither Sampson nor Addison had the decency to send a card and they'd known him for a quarter of a century.'

'To Derek' said Michelle, raising then draining her glass. Goodchild followed suit and they started on their second pints.

'So why did you want to meet me here, Mark? It's full of workers from the Department of Trade or Overseas Development Ministry.'

'I seem to remember you saying that you lived south of the river. If you play your cards right you might be able to entice me onto a train heading in that direction.'

'You're on but let's forget the train. There's a mini-cab office down by the Apollo theatre. We'll go straight to my place and avoid the commuter oiks, OK?'

'Fine. I've had enough of crowds to tell you the truth and the rolling stock on ordinary trains weren't designed for guys my size.'

'True. No matter what they say, size does matter.' She smiled sweetly up at him as she said this and was pleased that he held her eyes and gave her a wink of complicity.

An hour later they were approaching one of the highest points of what was still, technically, London; the television transmitting tower at Crystal Palace.

'How far on foot from here to your place?' he asked her.

'About five minutes. Why?'

'Could you pull over on the left please, driver?' asked Goodchild. The man did so. Goodchild paid him off and he and Michelle left the cab. Once the car had headed off back towards central London he allowed Michelle to lead the way towards where she lived. His eyes were in constant motion taking in their surroundings. They turned right at a major traffic island and found themselves in a narrow road lined with small bistro type restaurants which stood in contrast to the huge Victorian pubs they had passed after leaving the cab.

'What are you looking for Mark?' asked Michelle. 'You're acting as though you were on a counter-surveillance op.'

'No, nothing like that but I will admit that I never take a taxi directly to a destination – force of habit from working CT. When you asked the driver to head towards Gypsy Hill I remembered a conversation I had about ten years ago. Do you drink in this area at all?'

'Never. The only places I ever use on my doorstep are the take-aways.'

'Good. The conversation I had was a strange one. On one level it was quite superficial but the four guys I'd ended up talking to were obviously serious players in the world of security. One was army, one Foreign Office, one was GCHQ and the fourth was an investment banker. They all had a good collection of war stories and certainly knew names and events that the general public aren't aware of. The gist of the conversation that I was receiving was 'isn't it a good job that we are on the side of the angels because, if we were on the dark side, the authorities would have no chance'. I felt that I was at a job interview.'

'And you met these supermen how?'

'Derek Clarkson introduced me to them in the Red Lion one afternoon.'

'So what's the Gypsy Hill connection?'

'The Foreign Office type said he lived here and told me some pretty amazing stories – all of which checked out. See that large grey pub on the corner? It was a major money laundering centre. All the Irish building workers who did not have U.K. bank accounts used to turn up on a Friday to exchange their cheques for cash. That was only the tip of the iceberg though. The real purpose of the place was to funnel funds into the UK Muslim community and this was done by Philippino domestics – not all Islamists over here are of Pakistani descent you know.'

'And that lot have been well and truly infiltrated. Bloody hell! Anything else I should know about my neighbourhood, Mark?'

'Loads but we can do that later. What do you want to do about dinner?'

'Cantonese take away if that's all right.'

'Bring it on. I take it that you have an adequate supply of cold ones at your place?'

'Of course. A girl never knows when she is going to get lucky and drag a horny, thirsty stud back home.'

They loaded up on Chinese and went to Michelle's flat. It was the entire top floor of a Victorian detached house that had been professionally converted into two large apartments. Goodchild knew nothing about the finer points of interior design but, even to his eye, the place seemed to lack character. As a functional piece of architecture it was fine albeit a tad modern, minimalist and cold for his taste. No-one would ever call it a home.

The two of them opened all the foil containers and ate directly from them using either forks or fingers, whichever was most suitable for the dish being consumed. It became messy. The mounting pile of empty Heineken cans gave the kitchen area where they were eating the air of student digs. They laughed easily when they realised what they looked like.

'Can't imagine Oliver Addison getting down and dirty with General Po's chicken' said Michelle.

'I can imagine him getting very dirty with General Po though' said Goodchild.

'He's not is he, Mark? Addison bats for the other side?'

'I've no idea, Michelle. It was just a throw away line. If he is he keeps it to himself. I've never heard mention of a Mrs Addison though.'

'If all unmarried policemen were shirt lifters then that would put you in the frame, wouldn't it darling?'

'I am secure in my masculinity. Come to think of it though, all fours members of the Orion team are single. What does that say about us?'

'Well you're divorced from a bitch and I'm too young and intelligent to tie myself down – and we <u>know</u> we're both hetero. Chris scares the shite out of normal guys and anyone that sees her as a challenge to dominate is going to come unstuck big time. Truth be told, I know nothing about her private life or background. I don't pick up any sapphic vibes from her and I can usually tell. There are a disproportionate number of them in the police as I'm sure you know.'

'No comment. What about Martin? That psychologist said to me that he reckoned that Martin 'had issues' with his sexuality.'

'Come on, Mark. What do you expect from a psychologist with a name like van Dyke? Whatever Carver's personal problems are I'm pretty sure they don't stem from his sexual orientation.'

'That's the second time you've mentioned that you're not happy with Martin Carver, what's up between you two, Michelle?'

She drained her can of lager, crushed it in one hand and went to the fridge to get two more. It was obvious to Goodchild that she was playing for time whilst she debated with herself about the rights and wrongs of saying something derogatory regarding a colleague to a superior officer.

'As we are all off Orion now I suppose I can tell you. Remember when you sent us to Brighton to follow up the Jennifer Duncan lead?'

'Of course.'

'On the way back to the hotel three local druggies tried to mug us and sexually assault me. Martin had seen it coming and took control. Before I could move he put all three of them in hospital. We never called it in.'

'And your problem is what, exactly?'

'These arseholes had knives. Once Martin had knocked them out he went back and mutilated their hands effectively crippling them. That's GBH in my book, Mark.'

'What would you have done if you'd been on your own, Michelle?'

'I'd have badged them and tried to arrest them. If they had resisted I'd have kicked the main man in the nuts then put some serious distance between them and me – then I'd have called for back up. That's what police officers do, Mark.'

'Fair enough. Why didn't Martin exercise that option. I take it you discussed it later?'

'Fucking right I discussed it. He reckoned that if we'd declared ourselves it would have compromised the investigation. I reckon he gets off on being bloody Rambo. Anyway, I've not reported him and I never will. But I don't want to work with him ever again.'

The laughter had left the room and the two of them drank in silence. Michelle was waiting for Goodchild to give his opinion on Carver's actions that Brighton night. Goodchild knew this and was framing his reply carefully. Michelle was a woman of strong convictions and he did not want to alienate her with a glib response.

'I used to see things in black and white. It's one of the reasons I joined the police force. No-one is above the law especially police officers. And that used to work pretty well for me. I've not been a saint, Michelle. I've used my fists more than is allowed but I've never faked or planted evidence. I like to think I've been an honest cop and I've risen to where I am without compromising myself.'

Goodchild looked across the table at Michelle, aware that he was not expressing himself well, his fear of provoking her inhibiting his flow of words. She returned his look without expression giving him no help. He'd expected this.

'Fuck it – there's no way I can explain this without appearing patronising; it comes with my age, rank, experience and gender. You've seen film and photos of what bombs and bullets do to a human body. The great British public would puke their cornflakes if those images were shown on breakfast TV. 'Ten killed, one hundred injured' might be the statistic of the day but have you noticed that the journalists never describe what the injuries are? A man's had his balls blown off, someone is left with only one limb, another's internal organs are so fucked up that they'll never eat solids again or a person's face is so disfigured that they look like they've stuck their head into a deep fat fryer. Those are just the after the event images. I've been there just after it's happened and it's like a fucking abattoir. A dead human being with no clothes or skin left; another who's been so badly burned that the muscles contract and a six foot tall woman is transformed into a blackened child sized cadaver of indeterminate gender contorted into a foetal position. But all that's not the worst bit: sure, you have bad dreams for a while but the mind has a way of healing itself the same as physical scar tissue fades over time. The worst bit is when you have to talk to the killers, their helpers or those planning to commit such an atrocity. Not many officers can do that with the necessary detachment. Those who can't do not work in counter terrorism because if they did, they'd probably fire bomb a mosque in Leicester or Bradford. For whatever reason, I was able to sit in a room with the amoral pieces of shit who were involved in such crimes and talk with them reasonably and politely in order to gain a confession or useful intelligence. Then I'd go home and drink myself to sleep, ready to start again in the morning.'

'I hear all that, Mark. Are you excusing Carver's actions or do you think he was wrong?'

'I won't say he was wrong but I don't think he should be a policeman. If I were staying on in the force I'd make him find a new career.'

'You're leaving? When was this decided? They can't sack you, Mark!'

He shook his head and smiled wearily.

'I'm making the decision, Michelle – although it is a case of jumping before I'm pushed. I'll sign the Orion dossier off by Thursday – Friday at the latest and it's been suggested that now might be a good time for me to take some well earned leave what with the pressure of heading up a high profile investigation and the death of a close friend and colleague.'

'And you were going to let me know when? Not that you have to include me in your decisions, Mark. It's just that…'

'Sssh' he whispered putting a finger gently to her lips. 'I know that you've booked two weeks off as of Monday. I'd intended to tell you today and see what your plans were and ask if they might include a soon to be unemployed copper.'

'Well I was thinking about going on a Club 18-30 trip to Ibiza but that excludes you on age grounds, doesn't it?'

'Yes and the fact that I prefer music to electronic noise. I was thinking of a motoring tour of south west France. Fly to Toulouse, hire a vehicle and just follow the back roads. Good weather, gourmet food, fine wine staying in Chambres d'Hotes with the locals not the tourists.'

'That sounds lovely – and romantic. Room for a little one on this trip of your?'

'Well it wouldn't be very romantic if I were to go alone would it? You've got yourself a deal.'

Michelle ran round the table to embrace him and the laughter came back into the room. The embrace turned into an intense kiss and when they came up for air it was as a couple, comfortable in one another's company, knowing that the future held something for them.

'Does south London run to a decent red by any chance?' asked Goodchild.

'Go through to the lounge and I'll see what I can find. I need to tidy this mess up as well.'

'What mess? That's supper or breakfast to me.'

'Breakfast? Cold Chinese? You, sir, have been single for far too long.' As soon as the words were out of her mouth Michelle wished the ground would open up and swallow her. Goodchild stood stock still, staring at her impassively. Taking pity on her discomfiture, he took his cell phone from his jacket and spoke into it. 'Roger – Mark Goodchild. Hold the front page; I think some girl has just proposed marriage to me! Dunno, we were both drinking. If she says it again after breakfast I'll let you know. Ciao.'

'Bastard. 'Ciao' my arse. Get in that lounge if you want some wine.'

'Yessum boss.' Goodchild left her in the kitchen with a smile on her face. To kill time he turned on the TV and switched to Sky News. A talking head was going on about the imminent implosion of the Euro as a currency which could result in the return of the Deutschmark, French Franc, Italian Lira etc which could, in turn, result in World War Three. Goodchild mentally tuned this out as he read the scrolling banner at the foot of the screen. 'British singer Tony Guest accused of murdering American student in UK says Daily Post.'

'Oh fuck' he said softly to himself. He saw by the clock on the screen that the time was 2150hrs and switched over to ITV to catch their main bulletin of the evening 'News at Ten'. As the tail end of some puerile sitcom played out he went back to the kitchen.

'Leave the tidying up, Michelle. You need to come and watch the news. Oh, and bring the wine.'

Goodchild's seriousness when he uttered these words stopped her from making the smart comment that she had been about to throw his way. Pausing to pick up two glasses and a screw top bottle of Rioja, she followed him into the lounge and joined him on the sofa.

'I take it that you've not called me through to watch good news, Mark.' She said.

'Neither good nor bad would be my call at the moment. Sky had a breaking news line saying that my mate Roger's paper is going to print a story tomorrow about Tony Guest killing an American.'

'Well it was going to leak sooner rather than later, Mark. What's the problem?'

'We'll have to wait and see what the media have to say but the problem is that this announcement has come from the UK not the other side of the pond which is what I would have expected.'

'Shit, yes. And he's your friend, contact or whatever the powers that be decide to describe him as.'

'Exactly. Right; here we go. Let's see what the lovely Mary Nightingale has to say.'

The newscaster outlined the story which was being run in the next day's paper as an exclusive by Roger Tucker. She went on to mention that Tucker had sources who were members of the operation known only as 'Orion' and that further details regarding the creation of this 'elite team at the heart of the Metropolitan Police' would emerge in the days to come. A spokesperson from the American embassy then replied to questions in a live remote interview and confirmed all the details that Tucker's article contained. After very little probing he also admitted that the FBI were already in touch with the British authorities and that a dedicated team was being sent from Washington to London. The spokesperson politely avoided the question regarding extraditing Guest to stand trial in America saying that his Attorney General's office would be consulting on that. The openness of the American response to the interviewer's questions was in stark contrast to the Metropolitan Police's 'unable to comment at this time'.

Mary was replaced by Alistair who began to talk about the economy so Mark killed the TV.

'What's the earliest I can get hold of a newspaper round here?' he asked.

'About seven – why?'

'Obviously I need to see exactly what Roger Tucker's written in case Addison or some other bugger wants to haul me over the coals on this.'

'You can do that online you bloody dinosaur!'

'Damn! Of course I can. When will tomorrow's edition be on the web site?'

'I don't know; not yet, that's for sure. Why don't you give Tucker a call and have him show you the lie of the land?'

'I'd say that he's going to be a tad busy if he's put his name to a world wide exclusive of this nature. He'll probably be doing the quoted follow up story and preparing to face the TV cameras himself in the days to come. Anyway, he's been trying to contact me and I've not been taking his calls so I'd be wasting my time I reckon.'

'Bollocks, Mark. You've been heading up an investigation into a serial killer, successfully too, and organising his interrogation, processing, liaising with a foreign government and God knows what else. You're the one who's been busy not some bloody journo so stop acting like his friend and start being a police officer.'

Such intensity would normally have made Goodchild switch off but he had things that he wanted to say to Michelle this evening so he gave her his full attention. Before speaking, he bought a little time and lowered the tension in the lounge by pouring out two glasses of the, as yet, untouched wine.

'Michelle, I shall not be a police officer for much longer but as long as I remain one I'll act as professionally as I know how. The fact that the office has not contacted me, or you for that matter, when the shit has hit the fan tells me all I need to know. Once my report goes in this week I have no more input for Orion. When I return from leave we'll see what's what but my neck is really exposed here.'

'How do you see my position?'

'You're probably safe – as long as nobody knows about us. You've made a positive contribution to the Orion investigation and should be looking at a promotion to Inspector after Guest's conviction. The American angle is an irrelevance for you. No; you're safe is my view, Michelle.'

'All right, Mark – let's think this through. Blunt question; when you leave the force, what are you going to do?'

'This is the only thing I know, Michelle. For better or worse my police career has taken me into the world of counter-terrorism and security. These are both growth industries and I'd have no trouble at all finding gainful employment. The only question is whether it would be in the public or private sector.'

'What are the pros and cons from your point of view?'

'If I stay in the public sector there's the continuity of pension rights and all that good stuff and I also know the main players. I could cross over to Immigration or Revenue and Customs easily enough but where I could be of most use would be VX or Box. I don't know whether either of them would want me and the baggage they'd perceive me to be carrying.'

'Doesn't sound that promising if you don't mind me saying so. Where would you fit in in the private sector?'

'The only people I'd consider working for are Krohl or Control Risks. Hints have been dropped in the past that I would be welcome and the money is attractive. Then again, if I wanted money I'd join Blackwater, do a couple of tours in Kabul, and retire.'

'You fucking well will not! Blackwater? AKA 'the Velcro cowboys'! Their idea of operational security is wearing sunglasses at all times and carrying enough ammo to re-enact the Normandy landings. 'Peace through superior firepower' is not a very useful mission statement and Mohammad bin Flip-flop with his I.E.Ds is sending them, or bits of them, home in a bag on a regular basis.'

'OK not Blackwater then. There is a third option I've been thinking about.'

'Well I hope it makes more sense than Blackwater, Mark.'

'George W Bush made more sense than Blackwater. Moving on – I have been toying with the idea of starting my own business, MG Security Consultants. I have the expertise, I have the contacts and I can raise the start up capital – how hard could it be?'

'That depends on a few things. If you are made to be the scapegoat for what went on during the Orion operation well, who would want to hire you then?'

'That had crossed my mind. If they tried to hang everything on me I'd be stuffed on all fronts with nothing to lose. They would not want me in full-on revenge mode so don't worry that I'd end up as irreparably damaged goods. What else?'

'Mark – you are an old school cop; you've been dragged kicking and screaming into the 21st century. You were going to wait for the shop to open to read a newspaper for Gods sake! At the very least you'd need the world's most efficient, long suffering secretary.' She shook her head in amusement and drained her glass.

'If that's the least I need, what's the most?'

'A business partner. Someone who knew the same world as you but saw if from a younger perspective. Someone who was IT savvy but not a nerd and someone who would not put up with macho male bullshit.' She replenished her glass.

'Do you know anyone like that? Because it couldn't have been yourself you were talking about or job application techniques have changed a hell of a lot since I last made one.'

'I've even thought how to improve your company's name. MG are obviously your initials, right?'

'Right.'

'So all you do is put S for Stone at the beginning and there you go.'

'SMG Security Consultants? Sub Machine Gun? Not exactly subtle is it Michelle?'

'It caught your attention and, anyway, I doubt if subtlety is your forte. Also, what are the alternatives? If we use our initials it's a combination of M,S,M and G. MGM and M and S are already taken, S and M is either kinky sex or sales and marketing.'

'There's a difference?'

'Not so's you'd notice. M and M is just plain silly so, Sherlock, by process of elimination and eminent good taste we end up with SMG. I rest my case.'

Michelle left Mark on the sofa and returned with a second bottle of Rioja.

'Where do you get this shit from, Michelle?' he asked.

'It's on special offer at the supermarket.'

'Not the wine – the alphabet bollocks. Joking apart, I once had to sit through a seminar on 'branding the Met – a mission statement for London policing'. Two complete wankers spent an afternoon saying what you just managed in thirty seconds. Where did that come from or am I just lucky to be in the presence of genius?'

'I was not always in the police but that's a boring story for another time. Can I be serious before we do this next bottle?'

'Go on.'

'We'll have our two weeks in France together and I'm sure it will be fabulous. It's only when you spend time with another person 24-7 that you really know if you have a chance of making it as a couple. I'd like to have that chance, Mark.'

'A chance is all I ask, and all I give. Thanks, Michelle.'

They kissed long and slowly with passion restrained but their hearts hammering with emotion, that wildest feeling that is generated by a mixture of love and fear. She did not ask him why he'd said 'thanks' nor for what. She knew, for she felt the same.

They broke contact and drank. A woman of artifice would have used the moment to curl up against the big man to let him have the role of protector and most males would have played the part. Mark and Michelle were beyond games.

'Plan of action for tomorrow?' she asked him.

'Unless summoned, I'm going to work from home on the Orion report. You?'

'I'd planned on going in but there really is no reason why I don't do the same as you. You could work here you know. I'll use my PC and you can have my laptop – or are you still using pen, paper and a copy typist?'

'Very funny. Offer accepted. With us working together that should even speed things along.'

'An early night then, is it?'

'Oh yes; I owe you a set of severely damaged bed linen, madam.'

'Just as well I have some more of this for later on then. I'll be with you as soon as I've checked my doors and windows.'

Mark took his glass and made his way to the bedroom leaving Michelle to check her locks. Like most police officers and the occasional sensible civilian she followed a basic security routine which would foil the opportunist criminal.

Goodchild approved and trusted her to get it right. It had been a good evening so far and the lack of communication from Scotland Yard did not displease him. Orion had been a poisoned chalice from the start and he did not mind that others were to drink from that cup.

§

The cup was now overflowing and the spillage was landing squarely in Sir Alan Sampson's lap. Liquid flows in a downward direction so Oliver Addison was next in line for a soaking but his frantic splashings made him look like a drowning man who could easily drag others down with him so he was left alone and isolated.

As Monday evening became Monday night the American media had seized on the story and the angle they chose to pursue was the contrast between the American and British judicial systems. That British policing methods were archaic and inefficient in comparison to those of the FBI were taken as a given. Much air time was given to the definition in the UK of a life sentence and the fact that time off was given to criminals who pleaded guilty and then behaved themselves during their time inside prison. The fact that this rule did not apply in murder cases was hardly mentioned.

Then came the matter of extradition. The fact that Tony Guest was in a British jail on remand and therefore inaccessible was infuriating to the American fourth estate. They put these questions to Senator Lyall Lodge III at a press conference held in Washington DC at midnight UK time.

The senator, as a recently widowed man who had now lost his only child to a foreign serial killer, was known to be close to the President and was telegenic as hell, was catnip to the media.

He comported himself with dignity, pausing dramatically to take a breath and keep the tears at bay and spoke of justice (with a capital J). When asked if he had spoken with the Attorney General, the FBI Director or the President of the USA he replied that he was an American citizen the same as all others and did not believe that his office (or wealth) should entitle him to special treatment. This statement did not answer the question but nor was it a direct lie. The media knew this but John Q Public did not grasp the subtlety of the response as he worked his way through his six pack.

The ether between Washington DC and London fairly crackled with questions and requests from the Americans and vague explanations and promises of co-operation from the British.

Sir Alan Sampson and Addison had planned as well as they could but the intensity of reaction from the American media had caught them off balance.

§

Peter Balls was drunk. Not because of alcohol but because his paper was so far ahead of the pack that his competitors were reduced to begging him for information and the effect this had on him was euphoric. Everyone, including the Metropolitan police wanted to speak with Roger Tucker. He told all enquirers that his correspondent was at a private location preparing his next revelations. The only person he had given any hope to was a senior producer at Sky News. He had said that 'in principle' Roger would agree to be interviewed on air and that he would try and sort it out next time he spoke with the man. The one thing he did promised was that Roger would not be speaking with the BBC, the Socialist Workers Party, the United Nations or any other organisations living on a planet other than Earth.

The man in question was in a comfortable suite of a small hotel just off the High Street Kensington. After sending his copy to his editor he had immediately decamped to this discrete yet centrally located bolt hole that he occasionally used when he needed invisibility in London. From the outside, the Victorian brownstone gave no indication that it was a hotel; one needed to know of its existence and have been introduced to the management in order to obtain a room there. No business was conducted in its public areas and the unwritten rule was that no-one recognised anyone else they might bump into whilst there. It was more discrete than even the gentlemen's clubs of St James'.

Roger had been invited there by the late Dennis Thatcher whose political views accorded with his own. Dennis had never revealed any inside information that he might have garnered during his wife's tenure as Prime Minister but he had put Roger in touch with people who had been useful to him over the years. The journalist had been wary at first about the situation, suspecting that he was being used to disseminate someone's political agenda. As time went on he came to realise that Dennis just liked to share a drink with agreeable company away from prying eyes and receptive ears.

Despite the hotel's antique appearance it was technologically equipped to a standard that allowed him to work as efficiently from his suite as he could have done from home. Having assured Peter Balls that he would have a major follow up for the Wednesday edition he had taken the batteries out of his mobile communications kit and decided to communicate by landline if he really needed to talk to someone. At the moment he didn't nor did he wish to. Media types from all over the globe were trying to contact him and it was only a matter of time before various law enforcement agencies would be requesting a word with him. He did not known if the Met could locate him through his cell phone and BBM but thought it prudent not to risk it. If the Americans wanted to find him he was pretty sure they could, so his openness with Ryan at their embassy would, hopefully, pay dividends.

For the moment he felt secure and in control. He'd written the bones of his next article but the coming twenty four hours would decide the shape of the flesh he would add to skeleton – which was starting to take on a life of its own.

He'd written a front page exclusive with an international political dimension and was the man of the moment. He knew how quickly that could change and the thought that he'd made a promise to meet up with someone who issued death threats as a conversational aside was eating away at him. He really should have spoken with Mark Goodchild by now but his friend had let him down and he had had to act or lose the story. 'Damn the man' he thought. 'I gave him an opportunity to comment on the American information and he did not even take my calls'.

No, he had done nothing wrong professionally from his point of view so he shut down his computer and poured himself a generous measure of old Armagnac. He'd leave the rolling news on for a while then grab a full night's sleep. Tomorrow promised to be busy.

§

Another man drinking alone to his sense of accomplishment was ML. He was in his private pub watching the news with amusement. Roger Tucker had performed beyond all expectations. When one knew the facts behind a story, as obviously ML did, then the circumlocutions of the media and its interviewees took on an entirely different meaning. One could even extrapolate facts from someone's absence from the screen and even 'no comment' took on significance.

ML had one more important card to play in the immediate future before he shuffled the pack and dealt the final hand. He could not do much at the moment except set up a meeting with Ian Williams to pay the man for his work in Fuerteventura so he'd need to brush up his Rodney McNaughten persona once again. That would keep until the morning. ML wondered if Williams was bright enough to put two and two together once the story of Tony Guest having killed an American girl in Corralejo became public knowledge. A lot would depend on whether or not the Americans had any recent photos of Catherine to release. It all added a further element of uncertainty to the unfolding events. This did not disturb ML's equilibrium such was his confidence in his own ability to control and, if necessary, adapt to events.

He decided to sing something that matched his mood i.e. he was the person winning the battle of wits between himself and the law because he was better than they were. The selection of songs about ego and triumphalism were few and not to his taste ranging as they did from 'You're simply the Best' to 'We Are the Champions' – music for the masses. He set about arranging a less punk version of a song by the little known American Papa Roach; its title was 'Getting Away with Murder'.

Chapter Thirty Five

London can be a beautiful city in late October. The trees of the royal parks and the various gardens along Victoria Embankment perform their annual costume change of green to gold and the urban takes on a more rural aspect. Normally Chris Fearnley would have appreciated this especially after having spent four weeks in dry, dusty Fuerteventura. This particular afternoon saw her cursing as squally showers had stripped leaves from branches, fabricating a carpet of sodden vegetation for pedestrians to slog their way through. Autumn's golden gown had become a dirty raincoat.

Chris had been at New Scotland Yard for most of the morning composing a report on her activities on Spanish soil. She was having to tread a fine line and not reveal that she and Martin Carver had actually been pursuing a totally different agenda than they had been briefed to.

Carver's transfer to the Diplomatic Protection Group had been put on hold when the FBI had requested that he be their point of contact with the Met. At that stage of the investigation American requests were always viewed favourably so that, at a future date, the British authorities could not be accused of hindering the FBI's efforts. Jim Cooper, as the new head of the team following up the Orion work, was not best pleased but possessed the political awareness not to fight that particular battle. Chris had yet to meet Cooper and had expected him to haul her before him this morning. Instead she had found an email from him on her arrival requesting a formal report on what she had achieved during her time in Fuerteventura, this to be carried out 'as a matter of urgency'.

She had finished typing most of it by noon but wanted to run it past Carver first. He was also in London on this occasion, attending to paperwork which still managed to accumulate in an electronic age so it was easy to arrange a meeting for that afternoon. Her innocuous email suggested they get together to review the American aspect of the case and that she would see him 'downstairs at 1500hrs'. The location was not in the Yard building. Over the years she and Carver had developed a series of code phrases for their own use. 'Downstairs' referred to one of London's lesser known meeting places for denizens of the security services. Gordon's Wine Bar. Officially Gordon's was open to the public but one could be stood leaning against it and not know that it was there. Hidden between Charing Cross Bridge and Villiers Street, one gained entry by descending a short flight of stone steps into a public garden. In summer a band played there thus rendering electronic eavesdropping all but impossible. The bar was, in fact, a cellar with a very low vaulted ceiling and little external light. Even on the sunniest day candles were needed on the alcove tables and faces were difficult to make out. The décor consisted of framed front pages of yellowing newspapers from years long gone. The subject matter of these faded journals indicated the interests of the bar's clientele. Chris made her way to a table where Martin Carver was sat under a headline which read 'Minister for War resigns over call-girl and the KGB'. It was dated June 5, 1953.

'Hi, Chris' said Carver standing up. 'Looking good'. She did. A month of walking the streets of Corralejo where the temperature was always in the mid twenties Celsius and clouds were non-existent had give her skin an almost amber hue. This, combined with a regime of almost daily four mile runs and ocean swimming, had given her a glow of health and vitality. She took the compliment with a smile.

'Thanks. I feel it. A month of this bloody weather and pub food will soon get me back to my slovenly best. Drink?'

'Cold Guinness, please Chris.' She went to the bar and returned with a pint for him and a half for herself. She was not one of those female police officers who felt that she had to drink like a man to prove herself in a male dominated profession. Chris Fearnley had nothing to prove to anyone.

'What time did you get in last night, Chris?'

'Just before midnight. The flight was on time but I could not be arsed going home so I stayed at the Gatwick Hilton and put it on expenses. Money doesn't seem to be an object for the American side of the Guest investigation.

'Tell me about it! God knows how many agents the FBI has sent to the UK but new ones appear every week.'

'Well in Spain it's no different. They've a C-130 plane parked away from everybody else and they've built a village of portakabins next to it where most of them stay. They've a secure satellite up-link to the States and they've also taken an entire floor of the best hotel in town; they seem to hot bunk there and ablute as and when they can. These people are under serious pressure to produce, Martin.'

'I've noticed. OK. I've read between the lines of your emails and phone calls for the last four weeks. What's your real take on this, Chris?'

'The first thing I must say is that the Yanks are going to make us look totally stupid. They are not just looking into Catherine Taylor-Lodge's death; they are pulling Tony Guest's life apart and, as a result, finding information about the UK murders. You must have picked up on that, Martin?'

'Yes, but carry on. I'd rather just listed to what you have to say for the moment.'

'OK. Now, remember that the Americans were starting from square one and had not even seen the Orion file. When I met them in Spain they asked me about the music scene in the UK, what sort of a musician was Guest, what sort of person would be a fan of his etc etc. I answered as best I could and then they put Catherine's ID photos and class book photos in front of me. One of their guys commented that Catherine looked as though she might be at home in church or maybe at a folk festival but that she most certainly did not look like a rock chick. I had to agree. Then they produced a series of images of a totally transformed Catherine. I mean you would not think it was the same girl. Apparently this info came from your end of the investigation, Martin.'

'Yes. They spoke to her tutor and classmates who all mentioned that Catherine had come out of her shell after her mother's funeral. Some of the photos came from the students and some from CCTV in a pub.'

'And some from her Majesty's Government. They obtained images of her checking in at Bristol and arriving at Fuerteventura. They are still trying to find out how she travelled from the airport to Corralejo and also where she stayed. Quite a few of the agents speak Spanish so they did not need my linguistic skills but they have been pretty open with me so far and gave me copies of the new Catherine photos. I was allowed to be present when they searched the apartment where Tony stayed. They'd bought in their own forensic team and the results are interesting – for us anyway. The English guy who owns the place, and the bar Tony played at, came with us. He was adamant that no-one had been there since Tony had left so we did not know what we would find. The FBI played by the book and told their Spanish liaison officer what they were going to do so we had a couple of very serious hombres from the Guardia Civil with us too. On entering the place it was obvious that an effort had been made to tidy up – but tidy by a man's standards. I mean things like the bed had been stripped but the sheets had not been washed – they were still in the laundry basket. Glasses, cups and plates had been washed, left to dry but not put away. The shower stall, sink and loo all had hairs on them. If Catherine had ever been in that apartment the FBI would have found trace of her. The results are totally negative.'

'Begging the question, where did she stay.'

'Precisely. She was not registered at any hotel or hostel on the island. Even if you walk in off the street and pay cash a hotel will insist on taking your passport for 48 hours during which time the federales will check you out. She must have had a private arrangement to lodge somewhere but she had no known connections with Fuerteventura. She did not hire a car so I think that she stayed within walking distance of the Rock Café.'

'What about a taxi ride to somewhere other than Corralejo?'

'No; the Guardia have interviewed every cab driver who works there. They are all licensed and would not risk lying to the authorities. She must have either walked to where she was staying or someone gave her a lift. I'll come back to that in a moment. On a more positive note, I and the FBI have spoken with quite a few locals who remember seeing Catherine. The girl was stunning looking and stood out from the crowd big time. I've traced her shopping on her own for clothing and accessories. She did this on foot on and around the main drag in town which again points to her staying somewhere local. More interestingly I have sightings of her in the company of a man who is not Spanish. The two of them stopped for a drink in a bar that tourists don't frequent and the story is that she sang to one of the locals who had been smitten by her beauty. Then we find her in the bar where Tony was performing in the company of a guy, possibly the same one, for several hours.'

'Please tell me we have CCTV images, Chris.'

'No. Big brother has yet to land in Fuerteventura. I don't even have a description of the guy that amounts to much. The Spanish blokes only had eyes for Catherine and the rock bar is a zoo. I spoke at length to the waitress who served her there. All I've got is a clean shaven white male, late twenties to early thirties, smartly dressed but not Spanish. She couldn't even tell me if they were a couple or whether they arrived and left together. The girl reckons that she only saw them two, maybe three nights and then they were gone. She'd forgotten all about them until I showed her the latest photo of Catherine and that did jog her memory. She reckoned that they were just another young couple, if indeed they were a couple, who'd booked a short stay break at one of the cheaper hotels. We know that's not the case.'

'So we don't have much solid info yet. Did the waitress see if Catherine spoke to Tony at all?'

'I asked that of course but she could not say. The bar gets bloody well packed and anything's possible but, if they did speak, then she did not notice it.'

'Fair enough. What's your thinking on all this then?'

'Catherine's killer has somehow persuaded her to fly alone to Fuerteventura where he has access to a property. He's taken her out and about and he's done it at a time when Tony Guest is on the island and arranges for her to be in the same venue as Tony to help put the singer in the frame for her murder. Her remains are on the island somewhere and my guess would be the sand dunes of the national park.'

'Or under a pile of rocks on an extinct volcano. I've checked the island out online and there are hundreds of desolate spots where one could dispose of a body. I don't think we are going to find her remains – the killer has had plenty of practice already at corpse disposal. Have you shared your idea with the Americans?'

'Yes, but in an informal way. I've been spoon feeding one of their men and letting him take the credit.'

'So what are they doing with the information?'

'What they do best; number crunching. They are checking out every male who flew into Corralejo up to one month before Catherine arrived and cross referencing the names with those who were on flights back to the UK between the dates of Catherine's disappearance and the posting of her finger to the US embassy in London. I take it you know from where and when the package was sent?'

Yes. Manchester airport just after Tony Guest's flight landed.

The team I've been working with have been fairly open with me as well. Anything else?'

'They are compiling a list of empty properties and properties for rent; the Spanish authorities are helping with that but it seems too obvious for our man. He's far smarter than that. I've come to the conclusion that our killer must have help at a local level – not an accomplice, but a facilitator; someone who can get things done on the quiet, you know.'

'Of course. Wherever in the world that there's a sizeable expat community then you'll find a 'Mr Fixit'. I take it you've found him?'

'I think so. I only started looking in this direction a week ago and I've had to tread carefully. I don't want to risk spooking him or anyone he might be in touch with. The guy in question owns several flats which are not anywhere I'd choose to stay let alone an American millionairess but he does have contacts amongst the more affluent foreigners on the island. His business cover is that of being the owner of a small music bar called – get this – the Royalist.'

'English then?'

'As roast beef and Yorkshire pudding. I've spoken with Richard Waterman; if this investigation ever becomes a film then Ray Winston is the only actor to play him. He's a caricature of an east London villain but charming with it. He's got some previous, nothing too heavy. Handling stolen goods, bounced some cheques in the seventies. He's never done time, not violent and has never been into drugs so he's made a bit of money and probably cut some tax corners doing so but I reckon he has his little place in the sun and is happy doing a bit of this and a bit of that if the occasion presents itself. The locals all like him and he's never had any grief with the Spanish police, so, if I needed a roof over my head quickly and discreetly he would be the man I'd go to.'

'Does he have any known associates who are slightly less angelic than him?'

'No. He does not even go to play in Marbella. Strictly a medium sized fish in a small pond is our Richard.'

'How did you play it with him, Chris?'

'Good cop. Sat at his bar, started chatting and told him quite early on that I was with the Met, here to hold the Americans hands. The FBI presence was about to become well known anyway so a bit of honesty cost me nothing. I showed him Catherine's photo and I don't think he's ever seen her. In fact he said he was 'bleedin sorry he hadn't met a little darlin' like her'. He claims not to visit the Rock Café 'too noisy and not my cup of tea, musically' was his verdict. He promised to ask around his contacts to see if anyone had put her up but he wasn't hopeful. So that was that for Catherine. We had a few drinks, went for dinner and I eventually slipped in a question about what sort of people he helped to find accommodation for. This resulted in waffle and evasion – he was definitely uncomfortable and knows something. I chose to back off and steer the conversation back to somewhere that Richard could act the part of the rough diamond raconteur. The things I do for England.'

'If this Richard Waterman obtained our killer's accommodation if was probably done in all innocence, agreed?'

'Given his history and the impressions I got from talking with him, yes.'

'I also think that the killer knew Waterman from the past – he may well be a regular visitor to the island. I mean a total stranger would hardly be likely to walk up to some quasi-villain with a bundle of cash and ask for board and lodging. So, how did they contact each other?'

'Phone or email are the most likely.'

'Therefore we need his phone records and a look at his computer.'

'I've thought about this and there are problems. If I hand this info to the FBI they will probably throw all their computing power at it and possibly come up with something in five seconds flat whereupon a British subject may well end up on an FBI plane to God knows where but it won't be the offices of the International Red Cross. They might even try for an international arrest of whoever Waterman has been speaking to. We would not be getting police officer of the year awards in this lifetime if that were the outcome.'

'Suggestions?'

'Hold on; I've not finished with the problems yet. The Yanks are convinced that Tony Guest is their killer and they are going through the motions to prove that to be the case. They are furious that he's in our custody and not theirs. Anything that casts doubt on Guest being their man risks being filed in the shredding machine. In the meantime our efforts could alert the killer.'

'The bugger of it is that the records of Waterman's phone calls will be held by GCHQ but we'd need serious political clout to see them. We're talking about international calls, probably between two UK nationals and our unofficial efforts could not explain why we'd need info from Cheltenham as we already have Guest in custody. We've painted ourselves into a corner, Chris.'

'I've an idea; the American investigation will continue until they find Catherine's body and I agree with you – that's not going to be anytime soon. I'm sure I can get myself back to Fuerteventura to keep in with the Americans. Once I'm there, I re-establish contact with Waterman and steal his phone and get a look at his email records. What do you think?'

Carver did not reply straight away. He took a pull of his drink and went away into himself, envisaging scenarios in his mind. He had no doubts as to his colleague's competence in carrying out such an operation but he wanted to maximise its chances of success whilst keeping risks to her safety at a minimum.

'I think it's a good way forward but you're going to need back up. Whatever plan you have for getting hold of his phone and email records will entail you being exposed, not only to Waterman and his pals but also the Guardia Civil. They are almost definitely surveiling you, you know.'

'Yes, I've noticed that the same faces pop up from time to time. After a month in town my face is known too and the friendly locals all say 'ola' as I pass them. Just how friendly they are is an unknown.'

'Remember that the Guardia are almost a state within a state. They are experts at intelligence gathering and will have informers reporting back to them from all the different communities, including the British.'

'Yeah. I know how they operate but I've been open and predictable so far – just a dumb foreign blond. When it comes time for me to lose them I don't foresee any great problems but you're right; I'm going to need back up.'

'And that means me. Unfortunately I'm still tied up liaising between the FBI and various police authorities plus I need to be around in case Tony Guest feels the need to talk. How long are you back in London for?'

'I don't know. I'll have to wait and see how Jim Cooper reacts to my report. Why?'

'I'd like you to work up a detailed plan for obtaining Waterman's phone etc, including a timetable, and run it past me. We should be able to have something pretty solid together by the end of this week. You must be able to take a couple of days leave before you head back to the sunshine mustn't you?'

'I should bloody well think so, especially after Goodchild and Michelle managed two weeks away once Tony was banged up. How are you getting on with the FBI in Bristol, Martin?'

'Fine, I'd say but it's bloody hard work. They are used to descending on their locals from a great height and with the full power of the federal government. They are frustrated that they can't do that here. Add to this fact that the locals we have given them to knock on doors are not all of the highest calibre and we have some fairly pissed off agents. I'm sometimes being used as a glorified interpreter between the two forces. There is also an enormous cultural difference. I swear that when these guys graduate from FBI academy that they have their sense of humour surgically removed. Also, despite the fact that half the Yanks have Irish names, they won't drink! And don't even start me on the subject of handguns. You'd think we'd asked them to leave their testicles at home, not their pistols. Despite all that, they've made progress. Their computers have created a picture of how Catherine lived, who she spoke to, how she paid bills and where she used her credit card. Using the latest photo of the girl all the bars, pubs and restaurants in central Bristol were visited and we finally hit gold. On the Sunday afternoon before she flew to Fuerteventura she went to a large music pub and ended up singing on stage. Apparently she's quite good. But here's the kicker; she was in the company of an older guy who also got on stage to sing and play guitar as well. The musicians were interviewed and they stated that Catherine's friend was a professional musician, that he sang a country song in an American accent and used on the same accent when he spoke into the mike to address the crowd. They could not identify him when they were shown a photo of Tony Guest because the fucker kept his dark glasses on throughout the afternoon but size, race and age are about right. As far as the FBI are concerned it's another nail in Guest's coffin.'

'Shit. These musicians; do they know Tony?'

'They know of him but they've never met. They have been interviewed by Avon and Somerset Constabulary and it's all going into the FBI dossier should they ever bring Tony to trial. The time line looks like this: Saturday evening Catherine attends Tony's gig. We don't know where she spent the night and we're still interviewing taxi drivers. We then have a very brief CCTV image of her on foot with a guy mid-afternoon the next day about twenty yards from the music pub. I would imagine that they had lunched somewhere but we have not found out where yet. The locals are still searching. A barmaid from the pub remembers them drinking 'quite a bit of wine' but that they were not drunk when they left together. Catherine saw her tutor on the following Tuesday to say that she had some personal business to take care of in New York and would be gone for a week. The tutor had the impression that the girl was just being polite and was on the verge of quitting her studies. The FBI went through the hard drive on Catherine's computer and did not find anything weird, although they did comment that she must be one of the few females in the modern USA not to use any form of social networking. They found out that she had researched Fuerteventura online and had paid for her flight electronically. Apart from the images at the airports and the information from various Spaniards, that's all we have. She did not email anyone with the news that she had met someone new and was about the fly to Spain to meet him. And that's it as far as Catherine is concerned. My Americans have focused their attention on Tony but, with him not talking to anyone except his lawyer, are having a tough time of it. They have no trace of him or his vehicle in Bristol on Saturday or Sunday but there are loads of hostels where he could have stayed and paid in cash so he could have been there but left no trace or, as the FBI think, used a false name. The next positive sighting we have for Tony is when he arrives at Manchester airport where he left his vehicle. We have him arriving at Fuerteventura and a taxi took him to the bar his mate owns. He was expected and picked up the keys to the apartment and you know the rest. You can see how this must look to the FBI can't you?'

'I'll bet there were high fives all over once Catherine's companion was described as a professional musician. Jesus, this looks bad for him. What's your next move, Martin?'

'We have to play the long game, Chris. Between now and the start of Tony's trial I want a public appeal based on Bristol for the weekend on which Tony gigged there. Someone must have noticed where a girl as striking as Catherine had lunch and it's possible that whoever served her was not on duty when we canvassed the restaurants. I don't think it would take too much nudging for the Americans to request a slot on the next Crimewatch programme.'

'When's that due to go out?'

'Six weeks from now which means two weeks before the trial starts so we have the time – just.'

'And, who knows; your famous horse might begin to sing.'

'Exactly. I would not say that the media have lost interest in the case but the pressure has died down on this side of the pond at any rate. The politicians in New York and Washington are maintaining a surprisingly dignified silence and the American press are gearing themselves up for next year's presidential elections so we do seem to have some breathing space.'

'For now. As trial date approaches the reptiles will be back to rehash what they don't know and I predict that Tony will be tried in the court of American public opinion. You mentioned next year's presidential election. If this drags on without a solution on the American side then the whole Tony Guest affair could become a political football – with the British police being on the receiving end of a kicking.'

'Nothing we can do about that, Chris. We have our plan of action – let's stick to it. Anything else before you head off to see Jim Cooper?'

'This all started with an email to Goodchild's journalist buddy. Do you think it might be worth one, or both of us, having a word with him?'

Carver did not hesitate before answering. His reply came with a vehemence that surprised Chris Fearnley. She had only ever experienced icy control from the man.

'No way. Absolutely no way. This entire fuck up came about because Mark Goodchild allowed his pal access to a major police investigation and look at the result; Goodchild's career is ruined and so is Michelle's if what I'm hearing about them being an item is true. You and I are sailing very close to the wind to try and find the real killer. Then there's the small matter of an innocent man facing a lengthy prison sentence at Her Majesty's pleasure <u>if</u> he doesn't end up wearing a fetching outfit of Guantanamo orange. As for Mr Tucker – he's gone from the equivalent of journalistic stand-up to being a talking head on all matters legal, judicial and political. He was on the BBC the other night talking about 'the special relationship and how the Tony Guest case may 'impact' on it'. Jesus in his jim-jams! I'll just bet he'll be the first with a book out when this is all over, too. As the song goes 'My God How the Money Rolls In'.

'That's a no then, Martin?' said Chris with an amused smile on her face.

'Sorry – got a bit carried way there.'

'Don't apologise; that's the first time I've seen you display any emotion in the years I've known you. It suits you.'

'Yeah, I know. All the girls say I'm cute when I'm angry. That's why I maintain this placid exterior – to give womankind an even break.'

'Piss off, Martin. I can see this conversation degenerating into who you should never give an even break to. I've got to go. Catch up as and when, OK?'

'Sure. Give Cooper a knee in the nuts from me will you?'

'Career advice the Martin Carver way.' She shook her head as she made her way outside where the showers had diminished to drizzle. As she made her way along Victoria Embankment she tried to sort out what she had learned from the meeting and how she could incorporate it into her report to Cooper. Her mind kept returning to Martin's uncharacteristic outburst. She liked him. Actually she liked him as much as she was able to like any man and a lot of that was due to the fact that he had always kept their relationship at a professional level. He gave her space and truly listened when she had something to contribute. Then again, he was like that with most colleagues – even the idiots – and this was manifested in a calculating demeanour which a lot of people took for aloofness bordering on the rude. So to see him react to a simple question with an instant and heatedly expressed response had been something of a shock. Despite the fact that she liked him, she always felt that there was a dangerous side to him. His outburst made her think of a large dog that had been woken unexpectedly from its slumber to reveal for an instant its lupine nature before settling down to its domesticated role. She'd covered her unease with an expression of levity but he'd not been fooled. His mask had slipped and he knew that she'd had the briefest of glimpses at who lay underneath. And she knew that he knew that she knew ad infinitum. Would this strengthen or weaken them as a team was her overriding thought as she approached the Palace of Westminster.

Chapter Thirty Six

A month after Carver and Fearnley had had their discussion in Gordon's Wine Bar various meetings took place, not all at the same time, which were to define the manner in which events in the Tony Guest case would unfold.

The first was a small gathering called by the Attorney General of the United States and was held in his private office in Washington DC. Present were the Director of the FBI, Legal Attaché Ryan from London, England and SAC Ross Lopez who was in charge of the American end of the investigation in Fuerteventura.

The four men had spread themselves out at the top third of a mahogany conference table and had their stacks of evidentiary papers at their sides.

'I'd like to thank you all for taking time off from your busy schedules to attend today, gentleman' began the AG smoothly. As if they'd had a choice in the matter. He was the chief legal official in the government and only a Supreme Court Justice with a lifetime tenure could defy him. The elephant in the room that they all pretended was not there was the fact that he was the first black AG appointed by the first black President. Race is never far from the surface in an American political situation. 'This is an informal meeting to review where we're at as regards the investigation into the heinous murder of Catherine Taylor-Lodge' he continued. 'As such, there are no secretaries present, the meeting will not be recorded so we may all speak freely.'

No-one blinked an eye at such blatant bullshit. Speaking freely to a politician meant saying what he wanted to hear. For a law enforcement officer to go against the party line would mean press leaks and professional death. The three FBI officers maintained poker faces and waited for the AG to continue which he did.

'My people and I have gone through the dossier which you've submitted. An impressive body of work – as I would expect from the Bureau. I have only one question; Director Mueller – is there any doubt that this Brit, Tony Guest, is the murderer?'

If Attorney General Holder thought that he could intimidate Robert Mueller with such a direct question then he clearly had not done his homework. The man had taken up his post just prior to the 9/11 attacks and had worked tirelessly to defend his country since then – just as he had as an officer of the United States Marine Corps in the jungle of south east Asia where he had been awarded a Bronze Star along with his other decorations. He could have stayed as a partner in a prestigious law office and made more money than he needed but he was of a breed that believed in the concept of public service so he had served under George W Bush and continued to do so when his Democratic successor had requested it. After ten long years as Director of the FBI it would take a bigger man than Eric Holder to back him into a corner.

'There is no evidence that directly links Guest to Catherine Taylor-Lodge at this time' said Mueller in a tone devoid of any emotion.

'That was not what I asked, Director. I asked if there was any doubt that Guest was the murderer. Is there?'

'In the absence of evidential proof that they were ever together then the answer to your question is of course there is doubt' replied Mueller.

'So, after two months work in three countries at immense cost to the public purse you have produced this huge piece of paperwork but no guilty party, not even a body for a father to bury. That's not very impressive, Director.'

Ryan and Lopez sat like statues although each one of them was inwardly blazing at the implication that the Bureau was just a paper producing body of functionaries. Their boss was at bat and they were in the dugout, waiting.

'The letter 'I' in FBI does not stand for 'impress'. It stands for two other things. The first is 'investigation'; that's what we do and are continuing to do in this case. The second is 'integrity'. We do not take a bunch of circumstances and twist them until they fit the result that someone else requires. You are in possession of all the information that we and the British police have gathered. Answer your own question; is there any doubt? Yes there is. A better question would be how much doubt is there?'

'And the answer to that is what, exactly?' said Holder.

'Kevin, Ross – would you care to comment on that?' said Mueller to his subordinates.

'I've never set foot in England' said Lopez 'so I don't have a feel for the people there as Kevin does. My take on this comes purely from what is contained in the dossier you and your people have gone through. The facts are that Catherine went to a bar where Guest was playing on a Saturday night. The following week they fly out separately to Fuerteventura where he has an unexpected week's work. She attends the bar where he's singing two maybe three times. He comes back to England; she doesn't. Legat London receives her finger in the mail indicating she's dead. Finger was posted from the airport Guest flew into at around the same time as he was there. The British police arrest Guest for the murders of three English girls who have only ever been identified by their amputate fingers. COD was the same poison used on Catherine. When the British cops searched Guest's home and possessions they found a coaster with Catherine's number on it in his guitar case. We are told that Guest is likely to plead guilty to killing three English girls but he denies ever having met Catherine. We have no evidence, either forensic or electronic, to show that they were ever in touch with each other so out of motive, method and opportunity we are stretching just to prove the last one. Having said that, my instincts scream that he's our boy. We still have work to do to prove that, Kevin?'

'Thanks, Ross. Good summary. I don't want to take up time going over everything that my team has been doing in the UK. After all, you and your people have gone through the dossier.' This was the second time that an FBI officer had referred to the AG's phrase 'my people and I have gone through the dossier' and Holder was beginning to think that he did not enjoy the full respect of the Bureau.

'I've looked into the man's background and have constructed a profile of him. By all accounts he is liked by everyone. Charming, witty. He's married and a homeowner though he used to be a bit of a stud when younger. Hard to avoid it when you're on the road rocking most of the time. If we were investigating this guy over here then the Bureau's manpower would be deployed to examine every detail of Guest's life and that of his family, friends and acquaintances. On UK turf we are limited in what we can do. The British authorities have charged him with three murders and are looking into a further seven as yet unidentified victims. From what I've learned, the guy's going down for life. Over in jolly old England that can mean anything but I'm hearing that Guest will have a thirty stretch before he's eligible for parole. To sum up; I'm not convinced that his charming personality excludes him from being our murderer. Ted Bundy was charming. The nature of Guest's work indicates a narcissistic personality and one who has chosen to spend most of his time away from his home and his wife. He meets hundreds of women every year and an intelligent killer could cull the weakest from this mass without drawing attention to himself. But once we do look at him closely, the coincidences just keep on piling up. In my view he's either a huge victim of circumstance, someone's set him up or, and this is what I favour, he is our man. As Director Mueller and Special Agent Lopez have both said, our investigation continues.'

The Attorney General sat back in his chair and regarded the three men from the FBI in silence. The meeting had not gone as he had anticipated and he was not pleased at what he perceived as the lack of respect shown to him and his office. None of these three jumped up cops had addressed him as 'sir' nor by his rank. 'Time for some hardball' he thought.

'OK gentlemen – I am meeting with the President later today and I'm sure that the subject of the senator's daughter's murder will be raised. If all I can do is point to your dossier and say that 'your investigations are continuing' it's not going to cut it. Mr Ryan; you indicated that you were limited as to what you could do on UK turf. Do you require any help from the executive to make the British see things our way?'

Robert Mueller fielded the loaded question. 'It is not the Bureau's function to put pressure on foreign governments, especially friendly ones, to act as we wish. The co-operation given to my staff by both the British and Spanish has been exemplary. If you, having gone through the dossier with your people, think otherwise then, by all means have the President talk with Prime Minister Cameron. That's a political call. The FBI has no request to make.'

Which everyone knew, translated as 'knock yourself out, asshole'.

'Thank you for your time, gentlemen' said the AG. 'My office will be in touch.'

The FBI men gathered their material in preparation to returning to the Hoover building down the street. As they were doing so Holder left his own office and closed the door softly behind himself without the courtesy of a goodbye. The three men left on their own were wise enough to say nothing before gaining the security of their own vehicle. Robert Mueller spoke first. 'Well done, guys. You comported yourselves in a totally professional manner and that will go on record. I want you both to take a forty eight hour leave before you head back to Europe. My secretary will organise the paperwork on that at a later date. Anything you need?'

'I'm good, sir' said Lopez. 'The Spanish are helping us try and find where Catherine stayed and my folks are checking with

Kevin's about single guys who flew in and out of Fuerteventura during the relevant time frame. It's a numbers game, sir; as usual.'

'If I had control of the entire British police force it would help, sir' said Ryan. 'Checking all these different, single guys means talking to different constabularies throughout the country. That takes time and scarce manpower for the Brits. But we'll get there, sir.'

'You've got this TV show coming up soon, Kevin' said Mueller. 'Remind me what that's all about, please.'

'It's called 'Crimewatch' and has very high viewing figures. Basically we are going; or rather the British police are going to show photos of Catherine to the audience and try to find out her movements between the Saturday gig and her flight out to Spain the following week. We are also filming a reconstruction of her walk to the music pub on the Sunday afternoon. Ideally we can find out who the guy on CCTV with her is. Hopefully they lunched together and our guy paid by plastic.'

'Long shot, Kevin, long shot.'

'I agree, sir; but we have to try everything and be seen to have tried everything especially after the meeting we've just had. If someone from the White House calls you to find out what more we are doing then you can honestly say that we are using UK national television, prime time, in our search for proof in this case.'

'Good point, Kevin. Politicians love TV.'

The men duly arrived back at FBI headquarters and went their separate ways, the two agents for their 48 hour break before returning to Europe and Director Mueller to get back to the myriad problems that the Bureau had to deal with.

Three days later in London a meeting of the British government's cabinet had just ended. All the ministers and functionaries left number ten Downing Street with the exception of the Foreign Secretary, William Hague and the Home Secretary, Theresa May who has been asked to remain behind by the Prime Minister.

'Sorry I've not been able to give you any advance notice

about this' began David Cameron 'but time zone differences are sometimes most inconvenient. Obama gave me a call late last night. All very affable, chatting about the difficulties of dealing with certain European leaders etc etc but, at the end of our conversation, he raised an issue which I'm sure was the main reason he made this unscheduled call. He wanted to reassure his 'good friend and colleague' Senator Lodge that everything possible was being done to bring his daughter's killer to justice.'

'I don't believe my ears' said the Home Secretary. 'The heads of government of two major nations concerning themselves with the death of one girl.'

'You don't know how the American system operates at its highest level, Theresa' said the Foreign Secretary. 'Obviously Obama owes Lodge and the debt is being called in.'

'You're probably right, William' said Cameron 'and I think it would be useful if your department could find out the nature of their relationship. Anyway, we need to be up to speed on this situation so I've Alan Sampson waiting next door to brief us. Any questions? No? Good. I'll have him wheeled in.'

Shortly after, the green baize door to the cabinet room opened to admit the Commissioner of the Metropolitan Police, resplendent in full uniform with his cap tucked underneath his left arm. He advanced to the middle of the long table where the three politicians were sat. The Prime Minister rose and shook his hand.

'Good to see you again, Sir Alan. Please, take a seat.'

'Thank you, Prime Minister.'

He made his brief 'hellos' to May and Hague then, at Cameron's invitation, began to speak.

'As requested, I've put together a record of the entire Tony Guest case beginning with the email to the journalist, Roger Tucker and ending with the fact that there will be a major piece on Crimewatch next week regarding the American girl.'

Sampson opened a large briefcase and extracted three folders from it. Each was two inches thick and bore a light blue label bearing the words 'Top Secret'. He gave one to each politician.

'Now I know how busy you all are and this is an awful lot of information to process but it is what you requested, Prime Minister. I have also put together a more manageable summary which still amounts to four pages, then a one page fact sheet in bullet point form and finally a day by day timeline of events. Everything you have in front of you is a known fact. There is no speculative material at all.'

The Prime Minister and his two colleagues skimmed down the sheet of bullet points then speed read the four page summary. It did not take them long and they all finished at more or less the same time.

'I've a question, Sir Alan' said Theresa May.

As Home Secretary she was his immediate superior. 'This is a factual report of a complicated murder investigation. Why has it been graded Top Secret?'

The question was a good one. In general UK government documents are security classified as Top Secret, Secret, Confidential or Restricted each denoting the degree of harm to British interests or security if revealed to unauthorised parties. There are higher classifications than Top Secret and these tend to belong to the world of intelligence and nuclear weaponry. For a murder investigation to have a TS grading was out of the ordinary to say the least.

'There are two reasons, Home Secretary' replied Sampson. 'Firstly the deployment details if we suspect a terrorist device has been found should not be bandied about. The main file contains a lot of detail of Operation Longbow. However, of greater concern to me is the make up of the poison used to kill these girls. Without going into detail now, it's called KOLOKOL and, as far as we know, is only used by Russian Special Forces. It's what they used to assault the theatre in Moscow some years back that had been taken over by Chechen terrorists. They killed the terrorists but an untold number of hostages ended up in the morgue as well. I don't think it would be a good idea if the existence of such a substance on British soil became publically known – hence the classification.'

'Umm – thank you, Sir Alan' said May.

'Yes, thank you for that' said Cameron 'but I seem to be missing something here. This chap, Guest, has admitted to three murders and the Americans are telling me that they have a very good case against him for the student's killing. How the devil does an itinerant musician lay his hands on such an outlandish substance let alone know how to use it?'

'Prime Minister – if you want me to speculate I will but we could be here for hours and I know that you are all due to be in Parliament in ninety minutes and will have to prepare before that. In short, we've asked ourselves the same question and it is a line of enquiry that we are pursuing. The bottom line is that Guest will go on trial for the murders of the three English girls we've identified and he will plead guilty. The Crown Prosecution Service feels that this is the best way to proceed. If or when we manage to identify the other seven British victims we shall prosecute again. The difficulty lies with the American girl and that is why we are all here. The circumstantial evidence against Guest is very, very strong. We think he did it. However, if he did, it is virtually certain that the murder took place in Spanish territory and, as such, we have no jurisdiction. The CPS tell me that Spanish law on murder is very complex and on sentencing they focus more on rehabilitation than punishment. Officially murderers are subject to a 5-15 year term although this can increase in certain circumstances. In fact there is a British citizen currently doing a thirty year stretch for the abduction, rape and murder of a young Spanish girl. My thinking is that, after Guest has served his time here, the Spanish won't be too concerned about him and the Americans would then take over.'

'My thinking is that they will want to get their hands on him a lot sooner that that' said the Foreign Secretary. 'It's not very well known but around 30 UK nationals have been extradited to the USA in the past ten years.'

'We can cross that bridge when we come to it, William' said Cameron. 'What more can we do to aid the Americans in this, Sir Alan?'

'Nothing. Avon and Somerset Constabulary have supplied manpower to knock on doors in Bristol and the Met has sent an officer whom the FBI requested to liaise and facilitate. Another officer, an experienced member of the original team at the Yard, has been to Spain to do what she can but that is obviously limited in scope. It is someone else's country after all. Basically an American girl has probably been murdered in Spain so that is an issue for the FBI and Interpol. The problem is that the prime suspect is British and is about to disappear into one of Her Majesty's less pleasant residences for the foreseeable future thus keeping him out of American hands and hence the pressure building up from across the Atlantic.'

'That is about the size of it' said Cameron. 'Last thing before you go, Sir Alan. Can I say to Obama that our best people are making their best efforts in assisting his people in this matter?'

'Absolutely, Prime Minster.'

'Then I'll detain you no longer. Thank you again and I'll be in touch. Please let Theresa know if anything new comes up.'

Britain's most senior police officer gathered his things together and left the famous old room at a brisk pace leaving the politicians on their own once more.

David Cameron turned to Hague and May. 'All three of us need to digest the main file in its entirety I'm afraid. This case has the potential to cause us grief on so many levels it's not true. Firstly, police – media relations. Someone is responsible for lying to the public. Secondly, police – government relations. How can the Met close down central London without consulting the Home Office? Thirdly, how many young people are missing from home and what is being done to find them? Those three are for you, Theresa. William – state of play on our extradition treaty with the Americans. What could be the repercussions for Anglo-US relations if we refuse to hand Guest over to them after his trial? Bear in mind the influence that this senator might have. Both of you, keep this close. I don't want any leaks. All this effort may not be needed; but if it is I want us to be able to show that we have been keeping on top of the situation. Right – I'll see you in the house for a spot of socialist baiting.'

The two senior ministers left number ten. May's car was waiting for her whereas Hague only had to walk across Downing Street to enter the august building that is the Foreign and Commonwealth Office.

The accommodation above number ten is too small for a man with a wife and three young children so David Cameron had taken over the flat above number eleven which was nominally that of the Chancellor of the Exchequer. He'd put all thoughts of murderous musicians, Russian poisons and presidential pressure from his mind. That was for later. Right now all the man wanted was a quick lunch with his wife and new baby before crossing Parliament Square to defend, again, the government's stance on the economy.

Two hours later he returned from verbally battering his opposite number and went to his private office where he divested himself of jacket and tie. After going over his schedule for the next day with his Principal Private Secretary it was time for him to go through the various ministerial submissions which had been accumulating for his attention throughout the day. There would be more towards the end of the afternoon but he would deal with these there and then.

David Cameron was a young Prime Minister but almost all his working life had been spent in the political arena so he was able to see through the obfuscatory language employed in some of the paperwork to what the real situation was. This meant that he processed information almost twice as fast as his colleagues which was one reason he had the top job and they reported to him. Having been schooled at Eton and Oxford helped as well. Those who thought that a first class education should bar someone from high office were practicing the politics of envy. Thus it was that he found himself with fifty minutes spare before his next meeting so, literally and mentally rolling his sleeves up, he attacked Sir Alan Sampson's fat file. He quickly realised that he could ignore a great deal of it as it concerned technical reports in scientific language which he could not be expected to comprehend. The rest, especially when read in conjunction with the timeline, was fairly straightforward but one thing towards the end of the report did not make sense to him. The police officer who had headed up the investigation and who was responsible for a multiple murderer awaiting trial had been taken off the case. His three subordinates were still, in one way or another, continuing in their efforts. What had happened to Acting Commander Goodchild? He made a note to ask Sir Alan Sampson at the first opportunity. Apart from that the report was solid. He felt that he could tell the American President that his country was doing all that it could to assist the FBI and, if anyone wanted to ask questions in the House about this case, he was now in a position to answer with authority. Now all he could do on the American side of the case was to wait and see if the Crimewatch programme brought any new information to light.

Chapter Thirty Seven

The following Thursday at 2100hrs the BBC transmitted its Crimewatch programme. The show's anchor was the experienced journalist Kirsty Young and she herself presented the main feature which was the disappearance and death of the American student Catherine Taylor-Lodge. The BBC had trailed the show extensively and the public were aware of some of the background to the case owing in the main to Richard Tucker's articles so interest was high. Viewing figures would pass the five million mark.

Up to date photos of Catherine were shown as Young succinctly went over the details of the girl's last known whereabouts. CCTV images of Catherine and 'an unknown man' entering the music pub on the Sunday afternoon were used.

'Police would like to interview the man shown accompanying Catherine in these images' said Young. 'Did you see them having lunch in a bar or restaurant that Sunday? Did you see them having a drink in a pub or just walking somewhere in town? If you have any information please call Crimewatch, in confidence on 0800 555 111. Thank you.' The programme then moved onto the story of an Asian shop owner who as in intensive care having been hit on the head with an iron bar whilst defending his premises from feral thieves.

The programme ended at ten p.m. when the main news was shown. At 2235hrs there was a Crimewatch Update during which the presenters gave a summary of the results of their various appeals. Kirsty Young revealed that several calls of interest had been received regarding the American student's murder and this information was being given to the relevant police forces.

Across England many interested parties now sat down to take stock of the show's potential influence on the case.

ML had watched it from his home in Clerkenwell. When the presenter had asked the viewers if they had seen the couple having Sunday lunch together he instantly realised that he had made a tactical mistake. Because he had been in a rush to book a restaurant he had reserved a table in the name of the character he was playing that weekend, Dominic Lord. This was also the name he had used at the hotel where he had stayed in Bristol. He had, as usual, paid in cash but someone had written his name down when he made a reservation for two people. It would only take one member of staff to have remembered Catherine's face and the process of tracking one Dominic Lord would begin. The Passport Office would confirm his existence but he would only be one amongst many men with that name so it would take the police sometime to eliminate all the others as possibilities. On the other hand there were probably not a lot of Dominic Lord's flying into Fuerteventura during the relevant time frame so they could be onto that identity fairly quickly. Then they would run down the credit cards and driving licence details. None of this would help the authorities. All correspondence for his Lord persona went to a Pakistani owned newsagents in Deptford. He paid the man fifty pounds a month to act as a private post box for the inevitable bank statements and promotional litter that even a false identity attracts. He feared that the kindly Mr Munir was about to incur some serious unpleasantness from several government agencies. A larger concern was Richard in Fuerteventura. How would he react when the authorities asked if he knew a Dominic Lord was anybody's guess. He could play the innocent and say that they'd known each other for years and he had recently rented a property for him. Richard had never seen him with Catherine and may not have even seen the girl at all, despite the smallness of Corralejo, given the fact that he was rarely conscious before mid-afternoon. It did not matter. Once the FBI forensics people had a location they would examine it in microscopic detail and, even after all this time, find traces of Catherine and the cause of her death.

On the other hand, Richard was just as likely to say that he'd never heard of Dominic Lord such was his antipathy toward the forces of law and order.

One thing was certain. He could never use the Dominic Lord I.D. again and would destroy all documentation pertaining to him within the hour.

Roger Tucker watched the programme from home in the company of his wife who had returned from her extended stay at their Spanish villa. He would dearly have loved to be privy to the calls that the BBC had received but that was never going to happen. He'd also given up on trying to contact Mark Goodchild as his calls always went unreturned. By all accounts his friend was off the case now and his replacement just did not talk with journalists so Tucker found himself sidelined for the time being. The Americans owed him for keeping them in the loop before going to print and he had yet to call that marker in. He'd be speaking with Kevin Ryan soon he thought to himself. In the meantime life was good. He had a book contract and the first draft was finished. All he needed now was the outcome of the trial plus anything that the Crimewatch appeal threw up. His standing in the journalistic community was higher that it had ever been and his wife loved it. They were invited to all the best parties now.

Kevin Ryan had called his team into his office at the American embassy to watch the TV in case something broke which required them to contact Washington. Alan Sampson had promised to let him see any substantive information as soon as they had it. Ryan settled in for a long night.

Sir Alan himself viewed Crimewatch from the comfort of his own home. He'd left Oliver Addison in charge at New Scotland Yard who had, in turn, sent the new boss of Orion, Jim Cooper, to liaise with the BBC. Unfortunately for Cooper this meant a trip to the BBC studios in Wales and the joys of a Thursday night in Cardiff.

Mark Goodchild and Michelle Stone watched the show together at her flat in Gypsy Hill. Their vacation in France had been a success and just the break they both needed. He'd hired a car and shown her places she'd only vaguely heard of; Biarritz, Bayonne, Pau were some of the larger towns they visited phoning ahead each day to reserve a room for the night under the excellent Chambres d'Hôte system used in France. Towards the end of the first week Michelle realised that they were embarked upon a pilgrimage to French Rugby culture and pulled him up on that fact. Mark admitted it and drove her up the coast to Arcachon with its magnificent beaches and seafood restaurants – and no rugby. There they stayed for the last week of their leave walking, eating, drinking and making love.

Now they were back to what passed for normality for an officer of the Metropolitan police. Sometimes she stayed at his house but tonight, for no particular reason, they were on her turf. Neither had raised the subject yet but they both knew that they were heading down a path where it would make sense to live under one roof. They were not in a hurry though, which is the mark of a secure, adult relationship.

They paid scant attention to the item which had once consumed them. Michelle found herself used as a word processor on legs for Jim Cooper, her presence as a member of the original Orion team resented. Mark's situation was an awkward one. He still held the rank of Acting Commander. They could hardly demote him after he'd caught a man who confessed to three murders but he could hardly slot back in with SO15 with his elevated rank without seriously disrupting the system. The powers that be decided to send him out to the various different constabularies of the United Kingdom to address those officers who concerned themselves with counter terrorism. In reality he ended up giving the inside version of the Tony Guest capture. He was tacitly encouraged to carry out this task at a relaxed pace whilst a more substantive role was found for him and at first this suited him as he could plan his exit strategy from the service. However, it rapidly palled and the prospect of another six to twelve months of this make-work assignment was not something he relished.

Martin Carver watched Crimewatch at the hotel in Bristol where his FBI colleagues were staying. If the programme were to produce anything new for them to go on this is where the action would begin. He'd promised to contact Chris Fearnley as soon as anything new came in. She was back in Spain having failed to access Richard Waterman's computer or cellphone. The man was very wary of all police and behind the Jack the Lad exterior lay a shrewd mind. He'd also taken to disappearing for days at a time. She'd checked out his property with a view to a spot of breaking and entering but quickly realised that this was a non-starter. The man's penthouse was in an exposed position and just around the corner from the Guardia Civil station. The locks on the doors and windows were modern, efficient and could not be overcome without drilling. She and Carver had agreed that if Crimewatch came up with a name then she would confront Waterman with it and go from there.

There was one important player in the Tony Guest case who did not watch the programme and that was Ian Williams. Indeed, Williams was unaware of the existence of a multiple murderer who had been arrested on his return from Fuerteventura. This was because he had no interest in current affairs so did not buy a newspaper nor did he view programmes such as Crimewatch. His TV viewing was limited to the X Factor and certain musical programmes. His reading matter was work related only. The man lived in a little bubble of office, home, on the road work and the occasional musical evening in a public house, or sometimes a club. He did not chat online, did not Twitter, did not interact with others socially at all. He did spend a lot of time on the net trawling the pages devoted to conspiracy theories throughout history. It fascinated him but he had yet to make his mind up as to what was real and what was deluded fantasy. Just as he had yet to make his mind up regarding his own sexuality. He'd had sex with women but had always had to pay for it so he knew that his equipment functioned alright. He just had not enjoyed the experience very much. He'd never been with a male but, more and more, he'd found himself having a tight feeling in the pit of his stomach which threatened to spread south when he saw an attractive man. Sometimes he'd find himself crotch staring and have to snap himself out of it before the staree caught him. He was trying to summon the courage to visit a gay bar and just talk to someone about it but he did not dare do so in the town where he lived and worked. Perhaps Blackpool, which promoted itself as England's gay Riviera could be the answer.

If the solitary Williams had seen Catherine's face on the TV screen he would have remembered her and contacted Crimewatch. His information on how he had come to meet her would have been of use to the police but, because of the nature of his existence, that was not to be. Just bad luck.

But good luck exists too. If one thinks about it, the producers of Crimewatch were trying to find where Catherine and her companion had had lunch that Sunday. By making the appeal at nine on a Thursday evening the chances were that catering staff would be too busy actually working to be watching television so it was a pretty futile exercise.

Len Austin was the head barman at the Picture House restaurant and had served Dominic Lord and Catherine that Sunday. He watched Crimewatch from an armchair in his lounge with his foot placed carefully on a stool. He'd slipped on a wet cobble on his way to work two days before, badly spraining his ankle in the process. So it was that he was more or less immobilised at home rather than being on duty when the show went out. Len was a staunch supported of law, order and the Conservative party who missed Margaret Thatcher's no nonsense approach towards left wing scum who went on strike for a political gain. In his opinion Crimewatch served a useful social purpose and he was glad of an opportunity to watch it. His wife of twenty years, Stephanie, was of the same view. She was a Senior Nurse at Bristol Royal Infirmary on the Accident and Emergency ward and was sickened by the amount of time they had to devote to patching up the victims of random violence which was nearly always caused by drugs or excessive alcohol consumption.

The moment Catherine's photo filled the screen Len swore softly, almost inaudibly to himself. Stephanie caught his expression.

'What's wrong, love?' she asked.

'I've served that girl. Hold it down a minute. I need to listen to this.'

When the section on Catherine ended he asked his wife for a pen and paper so that he could write down the contact number which he'd just seen.

'Are you going to phone in, Len?'

'Yes. It's the only thing to do. I wish I hadn't been drinking wine though. They'll pick up on that.'

'Are you sure you want to get involved in this, love? You never know where it will lead to.'

Len Austin did not reply verbally. He looked at his wife for a long ten seconds before she smiled and answered her own question.

'Yeah, you're sure. Sorry, love. I'll get the phone.'

The BBC studio in Cardiff had dozens of trained staff to receive the calls that Crimewatch generated. All conversations were recorded and the drunk and deluded who phoned in merely to spout abuse would, at a later date, receive a police visit. Len Austin's call was answered immediately. After stating his name and recounting his story he was asked to leave his number and await a call back. The BBC staff had been trained to look out for leads which were solid and the girl who had spoken to

Austin judged his call as falling into that category. She raised her contact sheet in the air and the floor supervisor went over and retrieved the details. Once she had read it she passed it over to Jim Cooper who then phoned Martin Carver in Bristol. Carver called Austin and asked him to come down to the local police station. On learning that the man was incapacitated, Carver and an FBI agent named Tom Tracey drove across the city to his house to interview him. Bar staff, or at least the sober ones, tend to have good memories for names and faces so Austin was able to give a detailed description of the man who had lunched with Catherine. He was also adamant that the man was English which did not fit with what they had learned about Catherine's singing companion from later in the day whom everybody thought to be American. After half an hour with Len Austin, Carver and Tracey drove to the Picture House restaurant to try and find a name. The maitresse d' was a Polish woman named Anna Skierski and it was she who had been on duty the Sunday in question. Her memory too was good. When shown a photo of Catherine she immediately recalled her and her charming companion. Receipts for the day proved that their bill had been settled in cash but the reservations register gave up a name – Dominic Lord.

Armed with this information Carver and Tracey raced back to their base in Bristol and started the process of tracking this name. Carver's first call was to Chris Fearnley in Fuerteventura.

'Chris, it's Martin' he said from the privacy of a small office. 'Crimewatch has thrown up a name. Dominic Lord. Long story short; the barman in a Bristol restaurant remembered serving him and Catherine. The guy likes dry Martini cocktails apparently. No credit card details, just the name. I'm going to have the Yard check if anyone using that name flew in or out of Fuerteventura during our time frame but the Yanks will probably beat me to it. I'll let you know ASAP but you might want to hit Waterman now.'

'Well it's still relatively early in the evening over here so I think I'll do just that. How solid do you reckon this info is?'

'One hundred per cent. The barman is a pro and the girl who runs the restaurant was very switched on. The name is probably false but it's a start. Our guy has made a mistake I reckon. If he'd just shown up at the restaurant and asked for a table for two we would not have a name at all.'

'Martin; he could have reserved a table as John Smith. This might mean nothing. I don't think it's worth me bracing Waterman with this.'

'Shit, you're right. OK. Hang fire whilst I have flights checked out for Dominic Lord and I'll get back to you.'

Carver broke the connection and called Oliver Addison at New Scotland Yard. He was not surprised that Jim Cooper had already contacted the Deputy Assistant Commissioner but he was taken aback to discover that Addison had started a search of airline reservations in the name of Dominic Lord. The results were already in and the police now had credit card details and an address. Warrants were being issued and a team assembled to arrest Lord. Unfortunately they would get no further than Mr Munir's corner shop.

Armed with the information that a Dominic Lord had indeed flown into Fuerteventura, Carver called Chris Fearnley again to let her know.

'OK Martin - thanks for that. I'm heading off to Waterman's bar now to rattle his cage. I'll check back with you on the hour however it works out.'

'I'll be here. Good hunting.'

Chris put on a light leather jacket that she'd purchased locally and left her hotel room. She was staying in an old beach front hotel in what had once been the fishing harbour of Corralejo. It had few rooms and was not used by the major tour companies so she was spared the buffet dinners and plastic flamenco that the larger establishments provided. She opted to walk along the promenade as far as she could before it ran out and she descended onto the beach itself. Music and lights from the main street over to her right made their presence felt until she arrived at the street upon which Richard Waterman's bar was situated. Chris took a moment to survey the scene. Scores of young people were drinking and dancing in the Waikiki club – restaurant immediately in front of her. Further on there was a garishly lit American style eatery and, just past that, lay the small British music bar. She took a deep breath, held it for a best of three then exhaled and advanced to her target. She had a plan but it would have to be flexible. How Waterman reacted would dictate how she proceeded.

Chris entered the Royalist and saw that Waterman was sat on the customer side of the horseshoe shaped bar. He'd noticed her as she moved across the floor and raised a glass in greeting to her.

'Evening, Chris' he said. 'How are things going then?'

'They're going, they certainly are going, Richard.'

She ordered a bottle of Mahou beer which Waterman told the barman to put on his tab. After a pull on the bottle she looked him straight in the eye and began.'

'Richard; I'm here tonight in an official capacity. I'm not going to play games because this is too dammed important for that and I don't have the time. I'm not going to threaten to ruin the lifestyle you've created here nor am I going to make any promises to you if you give me what I want. We both know that the FBI are going to call the shots in this case. All you can do is damage limitation.'

Waterman had not blinked as Chris went through her little speech. When he spoke it was with an air of restrained menace.

'That sounds proper scary, darlin'. What the fuck are you talking about?'

'Someone known to you has become a person of interest to us in this case. Dominic Lord.'

She was gambling. She had no idea if Waterman knew Lord at all or, if he did, it could be by another name. She waited and watched as the local fixer calculated the pros and cons of continuing to talk with her. He decided to play for time.

'This is about the missing American girl, right? So why am I talking to a British copper and not the FBI?'

'They are lagging behind on this particular piece of information, Richard. You're a Brit. I thought I'd give you a chance to do the right thing before the Yanks go all federal on your arse and engage in a spot of extraordinary rendition. Shall I call them?'

'No need for that. Look, yeah, I know Dominic; I've known him on and off for five or so years. He's all right, he is. A bit posh but not a snob, like.'

'Tell me about your last contact with him, Richard.' Chris took out a pad and began taking notes.

'He phoned me from England about six or seven weeks ago. He wanted to rent a villa and a car for a few months 'cos he had some business to do out here. I sorted that for him and he came over. I picked him up at the airport, drove him to the villa and showed him around – alarm systems, air-con, keys all that sort of thing. He liked it but, bugger me, a week later he upped sticks and left again. He'd paid up front so he lost a packet on the deal. If I'd been able to let it out again I'd have been quids in.'

'Are you saying that nobody has been in these premises since Lord left?'

'I've not rented it to anyone. Dominic asked if I could arrange to have the place cleaned so I sent a couple of Pedros in to do that and they also give it a wipe down once a week just to keep it nice, like. This fucking dust gets everywhere.'

'OK, Richard. Where is this villa?'

'It's less than five minutes walk from here, just across the main drag.'

'Do you have the keys to it with you?'

'Yes.'

'Right. Let me think for a minute.'

Chris reviewed her brief notes and pondered her options. They were limited. She wanted to keep Waterman talking openly but once the American and Spanish authorities found out about his link to Dominic Lord they were likely to bully him into silence. There was no way she could not pass her information on to the FBI and they were going to want to talk to the source. Tough luck, Richard.

'Richard – you need to answer my next question truthfully. Was the rental of this villa totally legal, above board, taxes paid etc?'

'Yeah, course it was. I look after quite a few properties for foreigners and they pay me a fee for that plus a commission whenever I let them out. I declare all that income at the end of the year. It's kosher.'

'Leaving you free to add a bit on top as a cash payment finder's fee no doubt.'

'I couldn't possibly comment.'

'I'm going to call the FBI now, Richard. They'll meet us at the villa with their forensics team and they'll probably have a Guardia liaison officer with them. I'm going to go into bat for you and say that you have been open and cooperative with me and that you are happy to continue to be interviewed by me. That's the best I can do.'

'I'm 'happy' am I? I'm fucking well not you know. What if I just give them the keys and say I've told you everything I know already?'

'That would be a mistake, Richard. If you go that route your feet will not touch the ground and you'll be in a Spanish interrogation cell before you can say hijo de puta! I want to know everything you know regarding Dominic Lord but if you won't tell me in civilised surroundings then you can exercise your democratic right to be a twat and end up being charged as an accomplice to murder. Your call.'

Richard Waterman's lifestyle choices had placed him in some tricky situations before but this was way beyond his experiences. He realised that this sexy bitch from the Met could be a real ball-buster. She could also be the only friend of influence he had at the moment.

'You make a compelling case for continued co-operation, detective. We'll play it your way.'

'Good lad. I'll also need the names and contact details of the people you employed to clean the villa.'

Waterman went behind his bar and came back with a ledger. Chris wrote down the address of the villa and that of the couple who had cleaned it after Lord's departure. She then called S.A.C. Ross Lopez who was at the hotel the FBI was using. He answered after only two rings. Caller I.D. showed him who was phoning.

'Hi, Chris. What's happening?'

'Lots. The BBC have come up with a name for the guy who had Sunday lunch with Catherine just before she left England. We also have the same named person on a flight into Fuerteventura that same week. At this moment I'm with an English guy who lives in Corralejo and who knows our suspect and who rented a villa to him for his last stay here.'

'That's great stuff, Chris. I can't wait to meet this guy. Where's the villa? I need to get my forensics team down there ASAP. I take it the suspect's no longer there, right?'

'Whoa there, agent Lopez. One thing at a time. There is some bad news to go with the good. The name we have for the suspect is Dominic Lord and he's been coming to the island for years. Your people in London will be sending over his credit card and passport details soon. Someone will need to let the Guardia know all that and I reckon it would be best coming from you.'

'Yeah, I'll handle that. What's the bad news?'

'Lord or whoever he really is took out a long lease on a villa in Calle Carabela but left after only a week or so. The guy who let it out had it cleaned right after at Lord's request and it's been gone over once a week since then. I don't think your forensics people have much of a chance here, Ross.'

'All due respect to Scotland Yard but the FBI has the best forensics in the world and I have a top notch team here with me. If Catherine was ever in this villa they will find trace of her. Anything else I need to know?'

'Yes. The Englishman who let the villa is a local businessman of sorts. He has a record for false checks, handling stolen goods that sort of stuff. He does not wish to talk with the FBI and you don't have jurisdiction here. The Guardia can, of course, haul him in but I don't think that's in our interest.'

'So what do you suggest, Chris? You've met the mutt.'

'He's said that he'll continue talking with me and I think that's the way forward for now at least. He's not stupid and has been reasonably open with me so far. I haven't even begun to apply any real pressure either. What do you say?'

Ross Lopez was not happy with this at all. This was a Bureau investigation and they'd only let a Brit in on it as a matter of professional courtesy and to help smooth the way for their colleagues who were operating in the U.K. Once Chris Fearnley had realised that her linguistic skills were surplus to requirements, she had kept out of the way but dutifully attended all meetings Lopez had called. She's obviously been asking around on her own though. How else could she have come up with an address so quickly? On one level he was pissed that she had been developing contacts without telling him but, on the other, he had to admire her result.

'OK Chris, we'll play it your way for now. I'll want to know everything your guy says first thing tomorrow morning. Meet at the airport field office at 0730hrs.'

'No problem, Ross. How long before you can have your forensics people in town?'

'Fifteen minutes. Most of them are at the hotel with me. I'd hoped you guys would develop something so I pulled them in from the airport this afternoon.'

'Smart guy. I have to call my boss in London. Can we meet at the corner of Main Street and Carabela in half an hour? I'll have the key holder with me.'

'Half an hour it is, Chris? Good work.'

Lopez broke the connection. Chris Fearnley turned to Waterman who had changed from beer to top shelf scotch. He figured that it might be some time before he would be able to enjoy a decent drink again. Like ten to twenty years..

'Richard, I want you to clear the bar and close it' said Chris. 'You then have twenty five minutes to tell me everything you know about Dominic Lord and try to save your sorry arse. Move.'

Waterman did not hesitate. Only two tables were occupied this late in the year and he hustled the patrons out of the door with a promise of free drinks on Friday night. If he were still open on Friday he'd be glad to pay. He sent his barman home, locked the door behind him and turned off the external lights. He went behind the bar and poured himself a strong one.

'Another beer, officer? Or are you on duty?'

'A beer would be fine, Richard' she replied to his surprise.

'Now - tell me about Lord, starting from when you first met and leave nothing out.'

Waterman began to speak and continued for 15 minutes without interruption from Chris who was scribbling away in her notebook using a personalised form of shorthand. Neither of them had touched their drinks. Chris scanned her notes making small, coded additions in red. These were to indicate points which required clarification or expansion.

'Richard, that's a good start but I do have some questions for you. Right now though we have a date with the FBI. Word of advice. Do not be cocky, do not call anyone 'mate' or 'darling', do not crack jokes. These people have no sense of humour and it is in their power to take you away from me and place you somewhere you don't want to go. Got it?'

Chapter Thirty Seven

'Got it. Let's go then.'

The two of them left the bar by the front door which Richard locked behind him having first set his alarm system. They turned left towards Main Street which they crossed with ease there being little vehicular traffic at this time of night, then they headed south for thirty yards where they came upon three black S.U.V.s with darkened windows. On a street devoted to clubs, bars and restaurants they stood out like roller skates on the Pope. The FBI obviously were not doing subtle this evening. Another incongruous sight emerged from the passenger seat of the lead vehicle - special agent Ross Lopez clad in a grey two piece, white button down and maroon neck tie. Chris introduced him to Waterman and he politely shook the Englishman's hand. The three of them turned right into Carabela with the menacing S.U.V.s crawling behind them. Waterman looked at Lopez's serious visage and thought that this looked like a funeral cortege.

Arriving at the villa, the car carrying all the technical equipment reversed into the darkness under the pergola. FBI agents then got out of the vehicles and started to don blue, hooded overalls and matching overshoes.

'Mr Waterman' said Lopez. 'May I have the alarm code please?'

Richard explained where the box was situated and wrote the number sequence down on one of Lopez's cards. He also gave up the information regarding the three safes inside the villa.

'Thank you Mr Waterman' said Lopez. 'I believe that detective Fearnley is going to interview you now. Is there anything that you'd like to tell me before you go?'

Richard thought quickly. She'd already begun to interview him and obviously the Yank didn't know this. What sort of game was she playing?

'Ah, I'd rather just talk to a British police officer at this moment in time, sir' he replied in his humblest voice. Chris was proud of his acting abilities.

'Very well. I'll be in touch. My forensics team will want to talk with the people you used to clean this place. Would you organise that for tomorrow please?'

'Certainly, no problem. Where will you want to see them?'

'Here will be good. I'll let detective Fearnley know what time. Now, if you'll excuse me; I'd better let the Spanish police know what I'm doing before a neighbour calls this in.'

Chris took the hint and motioned Waterman back towards Main Street with a jerk of her head. The odd couple went back to the Royalist where they each took a drink and continued their conversation about Dominic Lord. After an hour of back and forth, Chris reckoned that she had squeezed the last drop of information.

'All right, Richard' she said. 'So far so good. I've calls to make and shit to organise so I'm off now. Play it straight with the Yanks tomorrow and you should be OK. But the Spaniards will be looking closely at you. Nothing I can do about that. Last thing; don't even think about doing a runner because the person chasing you would be me.'

Waterman looked at her eyes and saw she was not joking.

'The thought never entered my mind' he lied. 'I'll be here tomorrow for another shitty day in paradise.'

Fearnley left him in his bar and made her way back to her hotel. Once in her room she called Martin Carver in London to update him. There being nothing to do until the FBI forensics team had carried out their work, she showered and went to bed to be ready for an early morning with the Americans.

Chapter Thirty Eight

In England the hunt for Dominic Lord was underway. It became quickly obvious that the identity was false. The Passport Office came up with a photograph of the man which was very much that of a white Mr Average with no distinguishing marks. The passport had been issued prior to the introduction of the digital chip so no solid physical data was produced. It seemed that Dominic Lord had used a variation of what had become known as the Forsyth system of obtaining his documentation, after the author's explanation of how to do so is his novel Day of the Jackal.

One piece of false paperwork allowed more to be obtained and, thus, a new identity was created. It was a dead end for the authorities. As ML knew it would be.

Martin Carver had passed on the details of Chris Fearnley's interrogation of Waterman to New Scotland Yard. The team had then gone to work searching for an international restaurant reviewer who matched the Dominic Lord profile. Nothing came back immediately but they persisted. Carver did not hold out much hope on that avenue of investigation. This man was a ghost. He had just finished shaving when his cell phone rang. Such was his commitment to the case that he even took the damn thing to the bathroom. Caller I.D showed it was Fearnley calling.

'Morning, Chris' he said. 'Any news?'

'Hi, Martin. Yes. I've just spent three hours with the Americans. First off, they've already found traces of Fentanyl or Kolokol in one of the villa's bathrooms. I don't understand the science involved but they are certain that this substance was there and only there. Too much coincidence. This is where Catherine died.'

'What about trace of the girl herself?'

'Nothing yet. Say what you like about the Spanish but they do a very thorough cleaning job. And the killer has done his best to sanitise the scene as well. The forensics people are pulling the place apart and it's going to take at least a week before they're through. The Guardia are doing a house to house with the FBI and yours truly in tow. The one weird thing is that, although the villa has been almost immaculately cleaned, there is a paper shredder which had not been emptied. The FBI have bagged the contents and that will go back to the States for re-assembly.'

'Good luck with that. I hope it wasn't a cross cut. So what are you plans, Chris?'

'I'm staying here for a few more days at least in case anything breaks. I need to talk with Waterman later today to show him the Dominic Lord passport photograph and get confirmation that this is the same man who rented the villa. After that I don't see what more I can achieve here. We need a head to head you and I.'

'You're right, Chris and time's cracking on. It's less than two weeks to the trial and Tony Guest must be getting twitchy. I need to see him soon.'

'Can you wait until I return, Martin? I'd like to be present.'

Carver thought about her request for it was odd. In the scenario they had set up, he was the interlocutor with Guest therefore she had another reason for wanting him to delay his next meeting with the prisoner, presumably one she did not want to talk about on an international phone call.'

'Fine, Chris. If you're back before next weekend that works for me. Talk with you soon.'

'Thanks, Martin. I'll give you a bell when I know my flight details. Bye.'

She broke the connection and headed off to see Richard Waterman armed with the passport photograph of Dominic Lord that she had been given at the morning meeting.

In Bristol the local police force had canvassed every hotel and finally found the one where Lord had registered on the night that Tony Guest had last gigged in the city. Over the next twenty four hours every member of staff who had been present that weekend was shown Lord's photo. Nobody remembered him. The man had paid in cash, had not ordered from room service and had not used the hotel car park. Other than a fake address and an illegible signature in the register there as no trace of Dominic Lord. Carver and the FBI team concluded that they had done all they could in Bristol and headed back to London to make their reports.

In the capital Jim Cooper's enlarged Orion team was still plugging away trying to identify the seven British girls whose fingers had not been matched with a missing person. Michelle Stone was somewhat sidelined from this process. The team realised that Cooper did not want her there and they took their lead from him. This suited Michelle just fine. She'd showed them what needed to be done and the ball was in their hands now. The score stood at Michelle Stone 3 - Jim Cooper 0.

Chris Fearnley arrived back at Heathrow airport at nine in the evening the day before Carver was due to talk with Tony Guest. She strode through the herd of anaemic Brits like a sun-bronzed goddess from another world and was surprised to find Carver waiting for her at the arrivals gate. He was even holding up a hand printed sign that said 'FEARNLEY'.

'Hi, Martin' she said looking at him quizzically. 'Is something up?'

'Hi yourself. No; but when I checked what flight you were on I realised that we would not have much time together before tomorrow's visit. We have an appointment for ten a.m. My car's this way.'

They headed to the short stay car park with Chris carrying her two suiter in one hand and pulling her wheeled case with the other. He did not offer to help and she took no offence. Carver was a man who always wanted to have both hands free.

His vehicle turned out to be a white Range Rover turbo with windows dark tinted to the very limit of legality. Chris put her gear in the back then joined him up front.

'I assume that you want to talk about something that you couldn't mention on an open phone' said Carver.

'Correct. You can also assume that I would like a decent drink as well. You OK with that?'

'To tell the truth I'm probably at the limit already so I'll have to put the car to bed.' He paused briefly, thinking then continued. 'I've a fairly decent selection of hooch at my place if that's alright.'

A broad smile grew on her face. 'Mister Carver! After all the years I've known you I've never had the slightest clue as to your place of residence. The girl is intrigued. Lead on, sir.'

They drove east through the night towards Hammersmith into the centre of London keeping the river on their right. Up ahead in the distance the magnificent monument that is Tower Bridge was floodlit and Carver turned onto it to cross the Thames. Once they were on the south bank of the river he navigated his way through what had suddenly become a decidedly downmarket area. This was Southwark where the dockworkers used to live cheek by jowl. Further east it became Bermondsey, an even more depressed area with the demise of the docks but one man's poverty is another man's business opportunity – in this case the property developer. Carver turned down a cavernous ramp and, by pressing a button on his dashboard, opened a set of electronically controlled gates. He parked the Range Rover and showed Chris to a lift which was far too modern to have been part of the original structure. They rode to the top floor, exited into a dimly lit corridor along which they walked to a single door at the end.

Chris Fearnley was baffled. They were in one of the many former warehouses that had served the Port of London, storing all the goods that the British Empire brought home. In the late twentieth century they had been converted into apartments with some of them, depending on size and location, being worth millions of pounds. By the look of this place it was clearly at the top end of the market. The ceiling was high, easily fifteen feet and there were windows all along one wall which almost matched that. The view was superb, especially by night. Straight across the river was the Tower of London, with the bridge to its right, Customs House the left and Saint Paul's on its hill behind. She turned round to find that Carver was nowhere to be seen. He'd obviously left her to look around on her own so she did. She was just admiring the professionally equipped kitchen when he came back through a door at the opposite end of the open plan room.

'Sorry to leave you like that, Chris but I only had ten seconds to unset the alarm. Now, what would you like to drink?'

'Oh, how about something in keeping with your lifestyle, Martin? Vintage champagne?'

'I've some decent Bollinger but it's non-vintage I am afraid.'

'Martin; I'm joking. I'm not a wine snob; anyway I don't think that sparkling wine would hit the spot at the moment. I'd like a cold vodka, neat, with a lager chaser.'

'Good idea. Coming up. Make yourself at home.'

Whilst Carver busied himself at the bar and kitchen, Chris walked the sixty feet to where a suite of black leather and chrome armchairs and sofas were situated. She chose a place on the sofa so that she could enjoy the view over to the Tower. Presently he joined her with the drinks and some savoury nibbles. The vodka was in shot glasses. Chris sniffed at hers, took a sip and then downed it.

'That was good. What is it?' she asked.

'Grey Goose' replied Carver who then downed his own shot. 'So; what couldn't you say to me on the phone, Chris?'

'The Yanks think Tony Guest and Dominic Lord are one and the same man.'

'Are they mad? Lord's photo looks nothing like Guest. They've got it into their heads that Tony killed Catherine because of all the circumstantial evidence and anything that goes against that idea is going to be ignored. It's hardly what you'd call dialectic.'

'You're forgetting something, Martin. The Americans haven't met Tony yet and they won't see him until the trial next week.

Get me a refill whilst I grab something from my case, will you?'

When Carver returned with two more vodkas Chris had a buff, unmarked folder on her lap. After taking her shot, she extracted two pieces of paper from the folder. They were photocopies of Guest's and Lord's passport photos.

'These are what the Americans are going by, Martin. Take a look.'

'Shit. They are the same but slightly different. Wait a minute. Look at the issue dates. Tony's is nine years old. Lord's is only two. I wonder what Tony looked like nine years ago. Did you point that out to them?'

'No. I didn't want to be seen as a member of the Tony Guest fan club. Anyway they picked up on it themselves but dismissed it. Some arsehole said that people don't change that much in nine years.'

'I wish I'd been at this bloody meeting. There are two men who look similar but who flew into Fuerteventura on <u>different dates</u>. How are they explaining that one away?'

'Again, the point was raised and they admit that they don't know. Various theories were thrown around ranging from Tony having multiple identities and flying in and out in less than twenty four hours for reasons unknown, to Dominic Lord being an accomplice who delivered the poison to Tony.'

'Did you show Waterman the Tony Guest photo?'

'I did – without giving him any details. I asked 'can you identify this man?' He said it was Dominic Lord. When I showed him the Lord photo he went a bit cross eyed on me but said that that was Lord too.'

'This isn't looking good. Let's try and see things from the American's point of view. We have, in custody, a man who has admitted to killing three young women using the same exotic poison used in Catherine's murder. Then we have the finger amputations common to all four cases. Catherine was in the same bar where Tony was playing that Saturday night in Bristol.

That same night Dominic Lord is registered at a Bristol hotel. On the Sunday Dominic Lord has lunch in a Bristol restaurant with Catherine after which they go to a music pub and both sing on stage. The band that day describe him as good enough to be professional. The following week Tony, Lord and Catherine all turn up on different dates in Fuerteventura. She is seen at his gigs a couple of times and then disappears. Only Tony returns. Well, not quite. So does Catherine's finger. We arrest Tony for the murder of the three English girls and he owns up to it. During a search of his possessions we find a beer mat from Bristol on which Catherine had written down her mobile number. You track down the place that Dominic Lord rented in Fuerteventura and the FBI forensics people find trace of the Russian poison. Finally, the Tony Guest and Dominic Lord passport photos are very similar despite their different issues dates. Have I missed anything?'

'No. I reckon that you've just summed up the case for the prosecution of Tony Guest for Catherine's murder quite well.'

'Fine. Now let's see what contradicts it. The obvious weak point is that both Guest and Lord passports are on record as having been used by somebody or somebodies to fly into Fuerteventura round about the same time. I know the FBI are trying to square that particular circle but, to me, to say it's the same person is clutching at straws. Next weak point; the supermen of FBI forensics have, so far, found no trace of Tony at the villa and no trace of Catherine at his apartment. Thirdly – his lifestyle during his week in the sun. Music in the evening, drink with the band and hangers on until dawn then stagger back to his apartment to sleep it off. Fall out of bed, eat, soak up some rays and repeat until he returns to Manchester. When was he supposed to have an opportunity to meet the girl let alone murder her and dispose of the body? I've read the transcripts of the Guardia interviews with staff and customers at the Rock Bar and Tony isn't remembered as having any female company let alone a stunner like Catherine. That's me done. Anything to add?'

'It's thin, Martin. Very thin. So you can see why the Americans really fancy Tony for this. We have to find out who Dominic Lord really is or our boy is toast. And how are we going to do that when the Met isn't even officially on the case?'

'Difficult but I have some ideas I'm working on. There's one last thing. How much do I tell Tony tomorrow morning? I've led him down this path. Should I give him the chance to leave it and take his chance in court by changing his plea?'

'Morally, yes. Practically, no. We're doing this to keep him out of American hands, remember. We have to back ourselves to be able to find the real killer – we have a hell of a lot of info. It's down to number crunching now is my view. Up for it?'

'Too right I am, Chris.'

'That's that settled then. No more shop tonight. Let's talk about something else.'

'Pick your subject.'

'Oh, I dunno – how about 'how does a Detective Inspector own a multi-million pound riverside property in central London?'

'That's easy to explain. Catherine was not the only one to come into an inheritance although mine was not as straightforward as hers. All this came from my late cousin Morris. He'd made a pile in hedge fund management or some such bollocks and he willed the lot to me.'

'You must have been close.'

'I hardly knew him and what I did know I did not like.'

'So why you?'

He was my father's brother's son and had no other relatives. Unmarried, although if he'd split his millions amongst his girlfriends they might have ended up with fifty pounds each. I think the real reason he left it to me, other than me being the last of the Carvers, is that I sorted out a problem he was having with some drug dealers years ago. Stupid little sod really.'

'How did he die?'

'A speedball. A mixture of heroin and cocaine. How dumb is that? ODing when you have it all ahead of you. This apartment wasn't all he left me. There was an Aston Martin V12 in the garage. I sold that to some wannabe James Bond. There was also a respectable sum of cash in his bank account which is now in mine. That's the story, Chris.'

'It's part of the story. You obviously don't need gainful employment. Why are you still dealing with the scrotes that our job brings us into contact with?'

Carver stood and crossed the room to the bar, returning with two more lagers plus the Grey Goose in a champagne bucket full of ice.

'I'm not in the business of protecting the public' he said. 'I'm a hunter and my prey is scumbags, the bigger the better. I want whoever killed these girls, not for the sake of justice, but for my personal satisfaction. This is not what I told the recruitment board when I transferred out of the army, by the way.'

'I'll bet. Still, were you never tempted to cash in your chips, go travelling and find a beach to live on with hot and cold running dusky maidens?'

'I've done my travelling during my time in the army. As for the beach scene, yes, it's fine for a while but I need more stimulation than that and the job offers it. I know I'm lucky not having to worry about paying the mortgage and behaving myself so I don't fuck up and lose my pension. This affords me a certain freedom of action not available to most officers and keeps me free from the sort of stress that killed Goodchild's mate Clarkson.'

'Hmmm. I detect a distinct lack of female influence in your living arrangements, Martin. Are you house trained? Have you ever been married or serious about anyone?'

'No. I thought that it was a form of mental cruelty to commit your life to someone when you're doing a job where you disappear for months on end and each day may be your last.'

'So, a girl in every port was it?'

'Jesus, Chris! Back off a bit will you? No, it wasn't like that. I'd go on leave the same as civilians go on holiday and if I met someone I liked we'd do what adults do and then kiss goodbye. No false promises made, nobody hurt. It's how I've lived since I transferred to the police as well before you ask.'

'Are you seriously trying to tell me you don't have a procession of girls traipsing through this passion pad of yours?'

'You're the first person, male or female, I've invited to this place since I took it over a year ago.'

Chris took a long pull at her lager to cover the silence that had descended on the two of them and also to reflect on what Marin Carver had just said.

'Sounds lonely, Martin.'

'I'm alone, not lonely. There's a difference. But you know that, don't you?'

Chris looked down at the drink in her hand, avoiding his perceptive eyes, an air of deep introspection surrounding her.

'Yeah, Martin. I do know. But, then again, you're never alone with schizophrenia! Where's the bathroom?'

Martin directed her to one of the guest bedrooms which had en-suite facilities.

When she returned the muted sounds of the Moody Blues were emanating from the Bose speaker system. She resumed her place.

'Where were we Martin?'

'Uh, uh. I've done all the talking so far. What's Lecter's line in Silence of the Lambs? Quid pro quo, Clarice. Why do you do the job, Chris?'

'I detest scumbags, parasites and bullies. I get a real buzz putting them away. I'm a bit like you in that respect. If my work has a beneficial effect for society I regard that as a bonus but I'm not here to live up to some stupid bloody mission statement.'

'Have you a long term goal then?'

'No. I'll never achieve high rank. I'm no good – no; forget that.

I refuse to play the political game and it would be so frigging easy. Everyone knows that there are female officers who have been promoted way beyond their abilities all in the name of equality. It's going to bite the force in the arse one day in the same way as promoting ethnics has. So, to answer your question, I don't have a long term plan but I'm not planning on staying with the Met for ever and a day.'

'Any ideas as to where you'd like to go?'

'None. As I said, I get off on putting shit in a cage and where else can I do that? Plus I do have to plan for later in life, pay the mortgage and all that mundane stuff that you don't have to bother with.'

'There's one thing I've never asked you over the years when we've worked together. I always thought it was none of my business.'

'You're probably right so don't ask now, Martin.'

He poured two more vodkas and sat back in his armchair silently observing her. She'd tensed her body and, without really changing her position, adopted a defensive posture. Carver noted that she was rubbing the third finger of her left hand with her thumb. The finger bore no ring. She intuited that he was going to ask about her marital and emotional past.

'As you wish' he said. 'Do you have fresh clothes in your luggage?'

'Yes. I used the hotel laundry service before I left Fuerteventura. Why?'

'It would make sense for you to spend the night here instead of getting a cab to wherever it is you live. The spare rooms are both made up and we can have breakfast together before I head off to visit Tony.'

'Makes sense to me. Thanks, Martin. You sure you don't mind?'

'Not in the slightest. I'll be ready for seven thirty. See you then.'

He knocked back his last drink and headed off to his room leaving Chris to wonder why she had been so snappy with him.

She downed her vodka, picked up her lager and stood on legs which had suddenly become a tad unsteady. Realising that Grey Goose was stronger that it tasted, she focused and advanced to the huge window to gaze again at the nightime skyline of her city. 'Alone, but not lonely' Martin had said. 'Fuck, I wish I could pull that trick off' she thought to herself. Tiredness, the strange location, memories and alcoholic melancholy combined to produce silent tears which coursed down her cheeks. After a time, the duration of which she could not have said, she turned from the Thames and went to meet Morpheus.

The next morning, having showered and changed into clean jeans and a V-necked sweater of blue Merino wool, Chris entered the lounge to find Carver at work in the kitchen.

'Morning, Chris. Sleep well?'

'I think I was unfuckingconscious but I feel fine.'

'That's the advantage of drinking decent booze. I'm doing bacon and sausage. How do you like your eggs?'

'Sunny side up please.'

'Fine. Won't be long. Help yourself to coffee and juice.'

Soon they were sat across from each other at the breakfast bar working their way through a substantial amount of carbs and protein but all of the highest quality.

'That was just what the doctor ordered, Martin. Thanks. The Spanish just don't quite get how to do a fry up, do they?'

'No. Then again they're probably better at octopus than I am. Each to their own.'

At the end of the granite bar lay Martin's wallet, keys and cellphone. The latter began to vibrate.

He looked at the caller ID and was surprised to see that it was New Scotland Yard. He pressed green and answered 'Carver.'

A pause whilst whoever was on the other end spoke at some length.

'Actually, sir, Fearnley got in last night. I picked her up at the airport.' As Carver was speaking these words he was using improvised sign language to ask Chris whether or not he should reveal her presence. She gave him a thumbs up.

'Well I assume she'd turned her cell off on the plane and hasn't yet reactivated it. You can speak with her now if you wish. She's here.'

Carver was silent once more whilst the caller continued uninterrupted. Finally he was able to speak.

'I'll pass that on, sir. To whom will she report?'

Another pause.

'O.K. Will do. I'll get back to you once I've finished at Belmarsh. Yes, sir.'

'What's happened, Martin?'

'Unbelievable. That was Deputy Assistant Commissioner Oliver Addison in full panic mode. It seems that Jim Cooper drove into a herd of deer on a country road in Hertfordshire last night. He rolled the car and is in intensive care with a broken pelvis and a fractured skull amongst other things. The ICU has him in an induced coma and it's fifty fifty whether he makes it.'

'Poor bastard.'

'That's only part of it. Addison is a PR type and what's really worrying him is the fact that Cooper's blood alcohol level is treble the legal limit. The guy was hammered and if that fact gets into the press then the Met looks very bad indeed. He wants you back at Orion ASAP.'

'So who do I report to?'

'They haven't decided. Headless chickens springs to mind. The person with the best overview of the case is your mate Michelle but they can't put a sergeant in charge. The rest of Cooper's team are time serving muppets. Any thoughts?'

'Bring back Goodchild?'

'Makes sense but then the top brass would be admitting that they made a mistake in the first place. Then again, if we plus

Michelle push in the right way we may be able to swing it. Try and have a private word with her when you get in. I'll see you as and when. Keep lunch free; I should be back by then.'

'Will do. What's the best way to get to the office from here?'

'Cross the bridge and hail a cab. You'll be fine this time of day.'

'Great. I'll be off then. Oh shit. Look, can I be a pain and leave my case here? I'll pick it up later.'

'No problem.'

'Thanks – and thanks for last night too, Martin.'

Chris gathered up the few personal effects which she carried and left Martin to tidy the kitchen. He had to smile at that. None of the little peck on the cheek from Chris Fearnley. He reckoned her to be a woman who would kiss properly or not at all. Once the dishwasher was cycling he went to his window and looked down onto Tower Bridge. He spotted her almost immediately as she cut through the mass of grey suits the way a Bermuda sloop would cleave its way across the Atlantic.

'Why the fuck did you have to be a colleague?' he said aloud. He watched until he lost sight of her then went to prepare himself for what was going to be a delicate visit with Tony Guest.

Chapter Thirty Nine

Her Majesty's Prison Belmarsh is situated in the Thamesmead area in the London Borough of Greenwich. This lies to the south east of the city and was only a thirty minute drive for Carver so he used his own vehicle. As he parked the Range Rover he thought about the strangeness of the establishment. Basically it was a category A prison housing some of the nastier elements that poisoned British society. At one time it had been known as the UK's Guantanamo owing to the fact that suspected Islamic terrorists were held there without trial. Lawyers using the European Convention on Human Rights put a stop to that. The inmate population of just under one thousand consisted of the usual mix of murderers, rapists and armed robbers. There was also a young offenders institute on site. Go figure.

Carver went through the security checks which were somewhat less severe for a serving police officer than they were for the family and friends of the inmates. Finally he was shown into an interview room where Tony Guest was waiting for him on his own.

'Martin! Good to see you mate' said the musician as he stood to greet his visitor.

'Hi, Tony. You're looking well.'

'Yeah, it's the enforced lack of booze that accounts for that and I've got gym privileges which I take advantage of. Every cloud and all that. How've you been?'

'Busy, busy, busy. Mainly running around Bristol making sure the FBI does not extraordinarily render some innocent member of the public. I hear your wife's been to see you.'

'Yeah. She's a good girl is Gill. It's a fucking long way from Shropshire to here and her employers aren't the most sympathetic of people. But she's made it down twice.'

'How much did you tell her, Tony?'

Guest took his time before answering. His head slumped and his bravado evaporated like brandy in a sauté pan. Looking up at Carver he spoke seriously.

'She never asked me if I did it 'cos she knows me. She just asked if she could do anything for me. Hah! She's been doing that all my life. How I ever married a woman that good I'll never know. Anyway, I told her I didn't do it. I had to Martin. Obviously she then asked why I'm pleading guilty. I said I couldn't tell her yet but that I'm safer in here than out there. She's bright but didn't get it so I just whistled the opening bars of the Star Spangled Banner. Then she got it. So, all's good between me and the missus if you ever have to talk with her, Martin.'

'Fine. We can live with that. OK – to business. Does the name Dominic Lord mean anything to you?'

'No. Should it?'

'Don't know. Just a long shot. Think carefully.'

Guest took his time but finally shook his head.

'Sorry, Martin. Means nothing to me. Who is he?'

'He does not exist. It's the false identity of the real killer. Chris and I are getting close to him. Once we find out the modus operandi of how he creates his false identity it's only a matter of number crunching before we find other fake documents and, ultimately, who this psycho really it. We'll get him, Tony. You have to hold onto that fact come Monday.'

'Why do you say that?'

'The Yanks have decided that you killed their girl. Any evidence to the contrary they explain away as coincidence or cleverness on your part. The FBI are under huge political pressure to produce the killer and you suit them just fine. We have to keep you away from them or you could end up in fucking Shawshank. On Monday your barrister will say to the judge that you have been uncooperative, will not talk about where the three bodies are and as such he has received no instruction from your solicitor therefore has nothing further to add. I don't know what sort of lecture, if any, the judge will give but the outcome will be the same. He is obliged to sentence you to life with a minimum tariff of thirty years.'

Carver stopped speaking to allow Guest time to absorb the magnitude of what he was committing himself to. He'd calculated that he'd rather the man balked now in private than next Monday during sentencing. Tony stood and began to pace the small room running his fingers nervously through his hair. Presently he sat down.'

'I'm fucked. How did this ever happen?'

'First off – you're not fucked. I'm a cunts hair from cracking this case so you have to trust that as much as I'm trusting you not to reveal how I set this all up. How did this happen? Wrong question. Why did it happen? Someone thinks they've been very clever in jerking the strings of three different police organisations – and three of the best to boot. The Met, the Guardia Civil and the FBI! Talk about a death wish. Unfortunately, my friend, you are collateral damage in this nutter's game. But I'm a bit of a player too so hang on in there with me and we'll get through this. All right?'

'It'll have to be won't it. I'm shit out of options. It reminds me of the blues song 'If it wasn't for bad luck, I'd have no luck at all'.'

'Don't give me that sad loser shit. Just think; when you get out you can work on your Johnny Cash repertoire. Doing time, especially when you're innocent, gives a singer real street cred. We could even write something together.'

'Would that be before or after I sue the shit out of the Crown Prosecution Service?'

'There you go – positive thinking. Seriously now; is there anything you need that I can get you before Monday?'

'Nah. Just catch the motherfucker responsible for all this shit sooner rather than later.'

Carver left Guest feeling that it had gone as well as it could have. For a man about to receive a life sentence, Tony had stayed remarkably upbeat. Carver looked forward to celebrating with the man once the case was truly resolved.

As soon as he entered the Orion offices he could taste the atmosphere of gloom. All the officers bar Michelle Stone had been hand picked by Jim Cooper who now lay somewhere between life and death in Queen Elizabeth ICU. The fact that he had contributed to his fate through drunk driving would have become known to the team whether Oliver Addison had told them or not. This robbed them of the opportunity to display too much sorrow for him.

Carver could not see Chris Fearnley anywhere so he made his way over to Michelle Stone's work station.

'Hi, Michelle. It's been a while.'

'Hasn't it just.' Her reply was definitely on the frosty side. She had not forgotten what Carver had done to the three thugs in Brighton.

'I've just come from Belmarsh trying to get something from Guest. No dice. Could you bring me up to speed on what's happening?'

'Sod all is what's happening. These poor lambs have lost their shepherd so it has all ground to a halt. Not that it was exactly racing ahead when Cooper was here. Oliver Addison was here bright and early making all the right PR noises. Fat prick. He says he'll appoint a new team leader today. Chris is upstairs being debriefed by him now. I hope that doesn't mean that he sees himself as taking over. The man couldn't find his own arse using both hands and a mirror.'

'OK thanks for that. Any idea as to who will head up this part of the investigation?'

'None. But I pity whoever draws the short straw on this one. The brass are only really worried about your American girl. The seven British victims might as well be cold cases. This lot fill in an awful lot of forms but there's no dynamism, Martin. Look around you. There are forty officers in here and, apart from me, only two females. Empathy factor - zero. Without someone to push them they're all stood around with their thumbs up their arses and their brains in neutral.'

'What about bringing Mark Goodchild back?'

'Oh my god! You said the 'G' word. No. That would be too logical and the brass would lose too much face. I can't see it happening. This lot would take sick leave en masse at the thought of having to actually work.'

'So how the hell were they selected to operate the highest profile case the Met has?'

'These are all, and I mean all, people who have worked with or for Jim Cooper throughout his career. If they'd cracked this he knew they'd let him take the credit, get the promotions and then they'd follow his path. It's police work, Martin, but not as we know it. Heads up. Here comes Chris.'

'Hi, Martin. Addison wants a word with you now. We still on for lunch?'

'Yes. We need to get our heads together. I'll see you back here.'

Carver left the two women together and headed off to the top floor. Chris was aware that Michelle's relationship radar was operating at full power. Martin's lunch query had activated it so to forestall any embarrassing questions she said to her 'Between you and me, Addison's trying to get hold of Mark Goodchild and bring him back to London to get this investigation back on track. For some reason his cell's not working.'

'That's probably because he's driving through darkest Norfolk on his way to Norwich and there aren't that many relay masts.'

Chris looked down at the seated Michelle and evaluated her words.

'And just how do you know the whereabouts of Commander Goodchild, Michelle?' she asked.

The only thing that Michelle Stone hated about herself was

her tendency to blush at the slightest hint of embarrassment and she felt the slow burn creeping up her neck to her face now.

'Ah, well, Mark – Commander Goodchild has kept in touch with me because he still feels a responsibility about the case and he knew I'd been kept on and….'

'I hope you don't play poker, Michelle. You and Goodchild. Talk about still waters. Bloody hell!'

'Take that shit eating grin off your face, Chris. You've got it all wrong.'

'I have, have I? I'm not making any judgements here, Michelle. Good luck to you. Just don't get hurt.'

Michelle realised that she could not bluff Chris Fearnley. Her secret was out but she knew it would be safe in this woman's hands so she let it out.

'If anyone risks getting hurt it's Mark. I've never met a better man. I love him, Chris and I've moved into his place. No one knows yet. Can we keep it that way?'

'Of course we can. So how long has this been going on, as the crap song goes?'

'Christ, Chris. Can we have this conversation somewhere other than the bloody office?'

'Sorry. Not very sensitive am I? Anyway, it's none of my business. As I said, good luck to you. Are you going to be cool about working with him if he comes back though?'

'No problem. The job's the job and we are us. We try not to take police shit home with us – with varying degrees of success, but so far so good.'

'That's good, Michelle. Change of subject; what, if anything, is happening on the identification of the seven remaining victims?'

'You're asking the wrong person, Chris. Cooper did not like me being kept on the team and I was more or less ostracised by his lot. I've been given loads to do but it's all been make work stuff. If Mark comes back I'll push it the way I did when it was just the four of us.'

'Good to hear. Well, as there's bugger all going on here, do you fancy a drink?'

'I thought you were meeting Carver for lunch?'

Fearnley picked up a tone in Michelle's voice and analysed it. 'You don't like him, do you?'

'No. He scares the shit out of me and I don't think he should be on the force. There's a barely controlled violence in the man that makes me think he's one step away from being a crim. I'm not comfortable with him, Chris. Not comfortable at all.'

'We'll have to agree to differ. I'd trust my life to Martin Carver. Could you say the same about Mark?'

'Yes. No hesitation. Look, there are things about Carver you don't know, Chris. Are you getting, ah, close to him?'

'He's a colleague and a friend. That's it. And I don't use the word friend lightly so if you want to explain to me what I don't know about him, go for it – but spare me the innuendo.'

'It'll have to wait for another time, he's just walked back in the door.'

Carver approached the two female officers with a spring in his step and a satisfied grin on his face. The entire team was watching them.

'OK, Chris early lunch and it's celebratory. Fancy the Hispanola?' he asked.

'I've never been on it so let's go for it. I take it you've had good news from Addison' said Chris.

'Yes. Goodchild's back in charge and is returning as we speak. He should be here in a couple of hours so we'll have a bite to eat then write up our notes on the American side of the case and report to him at 1700 hours. Michelle – you know how he works. I suggest that you clear your decks and prepare for battle.'

'About bloody time. Am I to keep this info to myself or can I give these plods a heads up?'

'Keep it to yourself. Addison wants to make some sort of announcement. Ready, Chris?'

Fearnley slipped on a black leather jacket and the two of them headed out of the building towards Victoria Embankment leaving Michelle to organise her systems in preparation for Goodchild's return.

The Hispanola is a black and white steam ship moored between Westminster and Charing Cross. It has been tastefully converted into a floating restaurant and caters, in general, to higher level civil servants from Whitehall. In winter people dine below decks and it can be a tad unnerving for first time visitors as the ceiling is black velvet punctuated by bright pin lights to give the impression of a night sky. As river traffic passes the vessel it does rock perceptibly, thus adding to sensory confusion. The galley does turn out some memorable dishes and the service is both discrete and efficient.

The two officers were shown to a small table at the rear of the dining room. They were early for lunch and found themselves alone for the time being.

'This is spooky, Martin. I like it. Is it a regular haunt of yours?'

'Maybe twice a year. It's proven useful for discrete meetings in the past, both police and military.'

'It's as if time had stopped. I could imagine coming on board on a late winter's afternoon and by the time one left it would be dark outside.'

'Yes. That's happened to me and the immediate reaction is 'where the hell did the day go!'. I've always quite liked that.'

'Well thanks for organising something different. I really don't like the mundane. Shall we get business out of the way before this place fills up?'

'Good point. Where do you want to start?'

'Well, you need to know that Michelle is shacked up with Goodchild. She's just told me and they want it to be kept secret.'

Carver took a long pull at his gin and tonic whilst he evaluated this new information. Finally he spoke.

'That means one, or more likely both of them are going to quit the force. Which then means they are going to keep their heads below the parapet and play everything by the book. I was debating about letting Goodchild know what we have been doing with Tony Guest but that is a non-starter now.'

'Don't you think he'll work it out for himself anyway, Martin?'

'No. Well he might but he'll convince himself that everything's fine. Remember, he's in lurrv with all that entails and I'm sure he has a clever exit plan. Private security consulting would be my guess. If he admits that we're perverting the course of justice he'd feel duty bound to act and he does not want to go there. Ignorance, even feigned, is bliss so we'll keep him in the dark.'

'Perverting the course of justice? Christ, Martin. I had not thought of that. It can carry a life sentence. Do you know what you're doing?'

'There is no evidence, Chris. Our taped interview with Tony is our get out of jail card and I put some steel into his back today. He's ready for a thirty year sentence. It's up to us to solve this case and I reckon it's the American angle that will crack it.'

'I agree. We can't let ourselves get sucked into the British end of the investigation. We need to have access to the FBI's resources.'

'True – but what can we offer them in exchange?'

'I got on well with them in Fuerteventura and I did track down the villa where Catherine was probably killed. That's probably enough to buy us a seat at the table when they have a review meeting, surely.'

'The problem is that their legal attaché usually deals directly with Commissioner Sampson. We, for all out talents, are just slugs on the lettuce leaf of life.'

'Nice imagery, Martin. If you could stop thinking like a soldier with your rigid train of command we might get somewhere. I can't go over your head but you could contact the embassy and finesse a meeting couldn't you? Then you tell Addison that the Americans want to see us. We are the liaison officers after all.'

'All right. I'll give it a go after lunch which, if my eyes don't deceive me, is about to be served.'

They settled down to enjoy a rather good meal for what could have been considered a tourist attraction. At some stage during the lunch they paused in conversation then both started to speak at the same time. They laughed with the ease of old friends and verbally danced their way back on track. Chris was enjoying the man's company but could not remove Michelle Stone's words from her mind. The last emotion Martin Carver inspired in her was fear. On the contrary he gave off the aura of a man who would protect those in need of it and most certainly any woman who was in his company. Chris was sufficiently skilled not to worry about requiring protection but it was nice to have an equal around. She made her mind up to have a word with Michelle.

Lunch being finished Martin paid and the two of them headed back to the Yard.

'I never asked you, Chris. Where do you live? You're not going to have to haul your suitcase from my place to somewhere exotic like Croydon are you?'

'I don't think I've ever heard the words 'Croydon' and 'exotic' used in the same sentence before. No. I've a small flat in an old Victorian pile in Maida Vale. I rent, it's not too dear and I can walk to the office. It'll be nice to get back to my own little nest tonight.'

'Fine. Let's see how the afternoon goes and we'll sort something out later.'

They arrived back at the Orion offices to find low key chaos. Michelle was at her work station hammering away at the keys whilst the rest of the team had split into small groups and were conversing sotto voce amongst themselves.

Carver and Fearnley went over to Michelle.

'What's going on, Michelle?' asked Carver.

'Addison came and made a bollocks of a speech praising the sterling work of Jim Cooper – who is still not out of the woods but is 'in our thoughts at this time'. Then he announced that Mark is coming back to take over. He is due within the next hour but is meeting Addison before joining us. This lot are not happy campers.'

'Fuck 'em. I've work to do. Which deck can I take, Michelle? Preferably as far away from these pricks as possible' said Carver.

'I don't know how Mark is going to organise things. I reckon you should go into the goldfish bowl for the time being. Cooper's not going to be needing it and if Mark wants to use it he'll let you know PDQ.'

The goldfish bowl was a glass walled office that Cooper had evidently used as some sort of command post. It also had venetian blinds which could be closed for privacy.

'Excellent idea, Michelle. Chris – come with me please. I'll need your input when I speak to the legal attaché. Michelle – if any of these clowns, no matter what their rank, want to know what we are doing in the sainted Jim Cooper's office, tell them we're on a prearranged conference call with the FBI.'

'I love it when you decide to piss off the peasants, Martin' said Chris.

They went into the office to arrange a meeting with Kevin Ryan and his team. They left the blinds open and, sure enough, observed one of the more senior officers of the Orion team cross the room and start to give Michelle Stone a hard time. She obviously bit back and the man retreated to relate her story to his pals, having treated Carver and Fearnley to what he thought to be an intimidating glare.

The call to the American embassy did not go well. It took fifteen minutes before they were able to speak with the Legat and Ryan stonewalled them. The FBI were evaluating all the forensic evidence back at Quantico, they were studying the contact reports produced by the Guardia Civil and they were looking at the travel history of the Dominic Lord and Tony Guest passports. No meeting would take place until after Tony Guest had been sentenced so, in the hope that British justice moved swiftly, one had been provisionally arranged for 1400 hours the following Monday. Carver and Fearnley were invited.

With nothing else to do for the moment the two officers set about the process of catching up on their paperwork. Not only did they have to write up their reports on their respective work with the Americans but they also had to deal with minutiae of overtime claims, subsistence claims, travel claims etc; all the boring stuff that never appears on television cop shows. They'd both finished and were having a cup of tea when Goodchild appeared. On spotting the pair of them in the goldfish bowl he joined them.

'Martin, Chris; good to see you. Are you back on this end of the investigation too?' he asked.

'Not entirely, boss' said Martin. 'We have a meeting with the FBI on Monday afternoon once sentence has been passed on Guest. We'll know more then. The powers that be may want us to remain as liaison with the Americans or we might be cut loose back to Orion.'

'Or we might end up as press officers for Oliver Addison' said Chris. 'It's all up in the air. Anyway, for what it's worth, we've both written accounts of our adventures with the FBI for you to read as and when.'

'Thanks. I've created a new email account for all Orion related work. Please send your reports there.' Goodchild wrote the account details on a post-it note which he passed to Martin.

'Right, let's get this circus rolling.'

The three of them left the office together. Carver and Fearnley headed over to where Michelle was waiting. Goodchild took centre stage.

'Good afternoon ladies and gentlemen' he boomed. 'You all know who I am. I know very few of you. This will change. Your first task will be to email me details of yourselves, your professional history and what you, personally, have been doing since you have joined the Orion team. I want this done by close of play today. Once I've read through your details I am going to create three teams out of you which will operate eight hour shifts. Orion is going to be a 24/7 organisation until we have identified the remaining seven victims and given the CPS sufficient evidence to mount a prosecution. You've seen how it's done – now it's time to do it. If you have any questions you come to me with them. If, for some reason, I'm not available and it's urgent then go to DS Stone who will know how to contact me. Sorry, Michelle. I'm about to increase your workload. Finally, I've just been talking to the hospital where DCS Cooper is. He has had to undergo an operation to relieve cranial pressure caused by swelling of the brain. This is not a good thing but had to be done or he would have died. The operation went as well as it could have but he is back in an induced coma. Prognosis is still fifty-fifty. Sorry to be so blunt but I thought you'd want to know the state of play. Any questions? No? OK get on with your personal submissions please'

Goodchild walked back into the goldfish bowl, shut the door and began going through what had been Jim Cooper's computer. Whatever the latter's faults he had been a meticulous record keeper and Goodchild soon found himself wallowing in a plethora of detail. Deciding to leave that for later he opened up his new email account and was pleased to see that Carver and Fearnley had already transmitted their reports. Whilst their work did not directly relate to the search for the missing girls in the UK, it was obvious that the FBI were convinced of Guest's guilt in the death of Catherine Taylor-Lodge. 'Perhaps they have some evidence that they were not sharing with the Met' he thought. He stood up and stuck his head out of the officer door.

'Martin, Chris; a quick word if you please' he called.

They entered the office and took seats at his invitation.

'Thanks for your reports. Good work the pair of you. There's one thing bugging me though. The FBI are acting as though they are certain that Guest killed the American girl despite the fact that all the evidence is circumstantial. Now, I'll agree it's very strong circumstantial but I've worked with the FBI before and this is just not their style. They conduct investigations looking for incontrovertible evidence to gain a conviction. Here they seem to be looking for anything that will damn a pre-selected suspect. Question: is it possible that they know something that they are not sharing with us?'

'Intellectually anything is possible, boss' said Carver. 'But I think it highly improbable that they've held anything back from me. I'd have smelled it. Chris?'

'I agree with Martin, boss. We've been straight with each other in Spain and it's produced results.'

'I think what we're seeing here is the result of immense political pressure' said Carver. 'I don't know how fully you've been briefed by Addison but are you aware that David Cameron had the Commissioner over to Number Ten?'

'No. He did not tell me that. Are you sure, Martin?'

'Yes, boss. So guess who pushed Cameron's buttons to make him act? Has to be, Obama. All the FBI want is someone, anyone to lock up for life plus a hundred and ninety nine years. Tony Guest suits them nicely.'

'Fanfuckingtastic' sighed Goodchild as he realised the position he was in. 'Give me a moment here.'

All three officers fell silent as the senior man processed the information and worked out the various options available to him. The atmosphere in the room was like that of a chess match when one player knew that his next move would win or lose the game. Finally Goodchild came to his decision.

'I don't really need to be involved in the investigation of the death of an American citizen on Spanish soil but I would appreciate an informal briefing from you two should anything come to light which could aid Orion achieve its primary purpose. I want you to leave the office now and not even think about the case over the weekend. I'll see you in court on Monday morning and you can give me a call after your meeting with the Americans. We'll meet up for a drink whilst this muppet show gets its act together. You OK with that?'

Carver and Fearnley looked at each other, nodded then answered, more of less in unison.

'Yes, boss.'

'Good. Of you go then.'

The two officers squared their desk away bade farewell to Michelle Stone then left the building together. Once outside they paused, undecided as to what to do next.

'Informal briefing' said Chris. 'I'm getting a bad feeling about this, Martin.'

'Yes. We'll play it by ear and I don't see any value in discussing it until our meeting on Monday. Then we can plan. What do you want to do now?'

'Truthfully? It's early and I feel like a kid who's been let out of school. I'd like to get a little bit tipsy then buy us an Indian dinner then get a bit more tipsy and not have to think about this fucking case every waking minute. At some stage I need to retrieve my case but mañana is another day. Sound like a plan?'

'It's one the General Staff would be proud of officer Fearnley. May I suggest a venue for bhajis and balti's or do you have somewhere in mind?'

'No – suggest away. I'm just a curry whore.'

They headed away from the Yard, skirted Parliament Square then crossed the river via Westminster Bridge. Dark was falling and the London Eye lit their way along the south bank of the Thames. The river meanders and from time to time famous landmarks vanished from sight only to reappear again minutes later. Once more they found themselves approaching a floodlit Tower Bridge. As it was Friday, a lot of office workers had finished early and the riverside bars were filling up quickly so, the evening being balmy for the time of year, they secured a table on a terrace. Chris was entranced by the river traffic and did not hear Martin say anything but they'd hardly been sat for five minutes when a bottle of champagne arrived. She didn't ask, she just accepted and eased into the pleasure of the moment. She did see him do clever things with his smart phone and heard him reserve a tablet for two at seven that evening. Where, she did not know.

They drank in companionable silence each alone in their thoughts yet aware of the other's presence. Having finished the wine they continued to head east until they arrived at Tower Bridge and the eponymous (in translation) Pont de la Tour restaurant. The time was just past six so they were able to sit comfortably at the bar.

'Wine or a cocktail, Chris?'

'Let's stay on the wine shall we. I think I OD'd on vodka last night.'

Carver smiled and ordered a bottle of Louis Roederer which they sipped whilst listening to gentle piano.

'I've actually been here once before you know' said Chris.

'Really. When was that?'

'Summer of '97. That arsehole Bill Clinton was in town and that other arsehole, Tony Blair hosted a lunch for him here. Screwed up traffic all over the City. I'd been seconded to security and it was hilarious. No communication between the American Secret Service and anyone at all. The result was that by the time Clinton had finished troughing and reached his vehicle, half the motorcade was on the north bank when Tower Bridge opened up to let a ship through. Old Billy boy was stranded, his people were going spastic and no one at their Embassy was answering the phones. Happy days.'

'I'd never heard that story before. Bloody good one though. Time to move on if you're ready.'

'Yup. Where we going?'

'Just round the corner. The Bombay Clipper. Don't let the posh décor and the lighting put you off. The food is first class. It's one of the few restaurants where I'm a regular. It's also staggering distance to my apartment.'

'Let's go then, lover. I have a distinct need for some spice tonight.'

Her smile was wickedness personified and would have jellified the legs of a weaker man. Carver took it in his stride and with a pinch of salt. He did not want to read her signals wrongly and screw up what was becoming something more than a friendship nor did he wish to spoil their efficient professional relationship. Tonight would take care of tonight. On Monday they had a man's life in their hands.

Chapter Forty

The trial of Tony Guest had been expected to take place at the Central Criminal Court known the world over as the Old Bailey. The judge, in this instance the Honourable Mr Justice Walling had however decided to use the facilities of the Crown Court which abuts Belmarsh prison. He was aware of what was likely to happen having spoken with the counsel for defence and prosecution during pre-trial procedure and saw no reason to incur costs to the public purse by transporting the accused back and forth across London when, in all likelihood, the man would begin his sentence in Belmarsh anyway.

The press and TV were not happy with this, the former because they preferred the pubs of Fleet Street and the latter because the Old Bailey made for a better visual backdrop for their outside broadcasts.

The courtroom was packed, with strict security procedures being in place. Even the barristers had to pass through metal detectors such was the intensity of emotion aroused by the case. Goodchild, Carver, Fearnley and Stone were present as the original members of Orion who had gathered the evidence to place Guest in the dock. Kevin Ryan and an unknown bag carrier were there to show American's continuing interest in this man. Members of the three victims' families had secured an area in the public gallery to themselves. Chris Fearnley noted that Janice Hope's former employer, Fullerton Prosser, was sat with the families. 'Good man' she thought. Also in the public gallery was Roger Tucker who eschewed his right to sit with his colleagues in the area reserved for the media.

There was a subdued murmur of sound as the various participants in the drama conversed amongst themselves. This stopped at nine fifty five when Tony Guest appeared in the dock flanked by two burly security guards. He was wearing a dark blue single breasted suit over a white collarless polo. He was clean shaven but his hair, although washed, was long enough to touch his jacket collar and had not seen a comb in the recent past. Wearing a tie to show respect for his surroundings was obviously not on his agenda. As Kevin Ryan put it, 'Look at the guy – rock star chic.'

The dock itself was of modern construction, raised high against the rear wall facing the judge's bench and surrounded on all sides with toughened glass. No prisoner would escape from its confines nor would an aggrieved member of the public be able to assault him.

At ten precisely the clerk to the court ordered all to rise as the judge entered and took his place. Justice Walling was a small man in his late fifties but his short wig, red and black robes plus the royal seal above his head all served to increase his stature. His voice was that of a thespian and he used it to good effect moving proceedings along at a crisp yet comprehensible pace.

All that had to be said had been said in just under an hour. Guest had no defence; three independent medical reports found him to be sane and his barrister had received no instruction. Justice Walling began his summation.

'By your own admission, Mr Guest, you are guilty of the murder of three innocent young women. They are the primary victims of your evil. Your refusal to cooperate with the authorities by telling them how they died or where their bodies lie condemns three families to years of mental anguish as they seek to find some sort of closure. You are a cold, cruel person Mr Guest. Were capital punishment still available to the judiciary then you would merit it. As it is, I sentence you to life imprisonment with a minimum tariff of thirty years. Take him down.'

Carver was watching the public gallery. If anything were to happen it would happen now and he would have bet on any outburst coming from Jennifer Duncan's father, Malcolm. The former soldier did not move a muscle. His left arm was around his wife's shoulders as she sobbed against his chest. His eyes were fixed on Tony Guest's back as he taken back down to the cells. Carver imagined that they had superimposed cross-hairs on the convict's spine.

The brevity of Justice Walling's speech had taken everyone by surprise and there was a general air of 'is that it?' especially from two Americans who were more used to the members of the legal profession making self aggrandizing speeches, often of political content, at the end of a high profile trial. Kevin Ryan came over to the four British police officers.

'Good morning' he said pleasantly. 'That was quick. What happens next?'

'He gets to eat crap food with unpleasant dining companions for the next thirty years' answered Goodchild. 'Then he can apply for parole and a new judge will take a view but probably chuckle weakly and send him back to his cage where, eventually, he will die.'

'What about the appeals process?' asked Ryan.

'He pleaded guilty. Who's he going to appeal against – himself? That's it Mr Ryan. The next time we see Guest will be when we link him to the other dead girls and then we can all do this again.'

'Is there any way I can get to talk to this mutt, Commander?'

'Not if he does not want to Mr Ryan. As far as I can see, the only people he talks to are his wife and DCI Carver here.'

'Martin, would you try and set up an interview between me and Guest? It would mean a lot to us' asked Ryan.

'I'll certainly try but it won't be today. The prison authorities have to process him now that he's been convicted. I don't even know which prison he'll be taken to.'

'OK I appreciate that. I'll see you guys fourteen hundred at the embassy then.'

'Yes, see you then.'

The two Americans left the building which was steadily emptying. 'It's customary when we've put a major scumbag away to have a drink or seven. As far as I'm concerned we four did all the valid work on this one so I invite you to the Red Lion for drinks at noon.' Goodchild was in expansive mood as he made this announcement and it brooked no refusal.

'Always up for a celebratory' said Carver 'but Chris and I need to keep a clearish head for our meeting with the Feds this afternoon.'

'No problem, Martin' said Goodchild. 'An hour and a bit in the Lion, do your thing for Anglo-American relations whilst I kick arse at the yard and then we'll do some serious drinking. That fit in with your plans does it?'

'Absolutely, boss. Oh, oh. Six o' clock boss. Incoming press.'

Goodchild turned, slowly to see an approaching Roger Tucker.

'Congratulations, Mark' said the journalist. 'You got your man. Trebles all round at the Feathers is it?'

'Not now, Roger' said Goodchild in a voice that would make a pit bull cower. 'Why don't you go and talk with your American friends or find a TV camera to spout shit into?'

'For fucks sake, Mark….'

He did not finish whatever he meant to say. Mark Goodchild actually started to growl. Chris Fearnley reacted first taking Tucker by the tricep and walking him rapidly to the main exit. She was only using one finger and a thumb but the nerve hold had paralysed Tucker's left side and was so painful he could hardly breath let alone scream.

'You just missed an extended stay in hospital by one second, sunshine' said Chris. 'I know you were mates but he thinks you shat on him….'

'I never – I did…'

'Shut up. He'll call you when he's ready. Now fuck off and stay out of the pubs he uses.'

Roger Tucker did the sensible thing and left the court massaging his arm as he went. There was the usual media scrum on the steps outside so he allowed national television to ask him their usual banalities. He was booked for an in depth interview with Channel 4 news that evening and wanted to get a feel for which way the TV channels were leaning on the trials brevity and outcome.

Inside, Chris had rejoined her colleagues.

'I've a car and driver waiting out back' said Goodchild. 'I reckon we should all take advantage of it and avoid the media monkeys who will be clamouring for a statement.'

'Makes sense to me, boss' said Carver. 'I'm surprised that one of Addison's staff isn't here to claim glory for the Met on national TV though.'

'Addison will make a statement in time for the lunchtime news but it will be made outside the yard. I've flat refused to have anything to do with the media claiming that such exposure is incompatible with my counter terrorist duties.'

'Good body swerve, boss. Let's be off then' said Carver.

The four officers made their way to a rear courtyard where a black Ford Mondeo waited for them. Goodchild's bulk necessitated him taking the front passenger seat so Carver found himself sat between the two petite women in the back. Traffic was kind to them and they were in the downstairs bar of the Red Lion less than thirty minutes later.

Joseph Slattery gave them their first round of drinks on the house then left them to it. At this time of day they were the only people in the bar which suited them fine. As far as they were concerned, only police officers understood the importance of moments such as these. Not even Rachel Watkins and her team had been invited.

They celebrated, but in an oddly restrained fashion. Although they had worked as a team and would receive accolades because of a positive outcome to the case, each one of them was carrying a secret. Goodchild and Stone had not revealed that they were going to leave the force and he believed that no one knew of his relationship with her. Michelle had not had a chance to talk further with Chris and was therefore unsure as to whether or not she had told Carver of her new living arrangements. She had been watching him to see if he acted any differently towards her but detected nothing out of the ordinary – but Martin bloody Carver was not the type to tip his hand anyway.

Carver and Fearnley were living with the knowledge that they'd persuaded an innocent man to plead guilty to multiple murder in his own best interests. Even if they did catch the real killer, if their actions ever became known they'd be kicked off the force and be lucky to escape a prison sentence themselves. The fact that they knew about Goodchild and Stone (plus the fact that he did not know that they knew) added a further layer of duplicity to the group's dynamics. Chris would have described the situation as surreal; Martin would have called it a proper mind fuck.

After an hour of self congratulatory bullshitting, they ordered some lunch. Not because they were hungry but by way of soakage because this Monday had far to go and clear heads would be required.

The pub started to fill with its lunchtime crowd, a lot of them looking like middle grade civil servants in need of a Monday stiffener to ward off the shakes brought on by a weekend's over-indulgence. The denizens of the Treasury and the Foreign Office, both across the road from the Red Lion, were notorious topers. Goodchild settled the bill and the four of them regained the daylight of a London winter.

Carver and Fearnley hailed a cab which deposited them at the American embassy fifteen minutes before the hour. Looking up at the monstrous edifice, Chris shook her head in amusement.

'Do you think the Yanks will take that bloody ugly bird with them when they open their new embassy in Wandsworth, Martin?' she asked.

'Well it's big, brash, over the top and in very bad taste so I'd say it's odds on they will. Come on .'

They mounted the broad flight of concrete steps to the embassy's main entrance and were directed to Marine Post one, an armoured glass booth with some very serious looking young men inside it. They did not wear dress blues for this duty; they were clad in green camo BDUs and were armed for bear. This was just the first overt line of defence for the United States mission in London. Carver had a fairly good idea of what was out of sight so he spoke politely and kept his hands in view at all times.

Their names and police I.D.s having been checked against a list, they were directed to take a seat against a wall on the other side of the vast atrium that made up the entrance to the embassy. In under five minutes a clean cut young man who should have had 'Property of the FBI' stamped on his forehead appeared and gave them visitors passes to wear around their necks. He then escorted them via a lift and corridor to Legat country where he left them in a conference room with ten other people – eight male, two female. They had obviously been working all day to judge by the piles of paper on the large table and the smell of pizza and coffee in the air.

Kevin Ryan was at the head of the table and stood to greet them.

'Come on in guys. Glad you could make it. If you wouldn't mind taking these two seats on the left, we can begin.'

Carver and Fearnley sat where Ryan had pointed. Each of them had a yellow legal pad and pencils, red and black, in front of them.

'First off I'm not going to introduce everybody to you' began Ryan. 'At this stage it's not essential. That may change. What I will say is that all these people are FBI. There is no C.I.A. or State Department involvement in this meeting and all these people, even the ones you have not met, know who you are and the work you have both carried out with the Bureau thus far.'

The two British officers looked around the table and saw that there were indeed a few faces they recognised from Bristol or Fuerteventura.

'I'd like to thank you both for your contribution to our efforts in finding the killer of Catherine Taylor-Lodge and I've cleared it with Commissioner Sampson that your role as liaison continues' continued Ryan to their surprise. No one had informed them that their status had been formalised.

'Chris, Martin – I'd like to bring you up to speed with what we have been doing, what we are thinking and where we go from here. Firstly, we are ninety nine point nine per cent certain that the guy you sent down for thirty this morning is the guy who killed Catherine. Our goal is to make that figure one hundred per cent at which time the United States Government will seek his extradition to face due process in New York State. Failing that, Guest will be tried in absentia. These matters will be resolved at a governmental level and have no bearing on FBI or Metropolitan Police operations. We just find the evidence.'

As Ryan was speaking, Chris Fearnley was taking notes. Martin Carver sat immobile, listening and watching everyone's body language.

'We have been tracking the Dominic Lord identity, both passport and credit cards, going back a period of five years. What we have found is this. It is very rarely used. It showed three visits to Fuerteventura which ties in with what Richard Waterman told us. We also have three visits on the Eurostar to Paris followed by three flights from Vienna, Austria to Kiev, Ukraine return. Any comment on that itinerary?'

'Once in the Ukraine he could hire or buy a car for cash' said Carver. 'Then it's a straight run north to Russia or south to Georgia where he could organise delivery of the Kolokol. I'd guess Russia.'

'Thanks, Martin. That's the conclusion we came to as well. What we have to do is try and find out where Guest was on those dates.

His passport and credit cards were not in use but, if he won't talk to us, where can we go?'

'I've an idea on that but I'll have to move quickly' said Chris.

'And that would be?' asked Ryan.

Chris leaned over and whispered in Carver's ear. He nodded assent to whatever she had said.

'We can talk with Guest's wife, Gill' said Chris. 'She's been cooperative with us so far and acted as her husband's business manager. She has records of all of his engagements, bookings whatever so it should be quite straight forward to cross reference that data with the Dominic Lord travel dates.'

'Excellent. You'll do that how?'

'We already have copies of Guest's bookings so if you give us the Lord travel details we can start this afternoon. If there are any gaps then Martin or myself will travel up to Shropshire and have a word with her.'

'OK. That's covered then. Next thing; Quantico has reassembled the contents of the shredding machine found at Dominic Lord's villa in Corralejo. Most of it was crap, utility bills and suchlike but there is one thing that stands out. Have a look at this.'

Ryan passed over an A4 sheet of paper to the two British police officers. It was a photocopy of a fax and in the centre of the page was what appeared to be a business card.

IAN WILLIAMS
MARKETING CONSULTANT
07961 974157

'The name and the phone number match. This guy's home address is in some place called Preston in the north of England. We've not been able to find out much about him in the UK and it's a fairly common name. What we do have is a passport number and records of him entering and leaving Fuerteventura the same week that Catherine Taylor-Lodge died. He has very little credit card activity so we need some help here to find out more about who Williams is, what he does and how his card ended up being shredded in the villa where our girl was probably killed.'

'Leave that with us Mr Ryan' said Carver. 'This will take priority over checking Guest's itinerary over the past five years. It's way too coincidental for us to overlook. Anymore surprises today?'

All the Americans looked towards Kevin Ryan and a palpable silence invaded the room. Carver and Fearnley sensed it and realised that the Legat was deciding whether or not to let them in on something with which the FBI were not comfortable.

'Martin, Chris. This is Special Agent Mary Connor. She specialises in criminal psychology and has come up with something I feel you need to evaluate. Mary.'

Mary Connor was a mouse. Small, brown hair, hazel eyes, brown, sensible clothing and prone to quick, darting movements of head and hands. Her voice did not squeak but it was soft to the point of inaudibility. This made everyone strain to catch her words and therefore ensured that she was the centre of attention.

'I've looked at the name Dominic Lord' she began. 'We know it's a false identity so why did our man choose this particular name? Dominic is from the Latin dominus which translates as lord or master. Anno Domini 'in the year of our Lord' and all that. There is another Latin word for master; it is magister as in the magistrates in English law courts. Now, if we return to how all the events which culminated in Catherine's murder started we have the email to the journalist which was signed ML. I suggest that it is magister something. Any ideas?'

The room fell silent as the Americans all observed the two British police officers. Carver closed his eyes and reclined in his chair. Presently he stood and began to pace with his head bent towards the floor and his right hand massaging his right temple. His eyes had taken on the look that is sometimes referred to as the thousand yard stare. After a minute of this he snapped back to the room and retook his chair.

'I don't like this at all' said Carver.

'What? My linking of the words Dominic and Lord' said Mary Connor.

'No. On the contrary it is a very good insight. What I don't like are the implications. Have you pushed this any further Mr Ryan?'

'No. We're stuck with this. The guy sounds like some egotistical nut job to have selected such a name but, hell, the asylums are full of Napoleons and Caesars, right?'

'It's worse than that' said Carver. 'ML. Does Magister Ludi mean anything to you?'

The Americans all indicated a negative reply either verbally or with a shake of the head.

'It's not that obscure' continued Carver. 'The philosopher Herman Hesse wrote a series of essays collectively titled 'The Glass Bead Game'. It basically sets out the fundamentals of existentialism and its alternative name is Magister Ludi which translates as 'Master of the Game'. This fucker is playing with us.'

The FBI were, or pretended to be, shocked by Carver's use of language at a formal meeting and there was an embarrassing moment's pause whilst they got over the shock.

'I missed German philosophy 101' said an as yet unidentified FBI agent. 'What on earth is 'existentialism', Detective Carver?'

'It's a philosophical theory which states that man is responsible for his own actions and is therefore free to choose his development and destiny. That is the mind set of the man who killed Catherine Taylor-Lodge.'

'You've spoken with Guest, Martin' said Ryan. 'Does he come across as this kind of personality?'

'Yes and no. He's a performer. He gets on stage and struts his stuff and has been doing so for years. Since his arrest, however, he's sort of pulled into his shell and become and introvert, accepting his fate and is now looking at thirty years. Odd, to say the least.'

'Is he sane?' asked Ryan.

'You were at the trial so you know what the white coats said. I'm not qualified to answer that question, Mr Ryan.'

'But you have an opinion, don't you?'

'Of course, but it's irrelevant to the case. Look, we've a lot to be getting on with so I think DI Fearnley and I need to get back to base and start things moving. I'll put a team onto cross referencing Guest's gigs with Dominic Lord's travels. I'll personally find out all I can on Ian William and give you a call tomorrow morning. That OK for now?'

'Yes, thanks, Martin. Good meeting. I'll see you out.'

As Ryan escorted Carver and Fearnley to the door, the British policeman stopped and said 'Agent Connor? Good insight on the name. If you come up with anything more like that please give myself or Chris a call.'

The brown mouse turned pink and nodded in affirmation.

Carver and Fearnley took their leave of Ryan and hailed a cab on Upper Brook Street which had them back at New Scotland Yard in a frustrating fifteen minutes. Once in the Orion offices they went though a private debriefing with Goodchild who gave them the go ahead to proceed with the American side of the investigation as they saw fit.

Caver handed the Dominic Lord travel details over to Michelle Stone who then set about the boring yet essential process of checking them against Tony Guest's known performance dates. Carver and Fearnley started to investigate Ian Williams. The case had regained its momentum with even Jim Cooper's people finding new motivation. Goodchild felt optimistic that some of the seven missing girls would be identified and he could then leave the force with the job done as well as possible.

The Chinese have a saying: Just when everything in the garden is beautiful, an evil wind will blow weeds in to poison it. Or in English, shit happens.

In Clerkenwell ML was preparing his next move. He'd watched the predictable outcome of Tony Guest's trial and wondered as to how much complicity there was between him and the Metropolitan Police in pleading guilty and thereby escaping the clutches of the Americans. He's planned on pumping Roger Tucker for information but it was apparent that the journalist was persona non grata with his former friends in the police. The man had become a talking head on serial killers and was making no secret that his definitive book on the Musical Murders would be out soon. So ML had to find a new way to advance his agenda. It would be amusing to cause embarrassment to Tucker at the same time; and timing was the most important element in the exercise.

Tucker's newspaper was tabloid in format but aspired to quality in content. If he could make it look down market, amateur and less journalistically credible than one of the tits and arse dailies, how much fun would that be? What was required was the righteous wrath of the great British public directed against the police, the judiciary and the Daily Post.

ML took a pad of paper and started to work out time lines. By now the Americans, with or without the help of the Met, must have tracked down Richard Waterman and therefore the villa in Corralejo. The question was would they have found what he had left for them in the paper shredder? Spanish cleaning staff would not have touched a piece of (to them) unusual electronic equipment nor would lazy Richard. It was doubtful that he would have double-let the premises just in case 'Dominic Lord' returned to the island so it was probable that the FBI would have reconstructed Ian Williams business card by now. Therefore they would have had to have asked the Met for help in tracking the man down so, despite Guest's conviction, there were still loose ends to this investigation. Even if he were wrong in his calculations,

ML decided that he had nothing to lose by throwing a rock into this particular pool.

Taking a one time disposable cell phone from his stock, ML dialled the offices of the Sun newspaper in Wapping, east London and asked to be put through to the news desk. Once connected he activated an electronic device available at the Spy Shop on Park Lane which scrambles one's voice pattern so that Kylie Minogue would sound like Johnny Cash. This tends to get people's attention.

'News desk – Aiden Hartley speaking. How may I help you?' came a voice straight from the Thames estuary via twenty plus cigarettes a day. An old pro on his way out thought ML. Excellent.

'Are you recording this?' he asked.

'No; should I be?'

'Your call, but it's important. The Tony Guest case. You involved in that?'

'Yeah, we all are. Done and dusted now though innit? Hardly news Mr....?'

'You could not be more wrong, mate. Guest is innocent. He only pleaded guilty so's the bleedin' Yanks could not haul him off to the States to stand trial for the murder of the student bint.'

'How do you...'

'Shut it. The Yanks and the Met have another suspect – another Brit, and they're trying to track him down now. Initials are I.W and he's from Preston. That's all I have at the moment but this guy is a stalker and was in Fuerteventura when the American girl went missing.'

'I.W from Preston. Not much is it?'

'For fuck's sake – check I.W's flying to Fuerteventura in the relevant timeframe. I can't do all your work for you you tosser!'

'How did you obtain the info you have?'

'You are bleedin' joking aren't you, pal? If you're not interested I'll blow you off and let a proper paper have this. I reckon the Guardian would love to have a pop at that fascist from the Daily Post.'

'All right, all right. Give me an hour to verify a few things then call me back. I assume from the voice box you don't want to leave your number with me?'

'Clever boy. I'll be in touch.'

ML broke the connection and reviewed the conversation. It had gone well. He'd used the vocabulary of someone who had not had the benefit of higher education but he'd indicated that he was privy to a certain level of the police investigation. By referring to Roger Tucker as a fascist he had nailed his political colours to the mast. Hopefully Aiden Hartley would take him to be a low ranking, bolshie copper or clerical assistant with an axe to grind. Time would tell.

Aiden Hartley thought he'd seen and heard it all during forty years in journalism. He's never made it as a by line writer but he was a dogged investigator who made up in tenacity for what he lacked in sobriety. Even by Fleet Street standards the man was a legend in his own lunchtime. Now this had landed in his lap. He decided to do some research of his own before passing the information further up the food chain.

Most people would have called the Crimestoppers number that had been shown on the television show regarding the American girl's disappearance. Hartley had his own contacts at New Scotland Yard and was able to get through to the Orion offices directly. He played it straight with the young sounding detective constable with whom he eventually found himself speaking. After a few minutes of verbal fencing he started to press.

'Look, son. My number will be on your caller ID so you can verify that I'm phoning from the offices of the largest selling paper in the country. I've given you my name and I've told you that I'm recording this conversation. You, mate, are giving me the run around. Now, straight question; are you or are you not looking at another suspect in the Musical Murders case? A man who has the initials I.W, and is from Lancashire. A reply please or my editor calls your Commissioner.'

'I'm sorry, Mr Hartley but I have no knowledge of…'

'I'm being run around again. Is there anyone competent there who can answer this simple question before tomorrow's edition comes out?'

The young DC on the receiving end of the call wished Jim Cooper were there to take over. He looked across the open plan office and saw Martin Carver and Chris Fearnley were in conversation and not on the phone so he decided to pass the buck their way. Putting Hartley on hold he called across the room.

'Sir; I've got a journalist from the Sun on the line wanting to know if we are looking at another British suspect in the Guest case. He reckons it's someone in the north of England with the initials I.W. What shall I do, sir?'

'Put him through on 2332, please' said Carver who then strode into the goldfish bowl taking Fearnley with him. Goodchild was absent so the two officers took Hartley's call in private.

'This is DCI Martin Carver. I believe you have some information for me.'

'No, mate. I have questions for you. Are you looking for someone with the initials I.W. in connection with the murder of the American senator's daughter? The guy's a Brit and lives in Preston.'

Carver had the phone on speaker mode so Chris was able to hear both sides of the conversation. Hartley's revelations made her eyebrows shoot up. Carver remained calm.

'Mr Hartley; you are mistaken. I ask the questions and I may or may not reveal details of ongoing enquiries into multiple murders. You, of course, you may print whatever you want but it will be without verification from this office. Now; what incited you to make this particular enquiry?'

'I received a phone call about fifteen minutes ago. The voice was electronically disguised but basically the caller said that Tony Guest was innocent, he's chosen to be banged up so's the Yanks can't get to him and you lot plus the FBI are looking at some geezer from Preston with the initials I.W. as a suspect. My source said I.W. was a stalker and was in Fuerteventura when the American girl went missing. Any comment on that DCI Carver?'

'Do you have any idea who the caller was, Mr Hartley?'

'Oh come on, Officer Carver! Don't answer a question with a question. I'll just put that down as 'Scotland Yard made no comment' and you'll look right awkward prats on tomorrow's front page.'

'This is a current murder investigation and we would request the help of the press in its pursuit. Certain details, if made public, could be construed as being a hindrance to the successful conclusion on the investigation.'

'Is that a threat, officer?'

'No. It's an observation. Back to my question. Any idea as to who called you? Did you record the call?'

Aiden Hartley was experienced enough to read between the lines. A potentially huge story had come his way by chance and this guy Carver, for all his sang froid, was on the back foot. It would not do to piss the man off at this stage so answering his questions could only be to the journalist's advantage.

'All right then. I'll show you mine then you show yours. I don't know who called me and, yes, I did record the conversation. For what it's worth I'd guess the caller to be male, thirty to forty and blue collar socially.'

'And you're basing that description on what, Mr Hartley?'

'Vocabulary and forty years experience.'

'Fair enough. I'd like a copy of the recorded conversation, please.'

'And I'd like a shower with Kate Beckinsale – without the leather kit. My turn, Officer Carver. Are you and the Yanks looking for an I.W. from Preston?

Carver looked across the desk at Fearnley and held his hands out with palms up, silently asking 'what the hell do we do now?'. Chris mouthed to him 'tell him'.

'Very well, Mr Hartley. I confirm that we are still pursuing our enquiries along with our American colleagues into the death of Catherine Taylor-Lodge. We are in receipt of information which has made a British citizen from Preston a person of interest. I cannot confirm names or initials at this stage. I would emphasise that this information is sensitive and our investigators are at a crucial phase. As such, I would be grateful for sight of anything the Sun intends to publish prior to you doing so.'

'Are you mental? The Met censors the national press. What planet do you inhabit, Carver?'

'I'm not attempting censorship. We could not even request a D notice as this case does not come under any definition of national security. It would, however, be useful for us to see anything which you are going to print before anyone we may wish to interview reads it. I don't think that is an unreasonable request, Mr Hartley.'

'That's for my editor to decide. I'll give you a free one though, officer; the person who contacted me said that he'd call back in an hour's time. That's now forty five minutes away and I've some research to do. Anything you can give me that might help?'

'Not at this time, Mr Hartley.'

'What a surprise. Must crack on then. No doubt we'll talk again soon.'

'Thanks for your call. Goodbye.' Carver broke the connection and spoke to Chris Fearnley.

'He does not have Ian Williams' name yet so I don't see how he's going to track down I.W. from Preston. Airlines aren't supposed to give out passenger details – it's a privacy thing but the Sun may have a tame copper or travel agent who would pull up all the I.W.'s who travelled between the UK and Fuerteventura at the relevant time. We have to beat them to it, Chris and I'll have to dump that task on you. OK with that?'

'Sure and it shouldn't take too long. I've a name, a location and a phone number. Thirty minutes tops. What are you going to be doing?'

'I need to get this information to Addison. He's going to have a baby when he realises the Sun's involved. I hope Goodchild's with him. Work from this office and don't let those clowns outside know what you're up to.'

'I'm on it.'

Chris retrieved her laptop from the main office and set to work. Carver ascertained from Michelle Stone that Goodchild was indeed upstairs with Addison. A quick phone call and Martin headed off to join them.

Deputy Assistant Commissioner Addison was in full uniform whilst Commander Goodchild was still wearing the lounge suit he'd selected for the trial. The two senior officers were sat in a relaxed manner each with a tumbler of whisky in hand. They were quietly celebrating Guest's thirty year sentence and their self satisfaction set Carver's teeth on edge.

'Gentleman, sorry to burst in like this but something's come up you need to know about without delay.'

'Not at all, Martin' said Addison. 'Nothing can spoil today. Drink?'

'No thank you, sir. I've not had time to write up a record of the meeting which DI Fearnley and myself had with the FBI this afternoon but I'd like to make a verbal report now.'

'Come on, Martin' said Addison. 'Surely this can wait until tomorrow.'

'Well, it could, sir. But then you could read all about it on the front page of the Sun.'

'Tell us what's happened, Martin' said Goodchild.

Carver recounted the details of his meeting from memory. He was not interrupted. It was only when he got on to Aiden Hartley's phone call that the other two men realised the seriousness of the situation.

'What do we know about this Ian Williams character then, Martin?' asked Goodchild.

'Nothing yet, boss. DI Fearnley is hitting the databases now. You know the drill; electoral roll, NI number, passport details and travel itinerary. She'll have all that done in the next fifteen minutes or so.'

'Do you think the Sun will cooperate with us, Martin?' asked Addison.

'That's not my area of expertise, sir but common sense tells me that they will do their best to shag us senseless. The Met has been at war with News International for nearly two years. Rupert Murdoch's been dragged in front of a parliamentary enquiry, he's been forced to close one of his most profitable newspapers and sack his senior staff. If the Sun has an inside track into our investigation and can prove that Guest is innocent you can bet your pension they'll screw us. That's how I see it at any rate, sir. Your knowledge of the media may make you think otherwise.'

'This is a disaster' said Addison. 'I'll have to let Sir Alan know about this. Mark; I want you and Martin to pull out all the stops on this. If this story is true we need to get this Williams character before the gutter press. Do you think you can manage that?'

'Yes, sir' replied Carver. We appear to have more information than the Sun and our resources are superior. I wouldn't be surprised if DI Fearnley hasn't already found him so, unless there's anything else..?'

'Of course. Off you both go and let know the minute you have something. I've now got to extract the Commissioner from a meeting with the mayor. Bloody hell!'

Chapter Forty One

Carver had been right in his assessment that the Met would track Williams down before the sun newspaper. Hartley was still struggling with Google searches and had not spoken to his editor when Chris Fearnley was comparing the Welshman's travels with those of Tony Guest.

As Carver and Goodchild entered the goldfish bowl she was carrying on a conversation in a phone held in her left hand whilst using her right to access data from her computer. She noticed the men's entry and flashed a huge smile and a thumbs up.

'I suppose that's the famous multi-tasking I keep hearing about' whispered Goodchild.

'No, boss' replied Carver. 'That's Chris Fearnley in attack dog mode. Watch out you'll get bitten.'

Fearnley finished her call and printed off some readouts to add to the pile already on her desk. She finally sat down (in Goodchild's chair), took a composing breath and addressed the two men.

'We've finally had some luck. Ian Williams is not a mystery man like Dominic Lord. He was dead easy to track. Without going into his background too much for now what I have is that he runs a company called Williams Marketing Associates Ltd. There are no associates. It's a one man band with its offices registered in Fisher Street, Preston which happens to be his home address. He pays his taxes, has a just above average income, is single and spends a lot of time travelling around England. No credit cards, not even a company one. Williams operates either with cash or by debit card. By looking at ATM withdrawals I've placed him at five towns or cities at the same time as Tony Guest is on record as having played there. That cannot be a coincidence. I also have him flying in and out of Fuerteventura the same week as Catherine. I've not found out where he bought his ticket yet – it's not showing up on his financials nor do I know where he stayed but my buddies in the Guardia will give me that info. What do you reckon, gentleman?'

'Good work, Chris' said Goodchild. 'You mentioned luck; what is it?'

'Williams took the Virgin Express from Preston to London Euston first thing this morning. At three thirty he withdrew two hundred pounds from an ATM in Camden High Street. He's still in London and I reckon he's planning on making a night of it.'

'Do we have a photo of this character, Chris?' asked Carver.

'Passport Office promised it in the next ten minutes.'

'Boss, we can't let this guy slip through our fingers not after the FBI have dropped the name to us. I recommend we get an Armed Response Unit to Camden and then get all of Orion up there in civilians to saturate the area as soon as we have a photo of him. We've more than enough to pull him in for questioning.'

'That sounds like overkill to me, Martin' said Goodchild. 'I don't like the thought of this lot mixing with an ARU looking for a psycho who might be carrying a lethal gas on his person. If they only have a passport photo to go by, well, you know how iffy those can be.'

'I've an idea' said Chris. 'If your worry is having a positive ID on Williams why don't we use the counter-terrorism unit's technology to rack his cell phone? I could go to Camden and phone him to set up a business meeting, say I'd got his number from a website, keep him talking then ARU take him down when I have eyeballed the guy.'

'No' said Goodchild. 'I'm not letting an ARU loose in Camden during rush hour. The potential for civilian casualties is too high. We need to find another way.'

'Let's refine Chris' idea then' said Carver. She and I draw firearms and deploy to Camden. Chris phones him on his cell saying she's seen his website and she's looking for someone to market her fashion range in North West England. He'll ask where she's based and, surprise surprise, she's in London. Set up a meet and we'll effect the arrest ourselves. If we do this right, no one will even notice it happening but have a van load of uniforms round the corner just in case.'

'You happy with that, Chris?' asked Goodchild.

'Yes, boss. Martin and I have done this before you know.'

'I'll let Addison know that Chris has traced Williams and we will be arresting him today. I'm not telling Orion because someone has leaked to the Sun and we can't risk any more of that shit. Anything else?'

'I just need to have a look at this guy's website so I can talk sensibly to him – despite Martin's sexist assumption that I have a girly fashion range. He may specialise in what he markets.'

'One more thing, boss' said Carver. 'That journo at the Sun said his source was going to call him back about now. Who's going to follow that up?'

'I'll leave that with Addison. I've no time for chasing the bloody media. They'll call us when they want something. Let's just concentrate on bringing Williams in. Call me before you head out or if you need anything.'

Goodchild left them to head back and brief Addison. Carver and Fearnley descended to the sub-basement armoury where they were issued with their personal weapons, a Browning 9mm Hi Power for him and a Glock semi-automatic which suited Fearnley's smaller hands for her. They both drew light body armour which would not show under the winter jackets that the weather justified them wearing.

Carver then organised a track on Williams's cell phone with the counter-terrorism unit whilst Fearnley put together a Rapid Response Team of six uniformed officers who would deploy at her command. All this was accomplished without complications and they reconvened in the goldfish bowl just over an hour after they had started. Goodchild was waiting for them. Carver brought him up to speed and the senior man nodded approvingly.

'Well done you two' he said. 'Time to make contact then. How are you going to play it, Chris?'

'I've looked at his website and he claims that his company can market just about anything. My gut feeling is to go along the music and food route if, as seems to be the case, he keeps turning up in towns where Tony Guest was performing. The fact that he is in Camden is potentially significant too: there's a lot of music venues round there.'

'I can't fault you reasoning, Chris. Go for it.'

Once again Chris composed herself then punched in Williams' cellphone number using the desk phone which caller ID would show as number withheld. It was quickly answered.

'Hello' came a neutral male voice.

'May I speak with Ian Williams, please?' said Chris.

'Speaking. Who's calling?'

'Hi, Mr Williams. My name is Chris Cartwright. I found your company's number on your website. Are you free to talk for a moment?'

'Sure. What can I do for you?'

'I work for a consortium of businessmen who have launched a new chain of bar – restaurants called Sing For Your Supper. It's a bit difficult to explain in a few words but if you can imagine a cross of an open mike evening and an informal eating atmosphere then you're about there. It's gone down well on the south coast and we're now going to franchise it in the north and will need a company with specialised knowledge of the local market to help us. Does that sound like the sort of thing you could get involved in?'

'Absolutely. Where in the north were you thinking?'

'Manchester for sure. Elsewhere we don't know which is why we need a local marketing company. Could we arrange to meet sometime this week, Mr Williams? My people really want to push ahead with this.'

'Of course. Where are you based Ms Cartwright?'

'I'm in London but I'm happy to travel up to meet you in Preston.'

'London? I'm in London right now.'

'Wow! How lucky's that? Look, Mr Williams; first meetings are always exploratory, getting to know each other and they don't always result in a deal, right?'

'Tell me about it. Well I've finished my business for the day and was planning to go to a music gig in Camden Town. I don't mind meeting up this evening if that suits your plans.'

'Alright – sounds good to me. Where are you now?'

'I'm just wandering around near Euston Station. It's an area I know as my train always ends up here when I visit London.'

'Fine; there are plenty of taxis round there. How about if we meet in an hour's time in the White Lion pub in White Lion Street? That's in Islington and it's an easy run from there to Camden for later on.'

'White Lion. Easy enough to remember. How will I recognise you?'

'Five nine, short blond hair, black leather jacket, jeans and blue jumper. I'll be in the front bar sat by the window.'

'Right. I'll see you in an hour's time Ms Cartwright.'

'I look forward to it. Bye.'

'That went well' said Goodchild. 'I'm off to the tracking section. I'll call you if anything strange happens, Martin. Good luck and don't take any chances.'

'No, boss' said Carver. Chris Fearnley did not comment instead checking that her Glock was secure and hidden from view on her right hip. They hurried out of the building where an unmarked Ford was waiting for them.

'White Lion off Upper Street, fast as you can' said Carver to the driver. 'No lights and sirens, please.'

'Sir' the man replied with a nod then headed off at a brisk pace to their destination. As the car reached the end of the City Road, Carver had it stop at the Angel.

'OK Chris. We're half an hour early so I think you can walk the rest of the way. I'm going to check in with Goodchild then go and see the uniforms. I'll be with you as soon as chummy has entered the bar then we'll do what we do.'

'Don't be late or I'll just take him down on my own scoring one for the girls' team.'

'Yeah, right.' They both knew she was joking.

Chris Fearnley left the car then turned left into Upper Street. As usual it was busy with people waiting for buses or descending into the huge underground station to begin their commutes back to the suburbs. The street was also crowded with groups of youngish people looking for somewhere to drink or eat. There were countless venues in this popular area and Chris always found it bizarre that she was a stone's throw from Holloway Prison for women. She crossed the busy road at the lights then headed up the small street at the end of which stood the White Lion, a classic piece of Victorian architecture. Being off the beaten track it was much less busy than the establishments she had left behind her. She bought a coke at the bar then found a seat where the windows met the rear wall and from where she could observe both entrances to the large, oblong room.

At the appointed time a man entered the main doors to the pub, stopped and looked around. Chris affected not to notice him as this was supposed to be the first time she'd seen him; but she instantly recognised Ian Williams from his passport photograph. One word summed up his appearance; medium. Medium length brown hair, medium height and build, a mid brown suit that had High Street written all over it and a rust coloured polo neck to complete the ensemble. If he'd been wearing platform shoes he could have walked out of a nineteen eighties fashion shoot.

'This guy works in marketing' thought Chris. 'He looks like an ambulatory turd!'

Williams spotted her and made his way to her table. 'Excuse me' he said in a medium sort of voice. 'Are you Chris Cartwright?'

'I am. You, I hope, are Mr Williams.'

'Please, call me Ian.'

'Ian it is then.'

'Would you like another drink?'

'No, I'm fine for the moment thanks.'

'OK I'll just get myself one then.'

Chris observed his body language as he went to the bar. She was not surprised to see that he ordered a half pint of the weakest lager but she did raise a mental eyebrow when Williams took out a plastic bag that banks use for change and methodically counted out the exact number of coins to pay for his drink. He looked as dangerous as a doughnut. Experience had shown Chris Fearnley that appearances could, indeed, be deceptive so she continued to regard Williams as a potential serial killer and to discount his geeky demeanour.

Williams returned to the table and took a seat facing Chris which put his back to the room. Not a sensible move from a tactical point of view.

'Is this your local then, Chris?' began Williams which, as an opening line, is not much better than 'do you come here often.'

Chris played along. 'No. It's just somewhere I sometimes meet colleagues and I knew it was about equidistant from where we both were when I phoned you.'

'That was considerate of you.' Williams then proceeded to talk at Chris about his 'passion for marketing', the difficulties of running your own business, how poor the train service was in the north, how dreary the music scene was where he lived. The man was a lump of verbose negativity and Chris started to fantasise about the good she could do for the planet were she to empty the contents of her Glock into him. As Williams droned on, Chris caught sight of Carver as he entered the bar. She touched the right side of her face with her right hand then quickly stroked the tip of her nose. This conveyed to Carver that she did not perceive a physical threat from Williams and that they should move on him with immediate effect.

Carver strode across the room and appeared slightly behind and to the right of Williams.

'Chris! I did not know you were in town.' He said with his Mr Happy face on.

'Hi, Martin. Last minute business meeting' she replied. 'May I introduce Ian Williams of Williams Marketing Associates?'

'Good evening' said Carver extending his right hand. Williams stood to shake it and Carver's left hand appeared from behind his back to slap the rigid cuffs on in less than a second. Chris had moved away from the table and her hand was on her hip. She saw that there was no need for her to draw her weapon so she took out her warrant card instead.

'Metropolitan Police, Mr Williams' she said in a quiet voice. 'You are under arrest for the murder of Catherine Taylor-Lodge. You do not have to say anything. But it may harm your defence if you do not mention when questioned something which you later rely on in court. Anything you do say may be given in evidence. Let's go.'

Williams was in a state of shock and walked meekly to the front door. Carver had called the TSG as soon as the cuffs were on and their grey Mercedes van pulled up as the three of them arrived outside. The side door to the vehicle opened so that Williams could be placed in the sole seat used for transporting prisoners.

'Thanks, lads' said Carver. 'If you could take our friend to Paddington Green for admission they're waiting for him. After that you can go and spend your overtime in the boozer.'

'Certainly, sir' said a sergeant who was kitted out in full Robocop gear. 'Will you be joining us?'

'Not this time. Our evening is just starting but thanks. You pulled this together quickly and I'll make sure the Commander knows.'

Carver closed the door leaving the van to head off into the night. The unmarked Ford that had brought them from the Yard pulled up at the kerb. It was the same driver.

'Would you take us to Paddington Green please?' said Carver. 'That went well, Chris.'

'Yes. He made it easy with his choice of seating position though. Nice take down, anyway.'

'First impressions of the guy?'

'A wimp, a bore, not very bright, socially inept and he does not give off any murderous vibes – for what that's worth.'

'You don't have a good feeling about this, do you?'

'No. It's been too easy. An organised serial killer would not have fallen for my Sing For Your Supper bullshit. He would not have sat with his back to the room of an unknown place either. Remember, Martin – all of today's events stem from a business card which was found shredded at 'Dominic Lord's' villa. Are we being played here?'

'The thought had crossed my mind. Magister Ludi? It's possible. Right; here's how we are going to proceed. Forensics and techos are going over Williams' home/office right now. Goodchild has decided that we will conduct the initial interviews with you taking the lead.'

'Why me? I'm pleased to do it but you're senior here, Martin.'

'We're going to concentrate on Catherine and you were liaison in Spain. Plus you collated all the material so you've the best overview of the Williams and Guest aspect of the case. Just to let you know; in the spirit of Anglo-Americans co-operation, the FBI have been kept informed of our progress. Kevin Ryan is at Paddington and will be observing you.'

'No pressure there then. I suppose this means I can't threaten to shoot the shit's kneecaps off?'

'Keep you eyes on the road, constable' said Carver to the driver. 'DS Fearnley was joking.'

Goodchild was waiting for them when they entered Paddington Green station.

'Well done, you two' he said, 'Any problems?'

'None' replied Chris. 'He sat with his back to the room and Martin had the cuffs on him before he knew what was happening. I read him his rights and he came along like a lamb.'

'Fine. He's been strip searched and his clothing has gone to the Yard to be processed. I've kept the contents of his pockets here. Nothing much there. Wallet with two hundred and twenty pounds in it, plastic bag containing loose change, a debit card, train ticket for tomorrow morning to Preston, a copy of What's On in London, a set of keys and a cellphone. He's in a holding cell now.'

'Let's leave him there for an hour' said Chris. 'I need some food and I also want to look at the contact names on his cellular. We also need to sign these hand guns back.'

'The longer you leave him alone, the more likely he is to lawyer up, Chris' said Goodchild.

'Normally I'd agree, boss but I've spoken to him already and reckon I can avoid that happening.'

'OK it's your show. Get off to the canteen and I'll see you in interview one when you're ready. I'll sign the phone over to you then.'

Carver and Fearnley headed off in search of bacon sandwiches and tea. There was no knowing how long the interview would last so sustenance was important. After refuelling, they returned to meet Goodchild and found him in the company of Kevin Ryan.

The notes that Chris Fearnley had made back at the Orion offices had been brought over so she found herself some desk space and began to review them in conjunction with the contact list on Williams' phone. After ten minutes work she squared everything away.

'I'm ready to start now, sir' she said to Goodchild. 'I take it that Williams has been given a cup of tea or two?'

'Yes, he has.'

'That's nice. Could you have the biggest, ugliest uniform in the station escort Williams from the holding cell to the interview room please, sir?'

'Certainly. You'll watch from here?'

'Yes, sir.'

Interview room one did not have two way mirrors. It had cameras installed for a visual record of proceedings. Carver, Fearnley and Ryan were watching two screens on which they saw Williams enter the room followed by a shaven headed uniformed sergeant with the size and the attitude of a bear with anger management issues.

'Oh shit" said Carver. 'It's Igor.'

'Who the hell – sorry, what the hell is Igor?' asked Chris.

'He's a legend. Used to be in the old Special Patrol Group, now in Tactical Support. He always insisted on being first out of the van in public order circumstances. Lovely guy once you get to know him.'

On screen the lovely guy pointed at a chair and issued a one word command to Williams; 'Sit'. Williams sat. Igor stood above him and regarded his charge as though he were something that he'd wiped off his sole of his shoes.

'I've a question, Detective Inspector' said Ryan. 'You requested a big, ugly guy to escort the prisoner, obviously for purposes of intimidation, yet you were concerned that he was given a nice cup of tea. What's all that about?'

'The combination of warm liquid and fear means that Williams will very soon be needing to go wee wee. He's not going to like asking a woman for permission to go to the little boys room so he'll be in a state of some discomfort when I get round to talking with him. Advantage me.'

Goodchild entered the room.

'How long are we going to leave him there, Chris?'

'He's sweating already and looking twitchy. We don't want to be accused of intimidation so we should start now.'

Goodchild nodded his assent and Carver and Fearnley left the observation room. Entering interrogation one she thanked Igor who lumbered off with one last glare at Williams. The two police officers sat down facing Williams and Chris activated the recording equipment. She spoke in a clear, professional voice devoid of emotion stating time and date of the interview, identifying herself and Martin only as Detective Sergeant Fearnley and Detective Inspector Carver. Williams could not know who was who but would assume that as Chris was doing all the talking, she was the senior officer.

'Mr Williams' she began. 'You have been arrested this evening in connection with the murder of Catherine Taylor-Lodge. Do you have anything to say?'

'I don't know anyone called that. This is some kind of terrible mistake' stammered Williams.

Chris took an A5 colour photograph from her folder and placed it in front of Williams.

'Do you recognise this girl, Mr Williams?'

'Yes' he replied immediately. 'Her names Cath. She's American.'

'And how do you know her, Mr Williams?'

'We had drinks together a couple of times this summer in Fuerteventura.'

'For the record, Mr Williams had just identified Catherine Taylor-Lodge as a girl he met in Fuerteventura this year. How did you come to meet this girl, Mr Williams?'

'I was on the island working and my employer told me to look out for a single American female who was working for his competition. He said the Rock Café was the sort of venue where she was likely to be so I sort of got to know her.'

'I see. Who was your employer, Mr Williams?'

'I dealt with a gentleman called Rodney McNaughten but I think that he was a lawyer representing someone else.'

'And how did you meet McNaughten?'

'It was just a chance meeting in a bar.'

'Which bar?'

'Turnmills in Farringdon. We got talking and I told him I had a marketing company. He said that he might have need of someone in the future so I gave him my card.'

'Do you have his card, Mr Williams?'

'No, I remember now. He was embarrassed that he had run out of cards but it didn't matter 'cos he called me and we had a meeting and I got the contract.'

'When and where was the meeting?'

'We met in the bar at Euston Station. I don't remember the exact date but it'll be written down in my office diary.'

'I see. What was this contract for?'

'It was a very basic market research job. I had to go round all the bars and restaurants that advertised in the freebie publications on the island and find out what they were paying. Then I had to keep an eye out for this American girl.'

'And you found her?'

'No. I had a call from McNaughten asking for how I was getting on. I told him about Cath and, I remember this well because he used an inappropriate word, he asked what colour she was. When I said that she was white he called me off and said that the American was a Negress. He then told me to cut my visit short and go back to the UK to write my report.'

'Where are McNaughten's offices, Mr Williams?'

'I only ever met him three times, each time in London. I don't know where his offices are.'

'You don't find that odd, Mr Williams?'

'Look, I worked for one week in the sun and was paid for the two I'd contracted for plus my expenses. I'm not complaining.'

'How were you paid?'

'Cash. McNaughten had sorted out my flight and hotel mind you.'

'Where did you stay?'

'Oh God, I don't remember exactly. It was on the main street into Corralejo. Not a very smart place but it was OK to rest my head at the end of the night.'

'Did you ever take Cath back to this mystery hotel, Mr Williams?'

'No! No, it wasn't like that! We had a few beers, a chat and listened to the band.'

'On more than one occasion though, did you not?'

'Twice, in one week. That's it.'

'Come on, Mr Williams. She's a very pretty girl. You must have been interested.'

'I offered to walk her home but she refused. Said her place was nearby, she did, and went off on her own.'

'So you let this beautiful girl you've spent two nights drinking and chatting with head off into the night alone. You didn't follow her to see she was all right, did you?'

'No. A girl says no, it's no.'

'Get a lot of 'no's' do you, Mr Williams?'

'What's that supposed to mean?'

'Changing the subject for the moment. How well do you know Tony Guest?'

'I can't say I know him. I've heard him play many a time but we've never actually spoken.'

'When have you seen his act then?'

'Lots of pubs and clubs in England. My work means I have to travel a lot and if I stay overnight I get the local paper to see if there are any gigs happening. If Tony's in town I always go and see him.'

'You must have been well pleased to find that he was playing in Corralejo at the same time as you were there then.'

'Too right, I was.'

'You did not find it a bit odd, a bit coincidental then, Mr Williams?'

'Didn't cross my mind.'

'Right. When was the last time you saw Guest play, exactly?'

'Now you mention it, it must have been in Corralejo. I can't recall seeing him in the listings recently.'

'Is that the only thing you read, Mr Williams? The music listings in the local rag.'

'Well, yeah. If you buy a newspaper that can cost up to two hundred and sixty pounds a year.'

'Don't you watch television, Mr Williams?'

'Not a lot. I try not to miss Britain's Got Talent and the X Factor. Some of the Freeview channels have reruns of Top of the Pops from the seventies and eighties. I like those, I do.'

'So you don't watch the national news at all?'

'No; it's only news if its miserable and it's all lies anyway. What's my television viewing got to do with anything?'

'Interview suspended at nineteen thirty hours.'

Chris switched off the recording equipment and sat back staring into Williams' face. She gave nothing away as to what she was thinking but her unrelenting gaze had Williams squirming in his seat. Eventually he looked down at his lap and said 'This is all wrong, this is.'

Chris picked up the phone in front of her and said. 'Could you send someone to escort Mr Williams back to his holding cell, please? Thanks.'

The interview room remained silent but is was a serious silence, the kind one feels just before something unpleasant is about to happen. The door opened and a uniformed P.C, not Igor, appeared to take Williams away.

'We are going to check what you have told us, Mr Williams' said Chris. 'Right now police officers are searching your home and office. If your diary and phone records back up what you have said then everything is fine. If, however, we find that you have been lying to us, well, we will find ourselves having to examine your life in much more detail. Take him away, constable.'

Carver and Fearnley rejoined Goodchild and Ryan in the observation room. They all looked at one another waiting for someone to start.

'What's your feeling on this guy, Chris?' asked Goodchild. 'That was one weird story.'

'I'm not going to go with feelings, boss. I want to chase down the evidence. Who is this McNaughten fellow? Williams reckons he's a lawyer and a gentleman so what the hell was he doing in a place like Turnmills?'

'Sorry to interrupt' said Ryan. 'What is this Turnmills place?'

'It's a nightclub for the younger crowd up in Farringdon. Loud music, weird décor, several gay nights a week and open until silly o'clock in the morning. Anyone can get in so there won't be a members list to check. I wonder if Williams is gay.'

'Irrelevant at the moment' said Goodchild. 'I think Chris is right. We need to chase down all these details and see what the search in Preston turns up. This phone will also throw up numbers used by McNaughten so the techs are in for a long night. Do you intend having another crack at Williams this evening, Chris?'

'Yes. I'm going to crank up the pressure any way I can; see what else I can squeeze from him. He's being co-operation personified but I feel there's more to come.'

'For your information, the Sun is going front page with this story tomorrow and that will be announced on News at Ten tonight. That might help concentrate his mind.'

'Damn! The media circus hits town again' said Chris. 'I take it that Addison will be dealing with that?'

'Yes. Martin; you're very quiet. What are your thoughts on Williams?'

'I think he's innocent, a dupe in some sick bastard's game. Let's go back to what was said at the embassy this afternoon. Dominic Lord equals magister ludi. Does no one find it strange that the name of the person who sent Williams to Fuerteventura and pulled his strings was named McNaughten?'

'Shit, you're right, Martin' said Goodchild. 'We are being played.'

'Sorry, guys' said Ryan. 'I know the name. It came up in law school but that was a while back. Could you refresh my memory on it?'

'In 1843 a man named McNaughten tried to murder the Prime Minister, Robert Peel' said Carver. 'He mistakenly killed his secretary instead. At his trial he was acquitted as he was deemed to be insane and not able to distinguish between right and wrong. Since then, one of the grounds for an insanity defence has been known as the McNaughten rule. It applies in the UK, Australia, Canada, New Zealand and most U.S states.'

'I agree it's strange, Martin' said Goodchild. 'But what's his point? What's his goal?'

'We've just locked a guy up for thirty years and he is still our number one suspect in another eight murders, including Catherine. Tonight the main television news is going to quote a Sun exclusive saying that we are questioning another British national in relation to these murders. How are the Met going to look after that, boss?'

'Guest confessed to three murders but denies killing Catherine' said Goodchild. 'What if we have two killers? Maybe Williams planted Catherine's phone number on Guest during his visit to Fuerteventura. Chris is right. We have to squeeze this bugger till the pips squeak.'

'I need a time line, boss' said Chris. 'Going back five years I want to know where Guest was, where Williams was and where any documentation in the name of Dominic Lord or Rodney McNaughten was used. Finally, whenever the presence of two or more of these characters coincide, is there a trace of a fifth party that we do not know about?'

'You've got it, Chris. I'll head back to the Yard and get this moving. Call if you need anything else. Kevin; I'll see you to your car.'

Ryan would have preferred to have remained at Paddington Green but took the hint graciously.

'Thanks, Mark' he said. 'I need to report back to Washington. When are you next going to speak to Williams, Detective Inspector?'

'No later than twenty one fifty five hours. I don't want him to miss News at Ten.'

'Fine. Could we all meet up tomorrow for a progress review? The US media have stringers or full sized bureaus over here and the Williams situation will make the lunchtime news back home.'

'Good idea, Kevin' said Goodchild. 'I'll give you a call later tonight and we'll set it up.'

The American and the Englishman left the room together. Once they had gone, Carver turned to Fearnley and asked 'Now what do you really think, Chris?'

'There is no way on Christ's earth that Williams is an organised serial killer. He's a seedy little man with pretentions of adequacy but this McNaughten guy has manoeuvred him into our sights. We're going to have the media all over us, Martin but I can't see a way out. We'll have to follow procedure and carry on as though this muppet were a serious suspect. To be honest, I don't see any point in continuing to interview Williams but we have to dot the i's and cross the t's to cover out collective arses. Any ideas?'

'To repeat what I said before; we are being played. Why, I don't know nor do I care. Right now though, we are on the back foot and will remain there as long as ML uses the media to make us look bad. My belief is that we are up against a single, resourceful psychopath and we will catch him either by him making, or having made, a mistake or by good, old fashioned police work. The problems we have are that Goodchild is no longer thinking clearly and the Yanks plus our top brass are responding to political pressure. It's down to us, Chris.'

'Great; I love a challenge. Any suggestions as to how we proceed?'

'Well, we're committed to interviewing Williams tonight. I agree it's a waste of time but we have to go through the motions. Let me ask you a question. When you put the squeeze on Richard Waterman, what impression did he give you of Dominic Lord?'

Chris Fearnley did not reply immediately. She withdrew into herself and gave the question the consideration it was due. After a minute's thought she replied.

'Waterman's been around the block a few times and is no mug. He's impressed by Lord, views him as someone to look up to, a gentleman. A man of substance.'

'A source of money, in other words. A man who flies in and out, rents villas and hires staff. How would such a man travel, Chris?'

'First or business class of course.'

'But we don't have a record of Dominic Lord flying back to the UK when Catherine was killed so that means…?'

'Private plane!'

'Call your friend Richard now. Let's see if he remembers how his esteemed client Dominic Lord liked to travel.'

Chris retrieved Waterman's number from her cell and called him on the landline. The conversation was brief and ended with her instructing the man to forget that it had ever taken place. Hanging up, she turned to face Carver.

'You were right, Lord wangled a private flight to the UK and returned twenty four hours later the same way. Did no one think to check private aviation? Jesus!'

'It's just not something you'd associate Fuerteventura with. It's not exactly Monaco, is it?'

Anyway, it gives us something to chase down. Let's move it further. If you use a private jet, how do you get from the airport to your destination?'

'When Lord returned to Fuerteventura Waterman picked him up.'

'Yes, but what about the UK end? Unless he had a vehicle in the long stay car park then we are looking at a private hire limo service.'

'Or a black cab.'

'No. That does not fit with the private jet image and serial killers all have narcissistic tendencies. It's 'look at me' writ large. We need some donkey work done here.'

'I'll call Michelle. She's worth any six of those cretins in Orion.'

'Tell her to keep it to herself and give her a heads up on what News at Ten are going to announce tonight – if the boss hasn't told her already that is.'

'Right you are. Then it's time for a pre-supper drink before we have another stab at Williams. Up for it?'

'Always.'

Chapter Forty Two

When Carver and Fearnley returned to Paddington Green to resume their questioning of Williams they were in possession of much more information than before thanks to the efforts of Michelle Stone at Scotland Yard and the Lancaster constabulary in Preston.

They reconvened in Interview one at twenty one forty five hours. Williams was already there with a uniformed escort who Chris Fearnley dismissed. As she and Carver took their seats the Welshman started to speak. 'Look, I want…'

'Please do not talk until the recording equipment has been activated' said Fearnley. 'This is for your protection as I'm sure even a mug like you can understand.'

She then started up the machine and stated the date, time and names of those present.

'Now then, before you tell us what you want' she began 'let me give you some background information. Records show that you are quite often present in a town where Tony Guest is performing. Do you have any idea where he is tonight or has been for the last six months?'

'No. How could I?'

'Then you must be about the only man outside of a closed order monastery who doesn't. Look at this.'

She handed over a copy of the Daily Post which carried a full face photo of Tony Guest accompanied by the headline 'Musician Admits Killing of Three Girls'. In smaller type was the line 'Seven More Victims Still Missing'. 'See pages 4,5,6,7,8 and 9.'

'This has been one of the biggest news stories of this year' said Chris. 'Do you seriously expect us to believe that this is the first time you've heard about it?'

'I told you, I don't buy newspapers or watch the news I…'

'You frequent music venues all the time. Surely this came up in conversation.'

'I don't really talk to people at gigs. I drink on my own and listen to the music. That's it.'

'You work in marketing; communications skills are vital. You're telling me that this subject never came up in conversation.'

'I don't socialise with clients. I go in, study their requirements then make my report. That's what I'm paid for.'

'You must be great fun at dinner parties. OK. Watch this.'

Chris switched on a small television set that had been positioned so that all three people in the room could watch it. The familiar intro music of News at Ten filled the room and the authoritative tones of Mark Austin began to summarise the day's events. He led with the story that the Sun newspaper had received information indicating that Tony Guest was innocent of the murders to which he had been forced to confess and that police had arrested a Preston businessman in connection with the murder of an American girl in Fuerteventura which may have links to the 'fingers in the Park' killings earlier in the year. Aiden Hartley of the Sun was interviewed and, whilst not giving many details away, left the viewers in no doubt that his paper believed the story to be true and that a full account would be in tomorrow's edition.

Deputy Assistant Commissioner Addison appeared to make a brief statement to the effect that a man was indeed 'helping the police with their enquiries' into the murder of Catherine Taylor-Lodge and that the Metropolitan Police were liaising with the Spanish and American authorities. He then refused to take questions and hurried away from the cameras.

ITN devoted ten minutes to the story which raised questions about miscarriage of justice, the death penalty, the American judicial system and the competence of the Metropolitan Police.

The story ended and the newscasters moved on to the crisis in the Eurozone. Chris switched the set off.

'You're going to be famous' said Chris. 'Sooner or later the media are going to get hold of your name and your life is going to change. Anything you'd care to tell me at this point?'

'I think I need a lawyer.'

'You may well do and it is your right to phone for one now and to say nothing further to me. However, once you go down that route I shall charge you with murder, you will be remanded in custody to await trial and we are then obliged to make your name public. At the moment your status is someone who has been arrested and who is helping us with our enquiries. If you can convince me that you are innocent then you will be released without charge and that's an end to it. Your call.'

'What do you want to know?'

'Let's start at the beginning when you met Rodney McNaughten in Turnmills. Tell me everything you can remember about that and subsequent meetings or telephone conversations.'

Chris went over the same ground as before, interrupting Williams now and then for clarification of some point or other. It was classic police interrogation technique. Williams' answers would be compared to what he had said during his first interview and any discrepancies would be seized upon.

After forty five minutes of going back and forth, Chris terminated the interview and summoned an escort.

'That's all for tonight' she said. 'You're probably tired so this officer is going to take you back to your cell and organise some supper for you. By tomorrow I'll have a more detailed account of where you have been recently and we'll have another chat after breakfast. Goodnight.'

Williams stood up wearily. He looked drained both mentally and physically. As he was being led away he turned his head over his shoulder and said to Chris. 'I did not do this. I don't know what's going on but I did not do this.' There were tears in his eyes.

Chris took the two tape recordings out of the machine, placed them in evidence bags and signed the outside. One copy would be for the police and the other for Williams should he ever be formally charged.

'Poor bastard' said Chris. 'What now, Martin?'

'I'd better contact Goodchild then someone should talk with the Americans. Give me a few minutes will you?'

Carver called the Yard to learn that Goodchild had left for the day so he contacted him on his cell and gave him a quick breakdown of the second interview with Williams. Goodchild heard him out and then gave him authority to contact the FBI. They arranged to meet at Paddington Green at eight the following morning.

Ryan was still at his embassy and thanked Carver for calling him. After giving him a much less detailed summary of the interview he agreed to the American's request to be present at the next day's meeting.

'Do you think Michelle Stone's got anything on private planes and limos yet, Chris?'

'No. She'd have contacted us if she had. I'd bet she's with Goodchild right now.'

'This is bullshit. Their relationship is starting to have a negative impact of the effectiveness of this investigation.'

'There's nothing we can do without dropping them in it, Martin. As you said, it's down to us and we are, as they say, resource poor.'

'So let's get some more resources. When I was in the army we were forever scrounging kit from the Americans. I think we can apply that principle here.'

'How so?'

'Call Ryan and let him know that we think Dominic Lord was using private aviation as a means to travel between the UK and Fuerteventura. He'll not even need a request for help – he'll just pick up that ball and run with it.'

'I like it. Do we let him know our thinking on private limos as well?'

'No. He should be bright enough to work that out for himself and, anyway, we are better placed to chase the UK car firms than him.'

'You're right. Do you want me to make the call?'

'I'll do it, Chris. I'm still officially the liaison officer between our two outfits and it would look strange if my junior officer passed on this sort of material.'

'You're right again. If you catch him now he might even have something for us by tomorrow morning. Go for it.'

Carver called the American embassy and Ryan was still there. He briefly informed the FBI man of his thinking, emphasising that it was just an idea which they had not run to ground yet. The American duly thanked him and offered nothing further but, as soon as the conversation was over, he went into an adjoining office to get his team moving.

'Listen up people' he announced. 'The Brit cop who was here today has just been on the phone and he's come up with an interesting angle. He thinks that this Dominic Lord character may have been renting private planes to fly between the UK and Fuerteventura. I want that checked out now. There's no way he could pay cash for something like this so, if we find the company, we can trace his financials and maybe get an address for the mutt.'

'This won't take long, sir' said a young agent. 'I spent a couple of weeks on that island and, believe me, private planes are not an everyday occurrence.'

'Glad to hear it. Find the plane, find the crew and find the financials. I'm back at Paddington Green tomorrow morning and would love to show the Brits how to gather information. Right now I'm going to hit the sack. I'm staying here tonight and can be woken for emergencies only.'

He laid emphasis on the word 'emergency', leaving his team in no doubt that he expected them to deal with media enquiries and other ephemera.

Back at Paddington Green Carver and Fearnley signed out of the high security station and found themselves at a loose end.

'Fancy some supper, Chris?'

'Yes but I've got to get back to my place tonight. Tomorrow's important and when the Sun hits the streets the shit will hit the fan. God knows who we'll end up meeting so I need a change of clothes.'

'May I remind you that there is a suitcase full of female attire back at my place? Something needs to be done about that before my cleaning lady comes on Wednesday'.

'Buggeration! I totally forgot. Sorry, Martin. This case is becoming a bit all consuming.'

'No apologies required. Shall we find a cab?'

'Lead on, you silver tongued fox.'

As the two officers set off to wind down after what had been an eventful day, the other actors in the drama were reacting in their own different ways to the News at Ten bombshell.

ML was at his home and was well pleased with the media reaction that his phone call to the Sun had generated. He would wait for a few days to see how the different parties involved reacted before adding more fuel to the fire. If the great British public became convinced that Tony Guest had been pressured into confessing to murders which he had not committed then a bandwagon would start to roll. Inevitably the politicians of the left and the few newspapers still of that persuasion would leap upon it aided and abetted by the BBC. The Home Secretary and the Prime Minister would face tough questions in Parliament. Resignations would be required, perhaps that of the Metropolitan Police Commissioner himself.

If the Crown Prosecution Service then proceeded to trial against Ian Williams and he were found guilty that would be perfect. ML could then release proof of Williams's innocence and the whole fuss would re-ignite. The Americans would still not have solved the killing of Catherine Taylor-Lodge so would blame the incompetence of the British Police and judicial system in order to cover their collective backsides. This could run and run.

Another happy chappy was Aiden Hartley. He was the man of the hour and was holding court in one of his favourite watering holes, Ye Olde Cheshire Cheese in Fleet Street. There he and his journalistic drinking pals from the days prior to the advent of computers were ensconced in the front downstairs bar. It being winter a real fire glowed redly in the hearth, adding to the old world atmosphere that was definitely lacking from Wapping where most of England's newspapers were now printed.

'You know the best thing about your story, Aiden?' said a broken down hack whose nickname was Thirsty. 'The fact that I broke it?' replied Hartley to general laughter.

'Apart from that of course' said Thirsty. 'Can you imagine the scenes at the Daily Post? That insufferable arse Peter Balls has probably run out of swear words by now and the self anointed expert on serial killers that is Roger Tucker has enough egg on his face to make an omelette for every prostitute in Paris!'

'Tucker's a decent type, actually' said Hartley. 'We've raised a glass or two over the years and he's let me have the odd story when times were lean. I reckon he became rather too cosy with that super plod from the counter-terrorist section, Goodchild. Be interesting to see what angle the Post takes tomorrow.'

The man in question was at home with his wife trying to make sense of his fall from grace. Peter Balls had, indeed, gone ballistic when he discovered what the Sun was going to print. Enquiries made to Orion were referred to the Metropolitan Police press office which, in turn, merely quoted the brief statement as made by Deputy Assistant Commissioner Addison. The American embassy were quite happy to confirm that a man had been arrested in relation to Catherine Taylor-Lodge's murder but declined to comment on the claim that Tony Guest had made a false confession saying, quite rightly, that that was a matter for the British judicial system.

Roger Tucker's contacts at New Scotland Yard were decidedly cool towards him and Mark Goodchild still wasn't returning his calls.

On the other hand, television and radio stations were clamouring for an interview with Tucker so he was not returning their calls.

What really hurt was his final meeting with Balls. The editor had decided to pull Tucker's humorous piece which had been due to run the next day. It would be replaced with a boxed caption simply stating 'Roger Tucker is Away' as if he were on holiday. Balls dismissed him and gave him instructions to try and find something positive to say about the fiasco the Tony Guest story had become. As Tucker was leaving his editor's office with as much dignity as he could muster the great man said to the journalist 'It's all my fault. I should have known better than to entrust a major crime story to the fucking in-house comedian.'

So Tucker was feeling low when he arrived home and started to guzzle red wine. It fell to his wife, Sharon, to lift him up.

'Don't worry, love' she said. 'It's only temporary and you've all but finished your book.'

'Yes, of course. All I have to do is change the title for something like 'How to fuck up without really trying'. It's dead, Sharon, as dead as disco.'

'You're wrong. Roger. It's changed, that's the truth of the matter. What you need is a different intro to the book explaining that it's the story of how an honest journalist and an innocent musician were victims of a set up. Then see what happens with this new guy who's been arrested and there you have a new ending. Come on; your glass is always half full.'

Tucker looked down into his glass as if he were Nostradamus practising divination. Presently he looked up at his wife.

'You're right. I need to talk to my publisher first thing tomorrow and I also need to persuade Balls to keep me on this story. He'll love the 'attack is the best form of defence' angle. Thanks, kid. Now, in the immortal word of Bob Dylan – bring that bottle over here.'

'It's a long time since we were kids, Roger' laughed Sharon. 'Does this mean that, later tonight?'

'I'll be yours? Depends how much wine we get through.'

If Roger Tucker had moved from despair to optimism the same could not be said of the upper echelons of the Metropolitan Police.

Because the Sun had managed to keep its story to itself prior to letting News at Ten know, all other national newspapers had been printed and distributed. They were therefore left to play catch-up and were putting as much pressure as they could on various institutions to try and get an edge on their competitors.

Because of the political ramifications of the story, many journalists were calling the press office of Ten Downing Street which redirected them to their equivalents at the Home Office or the Justice Ministry.

Prime Minister David Cameron knew that questions would be raised in the House of Commons if not the next day then certainly on Wednesday when he was due for his weekly thirty minutes grilling known as Questions to the Prime Minister, or PMQ's. He therefore instructed his relevant ministers to be on top of their brief for this at the next day's Cabinet meeting.

This instruction in turn led to the country's top police officer, Sir Alan Sampson, having his evening interrupted and thence, on the 'shit rolls downhill' principle, to Oliver Addison.

Addison duly contacted Goodchild who informed him on the state of play, that Orion was still working shifts to identify the unknown English girls, that interrogation of Ian Williams would resume in the morning and that, no, he did not intend returning to the office tonight as he could see no point in doing so.

Not knowing how to proceed Addison did what he did best;

he wrote a report which he emailed to Sir Alan. He then sat down to plot the shifting of blame for this cock-up onto that bloody impertinent Goodchild.

His day then became worse when the press office called him up to say that the breakfast television shows were all demanding someone senior to interview at some unholy hour tomorrow morning. Knowing that Sir Alan would not touch that with a barge pole he realised that it was odds on that he would have to rise at sparrow fart to defend the Met's position on live TV. He therefore decided to spend the night in the office, thankful that he always kept a spare dress uniform for emergencies.

The phone lines were humming in Washington DC and New York City as well. Kevin Ryan's report had started to filter its way around the capital and Catherine's former home city. Because of the interest shown in the situation by the Attorney General and the President, the FBI had no option but to inform those two offices of the developments in the UK. There was no way to keep this information quiet given the sizes of the staff in the respective offices. At a senior level leaks to the press were used selectively to gain political advantage. This is usually done responsibly. Those lower down the food chain are not as discriminate and leak like a Pakistani sewage pipe in order to make themselves look important. As the time difference between London and the east coast of America is only five hours the 'breaking news' that a Britisher had been arrested in connection with the murder of the senator's daughter was hitting TV screens by seven in the evening, local time.

The American media then went into overdrive trying to obtain further information from London only to be told that they would have to wait until tomorrow when everyone had woken up. Not being used to rebuff's, a pissed off American media took a uniformly anti-British stance in its reporting. Tomorrow looked like being an interesting day.

Carver and Fearnley arrived by taxi at Paddington Green on the stroke of seven in the morning. Chris was wearing a lightweight navy blue trouser suit with a white cotton shirt. On a lot of women this would have looked mannish but it only emphasised her femininity. It also looked professional on the off chance that she found herself facing TV cameras. She had also retrieved her luggage from Carver's apartment meaning to drop it off at her own place when she had a moment.

Carver was wearing blue Levi's, a Guinness rugby shirt, a short, black leather jacket and had not shaved that morning. He had no intention of going on television.

They grabbed some coffee from the canteen and settled down in Interview one to await Goodchild's and Ryan's arrival. The small TV set from yesterday was still there so they passed the time watching Oliver Addison being beaten up on breakfast television.

'I've never understood the format of these programmes' said Carver. 'They start off with the most serious topic of the day then move on to something like 'is your pet psychic'. This is followed by some musician I've never heard of talking about their latest record, having survived rehab etc etc and it all ends with the sport and a useless weather forecast. Repeat at half hourly intervals. What bollocks.'

'It's television, Martin. They don't do 'in depth' in the morning. Given the average civilians attention span, thirty minutes is quite good. All they're doing is following the format of a tabloid newspaper; news human interest, pop and sport.'

'I suppose you're right. Addison's sweating a bit, isn't he?'

'He's not in control of the agenda, that's why. Plus this is live and he's having to think on his feet. Not his forte in my opinion.'

'Agreed. A poor performance and any chance he ever had of the top job is history. Have you checked on Williams yet, Chris?'

'Yes. He did not get much sleep last night but I'm told that he's reasonably calm. He's abluted and having breakfast now. I told them to wheel him in at eight thirty.'

'Good. Hopefully the boss will have some news from Orion for us otherwise we're just spinning our wheels here.'

At that moment the door opened and Goodchild walked in. He was in uniform, which was a rare occurrence, so he was anticipating the possibility of going in front of the cameras too.

'Morning, Chris. Morning, Martin.'

'Morning, boss' replied Carver for both of them. 'You're early.'

'I thought we'd have a chat before the FBI arrive. Martin; what's with the Serpico look?'

'Unless something dramatic breaks this morning I reckon I'm better employed going over to Belmarsh to have a chat with Guest – see what he has to say about the story in today's Sun. He will relate more to this look than a spick and span copper.'

'Fair enough, I suppose. What are your plans for today, Chris?'

'I'm hoping that Michelle will have something for us on private aviation and limos but I've not heard from her.'

'Yes, well, sore point that is. I've just come from the Yard – I wanted to see how the night shift had got on. Before Michelle left for the evening she handed her work over to two other DS's. They've got nowhere. They claimed that none of the aviation companies – no; forget what they claimed, it's all just lame excuses for a lack of drive and competence. I might as well have Community Support Officers on the case. Anyway, Michelle's back on it and will call me as soon as she has something.'

'I'll look forward to that' said Chris. 'In the absence of new information all I can do is show Williams what's in the Sun and go over yesterday's ground again. We are not going to impress the American's with that sort of effort.'

'How did your conversation with the FBI go last night, Martin?'

'I spoke briefly with Ryan and let him know our thinking regarding private aviation. I would not bet against him finding the flight details before us.'

'Oh, why's that?'

'If someone hires a private plane they have to file a flight plan. Imagine that you're a rich bugger en route to Nice from London and you receive a call saying that you're needed in Malaga. You'd simply inform the flight crew of the change in plan and pay for the extra mileage. Dominic Lord has been very good at staying invisible and I reckon that he'll have booked the flight using a company credit card and the only record that exists is when he actually landed in Fuerteventura. The Yanks still have people on the ground there who can get that information from the locals. We don't.'

'Shit, you're right! Did you tell Ryan about your idea on private limo companies?'

'No, boss. I thought I'd keep that for us but I expect Ryan's people to think of it anyway.'

'OK it's now seven forty five and Ryan's due here at eight. I'm going to get a cup of tea and I'll see you soon.'

Goodchild left the interview room. Carver and Fearnley had nothing more to say so they used the remaining time examining Aiden Hartley's article in the Sun looking for an angle to use on Williams. Just after eight Goodchild returned accompanied by Kevin Ryan.

For a man who had slept the night in his office and was under intense political pressure from his superiors, the American looked disgustingly fresh. After initial greetings he got down to business.

'DCI Carver; good call on the private aviation. We have a break. My people in Fuerteventura have a record of Dominic Lord landing by private jet on Tuesday and leaving again on the following Thursday morning, again by private jet. This ties in with what your bar owner said to us, DI Fearnley and gives us a window for Catherine's time of death. The company that flew Lord is a British one and won't give out any details of passengers to us. They keep quoting the data protection act to my guys. Anything you can do to help, Commander?'

CHAPTER FORTY TWO

'Too bloody right there is. Have you brought the details with you?'

'Sure. I emailed all this to you at the Yard this morning but I figured you might not have picked it up yet. Here's a printout.'

Ryan handed a single sheet of paper to Goodchild who excused himself and left the office.

'If you don't mind me asking' said the American 'but why don't you guys have portable email access?'

'We do' said Chris taking a Blackberry from her jacket. 'Just try and imagine operating one of these when you have hands the size of Commander Goodchild's.'

'Ah, right. He is quite a big guy.'

The 'big guy' returned with a grin on his face.

'DS Stone is about to ruin some chief executive's breakfast. I've told her that if they piss her about she can invoke the name of Sir Alan Sampson, who sits at God's left hand.'

'So what's next?' asked Ryan,

'Williams is due to be interviewed for the third time at eight thirty' said Chris. 'To be honest, I don't expect much. I've compared his first two interviews and they don't vary in any significant way. I'm going to let him read the Sun and see how he reacts then I'll take it from there.'

'In other words, you'll wing it.'

'No, Mr Ryan. I'll improvise and adapt as any competent police officer would.'

'Let's go next door to the observation suite, Mr Ryan' said Goodchild. 'Williams should be arriving soon.'

As the two senior men left the room Carver and Fearnley exchanged a look and he gave her a surreptitious wink. She raised her eyebrows, put on her most innocent face and mouthed the word 'moi?'

They took their usual places and awaited the arrival of Williams.

As one would expect at Paddington Green he was brought in exactly on time. He sat.

'Good morning, Mr Williams' said Chris.

'Hi'

The man was having trouble holding himself together. He'd developed a tremor in his right hand and his head seemed to be too heavy for him to hold upright. He'd shrunken into himself and was squinting despite the room's lighting being fairly gentle. Chris had to decide whether to go hard or soft on him and had to make that decision now. She reckoned the hard approach would make the wimp breakdown and the interview would be over before it started so she went in gently. She could ramp it up later.

'Sleep alright, Mr Williams?'

'More or less.'

'I understand. Not exactly the Hilton, I know. Have you been fed yet?'

'Yes. It's all very correct here, it is.'

'Good, good. Now I'm going to activate the recording equipment and we'll start the interview.

She went through the usual procedure then picked up a copy of the current edition of the Sun and passed it across the table.

'Now, Mr Williams; this is what has brought you to our attention. Please read the article – take your time then we'll talk.'

Williams pulled the newspaper to himself and began to read. His brow furrowed and he began to chew his lower lip. He turned from the lurid cover to pages four and five where what passes for in depth reporting in the Sun was carried. His nerves were fraying and he started to wipe his face as the anxiety mounted. Finally he finished and raised his eyes to look at Chris Fearnley.

'This is bad, this is' he said.

'It gets worse, Mr Williams' said Fearnley. 'Please turn to the editorial column. I've marked it with a post it note.'

He did so. Fully three quarters of the editorials were given over to Tony Guest's imprisonment and what its implications were for the British judicial system in general and the Metropolitan Police's efficiency in particular. Once again, he looked up to meet Chris Fearnley's implacable gaze.

'As you can see, Mr Williams, this case has become even more important than before. The reputation of the Police Service has been besmirched and, in the days to come, the cries for an explanation will become more strident. The opinion of many people here is that Guest is guilty of the English murders. Two reasons for that; he admitted to it in court and, secondly, we have not been able to place you and Guest together at the same time and place as when two of the identified victims disappeared. Having said that, some people think that you were aware of Guest's activities, that you are the ML who sent the initial email to Roger Tucker and that you followed Guest to Fuerteventura where you killed Catherine Taylor-Lodge intending that he would ultimately take the fall.'

'That's madness, that is! Who is ML? Who is Roger Tucker?'

'Sorry, I forgot. You don't read newspapers or watch current affairs programmes on TV. You nearly got away with it, you know. If the FBI had not been able to reconstruct your shredded business card we would never have even known of your connection to Catherine.'

'I did not have a connection as you put it!'

'You told us that you spent two evenings with her, Mr Williams. Detectives count that as a connection. Can you see how this is looking from our point of view? If you cannot explain yourself better than you have up to now then I'll tell you what's going to happen. Guest will stay in prison and you will stand trial for the murder of Catherine. The Americans will bring all their power to bear to have you extradited to New York and we will not stand in their way. Conceivably the Spanish could claim jurisdiction but I reckon that they won't want the hassle of opposing the USA. Look forward to wearing bright orange clothes for a while, Mr Williams.'

Williams had lost what little spirit he had left in him. For the first time he realised the seriousness of his situation. Fearnley and Carver sat back in silence and observed as Williams' brain processed the information it had received. It was a slow process but they were not in any hurry. Finally, Williams came out of his catatonia.

'What more can I tell you?'

'The truth would be nice. You claim that you were hired to go to Fuerteventura by a lawyer you met by chance at a nightclub. Well the Law Society has no record of a Rodney McNaughten anywhere in England or Wales. Explain that would you, Mr Williams?'

'I can't. Hang on; he booked my flight and hotel. Surely you could find a record of that?'

'We checked that. It was a package deal booked at Thomas Cook in Old Brompton Road, paid for in cash. You tend to operate in cash, don't you, Mr Williams?'

'Yes. I've never trusted credit cards and if you book things online you get your identity stolen.'

'It must be difficult living in the twenty first century with that sort of attitude. Right; moving on. Do you know a man called Richard Waterman?'

'No. Should I?'

'He owns one of the top music bars in Corralejo so I would have thought that your market research job would have brought you into contact with him.'

'Well it didn't. I'd only scratched the surface when Rodney McNaughten cut the contract short.'

'I see. What about Dominic Lord? Does that name ring a bell with you?'

'No.'

The door opened and Mark Goodchild came in the room.

'Commander Goodchild has just entered the room' said Chris for the benefit of the audio record.

Williams looked up at the unsmiling bulk of a Metropolitan Police Commander in full uniform and did a fair impression of a rabbit caught in the glare of a car's headlights. Goodchild passed a note to Fearnley who read it then handed it back. Goodchild left without a glance at Williams.

'Commander Goodchild has left the room' said Chris. 'This is the big question, Mr Williams and I want you to think carefully about it before you answer. How on earth did your business card end up in the shredding machine in Catherine's villa?'

Williams shook his head and started in on his lower lip again. 'I can't explain that...'

'Mr Williams; I asked you to think before answering. Now think.'

Williams took a deep breath, closed his eyes and put his head in his hands with his elbows on the table. After a minute he came up for air.

'First off, I never went to Cath's villa so I did not drop it. I did not give a card to Cath so it's not her's and I never gave one to Tony Guest. I did give out quite a few cards to business owners in Corralejo so it's possible that one of them is your killer.'

'And this mysterious business owner just happens to use the same exotic poison that killed ten English girls over a period of years? I don't think that one flies, do you Mr Williams? You had better come up with a more plausible explanation than that. Interview suspended at zero nine zero five hours.'

'For your information, Mr Williams, the contents of your office have been brought to London and a team is going through your paperwork and hard drive now. I'll see you this afternoon. Constable.'

A uniformed PC led Williams away and Chris stood up to stretch. Goodchild and Ryan joined the two detectives.

'What time do you want to start the next interview, DI Fearnley?' asked Goodchild.

'Mid afternoon at the earliest, sir. I want him to sweat some more whilst I go through the material that has been retrieved from his office. Your note said that we have details on the private plane that was used by Dominic Lord.'

'Yes. He had to pay by credit card so we now have banking details for Lord. All correspondence went to that Asian corner shop in the east end but there has to be a source of funds to back the card up. DS Stone has that under control. Anything you'd like to ask before we break up here, Mr Ryan.'

'Yes. Have any of you ever been involved in a real serial killer investigation before?'

All three British officers replied in the negative.

'Fine. I have. It's not always the case that the Bureau is called in. Murder, even multiple murder, is not a federal crime. But kidnapping and killing in more than one state is so we are trained to investigate these cases. Now nobody's said it in so many words, but listening to your interviews and watching your expressions I get the feeling that you don't think this Williams guy has it in him to be a killer. You could be wrong. If we were in the States we would consider there to be sufficient evidence to charge him with Catherine's murder and I'd bet the farm on a jury returning a guilty verdict. I'm going to say as much in my next report to DC. Be prepared for an extradition request is my advice.'

'Thanks for your frankness, Mr Ryan' said Goodchild. 'I'll see you to your car. I'll see you two at the Yard at one.'

Once Goodchild and Ryan had left Chris turned to Martin and said 'What a prat. 'Have any of you ever been involved in a real serial killer investigation before?' No, sir. Only the unreal ones I fantasise about. Yankee Tosser.'

'The FBI are used to lording over their state police forces. It does make them somewhat arrogant. When he asked his bullshit question I felt like replying 'no, I live in a country with a much smaller population of inbred psychos than you do'. The arsehole is going to recommend extradition is he? That may well come back to haunt him. Look, I've got to get back to Belmarsh and talk with Tony Guest. I'll see you back at the Yard as and when.'

'OK. I'm going to drop my gear off then go and see what progress Michelle has made.'

They split up at the front door to go in search of taxis. With the Americans about to put pressure on the British government to hand Williams over and the media moving up through the gears demanding explanations which could not be supplied, Carver and Fearnley were both aware that the fate of two men lay with them and that a killer remained at large.

Chapter Forty Three

Martin Carver sat in the bare box that served as an interview room at HMP Belmarsh. The plastic table had a rubber trim around its edge and was bolted to the floor. There was no way for it to be used as a weapon. On one side of the table was a padded bench, again secured to the floor, with enough room for two people to sit side by side. Carver was sat in a chair on the other side of the table. The only source of light came from a low wattage bulb in the ceiling which was protected by stout, steel wire. Even illumination was caged in Belmarsh. All the walls were grey, as was the ceiling and floor. It was like a sensory deprivation tank.

The door opened to admit a warden and Tony Guest. The prison officer left the room and locked the door behind him.

'Hi, Tony. How's it going?'

'I'm OK for now. They've got me in the hospital wing and are carrying out more psych tests on me. They said they'll decide where to put me at the end of the week. I don't know if they mean where in Belmarsh or where in the country.'

'If you stay here I'm going to make sure you're in with the nonces.'

'Fuck off, man! Why'd you do that to me?'

'Because you've confessed to killing three young girls and haven't given up their bodies. The hard men in here will target you.'

'I can handle myself, Martin.'

'Not in here you can't. It's not a fair fight you get. It's boiling water mixed with sugar thrown in your face. It's homemade blades and mass attacks. You can't survive that. I could get you transferred to Shrewsbury prison; make it easier for your wife to visit.'

'Thanks, but no thanks. She's a brave girl but this has hurt her. If I see her too often I'll be tempted to let her know what we're up to. OK put me with the poofs.'

'Have you seen a newspaper today, or watched the news at all, Tony?'

'No. Why?'

'Fucking arseholes. Have a look at this.'

Carver reached into his hip pocket where he had folded in four the relevant pages of that day's copy of the Sun. Guest devoured it with his eyes then looked at Carver.

'This is great, Martin! When do I get out?'

'I knew you'd say that. Slow down, mate. You have to stick with your story a little longer. The Yanks have lost interest in you now; that's the good news. The bad news is that the UK authorities are still convinced that you killed the English girls. On top of that, I don't think this new suspect killed anyone and that will come out sooner rather than later.'

'Martin, what the fuck is going on?'

'My belief is that there is a nutter out there who killed the English girls and the American one and has laid a false trail to your door and the other suspect's. Why? I don't know nor do I care; but we are close to catching him and he's made some mistakes that will lead us to him.'

'What happens if I tell my lawyer I lied and want a re-trial?'

'It's not certain that one would be granted. There is also the fact that the circumstantial evidence against you for the murders in Spain and England is very strong. My advice is to carry on as you are.'

'Easier said than done. Shit. When I saw the newspaper I thought that was it.'

'Yeah, I know. That's why I came to see you. I'm certain you're going to be asked by lots of people for your view on the article. Keep schtum, Tony.'

'OK Martin. Hey, I'll tell you what's really bad about being in this shit hole. I thought that the experience might inspire me to write something like Johnny Cash – you know?'

'Sure. Folsom Prison, San Quentin – all that good stuff.'

'Exactly. Well I opened my eyes today, my first morning as a bona fide convict and who came wailing through my mind? Tom Bloody Jones! 'I wake up and look around me, at four grey walls that surround me'. Hell, that must qualify as cruel and unusual punishment.'

'It's not unusual.'

'Fuck off, Martin.' Tony Guest, convicted murderer of three, facing thirty years inside, roared with laughter at Carver's witticism.

'Glad to see you've kept your sense of humour, pal.'

'It's what separates us from the beasts. Thanks for coming and letting me know what the score is. Have you any idea how long I'm going to be inside for?'

'It's complicated, Tony and I'd be lying if I were to give you even an approximation. Everything depends on us finding out who this Dominic Lord guy is. As I said, we're starting to pick up on his mistakes and I'm hoping that we'll have you out sooner rather than later. Hang in there.'

'Luckily for me they abolished hanging. But I take your point; I'm cool for now.'

Carver pressed a button on the wall and the same prison officer as before entered the room.

'I'm finished for now' said Carver. 'You may take the prisoner back to wherever you keep him. Is there someone available to escort me out?'

'If you would wait here, sir, I'll be back in a moment.'

Fifteen minutes later Carver was outside in the crisp winter air and decided to stretch his legs. This was not an area of London he was familiar with but his memory supplied him with a rough map so he set off in a north westerly direction and soon spotted the airplanes landing and taking off from London City Airport. Knowing that to be on the north side of the river, he angled left towards Canary Wharf passing the Thames flood barrier on his way.

Although he was only a few miles from his apartment as the crow flies, this was a section of the river that took great, meandering loops as the east end docklands headed towards the city proper. Historically, it was an interesting route but he did not have the latitude to indulge himself this day. The quickest way back to New Scotland Yard would be to use the Docklands Light Railway and the Tube but the frustration of changing lines always used to annoy him so he continued walking, sure in the knowledge that he'd pick up a black cab at some point. As it happened he did not manage to hail one until he was well inside the borough of Greenwich but traffic was kind to him so he arrived back at Victoria in time to have a pub lunch.

Just before one, Carver entered the Orion offices and was waved into the goldfish bowl by Goodchild. Fearnley and Stone were already there. The Commander closed the blinds on his office then invited the three officers to be seated.

'Whilst we've been playing silly buggers with the FBI' began Goodchild 'Michelle has been doing some good, old fashioned police work. Michelle; would you take over, please?'

She stood up and went to a flip chart which stood off to one corner of the room. She turned the covering page to reveal a list of dates, locations and initials which she had hand written in black marker pen.

'One of the problems we've had in this investigation' she said 'is that Tony Guest, because of the nature of his work and the fact that he is a disorganised piss-head, has been hard to nail down as to where he was at a certain time and a certain date. The information that Martin brought back from the man's wife is still being verified. Personally I think it will check out but some places will require a police visit because some folk are reluctant to talk about cash payments which may not correspond to their tax claims. I've only marked Guest as being present in a place when it can be proven through documentation i.e. flight tickets or payment records. I've applied the same criteria to Catherine Taylor-Lodge, Ian Williams and whoever is using the identity Dominic Lord. This chart is the result. Williams keeps meticulous records. He puts all his travel down as a business expense and I have bar receipts for items as small as a coke and a packet of peanuts. Another day's work and I can reconstruct his life for the past year at least, maybe even five years. For now I've concentrated on the period when Catherine appeared on our radar until the day her finger was sent to the American embassy. Finally, our Dominic Lord character has started to leave a trail. I'll go into that in a minute. If you look at the chart I think you'll agree that certain facts stand out.'

'First off Williams wasn't in Bristol when Catherine lunched with Lord' said Carver.

'How do you know that Lord was in Bristol on the Saturday though, Michelle?'

Lord booked the table for Sunday lunch at the Picture House. He was registered at the Cornhill Guest House on the Saturday night. Logically he'd met Catherine that evening and made a date for the next day.'

'OK. I'll buy that. So Williams first appears at London Euston. That was where he claimed to have met Rodney McNaughten for the second time.'

'Exactly. I've found a ticket stub for a return rail trip from Preston to London on that date, I've also turned up a bar bill from Turnmills where he claimed to have first met McNaughten.'

'What really jumps out' said Chris Fearnley 'is that you have Guest and Lord flying out on Thursday but Williams did not leave until the Friday. Therefore they are different people.'

'And Lord turns up everywhere' said Carver. 'What's the betting that it was Lord whom Williams met at Euston on the Monday and also whenever the two of them met to finalise expenses and paperwork?'

'You know what that means, don't you?' said Carver. 'That article in the Sun is only half correct. Tony pleaded guilty to keep out of the Americans hands but it does not follow that Williams is our man either. Whoever Dominic Lord is, he is pushing our buttons and we and the Americans are reacting accordingly.'

'Hold on a moment, Martin' said Goodchild. 'Let's not go rushing off looking for some mysterious master criminal when we have strong circumstantial evidence that puts one or both these guys in the frame. Remember what Ryan said this morning.'

'With the greatest respect boss, fuck Ryan. He and his bureau are under intense political pressure to solve this case; or if not solve it, convict someone. The big question is how the hell would either Guest or Williams lay their hands on Kolokol? Any defence lawyer worth his salt would rip holes in this scenario.'

'You said that Lord has started to leave a trail, Michelle' said Chris. 'What do you have?'

'He's started to use a credit card. When he flew back to the island on Tuesday 31st he hired a private jet. Likewise when he went Manchester two days later. Obviously the address is false but the bank account is real enough. Once the aviation company's bill had been settled there was some twenty thousand pounds left on the card. It has not been used since.'

'What's the source of the funds on the card?' asked Chris.

'It's a numbered account in Lichtenstein, which in turn was receiving funds from the Cayman Islands which in turn will not tell me anything. I'm stuck.'

'Well who's best at unravelling financials?' said Chris. 'SOCA?'

She was referring to the Serious Organised Crime Agency, a Home Office organisation that had been set up to produce intelligence on a variety of criminal activities ranging from drug smuggling, human trafficking and money laundering.

'I don't think so, Chris' said Goodchild. 'It's all been a bit of a disaster at SOCA – they were supposed to be the UK version of the FBI, God help us. They're being disbanded to be replaced by something called the National Crime Agency, next year I believe.'

'I've an idea' said Carver. 'We'll have to let the FBI know where we are in this investigation. Surely international financials are right up their street?'

'I'm not comfortable with that, Martin' said Goodchild. 'I don't trust the Yanks not to leak the fact that the useless Brits have gone to them for help.'

'Then get someone else to do it. I assume you'll have to brief Addison or Sampson at some stage today. They are going to need something for the evening news.'

'Devious, Martin; very devious. I like it.'

'There's one more thing' said Carver. 'Where are we on finding out how Lord travelled to Heathrow, Michelle?'

'I'm on that myself. When I googled London limo hire I got over seven million hits. I've concentrated on firms that specialise in airport transfers but there are still a lot of them. At least I have date, flight time and a name to work with. Once we've finished up here, that's my priority. I wouldn't bet on it but if this guy is picked up at his home address well, we've got him.'

'That's good work, Michelle' said Goodchild. 'How did Guest react to his new found fame, Martin?'

'I showed him a copy of the Sun and he thought about it for quite a while. He then said that he'd nothing further to add to what he'd already stated. When I asked him straight whether he was still admitting to killing three girls he went 'no comment' on me.'

'No surprise there' said Goodchild. 'OK I'm going to write this up then take it to Addison. You carry on with your limo research, Michelle. Chris and Martin; you're due to interview Williams again this afternoon aren't you?'

'Yes, boss' replied Chris. 'I'm going to take it easy with him this time. We've only got the right to hold him until tomorrow night before we either charge him or obtain an extension. I don't want him screaming for a lawyer.'

'Does he have any family who might raise a stink about his arrest?' asked Goodchild.

'Parents are deceased' answered Michelle. 'Two aunts and one uncle plus numerous cousins who all live in Wales. They don't appear to be close.'

'That's all right then. I'd like us all to keep our Blackberries turned on. If any one of us has anything new lets all be in the loop, as they say. Carry on and we'll have a round up at seventeen hundred.'

As the police were continuing there efforts, Aiden Hartley was trying to maintain his position as the man of the hour. Over the years he had bought enough drinks and lunches for members of the Metropolitan Police that he felt that he was owed a few favours. Indeed, he was not averse to passing over a plain brown envelope full of cash if it would advance his cause. Thus it was that he found himself in the Eagle and Child public house on the City Road in the company of middle aged Detective Sergeant Andy Holmes. DS Holmes was a bitter man. He knew that he would never rise any higher in rank and felt that he deserved more. He blamed his lack of progress on his surname. If he'd had ten pounds for every time someone had said 'no shit, Sherlock' to him he'd be a wealthy man. The fact that he was venal, rude, unpopular and a very heavy drinker did not enter into the equation in his mind. He was also a member of Jim Cooper's Orion team. Aiden Hartley and he went back many years so, when Holmes had seen that morning's edition of the Sun, he smelled a nice pay day and had contacted the journalist as soon as he had finished his shift.

After minimal pleasantries and promises of secrecy the two men spoke about the real reason for their clandestine meeting. It only took Holmes ten minutes to give up the name and personal details of Ian Williams, even telling Hartley where the man was being held for questioning. The journalist was pleased as this sort of information could be verified by his newspaper but he sensed that there was more to be had from the bent copper so he bought another round then excused himself.

He phoned his editor with what he had gleaned so far, requesting that Sun staffers call around for verification and saying that he would get back to him soon. With his star in the ascendant, Hartley's request was granted. He then rejoined Holmes at their corner table.

'So, Andy; how's the investigation going in general?' he asked.

'It's a dog's breakfast, Aiden.'

'In what way?'

'Look, it started off with Acting Commander Goodchild and his three buddies in charge. That was going nowhere so they got Jim Cooper to organise a proper team to do some real police work. We were working our nuts off when Jim had his car smash and they brought Goodchild back. He spends his time in his office with his same three mates making us do all the donkey work. What does that sound like to you, Aiden?'

'I hear what you're saying, Andy. But, to be fair, Goodchild does have a good working relationship with the Americans, doesn't he?'

'So fucking what? We're the Metropolitan Police not NYPD. Another thing; I don't mind tipping you the wink when information is needlessly being withheld from the press but there is no way I'd let you take part in an active investigation the way Goodchild did with Roger Tucker.'

'You are joking! He did not really do that did he?'

'I've read the entire file. How do you think Tucker got all the info for his bullshit articles?'

'Bloody hell! I've got to think about this. Same again?'

'Yeah; I've finished work for the day.'

Hartley went to the bar for more lubrication. The Tucker-Goodchild connection was a good story but it would have to be treated with care. If he were to bring a fellow journalist and a senior police officer down in flames it would not do his own connections with Scotland Yard any good. Then again, he was close to retirement so what did he care? He'd leave that one to his editor. Having rejoined Holmes he let the conversation lapse for a while and let the booze work its way into the policeman's system.

'Are you all right, Andy?'

'Yes, of course. Why do you ask?'

'If you don't mind my saying so, you seem to have your mind somewhere else. Something's bothering you.'

Holmes took a long pull of his drink before answering.

'You're right something is. There is going to be blood on the floor when the truth of how this investigation was managed comes out. I reckon they're lining Jim Cooper up as scapegoat.'

'That's daft. He had not had time to accomplish anything before his accident. If anyone's for the chop it's Goodchild.'

'Clever man is our Commander – sorry Acting Commander. There's a rumour running around that when Jim Cooper ploughed into a herd of Bambis he was pissed out of his mind.'

'Could it be true?'

'No way. Jim likes a drink as much as the next man but he'd never risk his career and reputation by being smashed then taking to unlit country roads at night. But if you throw enough shit around, some will hit the target.'

'And you reckon that Goodchild is the shit slinger not someone higher up?'

'Dunno. Believe it or not, Aiden, but I don't talk with people higher up the food chain than Goodchild. To the powers that be I'm just another cog in the machine.'

Holmes was too stupid to realise what he had just done. His jealousy of Goodchild had led him to tell a journalist that the Met were covering up the fact that a senior police officer who was in charge of a high profile murder investigation was a drunk driver. Hartley changed the topic of conversation to what should have been done to control the rioters who had run amok in several

English cities during the previous summer. This allowed Holmes to vent his spleen about ethnic minorities and the people who chose unemployment as a way of life. Jim Cooper was soon forgotten, and as soon as he could, Hartley made his excuses to head back to his office. He reckoned that he had enough material for three more days of front page coverage.

Back at the Sun's offices in Wapping the news desk had been working the phone with a vengeance. They were soon able to confirm that a Preston man named Ian Williams had been arrested and had undergone a second day of questioning in connection with Catherine Taylor-Lodge's murder. Companies House revealed details of Williams' marketing firm and reporters were despatched to Wales to interview the man's relatives. Money changed hands and photos were obtained. The next day's front page was building.

At the afternoon editorial conference a major decision had to be made. Should they only print a follow up piece on Williams or should they write a full blown article regarding dissension in the Met's ranks, incompetence in case management and a senior police officer hospitalised through drink driving?

They had not even made enquiries about whether or not Jim Cooper was under the influence because merely asking the question would tip their hand to the police.

The editor sat back and allowed his staffers to express their opinions. Only Aiden Hartley kept quiet. Finally the editor called the meeting to order.

'That's it I've heard enough...except from you Aiden. What are your thoughts on how we should proceed?

All eyes in the room turned to the veteran hack who was a legend in his own lunchtime.

'I've not heard back from whoever gave me the initial info and I'd like for us to go with something that might provoke this person into contacting me again. To that end I would like us to put together a piece of two elements but hold back the Jim Cooper information for later in the week. Finally I think we're all agreed that Guest is innocent so, let's lead with a Sun campaign 'Free Tony Guest'. Back that up with the Met's abysmal handling of this case. 'The British public and the ten victims deserve better' sort of thing. See how the powers that be respond then, if necessary, hit them with the fact that they put a drunk in charge of a serial murder enquiry.'

'I like it' said the editor. 'Anything else?'

'If you don't mind my saying so, you might want to think about a major editorial piece on how the Met is being run.'

'That had crossed my mind. Right – anybody disagree with what Aiden has suggested? No? All right – get to work. Aiden; would you stay behind for a moment?'

The staffers trooped out of the editor's office leaving the two men alone.

'Good work; no – fucking good work, Aiden. How sure are you of your contact in the Met?'

'I've known him on and off for twenty years. He's a loser but has managed to find himself at the right place at the right time to earn himself a few pounds. At the end of the day, he sought me out so we are lily white on this one.'

'Fair enough. How do you feel about revealing Roger Tucker's link to Goodchild? I know that you and he go back a bit.'

'That's true but right now I'm not thinking of him as a sometime drinking mate but as an employee of that pretentious rag the Post. Roger's done very well out of this case; he'll just have to take the rough after the smooth now.'

'Glad to hear you thinking that way, Aiden. I'm going to have to have the staff put the piece together and I'll edit it myself. It's going to go out as an exclusive under your name so do you want a sight of it before it goes to press?'

'No, that's all right. I was thinking of calling it a day anyway, if that's OK with you?'

'Fine by me, Aiden. I could have the final draft emailed to your Blackberry if you want.

'I'm afraid I don't have one – this new stuff baffles me to be honest. There are functions on my cell phone which might as well be Attic Greek for all I understand them.'

'All right, we'll leave it like that for now but I do think we should issue you with something a tad more useful than a basic cell. Well done again and I'll see you tomorrow.'

Hartley left the Sun's offices basking in the rare praise that had come his way. He'd even managed to keep a fair amount of the black money that he had been given to pay Andy Holmes. He hailed a cab and directed it to El Vino's in Fleet Street where he might just be able to have a late lunch prior to hitting the claret.

Back at New Scotland Yard the pressure was mounting. The fact that the Sun had been looking for verification regarding the status and whereabouts of Ian Williams indicated that the paper had a source, possibly within the Met itself. Lancashire constabulary had been in touch with news of a Sun stringer having turned up at Williams' office and that a TV crew from ITN was on its way. The media vultures were circling.

The Met's press office stonewalled (as was expected) but had to confirm Williams' name and why he had been arrested. The less information the police gave out, the more aggressive the press became. The editor of the Sun contacted Oliver Addison directly and hinted that he was in the process of checking out some fresh information regarding the management of the murders which could cast the Met in a bad light. If the police could just be a little bit more cooperative then perhaps this unpleasantness could be avoided was the message.

Addison made an attempt to ascertain what the fresh information might be but that was never going to work. As the day wore on, relations between the media and the Metropolitan Police deteriorated to the point of open hostility. The result was that the next day's front page of the Sun was given over entirely to a photo of Tony Guest with the headline 'AN INNOCENT MAN'. Brief details of the unfolding drama of the case were listed then further developed inside the paper. The article posed more questions than it revealed facts, but culminated with an invitation for readers to respond, either by post or online, to a Free Tony Guest Campaign.

It was now certain that David Cameron would face serious scrutiny at Prime Minister's Questions in the House of Commons on Wednesday.

Sir Alan Sampson summoned Goodchild to his office. When the Commander entered he saw that Deputy Assistant Commissioner Addison was also present. The latter looked as if he had not slept for a week.

'Take a seat, Mark' said Sampson. 'Drink?'

'No thanks, sir. I'm driving tonight.'

'Quite right. Very well. It is the view of our political masters that we have lost control of this investigation and are back to square one. Is there anything I can tell them to the contrary?'

'Yes, sir. Despite how things appear, we have a suspect for the American girl's murder. He may or may not also be the killer of the English girls but we'll resolve that later.'

'This is this Williams chap who is in Paddington Green?'

'No, sir. This is a third person who has come to our attention during the investigation. We have a name, travel and financial details but the man is using a false identity. We should have him soon, sir.'

'A third man?' exclaimed the Commissioner.

'This is the first I have heard of this, Mark. Why did you not inform me sooner?'

'I emailed a full report to D.A.C Addison just after lunch time today, sir.'

'Is that correct, Oliver?' asked the commissioner.

Addison took out his Blackberry and accessed his messages. There were a lot of them. After a while he looked up at his superior.

'Sorry, Sir Alan' he said. 'I do have a message from Mark. I haven't read it yet.'

'Why the devil not?'

'I've been tied up with media enquiries all day and the press office has been on at me for guidance too. I was not expecting an important communication from Orion this afternoon.'

'Never mind. Forward it to me now – I need to see it before I speak with the Home Secretary. Whilst that is making its way through the ether, Mark, would you bring me up to speed verbally, please.'

Goodchild clearly and concisely ran through the state of play, culminating with the fact that he had one of his most efficient officers chasing down the limo used to transport Dominic Lord to Heathrow.

'So to sum up, Mark. An innocent man confessed to three murders to keep out of American hands; we then arrested another suspect who is also probably innocent; we are now trying to find a third man who may have been misdirecting us from the outset and is probably the real killer. Have I got that right, Mark?'

'It seems to be the most likely scenario, yes, Sir Alan.'

'Are there any other scenarios, Mark?'

'Yes, sir. The Americans reckon that they could try and convict Williams on the evidence we have so far. If that is correct then Guest's confession still stands.'

'God Almighty! All right. For now Guest stays put. I want to keep Williams for further questioning – apply for an extension, Mark. Finally, find Dominic Lord.'

'Yes, sir. I'll get on that right away if there's nothing further.'

'No, that's all. Carry on Mark.'

Goodchild was glad that he'd decided to quit the police. There was a shit storm brewing and he knew that he was in its path. He wondered if Addison had a decent weather eye or had he developed tunnel vision through his absorption in all things media. Not his problem. He headed back to Orion to implement his chief's instructions and then head off home with Michelle. Let the next shift crunch the numbers.

At Paddington Green Carver and Fearnley had come to the same conclusion. Chris had conducted another anodyne interview with Williams but if the Welshman had felt no pain, her head was fit to burst. Once the man had been taken back to his cell she looked at Carver and said 'That is the last man on the planet you'd want to be trapped in a lift with.'

'He does talk a lot without actually saying anything, doesn't he? Perhaps he is a criminal genius after all and this is his way of disguising it.'

'To use a legal term, Martin – utter bollocks.'

'I know. I'm going to give Goodchild a call whilst you sign the recordings over then I'm out of here for a drink.'

'Got room for a little one?' said Chris making a pathetic attempt at looking small and harmless.

'As long as it's you' laughed Martin. Ten minutes later and they left Paddington Green to hit the streets.

Chapter Forty Four

Also hitting the streets, albeit in the early hours of the morning, was the Sun's new edition loudly announcing Tony Guest's innocence and demanding his release. The breakfast television channels all led with the story which was now assuming political importance with the BBC giving air time to civil liberties groups, various left wing commentators and Labour politicians; in fact anyone who had an axe to grind with the police or the Conservative led government.

At his home in Sans Walk, Clerkenwell, ML watched the results of his machinations with pride. He thought that he might even buy a copy of the tabloid for the chromosomically challenged to see exactly how much detail was correct. TV, for all its immediacy, was designed for viewers with a five minute attention span, maximum.

From what the two airheads on the red sofa were saying, ML did not have to do anything more to muddy the waters. Indeed, if things continued as they were, there was the likelihood of a media feeding frenzy which would result in metaphorical blood being added to the mix – and that was before the Americans joined the party. No, he'd leave it alone to develop. There were still other avenues open to him should he wish to take them.

At New Scotland Yard Goodchild looked over the efforts of the nightshift with no comment because there had been no progress. He briefed Chris and Martin on the decision to keep Williams in custody for a further forty eight hours. It would be her job to keep Williams calm until a decision on his status could be made.

'So now I'm a babysitter' she said. 'Great.'

'It's important, Chris' said Goodchild. 'It'll be over one way or another this week.'

Carver and Fearnley glanced quickly at each other on hearing that particular comment. Either Goodchild knew something they did not or he was indulging in unwarranted optimism –

otherwise know as wishful thinking. They took their leave of Orion to head over to Paddington Green whilst Goodchild, Stone and the day shift carried on with their enquiries. It was going to be a long day.

At one thirty in the afternoon everyone watched the lunchtime news on television in case a member of parliament came out with a question to the Prime Minister that might have a bearing on the case. This did not happen and David Cameron had a good day at the despatch box aided, it must be said, by the ineptitude of his opposite number on the opposition benches, a man who had been bought and paid for by the trade unions in order to become leader of the Labour party. The Prime Minister tore him to shreds for his obvious attempts to use the tragic deaths of eleven young women to score political points. Cameron's anger at becoming embroiled in a police investigation was evident and Goodchild knew that if he did not come up with something soon then the Met would feel the wrath of its political masters.

At three in the afternoon the break that they'd been working for arrived. Michelle Stone put her phone down, punched the air and cried 'Yes!'

'What have you got, Michelle?' asked Goodchild.

'The limo driver who picked up Dominic Lord for his private plane trip back to Fuerteventura. He's on his way here now, boss. Should be with us in about half an hour. How do you want to handle it?'

'Have you spoken to him yourself?'

'No. His name is Paul Chilcott, aged thirty three, married, two children at primary school. He had to go through an enhanced CRB check to get this job. He's never even had a parking ticket and has been with this firm for the past six years.'

'All right; you and I will meet him in an interview room and ask if he minds if we record it to help the investigation. Set it up, Michelle and well done. I'm going to let the top floor know.'

Goodchild retreated to the glass office to give the news to Sir Alan Sampson and Oliver Addison. Michelle alerted reception to the imminent arrival of Chilcott then reserved an interview room for her and Goodchild's use.

The moment that Michelle had exclaimed 'yes!' the whole Orion team had looked her way. Those who had not been on the phone themselves had been privy to her conversations with the Commander. Among them was DS Andy Holmes.

Goodchild and Stone were waiting in the interview room when a uniformed constable escorted Chilcott in. They stood to meet him and Goodchild made the introductions. The man was wearing a dove grey suit, crisp, white shirt with no tie and spotless, black brogues. He was a shade under six feet tall with neatly trimmed short, dark brown hair, clean shaven and a relaxed demeanour. The latter was unusual for a civilian visiting New Scotland Yard. The most striking thing about Chilcott were his eyes. They were multicoloured showing shades of green, grey and brown and they were very mobile, taking in every detail both of the room and of the two police officers. Goodchild could detect the intelligence behind those eyes and wondered why the man was a glorified taxi driver.

Once they were all sat, Goodchild started proceedings.

'Thank you for coming in at such short notice Mr Chilcott. You were obviously on duty when DS Stone phoned your office.'

'No problem, Commander' replied Chilcott in a pleasant voice which was neutral in accent.

'This is a totally informal conversation but it would help us if you would give your consent to it being recorded. Otherwise DS Stone will have to take notes.'

'Record away.'

At a nod from Goodchild, Michelle activated the equipment and the dialogue began.

'On Tuesday thirty first August you picked up a passenger named Dominic Lord. You collected him at the Holiday Inn, Kings Cross and took him to the VIP section at Heathrow airport. Correct.'

'Correct. Our company has an arrangement with Heathrow. The car is met and the client and his luggage are escorted inside. The client then goes to the VIP lounge whilst his passport and any bags are processed. In the meantime the driver goes airside to wait for the client; then we deliver them to their flight.'

'Can you give a description of your client please?'

'He was about my height but more muscular. He walks like a relaxed athlete. Hair light brown, longish but tidy. He wore tinted reading glasses so I don't know the colour of his eyes. He spoke very few words to me – some clients are like that – but the little he said indicated that he was educated and English.'

'Anything unusual about him at all, Mr Chilcott?'

'Before I answer that, I have a question. What is the police's interest in this man?'

'We need to interview him urgently in connection with the murder of Catherine Taylor-Lodge.'

'The American student. I see. Forgive my reticence but we take client privacy seriously but murder outweighs that. There was something very unusual about Mr Lord. I picked him up in the bar of the hotel as arranged. However, I saw him leave a house in Clerkenwell about thirty minutes prior to that.'

'Are you sure? How did that come about?'

'I'm certain. I always try to be ten minutes early for a pick up but this time I miscalculated the traffic and was forty minutes early. The hotel won't let a car hang around that long so I drove to Clerkenwell for a sandwich and a drink then I sat in the car to kill some time. I was about sixty feet away when Mr Lord left a building. He caught my eye because I noticed that he was not wearing any socks. Most people in London without socks tend to have a dog on a string but this chap was dressed for warmer climes. So, for some reason, he chose to walk down some fairly dodgy streets with a two suiter over his shoulder rather than be picked up at that residence.'

'Do you remember the address, Mr Chilcott?'

'The street is called Sans Walk; hard to forget that one. I'm afraid I didn't get a door number but I could point it out to you.'

'Bear with me a moment, Mr Chilcott.'

Goodchild went over to another table on which a flat screen computer sat. He logged on to Google Maps and located Sans Walk. It appeared to be quite a small street which lay between Clerkenwell Close and Woolbridge Street in EC1.

'Which side of the street was the house, Mr Chilcott?'

'North.'

'Michelle; I want a list of occupants and owners of all properties on the north side of Sans Walk. Check them against Lord's financials and I'll see you in ten.'

'On it, sir.'

Michelle Stone hurried away leaving the two men together. Goodchild switched off the recording equipment.

'You've been very helpful, Mr Chilcott. You've a good eye for detail and a good memory too. If you don't mind my saying so, you don't come across as someone who drives rich people around for a living.'

'It's an easy enough job and I'm not stuck in an office. It suits me for now.'

'I've got detectives on my team with less acute powers of observation than you, Mr Chilcott. What's you story?'

'There is no story. I'm sure that you've had a look at the Police National Computer to see if I've ever been in trouble and the answer to that is a no. I'm just a private person trying to get along, Commander.'

Goodchild looked at Chilcott trying to work him out. He

couldn't but he made a mental notes to have the man's past looked into at the earliest possible moment.

'Very well, sir. I've got to set some things in motion as a result of what you've told us today. Is there anywhere you were supposed to be this afternoon?'

'I had one more job on but that's been covered. My wife will be expecting me back at around six.'

'I doubt very much if you're going to make that, Mr Chilcott. You might like to call her.'

'What time do you think I'll be able to leave, Commander?'

'I honestly can't say. What I'd like for you to do is point out the building from which Dominic Lord appeared but it's getting dark and you saw him on a summer's afternoon. I don't want any mistakes being made here.'

'Understood. Alright; I'll hold off from calling home until you have a clearer idea of how you want to use me.'

Michelle Stone came back into the room with a sheaf of computer printouts in her hands.

'OK, boss. These are the results. Lord's financials do not match anybody on that side of this street. There are not too many residents so I did a CRB check on them all and also looked at the electoral register. This must be the most law abiding community in London. Everyone is clean, in employment and a UK national to boot. I've only come across one anomaly; all the buildings are split up into apartments except for number ten. This building is registered as belonging to Cromwell Publishing Limited whose offices are about half a mile away in the same post code. The company has a varied portfolio of international business to business magazines – quite boring stuff really – but, and here's the interesting bit, it was purchased by a major American corporation the same week that Catherine Taylor-Lodge was killed.'

'That cannot be coincidental' said Goodchild. 'Who was the original owner?'

'I don't know yet. I did a Google search on the company and have a list of its directors but there is no record of a chairman. All I know for sure is that it was founded twenty years ago. I could call the MD and pump him but I thought I'd have a word with you first.'

'Or contact Companies House. As a limited company the details have to be there.'

'Yes. I've already delegated that task. In my experience even the Met has to make a visit to the premises to make Companies House move faster than glacial. Something else struck me, boss. The name Cromwell Publishing – You do remember Oliver Cromwell's job title don't you?'

'Lord Protector. Bloody hell! We've got to find out who lives in that building. Right – I'm going to organise an entry team from SO19 and we're going in tonight. I want you to find the details of whoever sold the company and I want that info yesterday. Mr Chilcott. You and I are going to drive along Sans Walk so that you can confirm that number ten is the same building from which you saw Dominic Lord emerge. You OK with that?'

'Fine with me.'

'Right. Wait here, please. I've some organising to do. Michelle, I'll see you back in the office.'

Goodchild left the room at a brisk pace and entered the office just twenty minutes later.

'Any news on who lives in number 10 yet sergeant?' he asked Michelle.

'No, sir.'

'Fine. Call me as soon as you have something. Mr Chilcott and I are going for a drive. SO19 are deploying as we speak and are going in tonight whether we have a name or not. Any questions before I go?'

'Sir, I've worked this case from the start and I'd like to be there at the end. I've delegated the job of finding the homeowner's name. Permission to accompany you now, sir?'

If it had been any other officer who had made such a request Goodchild would have flatly refused it and told them to remain at their post. But it wasn't any other officer. It was his current and future partner, both in business and, hopefully, life, and, in truth, she had made a huge contribution to the investigation so he nodded to her.

'Very well, you have five minutes to brief your lot then we are out of here' he said.

'Thank you, sir' she replied and literally jogged across the Orion office. It only took her two minutes to brief the team tasked with tracing the property owner's name which left her three to visit the bathroom. Michelle knew Goodchild well enough to realise that he had factored in a loo visit for her.

Five minutes after Goodchild had agreed to her request the two officers and Chilcott descended to the garage where an unmarked Range Rover was waiting for them. Goodchild took the driver's seat with Stone sat next to him and they drove off into the dark.

'I've decided to approach Sans Walk from the west, Mr Chilcott' said Goodchild. 'If you ID number 10 as the property from which you saw Dominic Lord emerge then I'll loop around back to Farringdon where the entry team are assembling and you can wait there. Once we have this guy in custody I'm going to need you with me to make a positive ID. Could be a long night, I'm afraid.'

'As long as you get him that's all that matters' replied Chilcott.

They drove on towards the target. It was not far but the London traffic at this time of night made their progress a slow one. Which is how they came to be spotted.

ML never went directly home. He nearly always had a black cab drop him off some distance from his street at a different place each time and he would then walk in, no matter the weather, looking for anything which was out of place. An intelligence officer would call it carrying out counter-surveillance.

His taxi had dropped him off on Gray's Inn Road and he was just strolling along Calthorpe Street when he saw the black Range Rover in his peripheral vision. In an instant his mind registered that the windows had too dark a tint to be legal, the communications antennae on the roof and the lack of blue lights behind the grill. So – not a police pursuit vehicle; it would need it's flashers for that but an undercover police vehicle all the same. What were the chances of one of those heading in the direction of his home he wondered.

He did not panic, just continued on his way keeping the Range Rover in sight. Perhaps it would head off to Kings Cross.

But he saw the car turn south into Farringdon Road and he arrived just in time to see it make a left into the maze of smaller streets which made up the area of Clerkenwell where he lived. Too much coincidence. He knew that they'd found him.

He was not worried about capture and the loss of his primary residence was an inconvenience at most, albeit an annoying one. He entered a nearby cafe and ordered tea to give himself time to organise his thoughts. He reasoned that the Range Rover was doing a drive-by of his home for whatever reason, probably to see the lay of the land and to plan the evacuation of civilians prior to blocking the street for an eventual assault by armed police. Next question; where could SO19 assemble prior to effecting an eventual forced entry on his home? The logical place was the enormous car park belonging to Mount Pleasant sorting office. This was the largest postal distribution centre in Europe and was just across the road from where ML was taking his tea. He decided too make a recce to confirm his suspicions. Within two minutes he's seen all that he needed to. At the rear of the open air yard, almost hidden behind the large, red, articulated delivery trucks of the Royal Mail, six blue police vans were parked in shadow against a perimeter wall. Each of these could carry six to eight armed officers, dogs, driver and various types of equipment. Somewhere there would be a command and control vehicle but it was not in evidence at the moment. ML now knew that the game was up and hailed a passing cab. He still had time.

In the police Range Rover Chilcott turned his head as they approached number 10 Sans Walk. 'That's definitely the place where I saw my client leave from' he said.

'Well the fucker's at home watching TV' remarked Goodchild. 'Eyeball the first floor, Michelle.'

'Got it, boss. You're right. We've got him.'

What the two officers did not know was the ML had installed a system whereby the TV automatically switched on when the outside light level dipped below a certain luminosity. An added feature was that certain room lights would come on in a predetermined order to give the impression that the house was occupied. ML's thinking behind this was, quite simply, the deterrence of opportunistic burglars who might target a property which was dark over a prolonged period of time. Tonight he would use the system for a different purpose.

Goodchild, Stone and Chilcott made their way through Clerkenwell and entered the car park at Mount Pleasant where Goodchild sought out the head of SO19 unit Detective Chief Inspector Rod McNeill. The two senior men went to the mobile communications vehicle for a briefing.

'DCI McNeill. Quite simply the target is in his building and we are not going to let him go anywhere. He's very smart, absolutely ruthless so I don't want any of your guys taking risks. What I need right now are some shooters on the roofs overlooking number ten whilst I have a cordon set up around the immediate area. Organise that now, please. Then come back here.'

'On it, sir' said McNeill who jumped out of the articulated vehicle to go and implement Goodchild's instructions.

Goodchild's time in counter-terrorism work now proved its worth. With the minimum of fuss and phone calls he was able to have the area sealed off and secured. Plain clothes officers went door to door and discretely ushered the streets' residents outside the cordon, the majority of them leaving by their back door so as not to alarm the target.

Finally satisfied that he had his ducks lined up, Goodchild went to see Michelle Stone.

'Do we have a name yet, sergeant?' he asked.

'No, boss. Still working on it.'

'No problem. I'll just call him Dominic Lord. Do we have the landline number for the property?'

'Yes. British Telecom were pretty swift on that. In fact there are four different numbers, three sequential which I suppose would be normal for an office a fourth which is completely different and ex-directory. That must be for his personal calls.'

'Then that's the one I'll use. OK. As the Americans say, 'showtime'.'

'Have you informed the Americans, boss?'

'No. That's politics and Addison or Sampson can deal with it. This is a police op, Michelle.'

'Fine. Ready when you are.'

Whilst Goodchild had been organising his operation ML had been making his own preparations for what he saw as the end game. His first move was to call Roger Tucker at home. The journalist answered promptly.

'Good evening, Roger. This is the man you know as ML. Are you sober?'

'Yes, I am.'

'Sober enough to drive legally?'

'Yes. I was just about to sit down to dinner with my wife.'

'Well she'll have to keep it warm for you. The time has come for you to honour our agreement and meet me. You will not regret it. Take your car and park under Holborn Viaduct. You'll be met there. Your wife is bound to ask where you are going. Be a good chap and lie. Tell her you'll be back in three hours at the outside. Got it?'

'Look, I can't just....'

'Yes you can, Roger' interrupted ML. 'In fact you must if you wish to stay on my good side. But enough stick. Here's the carrot. I want to see you tonight to give you the whole story, names, dates and all. Be at the viaduct in twenty minutes or consider Sharon's dinner your last supper. Clear?'

'I'm on my way.'

'Alone.'

ML disconnected from Tucker. It did not matter if the man came or not. If he did it would be the icing on the cake, if not no big deal. What ML did need was a view of what was happening outside his home. To achieve this he simply phoned ITN and the BBC informing both channels that the Met Police were surrounding a property in Sans Walk, Clerkenwell and that SO19 were standing by to effect an explosive entry.

When the TV crews arrived on scene and were told in no uncertain terms that they were not coming through the cordon whatever the rights of a free press were, they responded by hiring two giant cherry pickers from which any action could be filmed. Back at New Scotland Yard Addison was having a nightmare trying to control a media which had lost all trust in his organisation. The chickens of the original cover up were coming home to roost.

Roger Tucker made his excuses to his wife and left his home with a feeling of predestination. He had made a promise to meet ML at a future, unspecified time but he had not really taken that promise seriously. He was now on his way to meet a mass murderer without any back up but he felt that he had no choice. ML's use of his wife's name during their brief phone conversation was not accidental. Tucker thought that if he did not keep up his side of the bargain then it was not just his own life that he was endangering. In a strange way he had come to trust the killer.

When ML had said that he would tell the whole story, Tucker believed him. Since the very first email communication it seemed that ML had a need to put some sort of message across to a wider public. Perhaps tonight would be his swan song.

Tucker found a parking space close to Holborn Viaduct, shut down his motor and waited. He had made good time and was well within the twenty minutes that ML had stipulated. As he waited he scanned the streets. This was one of the most interesting parts of London to him. He was equidistant from Saint Paul's Cathedral, Lincolns Inn Fields and Blackfriars Bridge. Not far to the north lay Smithfield's meat market. This was the heart of the capital city in so many ways if one but knew it.

As he sat thinking of the complexities of London's past he heard a tap, tap, tap on his window. A nondescript man dressed in a shabby grey suit was looking at him. Tucker lowered his window a few inches and enquired 'Can I help you?'

'Is you Mr Roger Tucker, sir?' asked the man in a working class London accent.

'Yes, I am.'

'Good. A gentleman's asked me to show you to his offices. Can you follow me please, sir?'

Tucker left his car and followed the grey man up Snow Hill, slowly, as his guide seemed to have a problem with his right leg which dragged more than it walked. They arrived at an arched doorway set underneath the viaduct in which a Judas gate was set.

'Here you are, sir' said the grey man. 'The gentleman said you was to go straight in.'

Tucker took a deep breath then turned and crossed the threshold. As he stepped into the semi-darkness he failed to see the grey man who had followed him and who now swiped a lead filled sap across the base of his skull. He did not even feel the blow. One moment he was standing, the next he awoke strapped in an upright chair, his ankles and wrists fixed with duct tape. In front of him stood the grey man who had suddenly become more colourful as he held in his hand a wicked looking silver bladed dagger. He was also wearing one of those ridiculous Guido Fawkes masks so beloved of would-be anarchists.

'Good evening, Roger. Sorry about that but I need your undivided attention for a short while. And it will, of necessity be short. Are you right or left handed, Roger?'

'Right.'

Tucker's eyes widened in terror as the man he knew as ML advanced towards him and placed the blade on the tape that secured his right wrist.

'Fuck no, please' begged the journalist.

'Now now, Roger. You won't feel a thing.'

With one quick movement ML sliced through the tape not even scratching Tucker's arm.

'I have no intention of hurting you, Roger. You'll need that hand to take notes of our little chat.'

ML went away into the gloom and returned with a cheap, spiral bound note book and pencil which he gave to Tucker. He then wheeled across the room a small table on which lay a small flat screen television set. This he placed where both men could see it and switched it on. He channel hopped until he landed on BBC News 24 and frowned. There was nothing on the breaking news about a police siege in central London.

Not wanting to waste time ML began to speak.

'I'm going to give you everything and I'll even answer a few, but only a few, questions. In this box' here ML indicated a tea chest which Tucker had not noticed 'are the personal possessions, including ID of the ten girls whose fingers were buried in the park. They are for you.'

'Question?' asked Tucker. ML nodded.

'Where are the bodies?'

'There are no remains at all. Everything had been destroyed and disposed of.'

'How?'

'God, this is tedious trivia but, very well. This place sits above the River Fleet which, as you should know, now flows underground into the Thames. Behind you is a manhole down which I popped the detritus. Not all in one piece, of course. I won't go into the messy detail of reducing a corpse to an unidentifiable soup involving, as it does, acid and a fine woodchipper but let's just say there were more poured than popped down the hole.'

'Why these particular girls?' asked Tucker who was glad that he had not eaten. 'Had they harmed you in some way?'

ML regarded Tucker in genuine bewilderment.

'Them – harm me? No, no, no, no, no. I chose them because they were the lost and lonely, without status and, more importantly, whom the police would ultimately give up on. The police claim that a case is not closed until they have solved it but, realistically Roger, given their lack of man power they have to prioritise and, sooner or later, a case goes cold.'

Tucker nodded his head as if to show that he knew exactly where this lunatic was coming from. 'Now for the big question' he thought to himself.

'I have to ask; why? Why did you do all this?'

'Finally, we arrive at what you really want to know, Roger. Some twenty years ago there was a young woman of whom I was rather fond. Let's call her Judy. I had just started my business, was doing well and we were happy together. Then Judy disappeared. No phone call; no letter. She just vanished. Judy had no family so I went to the police. Their ineptitude was incredible. Unable to trace Judy they turned their attention towards myself, insinuating that I was responsible for her disappearance. I employed a private detective to try and find her but his best efforts were thwarted by a total lack of co-operation from the police force. Judy was never found. Do you know how many people are reported missing to the police each day, Roger?'

'No idea.'

'Around one thousand. Most of them turn up within twenty four hours. Kids that wander off or are mislaid by their drunken, inbred parents. But dozens are never found. They vanish into the cesspools of our cities, never to be seen again. At least alive. And the police don't give a damn. So I've done what I've done to demonstrate to the world how bloody useless our police service is and how, unless there is a high profile victim, what little interest they take in missing persons. That is the story I wish you to tell.'

'So you've killed eleven people to make a point. What would Judy think of that?'

ML fixed Tucker with his eyes. The mask hid his expression but anger exuded all the same.

'You did not have the privilege of knowing Judy. But I tell you, she would have understood. Hello; we have TV action.'

Chapter Forty Five

In Sans Walk Goodchild was becoming increasingly frustrated. He had dialled all four of the numbers which he had for Dominic Lord to be met with an answerphone message from three of them and nothing from the fourth. From his observation point in the control vehicle he could see the television screen was on in the target's first floor lounge and that, from time to time, a light would go on in another room.

'What do you think`s going on here, Michelle'

'Automatic timer to put off burglars would be my guess' she answered. 'I don't think he's at home'.

'Good. I agree. I'm going to send the team in and we'll see what we will see.'

Goodchild keyed a code on a radio and was in instant contact with the head of the SO19 entry team.

'McNeill' came the unit's commander's voice. 'Rod – Goodchild. I'm authorising entry now. We've not made contact and we don't think the target is present. I reckon the lights are on an automatic setting but we cannot be sure. The guy's method of killing is a high morphine based gas so you may want to send a dog in first. This is one clever fucking psycho we are dealing with here.'

'You reckon he'd gas his own house? I doubt that. But I hear what you're saying Mark. OK. We will go in five. Any chance of getting those TV cameras off whilst we approach?'

'None. I've tried but the media are not playing ball with us because we've fucked them over too much. Sorry.'

'All right. We'll just have to do it fast in case chummy is watching the news rather than a DVD. Catch you later.'

Exactly five minutes later Goodchild and Stone could see the black clad officers of SO19 advancing along Sans Walk. They could also see them on their TV screens as the media networks transmitted closeups of the police officers in their Nomex gear and assault rifles. Six men approached the front door of number ten and, at a silent signal, the largest of them smashed the lock to pieces with an iron ram. He moved to his left allowing his partners space to rush into the property where they dispersed in a prearranged plan screaming 'armed police, armed police!' A German shepherd dog preceded them and all officers kept a distance to see if it reacted in an adverse fashion to the environment. When the animal appeared to be safe and well the men conducted a room to room search. Finding no-one the sergeant in charge radioed his commander.

'Sir; there's not a soul here. No gas so I suppose you can send the SOCO's in.'

'All right. I'm coming over myself. Wait there for me and Commander Goodchild, please.'

'Yes, sir.'

ML and Roger Tucker had watched the police assault on number ten Sans Walk along with a large TV audience who were expecting something along the lines of the SAS hostage rescue at the Iranian embassy in Princes Gate during the 1980's. When Rod McNeill, Goodchild and Stone advanced towards the property the TV cameras zoomed in on them.

'Is that not your friend Goodchild?' asked ML.

'Yes, that's Mark'

'And who's the tart with the tits by his side?'

'That's DS Michelle Stone. She's part of the team that's been investigating the girls' murders.'

'Ah, a female. They dig and dig and dig don't they? Never stop nagging at each little detail. I'll bet she's been most useful to your pal Goodchild. A pity they could not have been useful for Judy. Watch this.'

On screen, the three police officers entered the house. ML counted to ten then dialled a phone number. The effect was not spectacular; no huge explosion, no gouts of flame but suddenly the windows of number ten blew out. The top floor of the property fell onto the one beneath which in turn was detached by explosives to descend onto the one below and the pattern continued until the entire building had collapsed into the basement bar like a stack of cards. The only survivor was the dog which had bolted at the first bang.

'What the hell happened there?' shouted Tucker.

'The joints of all the floors at my home had been weakened and plastic explosives placed at key points. The phone call I just made set off the detonators in a controlled sequence. Something I picked up from the Israelis actually. So, game over, Roger.'

'You fucking madman. The Met will never give up on finding you after this.'

'Good luck to them. The useless cretins couldn't find a whorehouse in Hong Kong let alone me. Time to say bye bye. I'm going to tape your mouth shut, Roger. The knife I shall leave by the door. If you topple the chair over and do a bit of scrabbling you should be free within an hour. I'll relieve you of your phone. Can't have the boys in blue here too soon, can we? Right; I've a plane to catch. Anything else you'd like to ask me?'

Tucker looked at ML and shook his head.

'You've just killed a man I've respected for years. A man who once saved my life. Please just go.'

ML regarded Tucker and twirled his dagger in his fingers. It was obvious that he was debating whether or not to kill the journalist who had so blatantly judged him. It was equally obvious that Tucker was beyond caring. Finally ML turned his back and walked to the Judas gate where he placed the knife.

'Adieu, Roger. Not Au revoir.' Then he was gone.

In Sans Walk the scene was chaos. The police wanted to enter the ruins of number ten but the fire service would not allow them permission. The media were screaming for more information but the key players were lying beneath tons of masonry. Finally Carver and Fearnley arrived on the site to establish some sort of order.

Carver had seen more buildings demolished during his military career than he cared to remember and realised instantly that no-one was going to walk out of this scene alive. He spoke to the senior fire officer.

'Look, I know that everyone who went into that house is dead but it is a crime scene and there could be evidence in there which could help us catch the bastard responsible. Would you not damp it down if at all possible?'

'All right, sir. But if it starts to flame I'll have no option.'

'That's fine but it looks like this was a controlled demolition so I doubt that incendiaries are an issue. Here's my number. Let me know when you're going to recover the bodies.'

Carver handed his card to the fireman then went back to the command vehicle where Fearnley was on the line to New Scotland Yard.

'They are running around like headless chickens, Martin. They want you and me to front a press conference to explain this fiasco.'

'No way. That's Addison's job. I'm staying here until Mark, Michelle and the SO19 guys are brought out. Then I'm going to speak with the FBI and then I'm going on extended leave.'

Chris Fearnley looked at her colleague and tried to read him.

'I think I'll join you, Martin. We'll get this bastard.'

'Don't be so sure, Chris. He may be too good for us'

'What do you mean 'too good for us'? He's a crim, we catch crims! Come on Martin!'

'You don't understand, Chris. In the R.M.P we spend a lot of time tracking down soldiers who have gone AWOL. Most of them are dim and easy to find. A few are bright and it takes a massive effort to trace them. Now this guy has just destroyed a house which I reckon was worth about three million pounds. Somehow he found out that we had discovered his base and had a contingency plan for that eventuality. Army officers are trained to have a plan A, a plan B, an alternative and a fall back position. If all that fails you are in the wrong profession. This guy is at least that good. He'll definitely have an escape plan and we don't even have his real name yet to give the UK Border Control. What the fuck are they doing at Orion, Chris? It can't be that hard to get info out of Companies House.'

'Well if this hasn't concentrated their minds nothing will. I'll light a fire under them and call you when I have something. You'd better inform Addison that you're not wearing make-up tonight.'

'I don't think I'll get to make that call. Look who's coming down the road.'

Fifty yards away the unmistakable figure of London's mayor, Boris Johnson, was advancing towards them. He was accompanied by Commissioner Sampson and his deputy, Addison. Plus, of course, all the necessary aides that such important men require to carry their bags.

Carver entered the command vehicle and found an SO19 black balaclava which he quickly pulled over his head before going to meet the entourage.

'Are you in charge here?' the mayor asked him bluntly.

'I am for the moment, sir' replied Carver. 'Until a more senior officer comes on scene.'

'I see. Why are you wearing that bloody silly mask?'

'I'm a Detective Inspector who works in counter terrorism and I cannot have the media filming or photographing me. I've been on this case from the start and Commissioner Sampson knows who I am.'

'Right. We'll come to that later. How many dead?'

'I'd say nine, sir. The six members of SO19 who went in first. Their boss DCI Rod McNeill who entered the premises once he had been told that it was clear. Plus DS Stone and Commander Mark Goodchild who was in charge of the investigation.'

The mayor was visibly shocked. For once in his life he appeared lost for words. Finally he pulled himself together and said 'This is an absolute tragedy; nine police officers killed in cold blood in central London. Recriminations will be for later. Right now what is being done to apprehend the culprit?'

'The man who lived at this address and presumably booby trapped it, has multiple identities with documentation to back them up. We have discovered that he is the chairman of a company called Cromwell Publishing and the officer in the command vehicle is now tracking down his real name. Once we have that we can see if a passport exists in that name and issue the details to the UK Border Control force who will check carefully everyone trying to leave the country.'

'And how long will...'

Chris Fearnley stuck her head out of the command vehicle and interrupted the mayor.

'Martin - we have the name! Gerald Michael Player. Passport Office are running it now.'

Carver stood quite still whilst Sampson and Addison congratulated each other. Boris Johnson noticed his lack of enthusiasm.

'Something wrong, Detective Inspector?' asked the mayor.

'I reckon it's another dead end, sir. From the very beginning of this case this person has been using word play, especially regarding his pseudonyms, to keep ahead of us. I think that in his mind G.M. Player represents Grand Master Player as in chess. We'll check it out, of course, but I'm not holding my breath.'

Carver was correct. Within ten minutes the Passport Office had verified that they had not issued a passport in the name of Gerald Michael Player in the previous fifty years.

Boris Johnson headed off to where the TV cameras were located with their various interviewers clamouring for information. The mayor gave the media what few facts he had, delivered a couple of meaningless politicians' promises and said that the Metropolitan Police would be holding a press conference later that evening.

'Could you kindly smarten yourself up for this evening's press conference, DI Carver?' said Sampson. 'Uniform would be good.'

'Sorry, sir. I'm not going on TV. You have Deputy Assistant Commissioner Addison for that kind of work. I'm still running this operation now that Mark Goodchild's gone. Although, given the gravity of this incident, it would probably be better if a more senior officer were to front the conference.'

'It wasn't a request, Carver' said a visibly furious Sampson. 'I'm giving you a direct order. Now, are you, or are you not...'

For the second time that evening Chris Fearnley interrupted a senior government official.

'Martin. Orion needs to speak to you now. It's urgent.'

'Excuse me, sir. I've work to do' said Carver who turned his back on the UK's most senior police officer and entered the command vehicle. Fearnley passed him a set of headphones which he pulled on then keyed his throat mike. 'This is DI Carver. To whom am I speaking?'

'Detective Constable Tanner, sir.'

Carvers mind brought up the image of the youngest member of the Orion team. He'd seemed bright and willing but did find himself doing more than his share of scut work.

'All right, Tanner. What's so urgent?'

'A gentleman who will not give his name insists on speaking to you and you alone. He says that he has quote 'information vital to what happened tonight and the case in general' unquote. I don't think it's a hoax or a nutter, sir. First of all he dialled Orion directly and he knows the names of senior officers in the squad. He said he'd be happy to be put on hold whilst I tracked you down. I think you should take the call, sir.'

'How long how has he been on hold for?'

'Seven minutes. He's calling from a cell phone and obviously we've traced it. He's near Holborn Viaduct.'

Chapter Forty Five

'Put him through.'

A new voice came on line. 'Is this Detective Inspector Carver?'

'Yes it is. And you are?'

'Don't hang up when I tell you. This is vital. I'm Roger Tucker of the...'

'I know who you are, Tucker. You have two minutes of my time. Get on with it.'

'This evening I was taken prisoner by the man I knew only as ML. I was present when he pressed the button destroying that house and all those inside. Prior to that he gave me an interview in which he admitted killing the English girls and the American one too. I'm at the site where he claims to have disposed of the bodies and there is a box here containing the personal effects of the ten English victims. I've touched nothing. It took me an hour to free myself and this is the only call I've made but once I've finished I will have to call my editor. Questions?'

'Did he give you his name?'

'He did not.'

'Shit. Stay where you are, Mr Tucker; I'm on my way with some specialists. On no account re-enter the premises nor let anyone else in until I arrive – not even a police officer. This lunatic loves his games and booby traps. Got that?'

'Loud and clear.'

Carver ripped off his headset and said to Fearnley 'We're going to Holborn Viaduct. You drive. I've calls to make.'

'You want to take the command vehicle?'

'We are going to need it. Let's go.'

Fearnley switched on the blues and they sped south for the short journey. Carver's experience in the counter terrorism combined with the events of the evening enabled him to get his priorities right and the first one was the protection of the public. To that end he ordered the closure of all the roads leading to the ancient part of central London and the evacuation of the few residential properties which there were. He reflected ruefully that it was the third such evacuation that had been caused by this maniac. The next action he took was to alert the bomb squad that their presence would be required. Finally he called Orion and instructed them to find Doctor Rachel Watkins and tell her to bring her best people to Holborn.

Chris Fearnley was an accomplished driver and had made the journey in a shade under five minutes. Carver had her pull up in the middle of the road some fifty yards from the viaduct thus becoming the first part of the night's traffic control. She turned on the roof mounted spotlight and illuminated the darkness under the archway where two figures raised their hands to shield their eyes from the intense glare. Carver activated the vehicle's loudhailer.

'Mr Tucker. Would you and whoever that is with you please walk quickly towards this vehicle.'

Carver turned to Fearnley and asked 'Who do you think that is with Tucker, Chris?'

'No idea. He looks like some grumpy teenager and he's giving the journo grief. Tucker's still yapping on his cellphone. Ah, I get it. The killer probably relieved Tucker of his own phone so he'd had to beg or borrow another.

In the distance, from various directions, came the sound of sirens. Traffic noise in the immediate vicinity began to diminish as the police cordons were put in place. The two men arrived at the command vehicle with Tucker still speaking rapidly on the phone. Carver left his seat and indicated by cutting his thumb across his throat that the call should be terminated (although the gesture could be interpreted as 'I'll slice your throat'). Whatever meaning Tucker took he said 'Look, I'll have to call you back on another line' and ended the call. He handed the phone to the youngster and said 'Thanks for that'.

'Thanks for the fifty. Nice doing business with you'. Fearnley had been right.

After a quick check of the man's ID Carver sent him back

through the police lines which were now in place. If he decided to sell his tiny piece of the story to one of Tucker's competitors, well too bad.

'OK, Mr Tucker; come inside here for a chat. We may be interrupted from time to time as I'm organising a major operation but you'll have a grandstand seat – not for the first time either.'

'You're Carver are you?'

'I'm Detective Inspector Carver to you, sunshine. Now get in.'

'I told you what I know when I called you. I've been straight with you but now I've a story to write and need to be at my office.'

'Tucker. You are a pubic hair away from being arrested for obstructing a police officer in the course of his duty, withholding evidence in a murder enquiry and being phenomenally ugly in a public place. Now get in or you will not see the light of day for another forty eight hours.'

Tucker could see that Carver was serious and, sensibly, got in. Carver followed.

'Status update, Chris please' he said..

'Uniforms have nearly sealed the designated area. Five minutes or so for completion. Bomb squad are ten minutes out and will approach from our twelve. I've told them to hold at fifty yards until they have spoken to you. Watkins won't leave the Yard until she hears from us what the site is like then she can decide what kit to bring.'

'Bloody prima donna. Get onto her yourself and tell her to bring everything she could possibly need including her toothbrush and tampons. Otherwise, good job. Now, Tucker; how long were you in the company of the killer for?

'From the time I regained consciousness to when he left me bound and gagged, one hour ten minutes.'

'Well there's no way that can be recounted in a two minute phone call, can it? I want you to tell me everything that happened this evening starting with how you came to find yourself as this man's captive.'

So Tucker began to talk. Carver could hardly believe his ears when the journalist revealed that he had gone to Holborn voluntarily but refrained from interrupting. Tucker then moved on to what he called the 'interview' and removed the spiral notebook from a pocket. He'd managed to keep a nearly verbatim record of the conversation. His narrative was interrupted by the arrival of the bomb squad. Carver spoke to its commander and stressed the dangers that existed. He insisted that no more than one officer at a time was to enter the site and that only after sniffer dogs or robots had given a preliminary all clear. They'd lost enough men this night.

At the request of the bomb squad's commander, Tucker drew a diagram of the site's interior and labelled the various items. Finally he finished speaking.

'That's it Detective Inspector. There is nothing more that I can give you.'

'You can give me your notes for a start' said Carver. 'They constitute evidence and a criminal psychologist will need to examine them.'

'Good luck with that. I write in my own shorthand that even my editor can't decipher. Take a look.'

Tucker gave the notebook to Carver who flipped from page to page. It was clear that the man was telling the truth. What was written made Sanskrit look like primary school English.

'I see' said Carver handing the notes back.

'In that case I will require a transcript of this. How long to do that?'

'I'll make it my first priority once I'm back at my computer. I'll email it to you personally. All right?'

Carver looked at the journalist carefully. He could insist on having him taken to New Scotland Yard where he could translate his bizarre shorthand but that would be a petty victory and one that could come back to bite him. The Met was going to need a friend in the media in the days and weeks to come.

'Very well, Mr Tucker. You've been most helpful so I'll have a car take you to Wapping. Just a couple of questions first. When the killer said 'I've a plane to catch. Adieu not au revoir' do you think that was true or a diversion?'

'I don't know. He knew I'd be free in about an hour and, sooner or later, would pass that info on to you. I can't second guess him especially since he was masked.'

'And when he spoke of this girl who went missing some twenty years ago, 'lets call her Judy'. Same answer I suppose.'

'Same answer. Look, the guys a homicidal maniac, a psychopath of the first order. That does not make him stupid. He lies as easily as we breathe which is one reason why we have not caught him. Is that it?'

Carver suddenly felt weary beyond words. He had to remind himself that Mark Goodchild has considered this journalist to be a friend so he left the command vehicle and organised a car to take Tucker to his offices where he could file his story. Before he left he promised to email a transcript of his notes to Carver and to present himself at New Scotland Yard for a fuller debriefing the following morning at nine. They did not shake hands.

He returned to receive a status update from Chris Fearnley.

'Bomb squad say they are nearly finished. The dogs are spooked about something but it's neither gas nor explosives.'

'If the killer was telling the truth, it's most likely to be human remains mixed with acid. What else?'

'They currently have one officer inside wearing a blast suit and using a hand held x-ray to examine everything they can. The squad boss reckons that the forensics team should be cleared to enter in fifteen minutes. I've informed the charming Dr Watkins who is ready to go. She is going to bag and shift the box with the victims' possessions before anything else. We'll have the ID's by morning.'

'Some poor sods are going to have to make some difficult visits soon. That it?'

'The FBI chap at their embassy is trying to get hold of you. This story is breaking on their east coast breakfast news and they'd like quote 'some light to go with the heat' unquote whatever that means.'

Just then a middle aged man's face appeared in the door. Dressed in a smart navy suit accompanied with a light blue shirt and a golden yellow tie he did not look as though he belonged at a crime scene. The four uniformed officers ranging in rank from constable to sergeant who stood respectfully behind him indicated otherwise.

'DI Carver?' he said.

'That's me. You are?'

'DCS Gwynn. I've come to relieve you of command of this operation.'

'Very good, sir. On whose authority, sir?'

'Commissioner Sampson. Good enough for you?'

'Absolutely.'

Turning towards Chris Fearnley Carver said 'Let's go Detective Inspector. We are relieved.'

'Not so fast, Carver' said Gwynn. 'What's the state of play?'

'I've done an initial debrief of Roger Tucker and will do a follow up at 0900 tomorrow morning at the Yard. Bomb squad are about fifteen minutes from clearing the site. At that time Dr Watkins and her forensics team take over. That's it. Goodnight, sir. Oh by the way; we still have two innocent men in custody.'

Carver nodded at Fearnley and the two of them headed off north towards the police lines and Farringdon where their own vehicle was still parked.

'That was the famous Nell Gwynn' said Carver once they were out of earshot. 'Do you know why he's named after a seventeenth century prostitute?'

'Do tell.'

'Because he will fuck anybody to advance his career. Be wary of him, Chris.'

Arriving back at Farringdon they found the area to be floodlit and heavy lifting vehicles were moving towards Sans Walk. The air was full of dust motes caused by the collapse of the building and they both knew that demolition work would only add to this. It was like 9/11 in miniature.'

'Martin – there's nothing we can do here and I don't want to be alone tonight.'

'Nor me. Come on then. My place to get cleaned up and we'll raise a glass to them.'

They drove to Butler's Wharf in silence, each of them numb from the nights' events. Fearnley and Stone, whilst not exactly friends had been female colleagues in a male dominated profession and respected once another. Carver had operated with Goodchild on several occasions over the years and had learned a lot from the older man. He was furious that he had died in such a, to him, stupid manner.

Once back in Carver's flat they took long, hot showers to cleanse more than their bodies. When Chris emerged wrapped in a towelling bathrobe, Carver was in the kitchen area rummaging in his fridge. He had put on a pair of chino shorts and a plain white T-shirt. The man looked dressed for the beach.

'Do you want something to eat, Chris?' he asked.

'No thanks but you go ahead if you want. I just need a cold beer right now.'

'Take a seat and I'll bring it over.'

Chris went into the lounge area where she collapsed into the sofa and stared, unseeing, at the magnificent view of the city at night. Martin arrived with four bottles of Löwenbrau weeping with condensation as though in sympathy with the emotions in the room. They drank the first bottles quickly and in silence.

Picking up the next two they said quietly one after the other 'To Mark and Michelle'.

'You know, Chris – one of the things Mark and I could never

agree on was beer. He'll be screaming at me now for toasting him in what he used to call 'poof's piss fit only for German homos'. Well sorry mate but this house doesn't stock draught Guinness.'

She didn't reply. Nor smile. Chris Fearnley could do the black humour banter common to cops the world over with the best of them but tonight she was unusually introspective.

Finally she looked at him directly and said 'What the hell went wrong tonight, Martin? Why did Michelle and Mark enter that building?'

'The short answer is that she went in because he went in. And he went in because he wanted to see, feel the beast's lair. The reality is that Mark had taken his eye off the ball because he had fallen for Michelle. I reckon that if this op had come to a successful conclusion then the pair of them would have quit the force to do something else.'

'So you're saying Mark was unprofessional?'

'Not at all. He was unlucky. Look, we only found the house because that limo driver, Chilcott, had such good eyes. As far as Mark was concerned there was no way that the killer knew we'd found his base so setting up an assault was the correct procedure. The next piece of luck goes against him. If the killer had been walking home five minutes earlier or later he would not have seen their recon vehicle – and how many civilians could I.D. one anyway? The killer admitted as much to Tucker. Now Rod McNeill was a pro. Acting on the info given to him by Mark, the dog he sent in was trained to detect certain chemical compounds. We had no evidence to suggest that the killer was familiar with explosives and, anyway, the amounts he used were small and hidden at the top of the building. It was kinetic energy not blast that killed everyone. So from Mark's point of view, when McNeill's people gave the all clear, he did not foresee any danger. He felt frustrated and compelled to enter the building.'

'Would you have gone in?'

'No. No point and it's not a commander's function to do that sort of thing. That does not make me better than Mark because I'd have sent an entire forensics team in and we'd have lost them instead of SO19. It's called a no win situation and, at the end of the day, it's all down to luck.'

'Everything? Predestination, fatalism, kismet? Is that what you believe in Martin?'

'Don't go all philosophical on me, Chris. We make our own choices in life and in professions such as ours we have to plan and try to cover all bases but there is no such thing as a risk free environment. All you can do is your best but sometimes life just takes a bite out of you and there is sod all you can do about it.'

'Shit happens'.

'Indeed it does. More beer?'

'No. Cold vodka please.'

So Carver went to the freezer and returned with a bottle of Grey Goose and four shot glasses which he filled. The two of them drank and talked, finally being able to laugh about some of the things they had gone through with Mark and Michelle. A necessary catharsis.

At some stage Carver noticed that Chris was not joining in anymore. He blinked to focus his eyes and saw that she had fallen asleep, a light snore coming from her mouth. He also noticed that her robe was gaping open to reveal one beautiful, bronzed breast. After a moment he went to her bedroom returning with a pillow and a light duvet. He made her as comfortable as he could, kissed her lightly on the forehead and went into his own bed. He set his alarm for seven then fell into a deep, alcohol induced sleep.

Chapter Forty Six

Six months later Carver and Fearnley were sat in the beach bar restaurant of the Mount Lavinia Hotel near Colombo, Sri Lanka. The enquiry into the deaths of the nine police officers had ended and the two of them had taken a month's leave.

The trip had been Carver's idea and he was paying for it over only mild protestations from Chris Fearnley. They had flown first class Quatar Airways stopping off briefly in Doha en route and were now well rested despite the long haul flight from London.

During the journey they had avoided all police talk or, indeed, any reference to Mark or Michelle. But they both knew, and knew that the other knew, that some important decisions would have to be made.

As the surf crashed against the sand, Martin sat back in his wicker chair soaking in the Celanese sun, a man at peace with himself, Heineken in hand and a relaxed smile on his face.

'You've been here before, haven't you?' she said.

'Once. Army business. How did you know?'

'Oh, little things like the hands together bowing at reception and saying something in the local lingo that got the staff treating us like gods. What was all that anyway?'

'Just saying hello. The word is 'namast' and can't really be translated. Just remember that most of the locals are Buddhist and you won't go far wrong.

'And, if I may ask, what British army business brought you out here?'

'Simple absconder. A brainless prat called Simpson the Sodomite. A kiddy fiddler. Took me all of forty eight hours to find him but I managed to spin it out for a week.'

'You let him run around child molesting when he should have been in chains!'

'No. I broke his legs, had a holiday, traced him to the hospital then had him medivaced to Colchester. End of story.'

Chris laughed and chinked her bottle against his. 'It is a beautiful place, Martin' she said.

'Yes. Used to be the governor's residence during the Raj.'

A waiter arrived with their lunch; fresh water shrimps which were the size of small lobsters. When they'd finished he said to her 'Come on. Let's get our feet wet.'

They walked down to the shore and allowed the surf to foam up their shins as they looked out across the bay towards the capital. There was no question of swimming in that swell.

'You're not going back, are you, Martin?'

'Am I that easy to read?'

'No. You're infuckingscrutable most of the time which is bloody annoying for a girl. But I can see you relaxed and, Jesus, happy for the first time and I think you want to carry on having that feeling. You don't fancy the new role do you?'

'Liaison between the Met and the FBI to find the Player? No, I don't. The feds now have ML on their most wanted list and they will do their own thing with the world wide resources they can bring to bear. I'd just be the representative of the limey losers who screwed up.'

'So who were the winners?'

'Short term – the mayor and the Prime Minister. By sacking Sampson and Addison straight away and promoting proper coppers to their positions they enhanced their reputations no end. I'm also glad Roger Tucker has done well out of all this. He's actually a decent sort and kept the Mark and Michelle aspect of the affair to himself.'

'God, yes. When it came out that he was the executor to Mark's will; wow. You saw his home, didn't you?'

'Yes. It wasn't a surprise for me. A senior CT operative like Mark would have a safe room but some of the weaponry? Christ.

If Tucker had published that instead of calling me – well, Mark's reputation would have been for shit. No, I like him.'

'I'll tell you who I like. That old lawyer, Blenheim. When Nell Gwynn threatened to charge him as being an accessory to murder he just laughed in his face!'

'Yes, that was a special moment. 'Go away you silly little fascist and learn some law. Takes about five years. Then I'll sue the police service, you personally and whoever sold you your ill fitting clothing'. Priceless.'

'Seriously, Martin. If you're not going to take the FBI job what are you going to do? You're not thinking of going after Player on your own are you?'

'I've thought about it, Chris. Manhunting is what I used to do but I had a lot of resources behind me when I did it. To try and find someone like the Player solo is unrealistic. But you're right. I'm not going back. I'm resigning.'

'And what about Michelle and Mark. Their memories. Don't they count for anything?'

'They count as memories and that's how they'll live on. I'll raise a glass to them once a year and that's it. Look, Chris. Tucker showed me some paperwork from Mark's house. He and Michelle were getting out and were going to form their own security consultancy together – SMG Ltd if I remember rightly. They'd had enough of all the bullshit and had been lucky enough to have found each other. I don't think either of them would begrudge me some happiness.'

'So you're giving up?'

'I've given up, Chris. There's a sickness in society that I'm not allowed to deal with. Nurses killing babies, children killing toddlers, cannibals for Christ's sake! Remember the horror the public felt over Hindley and Brady? A lot of that was because of Myra Hindley's gender. 'How can a woman blah, blah, blah.' Then we get Fred and Rosemary West. They are perverts and it's only going to get worse. Creeps like them used to operate in the shadows. With the internet they can form international clubs of like minded freaks and prey on whomsoever they like. No, I've done my time so that good people can sleep safe in their beds at night. I'm going fishing.'

'Fishing?'

'Metaphorically speaking.'

'Alone.'

'I'm best alone.'

Chris Fearnley stood up and touched him on his shoulder. 'I'll leave you alone then Martin and go for a walk. See you at dinner.'

With that she strode off down the beach, her head held high. Carver watched her go and felt something leave with her. Then he noticed that the set of her shoulders had slumped that she had brought both her hands up to her face. The woman was shaking. 'What the hell?'.

He ran to her and spun her around by her shoulders to find her crying like a child.

'Chris! What the, what's wrong?'

'Me! I'm what's wrong! I agree with everything you say and I want to do the same as you and I want to do it with you but I can't.'

'You want to do what with me?

'Martin, I'm in love with you and I know you like me, but I cannot give you what a man needs from a woman so I'm now going to lose you and go back to my flat in Maida Vale and a job I don't believe in and, and'. She broke down, completely, burying her face in his chest and holding him as one would cling to a tree when a gale was raging.

'Oi. Would you say that again please.'

'What?'

'The 'I'm in love with you' bit'.

'Didn't you know? I'm in love with you.'

'That's good. Because I've been in love with you for nearly a year now, but being a thick guy, did not pick up any signals that my affections would be welcomed. So if I love you and you love me let's work out what this problem is and wipe away those tears. Sit.'

Chris obediently sat on the soft sand and Martin sat next to her. He took her right hand in his left and simply said. 'Problems don't exist; only solutions. Tell me.'

'I grew up with my mother on a council estate in Camberwell. I never knew my father. She lived on state benefits and, as I came to realise later, casual prostitution. One day she acquired a pimp who moved in with us. Uncle Andy I had to call him. Anyway, I started to grow tits when I was about eleven and Uncle Andy said that we could make a lot of money together by doing what he showed me people doing on a video. I told him to fuck off. Whereupon he knocked me senseless with one blow. When I came to the bastard was inside me, really banging away. Then he turned me over and took me in the rectum. I'll never forget his words. 'No use in risking a pregnancy, is there?' I was eleven. It hurt like hell and he said that for the next five years I could sell myself as a schooly and make a fortune. It wasn't so bad was it? I just nodded and got him some more whisky. Then I killed Uncle Andy by tying some string across the second top step of our stairs and waited for the bastard to trip and break his neck. Which he duly did. Mum died a year later from choking on her own vomit in her sleep after a night of booze and pills. I found the body. After that I grew up in a care home which was the making of me. I'm good at exams. Unfortunately I have a phobia about anything penetrating my vagina. I have no lesbian tendencies and, God knows, you meet enough dykes in the Met to have the opportunity. I've been out with guys and I get horny but, when it comes to the moment of truth, I freak out and want to puke. So that's what I can't give you, Martin and that's why I'm such a fucking mess.'

'That's it? Have you tried any professional help?'

'No. I'd have to admit to premeditated murder and psychiatrists are legally bound to report that. Wouldn't help at the promotion board, would it?'

'So, if I get this right, you'd like to spend the rest of your life with me if I can abstain from penetrative sex?'

'Uh, a bit medically put, but yes.'

'Children?'

'Can't stand the little shits. All noise at one end and no sense of responsibility at the other.'

'You're playing my music. Come on. We've got two letters to write and a boat to buy.'

'A boat?'

'Can't go fishing without a boat'.

As they walked back along the beach towards the hotel for the first time they kissed, slowly even tentatively. He put his arm around her shoulders and she curled hers around his waist. The partners were now a couple.

'Martin, how do you think the Player got out of the country?'

'Who says he did. Now drop that subject – for the time being.'

Both of them were right. The Player did not leave the UK immediately after the SO19 killings. He had several things to attend to not the least of which was the disposal of his Range Rover. With the police only having the vaguest of descriptions for him it was easy for him to hide in plain sight. He still had multiple I.Ds that he'd kept at the Holborn site plus ample cash funds which enabled him to travel and live anonymously. Hogmanay in Edinburgh had been a box that he had long wished to tick. So he did.

Ultimately he had to revert to the grey man persona and blend in with the masses in a large urban environment. This he found increasingly tedious, the boredom only offset by the amusement he gained from watching the television news as the Metropolitan police engaged in a prolonged bout of self flagellation. The solemn pronouncements emanating from the FBI reminded him that he was far from safe. Thus it was that it was not until the month of April that he felt ready to take the Eurostar to Paris and thence southwards to Nice to think about what the future may bring.

FINIS

www.ingramcontent.com/pod-product-compliance
Lightning Source LLC
Chambersburg PA
CBHW051053030726
47504CB00006B/1600